WARRIOR OF THE DROWNED EMPIRE

FRANKIE DIANE MALLIS

SEVEN QUEENS PRESS

Cover Art by Stefanie Saw

Interior Cover Art by Saint Jupiter

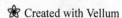 Created with Vellum

In memory of my father, David Gerald Mallis, September 29, 1950–September 10, 2024.

It was because of you I learned how to conduct research, and because of you I tapped into my deep and abiding love for academia, literature, and history. When I said I wanted to study ancient history, language, and mythology, you didn't blink. You supported me every step of the way, and then walked me down to the Classics Department at Cornell (after four and a half hours in the car with Enya). You were a part of the foundation in making this story possible, and one of my earliest stepping stones to bring me to where I am now.

In memory of my father, David Gerald Mallis, September 29, 1950–September 10, 2024.

It was because of you I learned how to conduct research, and because of you I tapped into my deep and abiding love for academia, literature, and history. When I said I wanted to study ancient history, language, and mythology, you didn't blink. You supported me every step of the way, and then walked me down to the Classics Department at Cornell (after four and a half hours in the car with Enya). You were a part of the foundation in making this story possible, and one of my earliest stepping stones to bring me to where I am now.

LUMERIAN OCEAN

N

ARAN

LETHEA

GRYPHON ISLAND

IA

...IERIAN EMPIRE

...ERIA NUTAVIA

LUMERIAN OCEAN
GLEM HARBOR
N
HA'LYROTZ PRISON
SEATHORNE FIELDS
CITY OF HARTON
ARAVIA
GLEMARIA

LUMERIAN OCEAN

N

OTURION
ARTMENTS

SEA TOWER

GRYPHON
ISLAND

GUARDIAN
OF BAMARIA

BAMARIA

ALSO BY THE AUTHOR

By Frankie Diane Mallis
Daughter of the Drowned Empire
Guardian of the Drowned Empire
Solstice of the Drowned Empire
Lady of the Drowned Empire
Son of the Drowned Empire
Warrior of the Drowned Empire

CONTENT WARNING

Dear reader, please be advised that this book includes the
following topics before you begin reading:

- grief
- misogyny
- violence
- sexual assault
- references to off-page rape
- recounting childhood grooming/attempted assault.

LADY OF THE DROWNED EMPIRE

Previously . . .

Lyriana is still reeling from the trauma of the events of Valyati: being forced to watch her friend Haleika transform into an akadim, before slaying her in the arena, and then witnessing the Emartis murder her father. And now, Mercurial, the immortal Afeya, finally has the leverage he needed to force Lyr into a bargain after she broke her oath with her apprentice, bodyguard, and love, Rhyan. To complicate matters further, Lyr must hide the fact that she's discovered Aunt Arianna's true identity: she is the black seraphim, the leader of the Emartis, and the one responsible for her father's murder.

With the Imperator rushing to consecrate Arianna as Arkasva and High Lady of Bamaria, Lyr watches helplessly as her country is taken over by the leader of the rebels, all while she tries to deal with the side effects of her deal with Mercurial. A piece of his soul, and a sliver of the light of the Valalumir are now inside her heart, linking her to him until she does his will.

But before the night is over, Lyr's most dangerous secret is revealed to her sisters and Rhyan—Lyr's the reincarnation of the Guardian of the Red Ray, the Goddess Asherah. Rhyan realizes

Lyr's true identity puts her in even greater danger, depending on who in the Empire knows of her celestial origins. Comments from his father, the Imperator of the North, years earlier makes him suspect that he's aware of Lyr's past life, and has been plotting to control her.

Meanwhile, Morgana meets with her secret lover, another mind-reading vorakh who helped her to better understand her forbidden magic. She's distraught that she missed Arianna's treachery, but learns that Arianna was able to keep her thoughts hidden through the Empire's most vile and precious secret. Instead of being taken to Lethea to be stripped, mind readers are brought to the Emperor to have their powers siphoned and sold off to the wealthy nobility as a way to guard their thoughts, and spy. Morgana never revealed this knowledge to Lyr and Meera because she has long suspected that something similar happened to their cousin Jules, a vorakh with visions. Morgana believes that Jules is alive and being kept as a slave like the other vorakh in the capital, and she's determined to find her.

Once the transfer of power to Arianna is complete, Lyr loses her title of Heir as well as the formal address of "Your Grace" but not before learning her longtime boyfriend Tristan is now betrothed to her cousin, Naria. Without her status and Tristan's political protection, Lyr is exceptionally vulnerable, especially as the Imperator of the South hints that many across the Empire seek her hand in marriage.

Since Mercurial put a piece of the Valalumir in her heart, Lyr's chest has been heating up in random moments, causing unbearable pain. Unsure if this is normal, she heads to the library with Morgana and Rhyan to research Afeyan deals. Amongst the scrolls, they discover an image of a snowy mountaintop, Gryphon's Mount in Glemaria, the place Morgana saw in Meera's most recent vision confirming that Lyr is Asherah's reincarnation. They believe this place may be crucial to claiming

Lyr's power and fulfilling her deal with Mercurial. Rhyan knows it as the spot where a white moonstone seraphim resides.

Soon after, plagued with guilt over the fates of Haleika and Leander, Rhyan leaves for Elyria to hunt akadim, and Lyr faces Tristan to say goodbye. Meanwhile Morgana seduces a servant from the capital named Namtaya. She sees Jules in Namtaya's mind—finally gaining confirmation—Jules is alive and being held captive by the Emperor.

When Morgana can no longer read Lyr's mind, Lyr returns to the library, believing this to be a side effect of her bargain. But the half-Afeyan librarian, Ramia, informs Lyr that Mercurial is missing, and anything that can endanger an Afeyan is something to fear. Lyr still needs answers but finds her mother's journal which reveals she had a recurring dream about Asherah at Gryphon's Mount. Her mother seemed to know she'd given birth to the Goddess and visited Rhyan's father for answers. In Glemaria, she discovered the moonstone seraphim had a lock on it, one that could only be opened by blood, soul, and key. Lyr realizes she has two out of three of those: she has the soul of Asherah, Asherah's blood thanks to the kashonim connection formed through her armor—Asherah's chest plate. All that's missing is the key—something Rhyan's father possesses. With all three, she will claim what her mother suspected was inside— the red shard, the remains of the Red Ray of Light guarded by Asherah, and her power.

Lyr meets with Rhyan's father, the Imperator of the North the next night, and finds the key embedded in the hilt of his sword. He offers it to her in exchange for bringing Rhyan back under his control. But when Rhyan returns from hunting he goes into a rage seeing his abusive father with Lyriana. Lyr leaves with Rhyan and helps him calm down before filling him in on all she's learned.

The following night, a strange girl from the capital appears in Cresthaven. She seems to work for the southern Imperator who has just negotiated a marriage contract between his son Viktor and Lyriana. Morgana realizes the strange girl is a vorakh invading her mind. She rushes outside with Meera, terrified of what secrets the vorakh might uncover, but they are ambushed by akadim, brutally attacked and kidnapped.

With her sisters' abduction putting the whole country on alert, Lyr is imprisoned by the Imperator for her safety inside the Shadow Stronghold. There she receives a ransom note. In exchange for Meera and Morgana, she must bring the object inside the Gryphon's Mount seraphim to the kidnapper—the red shard. But the key is still in Imperator Hart's possession. Lyr plans to negotiate, but Rhyan battles his father for her, stealing the key. Using his vorakh of traveling, he breaks Lyr out of prison, and they escape Bamaria to rescue her sisters.

Lyr and Rhyan head north for Glemaria, evading the soturi sent to find them. But they are caught by nine giant-sized nahashim, sent by Rhyan's father. Rhyan uses his vorakh to save Lyr from the snakes, jumping the two of them to multiple locations until he is drained of energy and susceptible to capture. Realizing the danger he's in, Lyr releases Rhyan's hand on his final jump, causing Rhyan to vanish without her.

Alone with the nahashim, she calls on her kashonim with Asherah, and defeats the snakes. But not before one gets its venom into her, causing temporary paralysis. Losing consciousness in Korteria, Imperator Kormac's country, Lyr communicates to Rhyan through the vadati stone that the soturi of Ka Kormac have found her.

Lyriana wakes up hours later, tied up and bound by Brockton Kormac in Vrukshire, Korteria's fortress. Brockton is the cousin of Viktor, the noble she's now betrothed to, and he is the son of the Bastardmaker, Korteria's warlord. Brockton interrogates Lyr, trying to get her to admit that not only have she and Rhyan broken their oaths to be together, but that Rhyan has a vorakh.

Lyr denies everything, but Brockton and three of his men

threaten her with sexual assault. Brockton strips Lyr of her clothing, only to discover that not only does she have a vadati stone, but it's full of blue light. Rhyan has been listening in the entire time. Brockton threatens to rape Lyr if Rhyan doesn't come. Seconds later, the windows smash. Rhyan bursts into the bedroom and kills the first three soturi he encounters. He frees Lyr who demands a sword, wanting her own revenge after Brockton touched her. But before she can strike, Brockton reveals that Jules is alive and will be endangered if anything happens to him. Lyr kills him anyway, and escapes the fortress with Rhyan. They seek shelter in Cretanya at an inn. Rhyan tries to comfort a traumatized Lyr, washing and bandaging her. He admits he'd been molested as a child by a Senator from Hartavia, and promises she'll get through this. But the idea that Jules is alive weighs heavily on them as they continue north.

Morgana and Meera attempt to escape their cruel akadim captors in a cave. They fail, but discover their blood hurts the monsters, something that will at least save them from assault.

Reaching the northern caves, Rhyan uncovers wall paintings depicting the seven Guardians. Auriel is pictured with Rhyan's eyes. The paintings reveal the significance of the seraphim in Glemaria—it's Asherah's tomb. Additional artwork reveals a message honoring Moriel as king. They've entered an akadim nest and are attacked. Lyr fights beside Rhyan, but discovers that her chest plate no longer hurts them as it once did. Even stranger, these akadim wear silver collars, while proclaiming their loyalty to Moriel as Lyr and Rhyan escape to a mountain cliff, but Lyr is thrown onto a frozen lake. The ice breaks and she drowns.

Lyr wakes in a warm cave to find Rhyan desperately trying to revive her. Since they nearly froze to death, he removes their clothing. Lyr is apprehensive, still traumatized from Brockton and Vrukshire, but Rhyan soothes her, and she recovers her body heat with him in the springs. Warm and drying off by the fires, Lyr is finally sure of how deeply she loves and trusts Rhyan.

They have sex for the first time. As their bodies join, the Vala-lumir in Lyr's chest lights up, and Rhyan has a memory of his past life. He's the reincarnation of Auriel, Asherah's lover, and Lyr's soulmate. Strengthened by this knowledge, they cross the borders to Glemaria and Asherah's tomb.

Morgana wakes in a new cave just as Meera has been taken to a spring for a bath. The demons try to get Morgana to bathe, too, insisting King Moriel is coming. But Morgana refuses, insisting that Moriel, the God is dead, and whoever did this to her should see the damage he caused, and bathe her himself. Moriel emerges. It's Morgana's secret lover. He reveals that he's her kidnapper and the reincarnation of the God. He also knows that Lyriana isn't the only Goddess to return—Morgana is the reincarnation of the Guardian of the Orange Ray, the Goddess Ereshya. Her lover plans to destroy the Empire beside her. But Morgana won't hear it. She's worried for Lyr, and realizes the vorakh she'd seen before her kidnapping, a mage named Parthenay, wasn't working for the Imperator, but was her lover's servant the entire time. And now she's on her way to bring Lyr and Rhyan to Moriel.

Morgana discovers the Afeya Mercurial has been imprisoned by Moriel. He warns that once Lyr arrives with the ransom, the shard of the Valalumir, he'll be able to draw on its strength to escape. He urges Morgana to break free, too, explaining that Moriel has linked his blood to the akadim, forming a kashonim that enhances his power, and breaks the small protection she, Meera, and Lyr had from the beasts.

Lyr and Rhyan fight the soturi guarding Gryphon's Mount—including Rhyan's ex-best friend, Dario. With all the pieces in place, Lyr attempts to unlock the tomb and fails. As Rhyan touches it, he falls into another memory of Auriel. He remembers carrying Asherah's lifeless body up the mountain, and using his magic to create her tomb.

The only way to open it was with blood, soul, and the key.

But not with Asherah's blood—with Auriel's. And because Lyr has Asherah's chest plate, and Asherah was kashonim with Auriel, they have Auriel's blood, along with the key, and Auriel's soul in Rhyan. The tomb opens, and Lyr retrieves the shard inside, as well as a stave that now has her name on it. She finally claims her magic power, and with the possession of the stave, is granted the magic of a mage, as well as a soturion. But before they can escape, Parthenay captures and delivers them to the Allurian Pass where Moriel, Morgana, and Meera await.

Moriel comes, revealing his current incarnation: Aemon, the Ready, Bamaria's Arkturion who she trusted. And what's more, it wasn't the red shard inside the tomb, but the indigo—Moriel's shard. He demands it in exchange for her sisters' lives. Due to Auriel's spells, the shard cannot be taken, it must be willingly handed over. Lyr has no choice if she wants to save her sisters—but then Mercurial breaks free of his prison, temporarily weakening Aemon, and creating a window of escape.

Rhyan helps an unconscious Meera escape the cave first. When he returns for Lyr, she's having trouble holding onto both the indigo shard and to him, necessary for a jump. Morgana tells Lyr to hand her the shard. The moment it's in her hands she uses her magic to create a protective shield so Lyr cannot touch her or the shard. Morgana reveals what she knows about the elixirs taken from vorakh by the Emperor, and that Jules is alive.

With their window to escape closing, Rhyan grabs Lyr and they travel without Morgana, or the shard, before Aemon can reach them. They fly away on a gryphon, and Mercurial finally appears. Lyr believes she's fulfilled her end of the bargain by claiming her magic power. But according to Mercurial, Lyr isn't done—she has to claim her Goddess power, something she can only do with the red shard.

He then reveals the reason her chest sometimes burned with heat since the contract was placed inside her heart, was because the Valalumir inside her was recognizing other Guardians. It only burned when she'd been touched by Rhyan, Morgana, and Aemon. And Meera who is revealed to be a reincarnation, too.

Mercurial lets them know they still need to fulfill their bargain by claiming the red shard, and that it will be the only way to fight Aemon, especially when Morgana hands him the indigo shard and unlocks his God power. He then offers one final warning to Morgana, the reincarnation of Ereshya. She will end up giving him the shard in the end, no matter how hard she fights back. And when she does, they are all in danger.

THE FIRST SCROLL: VISIONS

CHAPTER ONE

TRISTAN

Silver snaps covered the expanse of the dining table, their petals spilling from every one of my grandmother's crystal vases. The stupid shining flowers were too fucking bright beneath the crackling torchlights, their glare nearly as intense as the silver armor surrounding me. The soturi of Ka Kormac lined every inch of the Grey Villa's dining hall, their starfire steel blades at the ready. Never before had so many Korterian wolves entered our home. Never before had so many entered Bamaria either. Stationed here tonight, they were restless. The threat level was low behind our walls, and their auras reeked of boredom and disdain.

It permeated the air to the point of suffocation.

And it was giving me a Godsdamned headache.

I'd planned to turn in early tonight, for once. To maybe fucking sleep for the first time in weeks. It was supposed to be quiet in Bamaria. All the parties and celebrations around Lady Arianna's hurried consecration had ended. And at last, we'd come to the finale of events in which I'd been expected to appear.

Since the month's start, I'd been carried in a litter behind our new High Lady in countless parades. I was shown off, like some prized fucking show horse, all while holding the hand of Lady Naria, our new Heir Apparent. The whole time I was meant to look proud and besotted as she flashed her engagement ring to the eager onlookers. The ring my grandmother had chosen. I'd worn dozens of new robes the past few weeks, all afforded to me by the unfreezing of my accounts. And I'd shaken hundreds of hands as blessings and shouts of *tovayah maischa* were thrown at me. For weeks, I'd pretended I was happy, smiling blandly as the Bamarians applauded the beautiful couple. And I became an expert at keeping a sparkle in my eyes as they demanded we kiss. Which we did—every single time.

I stared down at my own hand, at the golden band that now adorned my ring finger, a ring with the sigil of Ka Batavia engraved in its center—a full moon above golden seraphim wings. It was a ring I'd thought of wearing for two years. Only I'd imagined Lyriana would be the one to slide it on my finger. Not Naria.

At least now it was done. Arianna was Arkasva Batavia, High Lady of Bamaria. The other visiting Arkasvim had left, retreating home to their own countries and affairs. The northern Imperator, father to the forsworn bastard, had rushed back to Glemaria immediately. I'd held my breath as the rest of them left.

All except for Imperator Kormac.

The southern Imperator remained, despite the shocking news of his nephew's sudden death back home. Brockton Kormac, an apprentice in our Soturion Academy, had been the son of the Imperator's brother, Korteria's Arkturion, the man known as the Bastardmaker.

And instead of comforting his family and Ka, going into mourning, or even attending the memorial held in Brockton's honor, the Imperator had chosen to extend his stay here. Tonight, he'd come unannounced to the Villa, demanding an audience with Bamaria's newly appointed Second, and Master of the Horse. My grandmother.

The title was laughably ridiculous. The old woman had never touched an animal in her life, much less a horse. But that didn't appear to be a requirement for the position. And so, when the Imperator's call came, my grandmother invited His Highness and all of his men inside without hesitation. As if I hadn't been tortured enough.

"More wine?" A servant who'd snuck up behind me was already pouring the red into my glass before I could refuse.

"Here," my grandmother demanded.

The servant scurried as she snapped her fingers. Beside her, my grandfather, Lord Trajan, polished off his cup in anticipation of a refill.

I glared at the freshly poured drink, having no desire for it, but with an unmistakably pointed cough from my grandmother, I picked up my glass, and took a sip. The wine was dry. Just as she liked it.

Everything was *always* as she liked it.

"You will not mind my saying," drawled the Imperator, "but you can understand the reasons I may doubt your abilities to … shall we say, *seal the deal*, Lord Tristan?" His blond hair was slicked back, his dark eyes raking me up and down from across the table. Pressing his elbows into the silver tablecloth, he leaned forward, his aura like a rough brush against my skin.

I resisted the urge to clench my fists in my lap, forcing myself instead to take another sip of wine.

Swallowing, I said, "I am not sure I know what you mean, Your Highness. There was no 'deal' to be 'sealed' as you say. But if I understand what you're insinuating …" I shook my head, almost in disbelief. Were we truly having this conversation? Tonight? In public? "Lady Lyriana was young when our courtship began."

Another cough from my grandmother echoed through the dining hall, before she took a sip of her wine, nodding at the Imperator.

His eyebrows furrowed. "I know it is crass to speak of such things, particularly before one so esteemed as Lady Romula, but I've heard rumors. Rumors that in two years of this," his lips turned up, "courtship, you two never *consummated* it. And correct me if I am wrong, but Lady Lyriana has not been *young* for some time."

My fingers were just inches from the silver scabbard encasing my stave. One move and I could have it in my hands, my magic pointed at him. In seconds, he'd be on his back and at my mercy.

But his wolves would have me at theirs.

Auriel's fucking bane. I hadn't expected to be hounded tonight by His Highness. And about my sex life of all topics—or lack thereof. But I lifted my chin, letting my disdain drip through every word I spoke. "Even so, I thought only marriages were consummated."

"A technicality." The Imperator laughed. "One my son will be sure to accomplish immediately with the lady."

I bit back a snarl.

"Once she is found, of course," he added. "And, trust me, she will be found and brought back to me. It's only a matter of time."

"Your Highness," my grandmother interrupted, "Ka Grey considers itself a beacon of morals for this country. Perhaps we are a touch old-fashioned." She pressed her lips together, the same exact shade as her wine. "However, my grandson knew Harren's Seat was unstable long before he himself admitted it. Tristan was never going to risk a permanent alliance with someone unlikely to secure the future of our Ka in Bamaria. It is the same reason he was never permitted to offer a ring." She lifted her glass to the Imperator. "In any case, all is well. The rightful Arkasva has her Seat, the ancient bloodline restored.

Lady Lyriana is in her appropriate station and should feel fortunate that your Ka has welcomed her. I imagine Tristan's *nobility* while courting the lady, may now be to your own Heir Apparent's favor," she teased.

I glared at my grandmother. The old woman was ruthless. Calculated. I'd always known this, but for her to be sitting there, discussing the merits of Lyriana's virginity, as if it were a gift for that swinish ass of the Imperator's son? For Viktor Kormac? She knew how I felt about Lyr—knew how I *still* felt despite my engagement to her cousin. This was ... there were no words for it. It was simply disgusting.

The Imperator's lips remained upturned in a smile I did not like. Since Valyati ... since we'd lost Haleika, there was nothing about this man that I *did* like. Just being in the same room with him had me on edge.

What I'd seen in the arena that night, the night Haleika died, would haunt me forever. The image of Lyriana forced to kill her, and the forsworn bastard forced to help—I'd had to banish it from my thoughts. Keep my mind clear of the memories.

I knew what I'd seen. But I also knew who was to blame. Knew who arranged the spectacle.

Him. Not Lyriana. Not her father. Imperator Kormac and his Godsdamned uncle, Emperor Theotis.

"Forgive me, Lady Romula, for speaking of such vulgarities before you, but they are a part of politics as much as they are life. You understand my concerns. I would see your country brought back to greatness, and to stability. Not just for your sake, and the friendship I bear Ka Grey, but because what happens in Bamaria echoes across the Empire."

"Then we are united, as we wish the same," my grandmother said, lifting her glass again in yet another toast. "Now that Lady Arianna is Arkasva and High Lady, we shall have that."

"Yes," the Imperator agreed. "Lady Arianna's consecration is of great comfort. But I am not yet assured, which is why I'm here." He shifted in his seat, his eyes darkening, and predatory, a wolfish curl to his lips. "After allowing a false Arkasva to govern for nearly two decades, and watching that rule end with a messy and public assassination, Bamaria remains fragile. And now, the late Arkasva's three daughters are missing? Including my own future daughter-in-law." His aura flared. "You'll have more than the Emartis revolting if things do not become secure soon."

Since Meera and Morgana had been taken by akadim, I'd been worried sick, my mind running in constant loops about their well-being. Lyr was gone too, allegedly searching for them. Gods. It had been weeks since they all vanished, including the forsworn. But for once, just once, as much as it hurt, I prayed the rumors were true. I prayed that Hart was with her, that she was safe. I prayed they all were.

I'd been summoned to Cresthaven following the akadim attack, and it had been immediately apparent that not nearly enough was being done to rescue them. The forces sent out had been too few, and had moved without urgency. Lyr had been locked in the Shadow Stronghold by Imperator Kormac, supposedly for her own safety. But mere hours later, she'd escaped. Something that was supposed to be impossible.

And then, of course, the forsworn bastard had been reported missing from his post.

Speculations had run high ever since.

It was *possible* she'd escaped; possible she'd bribed her way out. I'd almost had her freed with a bribe once before. But ... There was no answer to what had truly happened. No realistic possibility I was comfortable entertaining.

"I can assure you, Your Highness," my grandmother said, "I intend to maintain our special friendship. And, when my grandson weds the Heir Apparent, and your son finds his bride, we shall have more than friendship between us. We shall be family."

"In the loosest of terms, yes." The Imperator nodded, his eyes sparkling with an amusement that contrasted his frown. "I have always valued our friendship. And Lord Tristan has had an integral role in securing our shared interests here. We remain grateful for every vorakh he's brought to justice." His gaze flicked to me. "I hope you will continue to do so."

"Of course, I will." I always did. I tossed what remained of my wine down my throat, and slammed my glass on the table. "I would imagine you're just as *occupied* with stability in Korteria, as you are here, now that your Arkturion's eldest son has passed."

It had been a week since word spread of Brockton Kormac's murder, and yet his uncle was still here. Not showing any signs of grief, not even a hint of fucking sadness. If he had a heart, he'd have been long gone by now, back to Korteria. Then I could be left to grieve my own losses. To grieve Haleika.

"*Bar Ka Mokan,*" I added solemnly, lest I be accused of being antagonistic. I waited for His Highness to say the traditional words in response for Brockton, to say "his soul freed." To quell the unrest that I'd so clearly stirred amongst his soldiers.

He merely lifted his drained glass, the gesture so full of demand that a servant came running to his side with a fresh bottle of red. Another servant floated an unopened bottle of white to his seat, the wine almost smashing against the table in their haste.

"Do you think I haven't been back?" His eyebrows lifted. "I can move quickly through these lands, and silently when I need to. Do not presume to know my whereabouts. However, since you appear so keen to know my schedule, I return to Korteria in the morning. I'd have left sooner, if not for the absolute chaos here," he said pointedly.

The chaos he'd created with Haleika's death. Forcing Lyr to be the one to … to … I took a deep breath. It was still too soon, the memories still too biting. I couldn't think about that.

Couldn't allow the images to flow through my mind. They only brought forth the *other* ones, the ones I'd spent years trying to bury.

The worst ones.

The ones in my nightmares.

"Have there been any new developments in the investigation into Brockton's death?" I asked.

"I don't believe new developments can unfold in a story that has closed. Have you had any new developments on your cousin's transformation to akadim?" His black eyes turned to slits. "Or her slaying?"

My hand glided across the hilt of my stave. I flexed my fingers, before forcing myself to still. "It was a difficult, but important lesson for all involved," I said carefully. And then just like that, the lesson replayed in my head. Haleika's screams. The sound of her fear, her pain. "Wine!"

The Imperator delicately patted his mouth with the corner of his napkin. "I must prepare." He rose, and a dozen of his soturi stood at attention, their dark eyes all trained on our table. "Lord Tristan, if word does reach you of the forsworn bastard's where-abouts, despite his father's wishes, he remains under our jurisdiction. Whatever crimes he's committed in the North, he is wanted at present in the South. I, like many others, have reason to believe he is with Lady Lyriana."

"Why would word of his location reach me?" I asked. "We're not friends."

"Of course," the Imperator said.

"If you're asking for my help, perhaps you could tell me word of his most recent location?" I asked. "A clue as to where I might begin such a search." My heart pounded. Anything he told me now could lead me to finding Lyriana.

"This information," he said slowly, "is not to be shared with anyone. But, the two were spotted in Korteria. Quite recently."

Lyriana and Rhyan had been in Korteria? My stomach

dropped. Had they been there for Brockton's death? Was that what the Imperator was hiding? Was it ... was it possible they had something to do with it? By the Gods.

"As I said," the Imperator continued, "it is imperative when they're found, that you bring them both to me."

I nodded, my mind whirling, something clicking into place. This was why he was still here. Not to talk of peace. Not to ally with Ka Grey. But to assign me as his personal hunter. To play on my history with Lyriana. To bring her and the forsworn back to him.

All my years of hunting for him, and for the first time ... I felt sick.

When I was just a boy, he'd visit the Villa. Back then, I looked up to him. He spoke often of how he'd captured vorakh, how he had them bound and shipped to Lethea for justice. How each time it was done, Lumeria was made safer. Every time he came, he told me again of how my story and what had happened to my parents had moved him to be even more vigilant. To double his efforts. He said he'd imagined he was saving me, and finding justice for my parents every time another vorakh was arrested, every time one was punished. I'd told him that I wanted to help, to learn. I wanted to fight the vorakh, too. I wanted my justice. I wanted to avenge my mother and father. He'd smiled, and his own Arkmage from Korteria arrived to train me the day after my Revelation Ceremony. It was brutal. I'd barely slept, practicing over twelve hours a day with my stave. A week later, I caught my first vorakh in the city.

Watching him now, I realized I no longer held the Imperator in high regard. Only disgust.

We all stood to bow as he made his way out, his personal guards close behind. Once the last soturion cleared the entryway, I turned to Bellamy, my personal escort. I needed him to send word to Galen to meet me in the city. Forget sleeping.

After all of this, I needed a drink. A real one.

But my grandmother rounded on me, her speed startling after she'd spent the night moving with almost painful slowness. A blast from her stave pushed me onto a velvet couch.

"Grandmother?" I asked, struggling to sit up. But between her magic and the deep cushions, I kept falling back.

"What is wrong with you?" she hissed.

"Wrong with me? What is wrong with him? You know what he did! The role he played in Haleika's death! And yet you say nothing! You let him waltz in here and hold that over us all night! You don't force him to take any responsibility for the pain he caused!"

"Oh, no? Tell me. What responsibility would you have me give him?" She shook her head. "He was not in charge of the borders on Valyati. He did not let the akadim inside. And, most importantly he did not slay Haleika! That fault lies with Arkturion Aemon. With Harren Batavia. And most importantly, on your precious Lyriana and that forsworn bastard she bound herself to. Be smart, Tristan. Put your anger in the right place. And do it quickly."

"But—"

"But nothing! The business with Haleika is over. Done. We separated ourselves from that scandal as well as we could have. A Godsdamned miracle as it were. But then, on its heels, you cause another. How dare you let this get out!"

"Let what out?" I asked.

"The fact that you never bedded Lady Lyriana."

My skin heated, unsure if I was more shocked at her words, or her boldness.

"Not even once!" she yelled.

"So? So!" I was on the verge of exploding. "That was no one's business but ours."

She laughed coldly. "No one's business? You foolish boy. Everything you do is *everyone's* business. You are a lord of Ka Grey! Or have you forgotten? We have a reputation."

"A reputation?" I balked. "A reputation that I acted nobly? Are you not pleased that I lived up to the nobility's prudishly moral inclinations? The morals you said yourself we espouse?"

"My boy!" she snarled. "I have not and never will care what you do or do not do in your lovers' beds. But the Imperator cares, therefore the Empire cares. If this had remained between you two, it would have been of no consequence. But now? Now you look weak. Now you look indecisive. Unmanly. Especially after two years. By the Gods, tell me you bedded this one at least. Tell me you've bedded Lady Naria."

"Grandmother!" I pushed myself to my feet at last. "This is hardly—"

"Tell me," she demanded again, something dark and dangerous in her voice.

My chest heaved as I glared, my nostrils flaring. "How else do you think word got out that Lyriana and I hadn't ..." My fists clenched. "That we'd been ... waiting."

Fuck. I hadn't meant to reveal anything to Naria. It wasn't any of her business. But we were drunk, and I'd been ... in need. One inebriated confession that it had been a while for me—a very *long* while—and she put the pieces together. Told everyone in our circle. Which apparently meant everyone in my grandmother's as well. I'd barely wanted to touch Naria since. All the public displays of affection had been like torture.

"Good. Do *it* again," my grandmother commanded. "And do it well. Lady Naria, it seems, likes to talk. Let her. Let it be known without a doubt that you're together. That your actions will have permanent consequences. That we will be tied without doubt to Ka Batavia by blood. We almost lost our proximity to the Seat of Power before. And by the Gods, we will not lose it again."

"Almost lost?" I shook my head. "We've always been one seat away from the Seat of the Arkasva. Always on the Council."

"And yet, Bamaria has never been ruled by an Arkasva

Grey," she snarled. "The minute that Julianna," she spat, "revealed her vorakh, I knew it was over. Just a matter of time. And then in the midst of it all, we stumbled. The situation with your cousin could have been far worse. As it is, we had as great an outcome as we could hope for."

Anger propelled me forward, my aura pushing against hers, forcing her magic back. "You call this a great outcome! Haleika is dead!"

"And we are fortunate that her death has not interfered with my plans. The Seat of Power was always meant for us. Change is desperately needed. But, I'm not so foolish as to dismiss the fact that power must be granted, not stolen. Harren showed us that. And only when you put an Heir in Naria's belly," she said, her voice low, "only then will you guarantee the continuation, and success, of our bloodline."

I shook my head, too stunned at her brazenness to reply.

"Should Lyriana send word to you," she continued, "I expect you will use any means necessary to bring her in. Along with the forsworn."

"Why?" I asked. "Why are you so keen to give him what he wants?"

"It's a dangerous thing, my dear, to not have that man on your side."

I pinched the bridge of my nose. "It's been weeks since she vanished. They could be anywhere." And if they had been in Korteria—if they'd been there when Brockton was killed—they were certainly long gone by now.

"Do not fret," my grandmother said, "rumor has it the Emperor intends to draw them out, make them easier to find."

"Meaning what?" My belt suddenly felt too tight, my hands numb.

"Meaning, Tristan, that he gave this task to you. And you will complete it."

"As you wish." I practically spat the words. "I'll take my

leave. And I'll be sure to end my night in Naria's bed if it pleases you, Grandmother."

"Such a martyr." She laughed sweetly and sat back on the couch across from me, her eyes shrewd. "I thought I lost everything when I lost your father. We nearly fell into ruin when that monster—" Her lips tightened, the wrinkles around her mouth severe. "But you, Tristan, you have brought back hope." She frowned. "A rather fragile thing I possess. Do not break it."

I straightened my robes across my shoulders and left.

An hour later I sat in a bar with Galen. Urtavia was full of Lumerians from across the Empire, dancing, and playing instruments in the streets.

I stared out the frosted window until a bottle of whisky hovered above my shot glass. Our server tipped it over, and I watched dully as the golden liquid splashed, filling my cup and Galen's. Wordlessly, I drank, the alcohol burning against my throat.

We'd been doing this several times a week since Valyati. Barely speaking Haleika's name. Barely saying anything at all. Just sitting together. Drinking. Grieving.

We'd both loved her. Me as a cousin. He—as *more*. Discovering her affair with Leander had only intensified his grief instead of assuaging it.

Outside, a woman elbowed her way through the crowd, her face covered by the mask of a black seraphim. The symbol of the rebels, the Emartis.

She walked right into another woman—a mage. Within seconds an argument broke between them. Their staves were drawn, their auras emitting enough heat to melt the frost coating our window, until a soldier approached, shouting.

He wore golden armor with shoulders shaped into sharpened seraphim feathers. The armor of Ka Batavia. Armor I was seeing less and less these past few weeks.

Galen frowned, watching the soturion chase the masked mage down the street, easily catching her.

But then a soldier of Ka Kormac, his armor gleaming with silver, stepped between them. The mage had been on the verge of arrest. Now, she was clearly being instructed to hand over her mask, and walk away. Free to go with barely a slap on the wrist.

The two soturi, one in gold, one in silver, remained in a heated disagreement. A few weeks ago, a mage in an Emartis mask would have been arrested, taken right to the Shadow Stronghold. Now there was only the illusion of a reprimand. That mask would be circulating through the crowd again in minutes.

For now, there was no Arkturion to enforce the law, no one to back up Turion Brenna's decrees. The Ready was gone. And in his absence, our High Lady and the Imperator had all but signed off on the rebellion that had changed everything.

Galen's dark eyebrows deepened to a V. "Any updates on Lyr? Or Meera and Morgana?" he asked, pouring a glass of beer. "Did the Imperator say anything?"

I shook my head, ruminating over what had truly happened in Korteria. Four soturi were dead. Murdered. And she may have been there.

Was she okay?

"My lord," Bellamy said urgently, a hand on my shoulder. The glowing vadati stone in his ear was fading from blue to white. "We have a ... *situation.*"

Galen sat up abruptly. "I'll help."

But I was already on my feet, dropping three coins on the table. "I've got this. Next drink is on me."

A second later, I was outside, pushing through the crowds, pulling my winter robes closer. Bellamy murmured the details into my ear and I ran as a fresh bout of snow fell.

My hair blew back with a gust of cold air, and I turned toward it, moving past several shops that were open late. I recognized the street. It was almost where I'd apprehended the last monster—the vorakh dancer on Lyr's birthday. The recent months had been surprisingly quiet with little for me to hunt. I found myself practically itching for a fight.

The new crowd forming around me contained a mix of drunk and belligerent Bamarians. There were so many bodies I could barely see the vorakh. The revelers were openly spilling their drinks, dancing and toasting. The distractions were everywhere.

But it didn't matter. It had become instinct.

Follow the unique signature of their vorakh, the chill of their ice. Follow the pit in my gut.

I may have misunderstood my relationship with Lyr in the end. Underestimated my grandmother's intentions for our Ka.

But this?

This I knew.

A fresh snap of chilly air rushed against my skin, biting my nose and cheeks. Not the cold of the Bamarian winter, but the strange and peculiar chill I knew far too well. The chill that had haunted my nightmares since I was a boy.

The chill that came from a vision. It wrapped around my body, tightening like a vise. I was close. So fucking close.

The crowd clustered together, bodies pushing against each other to better see the vorakh.

"Move aside!" I demanded.

At last, I found my target. A mage. Female. Mid-twenties. Her dark hair was wild and unkempt, falling to her waist. She wore no cloak, nor sleeves, despite the season.

"I am Lord Tristan Grey," I said. The words I said every time. The ritual. A calmness washed over me. My focus narrowed.

Her eyes rolled back in her head, and she screeched toward the moon.

I aimed my stave at her heart, feeling the rage and anger that always rose to the surface.

She turned toward me; her knees bent as she swiped at an enemy that wasn't there.

"Just a baby!" she screamed. "Just a baby? No. No. No. I don't think so."

Just a baby...

My stomach hollowed, my heart stopping as the pit in my belly grew, and to my horror, my hand holding the stave began to shake.

"My lord," Bellamy warned. The crowd was growing restless, their auras spiked with the foul scent of fear. If I didn't apprehend her quickly, they would form a mob—the vorakh would only become more volatile. And more lives would be endangered.

I caught the vorakh's blank stare.

"I am Lord Tristan Grey," I said again, strengthening my voice. I'd said these exact words dozens of times. Had been successful with every utterance. I'd captured them all, conquered over their unnatural strength. I never failed.

She shrieked in response.

I inched forward. "You have been accused of possessing vorakh in the first order, the power of visions. I will bind you and hand you over to His Highness, Imperator Kormac. And then, you will receive justice."

"No. Just a baby?" Only the whites of her eyes showed, but a chill shot through my body, and I swore she could see me. "All grown up, aren't you?"

"Now," Eric, my other bodyguard, hissed. "My lord, take her down."

I tightened my grip on my stave, my fingers like ice.

"You'll regret it when he grows," she screamed. "When you see inside him like I have. When you learn what he is!"

Those words. Those *exact* words. The ones from my nightmares. From my memories. But she didn't—*couldn't* know. It wasn't possible.

Her dark irises rolled forward, her expression suddenly lucid, as she stared right at me.

Someone shouted from behind, "Arrest her!"

"Lord Tristan!"

"Kill it!"

The screams from the crowd were overwhelming, growing louder as they fought for dominance.

Yet all I could hear were those words. Not the ones uttered by the vorakh before me.

But the other one. The *first* one. The one that had haunted me my whole life.

And just like that, I was back there, back in my memories, in my nightmares. My body went cold.

There was blood. So much blood. More than I'd ever seen. I didn't know. Didn't understand. Because I'd never seen blood before. There'd been no hurt in my world. No injuries. No pain.

Only love. Comfort. Safety.

"Just a baby?" screamed the vorakh.

"Please," my mother begged. "Please!" She was crouched on the floor in front of me. A wall between us. She'd pushed me into the small cabinet beneath the table before the vorakh saw.

My father had fought her.

But now ... he was broken. He'd used his stave, casting spell after spell. But it hadn't been enough. The vorakh was too strong. Too powerful.

My father lay face down. His arms ... the arms which he'd hugged me with, the arms which had been so strong and had held me as he carried me ... they were no longer part of his body.

"Tristan," my mother hissed, she was crying now. Scared. "Close your eyes. Stay quiet."

But I couldn't close them. I couldn't stop staring through the crack, couldn't stop trying to understand. Couldn't stop trying to rearrange the images I was seeing—to put my father's arms back on his body. To wash away the blood. To make him stand up, to hold his stave, to make him speak, and fight.

To make him breathe.

"Close your eyes," my mother cried again, her voice so low I barely heard. "Don't say a word. You'll be safe."

"Ma?" My voice shook.

"Shhhh," she said.

The vorakh stalked forward, the ground shaking with every step she took.

"Tris—" My mother was cut off by a scream. Fingernails scraped against the floor as the vorakh dragged her away from me.

I clutched my knees to my chest, staring through the small slit in the door.

She'd looked like any other mage when I first saw her. Not particularly tall. Not even appearing strong. No red eyes. No claws. I'd even thought of her as pretty. She had a prominent beauty mark above the right corner of her lip that caught my attention.

But this wasn't the akadim I'd been taught to fear. Not the ones in the scary stories.

This was vorakh.

And this was so much worse. Her long black hair fell to her waist, her skin pale. And in that moment, her beauty faded.

Everything about her screamed death in my eyes.

"Please," my mother begged again. "No!"

"You've birthed evil. You'll regret it when he grows. When you see inside his soul like I have. When you learn what he is!"

"No!"

The vorakh wrapped her hands around my mother's neck.

"Where is he? Where's your son?"

"Not here! Not here, I swear."

I heard the crack. Heard the ripping sound. Saw the blood.

And then finally, finally, I listened to my mother. I did what I was told. I closed my eyes.

But it wasn't enough to save me. It wasn't enough to stop me from hearing. From knowing. From filling in the rest with my imagination.

My mother's head was rolling on the floor, rolling away from her body. Rolling ... Rolling ...

I blinked, pulling myself from the memory, coughing on bile, and gasping for air. Bellamy gripped my arm and I felt caught between both worlds, trapped inside two timelines. I looked down. My hands looked familiar, large and holding my stave, and yet they felt small. A boy's hands, weak, powerless.

"Yes. You!" the vorakh screamed; her eyes focused on me. "Finish what was started. Finish what was started!" She raced forward, pushing a mage to the ground, and punching another in the face.

I stumbled back as images of blood filled my vision. Her screams punctuated the chant of protective spells in my mind, the spells my father had desperately uttered. Until he didn't.

Close your eyes, my mother said. And right then and there with hundreds of onlookers, with an active threat before me, I fell prisoner to the memory and did as my mother once commanded.

I tried to open my eyes. To escape. To be here and now. But the memory continued to play out in my mind, visceral and terrifying, putting me back there in a way I hadn't experienced since that night.

The vorakh screamed, racing toward me. "I'll still get you!"

My eyes sprang open, my body somehow colder. I felt disoriented, like hours had passed. But then my mind righted itself, and I lunged forward, readjusting my grip on the stave, my knuckles white as I tightened my hold. Every muscle in my body tensed with pain.

I took a shuddering breath. It ended now. No more thoughts. No more feelings. No more memories.

No more fear.

I spoke the words, I chanted the spell, and watched in satisfaction as the black glittering rope erupted from my stave. It coiled around my target as I twisted my wrist, tightening her binds, pushing her hands against her body, trapping her legs together so she couldn't run.

By the Gods, no one would die by the hands of a vorakh again. No one would suffer like my parents had. I swore that every last monster would be sent to Lethea, even if I had to hunt them down myself. I'd see them all stripped, made powerless, and punished.

The vorakh's eyes rolled back behind her eyelids, her shrieking more frantic now, as she collapsed to the icy waterway beneath her.

I listened with satisfaction to the thud. The crowd cheered. The threat was over.

But then the vorakh opened her eyes, suddenly lucid, her body shaking beneath my binds. The chill of her vision was gone, her power was cut off. But I was still shivering as she watched me, her eyes roving up and down.

She recoiled, her nose wrinkling, as she turned her body away. "Too much yellow. Too much," she muttered. "Too much."

Utter nonsense. Vorakh madness. I snarled in disgust at her rantings. She was probably farther than Lethea.

"Well done, my lord." Bellamy pointed his stave at her prone body and lifted her into the air as the cheers grew louder.

A wave of dizziness washed over me. It was so intense, I thought I'd be sick.

And somehow, I was still cold, still shivering. My teeth were chattering, and wouldn't stop. Even as I burrowed deeper into my robes, even as I uttered a warming spell with my stave, winter clung to my body like a cold wet blanket.

"Please," my mother screamed again. "No!"

"You've birthed evil. You'll regret it when he grows. When you see inside his soul like I have. When you learn what he is!" The vorakh screamed, racing toward me. *"I'll still get you!"*

I clutched my chest, trying to shake the image. It was new ... foreign. A new part of the memory? Something tonight I had unlocked? I didn't remember her saying that all those years ago, nor in any of my flashbacks—never once had I recalled the vorakh uttering those words.

I'll still get you.

"Tristan? You okay, man?" Galen grasped my shoulder. I hadn't realized he'd followed me out here. "You're freezing. You're— Shit." He stepped back, looking almost afraid. "Are you okay?"

His brows furrowed, his dark eyes scanning me before he took another step back.

"Fine!" I growled. I needed to go. Away from the crowd, away from the cold, from the vorakh's evil ... from my own thoughts.

I *needed* Lyr. I—Fuck. No. Not Lyr. She was gone. And she wasn't mine. Not anymore—if she ever was to begin with.

"I need to go," I told Galen. "I need ... I need to see Naria." Galen frowned again, but nodded.

"All right."

"To Cresthaven then, Lord Tristan," Bellamy said. A white dome of light bloomed around me. I'd no longer have to deal with these people, or their little celebration. I rushed back to the seraphim port, ignoring the congratulations and accolades shouted as I passed.

I stared straight out the window, not speaking the entire flight. I remained silent when I passed through the fortress gates and front doors into the familiar Grand Hall of Cresthaven, the fortress of Ka Batavia. It was the place I'd come to so many times, especially in the last two years. My boots echoed against the floor. Colorful columns lined the hall all depicting the previous Arkasvim of Ka Batavia.

But instead of Lyriana's comforting curves appearing on the stairs, her dark hair spilling across her shoulders, her keen and seductive hazel eyes taking me in, I was faced with the slight, lean figure, and pale blonde hair of her cousin, Lady Naria.

My betrothed.

"My lord," she said sweetly. "I got word you were on your way. How was dinner with the Imperator?" That dinner felt like it was ages ago.

"He seemed rather informed about our ... intimate activities, Your Grace," I gritted. My chest heaved with exertion; icy cold sweat rolled down the nape of my neck. "I found that he was particularly informed about *my* activities before you."

"Or lack of?" she asked.

I practically growled in response.

Naria laughed. "I'm sorry. I didn't mean for everyone to know. It just ... slipped."

"Are you so sure about that?"

"Oh, come on, Tristan. Are you really that mad?" she asked, her voice whiny and childlike.

"Those details were private."

Naria shrugged. "Private or not, you still came here to see me." She twirled a finger through her hair, her engagement ring catching a glimmer of firelight.

"Only because I'd rather be partaking in such activities, than hearing about them."

"Good." Her lips spread across her face, and she blinked slowly, before glancing towards the grand staircase leading up to the Heir's wing. With a swish of her hips, she turned.

We reached her bedroom in seconds. My hands were every-where, pawing at her dress, sliding the straps down her arms. I pushed the material past her small breasts, before pulling the hem of her dress up her legs. I was so angry at her. And yet ...

"Tristan!" she yelled as my palms hit the bare skin of her thighs. "You're like ice."

"Then warm me," I growled.

I reached for my stave, uttering a locking spell to close the bedroom door. It clicked just as Naria's hands slipped inside my riding pants, pulling me free. I was so fucking hard and ready. Years of pent-up lust for Lyr had finally found an outlet. My robes and tunic were off next, and I lifted Naria against the wall as her legs wrapped around me.

One more spell. Just one more. Protection. I didn't fucking care what my grandmother said. This was enough. Fucking her was enough. Being engaged was enough. I wasn't having a baby on top of this gryphon-shit-show. Not yet. Not with her. Not until I was out of all other options.

I felt the thin barrier form around my cock, and then I slammed my stave on the dresser as I pushed inside of Naria.

She gasped, her heel digging into my ass as I punched my fist into the wall, pulling back and shoving into her again and again. I was rabid, farther than Lethea with desire. No other vorakh fight had ever left me this full of lust, this starved for warmth.

"Tristan," she yelled. "Gods."

I groaned, slamming into her now, over and over again, my hips setting a bruising pace.

Too much yellow. Finish what was started. I'll still get you.

"Tristan," Naria moaned. Then she yelled. "You're—ah!" She shivered. "You're ice cold. Fuck."

I knew I was. But I couldn't stop. Couldn't slow down. Couldn't be gentle. I needed to fuck Naria until I could forget, until I could no longer remember.

Until my body warmed.

You'll regret it when he grows. When you see inside his soul like I have. When you learn what he is!

I thrust again, and again. But I couldn't shake off the shivers wracking through me. Couldn't shake the monster's words. Couldn't forget the fear in the vorakh's eyes when her vision was over and she'd looked at me.

Right at me.

My body tightened, ready to come undone. The vorakh's face flashed in my mind. The one from tonight. And the one from my past. They were melding together, features shifting and combining. One with a beauty mark. One without.

When you see inside his soul like I have. When you learn what he is ...

Their voices united, taunting me.

I squeezed my eyes shut, my fist slamming into the wall as I came. My stomach clenched almost painfully with a final shudder, and I set Naria down, before I stumbled to the bed, grabbing hold of my stave, my body trembling.

Naria grimaced, but opened her closet door and reached for a spare blanket, tossing it on top of me.

"I'm going to take a bath. A hot one," she said, and slammed the door.

I chanted, seeing my breath in the air, as I summoned flames, pointing at every torch and candle in her room.

And only then, alone and freezing while surrounded by fire, did I realize why the cold tonight was so unsettling. Why the memory had been so vivid, so real. So hard to shake.

It hadn't been a memory.

I knew this cold because I knew how to hunt it. I knew how to find those who possessed it. Knew how to stop it.

My guts roiled violently and I leaned over Naria's bed, heaving up everything I'd drank tonight, and all I'd eaten. I coughed, nearly choking on bile, sweat coating my skin. My sick was all over the floor as the realization settled inside of me.

The vorakh that killed my parents had never said those final words. Had never said *I'll still get you.* And yet they'd been so clear in my mind. Like I'd been there. Like I was there still.

I'd been trapped in my memories before, but never like this. Never to the point where I'd forgotten my surroundings. Where I'd endangered myself. Where I'd closed my eyes in front of a Godsdamned threat.

And the memory had never shifted, not once in all the years I'd had it. There'd never been any new additions to my nightmares, to my dreams.

I curled my knees to my chest, still shaking with cold, as the realization hit me with a bruising force.

What I'd seen tonight, what I'd felt—it hadn't been a memory.

It had been a vision.

CHAPTER TWO

RHYAN

Snow fell on the mountain's top, coating the white seraphim. The flakes were so thick and heavy they were already blurring its form. I felt half-possessed with a need to clear the snow off, to keep the statue in pristine form. To honor it. To worship it. And yet I knew that the more snow that covered it, the safer it was. The more it would go unseen. Disappear. But then, so would she. Fuck.

I swore I wouldn't do this. I wouldn't fall apart. Not here. Not now. It wasn't what she wanted. What she needed. I'd promised her I was strong enough. Promised that I'd be all right. But I wasn't all right. I'd never be all right—not in this life, not in this body. Because she was ... she was...

My cry was soundless. A violent hurricane inside my blood and bones, trapped with no release.

I couldn't see through my tears. The tears that were freshly falling, and the tears that felt like they'd never stopped. Not since she ... not since Asherah ... Asherah.

My chest was rising and falling, my breath coming in harsh, broken waves. I pressed my forehead against the tomb, the carving just like the seraphim birds she'd so loved. The cold moonstone was almost soothing as I breathed against it. Soothing, until again I remembered its purpose. Remembered she lay within. The grief started all over, as fresh and painful as it had been when it happened. As it had been when, only moments ago, I'd laid her to rest.

"Mekara," I gasped. "My soul is yours." I ran my fingers along the bird's wing, along the place where I'd sealed the tomb. Her final resting place. The shard's final resting place. I'd woven enough spells, and cast enough enchantments that I knew beyond a doubt that no one could ever disturb it. No one in this world or the next would ever have access to that level of power, or that level of destruction again.

"Rakame." There was a flash of heat from above.

I jumped back, my eyes widening, boots slipping in a bank of snow.

I could hear her, hear her in my head again. Hear her calling back to me. Hear her clear and beautiful voice. Gods. It was all I'd wanted. To listen to her one more time. To see her. To hold her. And by all the Gods, one day I would. In Heaven. Or another life. Or maybe even in hell. It didn't matter where. Didn't matter when. I'd wait as long as I had to. Go wherever she went to find her.

But first I had to finish what we started. First, I had to honor her sacrifice, honor the risk she took to save my life. To save everyone's. Keep the shards separate. Keep them hidden. Keep them from ever coming together again, from ever falling into the wrong hands.

Especially this one. The most dangerous shard of all. The darkest. The indigo.

I pressed the red key into my belt, my eyes on the grooves where it locked into place. With a painful, ragged breath, I hugged the seraphim once more, my arms tight around its cold, lifeless form. This wasn't her. This wasn't life. She was gone.

Even if I could still feel her in my arms, feel her body against mine.

None of this mattered. Because I knew one truth.

Goddesses never died.

Not truly.

There was a caress of wind against me in silent response, and something surged inside my heart. A feeling of familiarity. Of home. Of her.

"Asherah, I still feel you." I placed my hand over my heart, eyes squeezing shut. "I feel you everywhere." My voice broke. "It should have been me. I should have gone first. Not you."

She'd taken on so much power, so much light. She'd lit up, holding far more magic inside of her than any mortal ever had. More than any mortal could, even one as powerful as she was. Asherah had glowed so bright, I would have sworn she'd returned to her original form. To her full Goddess strength. It saved me. Saved everything. But it had been too much for the mortal form of her body on this plane.

More wind blew, another breeze bristled through my hair. I couldn't say how, but I knew it was her. Not my imagination. Asherah had sent the wind from beyond. Even now I could feel her essence, her aura. Bright, warm, loving. Full of fire and life. She was still talking to me, still reaching out to be with me through any way she could find.

"Mekara, stay with me as I am. Stay with me while I am Auriel. Until the end. Until I'm not. And I will find you in the next life. And the one after. I will do so again and again, until the end of time. There's nowhere you can go where I won't find you. No face you can wear that I won't recognize. No form you can take that I won't love. Because I know you. I knew what you were to me that first moment I saw you. I will always know you. I swear." I pressed my fist to my heart. "Me sha, me ka."

I stepped back. It was time. Moriel's indigo shard would be sealed for eternity. It would be kept away from him, protected by Asherah, who would remain a Guardian, and a warrior for eternity, even in death.

I just needed to close my affairs on her red shard, and on the orange shard of Ereshya. I didn't know what had happened to the crystal which held the yellow ray Shiviel once guarded. He'd hidden it before we'd brought about his end—messy and painful as that had been. Nor did I know where the others were. I supposed they were all lost to the aftermath of the War of Light, lost to the Drowning. Lost to all of Moriel's other machinations by now.

Asherah had destroyed him. But even in death, he was treacherous. He, or one of his servants, would try to find the shards, restore the Valalumir, and finish what they started.

But they would fail.

Breath heavy, my soul weighed down with grief, I took another step back. I wasn't ready. I would never be ready—not for this. But it was time for me to take my leave. The sooner this ended, the sooner we'd be reunited.

I brushed the snowflakes from my hair, watching as the seraphim's wings began to vanish. I took another step, and I froze, my aura tingling with a sudden awareness.

I wasn't alone.

There was a flash of blue skin in the darkness, and cat-like eyes that peered through the shadows. Though feline, the eyes were peeking out from the head of a falcon—one attached to a tall Lumerian's muscular body.

I glared.

Mercurial held up his hand, revealing a star of gold and red light, shimmering and spinning against his palm.

Just as quickly as he'd appeared, he was gone, the light vanishing.

The ground shook suddenly, and a clap of thunder and light-

ning exploded with enough force, it felt as if it had broken the sky in half.

Not the sky ... My eyes widened. It had broken the tomb.

The seraphim statue was opening.

No. No!

"What have you done?" I yelled, searching for Mercurial. "You traitor!"

But the only response he gave was a bell-like laugh, muffled by the sound of stone grinding against stone as the tomb continued to come apart.

"I curse you!" I screamed.

But he only continued laughing as Asherah's tomb opened. "You already have."

"No! Stop!" I held up my hands, but they were strange to me now, lighter in color than I'd ever seen. Unblemished, roughened only by calluses. My hands, but ... not. There were no burn scars, no sign of the fall I'd taken, of the light burning through my skin. I tried to push my power out, to use what remained of my energy stores, but no magic came from me. It was stagnant. Still. Trapped within my body.

Every muscle straining, I tried to close the tomb, to reseal my spell. "No. No! Seal! Seal!"

The white seraphim came to life, stone no longer. It rose up on its hind legs, its wings spread out, sharp and ready to attack. Blood dripped from the pointed feathers. This wasn't possible. This wasn't happening. Then she stirred.

Asherah rose from the tomb. New, and different. Her body glowing with a light this world could no longer sustain.

I blinked.

No.

Not Asherah.

She was Asherah no longer.

And I was no longer Auriel.

My name was Rhyan. Lord Rhyan Hart.

No, that wasn't right ... Not lord. Just Rhyan.

And she was ... She was ...

"LYR!" I yelled. "LYRIANA!"

Her hazel eyes widened, her hair, which had been fiery red a second ago, was now almost black in the dark of the night. "Rhyan!" she cried in anguish.

I rushed forward, my arms outstretched and ready to hold her. "What happened to you? Gods, Lyr! Are you hurt?"

Snow had coated the ground as I worked, the mountain top covered by pure ice. But now, though the air remained frigid, the ice was melting into thick streams. The water was rising above my boots and knees, flowing down the mountain like the tides of an ocean. Rising and rising, higher and higher. Until our bodies were almost completely submerged, practically drowning.

"I'm sorry!" Lyr sputtered. "It was my fault. Mine. I'm sorry. I didn't mean to. I thought I was stronger." She held my gaze. "I thought I could stop it. But I couldn't. They've returned. All of them." Lightning flashed, and she closed her eyes. Her body was sinking beneath the water.

"Lyr!" I reached for her, but she was gone.

A wave rose from behind and crashed over me, drowning me, too. I couldn't breathe. I was submerged, my body was somehow rising and sinking all at once, floating in the icy waters, being taken by the tide, even as I swam against it. The waves were rushing and rushing until I was going over the edge of Gryphon's Mount. I flailed, reaching for something to hold onto, reaching for her. For Lyr. For my love.

But the waterfall took me. The ground below was rushing toward me, and I was falling. Falling. Dying. My hands thrashed, trying to stop it, to climb back up. To find her again. To do anything but fall. Anything but drowning.

And even as the end came, I couldn't stop fighting, couldn't stop searching for—

"LYR!" I yelled as my eyes opened in the darkness. "Lyr!"

My chest heaved, my breath coming in short, painful bursts against the cold air. "Lyr?" I reached blindly across the folds of the cloak beside me, but they were cold. She was gone.

I threw off my cloak. It had been wrapped around me like a blanket, my entire body shivering from the icy chill of the damp cave. Cold, even for me who'd been raised in winter. My heart was pounding too hard, and I clutched at my chest, seeing Lyr drown in my mind's eye again and again. I could see the waves take her. See them take me. My heart felt like it was splitting in two. It wasn't real. It was just a dream. Like the others I'd had, the ones that had tortured me when we'd been apart. When I'd missed her. When I needed her.

But that was a lie. Because this? This wasn't a dream. It had been a memory—at least, it started as one. My soul remembered what had happened, how we'd ended. My soul could never forget. She'd died. Asherah had died. To heal me.

To save me.

But it didn't matter.

Losing her had still destroyed me in the end. There wasn't a world I could survive in that she wasn't part of.

And now, every fiber of my being remembered.

CHAPTER THREE

LYRIANA

She's alive. She's alive. She's alive.

I paced back and forth across the cave as Morgana's words repeated in my mind. They'd been repeating in my head for the past three days. Ever since we escaped the Allurian Pass, ever since she betrayed us. Since Aemon betrayed us.

Since the whole fucking Empire betrayed us.

I turned before I reached the wall, just barely tempering my urge to slam my fist into it. My breathing was uneven, my shadow shivering in the faint torchlight as I walked. I continued on in my loop, completely possessed, utterly unable to stop, unable to slow my mind.

I passed Meera, still asleep and curled up on the floor, her frail body inside my cloak. She was also wearing my pajamas. There were few blankets in this cave   it wasn't one Rhyan had inhabited during his exile—but he'd been slowly scavenging for supplies. Every day he traveled through the countryside to patrol and spy, and every time he returned, he brought back the items we so desperately needed to survive. We had only a few belongings with us to start, the things Rhyan had initially packed for us when we left Bamaria. But Meera had nothing beyond what I'd given to her. Thankfully, Rhyan was slowly building a soturion uniform for her to wear and stay warm in.

I turned again, pacing down a short corridor that led away from her makeshift bed. It also took me away from the passage leading to the small corner Rhyan and I had claimed as our sleeping space.

After reaching the end of the cavern, I turned and found myself at my sister's side again. I paused, only long enough to hear her breathe, long enough to make sure she was still here. That she was still alive. Still safe.

Unlike Jules.

I suppressed a groan of frustration, not wanting to wake Meera, and began retracing my route again. Circling around, moving back and forth, over and over again. No matter how hard I tried, I couldn't stop. Couldn't tire my mind. I kept rushing through every small moment I'd overlooked these last two years, every lie I'd believed.

And every truth I'd been too afraid to face.

Before I'd killed that fucking bastard Brockton Kormac for assaulting me, he'd said Jules was alive. Said he'd ... said he'd raped her. Recently. He said she'd survived Lethea. That she'd survived for years. And some part of my soul had believed him. I knew Godsdamned-well he was trying to manipulate me, trying to stay alive. Rhyan had slain his three lackeys, and Brockton was next. We all knew at that moment he was as good as dead. Rhyan had sworn Brockton would die for touching me, and Rhyan never broke an oath. Brockton knew that, and he knew it didn't matter if his death came by Rhyan's hand or mine. Because the moment Rhyan had sworn, there was no stopping the outcome. And yet, despite the obvious manipulation ... I understood in my soul that he wasn't just saying those words. But I'd been too terrified to fully admit the truth, too scared of its consequences, too frightened of opening that door again. Of the fear.

Of the hope.

But when Morgana had said it—*confirmed* it ... Gods.

Two fucking years! Two fucking years I'd thought Jules had been dead. It had nearly torn me apart. The only comfort I'd ever found in that time was in the knowledge that her suffering had ended. That her soul had been freed, even if we'd never been allowed to utter *Ha Ka Mokan* when she was mentioned. Not that she was ever mentioned.

And it was all a lie.

I gritted my teeth, the rage simmering inside my stomach was making me sick as the truth hit me again and again.

We'd never had permission to acknowledge her, to say the words she deserved to have spoken in her memory. We'd never even been able to properly discuss her. To grieve for her.

But Jules's soul wasn't freed. She wasn't at peace.

And I was never going to be. Not until I got her back. Not until I made sure everyone who had ever hurt her had paid.

In full.

The Emperor. The Imperator. The Bastardmaker ...

Brockton had died too easily. Too quickly. I'd cried for him after—despite what he'd done to me. I felt guilty that night. Sorry even. I was going into shock over having taken my first life. At least, at having taken my first mortal life.

But now? Now if I could go back, I'd kill him again. And I'd do it slowly. Make it last. Make it painful. Tear him apart limb from limb. Remind him he was a worthless piece of gryphon-shit until he was a crying blubbering mess. I'd torture him until he'd lost all sense of himself. Until he was begging me for mercy, until he was crying out for the end.

But he was dead. And I had to focus on my immediate enemies.

Aemon, Bamaria's Arkturion, the warlord known as the Ready. He was the man I'd thought of as an uncle, as a protector growing up. And he was the deadliest soturion in Lumeria: the reincarnation of Moriel. A God. But he was so much worse. He was also vorakh—he could read minds. He'd been reading my mind my entire life. He knew my thought patterns, my darkest secrets and fears— my strengths, my weaknesses. He knew exactly how to manipulate me. And somehow, he could control the monstrous akadim. He'd found a way to siphon their power, to increase his own strength. To allow them to touch me despite Asherah's blood running through my veins. He was the reincarnation of the most evil of Gods to walk the Earth, one of the seven original Guardians. And he was the Goddess Asherah's worst enemy.

My worst enemy.

As soon as Morgana, the reincarnation of Ereshya, handed him the indigo shard, the light of the Valalumir that Moriel had protected, he'd be unstoppable. He'd have more than just his soturion strength and an army of akadim behind him.

He'd have the power of a God. The power of a Guardian of the Valalumir.

The same power the immortal Afeya Mercurial wanted me to have.

I placed my hand on my chest, over the star between my breasts. It was a faint gold, barely noticeable unless I met another Guardian and their touch came too close to the Valalumir burning inside. It was part of the red light Asherah had guarded. The light Auriel had put inside her when he stole the Valalumir and fell to Earth.

But it was also my contract with Mercurial. I was bound to the immortal, forced to carry out his will in exchange for his silence about my relationship with Rhyan. His price: I was to claim my power, and then grant him a favor of his asking. Mercurial would come for us soon. Would offer instructions, would demand I retrieve the red shard, the shard which would unlock my true form. My true power. With the shard in my possession, I would be remade as Asherah.

I rolled the stave up and down my palm. My stave. Asherah's stave. It was long and made of dark sun wood, unlike any I'd seen before. Starfire diamonds circled the top. After I'd found it in Asherah's tomb—in *my* tomb—I'd used the indigo shard to restore it. And now I was not only a soturion, but also a mage.

And soon, I'd be a Goddess.

Soon I'd have to fight Aemon. Fight Moriel reborn.

But Jules … Jules was alive.

I choked back something raw and visceral, emanating from my soul, something between a sob and a scream, just thinking of what she had endured, of what she might still be enduring.

Flames from a nearby torch crackled, and a small spring in the cave was trickling, the sounds echoing against the walls. My aura flared and my skin heated despite the cave's cold.

I closed my eyes, and I saw her. I saw Jules on the dais of Auriel's Chamber in the Temple of Dawn more than two years ago. Saw the eternal flame casting red light over her body. Saw her hold her stave for the first time, and the last. I watched as she dropped it and succumbed to her vorakh—as she saw her first vision.

I could still see the fear in her eyes, feel the terror in her aura, and I remembered how I sat there—sat and did nothing. How I let Tristan hold me back and whisper that she had to die, that she was a monster. I didn't save her. And I couldn't stop her experiencing years of torture and suffering, alone.

I'd barely rescued Meera from a similar fate when she revealed her own vorakh.

Lying a few feet away, my eldest sister made a small noise, a moan of distress. I opened my eyes, watching as she turned over. Her body stilled, and within a few seconds, her breath evened from inside her small alcove. For some reason, she preferred that to being closer to the fire where Rhyan and I were. I was unsure of the full extent of the horrors she'd experienced in her captivity. She swore she'd just been hungry, uncomfortable, and scared of the akadim. Rhyan had checked her over for any open cuts and injuries, but she was already bandaged up, rather crudely. And she was thin. So, so thin. They'd starved her. Reversing that had been Rhyan's main mission these last few days. The food he was bringing home to build her strength back up was working, but not fast enough.

I looked longingly down the corridor where he was fast asleep, tucked beneath his cloak in the dark. So close, but so far away.

Rhyan. My love. My best friend. My soulmate.

Gods, I just wanted to go to him. Run down the hall and crawl back beneath his cloak. I wanted to snuggle against him as his arms wrapped around me. I needed to feel his hand find its way to my belly, the way it always did when he fast asleep. I wanted to feel his comforting weight around me, on me, beneath me. I wanted to inhale his scent. But I couldn't go back there. Now that I had my magic, my aura was blasting my emotions everywhere without control. If my fidgeting didn't wake him, the swirling turmoil of my energy would. And Rhyan needed rest. He'd used more energy these last few weeks than he ever had. He was constantly fighting, and using his vorakh to get us across the Empire. Within weeks he'd crossed hundreds of miles, all while holding me. He definitely didn't need me disturbing him now. If anyone of us needed rest, it was him.

A hot wind pushed against me, hissing violently as it blew out several torches.

It took me a second to realize it wasn't the wind. It was me.

My aura. My emotions were out of control.

Fuck.

I ran for the mouth of the cave, my hands shaking as I crossed the protective wards. For a second, their magic hummed in my ears, vibrating with their strength. The wards had been the first spell I'd learned. I'd walked around the perimeter of the cave, my stave in hand with Meera by my side. She'd instructed me on exactly what pressure to apply with my fingers as I turned my wrist, helped me say the words with the right inflection, and focused my magic. I'd cast the spell twice. Partly to practice, partly because I didn't trust our enemies not to find their way through our gates.

Outside, the gryphon we'd acquired from the Allurian Pass opened one eye to watch me, making soft growling sounds as his chest rose and fell. One enormous wing shifted as he scanned our surroundings, and with a huff, he returned to sleep.

I stepped forward onto one of the few patches of ground not covered in snow. The wind blew through my hair, biting my cheeks. The wards of the cave continued to hum. Not knowing what else to do, I picked up a rock beside my foot, and with a cry, I threw it at a tree, listening for the sound of the crash. Then I found another, and another. I kept throwing them, hot tears in my eyes, my body shaking with rage.

"Lyr?" Rhyan's voice came from inside my shirt. A small blue light emanated from the vadati stone I wore on a necklace. "Lyr, where are you?" There was obvious worry in his voice.

I picked up another rock, still too angry to reply. Too angry to even care that snow was slipping between my toes.

The light from the stone faded. My eyes readjusted to the dark. A minute passed. Then I felt him beside me.

"Partner?" Even in the faint hint of moonlight, I could see his face was pale with worry.

I let out a shaky breath, and threw the rock with all the force I had, nostrils flaring as I listened for the sound of the smash against the tree.

"What utterly horrendous crime has that rock done to offend you?" Rhyan deadpanned. When I remained silent, he said, "It doesn't matter. I'm also mad at that rock."

I pushed my hands through my hair, growling in anger. *She's alive. She's alive. She's suffering at this very moment! And we're hiding out here in this fucking cave!*

He moved closer, his arms wrapping around my back. "Hey now. Are you all right?" he whispered. "Why are you awake?"

"She's alive," I said, my voice breaking. "And alone."

"I know," Rhyan said softly, somehow conveying a dozen emotions with two simple words. "I know." He hugged me tighter, snaking his hand to my neck, his fingers in my hair. "We're going to get her back. I swear."

I stepped out of his hold, and shook my head, finally voicing the fear I'd had the last few days. "How do you know? What if … what if when Brockton said that if *he* died, she died … I mean, do you think …?"

"No," he said definitively. "No. Lyr, I don't. The scum just wanted to live. Nothing more. The Empire has," his jaw tensed, "kept Jules alive for a reason. And whatever that is, it's not tied to him. It doesn't matter who his uncle is. If the Emperor decided something, then that's it. Brockton's not important enough to change things." Rhyan took a tentative step toward me, his expression unsure. His bronzed curls were mussed with sleep, and there were dark circles under his eyes, his jawline darkened from a day without shaving. He ran his knuckle against my cheek. "As soon as we know more, as soon as we're sure of where she is, we'll go and we'll get her."

I shook my head.

"I just …" My voice shook and I could feel my aura flare again with heat. I'd spent my whole life feeling the effects of everyone else's, it was so strange now that I finally had my own.

"What?" he asked.

My throat tightened. "Nothing."

He sighed deeply and looked me up and down with concern. "You're not wearing shoes."

"Neither are you," I said.

"Aye. True, but I'm northern, and used to the cold weather," he spoke with his exaggerated Glemarian accent, the lilts long and winding. He even puffed up his chest for effect. "My balls don't love it," he laughed, "but they'll be just fine." Then he shook his head, his expression somber. "You though?" he asked. "How are you keeping warm?"

"My aura," I said. "It's keeping me from freezing." I bit my lip, looking him up and down. "I'm sorry you had to come out here. I didn't mean to wake you."

"You didn't. I woke up on my own," he said nonchalantly, but there seemed to be something else he wasn't telling me. Something was wrong. Now his aura was swirling, agitated, full of raw emotion. The cold surrounding his body clashed against the heat in mine. He looked wearily at our surroundings, his right eyebrow lifting at our sleeping gryphon. His left eyebrow remained still. The scar his father had given him ran through it, ending at his cheek. He could barely move that part of his face, or show emotion through that eyebrow, though he wouldn't admit it.

"Lyr, come inside," he said.

"I can't." I shook my head. "I can't sleep. I'll just disturb you."

"You won't. And I don't care if you do. I want you to disturb me. I like sleeping next to you."

I bit my lip. "It's probably for the best anyway that one of us is awake. I'll stand guard."

"There's no need. Not with the protection spells you and Meera cast. And I patrolled the perimeter for miles. I checked twice. There're no threats nearby. None that we won't have ample warning for." Rhyan's hands ran up and down my arms. "You can rest. You *should* rest. We're as safe here tonight as we can be." He kissed my forehead. "Don't be afraid."

"I'm not afraid." My voice shook. "I'm furious."

He frowned, one eyebrow furrowed. "Do you want me to find more rocks for you to murder?"

"Rhyan, please. I just ... I ..." I groaned, throwing my hands in my hair. I knew what he was trying to do. To joke, to tease, to calm me down. To keep me from drowning. Something he'd done dozens of times before. He always seemed to know how to reach me when I was like this. So often, he'd become my anchor in the storm. But it wasn't going to work. Not this time. "I'm just—"

"You're what, partner? You can tell me. You can tell me anything."

"I'm just ..." My throat tightened. "So. Fucking. Angry. And I don't know what to do with myself—or what to do next."

I did want to throw rocks. I wanted to smash things. To fight someone. To scream until my voice gave out. To plot the ways I'd find Jules, and bring the Empire to its knees. I wanted to cause pain and violence. To find those who'd hurt me, who'd hurt her and everyone I loved. I wanted to find the Imperator, the Emperor, the Bastardmaker, Aemon, even my Aunt Arianna, and tear them all apart, limb by limb.

Rhyan's emerald green eyes searched mine. "Let me help you figure that out."

"You can't." I shook my head, the backs of my eyes burning again.

He took my hand, his thumb rubbing small circles into my palm as I stared ahead, fuming. "I can try." Rhyan's aura began to wrap around me like a cocoon, the cold finally smothering the fire in mine.

"Rhyan, please! I feel like I'm about to burst. I'm so—" I couldn't even finish the sentence. There were no words for how I felt. For the anger. For the rage. My aura was pulsing with it, my body trembling.

For a long moment, Rhyan was silent, simply holding my hand. The muscles in his jaw tightened, as his eyes snapped to me, some decision having been made in his mind.

"Come to bed with me," Rhyan said at last.

"I don't want to sleep."

"I didn't say *sleep*," he said pointedly, his voice low, commanding. "I said *bed*."

My stomach clenched. The fury that was boiling inside me now turned to molten lava rushing deep in my belly, sliding lower and lower.

"Come on. It's freezing out here. Your aura may be hot, but your body won't withstand the cold much longer. Now let's go. You need this. *I* need this." Rhyan threaded our fingers together, but still, I didn't move. "Partner." There was a warning in his voice. "This is a command from your apprentice. Bed. Now." He started to walk backwards, pulling me with him, but I dug my heels into the ground.

"Meera," I protested. We had a private section of the cave, our own little corner that had become our bedroom, but she wasn't sleeping that far away, and there were no walls between us.

"I'm aware." His good eyebrow lifted.

"So ..." I gestured helplessly. I hadn't exactly been in the mood since the Allurian Pass. But in the few moments our eyes had met in that specific way, the heat between us palpable, nothing had happened because we'd had no real privacy either.

"So," he stepped in toward me, "that just means you're going to have to be a very good girl," his voice lowered, "and stay very quiet while I fuck you."

My stomach tightened, my eyes meeting Rhyan's emerald ones, blazing with a different kind of fire. He pulled me against him in one swift movement, his hands on my ass, lifting me up as my legs wrapped around him. Gods. He was already so hard and thick, I instinctively rocked my hips against him, listening with satisfaction as his breath caught.

His hands dug into me, attempting to keep me still as he made a noise low in his throat. Then he walked us inside, the wards humming and echoing with their protective magic.

"If I recall, you're not exactly so quiet yourself," I whispered, biting his earlobe. His cock twitched between us.

"I see. Challenging me are you?" he asked. "Bad idea."

My stomach tugged, and a second later, my back hit our makeshift bed. I barely had time to place my stave on my travel bag before Rhyan was moving over me. His hands slid up my arms, pinning mine above my head as he thrust. My inner walls clenched and clamped down in anticipation of him inside me. Then he did it again, circling his hips, putting the exact amount of pressure my core needed to make me lose control.

His eyes met mine and he pushed even harder, grinding into me steadily as his hips rocked back and forth. I whimpered.

"Partner," he whispered, shaking his head. "You're already breaking the rules. Shhhh." He covered my mouth with his lips, his tongue licking the seam and deepening our kiss.

I gasped. "What rules?" My heels dug into the ground as my hips lifted, rolling up to meet his.

Suddenly he stretched over me, flattening my body as a mischievous grin spread across his face. "I forgot, I'm the apprentice, and you are my novice. So, it's my job to teach you. The rules are simple. Every noise you make, I stop. But if you're quiet, I fuck you. Now, are you going to be my good girl, and remain silent?" he teased. "Or …" He reached beneath my sleep shirt—his shirt that I'd stolen—and cupped my breast. It was already heavy, my nipple hard as his thumb ran over it, making me buck. "Or am I going to have to stop?"

"You better not," I hissed.

"Then you better follow the chain of command." He pinched, and I gasped before his lips found mine again.

His tongue slid into my mouth, massaging mine before he trailed kisses down my cheek and jaw, practically biting down on my neck. All the while he continued palming my breast, his hips grinding as my arms remained trapped above my head.

I wrapped my legs around him, locking my ankles against his

ass as he released me to draw my shirt up, his lips fastening over my bared nipple. Then he moved to the other. Pleasure rippled through me as his mouth wrapped around the peak, his tongue flicking before he sucked, while he continued rolling the first between his fingers.

I was trying desperately to stay quiet, but as he continued, the sensations began to build and build until it was too much, until I was overcome. "Gods!" I cried out before I could stop myself.

All at once, he pulled back, hovering over me. Not a single part of his body touched mine. I writhed, desperately trying to make contact with him again, to find more friction, more pleasure, but he held himself up. His arms were like an iron cage around my head.

He clicked his tongue in admonishment. "Partner." Rhyan's face was contorted into the stern expression he'd used for training me at the Soturion Academy. The cold, indifferent face of apprentice Rhyan. Though his eyes were the same as always, blazingly beautiful, and full of a desperate hungry desire, even as he shook his head. "You broke the rules. Now I have to stop."

I glared up at him. "I don't think you mean that."

"Don't you now?" His voice was dangerously low, a feral growl underlying every syllable. "What are you going to do about it?"

Without warning, I bucked, my legs kicking up, feet locking around him. He collapsed onto me as I trapped him within my arms and legs, flipping him onto his back.

"This," I said, breathlessly, and straddled his hips. I'd landed right where I'd needed to be, my center lined up perfectly over his length which was straining against his sleep pants.

Rhyan's groans of pleasure echoed against the cave walls. My lips curled. "Now who's breaking the rules?"

His chest heaved as he stared up at me, a wide grin spreading across his face. "Fuck. I keep forgetting how much stronger you are now." He rolled his hips up, pushing into me, and I stifled a moan. "You ready for me, partner?" Rhyan reached for the waistband of my pants—his pants—and my underwear, tugging them forward. "Am I going to find you wet beneath these?"

"Why don't you fuck me," I growled, "and find out." I was soaked with my desire. I didn't need anything else. Just him inside of me. I needed to feel every inch of him driving into me so I could forget, so I could feel something else. So this fury didn't consume me.

With a grunt, he jerked my pants down my ass. The cold air from the cave hit my exposed skin as I frantically pulled at his waistband, pushing it below his hips. Rhyan's cock sprang free, the head already beaded with the evidence of his desire. Wrapping my hand around him, I drew the moisture down his thick length.

"Lift your hips for me, Lyr," he hissed.

I did, my weight on my knees as I hovered over him. Immediately he was tugging my pants and underwear down one leg. I reached back to help, managing to wiggle my right foot out. Rhyan pushed the remaining fabric to the side. My sex lined up with his, as he gripped my hips, sliding me against him.

"So fucking wet." He gritted his teeth as I coated him with my arousal.

I leaned forward and whimpered into his mouth, the head of his cock pressed right to my core. My hand rested on his shoulder, as the other slid up and down his length between us. Then I lifted my hips higher, lining us up. Our eyes met and I gasped as he slid in, and in, and in.

My forehead pressed against his, sweat beading as my eyes squeezed shut. I stifled a groan, my hips slowly settling down onto his.

I gritted my teeth.

"Lyr? You okay?" he asked breathlessly, kissing the corner of my lips, even as he was struggling to remain still. "We haven't done it this way yet."

I hissed, but nodded, gently wiggling my hips, as my body adjusted. It almost felt like the first time he was inside me. But I could already feel him stretching me, my body remembering how to accommodate him. I sat up, rocking back and forth, stifling a whine. I was taking so much of him like this, taking him deeper than I ever had, but within seconds, I was moving over him.

"There you go," he growled in approval. "There you fucking go."

He thrust up into me, his eyes locked with mine as we found our rhythm, our hands clasping at my hips as I rode him, biting back every moan that tried to escape.

The pleasure began to tighten low in my belly almost instantly, the sensation of him inside me, against me, beneath me was overwhelming. I started panting, my body growing more and more desperate for release. It was too much. Too good. I bit down on my lip, whimpering helplessly as I rode a crest of pleasure and then another.

I was so close, so fucking close to the edge.

And then Rhyan wrapped his arms around my back, pulling me down against his chest, my sleep shirt riding up. I was immobile, helpless in his arms as he began pounding up into me, every part of him touching me exactly where I needed.

"Fuck," he snarled in my ear. "Fuck, Lyr."

I mewled desperately as another wave took me.

His hold on me tightened as I began to clench around him, on the verge of screaming.

"Are you going to come?" he growled. "Are you going to fucking come?"

"Yes ... Yes!"

"Bite my shoulder," he ordered.

I did, moaning into the salty taste of his skin, my eyes rolling back, toes curling, as my entire body tightened and then exploded with pleasure. Rhyan groaned and slowed his thrusts, still pushing into me as I rode the waves of my orgasm.

My eyes closed in bliss. A second later, he'd flipped me onto my back, and slid down my body, his mouth covering my core as he dragged what remained of my pants and underwear off.

"Need to taste you," he said, voice guttural.

I cried out the second his tongue made contact.

"Shhhh." He reached up, clamping his hand over my mouth, and then he slowly lowered his lips, my sex writhing helplessly and desperately against his lips and tongue.

I'd barely recovered from my first orgasm, and already I could feel another one rising, the pleasure cresting and ready to consume me.

Some unintelligible sound came out of my mouth, smothered by his hand, as he unleashed himself on me, licking and sucking, his fingers sliding in and out.

I kicked as I started coming again, my hips bucking, back arching off the ground. With a growl, I bit down on his palm. He didn't relent, his fingers only pressed into my face with more intensity as I shuddered.

Without warning, he crawled back over me, and shoved his pants below his knees. Holding my legs up, he lined me up with him and thrust inside, sheathing himself with one push. This time, there was no warming up, no going slow. His eyes met mine, wild, and on the verge of losing control.

"Fuck." His pace quickened, his rhythm leaving me breathless. I couldn't do anything but lay there as he fucked me, watching him, and realizing how safe I felt, even like this.

I loved him like this. Beautiful. Raw, and uncontained.

And mine.

His good eyebrow lifted suddenly, a cocky grin spreading across his face, his neck flushed with red. "One more?"

I whimpered again. I didn't know if I could. He pressed his

palm between my legs, adjusting his angle, and I barely stopped myself from crying out, shocked to feel myself tightening again. And then ...

My eyes rolled back, my legs shaking, as Rhyan buried his face in my neck, cursing and growling as he shuddered, and shook, spilling into me.

I sucked in a breath, barely recovered as I tangled my fingers in the soft curls at the nape of his neck, holding him against me. My heart was still pounding, but Rhyan's weight felt delicious over mine. I didn't want him to move. Didn't even want him to pull out. I loved being this close to him. Loved this new level of intimacy we'd added to our relationship.

I *loved* him.

He lifted his head, his lips finding mine kissing me with far more gentleness than he'd shown my core, his fingers now tangling in my hair, as our bodies remained joined. "Are you all right? Did I hurt you?"

"You didn't." I kissed him back. "I'm good. Really good. Might be a touch sore tomorrow," I said with a wink, and wrapped my legs back around him.

"Mmmm. I can apologize for that," he teased.

I smiled. Last time he'd *apologized*, he'd left me a sweaty, boneless, whimpering mess on the floor. And I'd loved every second of it.

"Partner," he purred contently. "So much for being quiet."

I scoffed. "I hope you're talking about yourself. Because I was following the rules," I said primly.

He chuckled, playfully biting my chin, before peppering my neck with kisses. "I think I'm going to need," he kissed my pulse point, "to explain," he flicked his tongue, "the rules again."

I laughed even as my toes curled again from his ministrations. "Well, you are my apprentice."

"Not being a very good one tonight, am I?" He licked the

spot he'd been kissing, then tugged my ear between his teeth. "I'm breaking all the rules now."

A moment later his lips found mine again as I tried to pull him even closer to me. His familiar scent of pine and musk was heightened like this. My heart rate started to calm down to something in the range of not-quite-normal, but no longer imploding. Rhyan's aura pulsed around us, forceful with feeling. The sensation reminded me of heavy snow falling at night, and a full moon making the frozen ground glitter.

The rawness of his emotions was everywhere, and his heart was still pounding voraciously against mine.

"What woke you?" I asked at last.

He lifted himself up onto his elbows, messy curls falling over his forehead, a frown on his lips. I cupped his cheek, finger stroking the scar, and pushing his hair back. Leaning into my touch, he sighed, silent for a moment before he confessed, "A dream. I dreamt of being Auriel."

I stiffened. "A memory?" He'd had two memories of himself as Auriel that I was aware of. One of me when I was Asherah, walking toward him on the beach before the Drowning. And then one at Asherah's tomb. He'd hinted to Mercurial that more of his memories had returned, but he hadn't shared those with me yet.

I hadn't wanted to press. My own memories of being Asherah so far were vague. Nothing more than small flashes, like looking at my hand on a beach. Seeing myself running into battle, a sword in my hand. Auriel walking toward me. But just those impressions alone had felt overwhelming to me. Rhyan's memories had been vividly intense, and much more detailed.

He nodded, his gaze distant. "The same one I had at the tomb."

I stroked his back, silently acknowledging what he'd seen. He'd carried Asherah's lifeless body to the top of Gryphon's Mount, and constructed her tomb of the white seraphim.

Rhyan started to soften inside me, and gently, with a small

noise between his lips, pulled himself out. Rolling onto his side, he slid his pants back up before reaching for me. His knee slid between my legs, as he hugged me against him, and drew his cloak up over us like a blanket.

"I remembered sealing the tomb again." He spoke lightly, but he tightened his grip on me, his thumb stroking my skin, a line of worry between his brows. "And ... I seemed to know where Ereshya's shard was."

"The orange shard?" The remains of the light Morgana would have once guarded. My heart thudded. "Where is it?"

There were seven lost shards of the Valalumir. No one had seen them in a thousand years—no one until the other night. When Rhyan was Auriel, he'd buried the indigo shard with Asherah in her tomb, hoping to prevent it from ever reuniting with Moriel. But now, thanks to me, it was with him again. As for the other six, Mercurial knew where the red shard was hidden. But that still meant the other five were lost and unaccounted for. Hava's violet, Cassarya's blue, Auriel's green, Shiviel's yellow. And Ereshya's orange.

I'd been so focused on finding the red shard, I hadn't considered the others. Where they might be, and who might be searching for them. I already knew. Aemon would be after them if he wasn't already. Which meant that as impossible as it sounded, we had to find them first. We would have to finish what we started a thousand years ago. Restore and harness the power of the Valalumir. Before he did.

Rhyan sighed heavily. "I don't ... I mean ... *I* don't actually know where Ereshya's shard is now. Auriel did, but his thoughts my thoughts? I don't know." He shook his head in frustration. "The information wasn't in the dream. Just the *knowing* that, at least back then—I—*he* had that knowledge. Maybe more of my memories will return now."

"Or Mercurial will tell us," I said bitterly. He had plans for me and the red shard. As for the other five, he knew their location, or at least knew how to find out where they were. Afeya knew everything. It was just a question of if he wanted us to know, and what else he desired from us in exchange for such information. Knowing him, such knowledge would not be given freely, but only for him to secure another deal.

Rhyan's hand swept over my hip, moving up my stomach between us. He pressed his palm between my breasts, to the place where my contract with the immortal had been sealed.

"Has it been bothering you?" he asked.

I shook my head. "Dormant."

Mercurial had said when it glowed, it was the light recognizing Guardians. He'd told me Morgana was Ereshya. And confirmed that Rhyan was Auriel, that Aemon was Moriel. But Meera had caused it to light up first. According to Mercurial, this made Meera a Guardian. But we didn't know which one. Three Guardians, Hava, Cassarya, and Shiviel, were still unknown to us.

I couldn't be sure, but I suspected she was either Hava or Cassarya reborn. The two Goddesses had stood alongside Auriel and Asherah. But Shiviel, Guardian of the Yellow Ray, had become Moriel's Second in the War of Light. He'd become a formidable monster of his own.

It seemed likely that all seven of the Guardians had been reincarnated. Why else had so many of us found each other already? But that meant we needed to find the others before Aemon did. Right now, we were three against their two. But since they possessed a shard, our greater numbers weren't working in our favor. Nothing would match Aemon's strength but another shard, another piece of the Valalumir.

"We're going to have to do what Mercurial says," I said, placing my palm over my heart.

"Fuck him," Rhyan growled.

"Rhyan, I have to claim the red shard to fight back. Between who I am, and my deal with Mercurial, I won't have a choice.

And you know it's only a matter of time before Aemon goes after the other shards." Saying it out loud seemed to make the truth of it more real.

Rhyan rubbed his hand up and down the length of my spine, the callused pads of his fingers soothing. "I know that's what he wants. I can feel what's coming. And I'll be with you the whole time. Fighting beside you. But don't worry about that tonight." His forehead pressed against mine, his lips finding mine for a slow, languid kiss. When he pulled back, I couldn't mistake the worry in his eyes.

"Rhyan?" I asked, reaching to smooth the crease of worry between his brows. "What is it?"

He shook his head, bringing my hand to his lips, pressing a kiss to my palm and sighed. "Gods. I hate this."

"What? What else is wrong?" I asked. His gaze was distant, full of worry and hurt. "Rhyan?"

"My father." His jaw tensed. "He's returned to Seathorne."

"What?"

The muscles in his jaw flexed as he nodded gravely. "We missed him on Gryphon's Mount by only a few hours that night."

"But that ... that doesn't make sense. He has to stay in Bamaria for Arianna's consecration." I shook my head desperately. "That's not for another week."

Rhyan sighed. "I didn't want to upset you. But when news of Vrukshire reached Imperator Kormac, they moved up Arianna's consecration—put the Laurel on her head before any other unrest could unfold. She's Arkasva of Bamaria now. It's been official for over a week."

My stomach dropped. Hearing Arianna was Arkasva, that she'd taken the place of my father after she'd murdered him, left a sob rising inside me. She was on my list of enemies. And someone I was determined to hurt. But I pushed my fury down. There was nothing I could do about that. Not yet anyway. But Rhyan, here at this moment, he was in real danger.

I searched his eyes. "If your father's back, we need to leave Glemaria. It's not safe for you here."

"It never was. We'll leave as soon as we can. But we need a plan, need to figure out where we're going. And how. Especially because I can't ..." he frowned, "I can't travel holding both of you at the same time." He looked away, embarrassed.

Rhyan had never carried two at once as he traveled. When we escaped the Allurian Pass, he'd gotten me and Meera out in two jumps, just to be safe. But now it was confirmed that his vorakh had its limits.

We'd tried having him jump only a few feet across the cave with both of us in his arms. It didn't work. Rhyan either remained in place, sweat pouring down his forehead from the effort, or he'd jump, taking only one of us, and leaving the other on the floor. Being able to only carry one person at a time had been fine when it was just the two of us. But now we had Meera, and not only did that remove traveling from our options for escape, we also had to consider that Meera wasn't physically trained to cross a country the way we were. She'd only just barely regained the strength she needed to get through the day after weeks of being starved and terrorized—forget hiking through the wilds and mountains of Glemaria in the snow. She was lucky to walk around the few feet of the cave without succumbing to exhaustion.

"I don't think we can fly either," he said. "It's too risky. There's going to be gryphons on constant patrol looking for us. He'll cover every area he can with scouts. We'll find a way. We always do." He nuzzled my cheek, making a noise low in his throat. "For now, let me get you cleaned up. And dressed. For as much as I love the feel of your naked body against me ..." He winked, and his hand slid down to my ass, squeezing. "It's too cold for you not to be covered up." He vanished, the cloak falling flat beside me where he'd been. He returned a moment later with a small washcloth that he'd dipped in the cave's spring. He pulled the folds of the cloak back, his eyes suddenly heated again as he reverently ran the cloth over my center, and then used a fresh towel to dry me, before he gathered up my pants and slid them back over my legs.

When we were together again beneath the blanket, my back pressed to his front, his hand reached for my belly. The spot he claimed as he slept. "*Mekara*," he whispered, snuggling against me. *My soul is yours.*

"*Rakame*," I answered. *Your soul is mine.*

After a few minutes, his breathing slowed, falling into the deep rhythmic pattern that told me he was asleep.

The wards of the cave buzzed faintly in the background, and the torches we'd posted for light crackled and spat. In the distance, the cave's spring trickled.

There was a howl of wind every so often, the high-pitched sound mixing with the low growls of our gryphon.

I tried to focus on Rhyan's breathing. To match his rhythm and join him in sleep. But I couldn't. Because mixed in with all of the noise, I swore I heard another sound. The hiss of a snake.

Nahashim.

I blinked, straining my ears. The sound didn't come again. I couldn't decide if I'd actually heard it, or if it was my imagination. The wards Meera and I had created were meant to keep them out, too. But nahashim always found their prey in the end.

And, so would I. When Rhyan's father sent nine nahashim to track and capture him, I slew every last one. I'd do it again to keep him safe. I'd relish it.

Just as I was prepared to do anything to rescue Jules.

Rhyan's chest rose and fell with slow even breaths against my back. He'd snuggled deeper into the covers, so his eyelashes fluttered against the base of my neck as he began to dream. I covered his hand with mine, my fingers lightly stroking up his forearm, as I eyed my stave and the gleam of my dagger in the firelight.

CHAPTER FOUR

MORGANA

I stared down at my feet, delicate and adorned with the golden straps of my sandals. The sand from the beach was sliding between my toes as the waves of the ocean gently lapped against them. The sun was setting as I held up my stave; the silver wood shone with just the smallest thread of gold from a suntree embedded within.

I was still getting used to using one. In the Above, as we now referred to it, we had no need for such things. Our magic, or rather, our will, simply was. But since we'd been cast down, pushed out from Heaven, more focus was needed, a tool to concentrate the mind, a way to direct the magic.

The waves crashed against the shore, rushing with far more ferocity than before. My toes were soaked, the waters were moving faster, the waves higher. The feeling was more visceral than anything I'd known. Everything was more visceral here. More alive. Brighter. Louder. Harsher. The water moved up my legs, darkening the orange color of my skirts. I could feel the material sticking to my thighs. I didn't like it. A thought while Above would have simply adjusted the fabric for me. We lacked such concreteness there. But here, I'd have to manually remove the offending cloth, knowing the water would immediately force it back against me. So much of this world was like that. Working against you. Unyielding. Disagreeable. A constant wind blowing in the wrong direction. Nothing on this plane was easy.

"Ereshya?" Moriel's voice was clear in my head.

"By the water," I thought. "Where you found me yesterday morning."

A second later his thick, muscled arms wrapped around me from behind.

"It's been decided," he said, his voice low. "It's done."

I'd been expecting this news, even though some part of me had hoped it wouldn't come to this. A part of me even now wished for a better outcome.

"Are you sure?" I asked, turning in his arms. My eyes roved over his silky black hair, his dark, endless eyes. They had not changed, maintaining the echoes of eternity they'd possessed when Above. "Are you sure it must come to this?"

His face was grim. "I am sure."

Darkness filled the atmosphere as he spoke. I could still feel his power, his strength, and the energy of his magic as easily as I had Above. But it was a small comfort against the rest of what we'd lost in banishment.

"The power of the Valalumir must be restored," he said. "It must be made whole, and returned to its original form before it weakens further. And we must continue to do what we swore we would. Guard the light." His arms tightened around me. "What are we, if not still bound by our oaths? The oaths we swore are eternal. I don't care what the others do. Or what the Council says. We shall not be forsworn. Even down here, we remain Guardians of Light."

My heart pounded at his proclamation. Lifting even as his words resonated. I hated being mortal. Hated the confines of this body. I could feel it trapping my mind and soul, squeezing me into this shrinking prison of skin and bones, caging what was once infinite. It felt wrong to bind such a thing.

But worst of all, I could feel it dying. Rationally, I knew it wouldn't be for a long time. Maybe even a thousand years if we survived the war, but it was dying nonetheless, dying in a way my first form could not. The knowledge made my heart pound too quickly as if it were beating for every breath I would not take. The thought of death, however far off in the future, terrified me. Almost as much as the idea of being killed. Because I could be now. I was mortal. And so was he. And all the others.

Except for one.

One of us had more power than we'd been afforded, more strength. The very one who didn't deserve any of it. The one who'd caused this, who'd forced us down here. Whose broken oaths had damned us all.

"Is it true?" I asked, squinting as a flare of the retreating sun cast itself forward.

"Is it true that the fool put part of the Red Light inside of her?" His hands ran up and down my arms and I turned again, leaning my back against his chest. This was also something I was still growing accustomed to. I was never sure if the strangeness of Moriel's touch came from the fact that we'd spent lifetimes not touching. If my mind couldn't move past the forbidden nature of such a thing. Or, if I simply could not accept the newness and physicality of my body. The way my skin felt, the way it sometimes hurt and burned, and the way it sometimes felt so good when he touched me that I wanted to scream and cry with gratitude. I felt like I was being constantly torn between pleasure and pain, satisfaction and yearning. It was all so confusing. And exhausting.

I missed being unbound, I missed the freedom of my ethereal body. The simplicity of it.

"Yes, he did," Moriel growled. "The light was dying in its etheric form, and all he could manage was a sliver of it into her

heart. He has ruined the Valalumir with his treachery, breaking what was once whole. Auriel has damned us again."

"But to restore the light," I said, "To restore the Valalumir from a crystal to its original form, won't we need to remove what's now inside Asherah? Is that even possible?"

"Of course, it is." His fingers dug into my arms. "Nothing new is created. Nothing is ever fully destroyed, only changed. What goes in, must come out, however tied to her it is. We'll remove it in the end."

"But she'll die." I frowned. "Won't she? If it's removed?" My throat constricted. I'd never begrudge them their affair. The idea of love, of a soulmate, of mekarim *... it sounded nice. More than nice, if I were honest. But I'd always thought of true love and soulmates as a kind of silly story. Something to dream about, to aspire to in the small moments of fantasy and dreams—not something to actualize. What made this even harder was the fact that for more years than I could count, Asherah and I had been close. Like sisters. I still found it difficult to do what I was doing now. To be here without her. To have chosen a side against her. To stay the course.*

I feared for her. For her mortality. For her soul. Just as I feared terribly for mine. But Moriel was here for me, like he'd always been. Moriel understood what I was going through—understood in a way that almost no one else could.

Asherah had caused this. Asherah had damned us. And much as I cared for her—loved her, even—I knew the truth. Asherah had to pay for her crimes.

"Only her body will die," Moriel said slowly as if contemplating mortality himself "As all bodies in this realm will eventually. Her soul though?" He pressed his lips grimly together. "That's another story."

I took a deep breath, trying to process again the idea of dying, of death. Of what she'd experience. Of how she'd change form, and what she would become compared to what she once was. I tried again to reconcile the fact that despite the love I bore her, this was bigger than us. There was no other choice.

"So, we go to war." The words were like wet sand in my mouth.

"We go to war." Moriel rested his chin on my shoulder, his hands moving to my belly, rising to the curves of my breasts.

My stomach tightened with tension, and pleasure. Always both with him. "How? They're all against us. Even the mortals. They worship Asherah and Auriel's sacrifice. They think the Valalumir is a gift. We can't fight them alone. Not with their support. Not with Asherah's power. We'd need an army."

"We have one." Moriel's words seemed to echo against the water, as his palms slid higher, rubbing against my suddenly sensitive nipples. They moved past my collarbone, and up to my face, until he covered my eyes. I sucked in a breath.

Did this pleasure come as a result of being untouched for so long? Or from the way my mortal body worked? Would it feel this way if anyone else touched me? Or was it just him, his hands, his fingers that wrought this reaction?

"Look, Ereshya," he whispered into my ear. "Let me show you." I closed my eyes and allowed his memories to enter my mind. The vision he showed me was dark, a scene in the middle of the night. My inner sight needed to adjust, but when it did, I nearly gasped. I was looking straight into the evil, red eyes of an akadim. A monster.

Every instinct in my body told me to run. To get away. I had to remember it wasn't really before me. It was Moriel's memory. Somehow that didn't make me feel any safer.

I braced myself, and looked back, looking the demon up and down. Another stood beside him, and another. I opened up my senses further, taking it all in. There was a row of the beasts, the akadim all standing at attention. And behind them, another. And another.

Despite my remembering where I was, that it was day, not

night, that I was safe in Moriel's arms, my chest pounded with a warning. I could not see how many rows of akadim had assembled. It seemed endless. The fear shot through me like an arrow. So many akadim. So many monsters.

"This is your army?" I choked out the words. I saw only death before me. Terror and violence. "Moriel, they're demons. They tried to steal the Valalumir." They were the reason we were summoned, the reason we were ripped from our families and made into Guardians. The reason we swore our eternity to keep it safe.

To keep it from them.

And, if the rumors were true, the reason why Auriel and Asherah fell.

"They may be demons," he said. "But they can be more. They were once our ruin. Now, they become our salvation."

I shook my head. "No. No. It's not right. We fought against them for millennia. Longer. We exist to counteract them."

"We did. Once. But no more. Now everything is different. Everything has changed. Now, the enemy is different. It unites us. Now we fight together." His hands fell to my waist.

My heart still pounded, harder than before, and my eyes closed again as I swept through his memories, trying to see things differently, trying to see them his way. To see the demons as ... not. As ... more.

"You don't agree," he said at last.

"No. It ..." Something crawled up my spine like a warning. "It feels wrong."

His aura darkened, and I could sense it storming around me, the sound of thunder crashing had me nearly jumping out of my skin. And I was reminded of how his energy would fill the Hall of Records.

"Was it right," he asked, "that I spent centuries diligently doing my duty, protecting the Light, only to be banished for another's mistakes? Another's weaknesses?" His grip on me

tightened. "Was it right that Auriel not only couldn't keep his hands to himself in Heaven, but had to steal the very Light we had sworn to protect? To bring it down here and ruin it? Was it right that I denied myself the feel and touch and taste of you for an eternity because I kept my oath? Was it right that the Council denied us the dignity of love and pleasure without cause, and then denied us our justice in the end?"

My throat went dry. "No."

"No." His voice hardened. "We are still Guardians of the Valalumir. Watchers of the Light. And though fallen, and forced to dwell down here, we are still Gods. We are still going to uphold our oath, our words. Auriel and Asherah may have forgotten themselves. The Council may have forgotten its point in existing. But I haven't. I intend to make amends for the wrongs they have done to us. By any means necessary."

"Any means necessary means akadim?" My voice shook. "Means allying with monsters? With mindless beasts?"

"Not allying," he said. "Controlling."

I turned back in his arms, staring into his darkening eyes. It was like staring into an endless night.

"Control?" I asked. "The akadim are leaderless. They answer to no one, not even amongst themselves. They have no ranks. No ruler."

"They do now. I am their mind. I am their Arkturion. They bow before me, and they call me Maraak.*" King.*

There was another flash in my mind, a memory of the magic he'd used to join their will to his. I didn't understand how he'd done it. But I could feel it down to the bones of this body that he had done so. I was as sure of this as I was that this form would one day wither and die.

"I will control them," he said. "I will keep them tempered, and useful. Keep them from destruction. They will have a purpose now. They will serve us, serve our mission. Whatever evil is inside of them will become obsolete. The good they do,

their assistance in the restoration of the Light will justify the means used to do so. Of this, Ereshya, I swear."

My body trembled. Even though the akadim weren't in front of me, the vision of them had been terrifying. The monsters had been banished to Lumeria on Earth so long ago, I never thought them to be much more than scary children's stories when I'd come into existence. Even after their attack in the celestial realm, I didn't understand their threat. And now, they were far too real, and sharp, and violent. Like all things in this world. Even if Moriel had control over them, I didn't trust them. Control could be broken. Control could be lost. Beasts were fickle.

"Do not be afraid, my lioness," he said. "You are a warrior, and a goddess. You are so much stronger than them, and you will be their queen. They will worship you." He pulled my hair back, his mouth suddenly hot against my neck, as his hands roamed lower, cupping my rear. "Me Maraaka." My queen.

"Rule by my side," he begged. "Rule with me, Ereshya. And I swear, I will kneel before you."

I sucked in a breath, Moriel's hands moved even lower, digging into my flesh, pushing himself harder against me, against this body that seemed to respond to his every touch, and every movement. My mind still didn't understand it, but my body craved more.

"Are you ready?" he asked. "Ready to fight?"

I drew in a breath, weighing his words. "If we fight and we win, we restore the Valalumir to glory."

He nodded.

"Then we can return home?" I asked, my hips moving against his. "We can plead to the Council. Restore our forms, our status." My heart leapt at the idea of being a Goddess again in full. Of leaving behind this flesh. Of shedding my mortality, of escaping death. The thoughts only heightened my arousal. Hope was blooming inside my chest. "We can resume our duties."

"No, my queen." He lifted my leg, wrapping it around his

hip, and I gasped at the newly deepened sensations. His fingers dug into my thigh, and he thrust creating friction between us. "We will not beg." Thrust. "We will not prostrate ourselves before their unworthiness." Thrust. "They banished us. And I will not forgive them, nor will I forget. Not until the end of time." He was working me into a frenzy now. "The Council is no longer valid." His voice deepened. "They have proven that time and time again with their decisions. We will stay here. We will make this our new realm. Our new Heaven."

I bit my lip, starting to moan.

"Yes, my queen. Yes. We will rule over everyone, over everything. And then one day soon, we will rule over them." He pushed the straps of my dress aside, his tongue smoldering hot on my neck. The material fell, pooling at my waist.

I startled awake, my chest pounding, my body covered in sweat.

Morgana. Morgana. Morgana! My name was Morgana. Lady Morgana Batavia. Previously Heir to the Arkasva, High Lord of Bamaria. Daughter to a father who was murdered. Killed by my aunt.

Morgana Batavia. That was who I was. That was my name. Not … Not …

I pushed my hands through my hair, black strands stuck to my forehead. There was a dripping sound, echoing in the caves of the Allurian Pass, soft sheets and blankets beneath me, and a chill in the damp winter air that blew through the stone corridors. A spitting fire crackled nearby.

But above it all, I still heard the cresting waves of the Lumerian Ocean. I still felt the heat of an ancient sun on skin I no longer possessed just as surely as I felt the lips of an ancient God kissing and sucking my neck, whispering an ancient name as an indigo-colored crystal sparkled beside me.

Ereshya. He was kissing—

Morgana! I was Morgana, born in the South of the Lumerian

Empire. I grew up in the country of Bamaria. I lived in Cresthaven. I was twenty-one years old. I had two sisters. One older, one younger. Meera. Lyriana. I had a cousin whom I adored. Jules. Another I couldn't stand. Naria.

I was a mage. I was a student. I was a noble. And I was a lady. I was real. *I* was real. And *I* was alive. Mortal. Not a Goddess. Not a Guardian. Morgana. Morgana! Not Ereshya.

Not Ereshya.

Not. Ereshya.

I gasped for breath, my chest so tight it hurt. An akadim growled in the distance, and I scrubbed at my eyes still seeing images of that beach destined to sink beneath the tides of the ocean.

Staring down at my hands, I saw larger ones than I was used to, elongated fingers, darker skin on my body, tanner than I had ever achieved in this life. Not the hands of Morgana. These were the hands of …

I thrust them under the covers and tried to breathe, still trying desperately to calm my pounding heart. Gods, I was so sick of this. Of everything. Of the damp, darkened corridors that plagued my days. The endless Glemarian winter. The smell of must and sulfur. The incessant dripping sounds that came at all hours. Worst of all, I was sick of the grunts of monsters roaming the caverns at night.

A dark shadow filled my mind. *Calm. Calm. This is only temporary. You'll have your own palace soon,* Aemon thought. *The finest in the Empire. Finer than anything the Emperor has ever dreamed of.*

I stared straight ahead, and grimaced, focusing on imagining an onyx wall around my thoughts, a dark labyrinth blocking him from entering.

But with a brush of his magic against me, the wall crumbled. His power was growing alarmingly fast every hour, just by being near the shard of the Valalumir I possessed. It should have strengthened my own power, too, but I hadn't figured out how to use it yet. Instead, I could only sense Aemon drawing more deeply from its magic. Siphoning its power as easily as he took oxygen with each breath.

Shadows darkened my room as he stepped through the threshold, his aura heavy with something that stirred inside of me, memories of an endless, and eternally starry night.

You could come out with me, he thought. *If you want.*

He sat on the edge of my bed, dressed as I'd so often seen him in his Arkturion armor and cloak. The gold seraphim feathers that curved over his shoulders had been shined and sharpened to perfection. Even his red cloak appeared brand new. For over a year, this had been the form in which I'd always ignored him. This wasn't my consort. The other version of him was. The one I was always waiting for, the one I saw in the darkness, the one who removed his armor in my presence.

The one I'd allowed to be someone else—someone secret.

"You haven't forgiven me yet," he said. "And I understand. But I need you to remember that we are still on the same side." He tilted his head, his eyes raking up and down my body leaving a shiver, pulsing in my core. They were his eyes, my lover's eyes, and they were Moriel's all at once. "Come with me," he pleaded. "Breathe fresh air, feel the sky above your head, the sun against your skin. Leave this cave you hate so much. It will be good for you."

I still refused to respond, attempting to keep my mind blank, to reforge my mental walls.

"Kitten," he admonished, "Your stubbornness does not serve you. You'll only wear yourself down trying to keep me out. You need your strength."

"Stop it!" I cried. "Stop invading my mind! Stop calling me that! Stop! Just stop!"

"Hmmmm. There you are." His lips curled into something

seductive and sinister. "Tell me. What would you like me to call you, if not kitten? What if I called you Ereshya?"

My heart beat faster, and something inside of my soul wanted to answer yes. Wanted to claim the name, to claim everything that came with it. His love, my power, the strength and rule of a Goddess. Of a Guardian. Even the memories I was having—the ones that felt more recent and real than my own as Morgana—they, too, wanted me to answer yes. Wanted to be Ereshya. My body remembered his body perfectly, and my soul wanted to hear another name on his lips.

An ancient name. My first name.

But I shook my head.

"You're remembering, aren't you?" he said. "Remembering who you were."

"So?" I snapped. "So what if I am? What does it fucking matter?" It had been three nights since I'd made my choice. Since I'd betrayed my sisters, and taken the indigo shard from Lyr. I hadn't handed it over to Aemon yet, even though it was once his. It was all that remained of the Indigo Ray he'd protected as Moriel. As much as he was pleased with my deception, I hadn't done it for him. I knew Godsdamned well what he was, knew he was dangerous. He'd led me and my sisters into grave danger just to get what he wanted. He'd forced us to become pawns in his game, and then had us tortured, and nearly gotten us and our bodyguards killed.

I had no intention of forgiving him for that. Not now. Not ever.

Nor did I have any intention of giving him what he wanted.

"It matters when your past memories return," he said. "That knowledge, those memories, they aren't harmless. They change things, they change you. When you remember who you are, who you were, you remember your truth. And when that happens, you can never be the same again." *Ereshya,* he purred the name into my mind, causing shivers to race down my arms.

"No," I said, carefully eyeing the Valalumir shard on the bed. I'd taken to sleeping beside it. Unnecessary since it had been cursed by Auriel for its protection. He'd made it so it could never be taken by Moriel, or anyone else, ever again. And thanks to my betrayal, because Lyr had handed it to me, it was mine. Until I surrendered it to him.

If I surrendered it to him.

Aemon had only asked me to relinquish my claim once since that first day. I'd refused, waiting for him to explode and attack me with all of his strength, and magic. Or worse, order his akadim to attack me for him. I'd braced for it. But he'd remained calm, and nodded as if I were being perfectly reasonable.

"As you wish," he'd said at my refusal. And then he turned away from me to talk at length with an akadim. I'd noticed this one in particular because he was different from the others. He had the same paleness in his skin, the same fangs slicing past his lips, and the glowing red of the beasts' eyes. But the similarities between him and the others ended there. He somehow looked less demonic than the rest. He was shorter, his hands were clawed, but almost finely so, and something in his face retained its mortality in a way I couldn't explain. He seemed intelligent, alert, almost as if he were halfway between being alive and akadim.

I waited the rest of that day and night for a second request for the shard, waited after Mercurial came and taunted me one last time that I'd made a mistake.

But Aemon didn't ask again. Nor did he try to take the shard from me by any other means. I was left alone, cared for with regular meals and private baths.

The crystal, made of pure indigo light from the Valalumir, shimmered next to me, right where I'd left it when I fell asleep.

You feel its power, Ereshya, don't you? he thought.

My fingers curled. "My name is Morgana. I am not Ereshya."

"You are both."

"I am n—"

"You are! You're not just remembering her. You're dreaming of *being* her." His voice was dripping with seduction.

I stilled. It was no secret, and yet I felt utterly naked hearing him say it out loud.

"Come now," he said. "I've known your mind a long time— you can't hide from me. You never could. Not even back then. Sleeping with the shard as your bedfellow is going to call out to the parts of you that remember. It's going to awaken Ereshya inside you. I know this, because it's bringing me back in time, too. Do you think it was just you? It wasn't. I was also there. I also felt it. Your leg wrapped around my hip. My hands sliding over your ass as the ocean rushed against our feet. My tongue licking the salt of your skin, your moans deep in your throat. Your nipples hard against my chest. You were so wet for me—"

"It was a dream!" I shouted.

"Yes, a dream." His eyes flashed. "But also a memory."

"And if I remember? If I forget I am Morgana and become Ereshya again, do you think that matters? Do you think if that happens, that I will then present it to you, and become pliable? That I could ever trust you again?"

"You were not so pliable back then either. As for trusting me again? You will," he said simply. "We go back millennia, you and I. Lifetimes have bound us together. But I will prove myself to you. And soon. You will not only know what it is like being Morgana. You will know what it is to become Ereshya. You will no longer just know me as Aemon, or *him*. But as Moriel, your king. Your consort. More of your memories will come now. More vividly, with more details. They'll come faster until you don't know where Morgana ends and Ereshya begins. You will forget which life you are living at times. Soon, there will be days and nights when Morgana will be the part of you that feels like a memory."

Dread filled me. Gods. I didn't want that. But something

softened inside of me as I met his gaze. "Is that how it is for you?"

He watched me carefully. "Sometimes. I have never not known a time when I didn't recall my past life as Moriel. I have spent years feeling like I was living between lives, losing moments of my life here and now, disoriented when I'd been transported back. Every year, more memories stirred, woke my soul even further." His eyes met mine. "Sometimes the most intense memories came when I was inside of you."

I shook my head. "Don't."

"What does it matter in the end? I am who I am. I don't have to separate myself from one life to the other. Nothing new is ever created. Nor is it destroyed—only changed. It's all just one continuous, eternal loop. Never-ending. Like a God."

My throat tightened again, my pulse pounding as I began to truly realize what that meant—the power he could unleash.

The power I could reach for.

"Trust me when I tell you," he said, "that the past not only mattered back then, but still matters now, matters even more so than before. There was never a time when I wasn't going to actively finish what was started. There was never a timeline or chance that this war wouldn't continue. My soul knew it then, and my soul knows it now. It was prophesied ages ago. This war was inevitable."

I shook my head. "Not all prophecies come true. And you forget, this isn't my war."

"Isn't it?" His aura seemed to pulse, his dark eyes sparkling with amusement. "You're foolish if you think it's not."

"I'm not. And it isn't," I said more urgently. "We're not them anymore. Don't you see? Memories are memories— they are the past. Irrelevant. They can remain where they belong. Nothing is forcing us to relive what happened! Admit this is a war that you do not have to fight." Because it was a war I could not bear. A war that would make my sister my enemy.

"Isn't it though?" he sneered. "Or did you forget all we've learned? Did you forget what the Empire would have done to you if you had been caught with your vorakh? Or Meera? Did you forget what they've already done to Jules?" His voice rose. "What they're still doing to her!"

I flinched.

"Tell me," he demanded, "how many nights did you search Bamaria, fucking every person you could find for answers? You cannot lie to me. I know you want her free, just as I do. Just as I want every vorakh freed from the enslavement of the Empire. Or is that not what you want? Not what you sacrificed everything for?"

I closed my eyes, my chest tight. I *had* sacrificed everything, before I'd known what I was doing. Before I knew the true cost. "I still want that." My voice was barely above a whisper.

"But you won't fight with me," he said plainly.

"I want to fight the Empire. The Emperor. The Imperators. I want to crush the system that enslaved our kind." Something inside me began to burn. "I want to hurt the people that took Jules away. That ruined my family. But not this. Not this other fight I know you're planning. To go against my sisters. To go after more shards of the Valalumir. To reinstate a war that ended centuries ago. *That's* the fight I don't want."

"And you think we can take down a thousand-year-old Empire with anything less than full power behind us? Without the power of the shards? Of the whole Valalumir? I need you to remember who you are—who you truly are now. Remember how we came together. Remember that we want the same things. That we have the same goals. Remember that even if I went about things in ways you did not like, it was for the greater good. We are meant to work together."

I scoffed. "That was before. Before I knew you were Moriel. Before you betrayed me, and my family." I couldn't let it go. Couldn't forgive him. Because if I did ... I lost myself.

"You found out the truth when you could handle hearing that information and not a moment sooner. Unless you want things to continue as they are, for the world to remain still, for your family and Ka to remain enslaved or worse, you will have no choice but to work with me. This is bigger than your own wants and needs. I tried to show you, to teach you. To prepare you. You grew up too privileged this time, and it was my duty to make sure you were ready."

"Ready?" I spat. "You tortured me!"

"And yet," he said, "in the end, you made the right choice. You betrayed your sisters. You kept my shard. Because you knew. You knew it had to be done. You knew your work had to be with me, and not them. And you are too afraid to admit it. Too afraid I'm right. Too afraid to admit exactly who you are." A liar. A Goddess. One who'd do anything to get my way. One who'd do anything to protect the ones I loved, even if I had to hurt them to do so. Because it was the only choice I had.

To take down the most powerful force in this world, we needed an even greater power. We needed a weapon unknown to them. A weapon they could not control.

And the longer I was in the dark of this cave, the more I realized the role I had to play, even if I was still railing against it. Because in the end, there was a simple truth about me. One I'd been running from for a very long time.

I wasn't warm and friendly like Jules. I wasn't graceful and mannered like Meera. And I wasn't patient enough to play the game like Lyr, bandaging every wound, smiling through the pain and sustaining half a life until the time was right.

I'd been born different.

I was meant to destroy.

And knowing that, knowing that I was not like them? That had been the hardest truth to swallow. Harder than losing my sisters. Harder than the look of betrayal in Lyr's face when she'd realized what I'd done. And the one in Meera's when she saw me for what I was—when I realized I'd have to give her up, that I might never see her again. I'd told her we could fight the Empire, told her there was a way. That we could figure it out. That despite Aemon's betrayal, we could work with him. I told her that Lyr wouldn't understand, but she could.

Except she didn't. Meera was against it. She wanted to escape, to go home. To see things right in Bamaria first.

How did I explain to her that it wouldn't matter what was happening in Bamaria if we didn't make a change at the top of the Empire? That it would never matter if the system of our oppression wasn't destroyed?

Maybe I could have tried to explain it better, maybe I hadn't wanted to. Maybe I'd wanted to send her away, to also take my revenge on Aemon. But it was done. The sides were drawn. And ever since, every second without Meera next to me—the first time in my life I'd ever been away from her—hurt.

Aemon pushed what remained of my blankets to the floor, his hand sliding up my leg. For a second, the heat from my dream returned, pooling in my belly with the knowledge that his touch brought pleasure, brought peace. That it was familiar, that he had brought me to ecstasy countless times before.

But I kicked out of his hold, rejecting his touch.

"Your choice," he said. "I'm leaving today. There's something I must do. If you do not wish to work with me now, then so be it. I give you this time to think. But you should use it wisely. I will return to you within a few days and I will expect an answer."

"You're leaving me alone. Here? With them?" I asked, suddenly panicked. I'd been walking amongst the akadim for days—fuck, I'd been with them for weeks since my abduction. By now, I knew they wouldn't hurt me. But they still terrified me. Even the smaller, more human-like one. "Are you going to lock me up, too?"

"No. That's not befitting of your station. Do not fear being alone with the akadim. You are their queen. Their *maraaka*. They worship you. They will fight for you. Die for you."

I took a shaky breath. I didn't want akadim to worship me. I wanted nothing to do with them. And yet … I feared being on my own with them.

"You won't be alone," he said, reading my thoughts. "Parthenay will keep you company."

Parthenay, that bitch vorakh who'd tricked me. Who'd led me and Meera into the trap that allowed the akadim to take us. She was also the one who'd captured Lyr and Rhyan, the one who'd brought them here. She was the one who ruined everything.

"Company?" I scoffed. "Seems more like my guard dog."

"She is both. You're prolonging the inevitable. The sooner you acquiesce the better."

I stared ahead. Hating everything. Wishing I could go back in time, back to when none of us were vorakh. Before Jules was taken, before a shadowed man whispered into my mind and slipped into my bed.

"Where are you going?" I asked.

"The capital."

I froze. "To Numeria? Wha—What are you doing there?"

He eyed me up and down, waiting a moment before he said, "Freeing a vorakh. One I've been trying to get my hands on for a very, very long time."

"Jules?" I asked, my heart pounding.

His eyebrows narrowed. "Not just yet."

"Because you don't have the shard?"

"Because it's not time, and I have other priorities. Something is coming. And if we are going to succeed, we need to be as prepared as possible. You took away one Lumerian with visions from my arsenal. So, I shall bring home another. One far more advanced in seeing the threads of the future than your sister."

"A chayatim?" I asked. They were the cloaked ones, the vorakh hidden in the Emperor's service.

Aemon nodded.

"Why now?"

His eyes fell on the shard. "It has strengthened me. Enough for this."

"Can't you free Jules?" I asked, hating how desperate and hopeful my voice had become. I was shaking with the request. "Please?"

"I will free them all. Every last one. I told you before, and I will tell you again. I do not allow vorakh to suffer. But even I have my limits, even I must play their games to achieve what we want—at least, I must while I remain without the shard."

My pulse thumped. I knew what he was doing. Manipulating me, wearing me down. I couldn't give in … couldn't allow it. Not yet.

His lips tugged, reading my mind. "We will take Jules away from Numeria—she cannot remain with them. But not yet. I only have strength for one. Unless you change your mind, unless you're willing to give me what I want, then I take my leave."

I almost wanted to say yes. If it meant freeing Jules. And if I was there, too … maybe I could redirect him from hunting my sisters.

Unless they were hunting me. My throat constricted, and I reminded myself that this man had kidnapped me, had held me prisoner in the most horrific conditions. I would not give him what he wanted. Even if the price was Jules.

"What if I try to run while you're gone?" I asked. "Go after Jules by myself? I'm a Guardian. A vorakh. And unlike you, I have the shard."

"And you will fail. Force alone will not be enough—not the kind of force you're describing. You'll only make it harder to free them in the end." He flexed his fingers. "But know this,

Morgana. If you work against me, I will send my akadim to hunt down your sisters. As well as Auriel's current incarnation."

"You've already done that," I gritted my teeth.

"I sent orders for them to be hunted and kept whole. No harm. But I don't need them to be brought before me in such a state. Nor do I much prefer them alive. That is a courtesy I extended to you. I can just as easily tell my akadim to bring them back in chains. As forsaken. I can have them returned as akadim. Or presented to you as torsos without arms and legs."

"No," I said, feeling my own aura intensify, pushing back against his. "You can't hurt them."

"And yet, you will not hand over the shard. You choose them over Jules."

"You're making me choose!"

"The Empire is making you!" he yelled. "You just don't see it yet. I can't make you do anything."

"No? Then how the fuck did I get here?" I growled. "I swear to you now, if you hurt them, you'll never see the shard again!" I took the crystal into my hands, slowly, sensually sliding my finger down its length as I'd done to him on countless nights. I twirled it before him, taunting him. "How long do you think before I can wield this against you?"

His nostrils flared, the room flickering with darkness as his eyes tracked the movement between my hands. The crystal began to warm, glowing brighter. It was recognizing him, recognizing Moriel.

But it was still mine. It still belonged to me until I said otherwise. And with that thought, its glow dimmed, and Aemon was released from whatever spell he'd fallen under. "See?" I sneered. "See how it answers to me?"

His hand wrapped around my throat, his fingers squeezing. "I will wait for you," he said. "For a time. But I have eyes on your sisters, and Rhyan. They are safe for now." He squeezed harder. "Safe from me, at least. But they are my enemies—and yours—

until they decide otherwise. You remember one moment in eternity now, but there's a thousand years' worth of war and hatred between us." Aemon released his hold on me and lifted my chin. "Talk to Parthenay if you get lonely."

He stood, looking down at me, his eyes shifting longingly to the crystal at my side. His aura intensified. Darkening, threatening.

His dark eyes flashed, and then he turned, leaving me once more alone, the monstrous growls of the beasts echoing against the walls. Only the faint light of indigo was my companion.

I turned the shard again, feeling its power vibrate and pulse in my hands.

His power would grow even more. I couldn't stop it.

But my power would increase as well.

I closed my eyes, feeling the shard's magic, feeling its strength, imagining it was mine. Imagining I knew what to do, that I had the power to wield it.

Something moved through me, a shock of magic.

You chose wrong, Ereshya. Again. Mercurial's laugh rang like a bell in my mind.

I tightened my hold on the shard, staring down an akadim who passed the threshold of my room, his pale skin mixed with the light of the shard made him appear almost blue.

We'll see about that, Mercurial. We'll see.

The beast grumbled, its red eyes tracking my every movement.

"Get out," I seethed, my heart pounding furiously. The akadim rushed off in fear, and my eyes widened. Once again, I was alone.

CHAPTER FIVE

LYRIANA

Meera frowned. "Gently, Lyr. It's a light movement. You don't need so much force. Like this." She demonstrated the spell again with her stave.

I took a deep breath, and repeated the words, my wrist turning exactly like hers. *Gently. "Ani petrova lyla."* Power rushed through me, my body suddenly alive with it. The lighted torch above me, and every other fire in the cave withdrew into the shadows, until each flame was vanquished. Smoke hissed from the dying embers as we were cloaked in darkness.

"You did it," Meera said happily.

"Again," I said, my eyes still trying to adjust to the black of the cave. I could hear her resheathing her stave in her belt.

"Lyr, you're casting spells perfectly. Really perfectly. You just have to soften your wrist-work."

"Please," I said. "Again."

Meera sighed, but she cast the spell for light. Within seconds the cave torches flared, the fires crackling and spitting. I squinted as my eyes readjusted. Meera stood before me, a slightly annoyed yet somehow still graceful expression on her face. We'd now surpassed a full week of living in this cave. Color had returned to Meera's cheeks, and her strength had greatly improved as she rested and ate regularly. She'd even started concocting different soups and stews with the vegetables Rhyan brought home after patrol, some recipes with more success than others.

Gathering more food was exactly where Rhyan was right now. He was doing his daily patrol of Glemaria, memorizing the schedules of the soturi on duty. He'd tracked their routes and patterns, and discovered the tiny holes that existed in the change of guard each hour. He was meticulous with patrol, taking notes on everything. It was helpful, but it also worried me. He was pushing himself to the point of exhaustion, often passing out upon his return.

I found myself missing him more and more. I wished we had more time during the day to be together. As well as more time at night ... But we had no choice. We couldn't make any mistakes leaving Glemaria. Not with his father inside its borders, nor with the additional legion he'd sent to hunt us down. By Rhyan's estimate, there were hundreds of soturi scouring the countryside for signs of him. And of me.

Not to mention his father's nahashim were constantly slithering the grounds. They couldn't go through the walls of the cave, we'd learned—not unless they caught direct sight of him, so he was careful to remain unseen, to jump from inside the cave and our wards to a great distance beyond every time he left. It was part of the reason he was so tired.

My heart thundered wildly whenever he was gone. I trusted Rhyan's strength, and I trusted his vorakh. But unlike the other countries we'd hidden across the Empire, the people here knew Rhyan. They'd watched him grow up as the Heir Apparent, the soturi had trained beside him, fought with him. He was far too recognizable, especially with his scar. Simply pulling up the hood of his cloak as he'd done before wasn't going to be enough.

We'd discussed the possibility of me going out with him, or even the idea of me taking over patrol so he could rest. But the constant jumps carrying me would only wear him out unnecessarily. And he knew the countryside best, knew the routes in the wilds that the soturi took. Even if I didn't get lost, it was physically impossible for me to cover the same amount of ground. And if my hood ever flew off my head in the sun my hair would turn red beneath—a dead giveaway to my identity. So, while he was out, I stayed with Meera. I focused on keeping up my soturion training, studying the magic I'd always wanted to learn, and testing her soups.

"I still want to practice," I said, rolling the stave in my hand. "The spell needs to be perfect."

"Why?" Meera asked.

"Why not?"

Meera shook her head, a sudden flare of irritation in her aura. "You're not in the Mage Academy, Lyr. No one's grading you. No one can even see you. So why this obsession with perfection when you're doing more than fine?"

"I like to do things right," I said. "I always have."

She made a sound of frustration, staring at the ceiling. "Then I need a break."

"Just watch me?" I pleaded. "You can sit down and rest. I'll practice some other spells. Let me know if you have any notes."

"I have a note." She placed her hand on her hip. "Take a break."

"I can't." My hand tightened around the stave.

"Are you worried about Rhyan?" she asked.

Exhaling sharply, I nodded. Meera noticed the way my mood shifted whenever he was gone. The way I anxiously watched the mouth of the cave, waiting for his return. "But that's not why I'm doing this. It's not a distraction. I need to practice. I need to be ready."

Meera folded her arms across her chest. "For what?" There

was a sharp command in her voice, a sudden resurgence of the girl who was once Heir Apparent, the future High Lady and Arkasva of Bamaria. A shiver ran down my spine.

"You know what. For everything I have to do," I said. "I'm still bound to Mercurial. And I'm going to have to face—" I stifled a groan. "Face Morgana and Aemon at some point. And—"

"And you're going to rescue Jules," Meera said flatly.

My heart pounded, my eyes locking with hers. "You know I am. I have to."

Meera laughed, the sound mirthless. "*You* have to? You?"

I narrowed my eyes. "What does that mean?"

"You keep saying I, not we. Do you really think you're doing this alone?"

"I …" I bit my lip. I'd been trying to avoid this conversation. "Meer, I've been thinking. And I think maybe it's best if you go home."

Her aura lashed out at me, stormy and icy. "What?"

"Hear me out. Rhyan and I need to buy time, legally. Everyone knows we left Bamaria, and that we're together. Alone. I know the rumors are out there, and who knows how far they've been twisted." I sighed. "We knew the risk we were taking when we fled. But now Rhyan is technically absent without leave, and I'm … I'm with him. And because of our kashonim, it puts us in danger. If we're caught, we could be found forsworn. Bringing you home, showing we did what had to be done, well, it lends credibility to our story."

"That's all? You really expect me to believe that? That's fucking gryphon shit, Lyr!"

"No, it's not!" I yelled. "It's true! Meera, we risked everything!"

"You think I don't know that?" Meera yelled. "You think I'm not fucking aware of everything you've risked and every-thing you've sacrificed to come find me? You think I've forgotten everything you've sacrificed the last two years?" Her voice rose.

My cheeks heated. "I know you haven't. It's … it's not the only reason. It's also strategic."

"Strategic?" Her eyes were red, as she stepped closer to me, her aura sharpening.

"Yes! We have no idea what's happening in Bamaria. What Arianna's up to. We need eyes there. We need to connect with our remaining allies. You're the best one to do that."

"Fuck that! And fuck Arianna. I might have thought so, too, before. But there's bigger things happening than who's currently sitting in a Seat we have no ability to claim."

"I know," I said, stunned. Meera had rarely cursed before she was taken.

"Do you?" She glared. "Because you seem to forget that I am the eldest sister. That I was groomed to lead. You may have spent the last two years protecting me, but I've spent my entire fucking life protecting you. I know what the vorakh did to me. I can't forget. And I know the cost you've paid. And Jules. I have to live with it. Every single day." Her voice broke. "But you? You were spared as a child from more than you know. The long meetings, the daily death threats we faced. Why else do you think you became so close to Jules? So you had a distraction."

"Stop!"

Meera shook her head. "On my ninth birthday, I was given a countdown to the day I'd rule. The night we lost Jules, I wasn't just going to come into my power and title. We were going to announce Father's abdication. That all changed the second my vorakh appeared." Her nostrils flared. "I should be wearing the Laurel of the Arkasva now. I should have been wearing it for two years. And maybe if I had, Father would still be alive."

The backs of my eyes burned. The grief, the loss of him was still too fresh. Too raw. And we both hadn't had any time to deal with it. To process, or even share our grief. Sometimes, I even forgot he was gone, until the memories crashed down on me. In those moments, it was like seeing him die all over again.

I shook my head. "Meera. No. You can't know that. What happened wasn't your fault."

"Isn't it? I know how guilty you feel over what happened to Jules. I know how it's tormented you. I had to watch as it tore you apart. And yet, somehow, you weren't able to see how much worse it was for me. To know that that night *I* was chosen. *I* was protected. A line no bigger than the edge of a knife is all that saved me. Do you understand the guilt I've carried? I was sitting there. Right there. Do you know what it was like? To know it could have been me? To always wonder if it should have been me? And now you want to send me fucking home to do nothing? Like before. I have lived the night we lost Jules a thousand times over," she cried. "I could have reached out and touched her—but I didn't. And then right after ... I still wanted to claim my full title. I wanted to go against Father, demand she be brought back. I had a list of plots to save her, bribes ready to go, names of soturi I trusted with the task. While we watched the Bastardmaker carry her away, I was plotting her rescue. Plotting to save her. Until I wasn't. Until I couldn't do *anything*, because I was too tormented by the visions—by the knowledge that not only would I never rule, but that every plan to quiet the growing rebellion was now useless because of me. In one night I had to accept the fact that I was so incapacitated I could no longer protect you. Like I always had. Like I swore I always would. Even worse, you had to take care of me."

"Meera." My voice cracked. I stepped forward, reaching for her hand.

She snapped it out of my reach, her nostrils flaring. "Don't."

"I'm sorry." I pressed my lips together. "I didn't see you. You're right. I should have. I'm sorry."

"You're sorry. So? What does it matter?" She shrugged. "Let

me guess. You still want to ship me back to Bamaria, keep me out of your way so you can protect Rhyan?"

"And protect you," I shouted. "Meera! I wake up in the middle of the night to watch you sleep. To make sure you're still here."

"Of course, I'm still here," she snapped. "I'm not Morgana."

I flinched hearing her name. We'd barely discussed her, barely let ourselves say her name out loud. It was like a dance between us, an unwillingness to confirm her betrayal.

"But, Meera, you're also—" I hugged my arms to my chest, my eyes hot with tears I refused to let fall.

"What? I'm what?" Her aura darkened. "Go ahead. Say it."

"You're … Meera, please," I begged. "I just want … I need you to be safe."

"And you don't think I can be? Because I'm vorakh? Because I'm a liability? Or is it because you think I'm too weak and fragile? You think I can't hear your conversations with him at night?"

I stilled.

Meera grimaced. "I know I failed you as your big sister. And as Heir Apparent. I know I fucked up by naming Arianna as our next Arkasva."

"You didn't though. Not once! No one knew about Arianna, not even Morgana. She could fucking mind read and she didn't know! She tricked all of us!"

"And yet, it doesn't matter. Because the truth is all over your face. I'm a powerful mage, I was trained to rule, one of the best in the Mage Academy. And even if I don't have my memories yet, I know I was a Guardian. I feel it in my soul. But still, still you don't think I'm enough."

My eyes searched hers, looking for the right thing to say. The right way to explain. "No. No, I—"

"Gryphon shit. Just—" Meera shook her head. "Forget it." Turning her back on me, she stormed off to her alcove, but not before she lifted her stave. Every remaining light in the cave was vanquished. Smoke filled my eyes as the darkness smothered my body. "Here you go," she called, her voice bitter. "Practice with that."

"Meera!"

But she was silent. I could feel more tears boiling. The air of the cave was suffocating, the walls too close to each other. I didn't want to be trapped in there anymore. I needed fresh air. I needed to get out. Get away. I followed the faint light that shined through the mouth of the cave, hearing the hum of the protection wards as I stepped outside.

I sheathed my stave at my hip. Rhyan had bought a mage scabbard for me on one of his outings. It was soft black leather that reminded me of his Glemarian armor. A sun had been stitched onto the front above silver gryphon wings, the sigil of Ka Hart. Inside, "L.B." had been painted in gold. He'd had it personalized for me from the vendor when he bought it. He'd shyly handed it to me, saying he wanted to make me smile. It had.

I took a deep breath, and prepared to move through the One Hundred and Eight postures of the Valya as my warm-up. Reaching my arms above my head, I stretched, then bent forward, my palms easily touching the snowy ground. My calves no longer burned the way they had months ago when I started training. But as I stretched now, I could feel even more ease in my legs. More energy. I pressed my hands down, my elbows bending as the stretch deepened even further. Slowly I breathed in and out, trying to clear my mind.

I rose up, my arms stretching back to the sky and I repeated my movements, bending again. There was a sudden shift in the air around me, an unnatural cold that seeped down to my bones. Yet there was no wind outside. The trees were still. My teeth chattered, and I turned, scanning the horizon. There was nothing. And then it hit me. The cold was coming from inside the cave.

Meera.

I turned, racing back, my stave out as Meera's scream pierced through the humming of the wards, as I yelled out, *"Ani petrova vala!"* Light flared against the stone walls, the torches flickering to life. "Meera!"

She was curled up inside her alcove, her body all sharp angles twisting in her cloak. The spring which had been trickling only moments before was now frozen, the ice crackling and popping.

"No!" she screamed, her face contorted with pain. "No!"

"Meera! Meera, it's okay! I'm here." I ran faster, sliding to my knees the last few feet, and reaching out for her.

She thrashed anew as soon as she sensed me, trying to fight me off. But I was ready. I overpowered her, pressing her back to the ground, careful of her head, as I pushed her back onto her bed of blankets.

"Meera," I yelled, "come back. Come back to me."

I held her face with both hands, pressing my forehead to hers, doing what I always did. The thing that always worked, that always helped when nothing else did: seeing my face, hearing my voice, being as close to her as I could get. Morgana and Father couldn't ever help her, but I could. I always could.

Blood gushed from her nose, her body shaking as it splattered onto her lips. I tightened my hold, my palms pressed to her cheeks.

A light flared where we touched, bright and golden between us. Suddenly there was warmth inside my chest. I looked down with worry, realizing the light had come from me. From the star in my heart. But taking my attention off Meera had been a mistake. As soon as I looked away, I was thrown backwards. Not by Meera but by some other foreign force.

"Lyr?" Meera sat up several feet away from me. She was completely alert and lucid, her eyes on me in a way they never had been during one of her episodes. When she looked at me during her visions, I knew she wasn't seeing me, only what was in her mind. But as she looked at me now, I could see the recognition in her gaze.

And I could the fear she felt. The fear she felt for me.

"Lyr!" Meera yelled. The cold in the room seemed to vanish as quickly as it came. Her vision had been the shortest one yet— mere seconds.

Shakily, I got to my feet, as something warm and wet dripped down my mouth. I reached for my face, and pulled my hand away, nearly fainting when I saw my fingers coated in blood.

But it wasn't Meera's blood. She hadn't even touched me.

It was my blood. It was my nose bleeding.

A feeling of profound weakness washed over my body. My knees buckled, and I sank to the ground. The stone walls of the cave and Meera's form blurred until they faded from sight.

I jerked, my stomach tugging as if I'd traveled, yet my knees were still pressed against the cold floor beneath me. Ice flowed through my veins, until my every limb was shaking.

"Meera?" I yelled. "Meera, what happened? Where are you?" I listened desperately. But there was no response. If she'd answered, I couldn't hear her. I couldn't even see her.

Because I was no longer in the cave.

My blood ran cold, fear overwhelming me. I was definitely outside. And definitely not in Glemaria. The air was far more humid and hotter than anything I'd felt in weeks. It didn't make any sense. I'd been on my knees, but now I stood. I was in the center of an arena, twice the size of our Katurium back home. Rows and rows of white stone seats were stacked on top of each other.

A limitless black inked its way across the sky bringing on darkness and night, as a faint crescent moon appeared. The crescent waxed, making its way through an entire month's worth of phases until it stopped, full and bright. A sharp popping sound around the arena's edge burst again and again as flames flickered to life atop hundreds of torches.

I turned and saw the seats had gone from a blank white canvas to a stadium filled with thousands of Lumerians, yelling and shouting in excitement. Each person was holding a purple flag with a golden Valalumir in the center—the sigil of the Emperor. I was in Numeria, the Empire's capital, in the center of the Emperor's arena. This was the Nutavian Katurium. Home of the Blade, the Empire's warlord. And Emperor Theotis—Imperator Kormac's uncle.

Three silver doors appeared across from me. Doors I'd seen once before—the same ones used to keep Haleika trapped as a forsaken. They'd only opened when she was released, moments before she completed her transformation into akadim.

I braced myself as the doors began to unlock, my feet widening, my muscles tense. Slowly I reached for my sword, but my hand scraped across a bare hip. My sword was gone, as was my dagger and stave. Not a single blade remained, not even a scabbard.

A thunderous howl ripped through the arena, before it changed into a wolfish growl. Two more howls answered its call.

I stepped back, my hands trembling.

Three silver wolves emerged from behind the doors, all giant in size. Each wolf was at least six feet tall, their fangs dripping, their eyes red.

The audience roared with bloodlust as I stumbled back, reaching helplessly again for a weapon I did not possess. My armor was gone, even Asherah's chest plate was missing. I fell to my knees, desperately searching for anything I could defend myself with. But there was nothing, just an endless field of dirt.

The wolves began to charge, growling and gnashing their teeth. I jumped to my feet and turned, not knowing what else to do. I ran. My hands pumped at my sides, my feet practically flying.

I was almost on the other side of the arena when a violet door appeared.

I ran faster. I had to get to the door, and get inside. Get to safety. The audience clapped and cheered as the wolves gained speed. But even at my fastest, running at a pace I'd only dreamed of achieving before, I was moving too slowly. The wolves' hot breath blew against my neck.

I was nearly there when the door opened. My heart stopped, my body freezing, as terror paralyzed me.

A shadow filled the threshold, before a fully grown lion emerged.

The lion roared, its eyes on me as it gracefully rose onto its back paws, mane flowing bright and red as fire. It snarled, and huffed, assessing the arena, before it roared and charged, running straight for me.

Just as I screamed, something shining on the ground caught my eye. An old-fashioned bronze shield appeared.

It was round with a stone glowing bright, nestled within a carving of a blazing sun. My heart beat faster and faster, something warm growing inside me.

I grabbed the shield, and the lion charged forward. Bracing myself, hands tightening around the metal, I prepared for impact as the wolves howled at my back. But just as I expected to be knocked over, the lion leapt over my head, and soared above me. I turned and screamed as the lion crashed into the opened mouths of the wolves.

The entire arena seemed to still, and the shield fell at my feet. The sound of its thud echoed, ringing in my ears. And I was suddenly, terrifyingly aware that something else was happening. No one was looking at the lion or the wolves anymore. Their attention had been drawn to a sudden show of lights dancing across the arena. Indigo, and orange. The heat in my chest flared.

The lion whined, its body stretched now before me, its belly exposed. Two of the wolves held the lion's paws in their mouths, their fangs piercing its flesh. Blood oozed down their chins as they pulled in opposite directions, stretching the lion's legs further, every step tearing its body apart.

"Lyr! LYR!"

I stilled. Something screamed inside my soul. That voice …

"LYR!"

Jules!

Jules was in my head. Jules was calling my name. Screaming. Gods, her voice! I hadn't heard it in years. Even in my memories, the way she sounded, the way she spoke had begun to fade. But it was her. I'd recognize her voice at the end of the world.

I spun around, eyes searching with desperation, but no matter where I looked, I couldn't find her. There was just the lion, being ripped in half, its face full of excruciating pain, its mane so fiery and red, flowing in wild waves.

Familiar waves.

My heart stopped.

Batavia red. The lion's mane was Batavia red.

Even during its torture, it stilled with a noble calm. Its eyes met mine, holding my gaze. And I saw what I hadn't before. Its eyes were human, alert, and intelligent. And this time, I saw the recognition in them, felt the knowing, felt the awful truth wash over me.

"LYR!" Jules screamed again, the sound heartbreakingly defeated. The lion's face fell.

The third wolf leapt from behind, its mouth open, before it bit down on the lion's head.

"NO!" I screamed! "NO! JULES!"

"LYR!" Meera's voice rang through the arena.

But I couldn't answer her. I couldn't find her. I could only see the lion dying. See Jules dying. I could only hear the fear and terror in her voice, the sudden finding and losing of hope. I could feel my heart breaking because I was too late.

Because I'd failed her. Because I'd lost her.

Again.

The vision faded, the arena disappeared and I was back in the cave, gasping, shivering. Meera was crouched before me, her hazel eyes wide. I was cold. So, so cold. Every part of me was shaking and trembling.

"I ..." My chest heaved, I couldn't stay still. "I ..." My teeth chattered. The images were still fresh in my mind, swirling around painfully to the point I thought my head would explode.

"LYR!" Rhyan yelled, his voice full of worry, from across the cave. He was back from patrol.

I wanted to answer, to tell them what happened, tell them what I saw. What I learned, what I knew. I tried to stand. But I lost my balance. And then I was collapsing, my body falling.

There was a frantic yell and something warm and sturdy settled behind me. The scent of pine and musk filled my senses, cool air from an aura wrapped around my body like a blanket. For one brief second, I felt a sense of safety, of being held. But then my head fell back as I lost consciousness.

CHAPTER SIX

RHYAN

I hoisted Lyr up into my arms and ran, my heart practically beating through my chest. Within seconds, I reached our corner of the cave, Meera trailing behind.

"Can you light the fire?" I asked urgently. Lyr's skin was so cold. She felt like ice in my arms. I'd only felt her body like this once before. When an akadim had thrown her onto a frozen lake, and she'd fallen in.

Meera's stave pointed at the small flames that kept our section heated. Within seconds the fires flared, flames licking beyond the stones at its base. The cave brightened, casting dancing shadows against the walls as the air began to warm. But not enough. Not nearly enough for what she needed.

I laid Lyr down on our bed, and hastily dragged her and the blankets closer to the fire. Then I knelt beside her, removing my cloak, and wrapping it around her shoulders. I took her wrist between my fingers, checking her pulse. Normal.

I pressed my ear to her chest. Her heartbeat was fine. She was breathing. And her nose had stopped bleeding. I rolled up her sleeves, my hands sliding and searching, but there were no injuries on her arms. Wanting to make sure I didn't miss anything, I unbuckled her belt, pushing back her tunic.

No cuts or bruises on her stomach.

Meera vanished and I anxiously pushed her tunic past her breasts. The Valalumir star was glowing with a faint golden light between the bindings of her shift.

Shit.

Ever since Mercurial had tricked her into the deal, the so-called contract had been torturing her. We knew it glowed and heated when it met another Guardian for the first time, when it reunited with another reincarnation of the Gods and Goddesses who'd protected the light. It had nearly burned her from the inside out when I'd touched her bare skin that first night. Morgana, the reincarnation of Ereshya, had also caused the light to burn. Though it was Meera who had been the first one to make it happen. Four of the reincarnated Guardians' identities had been revealed in this way. And as far we knew Lyr was Asherah, I was Auriel, Morgana was Ereshya and Aemon was Moriel. We still didn't know for sure who Meera had been—which meant three Guardians were unidentified, and two more reincarnations were out there somewhere.

The burning and glowing only seemed to happen the first time a Guardian came in contact with her, that had been Mercurial's explanation. But I still didn't fully trust him, didn't trust that he'd told us everything we needed to know. Because it didn't just glow the first time she came in contact with me. The light shone from her heart again the first time we'd had sex. I thought it was because of how close we were, how intimate. That had been well over a week ago. The two other times we'd been together in that way, again that same night in the spring, and then here in this cave a few nights ago, it hadn't happened.

Pulling her tunic down, I drew my cloak and blankets back to her shoulders, anxiously pushing her hair off her forehead. She looked … Fuck. She looked like she'd had a vision. But Lyr wasn't—*couldn't* be vorakh.

Gods. Please, no. Not her.

Meera returned, a small damp towel in her hands, her face contorted with worry. She sat on the other side of the bed and gently dabbed at her sister's face, wiping away the blood. Studying her closer, I realized Meera also had a bloodied nose.

"What the hell happened?" I asked, opening my belt for sunleaves.

"I don't know," Meera said. "I was having a … a vision. And then suddenly, I wasn't. It was like—" She made a sharp noise. "Like Lyr took it from me."

I blinked. "Lyr took it from you? It looks like she just had one, too."

Meera turned over the towel, and continued to wash the blood from Lyr with the clean side.

"Not exactly. She did have a vision," Meera said, and seeing the look on my face, added, "But …" She took a deep breath, her eyes moving anxiously back and forth. "This is going to sound farther than Lethea, so you have to hear me out. It was my first thought, too. But I don't believe she has a vorakh."

But all of her sisters had one, even Jules. It made sense that Lyr would, too.

Fuck. Gods, I didn't want this for her. She had enough to deal with. She didn't need this. Everyone I knew, everyone I'd cared about who had a vorakh, had suffered so much because of it. I couldn't bear it for Lyr to suffer, too.

But then Meera's words sank in. "What do you mean? What makes you think she doesn't?"

"Because it was mine. *I* was having a vision. At least, I'd started to. This was unlike any of the others I've experienced." Meera swallowed roughly, putting the towel aside, her eyes anxiously running over Lyr. "Whenever it happens to me, whenever I'm having one—" She bit her lip, shifting her body uncomfortably.

"What? What happens?" I prodded.

Meera took a deep breath. "When I'm having a vision, I lose track of my surroundings, and all sense of time. I can't tell how long a vision lasts. Ever. To me they always feel like hours. But most of them are barely a few minutes long."

I nodded, somewhat aware of this. Lyr had spent the last few years dutifully recording every vision Meera had.

"Okay," I said slowly, absorbing her words. "So this one didn't feel like hours?"

"No," Meera said, her voice hard. "This one felt like actual seconds. I felt the cold wash over me like always. I stopped being able to see the cave, or hear Lyr's voice, all the usual symptoms. And then I was in it," she shrugged, "in an arena. The Emperor's sigil was everywhere. And then it was over. I woke up to Lyr on top of me. And then she wasn't. Some force pushed her back. I went to her, and her body was cold, her eyes," she shook her head, "she couldn't see me. *She* was having a vision. There's no doubt about it."

"So she has vorakh," I said defeated.

"No. I don't think she does. Because, I felt warm the second my vision stopped."

I frowned. "Because it ended?"

"No," Meera said. "Gods. I'm not explaining this well. See, I'm never warm after a vision ends. The way Lyr feels now? That's how I feel for hours every time it happens. It's only been minutes. My body temperature is already back to normal."

I sighed. "Maybe because your vision was so short this time?"

"No." Meera gently touched Lyr's arm, the place beneath her sleeve where she currently wore the arm cuff hiding the time logs. "It doesn't matter how brief they are. The cold remains the same. Every single time." Her eyes met mine, imploring. "Except this time."

I frowned. Her logic made sense, at least, I wanted it to, but yet, I'd never seen anything like this before. It didn't feel like we had enough information to dismiss the idea that Lyr was vorakh. "You revealed your vorakh at the Revelation Ceremony?" I asked.

"Yes. And so did Jules," she said uneasily. "And Morgs. Didn't you?"

My jaw clenched. My father had secretly removed my Birth Bind months before the official Revelation Ceremony. But the vorakh was there, ready and bursting to be expressed the moment I was free. I absolutely did not want to get into the story with Meera, but I nodded. "I was there when Lyr claimed her magic. There was no vorakh then, but—I don't know. It wasn't a regular revelation. She had some memories of being ..." I pressed my lips together, unable to finish.

My chest ached. Ever since I remembered that I was Auriel, I couldn't say "Asherah" the same way that I had for my entire life. Because it wasn't just a name anymore to me. Her name felt like *more*. Underneath all the love I had for Lyr was all the love I'd had for Asherah, the love I had for her before she was Lyriana. I could feel it now, pulsing in my heart. Layers of love, and longing, and heartbreak. Lifetimes of falling in love with her soul again and again, meeting her for the first time, and recognizing her. *Knowing* her. I didn't remember the other lives yet, but I could feel them, feel their pulse running like an undercurrent through my veins, connecting us.

My heart was nearly bursting with it all.

I cleared my throat. "The night she claimed her power, she remembered being Asherah," I said. "But it wasn't a vision. It was a memory. Still, that doesn't mean she doesn't have a vorakh."

Meera looked thoughtful. "I know plenty of Lumerians

develop vorakh after their Birth Bind is removed. But I don't think that's the case with Lyr. We'll figure out what it means."

"I know we will." I tried to suppress a growl of frustration low in my throat. "But I'll feel a lot fucking better about all of this when she opens her eyes."

"She will. She has to."

I nodded, continuing to stroke Lyr's hand.

Meera made a soft sound with her throat. "You know, she's the only one whose touch ever really worked, that ever really helped me," she said wistfully. "Every time Morgana tried to—" She looked away, her aura shaking with a sudden grief. "We always said Lyr had a healing touch. But this time, she really did. The vision didn't just stop. All my symptoms were taken away, too." She shook her head, as if in disbelief. "I've never felt like this after. It takes hours to feel even remotely recovered. Hours to feel warm again."

A healing touch?

Something began to stir in the back of my mind as her words sank in. A memory that I couldn't pinpoint, or even fully recall. I couldn't quite decipher if it was from this life or Auriel's. There were moments lately when it all felt muddled. When my time-lines felt confused.

"What if she didn't take the vision from you?" I asked slowly, my idea barely formed.

"What do you mean?"

"What if she healed you?" I started to sift through lines of the Valya my mother had made me memorize as a boy. "Can-turiel created a light so beautiful and valiant, it shone day and night. The Valalumir, he named it. Every color of the rainbow could be seen inside, brighter than anything Heaven could hide."

Meera frowned.

I continued, "It never burned those who touched, nor blinded those who stared. Such was its beauty, the sun felt less fair … it offered heat, but did not burn … restored love, and one's will …."

"It removed harm from those hurt, and restored health to the ill," Meera finished. Her eyes widened. "Lyr has part of the Vala-lumir inside her now."

I nodded, my heart pounding as my dream the other night returned. Asherah had died. Asherah had sacrificed herself, healing Auriel. Healing *me* after the final battle. "The star in her chest was glowing when I arrived. What if … what if when she touched you, she healed you of your vision?" I asked.

"By the Gods. That would be amazing, but look at her." Meera shook her head frantically. "If you're right, I don't think she's simply healing. Not in a way where she can make the pain disappear. The energy of the thing can't just vanish. Everything that ever existed still exists," she said slowly. "According to the Valya, nothing that ever will exist hasn't already been created. So, the vision and its symptoms didn't go away. They still had to be expressed, the vision still had to be seen. So to heal me, she took it on herself."

My stomach dropped. I'd been taught the same philosophies. Nothing new was ever created. Nothing ever destroyed. But the way she was healing, taking it on … I didn't fully remember all the details yet, but this was starting to feel too close to what had happened before. Asherah had taken on other's suffering, carrying power and light too big for her mortal body to sustain. Healing Auriel, absorbing his injuries and wounds into herself. And dying. I bit down on my lip, the backs of my eyes burning. Because Meera was right—according to the Valya, my tutors and the scrolls I'd studied—everything that existed would always exist.

Goddesses never die. That's what Mercurial had told her. And if we were right, then Lyr wasn't vorakh … but in this moment, she might as well have been. Because she was suffering as greatly as if she were.

Meera leaned forward, tucking the blankets around Lyr's feet, making sure she didn't lose any more body heat.

"I should have thought of that," I said.

But Meera waved me off. "You're doing a really good job, Rhyan. I see the way you take care of her. You should know, I really appreciate it."

My throat constricted. "Thanks."

She gestured to the blankets. "Lyr always did that for me. And it always helped."

I nodded, tucking her in even tighter on my side.

"She's lucky to have you looking out for her," Meera said.

I frowned, my heart heavy as I watched Lyr's chest rise and fall beneath the blankets. "I'm the lucky one."

Meera smiled in response, then her face fell as her gaze returned to her sister.

"You know, I'm glad you're here, too," I said quietly. A tentative friendship had been building between us the past week. One that came with an awareness that it was our situation bringing us together, nothing more. But the friendship was budding all the same.

Moments passed, my anxiety growing until Lyr's fingers finally twitched and moved against mine. Slowly, her eyes fluttered open. I let out the breath I was holding and squeezed her hand, leaning closer so she could see my face.

"Hey, partner," I said, my voice gruff with emotion. "You're awake."

Lyr blinked rapidly, her beautiful hazel eyes taking me in and then seeing Meera by her side. "How long was I out?"

She squeezed my hand in return, almost as if testing her own strength. She'd squeezed my hand a hundred times before. But never with this much force—this much power. It was almost painful. She didn't know her own strength yet now that her magic was restored. It didn't matter. She could squeeze my hand as hard as she wanted. She could fucking break it for all I cared.

I was glad to feel it. It meant she was okay. It meant she was stronger than what had just happened.

"Not long. Just a few minutes," Meera said, her voice shaking. "Lyr? Are you okay?"

"I think so," Lyr said, her voice shaky. "I think I …" Her cheeks reddened.

"Had a vision?" Meera offered.

She looked away, her lips pressed together. Her panic was rising, her fear of being vorakh. "Yes. Does this mean—by the Gods, am I—"

"No," I said quickly, wanting to reassure her. "At least, we don't think you're vorakh. We've been putting the pieces together while you rested. Meera thinks you took on her vision."

Lyr started to sit up. Quickly I moved my hand to support her lower back, and could feel her shivering.

"Still cold?" I asked.

"Freezing."

"Sit with me," I said, shifting closer to the fire and pulling her onto my lap. I drew my cloak around the two of us. Lyr needed more body heat, but I didn't get the impression that stripping in front of Meera was going to go over well. Settling her between my legs, I whispered in her ear, "Hold the cloak closed in front of you." She did and I used the opportunity to slide my hands inside her shirt, wrapping my arms around her, giving her as much skin-to-skin as I could. She melted against me, sighing under her breath.

"That's better," she said. "Now tell me how exactly I took Meera's vision."

"Well to start," Meera said, "we're not even sure it was you. We think it was the light of the Valalumir inside you. It has the power to heal."

Lyr stiffened against me. "And you think that healed you?"

"Not completely. Just this once, but yes, I think so. Rhyan does, too. Our best guess is that the healing properties of the light allowed you to take it onto yourself. After you touched me, my vision stopped instantly, and I was warm. I'm never warm after. You know that."

"True," Lyr said slowly. "And I'm still cold. But not from you. I know how that feels." She shivered. "Or I thought I did. Gods. Meera, I'd felt your cold before, but it was never this intense. Is this always how it felt for you?" Her voice shook.

Meera smiled gravely.

I wondered how cold Lyr had been in the past few years by simply being near Meera, and felt rage boiling inside me. For so long she'd had to deal with this alone. I'd seen firsthand the wounds she'd had to dress by herself. I didn't realize there was another layer of suffering to what she'd endured.

"It's okay," Meera said. "I know what to expect each time. At least, usually I do."

"But the light was in me the last time you had a vision," Lyr said. "And I didn't heal you then, or take your vision on."

"The light was there," I said, "but your magic wasn't. Maybe that activated it."

"Maybe. Okay," Lyr said. I could see her mind beginning to accept our words, to rationalize and find the logic behind it as she always did. "Let's say that's the explanation." She shifted in my lap. "How do we know it was *your* vision that I had? And not my own?"

"Well, was this what you saw?" Meera asked. "An arena filled with the Emperor's sigil?"

Lyr nodded. "Yes." Her voice was quiet. Too quiet.

"What happened, Lyr?" I asked. "What else did you see?"

She took a deep breath, thinking for a moment before she said, "I was in the Nutavian Katurium. In the capital. There were three wolves in the arena chasing me."

I tensed, my blood boiling. "Ka Kormac?" I growled, completely unable to hide my fury.

"No. Actual wolves." Lyr stilled, her hand on my arm

suddenly tightening. "But ... Gods." She moved again, agitated. "Your visions are always symbolic, Meera? Right? I think that's who they were. The three wolves. The Bastardmaker, the Imperator ... and the Emperor."

Meera looked worried. "What else happened, Lyr?"

"I thought they were going to kill me. I had no weapons, just an old shield I found." She paused. "It came out of nowhere. It was ancient-looking, round and bronze. Just there on the field."

Something stirred inside me. A memory. I felt the ghost of a shield in my hands. Large, heavy. And just as quickly as it appeared, the thought was gone.

"So, I ran, and then ..." Her shoulders shook and I tightened my hug, pulling her even closer to me. "A lion entered the arena. It went after the wolves, trying to attack. But they caught it." She trembled. "They ... they tore the lion apart."

I ran my hands up and down her sides. Her aura was pulsating now with distress and grief.

"A lion?" I asked. "If the wolves were Ka Kormac, then, who does the lion represent? Do you know any Kavim with lions on their sigils?"

"No," Lyr said. "The lion didn't represent a Ka."

"Then what?" I asked.

"Not what. Who." Lyr shuddered. "I recognized the lion's eyes." She looked at Meera. And then, with a small, shaking voice, asked, "Do you remember her hair? I used to call it her lion's mane when we were little. In my vision, it was red. Batavia red. Remember the way she'd been lit up by the eternal flame in Auriel's Chamber? Remember how she looked? Just before? The lion had her hair at that moment. And I heard her voice in my head, for the first time in two years."

Meera's eyes searched hers, rapidly jumping back and forth before she cried out.

"By the Gods," I said, the puzzle clicking into place for me, too.

"The lion was Jules." Lyr's voice broke. "She's at the capital. I know it beyond a doubt. And she's being torn apart."

We'd suspected as much after Morgana revealed that Lumerians arrested for vorakh were taken and then enslaved there. The Emperor and Lumeria's most elite nobility were siphoning off their power, using it for their own benefit. We'd guessed she was being kept in the capital, close to the Emperor. But this felt like the confirmation we'd needed to make our next move.

"There's something else," Lyr said. "There were two lights that scared everyone in the audience. One was indigo. The other orange."

"Moriel and Ereshya," I said. Aemon and Morgana. Well, that was just fucking perfect.

Lyr nodded. "They're going after Jules, too."

CHAPTER SEVEN

RHYAN

Meera's face hardened, her eyes on Lyr, a dare in her expression as if she expected a fight. "If Jules is in the capital, then that's where we're going. All of us," Meera said pointedly.

Her gaze flicked to me, daring me to object.

Most of my interactions with Bamaria's former Heir Apparent had been in the last year, when she was weakened from visions. But I could see the flare of who she'd been before. The Meera who might have become Arkasva and High Lady.

Lyr's own aura still felt faint, but a sudden burst of heat rose off her skin as if in response.

"Yes. We're all going," Lyr said, and turned in my lap, her gaze intense. "Now we know for sure she's there. We're going to get her back."

"We will, I swear," I promised. "And if Aemon's headed there, too, maybe we'll take Moriel down as well." There was a violent edge to my words I couldn't hide. Ever since I'd seen that bastard whip Lyr, I'd barely been able to stomach looking at him. And now that I knew the truth, knew he was evil, my hatred for him had grown.

"We need a plan. We should leave Glemaria tomorrow. First thing," Lyr said. "We need to forge a path south to the capital. Then we'll find a way in."

My throat tightened, but as Lyr leaned forward, trying to stand, I let her go, my arms falling to my sides. She was steadier on her feet than I'd expected, but as I reached for her hand, the cold still clung to her skin.

"Lyr, wait," I said. "We can't just leave Glemaria."

Her hazel eyes flared with anger, the golden flecks molten. "What do you mean? That's what we've been discussing for days. We have to. It's been almost two and a half years. And every second we wait, is another second she's tortured."

I'd seen the determination and fire in Lyr's eyes, the moment the shock wore off, she'd become obsessed. Nothing was going to stop her from rescuing her cousin. Nothing was going to stop me from doing the same. I'd do anything for Lyriana. I'd crawl through the fires of hell for her. But this was more than that. Jules was my friend, too. I cared for her, too. She'd been there for me at a time when I'd had no one. I also needed to get her out of there. Needed to protect her.

And I fucking would.

But, not at the cost of Lyr's life. And if I knew Jules, she wouldn't want that either. She'd been just as protective of Lyriana as I was.

I squeezed her hand, still careful to keep my aura pulled back. "Partner," I said softly. "I'd go get her this second if I could. I'd travel into the Palace, jump into every room until I found her, kill everyone who'd laid a hand on her." My voice rose with the truth of my words, my rage boiling under the surface of my skin. "But it's not going to be that simple. There's going to be far more than the wards of the Palace and the Emperor's soturi guarding her. Especially now. I need to tell you both something I heard this morning. I think it's related to your vision."

Lyr's eyes widened, a quick glance to Meera before turning back to me.

I rose to my feet. "The Emperor's trying to do damage control right now. With …" I coughed, hating bringing this up. "With Brockton's death, and the fact that you're both missing, as well as Morgana, and … well, me … people are talking. Public perception is that Imperator Kormac doesn't have control over the South. Between the Imperator's failings, all the akadim attacks, and the unsecured transfers of power, rumors are spreading, and political protests are breaking out. Rioting, even. And it's becoming increasingly known that Aemon hasn't made contact with Lumeria in days. It makes the Emperor look like he picked the wrong man to lead. From what I understand, my father's at the helm of making sure these stories spread. If I know him, he's encouraging, if not outright funding, some of the riots. He thrives on civil unrest, especially if he can blame the violence on a rival. The Emperor plans to distract everyone while Imperator Kormac cleans up the mess," I said.

"While he tries to find us you mean," Lyr said, her eyes meeting mine. "Tries to find me."

"That, too." My fingers flexed violently at the thought. At the idea of Imperator Kormac getting his hands on her. On actually marrying her to that gryphon-shit ass of a son he'd spawned.

Over my dead body.

I nodded wearily. "In a month, at the end of winter, the Emperor will be hosting a Valabellum for Asherah's Feast Day."

Meera squinted. "What? A Valabellum? But those are … they're—"

"Barbaric?" I offered. "Old-fashioned?" I laughed, the sound grim. "My father did something similar after an akadim attack here. It proved to be quite a distraction." And a tragedy. It was the event that made me forsworn. I could feel my blood heating at just the thought of that day.

"Your father held a Valabellum?" Lyr asked.

My throat tightened, as I threaded my fingers through hers. She still didn't know the whole story. "Something else. An Alissedari. The fight takes place on gryphon-back. To end it, only one person has to die." I bit back a sudden burst of nausea. Memories of that day felt more visceral than they had in the year since it happened. They'd plagued me ever since we'd crossed the Glemarian border. That day was threaded into the scent of pine in the air, in the cold breezes I felt, and every time a gryphon roared. I squeezed Lyr's hand, remembering that what we were about to face was somehow worse. "An Alissedari *is* tame in comparison. I never thought I'd think of that event as merciful."

I felt suddenly wholly naked and vulnerable in a way that I hadn't been before with Lyr. Like she could see what had happened to me. And even worse, see the horrible things I'd done. See all the ways I failed. I had to tell her everything. She deserved to know. But I was still afraid this would be what made her see me differently.

"Are you sure?" she asked carefully. "The Emperor's really hosting a full Valabellum?"

"Yes. It was all anyone was discussing today, everywhere I patrolled. They're already recruiting soturi for the fights, and casting the roles."

"Casting?" Lyr asked in disgust. "Lumerians are auditioning for this?"

I nodded grimly.

The Valabellum was a reenactment of the War of Light, simultaneously a proper soturion fight, and a theatrical play. Dozens of battles would be staged throughout the arena. But unlike a habibellum, which was merely practice, this was a fight to the death. In the final event, seven soturi took on the roles of the seven Guardians. Asherah, Auriel, Cassarya, Hava, Ereshya,

Shiviel, and Moriel. Anyone could die in the lead up, and many would. Each fight represented one of the battles told in the Valya where endless numbers of Lumerians perished. There were no rules in the fight, no limits and many risked death by nightfall. But there was one death above all that was guaranteed.

In the final fight, whoever played Moriel was expected to die. Historically, it had been considered an honorable role to play. A worthy sacrifice.

It was a call back to the earliest days in Lumeria Matavia–when the Gods could still come down to earth at will. Dying wasn't a big deal back then, bodies could be shed and then regrown at will. Killing would have been a spectacle, brutal, and shocking. But ultimately meaningless, because the dead would reappear in a new body the next day. At least, for a while that was what happened. After enough time had passed, around the time the Valalumir had been created, the deaths began to stick. And those who'd planned to return to Heaven were stuck, living until old age in their mortal forms. Those who'd died, remained dead, their souls lost until they were reborn as another—with no memories of their past life. When Asherah and Auriel were banished, most Lumerians were already trapped.

"Those who are meant to die in the arena will no doubt be assigned carefully," I said. "I would expect the Emperor and his elites to have picked out their sacrifices before even announcing the games." The role of Moriel would be given as punishment. Some Arkasva would pay a lot of money to see their chosen enemy killed in such a way.

Lyr's face fell. "That means Lumerians from all over the Empire will be traveling to Numeria. Including the Imperators."

"There's going to be an increased presence of soturi every-where," I said, "and far too many of them know our faces. It's not just going to make it harder for us to get to the Palace, but nearly impossible to get inside," I said. "And even if I find Jules …"

Lyr swallowed roughly. "You'll have to get her out yourself."

I frowned, nodding. I couldn't jump holding two people at once, much as I'd tried.

"Even so, we need to get closer. We need to learn the grounds as soon as possible," Lyr said. "Inside and out. We have to know the schedule of everyone who works and lives there. We're going to need to get access somehow to the blueprints of the Palace, too. Find out exactly where they're keeping Jules."

Meera shook her head. "Blueprints like that aren't going to be available to the public."

"They're not," Lyr said. "But some were stored in the preservation rooms in the Great Library."

"Bamaria's out of the question," I said. "But, the Library of Glemaria has copies. I know where they're kept. They might not be up-to-date, or reveal every secret. But it's a start."

"Let's go then," Lyr said, her voice almost hopeful. "Can you bring me there? Now?"

"We can't," I said. "Not right now. Lyr, you're still not recovered from the healing you've done. You're freezing. I'm not taking you anywhere until your body temperature returns to normal. And I'm certainly not letting you out of this cave until you've rested. Now lie down."

She scoffed. "Are you serious right now? I can't do that. I won't. Now that I know for sure where she is? That I know we only have a month?" Her voice rose. "Morgana and Aemon are going to be there. And if we're not faster than them, we might never get her back."

Just like Asherah.

The thought came unbidden. A sudden memory unlocked. My Goddess was fiery and headstrong, protective to a fault. And she was quick to sacrifice herself for the ones she loved. For me. For Auriel.

Fuck. Hadn't that been all that Lyr had done the last two years? Hiding her cuts and bruises as she took care of Meera alone, as she healed her and protected her, vision after vision. Then she'd taken care of Morgana, too. Had barely slept those first few weeks of training while she was trying to be everything to everyone.

That same exact personality trait that had cost Auriel his soulmate.

The sorrow and grief I'd remembered in my vision and in my dream was now pulsing through me. The loss was ancient, but it suddenly felt too fresh and near. I could feel the loss of Asherah, and right at that moment, it felt as if I was losing Lyr. It was like a warning. One I would heed. I would never let anything happen to her again.

"We are going to rescue Jules," I said urgently. Lyr hugged her arms around herself, her face full of anguish, her eyes refusing to meet mine. "Lyr. Hey! Look at me. Look. Partner, look at me. We are!"

She looked but shook her head. "Really? Partner?" she spat.

"Yes. *Me sha, me ka*, Lyriana.*" I pressed my fist to my heart, tapping it twice before I flattened my palm against my chest. "We will. But we're never going to get her back if we don't do this right." My voice was harder than I'd meant.

Lyr's nostrils flared. "And who says you're the one to decide which way is right? That you're in charge? Because you were named my apprentice? But you forget, I have my magic now. I'm stronger than I ever was before. I can fight. You know I can."

"Not this second you can't!" I hissed.

"For just going to the library?" she yelled. "Gods, Rhyan." Her aura snapped with annoyance. "You're not actually in charge here." Her voice lowered. "I'm not in your bed right now."

"Godsdamnit, Lyr! I'm still your apprentice!"

"But not my Arkturion!" she spat. "I never signed up to be part of your legion!"

"That's not what I—fuck." I took a step back, trying to calm my racing heart before I said something to make it worse. "Lyr, listen to me. Please. We're not *just* going to a library. This isn't Bamaria, and we're no longer Heirs. Soturi from both ends of the Empire are hunting us. We have to be ready for anything, ready to fight. Get in, find what we need, and get out. This isn't a library visit. It's a battle. And anything can go wrong."

"Lyr, Rhyan's right," Meera said softly.

There was a dangerous flash in Lyriana's eyes as she looked at her sister. Something silent passed between them.

"Lyr?" I asked.

Her aura darkened, her face twisting, moving from anger to something that looked very much like heartbreak. "You didn't see what I saw," she said quietly. "The lion ... Jules ... the terror in its eyes, her voice ... " Her eyes watered. "We can't leave her like that."

She was closing in on herself. I knew that look. She was close to a panic attack. Forgetting to breathe.

"Lyr." I stepped into her space, and pulled her into my arms, rubbing my hands up and down her back, breathing slowly for her. It was a good sign that she let me, that she didn't pull away. Those were her worst times—when she wouldn't even let me help. When I had to coax her into receiving even basic comfort. She was so angry with me just now, I wasn't sure she'd let me. But thank the Gods, she did. I kissed the top of her head. "I swear on my life, we are going to get her back. All right? You trust me, don't you?"

She exhaled sharply, then her arms tightened around me and she nodded, burying her face in my chest. "I do."

"I trust you, too. We will succeed. But with a plan. The stakes are too high. If we're entering the capital, there can be no mistakes. We're not going to get a second chance. Neither is Jules. For her sake, we need to do this right."

Her arms tightened around me in response.

And I took a deep breath. "We do have to leave this cave before tonight though," I said. "My father's men will reach these cliffs by sunset, and I'd rather not test the wards against the number of soldiers I counted."

"Where are we going?" Meera asked.

"There's another cave I know. It's at the base of a cluster of mountains, outside the eastern villages. And it's close to the library. I scouted the landscape this morning and it was empty. It's farther east, which is good—the soturi I scouted are coming from the west. Once we're there, we'll be able to reach the border fairly quickly when we need to leave."

Which meant I'd have less far to jump. Something I needed to be mindful of with every move we made. Traveling now meant covering the distance three times. Once carrying Meera, once returning back for Lyr, and then a third trip, carrying her with me. It was starting to wear me down, far more than I wanted to admit.

"*After* we travel tonight, and I rest, we go to the library," Lyr said.

I offered a small smile. "As long as the coast is clear, we'll go. We'll look for the blueprints and anything else that might help."

"Thank you," Meera said. "I saw you brought some vegetables back. I'm going to make some stew for everyone to eat before we leave. And Lyr," Her eyes lingered on her sister, "Rest." Meera's expression hardened, before she turned and left us alone.

"How soon can we go?" Lyr asked, her eyes searching mine.

I slid my hand up through the back of her tunic, to the nape of her neck. Still cold. My fingers pushed into her pressure points, squeezing and kneading the tensed muscles.

"We're not going," I said firmly. "Not unless you actually rest."

She shook out of my hold. "Gods, Rhyan! You don't get to decide that. We're on equal ground here. Partners, remember? This isn't the fucking chain of command!"

"Lyr," I growled. Gods, we'd just gone over this. "Auriel's fucking bane." I froze. My chest tightened. It felt strange to say that now.

Lyr paled. "I am actually, aren't I?" She gave a shaky laugh, a nervous, profoundly sad smile spreading across her face.

"No. No. That's not what I meant. We *are* partners. And you're strong as hell. It's not about that. Okay? I just … please rest. With me. Do it for me. Because …" I swallowed, still finding it difficult to admit weakness, even in front of her. "Because I need it."

Her eyes searched mine, and I watched as she examined my face, frowning. Finally, she nodded in agreement.

Maybe I looked worse than I realized. It didn't matter. She'd agreed. I could practically sigh in relief now that she was safe in my arms again. Seeing her face covered in blood had distracted me from my own exhaustion. But now that everything had slowed down, I could feel just how affected I was, feel it down to my bones. I desperately needed to close my eyes. And I wanted Lyr's body wrapped around mine when I did, even if we were fighting.

I reached behind her knees, and scooped her into my arms, walking us both back to our bed. Laying her down, I carefully pulled the stack of blankets away from the fire.

Then I crawled in behind her, gathering my cloak over us. My arms wrapped over and under her, holding her against me, our legs tangled together.

Her breath began to slow, her shoulders delicately rising and falling. I reached beneath her shirt again, splaying my hand across her belly, reveling in how soft her skin was. In how she was finally starting to warm. She made a soft noise of satisfaction and snuggled closer against me. "I hate fighting with you," she murmured.

"I hate it, too," I whispered. "I'm sorry."

"Me, too."

My heart pounded, as I dared to ask the other question in my mind. "Lyr? Will you promise me something?"

"What?" She snuck her hand over mine, holding it beneath her top.

"With this new ability to heal ..." I trailed off, my eyes burning as it all hit me at once. What she could do now was amazing. Miraculous. And yet, nothing could be more dangerous for someone like her, someone who cared so much for the ones she loved. Someone who wouldn't hesitate to give her life for another. Someone who had died in a past life doing just that.

It scared me so fucking much. Both times she'd called on her kashonim with Asherah, it had drained her. And this? This was a direct connection to the Valalumir, a celestial force not even capable of withstanding the earthly plane. The Valalumir was the most powerful light in existence, but here, it was in crystal form, and broken into pieces, with one exception. The one slice of the Red Ray, burning inside Lyr, inside her incredibly mortal body.

Gods, I wanted to reach inside of her, toss out that damned contract, hug her to me and never let go. I wanted to keep her safe. Keep her warm. Forever. But I had to settle for this. Just holding her to me. And asking. Begging.

"Rhyan?" she said, her voice was heavy, already coated with oncoming sleep.

"Promise me something," I said. "Promise you'll be careful. That you won't overextend yourself with the healing. Use it sparingly. Only if you absolutely must. That's all. That's all I wanted to ask."

She didn't answer.

"Partner?" I said.

But she'd already fallen asleep, her breathing slowing, deep, and even. I leaned forward, suddenly aware that my own energy felt restored. My eyes had been drooping, but now I was all at once, completely wide awake. Like my tiredness had been taken. Like I'd been healed.

A small golden glow emanated from beneath her tunic.

Shit. My stomach turned, guilt and worry warring inside of me.

I laid my head down, and listened to her breathe, my heart pounding as I watched the fires burn.

CHAPTER EIGHT

TRISTAN

The snow had melted in Bamaria, but I was still cold. It was a week after the *situation*, but the chill I'd felt that night still clung to my bones. No matter how many fires I set, how much alcohol burned through my belly, I felt it. Felt the memory, felt haunted by the images I couldn't stop seeing in my mind.

"I'll still get you."

I blinked rapidly, reminding myself that it wasn't real. That it was over. That I had a duty to perform. A show to star in. I stood at that moment in the center of the Katurium, my silver belt shining in the late morning sun. The stadium was full of Lumerians, clapping and cheering as Naria gripped my hand. We'd walked out together, beaming. And now that we were standing here, our bodies stilled, the crowd was growing restless. I supposed after two years of openly courting Lyr, I now had to prove that that part of my life was truly over. Even after weeks of seeing us together, and all the political upheavals we'd endured, it was still my job to entertain them as I once had. To entertain them more.

I swore, if there were awards for performances like this—I'd be winning all of them.

But the yells from the crowd only grew louder, blatant with their dissatisfaction.

"We should kiss," Naria said. "They're calling for it."

It took all I had not to roll my eyes. But, as always, I did what I was supposed to do. I played my role, pulled her in close, one hand snaking down her ass, the other cupping her chin as I kissed her. Softly at first, a show of sweet affection. And then I deepened it, just the way I knew the crowd liked it. All at once, the cheers exploded, and I tried to imagine what this moment would feel like if I actually loved her. If any part of me gave a shit.

If I was kissing Lyr …

A set of doors opened. My chest seized with a sudden flare of panic. They were the same ones Haleika had been brought through, before she changed. Before she faced Lyr … We hadn't been allowed to see her, to say goodbye. She'd been kept in isolation. Then they put her in a box. A fucking box. That was how I'd last seen her alive. And every time I thought about it, thought of her lying in a coffin, alone and scared, her lover dead, knowing she was turning, and doomed, while passing through those very fucking doors … I wanted to throw up.

Naria squeezed my hand. "What's your problem?" she asked.

I took a deep breath, willing my mind to clear and blinked until my eyes dried. "Nothing. Just tired."

"Well, look a little calmer. Or people will talk."

"Maybe people wouldn't talk," I seethed, "If you'd given them less to talk about."

"It's not my fault your last girlfriend was frigi—"

I tossed her hand away. "She wasn't frigid! And she's your Godsdamned cousin."

"So?"

"So have some respect. For her, and for me. You might not

know this, but there's more to a relationship than fucking! She meant something to me. She still does." More than you do, I wanted to say, but I bit my tongue.

"You can be such a dick sometimes." Her eyes narrowed, her aura flaring with annoyance. She grabbed my hand again, playing off the moment like we were teasing each other. Smiling widely, she carefully stroked the golden diadem resting on her forehead.

The herald's voice rang out, announcing the entrance of Arkasva Arianna Batavia, High Lady of Bamaria. Cheers rang out from the stadium, but beside me, I felt Naria's mood change. The annoyance in her aura was replaced by fear as her mother's litter was carried across the field. She shrunk against me, her grip on my hand suddenly tight. Being in her mother's presence was the only time I ever saw her meek.

I hadn't noticed it before Arianna became Arkasva, but the change had been sudden, and there was no denying it. Arianna terrified her daughter. I didn't know why.

Maybe Bamaria would be great under this new regime. Who could say? What I did know was that ever since Arianna had taken her Seat, I'd felt uncomfortable in her presence. I couldn't pinpoint why. But seeing Naria's growing unease only made me think that something was strange about our new High Lady.

The cheers grew louder. Only a handful of soturi wearing the armor of Ka Batavia remained somber. Their gazes flicked to the ground of the arena, to the very place where Harren Batavia had fallen. My throat tightened—I hadn't let myself dwell on that memory either. Though surely others had to be thinking about it, too. I didn't believe Arianna would dare have a public appearance here so soon, nor would she dare to associate herself with those events. Not when those accused of murdering Harren Batavia had been her supporters. But the Katurium was the only place appropriate to host Valabellum trials. So here we were.

Arianna's golden litter, floating atop six mages, came to a

stop in the center of the arena. The mages stepped back, their staves pointed as the carriage lowered, and Arianna stepped out. We bent our knees, engaging in elaborate bows and curtseys.

"Welcome citizens of Bamaria! Welcome to our Valabellum trials. Rise."

As the applause died down, she came to stand between me and Naria, her aura pulsing. She took our hands and lifted them up, as if we were victors in a battle.

"I am so pleased to announce that my daughter, your Heir Apparent, and Lord Tristan Grey, the great vorakh hunter, shall be married the week after the Empire's great event." More applause followed. More cheering.

I shivered. I wasn't ready. Not to be bound to Naria. Not to be bound to anyone.

Especially not with my new ... secret. If that's even what it was. I was still trying to convince myself I'd imagined the vision, that it had been a fluke. That I hadn't become the thing that I hated, the thing that I hunted.

"What's with your face?" Naria asked.

"Nothing," I sneered, looking over at Arianna.

Arianna clapped. "The trials shall begin shortly. But first, I must bring you news." She paused dramatically. "As you know, several weeks ago, akadim entered our land, and stole Lady Meera Batavia and Lady Morgana. That night, Lady Lyriana was moved to a secure location, but vanished soon after. We now have reason to believe she was abducted by Soturion Rhyan Hart. He must be brought to justice for his reckless actions. A reward is being offered for the safe and speedy return of all three of my nieces. And a reward has been set for the capture of the once forsworn soturion. Let it be known, henceforth, Soturion Rhyan Hart has lost his political immunity in the South. Today, I strip him of his soturion title. I name him forsworn."

The sudden bout of angry shouting made me wish I'd taken Bellamy's offer of a sound-canceling spell. The hatred and prejudice against those named forsworn ran deep. I guess it didn't matter that he'd killed two akadim, that he'd protected everyone here from a greater tragedy. Fuck. I hated the guy—but even I could see the good he'd done.

I swallowed.

Would they turn on me as quickly if they knew? If my vorakh was exposed, would it even matter how many of the others I'd captured, how many I'd taken off the streets?

I'll still get you.

Arianna continued, "Before this terrible turn of events, we were to announce another most happy event—the engagement of Lady Lyriana to the Heir Apparent of Korteria, the son of our great Imperator, the grand-nephew of the Emperor. Lord Viktor Kormac." The crowd cheered at this, shouting out traditional wedding congratulations.

"I believe in my heart," Arianna continued, "my nieces are alive. And they will be found. Then we shall celebrate not one, but two weddings."

Naria groaned. "She might not even be alive, and still, she's taking attention from my celebration." She tugged me toward her, whispering in my ear, "With two weddings, you better remember you're marrying me, and not her."

"Trust me, Naria," I said, kissing her cheek. "You'll never be confused for her."

Her eyes twitched, unable to tell if I'd just offered an insult.

"As you all know," Arianna's voice rang out, "our great Arkturion Aemon Melvik, the Ready, has been tirelessly searching the Empire for my nieces."

This led to the audience screaming, "The Ready!" for a whole minute.

"But in his absence, we are without an Arkturion to defend us from the increasing threats. Though his silence has been concerning, I will not replace the Ready," Arianna said, her voice hardened. "For he is irreplaceable. I pray for his swift return. But until that day comes, we must be safe. It is my duty to protect you. Therefore, I have selected a new warlord."

The doors opened again. Arkturion Waryn Kormac appeared, his bulky body covered in his red cloak, the lifeless hide of a wolf strapped to his back. He marched forward, causing the wolf's head to bounce grotesquely with each step.

The Bastardmaker.

This time, the audience remained quiet, until a string of boos and curses rang out.

Without warning, soturi adorned in silver rose through the stands, rushing toward groups of protestors. Yells turned to screams of horror as anyone vocalizing their disdain of the Bastardmaker was grabbed and dragged through the aisles. One by one they fell, the wolves punching and kicking the objectors into submission.

I averted my eyes, unable to watch the violence. What was happening? Since when did they take people away just for expressing disagreement?

Bellamy and Eric both closed ranks, a dome of protection suddenly forming around me and Naria. But it was unnecessary, as Arianna revealed two dozen soturi standing in the shadows.

"Our continued partnership with Ka Kormac, and Korteria, is crucial to keeping us all safe," Arianna said.

I barely hid my scoff.

Partnership? Or occupation?

For years the soturi of Ka Kormac had been increasing in number in our streets, fully armed. No soturi were allowed to be armed outside their country. Except for the soturi of Ka Kormac in Bamaria. We had always been the exception.

Lyr had always been upset about this, and while I'd shared her concerns, I'd thought the numbers were bound to decrease again. But now? We were under the Bastardmaker's rule. Policed by a foreign Arkturion. Until the Ready returned—assuming that Arianna allowed it. After all, he was the one who originally prevented her from becoming High Lady—the Ready was the one who stopped the Emartis' first rebellion, and killed its leader, Tarek. He was the one who'd killed Arianna's husband. Naria's father.

I suddenly wanted nothing more than to leave the Katurium.

The Bastardmaker bowed before Arianna and kissed her hand, then hugged and congratulated me and Naria on our engagement. Again.

Once close enough, he pulled me aside. And all I could remember was that this man hadn't been so careful when he'd dragged Lyr from the temple the night of her Revelation. Seeing his rough hands on her … I'd wanted to punch him ever since.

"Lord Tristan," he grunted. "I have a message for you. From my brother." The Imperator.

"Of course," I said.

"He wants to remind you of his request. He says bring the forsworn bastard to him." His eyes flashed with malice. "Or else."

"Or else?" I asked.

He snorted. "Just do it. Don't wait for the Valabellum. A letter has been sent to your grandmother. You will head for the capital tomorrow to begin your hunt. Find the forsworn, and bring him to the Imperator."

"And Lady Lyriana?" I asked.

He grinned. "You'll bring her to her wedding bed."

My throat tightened as I swallowed back bile. "As he commands."

"Good."

"I am sorry for your loss, by the way," I said, unable to let it go. His son had died … or *sons* if the rumors were true. And he should be grieving, should be sad. He should feel fucking something. Like I did.

I stared, waiting. I needed to see some emotion in him, see that these men I'd followed my whole life were human. I needed to know that I'd been right to ally with them all these years. That I didn't have to worry about Bamaria, or Lyr. I needed some proof that these soturi, who had complete power over us—whose power I had helped increase, whose power my grandmother funded, had been for something good. I needed to know that I hadn't sold out my country.

"Brockton was a very strong warrior," I said. *"Bar Ka Mokan."*

The Bastardmaker squeezed my shoulder, painfully tight. Bruising. Tears pricked my eyes.

"Bring the forsworn, and Lady Lyriana," was his only reply. Then he shoved me back. I stumbled, caught only at the last second by Bellamy.

Another shout of protest in the audience was smothered, and two mages were dragged away.

"Oh," the Bastardmaker said as calm as ever, "If you find anymore vorakh out there," he eyed me up and down, and sweat beaded on the nape of my neck, "you know what to do."

"Of course."

His eyes pierced through me, and I felt faint. Did he know? Could he see it on me? Smell it? Was there some remnant of cold that clung to my aura? He looked away, and I almost sighed in relief, until his gaze fell on Naria. On *all* of Naria.

My hands fisted. But a moment later we were led off the field, to take our seats in the stadium. A set of doors opened to a hall lined with the contestants fighting in the trials.

I kept my head held high, never having interacted with many soturi before.

But then a familiar voice shouted, "Tristan! Hey!"

I froze, finding Galen dressed in his golden uniform, his sword shining and sharp.

Stepping back from my entourage, I grabbed his arm.

"The fuck, Galen. You didn't tell me you were doing this."

"I just decided."

"Well un-decide," I hissed. "If you're cast into the Valabellum, they could kill you."

His jaw was set. "I know the risk."

"Then stop this. Sit with us instead. I can have an escort bring you to our seats."

He shook his head, "I'm going to win," he said. "I know I can." He cracked his knuckles. "I intend to see inside the capital. To fight in the Valabellum. And I intend to look the Emperor in the eye." To seek revenge for Haleika.

"It won't change what happened," I said. "It won't bring her back."

"I don't intend for that." His eyes turned to slits, looking out in the arena, the sun casting a glow on his muscles, his aura pulsing with anger and vengeance.

He was going to win. I could feel it in my bones.

And it was going to get him killed.

CHAPTER NINE

LYRIANA

As the sun dipped below the trees on the horizon, we packed up our meager belongings, as well as the additional supplies Rhyan had gathered over the last few days. The sky was a burnt orange giving way into winter's looming darkness.

After I'd woken from a rather long and deep nap, we'd all decided that Rhyan would take Meera first to our new location. We were simply waiting for the exact moment to go. Once he had Meera settled, and took some time to restore his energy, he'd return for me. Not the best plan in the world, but the only one we had. Neither of us liked being separated, but we knew that if the soturi did find me, I had a far better chance of fighting them off on my own than Meera did.

I stood outside the cave with her as we waited for Rhyan to complete his final sweep inside. Meera was dressed like a soturion now. With her hood up, she blended perfectly with the pine trees. It was the first time we'd been alone since our fight.

We stared at each other, not speaking.

Finally, I said, "I'm sorry about earlier."

She looked away. "You should be."

"Meer."

She took my hand, wind blowing through her braid. "You're wrong about me."

"I know! That's what I'm trying to say. I'm trying to make up with you."

Huffing out a breath, she looked back at me. "I hear you. I just ... don't believe you."

I squeezed her hand back. "You're not weak, Meera. You know I know that. You've shown your strength and your resilience in ways I've never had to. You would have ..." The backs of my eyes burned as I considered that this future had been taken from her, taken from all of us. "You would have been a great High Lady and Arkasva."

A sad smile crossed her face, obvious doubt shadowing her eyes. "Thank you."

"I just ... I got used to protecting you."

"And I need to protect you, too. If you'll let me."

"You do," I said, my voice shaking. And I could feel it then. Something had broken between us a long time ago. I wasn't even sure when. And it wasn't fixed, not by this fight, not by this conversation. But this felt like a start. Meera was becoming more determined, like the Meera who should have been wearing the laurel. Maybe when we unlocked her memories, figured out which Guardian she was, she'd become even more powerful than she was now.

Her eyes scanned the horizon, tracking the wind moving against the pine trees surrounding our clearing. "I hate leaving you. Promise you'll be careful," she said.

"I promise. It's only for a little bit. I'll be fine. I know how to fight."

Rhyan stepped outside then, all of his belongings in a bag strapped across his shoulders. His soturion belt held his dagger and two swords. A third sword was strapped to his back. He pulled up the hood of his soturion cloak, the scar across his left eye darkening. "Are you ready to go?" he asked Meera.

"Ready." She hugged me tighter, and then stepped back.

Coming to my side, Rhyan took my hand, his eyes roving over me with studious precision. I wore my soturion cloak with my hood up, and my armor hidden beneath. We'd both begun wearing our armor beneath our cloaks since we'd left Bamaria to further conceal our identities. My belt held my dagger, sword, several small knives, and now also my stave.

"Partner." He took my chin in his hand, tilting my face up to kiss him as his hand ran down my side, past my hip. His fingers grazed across my weapons, reverently touching the hilts, before running down the leather scabbard that held my stave. "I'll be back for you as soon as I can. I'm not expecting trouble. But don't hesitate with these. If you need to defend yourself—strike first, think later."

The muscles in Rhyan's jaw worked as he reached for my hip, fingers digging into my flesh, like he needed one more touch. His chest rose and fell as he squeezed, like he couldn't bear to let go. His gaze held mine, his breath deepening. Then he released me.

"And stay with him." Rhyan walked over to the beast, offering a stroke to his beak. "*Tovayah,*" he said softly. "*Tovayah.* Keep her safe.*"

The gryphon's eyes landed on me, then rolled back, but he didn't move from his position. Rhyan caressed my hand again, before tugging me closer and kissing the corner of my mouth. He breathed into my neck, inhaling before whispering in my ear, "I'll come back for you, to this exact spot." His voice lowered, his good eyebrow lifted. "So be a good girl, and be right here when I return." There was obvious desire in his hooded eyes. But they were laced with anxiety. He stepped back, eyes lingering on me before he held his arms out for Meera.

"Both of you be careful," I said.

"See you over there, Lyr," Meera said.

I tried to communicate with her silently, reminding her that she might need to catch Rhyan when they landed. She gave me a nod.

He spoke quietly, and she screwed her eyes shut, her hands gripping tightly at his sleeves. Emerald eyes latched onto mine one last time, holding me captive. And then they were gone.

I took a deep breath, trying to calm my nerves. The last time Rhyan had traveled with Meera and left me, Morgana had betrayed us. We were now too far east to see the Allurian Pass. There was nothing but snowcapped mountains on the horizon. But I stared through them, wondering if Morgana was still there, wondering what she was doing, if she regretted her decision. But mostly, after everything, I wondered if she was all right.

Probably foolish to think about. For all I knew, she and Aemon were already making their way to the capital. To go after Jules. Or more pieces of the Valalumir.

Aemon had said he'd always known who he was, and had always been aware of his link to Moriel. It made me ill to think of what else he knew, what secrets he'd uncovered, and hoarded. I wish I had an idea of where we stood in his games, or just how far behind we were in learning what we needed to fight back.

I took a deep breath and closed my eyes. But I couldn't relax. The dwelling began to feel eerily quiet, and I realized it was the first time I'd been truly alone in this country, alone in its wilderness. I rubbed my hands up and down my arms.

The gryphon whined, pulling my attention back to him. He shifted his weight and pushed his head against my hand, jerking it to the side. I reached for his chin, but he pushed my hand away again, stepping closer and presenting his forehead.

"This is what you want?" I stroked the top of his head. He made a happy growling sound that vibrated through his body. Seemingly satisfied, he stood up, and shook out his feathers, blowing gusts of snow that had accumulated on his fur onto me.

"Really? I give into your demands for head rubs and this is how you repay me?"

But then a strange feeling crawled up my spine.

The gryphon stilled, his wings pulled back to his body, his posture defensive again. He snapped his head back and forth, observing as I silently slid my hand to my hip, and wrapped my fingers around my sword hilt. I held my breath, my ears straining.

A branch snapped.

The gryphon snarled.

A moment passed, and then another.

I felt it before I heard it. A faint rumbling against the ground. The dry, crunchy snow was covered in a thin layer of ice that began to crackle as something slithered across it with a hiss.

Nahashim.

The same one I'd heard the other night. If I ran inside the cave, it would follow, and I'd be trapped. It was the reason Rhyan wanted me to wait outside—to ensure I had a way to escape, to avoid being cornered.

I withdrew my sword. The snake was growing louder, getting closer. I unsheathed my dagger with my left hand, widening my feet, my knees bent. And with weapons in both hands, I waited.

A small shadow danced behind a tree, before the nahashim slithered forward, its black scales shining in the remaining light. The snake stretched, revealing its full height, its head just reaching my waist.

I lunged, my dagger poised to strike.

But I missed the snake as it dodged.

Advancing again, I tried to lure it into a false sense of security by lowering my blades. Its black eyes watched curiously as its body undulated. I took another step forward, and again I struck. My blade hit the tree, snapping a piece of bark.

I stepped around the tree's trunk, away from the cave. The snake stilled. I lunged. And missed.

Again, the snake slithered back, taunting me.

With a roar, the gryphon rose up on its hind legs. Its front legs kicked in annoyance, its sharpened talons slicing through the air.

"Shhh," I said, my heart pounding. "It's okay. *Tovayah.* Just one small nahashim." But the gryphon wouldn't settle. "Shhh," I tried again. Fuck. All I needed now was for the gryphon to make enough noise to alert Imperator Hart's soturi that I was here. "*Tovayah,*" I said, my voice low, attempting to mimic Rhyan's. The gryphon's talons hit the ground and I turned back to the snake.

Its mouth snapped, revealing fangs dripping with venom. My arm tingled, remembering the feeling of being stabbed by its fang the last time, as well as the coming paralysis. But with a deep breath, I charged forward, dagger lifted. At once, the nahashim retreated, its shining scales gliding back across the snow.

Another branch broke. And then another.

I stilled.

Tiny vibrations shook the loosened patches of ice on the ground, and without warning, the nahashim spun on its coiled tail, advancing. I thrust my sword, the point aimed at its throat. But it rolled just out of reach. Hisses hummed against the ground, the sound now coming from every direction.

A second nahashim slithered forward, and then a third, and a fourth. Within a few seconds there were dozens around me, all small, but still venomous and just as dangerous. Especially in these numbers.

Carefully, I stepped back, my heart pounding. Their scaly bodies undulated as they continued to advance, their hisses growing louder and louder until they became low, feral growls. I tightened my grip on my weapon as the snakes bared their fangs. I was trapped.

Frantically, I tried to decide my next move. But a violent roar erupted and I ducked just as the gryphon leapt over my head. Snow and ice exploded as its paws slammed before me. With a screeching roar, it attacked the nahashim, the powerful muscles in its legs rippling. His talons sliced easily through the bodies of those nearest, tossing them aside.

Some snakes started to retreat, but most were gliding purposefully toward the gryphon, venom dripping from their open mouths.

I rushed forward, using their distraction to my advantage, my sword slicing through the bellies of each snake I could reach. Their bodies fell in pieces, twitching and jerking, before they stilled beside a snowbank. The gryphon roared, turning so suddenly, his tail knocked me aside. He steadied himself just long enough to face me. But beyond him, I could see more nahashim coming—the larger ones, the kind that could incapacitate, and carry me back to the Imperator.

With another whine, the gryphon nudged his head against my hand, flattening his belly at my feet. I stared as his tail twitched in agitation, and he emitted a squawk that ended in a roar.

I was about to yell at the gryphon to get up, to fight before he was bitten. But then he snarled, his tail moving frantically. I realized what I had to do.

Grabbing hold of his fur, I climbed onto his back. I'd barely gotten a grip when he rose up on his paws, his front talons kicking out as his wings flapped, blowing my hair into my face as he took off. We were moving so fast, running straight for the mass of snakes and trees. We lifted off the ground and I squeezed my eyes shut, my heart plummeting.

I started sliding off, shocked at his speed. I wasn't used to flying this fast, nor riding bareback. Fuck—I wasn't used to riding gryphons at all! They were nothing like seraphim. His wings flapped, and he flew even faster, the ground falling farther away from me.

"Shit! Shit!" I was losing my grip, slipping as he continued his vertical ascent. But then his body righted, lying flat, and I collapsed against his fur, my entire body shaking with cold and fear as we soared above the trees.

I had to tell Rhyan what happened, tell him not to come back.

Icy wind bit at my nose and cheeks, licking at my fingers as I tried to wrangle the vadati stone from inside my armor. But I couldn't maneuver around the metal and maintain hold of the gryphon. Tightening my grip with one hand, I loosened my belt, letting the folds of my soturion cloak fly free. Then I reached beneath my tunic, ripping the chain from my neck.

"Rhyan!" I screamed into the stone. "RHYAN!"

"Lyr?" he answered immediately. "What's wrong?" The wind was so powerful, I could barely hear him.

"Don't come back!" I yelled.

"What? Why?" The stone brightened with more blue light. "Lyr? Where are you? What happened?"

"Nahashim! They attacked at the cave."

"Fuck," he said. "Are you hurt?"

"No!"

"Okay then I'm—"

"No!" I yelled. "Don't. I'm safe. Flying."

"You're … you're flying? On the gryphon?"

"Yes, yes," I said, trying not to show my panic. "Now, help me. Tell me what to do."

The gryphon screeched and any body heat I'd managed to maintain was sucked from me as something flew into my peripheral vision. I screamed. A nahashim was *flying* beside us. The Godsdamned snake had grown wings.

Fuck! These things really could do whatever it took to find their prey. It was several yards behind us, but it was catching up, far too quickly despite its tiny body moving against the wind.

"Lyr? LYR! What happened?" The stone lit up with a fresh blue light in my hand. "Are you okay?"

"Lyr!" Meera's voice. "Lyr, answer! Now!"

"The nahashim," I said, panting. I could barely breathe. "It can fly!"

There was a string of unintelligible curses on Rhyan's end, and the gryphon picked up speed. I was having trouble focusing on my surroundings. The trees below me were just a blur of dark green pine topped with snow. But everything was quickly fading into the darkness as the sun continued to fall below the horizon. I had no idea how to direct the gryphon, or where to go.

"What do I do?" I yelled.

"Get closer to the gryphon's head," Rhyan ordered. "Go. NOW!"

Snowy wind began to blast against my face, but I did as he ordered, my thighs squeezing over the gryphon's thick spine as I inched forward. "Okay," I yelled. "Now what?"

The nahashim's wings looked so thin and wiry, barely more than snake skin. But it was flapping with so much ferocity, it was going to be beside us in no time.

"Lyr," Rhyan said. "I need to know where you are. I need descriptions of your surroundings. Landmarks. Details. Anything specific. Anything you can tell me."

"I can't. It's all blurry. Trees. Mountains. I don't know. I don't even know which way we're flying. Everything looks the same."

"You didn't go far from the cave. Do you see a flat mountain-top? Look for a peak shaped like a blunt triangle. You shouldn't be far from it."

"Rhyan, I can't see anything," I gritted. "We're moving too fast. It's too dark." My cloak was beginning to strangle me as it flapped, the cloth twisting around me in the wind.

"Tell the gryphon '*sandar*.'"

Slow. I looked back at the nahashim. It was going to catch us if we slowed down. But I didn't know what else to do.

"*Sandar*," I yelled. "*Sandar*."

"Did he slow?"

"NO!"

"Try again. Rub the back of his head!" Rhyan urged.

Breathing through my mouth, my chest heaving, I did. *"Sandar!"* At first, nothing happened. But then the gryphon's wings swept down the length of his body, like sails on either side of me, and they stilled. The gryphon squawked and we angled upward. "Shit!" We were going higher, further from the trees, up to where the air was so much colder. But he was flying slower.

Slow enough for the nahashim to reach us. Something the gryphon seemed aware of as it suddenly panicked and flapped its wings. He angled down again, picking up speed. My heart dropped and I yelled.

"Lyr, breathe. Breathe. I need you to look. I need you to find the mountaintop. Flat. Triangular. It's huge. You'll see it, I promise, even in the dark."

I took a shaky breath and searched the grounds. But I saw nothing.

"Lyr, do you see it?" Rhyan asked.

"Not yet." I scanned over the blur of trees, forcing myself to focus, to make sense of the shadowy images rushing beneath it.

"Fuck. Lyr, do you see anything? Any identifiers? Come on. I need you to tell me something—anything you see so I can come to you."

I looked, desperately, on the verge of tears. And then in the distance, moving closer, I spotted a flatland above the pine, a mountain fitting Rhyan's description.

"I see the triangle!" I yelled.

"Good! Hold the stone to the gryphon's head, and hang on. Okay? I'm coming to get you."

I didn't question his orders. I held the stone up, faintly hearing Rhyan's voice shouting commands in High Lumerian.

The gryphon turned, and I patted its head again, watching as the nahashim picked up speed, hissing in the wind just behind us.

The mountaintop seemed to grow larger as we approached,

and the gryphon's body angled, soaring higher, its body slowing. I peered down, and could just make out the shadowy figure of a soturion in a green cloak.

Rhyan. He was on top of the mountain.

More shouts came from the stone, and we dropped suddenly. I screamed, my heart in my throat. We were falling.

But it was just the way gryphons descended.

Way too fucking fast.

I leaned forward, holding on as the peak came closer and closer. My breath came short as I tried to convince myself that we weren't going to crash. That we were going to be okay. We *had* to be okay.

But when I looked down again, Rhyan was gone.

Before I could scream, something slammed against my back. A warm hand gripped my waist, locking me against an armored chest, and the scent of pine and musk filled my senses.

Rhyan had jumped onto the gryphon.

"I'm here, Lyr. I've got you. I've got you," he said urgently, pulling me even tighter against him. "You did good." He sounded out of breath, his chest heaving against my back. "You did real good! Fucking proud of you, partner. Now hang on."

I sank back against him in relief, my muscles suddenly useless like jelly.

He directed the gryphon past the peak, soaring over a stretch of suntrees, before we began our descent.

"Almost there," Rhyan said. "We're going to meet Meera at the cave."

My heart lodged itself in my throat as we began to fall again, but Rhyan kept a steady hold on me.

"Partner," he said, still breathless against my ear. "You're okay now. Hard part's over." One hand reached for the gryphon's head, and we slowed, just enough for the descent to feel bearable.

The gryphon snarled as we touched the ground, snow

exploding like dust around us as more flakes fell in thick, steady clumps.

Rhyan dismounted at once, extending a hand to me as I followed him with far less grace. My boots hit the ground at an awkward angle and I stumbled into Rhyan's arms. He immediately pulled me against him.

"Shhh. Shhhh," he said. "Steady."

My chest heaved, my breath coming in rapid spurts. "I need to tell you something," I said shakily, as my boots sank into the snow. I pulled back, just enough to meet his gaze. "I really don't like flying gryphon-back."

Rhyan's jaw dropped in mock-astonishment. "Lyr!" he scolded, then lowered his voice, "Not in front of the gryphon! You'll hurt his feelings."

Then the nahashim fell. Its body landed in a tightened coil, barely a few feet away from us.

Rhyan snarled, instantly serious, as he withdrew his sword. "Get in the cave. Wait with Meera."

The black snake unfurled itself, hissing wildly, baring its fangs. The wings it had just grown disintegrated to ashes in the snow.

Rhyan slashed, his sword singing as it pierced the cold air. The snake danced, slithering and sliding its body away. Rhyan advanced.

"Don't!" I yelled. "That's what it did to me, before it led me into a nest and I was surrounded."

"Lyr, it saw us. It's going to report to my father. We can't just let it go."

"We can if it's a trap!" I yelled. "Let's go inside, we'll ward the cave. When it's clear, we'll move again."

But Rhyan stilled, his gaze focused as his stance turned predatory. Fresh cold energy from his aura swirled around me as the snake continued to slither away.

"Rhyan, come on. I don't like this. Something's wrong. You know it. Nahashim don't retreat," I said.

"They're not supposed to grow wings either," he muttered.

I shook my head. "Why grow wings to follow us here if not to—"

He gave me a sharp look, his jaw tensed. "I—" He frowned. "Fuck," he muttered under his breath. "Just ..." His eyes moved rapidly back and forth. "Wait here." He sounded distracted. "I need to scan the perimeter beyond the cave."

"Rhyan!"

But he squeezed my shoulder. "Lyr, listen to me. I'll be just a minute. I can handle myself. Go inside, and check on Meera." His jaw clenched. "I need to do this, and I need you safe and out of sight. Go." He stepped back, his cloak blending into the trees, making him difficult to see as he walked into the shadows.

A sense of unease gripped me. Why had none of the other snakes taken on the ability to fly?

Because they weren't meant to.

They'd been the trap. The snake hadn't been sent to retrieve us. It had been tasked with finding our location so it could report its findings, so whoever it answered to could come find us. And it had only stopped attacking because whoever had sent it was close.

"Rhyan!" I yelled into the vadati. "Rhyan, come back right now!"

Blue light filled the crystal. "Lyr, it's okay. I'll be back soon. I'm—shit!"

"Rhyan? Rhyan, what happened?" The stone went white. "Rhyan, answer me. Rhyan!" Fuck. I took off, running in the direction he'd gone in, leaping over snow piles and fallen branches.

He said he was checking the perimeter, so I started turning, trying to find a path that circled around the cave. But as I continued to search, there was no sign of him.

I didn't want to yell his name in case whoever had sent the snakes were near. So instead, I yelled, "Partner? Partner!"

I ran farther, faster, weaving in and out of the trees, my eyes wide and searching.

"Partner?" I yelled.

Then blue light filled the vadati. "Lyriana!" Rhyan's voice shouted.

"Rhyan! Gods! Are you okay?" I moved forward, pushing through the branches to find him. It was so dark, I could barely see where I was going. "Where are you? Are you hurt?"

"I'm perfectly fine. Stay exactly where you are. Do not move. I will come to you."

I paused, biting my lip as I searched for any sign of him in the gaps between the trees. My stomach started to sink, thinking of the nahashim. But within seconds, I could hear the sound of boots crunching in the snow.

Rhyan's familiar form came into view, emerging from behind a cluster of pines. He walked forward at a quickened pace. Not injured. Not captured.

I raced forward, relief rushing over me. "Gods. You scared me!"

"You don't have to be afraid. I'm here." He remained still, letting me reach him and throw myself into his embrace. For a second, he seemed stunned, his body stiff and unyielding against mine. But then slowly, his arms wrapped around me, his hands patting my back.

"We need to go," I said. "The snake is reporting to someone nearby."

"You figured it out," he said.

Something was wrong. His voice was his, but the way he was speaking felt odd to me. He sounded so formal, completely devoid of his usual spark. I couldn't detect any of the usual care he infused into almost every word he spoke to me. Stranger still, he remained stiff, not actually hugging me back. He was awkwardly patting my shoulders, while I was holding onto him as if my life depended on it. On the gryphon, he'd pressed me against him like he was trying to meld our bodies into one. And now, he seemed like he couldn't keep enough distance between us.

I took a deep breath and it hit me. His scent was all wrong. Clean. Pine. But … unfamiliar.

I pulled away, staring up into his eyes, checking over his face for any sign of injury. But it was still so dark, I couldn't see him clearly.

"Rhyan? Is everything okay?"

His eyes met mine in the moonlight, but … I felt like I was seeing a stranger. Rhyan's eyes were empty of recognition. I couldn't explain it. They were just as emerald as they always were, but they weren't *his*. They lacked his warmth. His spark. His love.

Which made no sense. I was being silly. It was just dark, and I was still unsettled from my flight, and yet—

The scar that ran through his left eyebrow down to his cheek —the scar his father had given to him, the scar that I had traced a hundred times—was gone. The skin there was perfectly smooth and pristine. And I realized he looked younger. Softer. Like the Rhyan I'd met over three years ago. I remembered suddenly seeing him for the first time in Urtavia on my birthday this year. I'd noted all the ways he'd changed since the summer we'd kissed. How he'd looked older, wearier, tougher. And scarred. Now, it was as if none of that had ever happened. As if he'd gone back in time.

"Your scar." I reached for his face, my fingers tracing the place where it had been. He flinched. "It's gone."

"LYR!" Rhyan screamed. But his mouth hadn't moved, his voice was coming from behind me.

I turned my head.

"That's not me! Lyr! Run!"

I faced the Rhyan in front of me again and jumped back, seeing his armor for the first time. Strapped across his chest was his old Glemarian chest plate adorned with the sigil of Ka Hart. The sigil that marked our kashonim was gone. And he was wearing it outside his cloak, the way it was supposed to be worn. Not the way we'd been wearing ours since we'd been on the run.

My mouth opened to yell, but Rhyan lunged for me, his hand around my neck, a stave pointed at my chest. Black rope coiled, springing forward and wrapping around me. Binding me. My chest seized. It was just like when Tristan had bound me. The panic I'd felt rushed back. I'd trusted him at the time, loved him, and he'd hurt me.

But … but Rhyan didn't have a stave. He wasn't a mage. And no matter what, under no circumstances would Rhyan ever hurt or do anything like this to me.

"Don't touch her!" he screamed.

"Don't touch her," came a taunting voice with a thick Glemarian accent. One I'd heard before. "By the Gods, Rhyan. So many demands."

Dario emerged from the shadows of the trees, pulling Rhyan forward. The real Rhyan. The Rhyan who still had his scar, who still wore the armor that showed our kashonim, peeking out from his opened cloak. He'd been bound in rope, his neck red as he struggled to break free.

I shook my head. "What is this?"

Staring back at the scarless "Rhyan" before me, he waved the point of the stave up and down his body. The golden-brown curls on top of his head straightened, lengthening into dark auburn locks. His green soturion cloak and black leathers were replaced with the blue robes of a mage. A stranger stood before me, one who possessed a kind of cruel sternness to his beauty. His eyes were dark, his skin pale in the way of most northerners. Looking me up and down, his eyebrows drew together over a large, gryphon-like nose.

Something began to niggle in the back of my mind—a description Rhyan had given me of one of his best friends.

One who looked like a gryphon.

"Who ... who are you?" I asked.

"I see Rhyan hasn't told you about me. Who am I, or the special skills I possess with glamour." He glanced at Rhyan, wind bristling through the dark auburn of his hair, his eyebrows still knitted together. "I think I'm rather insulted." He returned his gaze to me and bowed, too low, the gesture mocking. "Allow me to introduce myself to you, my lady. That is your correct title now, yes? Lady? Not Your Grace."

"Yes," I seethed.

He dipped his chin. "I am an old friend of Rhyan's. Lord Aiden DeKassas, at your service," he said. "I am the official apprentice to Glemaria's Master of Spies. And you are both wanted for questioning. It is my duty to bring you before His Highness, Imperator Hart, High Lord of Glemaria."

CHAPTER TEN

LYRIANA

Aiden. This was Aiden. I remembered now. Rhyan had wished for a pet gryphon as a boy. He told me he would have named him Aiden. But then he met a real Aiden, and he became one of his best friends, and the desire for the pet was gone. Now, Aiden, the mage, and his friend, had us both bound, while Dario, Rhyan's other best friend, looked murderously at us.

Rhyan struggled against his ropes, grunting and yelling. "Aiden. Aiden please, listen to me. Don't do this!" he begged.

Aiden's mouth tightened, his expression pained, but it was Dario who sneered and said, "Oh I think we will do this."

"I owe you both an explanation. I know I do. But you have to let us go. You don't know what's going on," Rhyan said, his voice desperate.

"Funny thing that is. We never seem to know," Dario said. "Come on, Aiden."

I was already struggling against the rope, trying to break it. Rhyan had done it before, and I had my soturion strength now. I was stronger than I'd ever been. But as my muscles strained, and I pushed against my bonds, using everything I had, the ropes only cut into me more sharply. It was impossible. Aiden had tightened the ropes around me with a vise-like grip. And he was keeping his focus trained on them, not letting them loosen an inch no matter how hard I fought.

I'd been bound before, but never like this, never with my power intact. And all at once, I understood how truly torturous it was. When Tristan bound me on Imperator Kormac's orders, it had hurt. The ropes were too hot against my skin, but mostly I'd been terrified of what was happening. The situation itself had been far more horrifying than any pain I'd felt from the binding.

This time, though, was so much worse. I was in agony. But Rhyan? Gods! Rhyan had gone months like this because of his father's cruelty. He'd gone months like this just to protect me.

"At least, release him!" I shouted. I couldn't stand to see him in the ropes now that I could fully understand what they did to him, understand how they'd been used against him. They were his own personal kind of torture. "Take me instead. I won't fight back, I swear."

"No," Rhyan growled. "No! Your quarrels are with me. Deal with me. I have a lot to answer for. To both of you. And I will answer. I swear it. It's me you want. Me who my father wants. Not her."

Dario laughed. "Our quarrels? That's how you're referring to what's between us now. *Quarrels?* What a fucking polite choice of words. But then again, what else should I expect from the smooth tongue of our old Heir Apparent?" He shook his head. "But you're right on one thing, *friend.*" Dario's accent deepened, the lilt that I found so beautiful sharpening into a vicious threat lacing each syllable. "You do have a lot to answer for. A fucking lot. And trust me. We will be getting every one of those answers from you in kind."

"Dario!" I yelled. "I beg you. You were his friend. Don't do this to him."

"Lyr," Rhyan said, a warning in his voice. But I could see how much this hurt him, the pain and panic in his eyes.

"*Was*, I believe is the important word, my lady." Dario scrunched his nose. "Past tense."

Rhyan squeezed his eyes shut, his face contorted with pain.

I gave up on reasoning with Dario. "Aiden," I pleaded. He seemed more reserved, possibly more level headed. "Please."

"Unfortunately, I cannot abide by your request." Aiden spoke formally, his accent barely there. His lilt was stifled in the way Rhyan often hid his, except for the moments he lost control of his emotions. There was a stillness to him—one I'd sensed when he'd touched me before.

"You see," Aiden continued, "Rhyan has a small tendency to sneak away. And kill the people you love on his way out." His voice hardened. "We will not be releasing you either, my lady. Maybe you misunderstood me. I'll explain again. And slowly. You will both be brought in for an audience with His Highness, Imperator Hart."

"Aye," Dario said. "Enough with this." He glanced around the darkening woods. The trees went on for miles. And we were in the center of it, vulnerable and exposed. Something unspoken passed between Dario and Aiden. "You'll have time to consider what you'll say to His Highness. We're too far for safe passage tonight, especially with two prisoners. Too many reports of akadim lately. We'll find cover for the night."

I locked eyes with Rhyan. Once we reached shelter, we could form a plan and find a way to break free. He watched me carefully, his jaw muscles tensed, his expression unreadable.

"Let's go then," Aiden said. "I saw the entrance to a cave nearby."

"Rhyan," I whispered. I needed to know if it was the one where Meera was waiting for us to return.

His widened eyes seemed to confirm.

Shit.

"If you don't shut it, Lady Lyriana, I'll be having Aiden add a binding to your mouth," Dario snapped.

I glared, but nodded. The last thing I wanted was a gag on top of my bindings.

"Come then, my lady," Aiden said formally. He walked ahead, and tugged on the rope. I had no choice but to follow, taking tiny, awkward steps—all I could manage with the bindings.

As we walked, the sky blackened, the faint glow of the moon and twinkling stars, our only source of light. But then a small flame appeared, crackling and spitting, floating before Aiden. For him to be producing light like this, to power and sustain it purely by his magic, he had to be a ridiculously accomplished mage. Which, I should have guessed. His impersonation of Rhyan had been nearly perfect. It made him incredibly dangerous.

And Dario, according to Rhyan, was an extremely vicious soturion. I shouldn't have expected anything less. These men hadn't just been friends with Rhyan before he was forsworn, they were part of the elite of Glemaria. Some of the best fighters in the country, if not the entire Empire.

Aiden turned, leading us through a small clearing. I kept my eyes ahead, watching the ground carefully, making sure I didn't accidentally trip on a loose rock or stick, until we came to a glade that led to another secluded cluster of trees. Beyond that was a small rounded clearing, and then the cave Rhyan had brought Meera to. I looked up, and sure enough our gryphon was flying above in lazy circles.

"Patrol?" Aiden asked, watching the gryphon's flight pattern. "Could we use it for passage to Seathorne?" I held my breath.

"Wild," Dario said, dismissively. "Too much effort to tame now." He slowly eyed the horizon and shivered. "Let's get inside."

We took the remaining steps, passing through the cave's

entrance without any problems. It was a bad sign. We shouldn't have been able to enter, not if Meera's wards were in place. Which meant she hadn't put them up yet, waiting for me and Rhyan to return.

"Your accommodations for the night," Dario said grandly as Aiden led us inside. "I'm not sure if this is the kind of place that fits the lifestyle you're accustomed to, my lady. But alas, I don't actually care."

I took in our surroundings. It was smaller than our last cave. And there was a distinct smoky quality to the air of a recently extinguished flame. But Meera was nowhere to be found. Nor was there any sign of her, or our things.

Aiden helped me to sit down against the wall, and on the other end of the cave, Dario pushed Rhyan onto the floor. I was about to shout, but Rhyan brought himself up to a seat, leaning his head back against the stone wall, his eyes closed.

Outside a wolf howled, and snow fell, the wind blowing in through the cave's interior. Aiden's eyes were on me as he moved to the center of the space, using his stave to pull out logs and twigs so he could transfer his fire.

A few pieces of wood rolled to his feet, followed by a stack of sticks, already neatly tied together. Their tips were charred, the acrid smell of smoke still clinging to them.

My eyes met Rhyan's, full of alarm, as Aiden bent over, brushing his fingers against the ashes.

"Still warm," he said, dropping his flame onto the pile. The fire he'd sustained burst to life, twice as large as it had been, the flames sputtering in every direction. "Looks like we've got company."

"Put up the wards," Dario said. "No one in. No one out."

"On it." Aiden kept both eyes on me and Rhyan as he pointed his stave at the entrance and performed the warding spell. If Meera was outside, she'd never find her way in—and without a vadati I couldn't contact her. She would be alone—cold, scared. In danger.

I tried to remember to breathe. To inhale, and exhale.

Aiden crouched before me, his keen eyes assessing. "Let's speed this process up. Is it just the two of you? Or is Dario going to find someone back there?"

"No," I said, my pulse vibrating. "He won't."

"You're lying." Aiden tilted his head, bringing his face even closer.

"I'm not."

"Easier if you just tell me the truth." He pointed at my heart. "Otherwise, we can do this the hard way. I can make you talk."

Rhyan shifted violently in his seat, a growl under his breath. But any threats he was about to make were stilled when Dario returned from the depths of the cave, clutching our belongings in one hand, and Meera in the other.

CHAPTER ELEVEN

LYRIANA

"And this is?" Aiden sounded bored as Dario hauled Meera out from the passage.

Bastard. Had they both fucking known Meera was here the whole time?

"I am Lady Meera Batavia. Heir—" She clamped her mouth shut. "I am the niece of the Arkasva, High Lady of Bamaria."

Dario dragged Meera forward, while Aiden bound her.

There was a flicker of pain in her eyes as the heat of the ropes touched her skin, but she otherwise accepted the binding with her usual quiet grace.

"You were taken, weren't you?" Dario asked. "Kidnapped by akadim?"

"I was," Meera said, her chin lifted.

"And you survived?" Dario's eyebrows narrowed.

Meera made a show of looking down at herself. "Clearly."

He laughed. "And your other sister? Lady Morgana? She's not hiding back there, too, is she? Disguising herself as a rock?"

"I believe you already know the answer," Meera said, her voice sharp.

"Yes, but I'd like to hear it from you." He winked. "It allows me to form some trust, give you less of a rough time while we're together."

"I doubt that." Meera's face hardened. "My sister's not back there."

"Where is she?" Dario demanded.

Meera's nostrils flared. "Yet to be rescued from our captors." She looked Dario up and down and then amended, "Our *previous* captors."

"And where exactly were these captors holding you?" Aiden asked. He circled Meera, and her eyes tracked his movement, watching his stave. "What brought you all the way to the North after your escape? What are you doing in Glemaria?"

Meera lifted her gaze. "The akadim held me prisoner in the Allurian Pass."

Aiden frowned. "That's the other side of the country."

"Maybe that's why you missed the army of monsters invading your territory," I snapped. "You have an akadim problem that your Imperator's doing nothing about."

Aiden's eyes snapped to Rhyan's. The mage folded his arms across his chest.

"Look who thinks they know so much about the Glemarian border patrol. Most likely the akadim were made beyond the mountain, in the non-magical realm," Dario said. "That's where most monsters in the North come from."

"Would that not count as a border?" Meera asked.

Dario's nostrils flared.

The Allurian Pass was on the western edge of the Empire. Aemon was definitely venturing into the human realm and taking the people there to add to his army. It was the only thing that made sense. Reports of akadim activity had grown recently, but the reports weren't reflective of the numbers he had at his feet. We would have heard about it if that many people were going missing on a regular basis. Now his choice of the Allurian Pass made sense beyond its proximity to the indigo shard. It was an easy place for him to slip into the shadows and build his army of monsters.

"I've answered your questions," Meera said. "You can plainly see I have no weapons as I am a mage. I hope you intend to release me. I was preparing for my travels back to Bamaria to recover from my ordeal. My aunt, Arkasva Batavia, and His Highness, Imperator Kormac, sent soturi to rescue me. To bring me home. Lady Lyriana and Soturion Rhyan were part of that mission. We are expected in the South. I would appreciate it greatly, as would my High Lady, if you allowed us to continue on our way."

Dario folded his arms across his chest, the corner of his lips lifting. "Interesting. Last we heard, *Soturion* Rhyan was wanted by Imperator Kormac for abandoning his post with Ka Batavia. Not to mention he's also wanted by Imperator Hart for an assortment of crimes in the North. Far too many to list."

"And Lady Lyriana?" Meera challenged. "She's not committed a single crime. All she did was rescue her sister. She's my protector and my escort." Her eyes softened.

"She assisted a forsworn in banished territory. She's also wanted for questioning," Dario said.

"Where I was being held captive!" Meera shouted. "Rhyan was on a mission to fight akadim from the South—surely that grants him immunity?"

"Hmm." Dario shrugged. "No, it doesn't. Both Imperators seem to have taken an interest in his … affairs." His dark eyes flicked to me. "And your sister's."

Rhyan sucked in a breath, his jaw tensed.

Dario took notice. "Interesting. Unfortunately, I must do as my Imperator commands and bring them before him," he said. "If they're as innocent as you say, they have nothing to worry about. Though considering they both attacked His Highness's soturi on Gryphon's Mount, they maybe should be worried."

"And me?" Meera asked. "Am I wanted for questioning?"

Dario's eyes narrowed. "We've been ordered to bring in anyone we find assisting them."

Aiden had paused before Meera, looking annoyed at the entire situation.

Suddenly, she lunged forward. She was bound, but her hand was perfectly in line with Aiden's stave.

"No!" Dario yelled, and pushed Aiden aside, just before Meera reached him. She'd been so close.

Aiden hissed through gritted teeth, his fingers tightening over the sun and moon wood. "Did you really think that would work?"

"Worth a try," Meera said, as Dario gripped her shoulders and sat her against the wall beside Rhyan.

"Can we not with these stupid games?" Dario said, rolling his eyes. "This whole thing is a fucking headache I don't need."

"I've heard you're used to those!" I snapped, remembering how Rhyan often described Dario as being too drunk to get out of bed for training. "Particularly in the morning."

A surprised laugh escaped his lips as his head snapped to Rhyan, who was staring down at his lap. "Myself to fucking Moriel." Dario pulled out his dagger, and tossed it in the air, catching the hilt and tossing it again. "Sure. He told you I enjoy my drink. That I enjoy actual fun, unlike some present company. But did he tell you anything real? Did he ever tell you about the tournament? The Alissedari that he simply *had* to win? You know how someone wins an Alissedari, don't you?"

Rhyan's face fell, all the color drained.

I've killed before ... My own people when I fled. I killed one of my friends with my bare hands. My friend.

The words he'd spoken to me once in despair, the first time I'd woken him from one of his nightmares.

Now Rhyan was staring ahead, tears in his eyes.

"Look, you can see it all over her face," Dario sneered, his accent still heavy. "She doesn't know. We've got time to kill. How about a bedtime story?"

Rhyan's lips were quivering, his chest heaving.

"Stop it," I said. "Just stop it."

"Why? Don't you want to know these things? You should, especially if you're going to listen to his stories about us. You might as well hear one of ours." Dario clapped his hands, like he was on stage. "Time for the tale of the Alissedari."

"Dario, please," I said again. "Don't do this now."

"No? No. I think now's perfect," Dario snapped. "Once upon a time there was a boy named Garrett. Garrett." He paused, letting the name hang in the air, echoing against the walls. "Did he ever mention that name to you, my lady?"

I lifted my chin, my lips pressed tightly together. Rhyan had mentioned Garrett once. Only once. When he thought I was asleep. I felt hollow.

"No?" Dario lifted his eyebrows. "Well, Garrett was one of Rhyan's best friends. Like we used to be. His father served on the Glemarian Council with Rhyan's. Like my father used to, before he was killed." He paused, looking murderous. "Garrett was a soturion—quite a good one, actually—could have been Arkturion one day. He trained with Rhyan. At least he did until the Alissedari. You're from the South," he said, as if this was an insult to my intelligence. "I should have clarified before. But just in case you didn't know, an Alissedari is a tournament fought on gryphon—"

"I know what it is," I seethed.

Dario held his hands up in mock surrender. "Oh, she is *learned*. Well, then you must know how this will end, since you already know the victor is created in one of two ways. They're the last one standing, or, the first to kill. Guess which way our dear friend won? Go on, my lady. Guess which way."

I killed one of my friends with my bare hands. My friend.

"They'd promised they'd work together," Aiden said, suddenly taking over. "To protect each other. And after they claimed their gryphons, they arrived at the stadium at the same time. Together." He was now choking back tears. "We thought they'd be okay. They'd be safe. That Rhyan would never—" His chest heaved, his neck red. "But then Rhyan had to win. Couldn't lose now, could he? No. He murdered Garrett. Murdered him right in front of us. In front of the whole fucking country." Tears streamed down his face, his cheeks red and mottled.

A tear rolled down Rhyan's cheek.

"You killed him." Aiden spoke in a hushed, broken whisper. "You killed him. Our best friend. My love."

By the Gods. That was why I could feel so much grief in his aura. So much more anger than Dario possessed.

Rhyan had never told me. He'd been in too much pain. Felt too much anguish to speak. I remembered when he'd confessed to killing his friend. His nightmares had been so terrible, his aura had started a blizzard—one that nearly froze us. But even that had been too much for him. He'd been unable to confess the rest. To offer any details.

Aiden sank to his knees. Rhyan was openly weeping. And for a second, I was wrapped up in Aiden's grief. To lose your love, I couldn't imagine it. Couldn't bear it. Just the idea of Rhyan being hurt sent me into a rage. But losing him completely … I pushed the thought away.

Gods. It was a horrible story, especially the way they told it. They made Rhyan sound like a cold-blooded killer, like a monster, like his father.

But I knew Rhyan. I knew without a doubt, there was more to that day. That as impossible as it seemed, he'd killed Garrett because he was trying to do the right thing. He was always trying to do what was right, and then he beat himself up over every little thing that went wrong, even those things that were out of his control. I couldn't even imagine what Garrett's death had done to him. What it was still doing.

My arms ached with the need to go hug him, to hold him, to comfort him. To listen to him as he finally confessed the truth. But Aiden had gone still, and risen back to his feet. Everything in his aura and demeanor was harsh and guarded.

Rhyan shook his head, looking desperate. "I wanted to tell you, Aiden. So many times. I—fuck. To say I'm sorry isn't enough, but it's the only words I have and I should have said so before. But I … I am sorry. More than you know. I think about him … I think about Garrett …" His voice was hushed, too much emotion to speak louder than a whisper. "Every day. Every fucking day," he croaked. "But there's … there are things you don't know. Things that—that …"

"I know. I know what I saw. And you think about him every day? I hope you fucking do. Because I do. And you know what else I think about?" Aiden asked, crouching down before Rhyan again. "Not the way he looked after you'd killed him. Or the way he lay lifeless in your arms. It's the last night we were all together that haunts me. The day your nose was broken. You remember that, don't you?"

Rhyan's eyes widened, and he nodded slowly.

"I fixed it! Healed you! Mended your bones while Garrett sat at your bedside. Were you plotting it then? Deciding that in order to win, you'd sacrifice your friend? Did you always plan it would be Garrett, not Dario? Did you ask your father to separate Dario and Garrett at the tournament so he wouldn't stop you?"

Rhyan sucked in a breath, his eyes watery and distant, lost in memory. Then his head fell forward, his shoulders shaking. He looked so helpless. I was desperate to inch toward him. To at least brush my fingers against his, to offer whatever comfort I could. But Dario gave me a look that made me freeze.

"I took care of you. My last day with him, with the love of my life, and I was at your bedside," Aiden said, his voice low.

"Then I watched you wrap your hands around his neck. And for a year, for a whole fucking year, all I've wanted was to do this!" His hand fisted over his stave and then—

"No! Don't!" I screamed.

There was an awful crunching sound, followed by an agonized yell of pain from Rhyan. Aiden had broken his nose.

"Rhyan!" I yelled.

"Fuck!" Rhyan's head snapped back, banging against the stone. His chest heaved, muscles straining painfully against the ropes, as his shoulders shook. Then slowly, he lifted his head, bringing it forward. There were tears in his eyes, blood gushed freely from his nose, as his fingers twitched helplessly at his sides.

"Stop it!" I yelled. "Don't touch him!"

"Or what, my lady?" Aiden stepped back, his hands shaking, his aura wild as obvious flares of anger and grief battled for dominance.

"Are you okay?" I asked Rhyan, my voice shaking.

Dario sneered. "Yourself to Moriel. He fucking deserved it."

"Fuck you!" I shouted, struggling to get to Rhyan's side.

"Fuck me?" Dario placed his hand over his heart. "I don't think so. Not tonight anyway. And I would refrain from commenting on the situation. Because there's one glaring detail about that night you won't comprehend. The one where you weren't even fucking there!"

"I couldn't care less what happened right now," I growled. "All I know is he's hurt!" I glared at Aiden. "And your *friend* is the one who hurt him."

"Lyr." Rhyan's eyes were bloodshot, his mouth tight with pain as he shook his head in warning. "Don't. Don't. It's okay. I'll be all right." Suddenly his eyes widened, staring behind me. "Fuck!" He strained as he shouted, his voice full of command and warning. "DARIO!"

A low growl echoed across the cave. I turned my head,

stomach twisting in horror as an akadim, completely impervious to magic, walked right through Aiden's wards.

The beast was so tall, the top of its head nearly brushed the ceiling. It was completely naked, wearing only a silver collar around its neck. We'd seen those collars before. It connected him to his master, and let them share power in a kind of twisted kashonim. This wasn't any old akadim who'd stumbled upon us. This was one of Aemon's monsters.

One of Moriel's.

Dario grabbed a torch from the wall, and raced toward the flames to light it. Then he withdrew his blade, his black curls shining in the firelight.

"Aiden," Rhyan yelled, spitting the blood that spilled onto his lips. "Aiden. Unbind me! You must! Unbind me, now! Aiden!"

But Aiden was frozen, his aura filled with fear, as he watched with stunned horror as his friend approached the akadim. He grasped his stave, his knuckles turning white. His face had paled with the same look of terror I knew I'd had when I'd first seen akadim up close. Despite how seasoned Rhyan and Dario were at fighting, Aiden was a mage, not a warrior. This was probably the closest he'd ever been to an akadim. Maybe even the first one he'd ever seen with his own eyes.

"Aiden!" I yelled, my entire body vibrating. "You have to unbind us! Or we'll die!"

The akadim growled, and swiped sharpened claws at Dario's chest. He backed away, just enough for the beast's nails to graze his armor. With a yell, Dario launched the torch at the akadim's head, but the beast swatted at it, sending the flames flying back in my direction.

"Lyr!" Rhyan screamed.

The torch hit the wall beside me, the fire catching on loose twigs. The sticks blazed instantly, the flames licking at my leg. Shit! Shit, I was going to burn. Angling my boot away, I repositioned myself, and kicked out, stomping on the flames until smoke rose beneath my foot.

"AIDEN!" Rhyan roared, sliding his body toward mine as if he could pull me back from any further dangers. "Aiden! Unbind us." His voice filled with panic. His muscles strained to near bursting, his fingers touching mine. "NOW!"

Dario yelled as he raced for the akadim. But it grabbed him, hoisted him into the air and tossed him into a wall with a sickening thud. His vadati stone smashed to pieces beside his head.

Another growl echoed through the cave, this one louder and deeper. A second akadim, its body thicker and more muscular than the first, had entered, wearing the same silver collar around its neck. Another one of Aemon's soldiers.

These were a new breed. When I first fought akadim, I'd been protected by Asherah's chest plate. Her blood was like torture to them, because she'd been a Guardian. That had saved me when I had no magic. But now the undead who served Aemon carried his blood in their veins, the blood of a reincarnated God. They could touch me now. As well as Rhyan, and Meera.

And worse, they had the potential to activate the Valalumir inside me. Aemon's blood, the blood of a Guardian could do that.

We absolutely had to get free.

"Aiden, do it. Release them," Dario finally commanded, pulling himself to his knees. His pants had torn at his knees above his boots, and blood was dripping from his forehead, his face covered in soot. With a grimace he was back on his feet, repositioning the hilt of his sword between his hands. "Now!"

Aiden blinked rapidly, then pointed at me with his stave. There was a blast of light, and at last I felt the ropes drop from my body, my magic and strength rushing back through my limbs. I felt like I'd been underwater, and I'd just risen to the surface, and could breathe again. I jumped to my feet, immediately racing

to the corner where they'd thrown my armor and weapons as
Aiden unbound Rhyan and Meera.

The mage's eyes darted between us as we brandished our
swords, bodies tensed to fight. He took a step forward, like he
was going to help, but I snatched Meera and my stave off the
ground first, pushing her behind me. Aiden's chest heaved, his
hands trembling at his sides as the akadim roared.

"Aiden," Rhyan said firmly. "Aiden, listen to me. I need you
to take Lady Meera to the back, and stay hidden until the threat
ends." He held his friend's gaze, offering him the confidence
he'd given me so many times before when I'd needed it. "Okay?
You've got this. You're strong. Keep her safe."

Aiden's throat bobbed, but to my surprise, he nodded, his
eyes blazing. "On my life." He pressed a fist to his heart twice,
before flattening his palm. Meera took his hand, offering a reassuring squeeze, and he nodded. He placed his other hand on
Meera's elbow, his eyes meeting mine before disappearing with
her into the shadows.

I held my sword with two hands, my eyes meeting Rhyan's.
Dario raced for the first akadim, jumping and striking its arm.

For a second, Rhyan pressed his side to mine, a brief reassuring touch we'd both needed. Then his voice was low in my
ear, strained from his broken nose. "Attack its right flank. I'll go
left. Strike deep. No holding back."

My throat tightened, but I nodded, tightening the grip on my
sword. Rhyan's lips curled back, his body preternaturally still,
ready to attack. I took off towards the right. He ran left. The
akadim's eyes flashed on me, his claw at the end of a giant,
muscled arm thrashing. I leapt, swinging my sword across his
body. The blade struck his skin and the hit reverberated through
the hilt and up the nerves in my arms. I resisted the blade's incli-
nation to bounce back, slowly piercing through the rough skin to
the thick cords of muscle. Gritting my teeth, I pushed, straining
as hard as I could without losing my grip. Blood spurted from

his arm as my feet touched the ground, my sword still in my hand.

The akadim growled, and before I could attack again, Rhyan made his second leap, the tip of his blade arcing downward. The beast's arm hung limp from its shoulder, less than a tendon keeping it from falling off.

It sank to its knees, groaning in pain as its severed arm hit the floor with a sickening thud.

Rhyan readied his sword again. But then a blood curdling scream rang through the cave. The first akadim had lifted Dario into the air by his neck, strangling him. Dario kicked helplessly, and stabbed at the akadim's arm with his dagger, but it was no use. The akadim squeezed harder, ripping Dario's armor away from his chest. He was stripping him for access to his heart.

To eat his soul. To turn him forsaken.

"NO!" Rhyan roared.

"Go!" I shouted. I could see the pain in his face, the warring needs to protect both me and his friend.

Rhyan stared hard at me, his eyes assessing.

"Just a fucking rope," I said. "Go!"

He ran for Dario just as I launched myself forward. I'd kill this akadim on my own.

The beast swayed, blood flowing freely from his severed shoulder. I bent my knees and jumped, lifting higher than I ever had. And with a thrust, I drove my blade into its heart. He howled, his remaining arm scrambling to grip the hilt. Gritting my teeth, I pushed and shoved until I felt my sword meet the barrier of muscle on his chest, tough and thick. My boots found purchase against his thighs, and I pushed the blade in even further, forcing it past the beast's muscle and bone.

On the other side of the cavern, I caught Rhyan launching himself onto the akadim's back. He wrapped his arm around its neck from behind, and withdrew his sword. Rhyan drove the blade through his back. He grunted, until the blade burst through the front of the akadim's chest. Dario fell from its claws, hitting the ground with a sharp thud.

I jumped back from the akadim before me, my blade still embedded in its chest. Rhyan yelled at Dario to get out of the way, but he just lay on the floor.

"Dario!" he yelled.

His chest rose and fell—he was alive—but otherwise, he wasn't moving.

The giant swayed and tipped forward. His eyes going blank as he began to fall, the blade's point positioned right where Dario lay.

I bit back a scream as Rhyan yelled out.

"DARIO!"

The akadim fell. Dario was going to be impaled. Rhyan leapt from its back, his feet barely touching the ground before he dove forward, wrapping his arms around his friend. They rolled off to the side, their legs tangled, just as the sword and beast smashed to the cave's floor.

I raced forward again. My beast was still alive—and my sword was in its chest. I needed to pull it out and strike again.

"*Maraak Moriel*," it growled, its collar shining in the firelight.

King Moriel. Aemon.

It grinned as it grabbed hold of the hilt of my sword, swatting my hands away. I fell back.

The akadim roared, spitting blood laced with its putrid breath against my face. Its red eyes narrowed to slits, fangs protruding from its mouth as it pushed my sword deeper into his chest, mocking me, making sure I knew that I'd missed his heart.

My chest heaved, as I prepared for my next move.

"*Maraaka Ereshya*," it said, licking its lips. Queen Ereshya. Morgana … I stumbled back.

My eyes burned. Aemon's betrayal was one thing. But Morgana's? Was it possible? Could it be that she hadn't just taken the shard, but that she was being worshiped by these monsters, too? That she was ruling over them? Commanding them?

No, no. She couldn't. She wouldn't.

But she was.

"You fail," it growled. "Lost your sword. Can't kill me now."

"Don't be so sure about that," I said, unsheathing my dagger. My name flashed across the steel in the firelight.

The akadim laughed, mocking the size of my weapon. But a second later, I'd launched myself forward. While it protected its heart, I shoved my dagger through its hand.

The akadim screeched, arm flailing, giving me the few seconds I needed to unsheathe my sword from its chest. I struck again. And this time, I didn't miss the heart.

Some animalistic sound echoed against the walls as the akadim's eyes widened, then went dark. It seemed to be still, suspended in movement for several agonizing seconds, before it toppled forward, my sword crashing onto the floor beneath it as I stepped aside.

Across the cave, Rhyan still held Dario in his arms, trembling with shock. His face was red, like he was still trying to breathe after being choked. But Rhyan's eyes, puffy, dark and swollen, were on me, looking me up and down, assessing that I wasn't hurt. That I was safe.

He lifted one arm, his palm outstretched to me, and I ran, dropping to my knees to hug his side. My arms tightened around him like I needed him to breathe, and for a second, I let myself sink into him, my face buried in the warmth of his neck.

Rhyan crushed me to him, his hand a steadying presence on my back, pulling me somehow closer. I lifted my head, our foreheads pressed together, and he let out a sigh of relief. He moved, his lips brushing softly against my forehead before he pulled back, his eyes heavy as they met mine. "Lyr," he said, his voice choking up. "Are you hurt?"

"No." I buried my face back in his neck, trying to catch my breath. To breathe in his scent, to feel he was alive. To revel in the knowledge that somehow, again, we'd survived. "You?" I asked, squeezing him.

"Just my nose," he said roughly, his fingers squeezing the back of my neck.

Dario took several deep breaths as he shifted himself to sit on the floor.

"You got to breathe, Dario," Rhyan said. "You hear me? You're okay. You survived. Take a breath." Rhyan reached for him, but the soturion ignored his gesture, standing on his own, some unspoken conversation happening between them.

Dario's eyebrows narrowed, but he nodded.

"We need to patrol the perimeter," Rhyan said. "See if more are coming. You're all right?"

His face was contorted in pain, but Dario gave a firm shake of his head.

Aiden and Meera emerged from the darkness of the passage, their faces pale.

The moment she saw me, Meera ran from Aiden into my arms. "Lyr," she cried. "You're okay?"

I nodded. "We all are."

She looked with disgust at the dead akadim, her eyes lingering on their collars. "Aemon sent them." Her voice was quiet, too low for the others to hear.

I nodded, the backs of my eyes burning. Not just Aemon. Morgana. But I couldn't bring myself to say it yet. To hurt Meera even more than she already had been.

Maraaka Ereshya.

"Let's go," Dario said. "Rhyan and I will secure the perimeter. Lyriana, I need you to protect Aiden and Meera."

I nodded. "I will."

Heart thundering, I watched Rhyan and Dario grip their

swords and head outside, their bodies vanishing into the falling snow.

I stood before Aiden and Meera, my body tensed, and my ears alert. A minute passed before Rhyan and Dario burst inside the mouth of the cave, their chests heaving, eyes wild.

"The fuck!" Dario roared, bending over, his hands slamming into his knees as he caught his breath.

Rhyan pushed his hair back, grimacing, his face red. "There's a dozen out there. And more are coming. We're surrounded on all fronts."

Meera shook beside me. "They're trying to bring us back."

"Or kill us." I reached for Meera's hand, watching as Aiden turned to Dario and Rhyan, his face ashen in color.

"Maybe," Meera said quietly, "Maybe we let them take us. They … they didn't hurt us before. Morgana wouldn't—"

"NO!" I shouted.

"We're trapped then." Aiden looked ready to panic.

Rhyan stared outside, and straightened the strap across his chest. "No. We're not. We have a gryphon, big enough for all of us." His accent was rough, the posh noble lilt he'd practiced completely gone. He looked between Dario and Aiden. "Give me thirty seconds. I can find him. I'll get us out."

Dario scoffed. "Right. Like we're just going to let you walk out of here."

"Are you fucking serious?" Rhyan spat. "You know I'll come back!"

Dario's face reddened, his eyebrows narrowed.

"I swear on my Godsdamned life!" Rhyan shook his head. "*Me sha, me ka.* We'll fight about this on the gryphon. If you want to break my arm next, be my guest. But by the Gods, I won't let anyone here die tonight."

A roar called from outside the cave. Another answered. The akadim were getting closer.

Rhyan rushed to stand before me, his breath coming short. I

reached for his shoulders, my fingers pressing into the leather of his armor. His green eyes fell on mine, blazing with light. There was something desperate in the way he looked at me. Like he was memorizing my face.

"You'll come back," I said breathlessly.

His jaw tightened. "I will always come back for you." He reached for my neck, his fingers brushing softly against my skin. Then I felt him grip the chain I wore, his hand sliding down toward the clear, white vadati stone. He pressed it into my palm, and leaned into me, his breath against my ear.

"Be ready," he commanded. This was the voice of an apprentice now, ordering me to follow the chain of command. "The gryphon won't fit inside. I'll fight my way to the cave's mouth, get as close as I can. When I call for you, come."

I nodded. "Be careful."

He pressed his fist to his chest, his knuckles brushing against mine. "*Mekara.*"

"*Rakame,*" I whispered back. My throat felt too tight for words.

And then he was gone, his figure swallowed by the darkness beyond the cave.

CHAPTER TWELVE

LYRIANA

I stared at the snowflakes tumbling inside the mouth of the cave, my heart pounding. Rhyan was no longer visible.

"Fuck!" Dario slammed his fist into the wall. "Fuck!"

"He'll be back," I said, my throat tight. One akadim could be life-ending. And Rhyan was surrounded by them. Vorakh or not, he wasn't immortal. Not in his current body.

"He will," Meera whispered. "He's strong."

I nodded, biting my lip to keep it from shaking, but worry seized every inch of my body.

"Here," Aiden said, handing me a torch.

I gripped it so tightly my fingernails dug into my palm. I stared down at the vadati now hanging over my chest, clear and dormant. And as the seconds passed, it remained so.

An entire minute came and went, a sick feeling welling deep inside me. Still, the vadati was silent.

"We need to move closer," Dario said, his eyes on the stone. His face filled with determination as he raised his sword, and jerked his chin at Aiden. "Be ready, we don't know what's out there." His eyes met mine and we instinctively stepped in, our bodies shoulder to shoulder, our swords out and ready to protect our people.

"Stay close to me," I ordered Meera. "No matter what."

I started to hold my breath, my hand nearly slipping down the length of the torch with sweat. Then a familiar squawk that ended in a roar drowned out the growls of the akadim.

The gryphon.

"Lyriana!" Blue light from the vadati emanated against my armor and filled the cave.

"Rhyan," I yelled, my hand tightening around the hilt of my blade. I turned to Dario. "We're coming."

"No. Wait!" Rhyan roared, the sounds of battle, grunts and growls filling the stone.

"Rhyan?" I asked.

"*Himai!*" He commanded just as a gust of wind filled with snow blew into the cave. A low growl echoed against the walls and a dark shadow filled the entrance. The akadim's outstretched claws reached for us as it began to roar, its eyes glowing red. It was massive. A giant even amongst akadim. There was no way I could reach its heart. I wasn't even sure I could cut off its arms.

It rushed forward, and Meera screamed. I raised my sword, my hand shaking and pushed Meera behind me. I aimed for my hit, but my sword bounced off its skin. And I fell back onto my ass.

Meera's arms wrapped around me from behind, lifting me up as I scrambled to my feet, reaching for my sword.

The akadim roared, its teeth gnashing, its claws nearly reaching where Meera and I stood. And then it stopped, and stilled, eyes widened in horror as something ripped through its heart.

A beak.

The gryphon had impaled the akadim from behind. Blood rushed down its belly, as the red light left its eyes.

I jumped backwards, moving Meera aside, just as the

demon's body slid lifelessly to the floor. The gryphon's beak opened and closed, shaking off the blood, then looked at me expectantly, like it wanted another head rub.

"Good boy," I shouted, my voice too high. "Good fucking boy. *Tovayah*." Then I urged everyone forward. "Go."

But another akadim was barreling toward us. And this one was even bigger, its giant head grazing the cave's ceiling. I reached for my blade, distantly aware of Dario running toward the beast—until its head rolled off, and one of Aemon's silver collars spun on the ground.

The moment the giant's body collapsed, Rhyan's boots touched down behind him. His knees were bent, the point of his blade against the stone floor. His shoulders rose and fell before he stood, sliding his blade into its belt.

"Get on," he roared. "They're coming!"

Rhyan was already running for me, pressing his forehead to mine, his arms tightening behind my back. Then he turned, his face hardened for battle and he sprinted back. Meera and I ran after him while Dario tugged Aiden outside.

The gryphon had backed away from the cave, and already akadim were attacking from all sides. Its talons thrashed as it screeched. Dario hoisted Aiden onto its back with one hand, while stabbing an akadim with another.

The gryphon rose up on its hind legs as we made it outside. Miraculously, we had a clear path, only a few feet to run before we'd reach it. Rhyan looked back. Right as he did, an akadim stepped in between us. I shoved Meera back, and widened my stance. This one had been a woman when alive. A soturion. Her position mirrored mine perfectly, revealing her training. She looked me up and down with red eyes, her fangs protruding from full lips. I feinted to the side, but she remained still, already guessing my move. I made it anyway. I launched my torch at her face. She was barely an inch clear of the flames, when Rhyan jump-kicked her, pushing her into place. The fires flared instantly, spreading down her body as she screamed in pain, arms flailing.

I froze. She looked mortal at that moment. Merely mortal. And scared.

Her screams of pain, the ghosts of her soturion training … She reminded me of Haleika.

My eyes met Rhyan's and I knew he was thinking the same thing. Remembering the arena, the horror. I could still see it so clearly. Still hear Haleika's final moments.

"Lyr," Meera shouted, pulling me back.

Chest heaving, I trapped Meera's hand in mine and ran. We were getting on that Godsdamned gryphon and we were getting out of here. Lifting her in my arms, I pushed her onto the gryphon's outstretched wing. She reached for his feathers, hoisting her body up.

Dario screamed from the opposite side of the gryphon. Akadim were climbing aboard.

Rhyan vanished and reappeared on the gryphon's back, just in time to grab Meera's arms and haul her the rest of the way up. With a quick glance at Dario and Aiden, he jumped again, his body reappearing behind mine. He reached around my waist, his head pressed to the back of mine. My stomach tugged and I landed face first in a heap of fur and feathers on the gryphon's back.

"Hold on," Rhyan ordered. The gryphon was frantic, slashing and moving, avoiding attacks from all sides.

Blearily, I saw Dario kill an akadim, but already, he was facing another climbing up the flank as Aiden scurried back.

"Go. Now!" Rhyan yelled. "*Vra. Mahara.*"

The gryphon's talons fell forward before he roared and lifted back once again onto its hind paws. One wing raised into the air, he roared in pain, blood dripping down his bronzed feathers.

"Hold on!" Rhyan shouted.

An akadim launched its body up, landing right beside me. I

screamed, just as Meera slid her body forward, her boot slamming hard enough into its face it fell backwards.

"Shit." My eyes widened. She'd gotten stronger.

A second later we were moving. I pulled her against me as Rhyan threw himself at Dario's side. Together they cut off the akadim's head, and kicked its remains from the wing.

"*Mahara*," Rhyan commanded.

Both wings were in the air now, the gryphon's body leaning dangerously far back, and then we were running, racing from the akadim, and lifting into the air, flying higher and higher.

"Come here to me," Rhyan whispered in my ear, arms circling around me.

I turned in his arms, sparing a quick glance for Meera who was miraculously unharmed. Then I began scanning Rhyan for injuries. He had a few cuts and tears in his pants and tunic, but the blood was already dried, the wounds already closing. The worst injury was to his face.

"Your nose." I frowned, and gently pushed his curls from his forehead. He flinched, and then sighed at my touch, his head pushing against my hand.

"It's okay," he said, but he was grinding his teeth as he spoke.

He'd most likely been able to ignore the pain during the adrenaline of battle, but now I was sure he was feeling all of his injuries at once.

Slowly, I began to lower my hand, fingers grazing against the swollen skin of his forehead. His eyes closed and he shivered against my touch with a long, painful breath.

I reached the bridge of his nose, and my hand stopped, my heart pounding and my chest warm.

I didn't know how to do it—only that I could. And all at once, I could feel heat spreading in my hand. Could feel my chest warming as the light of the Valalumir glowed beneath my armor, lighting up my palm.

Rhyan's eyes sprang open in horror and he grabbed my wrist, pulling it away. "Lyr, no!"

"What?" The light inside my chest went out. "Why?"

"Don't," he said, his eyes widening. "Don't heal me."

"It's okay," I said. "I can do this."

"But I don't want you to," he growled, suddenly shifting back from me.

"Rhyan!" I looked anxiously around us, but Dario and Aiden were too far to hear, their heads bent to each other in deep discussion. "You need to be healed. We … we don't know what we're going to face next."

"Exactly." He took both of my wrists in his hands, his touch gentle, but firm enough that I'd have to struggle to break free. "It's fine. It will heal on its own."

"But it can heal faster. What if we have to fight again tonight?"

"Then we fight! Lyr, this is exactly why I won't let you! If you do this, you'll take on this pain. And it will weaken you. There's no way in hell I'd risk that."

"But right now it's weakening you!" I said.

"No, it's not." His mouth tightened, his under eyes dark bruised shadows. "You saw how many akadim I just killed. I don't want you taking this pain on. Okay? Swear to me! Swear you won't heal me."

I searched his eyes, breaking free of his hold. He let me, but I kept my hands in my lap. "I can't stand to see you in pain."

"Neither can I stand to see you!" He took my hand in his.

"I can handle it," I said. "I'm strong enough."

Rhyan shook his head. "No. They needed to do it—it's mine to bear. Not yours."

"But—"

"Lyr, stop. Please. You can't."

"Rhyan!"

"Lyr, listen to me. When we went to bed earlier …" He

squeezed his eyes shut, his expression miserable. "You healed me. You took my exhaustion away."

My jaw dropped. "I …" I'd thought my chest had heated as I laid there in his arms. But I thought it was just a remnant of his touch, a reminder that he was a Guardian.

"I'm sorry," he said. "I should have told you earlier. That's why you slept so long. Okay? That's why. You healed twice today and it's worn you out both times. Lyr, we don't know enough about this yet. I don't want you using it again until we know how it's going to affect you. And right now, I need you ready to fight whatever comes next."

"And I need you ready to fight," I said.

He breathed out slowly. "I am."

I was about to demand a compromise, for him to let me heal him when we landed and knew we had time to rest. But there was a sudden flash of light in the sky, and the gryphon screeched, its body turning violently away. My hand shot out for Meera, as Rhyan wrapped his arm around me, pulling me back against his body.

"What is that?" Meera asked.

The muscles in Rhyan's jaw tightened. "It's Aemon."

I looked back, seeing the glowing blue lights beneath his ashvan horse, Aditi. Aemon's red Arkturion cloak flew out behind him.

"The fuck?" Dario yelled. "Who is that?"

"Not Glemarian," Aiden said, his eyes clocking Aemon's every move.

Aemon's aura was expanding, its violent deadly essence reaching toward us.

My eyes met Meera's, who'd leaned forward, her body straining to see him. I didn't have to ask what she was looking for. Because I was looking for a glimpse of her, too.

Morgana.

There was no sign of her though, and I couldn't decide if I was disappointed or relieved.

Maraaka Ereshya.

"What the fuck is he doing here?" I gritted.

Meera's eyebrows narrowed. *"Listening."*

I squeezed my eyes shut. Fuck. Of course he was. That was what he did. He'd been able to manipulate us when we were in Bamaria, able to push us toward everything he wanted. Knew how we'd react, knew our exact thoughts each time. Because he'd listened to everything.

Without a doubt, he knew what we were up to. Knew we were going to Numeria, that we were going to rescue Jules. And knowing him, he'd find a way to use that against us.

"It's a good sign," Rhyan said quietly. "He's not attacking. He's revealed he's here, and he didn't have to."

"So, he's sending a message?" I asked. "That the akadim were his?" My hands fisted at my sides, seeing their collars in my mind. "We already fucking knew that."

Rhyan nodded. "He fucked up though. Because he just showed us something I don't think he meant to. He isn't any more powerful than last time we saw him. Morgana hasn't given him the shard yet."

I shuddered with relief, not realizing how desperately I needed to hear that. To hear that Morgana hadn't brought back the full power of Moriel. But was that because she was truly on our side?

Maraaka Ereshya.

Or was she keeping it for herself?

"Do you think we'll know?" Meera asked. "When he does take the shard?"

"I think we will," Rhyan said. "I think he'll want that."

"The fuck's going on?" Aiden interrupted.

Dario's eyes narrowed on the three of us. "Don't know. But he's gone now. We'll report it." He reached for his belt, but then cursed when he remembered his vadati had been smashed in the fight.

Aiden's eyes narrowed on us. "We should look further into it," he said.

But Rhyan sat forward and said, "It's not fucking important right now. The real question is how you're going to get the warning out about the akadim."

"Akadim reports go to Arkturion Kane," Dario said darkly.

"Kane?" Rhyan paled. Kane was the man Rhyan's father wanted me to marry. The Arkturion who was supposed to make the Bastardmaker look civil. Rhyan had let his father torture him just to keep him away from me.

"Yes, Kane," Dario snapped. He looked down his nose at Rhyan, his sneer full of condescension. "You remember him."

Rhyan's mouth tightened. "Dario, listen to me. We can't go to Seathorne. We just can't. Say we escaped—say we fought and overpowered you."

"And why would I do that?" Dario jerked his chin at us. Aiden nodded in response.

I was too slow to understand the signal. But Meera wasn't. She'd jumped to her feet, wobbling to the side as the gryphon's body shifted beneath us, her stave out and pointed. Aiden was faster. Black ropes sprang from his stave, overtaking the light emanating from hers. He bound her within seconds. Rhyan lunged protectively in front of me, his body blocking me from view. Aiden bound him anyway, then bound me, too.

My skin itched the second the ropes made contact, and my chest tightened.

"Maybe you misunderstood," Dario said. "We were always going to Seathorne."

My heart sank. "Why? Why stick to the plan? Rhyan just fought for you—with you! He protected you! Doesn't that mean anything?"

"That we fought together? Just like old times?" Dario spat.

"What did you think happened here, my lady? That we made up? That it's all better? We stopped a fucking threat. Nothing more. Rhyan did his duty—the least he could do. Now we're going to report it. And then I'm going to do my duty and bring you before my Imperator."

"You would have died without him," I said through gritted teeth. "Rhyan killed your akadim when you couldn't. He fucking held you when you were laying there in shock! You owe him. He saved your fucking life. And you Godsdamned well know it!"

Dario smirked. "Aye. But we saved yours first, freeing you from the ropes."

"Ropes you put us in!" I shouted.

Rhyan only shook his head beside me. "Lyr. Don't."

I rose to my knees, trying to get between Rhyan and Dario. He could bring me before Imperator Hart. I didn't care. But I was going to be damned before I subjected Rhyan to the place where he'd been helpless and tortured. "Doesn't anything he did matter? He was your friend, and by the way he acted tonight, he's still your friend. He'd never do this to you if the roles were reversed."

"If the roles were reversed Garrett would be alive! My father would be alive. You don't want to play this game with me." Dario's eyes darkened.

"Bring me then," Rhyan said calmly. "Let me answer for my crimes. Let me receive justice if this is what you need." His eyes fell on Aiden. "But you both know what Kane is. What he's capable of. Please. Don't bring Lyriana and Meera into that. They're innocent. I beg you."

Something lifted in Dario's aura, and my heart nearly skipped a beat. He was listening. Rhyan was getting through to him.

Just as quickly as he seemed to shift, his aura darkened again, pulsing with something angry, and rageful. "Kane's who we report to." He stalked forward, hand on the hilt of his sword.

"We could have reported the threat to my father. The Master of Peace, remember? But you killed him, too."

I could feel it coming. Dario was going to strike.

"If you touch him—" I snarled.

"You'll what?" He grabbed my shoulders and pushed me easily aside, hovering over a kneeling Rhyan.

The wind howled, and I desperately tried to get back. To find a way to fight. Aiden had stilled, watching the exchange with the focus of a hawk. Meera started shouting, and I was pleading, begging. But Dario wouldn't be deterred.

"Aiden got his. I want mine. You promised to answer for your crimes. So, let's start. You said I could break your arm." He made a clicking noise with his tongue. "Not going to work while you're bound."

My breath came short, my heart fluttering with panic. I knew what was coming next. And from the way Rhyan's face paled, his breath coming short, he knew it, too. Dario fisted his hand around the hilt of his dagger, the gleam of the blade caught in the moonlight. "Noses don't break twice? Do they?"

The crunch sound was awful. And I screamed as Rhyan fell unconscious.

Meera and I were both rushing for him, awkwardly crawling on our knees, our arms bound, our power gone.

"You bastard," I yelled. "You fucking gryphon-shit bastard!"

My fingers itched, desperate to touch Rhyan, to soothe him, to heal him. His eyes were swollen shut, his nose bleeding fresh blood again. The gryphon shifted and Rhyan rolled into me, grunting softly.

"He'll fall off," I said at last. "How will you explain that to your Imperator? I assume he asked you to bring him back alive?"

"Put his head in her lap, free her hand," Dario ordered Aiden, his gaze distant. "Hold him then. Keep him from falling."

I wanted to punch him. But I also saw a flicker of regret in his eyes. I just hoped I could use that to my advantage.

"*Vra*," Dario commanded the gryphon. "We'll stop at the nearest post to report the attack. Then we head straight for the Imperator."

I brushed Rhyan's bloody curls off his forehead, willing my hand to warm, for my heart to glow. I wanted to heal him. I needed to.

His eyebrow furrowed beneath my touch. But no heat came. There was nothing else I could do. I could only sit there and try to hold him. Keep him safe, and allow him to rest until sunrise. Until we faced his father.

CHAPTER THIRTEEN

MORGANA

"Hello, kitten."

My throat went dry as I heard the click of my bedroom door closing. The bolt sliding into place. My heart was beating too quickly, sweat was beading on my forehead and neck, I was suddenly terrified I'd made a mistake.

A stranger was in my room with me. A stranger who knew my secret. A stranger I could not see.

"Shhh," he said. "Don't be afraid. I told you, I came to help you."

"You also told me men lie."

"And have I lied to you yet?"

I'd been trying to be strong. Trying not to cry from the pain, from the doom I felt from my vorakh. But now that someone was here, someone was speaking to me, soothing me, even if they had ill-intentions, it was enough for my guard to fall, my vulnerability to surface. I'd been acting strong for too many hours. I couldn't do it anymore. I broke down, tears rolling down my face. Just because I wasn't alone. Because a ghost of help had arrived.

It was so fucking stupid.

"No, kitten. No more tears. I'm going to take the pain away. I swear."

He stepped closer, his face and form hidden in the shadows. A hand reached out and cupped my cheek, a calloused thumb stroking my skin.

I sniffled. "How? How do I make it stop? How do I stop the noise?" There were still so many thoughts in my head, pounding, invading. A sentry on duty. A soturion flying on ashvan. Another guarding the wall to the fortress. Everyone's mind was whining incessantly. And loudly.

"Like this," he thought.

He leaned toward me, and I reached out a hand, touching metal. Armor. A soturion. I reached for his shoulder, my arms shaking. He was taller than me, and my heart pounded even harder when I made contact. My body may have been innocent of another's touch, but my mind wasn't. I knew what we were doing. I knew what came next.

"You've never done this before," he said, not in the way where I knew he'd heard my thoughts just then. But as if he'd known for a long time.

"No," I confirmed.

"I'll show you. Teach you. Then you won't need me. You'll be able to do this whenever you want, with anyone you want—whenever you need to."

He leaned in, his breath against my cheek, and then his lips brushed mine. They were soft and full and left shivers running down my spine. I sighed. And he did it again, then pressed his mouth to mine, both hands cupping my face, wiping away my tears as his thumb stroked my cheek.

I kissed him back, liking the feel of him. And then emboldened, nibbled on his bottom lip.

We stayed like that a long time, taking turns slowly kissing the other, exploring as my breaths came faster, and our bodies pressed closer.

My heart kept pounding, louder and louder, first with a warning. Then excitement. Need. Fear. And then ... desire.

Suddenly his mouth moved more frantically against mine, and his hands roamed lower, squeezing my ass, and pulling me into him. He removed any space that still existed between us and I was more than aware of his erection, pressing between my legs. I stifled a groan. I'd never truly felt one before. Not purposefully. And never ... there. I could feel myself pulse in response.

"Go ahead," he said, grinding into me. "Take your pleasure. Use me."

I froze, suddenly self-consciously unsure what to do.

"You know what to do," he purred. "I've heard you pleasure yourself at night. Many times."

My cheeks reddened. I started to pull away. "No."

"Kitten. You can use me, use me like you use your hands." His voice in my mind was suddenly deeper, huskier, "I want you to."

I closed my eyes, even though I couldn't see anything. Even though he couldn't see me.

"You spied on me? When I ..."

"No. It's a hazard of this power. Can you stop yourself from all you hear now?"

I bit back a retort. He was right, and yet ...

"Don't be embarrassed. I've loved every time you've done that."

A blush crept across my cheeks, and I started to roll my hips, sucking in a breath as the heat there became more, and more. I arched my back, my hips undulating, seeking him again and again.

"Good kitten." He wrapped his hands around my neck, stroking my skin as he moved to my shoulders, to the straps of my dress pulling them down, before at last, he palmed my bare breasts. They felt heavy in his hands, his thumbs sliding across my nipples until I cried out.

And only then, did I realize the voices had grown quiet. They were still there. My head still hurt, still pounded. But it was … less. The sounds faint. Distant.

"You see?" he asked, and kissed my cheek.

I could only pant in response.

"You need more. Come."

He swept his arms beneath my knees, and carried me to the bed, laying me back before he crawled over me. I could hear his armor coming off. Metal hitting the ground, straps unbuckling. Cool air rushed against my skin, until his mouth fastened on a nipple.

And then he was lifting the hem of my dress, pulling the skirts above my waist, and slowly removing my underwear. He didn't say anything as he slid his hand back up my leg, fingers grazing over my center, touching me there for the first time. His fingers moved in a circle, until I gasped and he pushed inside. I tightened around him, suddenly afraid.

"Shhh," he thought again. "Don't you feel it? Feel the peace. Feel the quiet?"

"Yes," I thought.

"Good." He returned to kissing me, moaning against my lips as his fingers started to slide in and out of me. The pleasure was starting to build, the way it did when I was alone. And before I could stop myself, my hips rocked to meet each thrust of his hand.

"You want faster?" he thought.

"Yes." I groaned, shocked at my response. Shocked at how good it felt. "Gods, yes." He did as I asked, giving me more, giving it to me exactly where I wanted it, where I needed it. And then I was losing control. Pleasure, raw and wild, fired through my limbs. The voices that had plagued me quieted even more. There was a silence in my head that I hadn't felt in hours.

His tongue swept into my mouth, swallowing my cries as I came, my body shuddering around his fingers.

I'd just barely come down from the release when he cupped me roughly between my legs, then slid two fingers back inside, languidly stretching me, before adding a third. "Morgana, you know what comes next."

"What?" I asked, even though I knew the answer. I still needed to hear it.

"I'm going to fuck you," he whispered.

I clenched around him, nervous again as I heard his belt unbuckle, and his pants slide down. My legs shook as he crawled on top of me, spreading me further. I could feel the soft hairs on his legs against the smoothness of my skin.

"Wait. I don't know. I'm not sure," I thought urgently. I still hadn't seen his face. I still didn't know his name. Or if I was making a mistake. How had I gotten here? What in Lumeria was I even doing? This was a stranger. This was the last thing I expected to happen today.

"It's okay. I'm going to take away the pain, remember? Take all the pain that lingers."

The high of my orgasm was starting to subside, and I could feel the torture of my vorakh already returning. The pounding headache amping up again with slow, steady beats. The inane thoughts of every person still awake in Cresthaven driving into my skull.

My mind was twisting, scared of what I was doing. Scared of who he might be. Wondering if I should wait, if this was supposed to be more special, more meaningful. Just ... more. And yet ... What did it fucking matter? I'd been wanting to do this, hadn't I? And I wanted the pain to stop. Who cared who he was? Who cared how this happened? As long as it did, as long as the silence came.

"Okay," I thought, and lifted my face, seeking out his lips in the dark.

"When I'm inside you," he thought, "it will be different. We won't be able to communicate like this. If you want something, if

you need anything ... you're going to have to tell me. Out loud."

"You won't read my thoughts?"

"That's the point. That's the whole Godsdamned point." He stroked my center.

"Will you tell me your name?" I asked.

He shook his head, "Ready?" He seemed to laugh. "Ready to make the noise stop?"

Swallowing roughly, I nodded. "Ready."

He grinned against my lips and lined himself up at my entrance, gently rubbing his length up and down my core. My breath caught, my heart thundering, and then suddenly, he pushed inside.

I cried out.

"Fuck," he grunted. "You're tight."

I could barely breathe. My mouth opened. It was so much at once. And he was everywhere, filling all my senses. All my awareness. I could feel him on every inch of my skin. Covering me, inside of me, becoming part of me. His aura enveloped us, a forceful shadow that felt like the power of death.

But as he slid all the way in, like a Godsdamned miracle, my mind was quiet. The voices had stopped. My headache was gone.

By the fucking Gods. He'd told the truth.

He was still, allowing me to adjust to his size. It hurt. But ... the other pain I'd been feeling for hours—that had been worse. And that was gone. Never before had my mind been so quiet, my thoughts so at peace.

I nodded up at him, urging him to move. His hips rolled back as he thrust in and out. The more he did that, the better it began to feel. The more my body welcomed him, stretched to accommodate the thickness filling me.

He rocked into me, a hand reaching for my leg as he slid deeper inside before pulling back, and thrusting again.

"How does that feel?" he asked, tenderly reaching for my face. He pushed my hair back. "How are you doing?"

"Good," I whimpered. "It's good."

"Are you sure? Are you sure you're okay?" he asked, his voice holding more concern for me than I'd expected. It was so different from the seductive voice he'd had before. It was almost as if he meant it—as if he cared.

Before I could answer, an ashvan raced past my window, leaving behind enough of their glowing blue light to illuminate my lover's face. Just for a second.

He saw the moment it happened. The second I recognized him, and stilled, his muscles tensing.

His long dark hair fell past his shoulders like black silk, and his eyes were made of pure indigo.

"Moriel?" I said, my heart pounding.

"Ereshya," he said, and kissed me.

I woke up with a gasp. My body was overheated. I was Morgana. I was Morgana. Not Ereshya. But that dream … It wasn't a dream, not exactly. That had been my memory of my first night with Aemon—almost. Until the end.

"Interesting," Parthenay said, her voice snide. She leaned against the roughhewn stone of what amounted to the doorway to my bedroom. "You woke just before it got *really* good."

"Get the fuck out," I said, trying to control my breathing.

"But you had us all so entertained."

My throat dried as I turned my head. Half a dozen akadim were in my room, hidden in the shadows of my peripheral vision. They were all kneeling on the floor, some with their hands hovering between their legs, watching me with red, hungry eyes. There was lust in them, a monstrous kind. But also fear. Fear of me. And reverence.

I was their queen now. A title I never wanted. Especially not over them.

"What are you doing?" I asked, trying to keep my voice from

shaking, from showing weakness. "No one is supposed to come in here."

"We were drawn," Parthenay said innocently.

"Gryphon-shit! Just because you invade my privacy doesn't mean you get to drag all of them in here, too."

"Trust me," she chuckled, "I didn't. Though, unlike them, I did have a front-row seat to what you saw. You know, I always wondered what it was like to get fucked by a king. By a God. Now you've shown me. Twice. But them? They came from your own call. They sensed the desire leaking off you." Her stupid hateful face contorted into one of mock passion. "Oh," she cried out, one hand on her breast. "Oh, Moriel."

"*Maraak*," chanted an akadim.

I stood from the bed enraged, my pulse pounding too quickly. I grew more used to them every day. I had to. But each morning was a fresh shock, like it had been during my captivity. It didn't matter that they considered me their queen, that Aemon had sworn they wouldn't hurt me. They were hateful, horrible, soul-less things.

I took a step forward. "Get out. All of you. Now!"

The akadim rose, bowing before me. "*Maraaka*," each one said as they exited my room, their faces downcast. At the tail end were three demons, smaller than the rest. More mortal in appear-ance. Their eyes were red, their fingers clawed, their necks adorned with the silver cuffs linking them to Aemon. I could almost sense the power, the strength and violence inside them. It mixed seamlessly with their intelligence. But they were still monsters.

And even though I knew they wouldn't hurt me. Knew they called me queen, I hadn't expected them all to listen to me so willingly, to be so docile.

"Why? Why wouldn't you expect that?" Parthenay asked. "*Maraak* Moriel has named you queen. They show their devo-tion daily."

"I know plenty of queens in history who weren't respected, nor obeyed. A title alone is not something that protects you, and certainly not against akadim."

"It protects you," she said, a note of jealousy in her voice. "They hunt in your name."

I scoffed. "And did I ask them to hunt for me?"

She shrugged disinterestedly. "Maybe not. But you have the shard."

"The shard you're babysitting?" I asked.

You're the one sleeping with it in your bed, she thought. *You're paranoid. You know I can't take it from you.*

Then why cast your shadow in my door, I thought. *We both know you're here to make sure I don't leave.*

She smirked, her mind suddenly quiet.

There was something else in her mind, something she was trying to hide from me.

I shook my head, trying to glean the thought from her. But I was faced with her own onyx wall, protecting her secrets.

She'd been taunting me for days. Coming in here, or thinking thoughts to me at all hours to drive me farther than Lethea. She mocked my thoughts and fears. Tried to unsettle me over my relationship with Aemon. Or King Moriel as everyone referred to him. She made my meals, and she ran my baths each night. Always with a snide remark. I thought it was jealousy at first, that Aemon was … well, not mine. But more mine than hers.

And then I wondered if I was clouding my own judgment. If my own distrust of her had made me paranoid. I associated her with my kidnapping. With her capture of Lyr and Rhyan.

But slowly, I was starting to realize that was just a distraction. She was doing her best to throw me off, to keep me from realizing what she was truly protecting.

Not me.

Not the shard.

But my ability to use it. The ability I'd been trying to tap into for days while Aemon was gone.

Her eyes narrowed, clearly reading my thoughts. She stormed out of the room.

I'd been determined to figure it out since I'd last seen him. I'd been holding the shard, trying to keep my memories of Ereshya at bay, while getting closer to the source of the crystal's magic. I wasn't sure what I was doing. But I knew that each day I felt more aware of its ancient magic, felt more of a spark inside me when I touched it. If Parthenay and Aemon were worried about me being able to do so, then it meant only one thing. It meant I could.

It meant I was close.

It didn't matter if Aemon had a claim on the crystal, if it wanted to answer to him. Because I now knew, it could answer to me.

I picked it up off the bed, feeling its weight in my hands, and stared, letting my eyes go slack. The shard began to glow. Indigo light filled the room, and colored my skin until I was as blue as Mercurial. I closed my eyes.

I am Ereshya, I thought. *Guardian of the Valalumir. Servant of the Council of Forty-Four. Goddess of the Orange Ray.*

I opened my eyes. The crystal in my hands began to heat, brightening, and the tiredness I felt from waking was gone. I had been hungry, about to demand breakfast. But now, I was satiated without needing food. Even more light spilled between my fingers, casting a vibrant sea of color against the stone walls. Lifting my arm, I held up the shard with only one hand, like a scepter. Like I truly was queen. It was large and heavy, and I'd always needed two hands to hold it. Now one was all it took. I felt stronger. Powerful.

Like a Goddess.

Like Ereshya.

I walked out of my room, and into the main hall. Aemon's

Throne Room. *My* throne room. A large expanse of the Allurian Pass with a throne, and little else, but tons of akadim roaming around. All wearing the silver collar he'd given them, forming his own kashonim.

What if I did that? What if I bound them to me?

My chest tightened. *No.*

That still seemed wrong. Like I'd be taking it too far. I knew my sisters didn't understand, knew they felt I'd betrayed them. But I wasn't like Aemon. I wasn't a monster. I didn't want to be. Maybe I didn't need to go that far, didn't need to mix my blood with the akadim. I just needed to prove I could command them. Prove I could get what I wanted.

If I could control them, control them long enough to bring the Empire down, I could free Jules. I could find my way back to my sisters. To my family.

Parthenay walked past, her eyes widening at the shard, glowing against my skin.

"What are you doing?" she asked.

"How dare you address me so informally," I said.

"He left me in charge," Parthenay said. "I'll address you how I want."

"And he left me queen." I turned away from her, ignoring her shout of "stop" in my mind.

Nearly a hundred of the akadim were in the room, all in disarray. Some eating. Some fucking. One had even dragged in a helpless girl, crying. Human. She had no aura. She'd come from the non-magical lands.

They'd been doing that for days. Sneaking out of the Pass beyond the Lumerian border and feasting. Half of their victims had been torn to pieces, made a meal of in all ways. The other half had been turned into akadim. Those were the ones without collars.

"Akadim!" I yelled. *"Ani Maraaka Ereshya."*

They froze, turning slowly to face me, listening intently. I recognized the ones who'd been in my room falling to their knees.

Parthenay's eyes widened. "You don't know what you're doing," she hissed.

"I think I know exactly what I'm doing." Then I raised the shard. Its glow lit the room, making lights dance across the gray stones. The cavern appeared to be flooded in deep indigo waters from the crystal. A deep, dark light, but still too bright for the akadim, who hid their eyes, hissing in pain.

"*Teka!*" I commanded. "*Teka el me. Teka el ra Maraaka.*" The order for them to kneel before their queen seemed to echo off every wall, until there were a thousand commands in the air. My voice. Ereshya's voice. I could no longer tell the difference in the echoes.

Several seconds of silence passed, and then all at once, they did as I commanded, falling to their knees in supplication, claws spread and heads lowered. Some even placed their faces against the floor.

I couldn't help but feel stunned that they'd listened. But even more than that, I was afraid of what I'd done. Of what I'd commanded. I remembered … remembered being Ereshya. Remembered fearing when Moriel had done the same. I hadn't dreamed it yet, but I could see in my mind's eye as clearly as I could see the monsters before me, thousands falling to their knees and shouting his name.

Now … they fell for mine.

Moriel can still overrule you, Parthenay thought. *You are second to him. Do not be so bold as to think he won't punish you when he returns.*

Will he? Will he punish his queen? Will he punish the Goddess he has taken to his bed again and again? Life after life?

Parthenay's mouth tightened, her nostrils flaring.

Or will he punish you? I thought. *I am the one who possesses and commands the shard of the Valalumir. I am the one who can take possession of another.* I stared down at her. *And you'd do well to remember, I am second to no one. You are bold to think he won't punish you. Or that I won't.* And when she remained defiant in her stillness, a sudden wall erected around her thoughts, I narrowed my eyes, pushing against her defenses. *Parthenay?* I crooned in my mind. *I do believe, I said,* Teka.

She flinched, her face giving away her surprise. Glaring, her lips curled in anger, the golden Valalumir tattoo on her cheek—the sigil of the Emperor she'd once served—had turned indigo.

I pointed the shard at her, still marveling I had the strength to hold it so easily. And then I lowered it.

Parthenay fell to her knees.

"We are at your service, your majesty," Parthenay gritted through her teeth. "How may we serve you?"

"That girl," I shouted, pointing at the one they'd dragged in. "Release her. She's to be my new maid. And my maids are *not* to be touched."

There was a collective grunt from the akadim who'd surrounded her. I could feel their dissatisfaction at the command, could feel her fear. She was blonde, with pale skin. Pretty blue eyes. Eyes that had never seen such horrors before. At least, I could spare her from seeing more.

"Come," I said, extending an arm out to her.

Shaking, her eyes roaming wildly around the room, as if expecting to be struck down at any moment, she stumbled forward in torn, ragged clothes.

You're no better, Parthenay thought. *You still command over them. They have their ways. They have to eat.*

They have to do what I say! I snapped. Then out loud, I looked out over my monstrous court. "I'll take breakfast in my room. Alone. She'll need a meal, too." I took the girl's hand, glaring at Parthenay. And then left, without looking back.

CHAPTER FOURTEEN

LYRIANA

The pine trees and the horizons of Glemaria were still cloaked in the black shadows of night, but the snow tipped mountain caps were just beginning to glow beneath the red-orange light of sunrise. I looked over Gryphon's Mount, my entire body sore and aching. We were still flying. I'd spent the entire night awake.

Rhyan's still head lay in my lap, his breathing labored and loud through his twice broken nose. Both of his eyes were blue and purple with bruising, and an inflamed cut above his left eye had begun to scab. I ran my fingers through his hair. His curls were soft, but had elongated into waves from my stroking them all night. I'd been hoping some of the Valalumir's magic would escape my binds, but my magic had been stuck inside of me.

Beside us Meera sat, her bound body stiff while one of Aiden's conjured fires floated between us. It had kept us from freezing all night. Not long after we'd escaped the cave, we'd landed at an outpost. Three sentries surrounded the gryphon, their swords pointed at us as Aiden and Dario went inside to relieve themselves and make their reports.

But once we were airborne again, we hadn't stopped. I expected we would have arrived hours earlier. But the akadim attack had left the gryphon's wings injured, and our flight had been slow and laborious.

A sudden drop of my stomach told me we were descending, and sure enough, the gray towers of Seathorne came into view, rising above the mountain. I shifted my hand to Rhyan's chest, my fingers grasping at the strap of his sword belt, desperately trying to keep him close. And to keep myself from panicking. With the appearance of the turrets protruding from Imperator Hart's fortress, all lingering hopes of escape were dashed.

I squeezed my eyes shut, the wind blowing snow into my face, until the gryphon's paws hit the courtyard, offering a clear view of the stone promenade of Seathorne.

Rhyan stirred from the impact."Lyr?" he murmured, one eye barely opened.

"Hey," I said, trying to smile.

He struggled to sit up, and forced both eyes open. He looked awful, and I knew he was in far more pain than he was willing to admit. His fingers wiggled at his sides beneath the crisscross of ropes around his arms, as his jaw set, his expression fully alert.

"You okay?" he asked, his eyes already scanning the scene before us.

I shook my head. "How are you feeling?"

"Don't worry about me," he said gruffly, then stilled, taking in the towers before us. His mouth tightened, the muscles in his jaw twitching as he watched Dario and Aiden. They were huddled together by the gryphon's shoulders, staring cautiously back at us. Aiden's hand was on his stave, the point aimed in our direction. But they were too far to hear our whispers.

"Fuck. We don't have time," he said urgently. "Listen carefully. You cannot trust my father. Whatever he wants from you, you must refuse. Whatever kind of deal he tries to make, Lyr, swear to me, you will not accept."

I bit my lip. The last time I'd seen his father he'd tried to force a bargain. In exchange for the key to Asherah's tomb, the key to my magic power, he'd wanted me to come to him here, to bring Rhyan back under his authority. And he'd wanted me to marry Arkturion Kane. When I'd refused Imperator Hart's offer, he'd nearly crushed my hand.

Now we were here, exactly as he'd wanted.

Fighting wouldn't be an option. Not a fair one, anyway. The battle would be political, and steeped in legalities. I was still a noblewoman of Ka Batavia. But that was worth less than it ever had been while my father's murderer sat on his Seat. My only other political advantage came from my forced engagement to Viktor Kormac—Imperator Kormac's Heir Apparent. I was only a ceremony away from becoming the grand-niece by law to the Emperor. Imperator Hart couldn't interfere with that. But the only way I could use it in my favor would be to surrender myself to Imperator Kormac.

Then I'd be married to Viktor.

Over my dead body.

"Lyr, please," Rhyan begged. "Swear to me. A bargain with my father is worse than one with the Afeya. You don't …" His throat bobbed. "You don't know what he's capable of. He'll separate us, and he'll hurt you. It won't just be physical. He'll come after you with any ammunition he can find." He sighed. "He'll use me and Meera against you."

I shook my head. I already knew that. "I might have no other option. What am I supposed to do if your life's at stake?"

"Let me protect you. And protect Meera. Let me be the one to keep you safe. Remember, I escaped before. I will do it again, and I will make sure you're both with me. I will get you both out, I swear I will, even if it's the last thing I do."

"No," I said. "Don't talk like that. We stay together. We leave together."

Rhyan nodded, his fingers dancing against my palm. "We stay together."

Dario and Aiden stopped talking, and began descending from the gryphon, motioning to the growing presence of the soturi who surrounded us.

"Do not admit anything to him, okay? He knows we were on Gryphon's Mount—he knows we were at the tomb— Dario will have reported us. But everything else that has happened since— including that you have magic now and that you can—" His eyes dipped to my heart, his mouth tight. "He can't know."

I nodded, my eyes darting to Dario.

"He ..." Rhyan looked pained over what he had to say next. "He won't just hurt you. He'll find pleasure in it. Don't show strength. Be meek. The more of a threat he sees, the harder he'll work to break you."

I shook my head. "Doesn't he already know that I'm Asherah?"

Rhyan's eyes closed slowly, and he winced. His father had never said the words directly, but he'd told Rhyan once I'd have a dangerous power that needed to be controlled. If he knew that, what were the odds that he also knew Rhyan was Auriel? I suspected that was the true reason he'd kept him alive all these years, the real reason he wanted him back.

"We can't help what he knows," Rhyan said. "But we certainly won't offer confirmation. Nor will we give him anything more." I nodded.

"Hey!" Dario yelled. "Enough."

I made a point of snapping my mouth shut as I glared at Dario.

He sneered, pulling his dark curls off his face and tying them back with a leather strap. The echo of boots marching across the courtyard sounded, and I braced myself.

But instead of the violent hands of a soturion hauling me to the ground, a rough, elderly voice, thick with a Glemarian accent shouted. "Rhyan? L-Lord Rhyan? Is it you?"

Rhyan stilled, his face even paler than before as he turned to look at the elderly man. He wore dirty gray coveralls, and had marched straight through the wall of soturi standing guard. He carried a large bucket with the distinct scent of raw meat clinging to it.

"Artem," Rhyan rasped.

"The hell happened?" Artem shook his head. "You weren't supposed to come back," he said quietly.

"Artem," Dario reprimanded. "We sent for you to attend to the gryphon, not make small talk. It's too fucking early."

"Aye, well, maybe choose a different time of arrival," he snapped. "Lord Dario." He lowered his chin and slapped his knee. Moving toward the gryphon's head, he cooed, calling him a good boy before he laid down his bucket. "Poor beast," he muttered, his hand gentle on one of the injured wings. But his eyes were on Rhyan as he asked softly, "What happened to him?"

The gryphon flattened himself to the ground and eagerly attacked his breakfast.

"Akadim," Dario said, securing the gryphon's rope to an anchor.

"He's hurt," Artem said, his eyes still on Rhyan, and full of sympathy.

"The gryphon is," Dario said pointedly. "Hence why you were sent for."

Rhyan's breath came out ragged, watching the old man.

"You know him?" I asked Rhyan quietly.

His throat bobbed and he nodded. "Stables master," he muttered. "Taught me how to work with gryphons—with all the animals."

Artem returned to the gryphon's face, running a soothing hand over his beak. A wave of sadness washed over me as I realized everything Rhyan had lost. His home, his family and Ka, his friends, his teachers.

I squashed the thoughts as the sentries began pulling us off the gryphon to the ground.

"Hey," Rhyan shouted. "She's bound, she's no threat to you."

"Fuck off." The soturion gripping me squeezed my arm even tighter.

My eyes burned, but I kept my head up straight.

"Inside," Aiden ordered.

Soturi in black leathered armor, all bearing the silver gryphon across their torso flanked us. We were quickly separated from each other, and marched from the promenade through the front hall of Seathorne.

The inner walls were just as plain and modest-looking as the outside. The hall was grand only in scale, with ceilings several stories high, intimidating in their structural height, possibly originally sized for gryphons.

As we were ushered deeper into the hall, I found more paintings of gryphons and sculptures lining the walls of Seathorne. The soturi pushed us between two silver statues– both life-sized and grandiose.

"Against the wall," sneered a soturion, shoving Meera back. Three men guarded each of us—all flanked by a dozen more soturi of Ka Hart, poised and ready, their daggers out.

"My name is Lady Meera Batavia," Meera said, her voice full of the affect of an Heir Apparent. "I have done nothing to deserve this ill treatment. I demand an audience with His Highness at once."

"Where do you think you're going?" her captor snorted.

"Then unhand me," Meera said. "He'll be displeased to see me like this."

"Don't listen to her," Dario said. "All three are wanted by His Highness."

Meera opened her mouth again, but was quickly silenced as her soturion grabbed her shoulders.

"Now no trouble from you," said the man before me, and before I could muster a response, he slammed my cheek into the stone wall.

"Get your hands off her!" Rhyan growled. He was instinctively moving toward me, but his guard slammed his entire body back.

"No! He's hurt," I said. "Can't you see his face? He's bound! You don't have to shove."

"I'm about to shove myself into you just to shut you up." A rough hand gripped my neck, turning me around and pushing my face against the wall. The stone scraped against my cheek. Another hand ran over my body, and I tensed, my heart thumping. I could hear the unclicking of my belt buckle, and the sudden lightness around my chest and shoulders as my armor was unclasped between my bindings.

No. No.

I squeezed my eyes shut hearing the snap of every buckle, and each subsequent closure come undone. Each one seemed to echo. Piece by piece, my armor, my belt, sword, dagger, and knives hit the ground.

Powerless, I pressed my cheek to the cold stone, trying to keep my entire body from shaking. But I couldn't help it. Couldn't stop remembering Vrukshire. I strained against the ropes, desperate to claw my way out.

Then my captor clapped his hand against my hip, and I froze, my eyes watering. There was nothing more he could remove from my body beyond my clothing. He'd already threatened me. Heart pounding, I waited. He moved closer and closer. Suddenly, my hip warmed beneath his touch, his fingers squeezing me with propriety.

My breath came short.

We're going to fuck your girl. We're going to do it until you get here.

No! No! No!

"Partner."

I opened my eyes and found Rhyan's face a few inches from mine, also smashed against the wall, his swords strewn at his feet. I wasn't in Vrukshire. I wasn't trapped by Brockton, or Brett, or Geoffrey, or Trey. There were no wolves here.

But we weren't free. Not even close.

"Breathe," Rhyan mouthed. "Breathe."

I did, meeting his eyes. I sucked in a breath just as I was hauled backward. Weaponless and relieved of my armor, I was dragged beside Rhyan and Meera down the halls of Seathorne.

To Imperator Hart's Seating Room.

Dread built in the pit of my stomach when we finally stopped before a set of looming double doors. A gryphon with his wings outstretched had been carved into the wood. A sentry, the herald I supposed, stood in the center and stepped aside upon our arrival, speaking quietly with Dario who shared our names and titles. The herald's eyes swept across Rhyan's beaten face, his lips lifting into a smug smile that I wanted to punch.

But Rhyan hadn't noticed. He looked lost, his eyes haunted like he was imagining the last time he'd been in there. Then he snapped to attention, his gaze focused on me.

A soturion I hadn't noticed before moved suddenly out of the shadows, smirking at Rhyan. "Welcome back, Your Grace," he jeered.

Rhyan growled low in his throat, his jaw tightening, then suddenly, he paled and turned to me. "I'm sorry," he mouthed. "Lyr, I'm sorry."

I shook my head.

The doors opened, and the herald announced our names as an aura powered with a hurricane-like force flowed into the hall. And then, we entered Imperator Hart's Seating Room.

CHAPTER FIFTEEN

LYRIANA

The Seating Room of Imperator Hart was cold, sterile, and plainly decorated, with little more than rows of benches made of simple wood to fill the space. It reminded me of the hall. Not adorned with jewels, or anything ornate. It was not befitting of the fortress of an Imperator, save for the fact that it was large and expansive. The gryphons, both real and carved, had been the emphasis in the fortress entrance, the symbol of Ka Hart's power. I thought this room meant to convey the same. With the exception of green tapestries, each adorned with the silver sigil of Ka Hart, the walls were bare. The layout and simplicity of the room forced my attention ahead—and that's when I realized the true aim of the decor. To make the one point of interest the dais and the Seat, to force everyone's attention onto its occupant.

Imperator Hart.

His dark beard was neatly trimmed, his eyes amused, dancing with the vicious cruelty I'd come to expect from him. He wore his golden Laurel of the Arkasva, and the black cloak with the golden border that marked him as Imperator. The hilt of his sword gleamed as did the Valalumirs on the straps of his soturion belt. The sun remained faint as it began to snow again outside, but the torchlights made him glow, highlighting every ornament of his power.

Only one thing was missing from his array of adornments— the red key to Asherah's tomb. The key Rhyan had stolen.

The closer we got to the Imperator, the harder my pulse thrummed. Beyond the lack of decor, the room was unnaturally empty. No nobility. Not even Imperator Hart's personal guards were present. Which meant only one thing—he didn't want witnesses.

My heart beat harder, my rage and fear beginning to boil and fester in my gut.

Rhyan had been walking beside me, his steps keeping pace, but as we made our way to the foot of the dais, and the air thickened with his father's power, he pushed ahead of our guard. His hands clenched at his sides, his body angled protectively in front of me and Meera. A movement his father's eyes clocked, but immediately ignored as he nodded to Aiden and Dario who both bowed low.

"Lord Aiden." Imperator Hart's voice was deep. "Lord Dario. Rise." Then with a flick of his eyes, he disdainfully added, "I understand bindings make bowing and curtseying difficult. But it does not excuse you from such formalities." He coughed, leaning forward, his eyes narrowed as Meera and I made attempts to curtsey. Rhyan however remained standing upright. But the Imperator ignored Rhyan. Instead, he gestured for Aiden and Dario to join him at the base of the dais.

They stepped forward with straight backs, and in unison uttered, "Your Highness."

Imperator Hart's lips lifted into an unamused smile. "I did not expect the capturing of a reckless, weak forsworn, and a powerless girl would require such effort. Nonetheless, you two shall be rewarded for your services." He leaned forward even further, his hateful eyes finding mine before raking me up and down.

"Welcome to Seathorne, Lady Lyriana. I am pleased to see you have found your way here. It seems you've taken up my offer to host you after all. A good thing. I didn't spend as much time with you as I would have liked in Bamaria. I believe we had more important things to discuss. But our dance, if I remember," his glare fell to Rhyan, "was quite rudely interrupted. You are blocking my view, Rhyan. Move aside."

Rhyan shifted his weight between his feet, the only sign of his agitation, but he remained standing before me. The Imperator snapped his fingers. Suddenly Dario appeared next to Rhyan, and with a grunt, shoved him, leaving me directly in Imperator Hart's eyeline.

I sucked in a breath, watching as Rhyan's hands fisted, his knuckles white with tension.

"Now my lady," Imperator Hart continued, "as I was saying, I desired more time with you. Something we can now achieve."

"I thought we'd spent more than enough time together," I said, infusing as much sweetness as I could into my voice, but even I could hear the undertone of my hatred. "I had no idea I left you wanting."

He made a noise low in his throat—something between amusement and disdain. "Your courtly charms are just as I remember, my lady. However," he drummed his fingers against the Seat, "let me also remind you that as much as you do not wish to be here, plainly evident by the dour look on your face, I do not care. It will help your cause greatly by remembering that you're in Seathorne now, not Bamaria. Such impudence may have been tolerated by your dead father, but you will address me as 'Your Highness.' Every time you speak."

I glanced around the room, eying the tapestries. "Trust me, the … *decor* alone is enough reminder of where I am. Your Highness," I practically spat.

"May I ask, how your grip is?" His voice was unsettling in its casualness. He was holding his hand up and stretching his fingers as if to demonstrate his meaning—as if I couldn't understand his words—or recall what he referenced. "Improved since last time?" he asked.

My fingers flexed uncomfortably, viscerally remembering the pain he caused at Arianna's ball. Fucking bastard. He had no idea the strength I possessed now. I could throttle him right then.

But Rhyan turned to me, a swift warning in his expression, his head shaking.

I relaxed my hands at my sides.

"Perhaps not?" his father asked.

I lowered my chin, my insides boiling. But he had already moved his attention to Meera.

"Now, I did not expect to see you, Lady Meera. I have prayed for your safe return. A miracle that you stand before me now. May I ask?" His eyebrows lifted in amusement. "How is it you stole away from your captors alive? And ... with your soul still intact?" He stroked his beard. "It's been my understanding that if akadim take prisoners, those taken do not remain prisoners for long. And not because they find freedom."

I tensed, and felt Rhyan's body still beside me. We were getting into dangerous territory.

"I thank you for your prayers, Your Highness." Meera smiled, speaking in a voice I'd heard her use a thousand times before in Bamaria—the practiced, calm voice of the Heir Apparent. But now there was a force behind her words, as if she were Arkasva. "They proved most effective by evidence of my being here. To answer your question, I admit, I was not conscious for most of my captivity. A miracle in and of itself to spare me of the many horrors I could have witnessed. I believe there was a plan in place for me, one that created a delay, and fortunately did not come to fruition. I was rescued first."

"A plan. I see. And were you spared of all their ... *violence*?" His lips curled around the question.

Meera's eyes narrowed. "Yes, Your Highness." She looked down at her body as if that were proof. "I sustained cuts and bruises. I was underfed, and left in horrid conditions and squalor for days. But no lasting physical harm. Thank the Gods."

"Truly? They did nothing else to you?" His eyes sparkled. "Nothing more intimately violent?"

"Your Highness?" Meera asked, her voice suddenly high.

"Did they rape you?" he asked bluntly.

Meera's mouth fell open. I felt like I'd been punched. The fact that he would ask so crudely with so much obvious excitement eking off his aura. Even Dario looked offended.

"Well?" Imperator Hart asked, now impatient.

"They did not," Meera said, her voice shaking with anger.

He tilted his head to the side, not even bothering to feign his disappointment at her response. "A relief. And your sister? Lady Morgana? I see she is not here with you. Am I to assume that she remains in captivity? Or ... worse?"

I took a deep breath, at least I tried to. Meera, however, seemed to be keeping her composure under Imperator Hart's glare.

Meera nodded. "When I last saw my sister, she had suffered no more than myself. We were kept apart, though in similar conditions." Her voice hardened. "Soturion Rhyan and Lady Lyriana did all they could in their rescue, and they deserve all of the honor afforded them for saving me. But despite their efforts we could not rescue her. Not yet. Morgana was held under greater security. I pray her situation remains stable, and I pray even more deeply for her rescue as soon as possible."

"I pray to the Gods as well." He smirked. "Fortunate that you found their favor. Who can say why a God, or Goddess may save one life, but not the other." His eyes bore into me. "Surely, Imperator Kormac's soturi, and the legions under the Ready's command will soon find success. At least, I pray so. But for now, you are quite a long way from home. Correct me if I am wrong, my lady, but your abduction was from Cresthaven, was it not? How is it that you came to be in Glemaria?" He sat back, his fingers steepled below his chin. "You see, a crime was committed in these lands by my son, and your sister. And I must know, were you also present for it? For their theft on my property? Or was your entire kidnapping some sort of elaborate ruse? An excuse for them to come and steal from me?"

Meera's lips tightened. "I was not present, nor am I aware, of any crimes having been committed. As for your accusation of my kidnapping being a ruse?" She scoffed, expressing her offense, and somehow conveying the ridiculousness of his question. "I can assure you it was not. I was brutally taken from Cresthaven, our escorts fell defending us. I know they'll bear witness. I was brought to Glemaria by my captors."

Imperator Hart nodded. "And yet, you survived long travel with the akadim. With no lasting harm, nor more intimate forms of violence. Forgive me, but this is most unusual behavior for the demons. Your story is … well … almost unbelievable."

"It's the truth," Meera said.

"Of course. But I must ask these questions so I can present your case to my Council. Now your rescue, what day was that?"

"I …" Meera balked. She knew Godsdamned well that her rescue had occurred only hours after the "crime" he was referring to. "I'm sorry, Your Highness. What day was I rescued? It's been only a few days," she said, and I knew she wasn't sure how to play this. "Forgive me. I've been disoriented from my ordeal."

"Perhaps I can help you remember," he said gently. "You were rescued a week ago. Exactly a week and a day ago."

I stiffened. He'd known. He'd known this whole fucking time. The nahashim had been spying all along. Gods. Was it a miracle we'd spent so many days evading capture, or had he been baiting us this entire time? He'd had hundreds of soturi searching for us. Why, if he knew where we were? Unless they weren't supposed to find us.

"Did that help, Lady Meera?" His nose crinkled, his expression full of derision. "Do you remember now?"

"Y-yes. It's been a week and a day."

Imperator Hart stroked his beard. "So, after your kidnapping, and your ordeal of terror and hunger, and the knowledge of some murky akadim plan that had not yet come to pass— one that involves your dear sister who is still in captivity—you ...?" He shrugged, frowning. "Help me understand, my lady. Because if I were in your shoes, I'd have come straight here, come straight to an Imperator with legions at his beck and call. I would have asked for soturi to aid in my sister's rescue and return. I would have alerted my country and Ka to the fact that I was alive and safe. After being hurt and starved, I would have sought shelter, medical attention, and nutrition. All things I can provide here. All things that you as a noblewoman would have been entitled to. And yet ..." He eyed her up and down. "You did none of those things."

"I was weak," Meera said. I could see her flailing as she tried to remain composed. "As I said, I was starved. I needed time to recover. And to—"

"To hide with your criminal sister and my forsworn son?"

"To rest. They saved me," Meera said defiantly. "It is thanks to them that I am alive. They've been nursing me back to health."

"In caves? With stolen food? Stolen clothing?" His eyes moved up and down Meera's soturion cloak with disgust. "Sounds more like they were keeping you hostage."

"No," Meera cried.

Imperator Hart scoffed. "Then you were aiding them. Helping two criminals evade my soturi. Which is it, Lady Meera? Are you in league with them, or are you still in some form of captivity that requires my intervention?"

"Neither." Meera lifted her chin. "I am a noble of Ka Batavia. Niece to the Arkasva and High Lady. Thousands of soturi are looking for me right now, all under Imperator Kormac's orders in the South."

"But you are in the North, my lady. Not the South." Imperator Hart narrowed his eyes, peering down his nose. "I am surprised you have allowed for such precious resources to go to waste as you hid. Resources that could have been used to rescue Lady Morgana. Unless you don't want her to be rescued for some reason?"

My chest tightened.

"How could you say such a thing?" Meera asked, her voice shaking with anger.

Imperator Hart shook his head. "I'm simply trying to understand these most unusual circumstances. Congratulations, by the way, on your aunt's ascension to power. A pity you missed her consecration."

He sighed dramatically, shifting his head from side to side as if weighing his options. Rhyan's nostrils flared, and I imagined he'd been forced to sit through such a decision- making process many times before.

Finally, Imperator Hart straightened, his eyes dancing with a decision I was sure he'd made long before we entered the room.

"All right, I have decided." He gestured for Meera to step forward.

"Your Highness," she said, following his orders.

"I shall take you at your word, Lady Meera. I shall believe that you are innocent of all suspected crimes. Clearly, you are too weak to have committed any. You also appear far too traumatized to travel. The choices you've made in the aftermath of your captivity tell me that you are not yet well. You cannot even seem to grasp what day it is. Or whether you are in the hands of criminals or not. You are in need of rest, medical attention, and care. I'll send word to Imperator Kormac and Arkasva Batavia that you are here. Then you shall remain in Seathorne at my pleasure, as my most special guest."

"I …" Meera started to protest, but Rhyan caught her eye, carefully shaking his head. "Your Highness," she said carefully, "I thank you for providing a space for me to recover. When I am well, I shall return home with my escorts."

"We shall have to assign you some first," he said. "When the time is right."

"May I ask, Your Highness," I said, throat tight, "What happens if Imperator Kormac requires us at home? Or we are called back by Arkasva Batavia? After all, we are still the subjects of Bamaria, and remain under the jurisdiction of the South and Ka Kormac."

"Worried about your future father-in-law?" Imperator Hart laughed. Then his eyes flashed. "You're under the jurisdiction of the North when you're in northern lands. I have every right to keep you. Never mind the charges of trespassing and theft. I have more than enough grounds to accuse you two of something far more severe. The breaking of your sacred soturion oath."

My heart stopped.

"And before you try to claim Rhyan has any rights under Ka Kormac, you should know that while you hid in a cave, evading my justice, and stealing from my people, your aunt revoked his political immunity. He no longer has the right to seek asylum in your country. Further, he is now suspected of being in league with the akadim and kidnapping you."

"What? That's ridiculous! That's—"

"My lady!" he snarled. "You forgot to say, Your Highness."

I pressed my lips together, and stared back in defiance. Fucking bastard. I took a deep breath. "I didn't realize you needed to hear your own title repeated back to you so many times."

He tilted his head. "Careful now. While you do amuse me,

my patience for you grows thin. You will not win my favor unless you can offer something *sweet* in return."

Rhyan's shoulders stiffened, his face pale.

"And believe me, girl," his father continued. "You will need my favor before the end."

My fingers clenched, but I remained silent. My body still.

"I know you think you want to leave here," he said, "but I'd strongly reconsider. Your allies at home are not what you remember. Since the disappearance of the Ready, you have a new Arkturion in charge."

"A new Arkturion?" I asked.

His eyes flashed. "Arkturion Waryn Kormac now leads the Bamarian legions."

The Bastardmaker. The fucking Bastardmaker.

"And your former betrothed, or ... *companion* as I hear it," he smirked, "has been ordered to hunt you down and bring you before Kormac himself."

Tristan? Tristan had been sent after us?

"Now, I have other matters to discuss. Lady Meera, you're to be brought to the medical wing, to be checked properly for injury. *Inspected.* Inside and out. Particularly for any signs of a black mark. I must be sure you're not forsaken. Lord Aiden, please escort the lady. Do not let her out of your sight."

"No! Wherever she goes, I go!" I yelled in panic.

"Lyr," Rhyan hissed.

"Please," I said. "I'm her escort!"

"Suspected criminals may not be escorts for nobles." He waved his hand in dismissal.

The backs of my eyes burned as Aiden took hold of her arm, his stave pointed at her.

"Meera!" I shouted.

She looked back at me, a determined look in her eyes, and nodded. "It's okay," she said, before she let Aiden lead her away from the dais.

But the doors opened before they could reach them. And the herald's shadow filled the threshold as he shouted, "Presenting Lady Hart, wife of His Highness, Arkasva Hart, High Lord of Glemaria, Imperator to the North."

I stilled. *Lady Hart?* Imperator Hart had remarried? When?

My gaze immediately fell on him, my heart pounding. Rhyan's eyes had reddened, and there was an expression on his face I couldn't quite read.

"Did you know?" I mouthed.

His jaw clenched, and he nodded, his eyes downcast, his hands trembling at his sides.

"My son didn't tell you he had a new stepmother?" Imperator Hart asked, closely watching our exchange.

"Lyr," Rhyan whispered, still barely looking at me. "I'm sorry," he said, his voice so quiet I could only just hear. "I'm so sorry."

I frowned, and looked over my shoulder. Just as Meera and Aiden vanished, Lady Hart appeared in the doorframe, gracefully stepping forward.

Three things became clear at once. First, Lady Hart was far too young for the Imperator. Rhyan's *stepmother* appeared hardly older than me.

Second, she was incredibly beautiful. She had large dark eyes, and shining brown hair pulled back by a silver diadem. Her skin was pale in the way of most northerners, but with distinctly pink cheeks and lips. She had the kind of beauty that conveyed a sense of warmth and intelligence.

And third, she was incredibly far along in her pregnancy. She entered the Seating Room, walking slowly, almost painfully slow, wincing every so often, her hand wrapped protectively around her swollen belly.

Rhyan's shoulders shook, and a small gasp escaped his lips as he watched. When she finally reached the dais, Rhyan's father stood and helped her up. She was out of breath, drained from the long walk down the aisle. But instead of offering her a chair, or even something to lean against, he left her standing alone, and returned to his Seat, settling back, his legs spread wide.

Dario, the only soturion who remained in the room with us, started forward, as if he meant to help her. But then he stilled, stepping back as if he'd remembered himself.

Lady Hart's eyes went to Rhyan's almost at once, staring at him for a long time. A wave of emotions I couldn't read flashed across his face. Something unspoken passed between them.

Who had she been to Rhyan? A friend? A classmate? Based on her age it seemed likely. From the look she'd given him, they'd been more than just acquaintances. It was also clear that he'd known that she'd married his father. But he'd never told me. Why? And why did he keep apologizing?

Imperator Hart grinned. "Please present yourself to my wife, Lady Kenna."

I swallowed, not recognizing the name, my heart thumping. "Lady Lyriana Batavia," I said. "I would curtsey, Your Grace, but I'm a little tied up at the moment."

Kenna's eyes lit up, looking between me and Rhyan, like she saw what lay between us. She smiled. It was a smile that felt oddly genuine, but then her face bore the neutral expression of nobility. "It's good to meet you, Lady Lyriana." Unlike her husband, she spoke with a soft Glemarian lilt. So, she'd been born here.

"My wife," he said, "is the eldest daughter of Arkturion Kane of Ka Gadayyan. A warlord that many argue is more powerful than the Ready. She comes from a very ancient bloodline. Like you, my lady."

"How fitting," I said, "For an Imperator."

I looked at her again more carefully. Kane's daughter. Shit. Was she dangerous? Was that why Rhyan was upset? Was this why he'd never mentioned her?

"More fitting than you know, Lyriana," Imperator Hart

continued, his voice rolling over the informal use of my name. "Lady Kenna was marked for Ka Hart for quite some time. Didn't my son tell you? She was once nearly betrothed to another member of my immediate family."

"Your immediate family?" I asked, frowning.

A red stain crept up Lady Kenna's neck, but she stared at me with an almost daring boldness as my mind tried to sort out the Imperator's meaning. He had no immediate family beyond his deceased wife. And Rhyan.

And Rhyan …

My heart sank. Kenna looked past me as Rhyan's face paled.

"You didn't know?" Imperator Hart asked, his eyes now sparkling with delight. "Until he was forsworn, Lady Kenna was Rhyan's lover."

CHAPTER SIXTEEN

LYRIANA

His lover. *His lover*. Lady Kenna was Rhyan's lover.

Hello, lover.

Nausea whirled deep inside of me. My chest tightening, a wheezing feeling stirred in my gut like I'd been punched. I couldn't catch my breath. The backs of my eyes burned like I wanted to cry. But I wanted to throw up at that moment even more.

I knew he'd courted as Heir Apparent. Knew he'd been courted many times. There'd been others before me. Of course, there'd been. But … I hadn't imagined anyone significant. Hadn't imagined anyone I'd come face-to-face with. Any previous bursts of jealousy I'd felt for the women who'd been a part of his past had been quickly squashed by their anonymity. By the fact that none had been mentioned by name or in detail. Because it was the past. Because it didn't matter. Because he was mine.

Maybe this was nothing. She was someone insignificant. Someone Imperator Hart was using to come between us. But my gut kept churning, and at that moment, caught so off guard, it physically hurt to look at Rhyan.

"By the expression on your face, Lady Lyriana," Imperator Hart said, "I surmise my son did not tell you about Lady Kenna."

I blinked slowly, my face tight. I tried to take a breath, to remain calm. This was a manipulation. Nothing more. Nothing Imperator Hart said or did could be trusted. I knew that. I knew that too fucking well. And I trusted Rhyan—more than anything in this world. I'd talk to him before I came to any conclusion. Even if this was making my stomach hurt. I knew what I had to do. And though my throat was raw, I straightened my shoulders, and plastered a smile across my face.

"A happy surprise," I said. "Congratulations, Your Highness. *Tovayah maischa*, on your happy news. And to you as well, Lady Kenna." My eyes dipped to her belly.

Imperator Hart frowned, displeased with my response.

Godsdamned fucking bastard.

Rhyan's chest heaved, a worried look in his eyes as his gaze moved back and forth from his father to me.

"Do you remember?" his father asked Kenna. His voice had softened to something almost sickeningly sweet. "Back before we wed, my love?" His aura darkened, and his eyes narrowed. "How many months it was? Hmmm?"

"How many months?" Kenna looked confused. "Months of what, Your Highness?"

"How many months," he gritted, "was my son fucking you?"

I couldn't hold back the gasp that escaped me. Nor could Dario.

"Your Highness." Kenna blinked rapidly, her hand moving protectively over her belly. "I can barely recall such a thing. It's a distant memory. I'm your wife now, and that's all that matters to me. That, and that I am carrying *your* child." She smiled, but the fear was clear in her eyes.

"A simple question. How many months?" he asked again, his voice hard and loud, ringing throughout the empty room.

My stomach roiled, and I wanted to throw up. I knew this was my fault. I hadn't responded the way he wanted—hadn't acted hurt enough. But by the Gods, I didn't want to know the answer. I didn't want to hear about it.

Kenna's chest heaved, her eyes widening with alarm. Rhyan's jaw tensed, his neck turning red.

"Tell me how long he fucked you for." He reached for her arm, wrapping his fingers violently around her.

My hands clenched.

"Your Highness," Dario started, but a sharp look from Imperator Hart, a pointed blast of his aura, and Dario stepped back, staring at the ground.

Kenna pressed her lips together, but the Imperator's hand twisted, tightening around her arm until she let out a cry.

"Stop!" I yelled. But he only jerked Kenna toward him.

"Seven!" Rhyan shouted, stepping forward. "It was seven months."

My eyes watered as I looked at Rhyan. He turned back to me, his face red, his jaw clenched. Seven months. That was longer than we'd been together.

"I'm sorry," he whispered, then looked up at his father with death in his eyes. "Are you satisfied? I can only assume from the size of her belly you've outdone me."

Gods. I needed to get out of here. I needed to break free of these damned ropes. I pinched my own fingers together. It was all I could do to keep from crying. But tears still welled in my eyes.

Something I realized that Imperator Hart had noticed. As had Rhyan. His face tightened, and fell. I knew he felt awful. But I still couldn't look at him. Nor could I face Imperator Hart who had finally released Kenna from his hold.

She started to reach for her arm, for the spot I was sure was already bruising. But then she straightened, hands at her side, shoulders pushed back. Her noble training kicked back in and she stared pointedly out the window.

Imperator Hart stroked his beard. "No need to be embarrassed, my love. It's in the past," he said gently. "I just thought that since it was the first time we were all together, I should remind you. Rhyan's my prisoner. And nothing more than your stepson."

Kenna's eyes flashed with anger, her neck reddening. "I'm well aware of his criminal status. My focus is only on *my* son, the one who will be here soon. And on you, Your Highness." She was speaking carefully, formally, but still with that Glemarian lilt.

"Good," his father said. But he still looked unsettled. I wasn't supposed to show strength. I had to remember that. The more power I showed, the harder he'd try to hurt me.

It was all a game for him. A game I had to play. I let my face fall, allowing one tear to roll down my cheek. But then another fell. And another. And I couldn't stop.

Shit.

"Lyr," Rhyan whispered.

But I shook my head. I couldn't look at him, not now. Not in front of his father and not in front of … *her*.

"Now, I have some questions for you, my lady." Imperator Hart grinned, obviously happy now that he'd gotten a reaction from me. "When I entered Bamaria, I possessed a certain red jewel on my sword. Ancient and priceless. I offered it to you. But you refused me. And instead of negotiating, you sent a thief to rob me."

I stared ahead, my chin trembling. I was unsure what to say or do. I couldn't deny his words. But I couldn't agree with them either.

"And then the two of you came here, attacked my soturi, and used the jewel to open an ancient artifact."

"And how would you know that?" Rhyan asked. "As I recall, we knocked your soturi unconscious." His eyes flicked to Dario.

"Hmmm." Imperator Hart almost sounded amused. "That you did. In fact, the two of you knocked out every sentry on duty that night."

"Last time I checked," Rhyan said, "an unconscious soturion could not bear witness. I'll admit, I did steal the jewel from you, and we did climb Gryphon's Mount. But that's all. Perhaps, we simply came for the view."

"Lying to me is a mistake. Do you think I don't know? You had no right to break into the white seraphim. Ah—" he held his hand up, "No interruptions. You opened it. And you took what was inside." His aura thrashed. "Where is it?"

"We took nothing," Rhyan said. "There was magic around it, an old spell. It created flames. And that's it. We took nothing."

"Challenging me, now?" his father asked, his voice deadly low. "You see, besides sentries, I had some eyes on the mountain. They saw everything. And they whispered what they witnessed back to me."

By the Gods. He'd had nahashim there that night, too. Not to take us, but to spy. Fuck. Fuck! He knew we'd opened the tomb, knew we'd taken the shard. Which meant he knew that I had magic.

The puzzle of the last few days began to come together. All the soturi hunting us all week, the legion he'd sent to find Rhyan who'd been moving steadily closer but not close enough. The nahashim that had stalked outside of our cave, and told him exactly which day Meera had been rescued. None of it had been to capture us. He'd let us know he was watching because he was herding us, pushing us where he wanted. I'd been right. The nahashim at the cave had been a trap, leading us not just to any soturi—but to the men he'd *wanted* to find us. The ones he'd trusted.

Aiden and Dario.

Imperator Hart clapped, and the door opened.

"Soturion Baynan Gadayyan," announced the herald.

A soturion entered carrying a long wooden tray covered by green cloth. As he moved closer, I realized he'd been the soturion who had unsettled Rhyan outside, the one who had jeered at him. His hair was brown, shiny, his skin pale, he looked like ... of course. Gadayyan. He was related to Kenna. To Kane.

"These are all their effects? Nothing missing?" Imperator Hart asked.

"All they had on their persons is here, Your Highness," said Baynan. "You have my word."

The Imperator eyed Dario carefully. "You took everything? All their belongings?"

"Aye, we did, Your Highness, I swear."

I stilled. I knew what he was looking for. The key to Asherah's tomb. The shard of the Valalumir.

"Take it," Imperator Hart ordered. Dario stepped forward, retrieving the tray and presented it to Kenna.

We were forced to wait in stillness as Soturion Baynan left the room, and then Imperator Hart removed the cloth, revealing all the armor and weapons his soturi had stripped from us. Including the stave holder Rhyan had bought me with my initials inside. And my stave.

He took it in his hand, twirling the mix of dark sunwood. I resisted the urge to run up there and claim it. It had been mine for centuries—for lifetimes. The source of my power and my magic, the power I'd been denied.

"Where did you get this?" he asked, his eyes wide and mocking as they waited for an answer he knew I'd refuse to give. And when I remained silent, he said, "Fine. I care not." He tossed it onto the tray. He picked up the key to Asherah's tomb, the red jewel, and he pocketed it in his belt pouch. "I have a use for you, my lady, one we shall discuss in private."

"You don't need her," Rhyan said. "You want me. Let her go, and you can have me."

"Dario." Imperator Hart waved. "Restrain him."

"He's … he's already bound, Your Highness," Dario protested.

"Are his feet?" Imperator Hart snapped. "He's like a wild animal. Now hold him back."

Rhyan seethed, baring his teeth as Dario's blade pressed against his neck. "Afraid I'll tear through your ropes. It wouldn't be the first time."

"Yes. Well, we can't have that now, can we?" Imperator Hart turned to me. "Would you like to play a game, Lyriana? To prove your worth here as a guest? And to save Rhyan from further harm?"

"Guest, Your Highness? I thought I was a criminal."

He shrugged. "You certainly have been in bed with one."

I stiffened.

"Rhyan will go into the dungeons where he belongs. But you, Lyriana, you have an opportunity here to remain above ground, to sleep in guest quarters. Something I think you will want. Because it's the only way you'll see your sister again."

I exhaled sharply. "What must I do?"

"Tell me the truth. You took something else from the statue. Where is it?"

The shard. Sweat beaded the back of my neck. "I don't know. It was stolen," I said. "I don't have it."

"Someone else does," he said.

I nodded, shaking.

"Who? Answer, and do not play dumb with me."

"I don't know," I said. "I swear." And I was telling the truth. I had a damn good idea. But I could honestly say that I didn't know if the shard lay in Morgana's hands or Aemon's.

"Perhaps someone can help you find the information in your mind?" He looked over his shoulder. "Arkturion?"

"No!" Rhyan shouted. He tried to lunge forward, his lips pulled back, but Dario restrained him, digging the knife into his neck.

"Dario, stop it. Don't hurt him!" I yelled.

Rhyan seethed, his chest heaving. "You traitorous bastard!"

Dario growled, "At least, I'm not a murderer."

"Fuck you," Rhyan said, his voice low and defeated.

A back door behind the dais opened, and a tall, looming figure emerged.

Arkturion Kane.

He was somehow simultaneously exactly what I'd imagined, and far, far worse. Thick and muscled, he was like an oversized, paler version of the Bastardmaker, with the same lascivious smile, only more angular. His face was like a rectangle in shape, his torso as well. His hair was a mix of brown and gray that might have once been the same color as Kenna's. His Glemarian leathers were polished to shine, and his red Arkturion cloak was freshly pressed.

He bowed before Imperator Hart, and offered a quick, but dismissive look at his daughter before he turned to me and grinned.

"Lady Lyriana, we meet at last." His rough voice held a hint of amusement. "I've heard many things about you." He stalked toward me, nothing but hulking muscles, every angle of his face sharp and cruel. But before he reached me, his gaze fell on Rhyan, and he laughed. "Not even back a full morning and you already broke your nose?" He made a fist, his hand almost giant in size. I couldn't even imagine the damage he could do with a single punch.

"It seems he cannot help himself," Rhyan's father said. "Now, my lady. How about we make you more comfortable? Then you can answer the Arkturion's questions. Kenna, remove her binding."

"W-What?" I stammered, and my eyes met Kenna's. She

looked just as bewildered. But she nodded and pulled out her stave, a traditional mix of pale sun and moon wood. As she quietly chanted under her breath, I felt the hold of the ropes weaken, and vanish. For the first time in hours, I was able to move, to flex my arms and feel my power surge up inside me.

"That was a show of goodwill," Imperator Hart said.

"Lyr," Rhyan hissed. "Don't trust him."

"Must we bind your mouth as well?" his father asked. "Dario —one more word from my son …" He didn't finish the threat, only lowered his eyebrows. It was enough.

"Now, we can do this the hard way, or …" Imperator Hart's eyes darkened. "Who has the shard?"

I refused to answer. Because my power was mine again, and Asherah's chest plate was in view. A plan began to form in my mind.

"You stole a crystal from my land. Who has it?" Imperator Hart asked. "And I warn you, you're running out of time to answer peacefully."

Arkturion Kane circled around me, his body so close that his cloak touched my clothes, his breath brushed through my hair.

I began to chant. *"Ani petrova kashonim, me ka el lyrotz, dhame ra shukroya."* I was sweating, my body already heating. *"Aniam anam. Chayate me el ra shukroya. Ani petrova kashonim."*

"What in Moriel are you doing?" Kane barked. "Your kashonim is bound."

But it wasn't. Not the one I wanted.

I took a deep breath, my heart thundering. It didn't always work. I'd called on her before with no answer. But this time I felt it—the surge of power rushing through my body. My hair blew back from my face. My skin glowed red and then gold. I'd barely slept the night before, but I felt as if I'd just woken up. Every inch of my body felt strong, energized, and ready to attack.

I didn't stop to think. I ran. My eyes on my possessions.

"LYR!" Rhyan screamed and then grunted in pain as Dario elbowed him in the guts.

I touched the dais, our weapons within reach. One blade to Kenna's neck and she'd be forced to remove Rhyan's bonds. That would be all it took before he jumped to me. We were getting the fuck out of here. And then we'd get Meera.

My fingers brushed the hilt of my dagger. But then a rough hand grabbed my neck from behind, and I was pulled back and slammed to the floor. Kane grabbed my hips and turned me over, smashing my back to the ground, my head just inches from cracking against the dais.

I saw stars in my eyes as Kane hovered over me, his eyes full of violence. But before he could touch me again, I kicked, my boot hitting his stomach with enough force that he fell backward.

I started to roll over when suddenly his entire body slammed over me.

I screamed.

Rhyan was roaring, even Kenna shouted for him to stop.

I kicked helplessly as he pushed down over me, reaching for my arms. I freed one hand, and made a fist. And with everything I had in me, knowing what he'd done to Rhyan, what he'd try to do to me, I punched him on the nose.

There was an awful crunching sound, and he screamed as blood gushed.

"You bitch," Kane growled.

He shoved a knee between my legs, both hands around my neck, strangling me.

But I was already reaching for his eyeballs, prepared to gouge them out.

Suddenly, my body seized. My chest warmed. I was on fire. Everything inside of me was burning, heating and lighting up. I couldn't feel Asherah's power. Something else had overwhelmed it, had come between us. A golden light glowed beneath my tunic.

"What the fuck!" Kane released me, but I couldn't fight back.

I was screaming. My body was engulfed in flames. I was burning, on fire. I couldn't take it. It was too much. Too painful.

"By the fucking Gods," Imperator Hart said.

Kane's eyes were searching for the source of the light. He reached for my tunic, and ripped it open down the center.

No!

"LYR!" Rhyan screamed. He'd fallen at Dario's feet, knees slamming into the floor. He was still bound, still tied up. His eyes were blank, his hands opening and closing like they had when he'd fallen at Asherah's tomb. When he had a memory of Auriel.

And then I realized too late what was happening. What had triggered the Valalumir in my chest to ignite. Kane's touch.

Kane was a Guardian.

CHAPTER SEVENTEEN

RHYAN

"LYR!" I screamed. Dario's knife was pushing onto my neck. But I didn't fucking care. Because Kane was on top of Lyr, her shirt ripped open, and her heart alight. I swore on all the Gods. He would not hurt her. He would not touch her!

Every muscle in my body was straining, fighting. I was using everything I had, every last store of power inside me. And at last, I heard it. The sound of the first tear of the fucking ropes. Then there was another. And another.

"LYR!" I screamed again, but a wave of dizziness washed over me. My vision blurred and I fell to my knees.

I was in my father's Seating Room. In hell. And Lyr ... Lyr was there. Lyr needed me.

And then she was gone. And so was everything else. I was being pulled away, losing control. Losing my sense of reality— of this life.

No! No!

I blinked, disoriented. Kane was before me. But ... not Kane. He wore ancient looking armor as we battled. A yellow crystal hung from his neck. He heaved his sword overhead. It was a killing blow. But I dodged as he slammed his blade down. Every muscle in my body was agony. I was bleeding, injured. More than that. I was dying.

I glanced down at my hands, burned and scarred from the fall. I could barely hold onto my sword. I was so weak.

"Too slow, Auriel. Always too slow," he taunted.

I gripped my blade, fighting to keep it from slipping through my sweating hands. I could do this. I had to do this. And I used all I had left to straighten my body, to stand up tall. One more hit ... I just needed one more.

But right then, I realized, I wasn't alone. Asherah watched from behind a stone column, her red hair gleaming in the torchlight. Her eyes were full of fire, her stave drawn. I nearly fainted at the sight of her.

She'd come. She'd found me. Her gaze met mine, holding me, steadying me, and then she nodded. The blue light of her magic sparked forth, followed by a glow of red. Asherah's red, the light of the Valalumir she still possessed. She rushed forward with a war cry, and her stave vanished, replaced by her starfire sword.

Shiviel stumbled back, caught unaware.

I readjusted my fingers along the hilt, my grip finally tightening, and together, Asherah and I plunged our blades through Shiviel's body, cutting through his armor, slicing him in half.

My body was flung backwards and Asherah screamed.

I snapped back to Seathorne, back to my father's Seating Room. He stood on the dais, a look of triumph on his face.

Lyr was unconscious on the ground, her tunic torn open by that fucking bastard Arkturion Kane. The golden light of the Valalumir in her heart was just beginning to fade. And hovering over her, his face full of hatred, was the Guardian of the Yellow Light. The reincarnated God.

Kane was Shiviel.

THE SECOND SCROLL: SEATHORNE

CHAPTER EIGHTEEN

TRISTAN

I rolled over in Naria's bed, barely awake as the sun streamed through her windows. There was a loud knock on the door. Soturion Markan entered. His eyes met mine with a familiar fury. The bald guard had protected Lyr since she'd been a baby, hiding in her shadows for our entire courtship. It felt so stark to be here in her home, in her wing, with her guard, but not with her.

Instead, it was Naria lying naked beside me. Naria whose snores of sleep I'd become intimate with. In recent days, the sound of Naria's theatrical whines as she came had replaced my memories of Lyr's hushed sighs. It was as if Naria had simply taken over Lyr's life with Arianna's ascent to power. None of this felt real. None of this was what I wanted. I was collateral, a game piece to move about the board as my grandmother saw fit.

"What?" Naria groaned, tossing her arm over her eyes. "What is it?"

"Your Grace," Markan said. "I am sorry to disturb you."

"Then don't." She rolled over, pulling a pillow over her head.

"I was sent by Arkturion Waryn to request a meeting," Markan said. "With you, Lord Tristan."

I sat up straight, clutching the blanket so tightly my knuckles were white. "When?" I asked.

"He'd like to see you at once."

Fuck. It was too early to face the Bastardmaker. "Where shall I meet him?"

"He's in the main hall, having breakfast. A meal has already been ordered for you."

Groaning, I slid out of bed. I was expected to leave for Numeria today, to follow the Imperator's command to go hunting for Rhyan and Lyr.

But I hadn't packed. I hadn't even begun to prepare. Instead, I'd spent the night trying to convince Galen not to go to the Valabellum. The Godsdamned fool had won the trials. He'd been crowned victor by the Bastardmaker himself along with a dozen others, half of whom were Ka Kormac. He'd be leaving for the capital in another week to participate in the next set of tournaments, the ones that would determine his role in the Valabellum. And that would decide if he *might* die on Asherah's Feast Day— or if he *definitely* would.

Idiot.

"What does he want?" Naria asked, throwing her pillow to the ground. She sat up, letting the blanket fall to her waist, her nudity on full display in the morning sun.

I turned away, opening the closet. "You know what," I said. "I have to leave today."

She crawled out of bed, coming to stand behind me.

I pulled out a fresh set of towels and laid them on the dresser, catching her eye in the vanity mirror. She wrapped her arms around me from behind, her bare breasts pressed into my back.

"You shouldn't have to go," she said. "I don't understand. Why are they sending you anyway?"

I shook my head. Good fucking question. "I'm a trusted confidant for the Imperator," I said blandly. "And I know Lyr."

"So? I know her, too."

I pulled out of her hold. "I need to get ready."

Naria shook her head. "But, you're a vorakh hunter. Why would they send you after Lyriana and Rhyan unless ..." She shrugged, scrunching up her nose. "No. That's stupid."

I froze. Was it possible? Not Lyr. She had no magic. She'd been tested by the Examiner from Lethea. But Rhyan ... How had he gotten her out of the Shadow Stronghold? How had he done it when I'd failed? The question had plagued me for weeks. Was it possible that he was vorakh? That he could travel?

I'd never encountered one of those before. I couldn't even imagine how dangerous someone like that could be. Surely, Lyr wouldn't allow someone like that to be free in Bamaria, to go unreported to me and the Empire?

But then the truth sank in all at once. Yes, she would.

I remembered all the times she'd mentioned Jules the last few years. The hurt in her eyes whenever the topic resurfaced, the way she seemed fearful after I'd hunted.

Jules had been her cousin. I could understand that sorrow. But she'd been a monster in the end. And I didn't think I could ever forgive that.

At least, not until Haleika. She'd become a monster, too. But that hadn't stopped me from seeing her as my cousin. It hadn't stopped my love for her. Hadn't stopped me from wishing, deep down, that they wouldn't kill her. That we could have kept her alive. Found a cure, done something— anything—to let her live. She hadn't deserved that ending.

None of it had been her fault.

I stared at my reflection in the mirror.

You'll regret it when he grows. When you see inside his soul like I have. When you learn what he is!

What did that make me? Was I a monster, too? How long until my vor—no. No. I couldn't finish the thought. Couldn't even think of the word. Because it couldn't be true. I'd had my Revelation Ceremony. Proved myself in the temple that I was worthy of my stave. I'd been the one hunting down the monsters for years. I didn't belong in Lethea. I was the one who *sent* vorakh to Lethea. I ran my fingers through my hair, shaking off the thoughts. Even if it were true, it would be fine. I just had to keep it under control until I knew what was happening. Keep it hidden.

"Just stay," Naria said. "We're all going to the capital soon enough. It's going to look strange if you're not traveling with us."

"Haven't we dry-fucked in front of enough people for them to believe our engagement?"

"We don't need anyone to believe a thing. We *are* engaged, Tristan. That's the point. But people will still talk about other less pleasant things. Things we don't want discussed. You know how unsettled everything is here."

She was right. There'd been even more arrests after the trials. The soturi of Ka Kormac were everywhere last night, arresting anyone who even looked displeased with the announcement of our new Arkturion. Every time I looked up, some other mage or soturion was being dragged away, bound by mages working alongside our soturi. I'd never seen anything like it. I'd thought there'd been a lot of arrests after Harren's assassination. But those numbers were nothing next to what I expected had been brought into the Shadow Stronghold the last few days.

And even worse, so many soturi of Ka Kormac had arrived, that they were reporting we'd run out of housing. Bamarians were now being asked to take in the soturi, to offer them rooms in their homes. A request that would surely lead to more revolts.

But we weren't supposed to mention that. I shrugged at Naria. "Well, you do have the ear of our High Lady. She's the one with final say over my travel plans. Isn't she? Go ahead. Make your wishes known to her."

"The fuck does that mean?" Naria asked.

I whirled around. "You know Godsdamned well what it

means." Black seraphim were being painted all over the city. Alongside wolves. And no one was doing a fucking thing about it. Instead, everyone was being arrested.

"No," Naria said. "I don't know."

"Really? Really! Who's policing the country, Naria? Who's making the decisions for Bamaria? Your mother? Or is it our new Arkturion? Or maybe it's Imperator Kormac?"

Naria flushed. "Of course it's my mother."

"Great." I folded my arms across my chest. "Then go to her. Tell her I should stay. Tell her I should travel in your litter, and wave to the commoners as we go north to the Valabellum. We can stage a performance in every major city we enter, so no one talks about the Emartis, or the protests, or how many fucking soldiers are currently armed inside our borders. Maybe we should put our bed inside of a room made of glass—let them all watch me fuck you. Would that drive the conversation where you want it?" I pulled back the curtains, and gestured at her naked body. "We could start right now with Cresthaven's sentries. I'm sure a few wolves will also catch the show."

There was no response. Naria only bit her lip, her eyes shifting quickly back and forth across the room. Then she slammed the curtains closed, and wrapped her arms around herself. "Never mind. You fucking asshole."

I took a deep breath, and tentatively reached for her shoulder, feeling exactly like what she'd called me. "I'm sorry."

She rolled her eyes.

"I am," I said. But she didn't bite. She was still closing in on herself. "I didn't mean … Forget what I said. I'm not upset with you. Are you all right?"

Her eyes shot up, her lip curling with anger. "Really? My betrothed acts like he can't stand me half the time, and then he says the cruelest things. He's leaving me alone so he can go hunt down his ex-girlfriend. My cousin. And now I have to cross the Empire alone, with my mother. Of course I'm not all right."

"I'm sorry," I said.

"Please," she said. "I'm not stupid. I know what I'm doing here. And I know how you actually feel. But I—" She swallowed roughly.

"You what?"

"I guess I'll just have to go by myself to the capital. Maybe I'll get one of those glass rooms and fuck myself in it. I can do a better job on my own anyway. See you there."

"Naria," I said, but she'd turned away, reaching for a silk robe. "Naria?" I rushed in front of her, reaching for both of her shoulders, and stared into her eyes. But she stared down, shaking her head.

We'd had a genuine flirtation years ago. I was well aware that she'd had a longstanding crush on me but I'd never taken it seriously. She'd openly courted Viktor Kormac, amongst others of the nobility. This was the first real show of emotion I'd seen from her. The first time I'd felt any level of vulnerability or intimacy, despite the number of nights I'd spent in her bed.

Naria shrugged out of my hold. "You don't get to judge me for how I choose to navigate my golden chains. I've never judged you for yours."

"You're right." I took a tentative step forward, as Naria's eyes narrowed. "Can you answer one question for me?" I asked. "Truthfully?"

She remained still, watching me carefully, something dark in her aura pulsing. "That depends," she said.

I folded my arms across my chest. "On?"

"If I want to be truthful."

"Are you afraid of your mother?" I asked.

She practically barked in response. "This is what you want me to answer truthfully?"

"Yes."

Her aura swirled around me, nothing but a heavy shadow as

her eyes narrowed. "What you're asking me, Tristan," she said, her voice now hushed, "is treason. Go take your shower."

But I stood there, watching her, my heart pounding. "You change," I said quietly. "When you're around her."

"So do you," she sneered. "Around your grandmother."

"I know."

"Then you have your answer." Naria shook her head. "Don't ever ask me that again. And don't pretend you care about me when you don't. I'm not stupid. I know what this is. And I'm choosing to meet it my way."

"I …" I frowned, exhaling sharply. "I don't want to see you hurt. And whether you believe me or not, I do care about you. Though you don't make it easy."

"Like I said. My choice. Are you satisfied? The Bastardmaker's waiting for you."

"I'll abide by your wishes. I won't ask you again," I said, releasing her from my hold. "I'll see you at the capital."

"Whatever." She tightened the ties of her robe, and opened the balcony door. It was still too cold outside, but the sun's warmth had returned.

"If you ever do want to talk to me though," I said. "I'm here."

Naria slammed the door in response. I grabbed my towels and headed into the shower.

Once I got the water running, the temperature to where I liked it, I stepped under the spray, and closed my eyes, trying to understand again what the fuck was going on. I even washed my hair twice, just trying to prolong the inevitable. But just as I was about to turn off the warm water, the temperature dropped. My guts twisted as the shower began to pour ice cold water on me.

I screamed in shock, and then I was gone.

No! No! I was in the shower. I was in Cresthaven. I was Lord Tristan Grey. I was an adult. I was a mage. I was not a child. This wasn't happening. And I wasn't … I wasn't …

I stared down at tiny hands. My hands, the way they used to look when I was a boy. I was painting. Every picture was the same. Every color of the rainbow. Just me splashing the colors all over the paper. Again and again. I had a gallery of rainbow paintings hanging from the walls of my bedroom.

"Tristan?" my father walked in, twirling his stave. "What are you painting now, buddy?"

"Colors," I said, my voice young and small. "Just colors."

He chuckled. "Which one is your favorite color?"

"I don't know." But the different colors seemed to fade, until only yellow remained. Maybe that was the answer.

But before I could tell my father, two swords appeared. They were floating in the middle of the room, then growing and expanding until they were too large to fit the space. They sliced, cutting through the walls. The Villa was falling apart before they cut through my father, through my pictures.

I reached for him, but my father was gone.

That's when I remembered. He was dead. He'd been torn apart. My mother, too.

I was in a box. Completely dark. I couldn't breathe. I needed to get out. To escape.

Suddenly the lid opened and light flooded me. I looked up, blinking rapidly as my eyes adjusted. And I saw myself. I was an adult, the same age I was now. And I was fuming, my neck turning red, something violent and angry firing through my aura.

I blinked again, and then I was myself, I was Tristan. I was standing outside the box. But as I looked inside I could see, it wasn't me as a child who'd been trapped in there.

It was the vorakh. The mage who killed my parents.

She rose to her feet, laughing hysterically, long limbs climbing out.

I stepped back, reaching for my stave, ready to utter the words. The ritual. But my stave was gone.

She wildly tossed back her long black hair, then she looked at me with her dark eyes, as a smile widened her face, her beauty mark pronounced over the right corner of her lips. My eyes focused on it, like it was an anchor that would keep me from panicking.

"You're grown," she cackled. "I've seen inside your soul. And I know who you are. You can't run from me. I'll still get you."

I tried to yell. To tell her she was dead. Rotting in hell. But my voice didn't work, and she only laughed louder, and louder.

There were screams, hundreds of voices crying out in anguished terror.

Then I saw a flash of light. Orange. Indigo.

I sputtered out water, my entire body shivering.

The glass door swung open and Naria stared down at me.

"Myself to Moriel," she said. "I thought you were having a fit."

"I-I …" My teeth chattered. I was so, so cold. I could barely talk.

"Did you fall asleep in there? It's been half an hour. The Bastardmaker keeps sending messengers to my room."

"Can you …" Fuck. Fuck! I was too cold to move. My entire body ached. How was this happening to me? How was this possible? What did it fucking mean?

"Can I what?" Naria asked.

"T-turn off the water," I said. "Towel?"

She shook her head, but leaned forward and shut off the spray, then tossed a towel at me.

"Th-thanks," I said.

Naria's eyes narrowed, and for the second time ever, she seemed to show some genuine emotion. "You're not okay. Maybe instead of this meeting, we should take you to the healers."

"NO!" I yelled. "No." If they took me there, I'd be at risk.

They would figure out what was wrong with me. Know what I was. Turn me in. Send me to Lethea.

Like I'd done to the others.

Maybe that was what I deserved.

Naria sighed. "What do you want me to do then?"

"Tell the Bastardmaker I'll be down shortly."

"I'll let the next messenger know."

I leaned against the tiles, and closed my eyes, my body shivering, the vorakh's face laughing in my mind.

CHAPTER NINETEEN

LYRIANA

I groaned, my entire body aching as I opened my eyes. The fiery feeling of the Valalumir was still pulsing through my skin like a living memory. I clutched at my chest, my breath catching, then ran my hand down my tunic. It was no longer ripped. A silver thread down the center held the pieces together in neat, even stitches.

I tried to take a deep breath despite the pain, and get my bearings. My head was resting on a soft pillow, and thick, woolen blankets covered my body. I was in an actual bed. The first bed I'd slept in in weeks. I couldn't remember the last time I woke up in one—or the last time I'd woken up alone, without Rhyan. He'd been a constant by my side since we left Bamaria, always snuggled against my body, his arms wrapped tightly around me.

A small fire burned a few feet away. A fire in a real fireplace, not just one haphazardly built inside the loose stones of a cave. Behind the bed were frosted windows with open curtains. Night had fallen. Torches protruding from the snowy towers reflected in the glass, and a gryphon growled from beyond, its outstretched wings flying across the mountainous horizon.

My heart pounded as I sat up. These weren't the dungeons. But a bedroom. A high-ranking noble's bedroom.

Blinking, and on the verge of panic, I took in my surroundings, the feel and scent of the space around me. And it was then that I knew without a doubt, this was Rhyan's room.

The bedroom he'd grown up in.

"Are you all right, Lady Lyriana?" Kenna sat in an armchair beyond the fireplace. She looked uncomfortable, stiff, and tired. She'd clearly been on guard.

"You've been here the whole time?" I asked, unable to keep the anger from my voice. Then added, "Your Grace."

"Aye, I was," she said softly. "I fixed your tunic for you. Used a sewing spell while you were asleep. I hope you don't mind."

My cheeks burned as I realized I'd been carried unconscious through Seathorne with my shirt torn open. Exposed. Again. In front of Rhyan's father, in front of Kane and Dario. And Kenna. I looked down at the silver thread. But all I could see were Kane's hands, see him ripping the fabric, and all I could remember was the feel of terror and humiliation washing over me, the pain of the fire that burned in my heart.

But aside from the horror of meeting him, there was also the small bit of knowledge I'd tucked away. He was a Guardian. A fucking Guardian. Only Hava, Cassarya, and Shiviel were unidentified. According to the stories, Shiviel was the only one of the three to join forces with Moriel. He'd turned on Auriel and Asherah just as Moriel and Ereshya had. And if I had to guess, I'd put money on it: Kane was the reincarnation of Shiviel. The one God said to be more monstrous than Moriel. And he was in charge of Glemaria's legions.

"I've been watching over you," Kenna said. "Imperator Hart asked me to stay, he said you'd want a female companion. You don't have to worry about when you were unconscious. You haven't been disturbed here. I swear."

I stared down at the bed—Rhyan's bed—realizing suddenly why I was here. Not out of kindness, nor because I was a "guest" of Imperator Hart's. I was here as a unique form of cruelty. A reminder that before me, Rhyan had a lover. For seven months. Seven *fucking* months. Far longer than he and I had been together. And now, I was trapped with her.

Gods. I could feel him everywhere. Calm, soothing colors filled every corner from the curtains to the couch cushions. They were in the soft fabric of the pillows and bedspreads. So much muted green against the dark wood of his furniture. Everything was neat and tidy, just the way he'd kept things in his apartment. The way he arranged our practice weapons in our training room at the Katurium. Even the way he somehow managed to make living in a cave look purposeful. The ghost of Rhyan was etched into every inch of the room.

Including the bed. Where he'd slept.

With Kenna.

My throat dried painfully, and just like that, my imagination ran away from me. I could see her in my mind, see her as she would have been. Her belly flat, her body lean and lithe—the opposite of mine in every way. I could see Rhyan naked. I could hear the sounds he would make when he lost control, feel the specific way his hips moved, the way he kissed, the way his eyes locked with mine when he was deep inside me. Gods. That knowledge was private. Intimate. His. Mine. Ours. A secret we carried between us.

But it was a secret Kenna had been privy to as well.

In this bed, right where I lay, for seven months, his eyes had locked with hers.

It would have been kinder for the Imperator to lock me in the prisons. But he wanted to hurt me, to break me. And I had to remember that. He could do it physically if he wanted to—and I had no doubt he would soon. But emotional torture was where his expertise lay, combat through mental warfare. Humiliation was just as sharp a tool in his arsenal as his sword.

I couldn't let him get to me—especially not over something as inconsequential as this. I always knew he had a past, just as he knew I did. And it didn't matter. It wouldn't change anything between us. I'd just been caught off guard. But knowing Rhyan had kept something this big from me, was worrying. He also hadn't told me about Garrett. Why? What else was he hiding from me?

I pushed away from the pillows and threw off the covers, swinging my legs to the side, my feet touching the soft carpet as I tried to think of anything but this bed, anything but who had slept in it.

In a corner, I found a set of old weights, and some blunt practice swords. Rhyan's old weapons. Above them was a painting of a gryphon soaring over Glemarian pine trees. I blinked back tears and caught my reflection in his mirror. Dark circles were under my eyes, and my hair was a mess, frizzy and wild, half of the waves sticking out from my loose braid. There was no shine like Kenna's. I looked paler than I'd ever seen myself.

"You know where you are, my lady?" Kenna asked.

"Seathorne? Or did you mean Rhyan's bedroom? Because yes, I can tell."

Kenna nodded. "You must be thirsty." There was a creaking sound, and I turned to see her struggling to lift herself from the chair and heading to Rhyan's desk. An old jar of ink, and several scratch pens were laid neatly in the corner. There was also a jug of water and several glasses.

"Don't," I sneered, and strolled from the bed. "I can get my own water."

"Because you're mad at who I am?" she challenged, her accent deepening. "Or because you don't trust me?"

I glared. "You're farther than fucking Lethea if you think I can trust you." My guts roiled. "How could I when you're—"

"Please." She shook her head emphatically. "Don't be upset about that. That's been over for a very long time."

Over between her and Rhyan. My cheeks burned. "I was going to say you're married to the Imperator."

Kenna's face paled. "Right. Well, that … is an ongoing matter."

"Let's also not forget I just broke your father's nose."

I snatched the jug from the table, refusing to look at her as I poured, filling two glasses with water. She reached out a hand to help, but I kept pouring, eyes on the fall of liquid into each glass, watching the way they reflected light from the fire. From the corner of my eye, I saw her lower her hand and step back.

She was so Godsdamned pretty. I had thought so when I first saw her. But here, away from the Imperator, it was even more obvious. It didn't help that something about the intelligence and kindness in her face made me want to like her. Made me see why Rhyan had. There was a spark in her brown eyes, and something in her aura that would have drawn me to her if we'd met at court. But whether or not I could trust her—that was an entirely different matter.

"My point is," I said, "There's no need for you to wait on me when you're this pregnant. Sit."

She frowned. "I'm not the one who passed out."

"Well between the two of us, I think I had the more eventful morning." I slammed the jug on Rhyan's desk, and slid one glass toward her.

"Thank you," she said.

"Where's my sister?" I asked.

Kenna took a sip, her brown eyes watching me carefully. "She was moved from the medical wing to her own guest room. She's in a hall not far from here. Dario sent word. He's keeping an eye on her with Aiden."

"Oh, that makes me feel so much better," I snapped, not even trying to hide the disdain in my voice.

"It should," Kenna said. "Not everyone here is trustworthy. But they won't hurt her."

I rolled my eyes and scoffed. "They bound us. They nearly got us killed out there, and then they broke Rhyan's nose. Twice by the way," I said. "And now we're trapped here as prisoners, because of them. I wouldn't exactly call them trustworthy."

Kenna sighed. "I heard about that, and I saw the condition of Rhyan's face down there," she said diplomatically. "But you can trust them when it matters. I consider them friends, they don't harm for fun, nor do they harm those helpless to fight back."

"Helpless to fight back? They broke his nose!" I yelled. "When he was fucking bound! So, how's that for being helpless to fight back? They could barely be trusted to free us from our bindings when akadim attacked. And remind me, but I'm pretty sure it was Dario holding down a bound and helpless Rhyan this morning on your husband's Godsdamned orders. *Friends*," I sneered.

Kenna frowned. "I know how it looks. But they have a long history together, and many duties here. Oaths they must fulfill. I can't say more, but you should believe me when I tell you that deep down, they do love Rhyan."

I almost laughed. "Do they? They have a very strange way of showing it," I said, unable to keep my emotions from causing my voice to shake. "Same with you."

Kenna stared at me directly now, a kind of blunt openness to her face.

"A lot happened between them that you weren't here for. I would leave them to work it out on their own." Kenna finished drinking her water, swallowing almost defiantly before she answered. "As for the rest, we all have a duty to the Imperator. I am limited in what I can and cannot do, just as they are. I have my own people to protect. I will not apologize for it."

"I don't recall asking you to."

"Look, despite the chains my position places around me, I'm trying to tell you that you can trust me."

"That's what this is?" I almost laughed.

"Lady Lyriana, I swear to you, my intention is to protect Rhyan. Just as it's yours. The sooner you realize it, the better for you, and the better for him. You are in the Imperator's nest now. You need allies. We have the same goals."

"Really? Where is he now, then?" I asked. "What has your *husband* done with him?"

Kenna flinched. "He's in prison. In Ha'Lyrotz."

It was where they'd kept him before. My throat tightened.

"Has he been seen by a healer?"

The look on Kenna's face told me all I needed to know.

I bit my lip to keep from crying. If Kane hadn't been a fucking Guardian, if his touch hadn't incapacitated me, we might have made it. I'd been so close to the weapons. I would have held a knife to Kenna's neck until she unbound Rhyan. Then he could have jumped to me as I grabbed our things— and we'd be gone.

I held Kenna's gaze. "Speak truthfully then if our goals align. Is he okay down there?"

Kenna shook her head. "No. We need to get him out."

"I don't suppose you have the key?" I asked sarcastically.

"I did," she said quietly. "Once."

"What do you mean, once?" I asked.

She retreated to the chaise, carefully sitting back down, and readjusting her green gown across the swell of her stomach.

"I freed him last time," she said. "When he was named forsworn after his mother died, I brought the key to his body-guard. That was partly how he escaped the prison."

"You freed him?"

She nodded. "I helped. I was already engaged to his father by then, though Rhyan didn't know it. I didn't really have a say in that matter." Her voice hardened. "I used my position as the Imperator's betrothed to gain access. Soturion Bowen, Rhyan's old bodyguard, *Bar Ka Mokan*, did the rest."

"Bowen died?" I asked, realizing the words she'd spoken. "His soul freed."

Kenna's face was grim. "He died helping Rhyan escape."

I closed my eyes. I had no idea he'd died that way. It was something else Rhyan had never disclosed to me. Though he'd never mentioned Bowen either.

"Does he know what part you played?" I asked Kenna carefully. "Your husband?"

Kenna rested the top of her head against the back of the chaise, and groaned. "Please ... can we not refer to him as that?" Then she looked back at me. "And yes, he found out that night when Rhyan was escaping. I was punished accordingly. Probably why he dragged me in there today to do what he did."

"I thought that was to hurt me."

"Oh, it was. Rhyan, too. His father loves killing two birds with one stone. Or, in our case, three." She smiled sadly, looking away.

I was beginning to see what had been obvious from the moment Kenna appeared. Imperator Hart was hurting her just as he'd hurt Rhyan's mother. It made me want to trust her—and yet —it was also the very reason why I couldn't.

"Poor Rhyan," she said. "The look on his face when he couldn't get to you, couldn't save you ... Being in that room must have been torture for him. That's where it happened, you know. Where his mother died." Her lilt had intensified as she spoke, her eyes watering.

My eyes widened. "In the Seating Room?"

Kenna nodded sadly. "In the exact spot you were standing. I was there." She met my gaze. "I saw what the Imperator did to her." Kenna sat forward. "I know you have no reason to trust me. And I understand. Believe me, I do. But I am not your enemy.

And I am sorry for what happened to you. The way you were treated by the Imperator, and … by my father."

"You're right," I said. "I have no reason to trust you beyond your word. I want to—but what I don't understand is why Imperator Hart would leave a potential ally alone with me?"

"He left you alone with someone he expected to hurt you. You've met him before, haven't you? Seen how he works? That's why he's trusting me to be here. I was Rhyan's *lover.* Remember?" She rolled her eyes. "He hasn't seen past that, hasn't seen or considered what else I could be—or the possibility that you could move past it either."

The fire crackled as a log shifted. I turned around, finishing my glass of water, while trying to breathe. Trying to think. I needed to prepare for what was next. Figure out how to help Meera and Rhyan. How to escape Seathorne. Not only were our lives at stake, but we only had a month to get to Jules. A fucking month to infiltrate the capital. And now Aemon knew where we were going.

What if Kenna hadn't just been sent to upset me? But to betray me?

I stared out the window, taking in how dark the night's sky was. Hardly any torches could be seen on the horizon with the snow still falling.

"What time is it?" I asked.

"Nearly seven," Kenna said.

I'd been unconscious the whole day. Twelve hours. Twelve hours Rhyan had been alone and imprisoned. Twelve hours Meera had been in isolation. And twelve more hours Jules was at the capital and I had no plan to rescue her.

"Imperator Hart has requested dinner with you. He has more questions. I was instructed to help you get dressed for your meeting. He'll call for you in an hour. Your clothes have been set out. I'll show you the shower and I can help you into your dress."

I stiffened.

"The ties," she said, "are not the ones you're accustomed to lacing in Bamaria. I'll help you, if you want me to."

"I'm not wearing some dress picked out by your fucking husband," I said. And my discomfort aside, I certainly wasn't going to be dressed up like a doll by Rhyan's ex-lover.

"Lady Lyriana," she said, her voice pleading.

But before I could respond, there was a violent pounding on the door. Kenna froze, her eyes widening. The shift in her aura was palpable. Full of fear and apprehension. It felt like I'd suddenly risen too quickly to an altitude that made it hard to breathe.

"Let me do the talking," she said quickly, moving protectively in front of me.

The door slammed open, and Kane strolled in, his red Arkturion cloak swishing with each step, his elbows bent, hands fisted. His aura filled the room at once, overtaking any sensation of Kenna's. It was violent and angry. And powerful. I had no doubt now in my mind of who he was. This was the reincarnation of a God. Of Shiviel. Glemaria's warlord.

The man who tore open my tunic.

The man whose nose I had broken this morning.

My throat was dry as I studied his cruel face. He'd fully recovered from what I'd done. There was no color under his eyes, no hint of swelling anywhere.

Looking me up and down, one corner of his mouth curled into a lopsided sneer.

"Thought I heard you finally awake," he grunted.

Kenna nodded to her father, angling her body to keep me behind her as Kane pushed further into Rhyan's bedroom. "Yes, Father. She just woke up. We're about to prepare her for dinner with His Highness."

"You don't look like you're preparing," he said.

"She just needed some water. Are you feeling better?" she asked.

"I wouldn't have to feel better if this little bitch hadn't punched me."

"Father," Kenna said, "Let's put that past us."

"Or maybe I should pay her back," he said, his voice low. "I promised not to touch *her*. At least not yet. But Rhyan's all alone in the dungeons."

My hands flexed into fists. I'd never before wanted to so violently hurt someone I'd just met. Then again, in some ways, I supposed I'd known him for an eternity.

"I was thinking," he said, "Rhyan's nose is already broken. Maybe I should give his right eye a scar to match the left."

"You will not touch him," I snarled.

"Or else you'll do what? Fucking nothing, because you know you're too weak. One touch from me and you were on the ground. Not even your fancy mage light could save you."

Fancy mage light? I blinked. The Valalumir. The very thing that had confirmed his true identity. He didn't know what it was, didn't know he was a God. And he wouldn't. That kind of knowledge could be dangerous for him to have. But Imperator Hart—I had a feeling he knew. I wouldn't be surprised if he was aware, or at least suspected, everyone's true identity. And all at once, I wondered if his marriage to Kenna was less about hurting Rhyan, and was more of a way to control a reincarnated Guardian.

Kane's eyes flashed. "Get fucking dressed. His Highness doesn't want to wait, and you stink of gryphon shit. So, here's what you're going to do. You're going to get in that shower, and give yourself a thorough, long scrub. And then you're going to put on the dress you were told to wear. No complaints." A slow smile spread across his face. "I have the key to your sister's room."

I stopped breathing. My body was numb.

"She'll be ready," Kenna said. "Please. Let me help her into the shower. Tell my husband I'll see him shortly."

Kane's eyebrows furrowed, his angular face twisted in agitation before he huffed, and turned around. "One hour." The door slammed shut behind him.

I gasped, nearly falling over, my hands slamming into the desk. It was Kenna who caught me, her hand on my back, steadying me.

"It's all right. Take a deep breath," Kenna said softly. "Don't fret for your sister. It's known all over the fortress she's here. The whole Empire is going to know soon, remember? He wants everyone to know it. He's going to hold that over the head of the southern Imperator. No harm will come to her for that reason alone."

I shook my head, the backs of my eyes burning. "You don't know that."

"I do." She looked away, swallowing hard. "She's going to be paraded around so the stories can spread."

I wanted to cry. She'd be kept alive. But that didn't protect her from the wounds no one could see. The ones concealed by clothing. The ones she'd carry inside.

"Be strong," Kenna said. "As a guest of Seathorne, she does have some protection."

"Guest?" My voice shook. "Be honest. Say hostage."

"The words are interchangeable as far as His Highness is concerned. Now please, I really do want to help you."

She returned to the table, refilling my glass of water and bringing it to me.

I took it from her, grateful.

"Do you trust me yet?" she asked.

I searched her aura. Nothing felt off about her. She was logical, something I always appreciated. She had pleaded in my favor in the Seating Room, and had protected me from Kane just now.

I shrugged. "I might be starting to. Reluctantly. A little."

She smiled. "I'll take 'reluctantly' over not at all."

I shook my head. "Why are you being so nice to me?"

"Why wouldn't I be?" Kenna asked.

I could only stare in response. "I'm the disgraced daughter of a murdered Arkasva. I brought Rhyan back to the one place he should have never come. Plus, I'm an enemy of the Glemarian Council. Scorned by two of your closest friends. Clearly despised by not only your husband, but also your own father. And … well, I haven't exactly been that nice to you."

"It's okay. I don't put much stock in first impressions." But when I didn't smile at her joke, she sighed, and said, "I am taking an enormous chance here. I am risking everything by choosing to trust you. But I do. Because there is only one recommendation I need in order to know I'm making the right choice —you have the trust of the one person we have in common."

"Rhyan."

Her eyebrows lifted in confirmation. "Drink," she said.

I did, thirstier than I'd realized. And before I could think, I asked, "Are you in love with him?" I wasn't worried about them. Or their past. Not for a second. Rhyan was mine, my love, my soulmate. I didn't doubt that. But if I was going to trust her, I had to know the truth.

"No," she said. "And I never was. Nor was he ever in love with me. Even when we were … together, he was trying to find his way back to you." She smiled sadly.

I thought of his confession to me before we'd had sex the first time. How he'd always loved me. How he'd fallen for me years ago. But hearing that Kenna existed, and how recently they'd been together, the smallest of doubts had begun to take shape in my mind. Not about us now, but maybe about how he'd felt before. About the truthfulness of his grand claims.

"He never said the words directly," Kenna continued, "but when he visited Bamaria all those years ago, I knew something happened."

My eyes watered thinking back to the night of the Summer

Solstice. To our first dance, to holding hands and sneaking into the woods. Leaning back against the suntree, Rhyan's breath against my lips, the way he softened and was finally vulnerable with me, whispering secrets in the dark.

I want to kiss you. Can I?

"We kissed," I said, and suddenly my longing for him felt like a crushing weight.

"More than that happened," Kenna said. "He was different when he came back. He was in love. Did you know that for a year, he wouldn't even look at another girl?" Kenna shook her head in disapproval. "His friends gave him such shit for that, but I recognized what was going on. Then, a little while later, something else happened. He changed. It was kept quiet, but his father had ... well ... he'd made it known that he was to resume *courting*." Her voice was strained.

I didn't like the way she said "courting", like it meant something else here.

"Not long after," Kenna continued, "my father was in negotiations for a marriage contract between me and the Senator from Hartavia."

"Hartavia?" My mind began to whirl. "The Senator?" I nearly shouted.

"You know of him?" Kenna asked darkly.

I knew exactly who she was referring to. He was the man who'd molested Rhyan as a boy. He was a fucking monster.

I nodded. "I've heard things."

Kenna bit her lip. "He scared me. And that night ... I went to Rhyan. He didn't know what was going on, just that I needed a friend to talk to, but ... one thing led to another, and that ended the negotiations. It wasn't love between us. I knew going in that I didn't love him, not like that. His heart was taken." She nodded to me. "But the relationship we had saved me ... for a time. Our fathers liked the prospect of us as a couple, and," she sighed, "as a political statement. It allowed Rhyan to relax from all the intrigues of Court. He no longer had to face the women his father paraded in front of him. But in the end, we really were just friends—friends who became a lifeline for each other."

"Okay," I said slowly. "But you were … " my chest tightened, "you and him?" I gestured to the bed.

"Yes," she said bluntly.

I bit my lip.

"Do you know, when he was dreaming, when he thought no one could hear, he'd say your name in his sleep. That's how I knew it was you still, after all that time."

Something lifted in my chest. "None of this bothered you?" I asked.

Kenna smiled and shook her head. "I knew his heart, and I never had plans to make a claim on it. We were just …" Her eyes watered then, but she blinked back her tears. "We were just trying to survive Glemaria."

I knew what the men here were like. I knew how they treated women. The way his father treated his mother— the way Kenna had been treated in front of me already. And I knew far too well how they treated Rhyan. Imperator Hart wanted to hurt me. And he would expect others to do the same. Even if Kenna was meant to get my trust, and betray me, he'd never come up with something like this. Something this selfless, this understanding. It wasn't in his nature. It made me completely believe her.

"When I last saw him," she continued, "I made him promise that he'd find the love he was always looking for. You. I'm glad he did. I risked a lot to save him that night. Because I wanted better for him." She looked away, something in her aura shifting, then calmed. "He needed to be freed. For Glemaria. And so … here we are."

I swallowed roughly, starting to like Kenna despite myself.

"I believe you. And, I want to trust you."

"Well, whether you trust me or not, we're out of time. Let's start by getting ready," she said.

"I ..." She'd been honest with me. "I'll accept your help getting dressed. But you should know something. I find it ... difficult for people to touch my clothing. I need ..." I bit my lip, "I need to know what you're doing. I need to know you're not going to rip or take anything off ... not that I think you would, but ... I just," my cheeks heated, "I need it all the same."

Kenna tilted her head to the side, her eyes softening. "You have my word. I'll show you to the shower. Then I promise, I will only be adding clothing to your person. I'll keep you informed of what I'm doing as best I can so you're comfortable." Her mouth tightened. "But, if you are not dressed properly for dinner within an hour, I cannot promise that Rhyan will not pay for the insolence. And I will not allow him to be hurt any more than he is. Are we understood?"

I looked Kenna up and down, feeling the weight of her question. It wasn't about getting dressed—but if we were going to be allies. I nodded.

"We're understood," I said, and stepped forward, taking her hand in mine. "Help me."

CHAPTER TWENTY

LYRIANA

Sometime later, I stood before the mirror in Rhyan's bedroom as Kenna finished lacing my gown. It looked a lot like hers. Glemarian green in color, with suffocatingly long sleeves that flowed past my fingertips, and an extremely tight bodice that flared at the waist. There were no slits below my hips to allow for movement, or the cooling breeze like we had back home, but rather extra layers built into the skirts to add warmth.

The sleeves were so tight against my arms, I'd moved my golden arm cuff to outside the dress. And to top it all off was my new Glemarian hairstyle, courtesy of Kenna. I washed my hair in the shower, feeling admittedly cleaner than I had in weeks. Then Kenna used her stave to summon heat to dry my waves. She pulled some of my front pieces back into a Glemarian styled braid that blended into the rest of my hair. It was … pretty. But not at all like me.

I supposed that was the point. I was supposed to be who Imperator Hart wanted me to be. And as much as I could stand it, I would. But only to get Rhyan and Meera out.

There was a loud knock at the door, and a soturion stepped inside.

"Your Grace," he said, bowing before Kenna.

I'd turned my head as if he were addressing me, then froze. I had once again forgotten I no longer held that title.

"Lady Lyriana," he grunted a moment later, "you're to follow me."

"Just a moment, soturion." Kenna pulled my loose hair off my shoulder, and leaned close, whispering in my ear. "Don't act unaffected by what he's done. You need to put your pride aside. He sent you here to punish you. He *wants* a reaction. If he thinks it didn't work, if he doesn't get what he wants, he'll do worse." Her eyes moved pointedly to the bed in the mirror's reflection. A reminder of my punishment. Of being forced into the same room as Rhyan's old lover.

There were knots forming in my belly, but my eyes met hers, understanding her meaning.

It was the same advice Rhyan had given me.

Kenna took my hand and squeezed, then stepped back, her expression neutral with the indifference of nobility. Throat dry, I walked out, surrounded by five soturi, each giving me a harsh look. The soturi kept a brisk pace, one that normally would have been easy for me to match. But my legs felt stiff after hours in bed, and I wasn't sure if the chills across my skin came from the coldness that seemed to seep through the stones of the fortress, or from knowing I was about to see Imperator Hart once more.

I didn't know what to expect, but it wasn't to be taken to a set of private stairs and led to one of the upper floors leading to the towers. When I'd been told dinner, I'd expected we'd be heading down towards the dining halls on the main level. I'd expected we'd be in public—and I'd have some safety granted from the eyes of others. But I was isolated and alone. My anxiety rose as we climbed higher and higher, going in circles as the stairs wound to the point of making me dizzy.

We stopped before a silver door, an emerald green gryphon carving in its center. A soturion knocked, and then announced me.

After experiencing the bleakness of the halls and the Seating Room, I nearly gasped as I was brought inside a shockingly elaborate dining room. Silver platters covered a white marble table in the center. Hundreds of crystals dangled, glowing, from the ceiling like stars. The amount of magic that would have been needed to sustain the lights inside each one would have been immense and had to have been the work of at least a dozen mages. Everywhere I looked, I noticed more details. Elaborate velvet tapestries, and carvings of gryphons within precious metals. Gemstones twinkling inside each corner.

I supposed opulence was reserved for only the Imperator's private quarters. And the Imperator alone.

Well, he and whoever else he invited to dine with him.

The soturion on guard inside the room saluted the five sentries behind me, and then all at once they exited, closing and locking the door.

Shit. I was alone. No guards, no allies, and no way out. I rushed back to the door, and despite knowing my efforts were futile, I tried to open it. But the doorknob felt as if it had been magically sealed shut. There were no witnesses in the Seating Room. But at least then there'd been Rhyan. Even Kenna had been a comfort. Now? I'd be completely alone and helpless with Imperator Hart.

I walked back toward the table, unsure if I should sit or stand. The tower began to hum, the floor shaking. I gasped, reaching for a chair, terrified the tower's entire structure was about to fall. But then the shaking stopped and a door on the opposite side of the room opened. The Imperator appeared. He stood inside what looked like a closet, the floor of which swayed ever so slightly. My eyes widened.

"It's called a lift. You've never seen one before?" he asked.

Taking a deep breath, I pushed my shoulders back, and willed my hands to remain still at my side. "I have. We have something similar in the Great Library—there is a floor that moves, taking you to the lower levels of the pyramid. But it doesn't look like yours." I'd only been in it a few times. It required a mage to move the floor up and down between the library's levels.

"Hmmm, right. I've seen the one you're referring to. On your little tour years ago. This is different. It's a human invention—popular beyond the border. It relies on rope. Perhaps the most interesting thing they've come up with. There, they have men stationed at the bottom, pulling the rope to make the lift go up and down. But here, the mages can do that with their magic. It allows me to rise and descend from the towers with ease. After all, these endlessly tiresome stairs can be such a bother, especially when you have more important things to do." He eyed me carefully. "They weren't too much for you though, my lady. Now that you've claimed your magic power?"

I sucked in a breath. "They were fine," I said.

"Good. We'll be keeping that quiet, just between us. No one needs to know what power you possess. Hmm?"

I nodded.

"And your room?" he asked, his voice filled with false sweetness and concern. "One of our nicest, of course. Was the bed as comfortable as you'd like?"

I could feel my pulse jumping. I was ready to retort back, to go on the defense. But Imperator Hart never reacted like you expected. So, I took Rhyan's—and Kenna's—advice. I looked down, allowing myself to genuinely feel the jealousy and hurt that had plagued me when I'd heard who Kenna was—when I'd woken in Rhyan's bed. I let myself feel the uncertainty that had washed over me at learning Rhyan had a long-term lover that he'd never told me about.

The knowledge that she knew his body. The knowledge that

he'd been intimate with not just me, but her. In that very room. On the very bed I'd slept in. For seven months. Fuck. I didn't have to try too hard to feel upset.

I looked back at the Imperator, and swallowed roughly. "It smells like him," I said, my voice shaking. I'd spoken the truth.

"Smelled like her, too. Can you stand it?" he asked sympathetically. As if we were in this together. As if either of us had been betrayed. He was the only one wrong in this situation, twisting everything and manipulating us for his own pleasure.

I shook my head. "No. Perhaps, if I am to continue staying there," I said primly, "the sheets might be replaced, ones without his scent lingering."

He smirked, and nodded. Good. If he thought he won this round, he'd let it go.

"Of course, my lady. Fresh sheets will be made available to you," he said, his voice suddenly charming. "I believe we can even procure some Bamarian soap to soak them in. Thank you for joining me for dinner. Have a seat."

I stared at the table, reluctant to follow any orders. "Why do I not have an escort?"

"I have things to say to you. Things no one else should be privy to. Sit," he commanded, walking around the table and pulling out my chair.

I kept my eyes on him, trying to remain alert to any hidden dangers or tricks, to guess his game before he won. But I could see nothing else to do but take the offered seat.

"Are you hungry?" he asked, pushing me in toward the table. Then sitting across from me, he made an elaborate display of unfolding his napkin and laying it across his lap. His eyes bore into me, his lips tightly pressed together behind his beard, as he waited for me to do the same.

I unfolded my napkin.

"I do like this color on you," he said, eyeing me studiously. "And this style of dress. It's surprisingly becoming. You should always dress this way. You look far more proper than you ever did in Bamaria." He twirled his finger in the air. "This way, you leave a little something to men's imagination."

"I prefer it when men have no imagination," I said. "No matter what I choose to wear."

He laughed. "We do things a little differently here. Something you ought to get used to."

"And why might that be?"

"You're going to be staying here for quite some time. Might as well acclimate."

The hell I would. But I smiled sweetly. "My Imperator will not like that."

"No," he agreed, leaning forward to pour me a glass of wine. "He will not. But I think, you'll agree that staying here is your best option. I don't think you'll have a choice."

"Did I ever?" I asked.

Wind howled outside, the sound louder than I'd ever heard. The tower shook again.

"You always have a choice, my lady. I can't say they're good choices, but they exist. Why don't you uncover your dinner? You must be hungry."

I kept my eyes on him, on his dark beard, not trusting him, and far too aware of his hateful aura. It felt visceral in a space this small. But I reached forward, and lifted the lid.

I'd barely uncovered the plate when something dark moved across it. My body jerked and I screamed. "Fuck!" I threw the lid across the room, pushing my chair back so fast, I almost fell over.

Slithering up from the center of my dinner plate was a black nahashim—the very same snake that had grown wings and chased me through the skies. The snake that had led me here.

"Don't be scared," the Imperator crooned. "He won't bite you. Unless I ask him to."

I remained still, not wanting to get near the snake. Imperator

Hart made a shushing sound as he stretched his arm across the table. The snake slid across his leather cuff, and wound its way toward his elbow.

"Do you remember him?" he asked, his lips lifting into a curve.

"We met last night, I believe. At least, I saw him last night for the first time," I said, trying to get my breath under control. "I didn't realize they could fly."

He chuckled. "They can do whatever it takes to fulfill their master's orders. Even ... *travel*. But you knew that." He eyed my position, far from the table. "Pull your chair in. Now."

Reluctantly, I obeyed.

"Last night was not the first time you met," he said. The snake's shiny black scales stretched and retracted as its body settled over the gryphon etched into the Imperator's leathered armor. "The first time, he was so tiny that he fit," he paused, patting his belt below the table's edge, "right here in my pocket. You remember?"

The nahashim he'd forced me to touch during our dance in Bamaria. My chest tightened.

"I trained him to follow your scent in particular that night."

My skin crawled. I wanted to bathe, I wanted to erase my scent, and any signs I'd been in the room. His actions that night at the ball had felt devious enough, forcing my hand to touch the snake. But this? Fuck.

"He's grown since then," I said through gritted teeth.

"He has. Beautifully. And he will continue to grow. Quite fortunate, don't you think? All the fully grown nahashim I'd bred and raised since infancy were killed. By you. All nine of them. Back in Korteria."

My breath caught. I *had* killed them all in Korteria. The very same day I'd killed Brockton. But he couldn't know that. It was impossible. No one but Rhyan knew that.

"I don't ... I don't know what you're referring to," I said, my heart hammering. "I was not aware you had nine nahashim, nor was I aware they'd been killed. We were never in Korteria."

He was silent for a long moment, his eyes raking me up and down.

I could feel my pulse pounding against my skin, threatening to burst out of me.

"You're quite good. Quite an actress. Though, you have some tells—your eyes. They've never been that convincing. Too honest." He grinned, and leaned his elbows on the table, his fingers steepled beneath his chin. "Let's play a game, shall we? A game of possibility. I can choose to believe you. Perhaps my nahashim suddenly felt the need to fight each other like Brockton Kormac and his friends. Or," he raised his voice, anger pulsing through every syllable as he sat up. "Perhaps, you were seen in Korteria by four wolves, including Brockton. Perhaps, they saw you in the very spot where the corpses of my nahashim were found. Perhaps, they saw you kill my pets, the very same day you killed all of them. Perhaps." Imperator Hart's aura darkened. "Do you understand what I'm referring to now?" he asked.

I swore I could hear my heart drumming. My blood was now pulsing in my ears. I swallowed roughly.

"I am sorry for your loss, Your Highness. Just as I was … saddened to learn of the soturis' deaths. It was a terrible tragedy for Ka Kormac. My sympathies go out to Imperator Kormac on the loss of his nephew and the three members of his soturi."

Imperator Hart held my gaze unblinking across the table. Without losing eye contact, he reached for his wine glass, and took a long sip. "What did the wolves do to you after you killed my nahashim?"

"N-Nothing." I shook my head. "How could they do anything? We never entered Korteria. Like I told you," I lied. But I could still feel it. Feel the way the air hit my skin when they'd stripped me. Feel the shame and fear that pulsed through my veins when their eyes were on my bare skin. Remember the threats they uttered through the vadati stone to Rhyan. The disgusting way Brockton's hand felt as he grabbed my breast.

... we're going to fuck your girl. We're going to do it until you get here.

Imperator Hart didn't respond, just stared at me with this dark look in his eyes that told me I had to go on, that I had to keep explaining.

I continued, "I had only one objective when I left Bamaria: find my sisters. We took the eastern pass from the Elyrian border, heading north." A truth. "We were never near Ka Kormac's territory." A lie. His Godsdamned nahashim drove us there. "I cannot answer any of these allegations."

Imperator Hart sighed loudly. "Shame. Witnesses say otherwise. You're lying, Lady Lyriana. I know for a fact that you're lying. My nahashim tracked you to Korteria, where you were captured by Brockton and brought to Vrukshire for questioning. Imperator Kormac himself reported to me the presence of the nahashim corpses."

"He … he reported the snakes to you?" I asked, trying to sound interested instead of guilty.

"Oh yes. And so much more. It seems Brockton kept you tied up for the entire day. Sometime after nightfall, there were screams from his bedroom, the sound of glass smashing. The Bastardmaker's son had an appetite for some, shall we say, less than savory things. He had special locks on his door to protect his … meals. According to my sources, by the time the servants pried the door open, they found three dead wolves."

Three? My heart stopped. Three? No. No. No. Not three. There were four.

"I believe their names were Geoffrey, Trey, and Brett. All dead. And then they found one *nearly* dead Brockton."

Nearly dead? By the Gods. I'd … I'd stabbed his heart. I felt the sword go in—felt the sickening give of my blade pushing through muscle.

I'd seen the life leave his eyes with my own. I'd been sick over what I'd done, and then sick I hadn't done enough and now ... Fuck! I felt farther than Lethea. My hands grasped for the edge of my chair, desperate to hold onto something, to keep breathing, to stay in my body. "We ..." My throat tightened. "We heard word in our travels that he passed away." Was Brockton alive this whole time? By the Gods. I couldn't breathe.

"Of course, he passed away," the Imperator said dismissively.

I resisted the urge to clutch at my chest. I was on the verge of hyperventilating.

The nahashim slithered across Imperator Hart's shoulders to his other arm, poking its head in his face.

"You gave him a mortal wound," he said. "Unfortunately for you, the promise of death by your hand was not instantaneous. He survived. Long enough for the door to be opened, long enough for him to say your name to the poor fool who found him. You should be honored. His final words before death were 'Lyriana Batavia.' How many can claim that for themselves?"

"He ..." I took another labored breath, barely able to hear over my heart pounding. "He accused me of killing him?" I tried to sound innocent and surprised, but the beats of my heart were growing with intensity.

"Brockton was a fool. I know he thought he could play his twisted games with you, and no one would ever know. But servants talk. They all knew you were there all day, even if none of them actually saw you. I can only assume they knew my son came to rescue you. From the descriptions of the wounds, I'd surmise he was responsible for the first three kills. Only an inexperienced soturion would leave an opponent still breathing. Always, always finish the job, little slayer." He smirked. "My son has many faults, but he certainly knows how to take a life. I've seen him do it. Out of curiosity, what caused him to stand down? What could have happened to make him, a well-trained killer, pause and allow you the final kill?"

If you kill me, I won't get to tell you about how I fucked her.

My skin crawled.

"You can tell me, Lady Lyriana." His father's voice softened. "Did something happen? Was this revenge? Did he touch you? Something more?" His eyes turned to slits, shining with the same excitement he'd had when he questioned Meera. "Did he try to fuck you?"

"You mean rape!" I spat.

Imperator Hart laughed, and the nahashim hissed. "Ah. Now we are getting somewhere."

Fuck. Fuck! How did I keep walking into the traps this man had set for me? At last, I reached for my wine and took a sip. I swallowed roughly, but I kept drinking and drinking, until I emptied the glass.

"Did he rape you? Or was my son fast enough to stop him?"

"What do you care?" I said, my voice hushed. I slammed my glass on the table. "Rhyan stopped him. Not that it matters now. Because none of what you're saying is of consequence. The official story of Brockton's death at the hands of his friends has been publicized across the Empire. Acknowledged by his Ka. By his own Imperator and Emperor. There is no active investigation, and no calls for my arrest, and certainly no calls for Rhyan's either—at least not regarding this."

"No calls for your arrest?" he taunted. "Lord Tristan is not merely hunting Rhyan. He's hunting you. Do you not yet understand all of this? Did you think you got away with it? You have not. The fate that awaits you at the hands of Imperator Kormac will be far more dire than you can imagine. And that, my lady, is precisely why there has been no public call. And why there won't be. Every single witness to Brockton's murder has spoken, and given their testimony. And do you know where they are now?"

My vision swam. "In Vrukshire?"

"Not anymore." He grinned. "Every last one has been executed."

"Executed?" All those servants were dead? Because of me? "By who?"

He looked at me pityingly. "Who do you think? Imperator Kormac."

"But they served him." My mind was whirling, unsure how to play this, unsure what it all meant. Only that we were fucked. That they knew, and something worse was coming.

"Imperator Kormac came home, and did his investigation. He knew of my nahashim, knew who they sought. He saw the wounds on his soturi. He knows which men died by the hand of my son, and which one died by yours. He's quite insulted by that you know. He had higher hopes for Brockton than to be taken out by a powerless girl. In any case, he learned all he needed to in a single morning. And then he eviscerated the evidence."

I shivered. "Why?"

"No witnesses, no crime, at least as far as Imperator Kormac is concerned. But I wouldn't look too relieved at this revelation. You have not been exonerated."

I knew there was no such look on my face, but I nodded for him to continue, barely able to stop myself from glaring.

"I can assure you that he desires his revenge greatly. Both he, and the Bastardmaker. It was *his* son and heir you stuck your blade into, after all. The thing about wolves is they are pack creatures. Loyal, and vengeful. And hungry. They will not rest until they sink their teeth into you, biting and tearing you apart until they are satisfied. Perhaps while my son gets to watch."

My eyes widened, my hands shaking.

Imperator Hart chuckled. "Oh, they'd love that. Kormac wants to find you—and, he wants to keep your crimes secret. You should be worried about why. He could easily send you to prison, execute you for murder. It's the legal way to do this of course." He shrugged. "An option that may offer him a moment of satisfaction. Or ..."

The snake hissed again, and the lights in the crystals above us twinkled as the wind howled and another rumbling through the tower made my stomach turn.

"Or?" I asked.

"Or he can keep you above the law, and use you to his advantage. Use your blood, your lineage," his lips turned, "not to mention your womb. A perfect way to legitimize his claim on Bamaria. I think we all know that you are far more useful to him alive, as a docile bride for Lord Viktor, than you are dead. By having you as a daughter-in-law, he has a claim to take your country for himself. It wouldn't be the first time he's taken something that isn't his. Think about when the Emperor had the Blade murder every last child of Ka Azria. What happened once they were gone? Imperator Kormac put his puppets, Ka Elys, in their place."

Ka Azria ... The ruling Ka of Elyria who'd been murdered for concealing vorakh. By the Gods.

My blood ran cold, my eyes locking with Rhyan's father. The puzzle pieces I'd spent years collecting were now snapping together. By eliminating the ruling Ka of Elyria, the only Lumerian country to share our border, the Imperator had created a clear path to enter Bamaria. My whole life they'd been using it. Entering easily, bringing more soldiers every time. And Ka Elys never stood in their way, never challenged the entry of an armed legion. Ka Kormac's soturi already had the backing of the Emperor. It wouldn't be long before Imperator Kormac controlled the entire southern border. Korteria, Elyria, and Bamaria would all be under his complete and total rule.

I wanted to throw up. It had been in front of my face the whole time. Ka Azria hadn't been a cautionary tale to warn others of concealing vorakh.

They'd been collateral damage in Ka Kormac's quest to control the Empire.

Imperator Hart blinked slowly. "You see the gravity of the situation then. Emperor Theotis is not long for this world. And if things continue the way they are, you will not just be facing Imperator Avery Kormac, Arkasva and High Lord of Korteria. You'll be bending a knee to His Majesty, *Emperor* Avery Kormac, ruler of all Lumeria."

I squeezed my eyes shut, trying somehow to find composure. Gods. The Imperator was monstrous enough with his outrageous levels of power—for him to become Emperor …

But no. He couldn't be allowed to ascend to the throne. The Emperor would be chosen from another Ka. That was the legal precedent. The way it was always done. No two Emperors in a row could serve from the same Ka, or from the same country. It was the law.

But … Fuck. It wouldn't matter. I knew firsthand *just* how well the Imperator followed the law. Knew what little regard he had for precedent or tradition. How little resistance he faced from those he controlled. He was as good as the Emperor now. And if nothing changed, he always would be. He and his progeny would rule our lives forever.

I stilled, my eyes narrowing. "I wouldn't be the only one to swear my allegiance. If this happened, he'd no longer be your equal. He'd be your Emperor, too. You'd be bending your knee as well, *Your Highness*."

Imperator Hart lifted his wine glass in response, his lips turned up. A grim toast. "You see my problem, then. I did not become Imperator of the North to find myself bowing before my incompetent counterpart. Now, considering what we know, I have two options to move forward."

After taking a long sip of wine, he sat back, readjusting the golden Laurel of the Arkasva atop his head, and refilled my glass. He gestured for me to drink, but I couldn't move.

For a moment, he eyed my goblet, but then he shrugged, running his fingers along the golden border of his cloak, so it laid just-so on his shoulder. "My first option here is that I fall in line with Kormac's story. Pretend Brockton and his little wolves had a big bad fight that led to their unfortunate end. I can pretend my nahashim weren't in Korteria. Pretend you and my son weren't there either. It seems the likely option—I expect word of your arrival to Seathorne has reached His Highness's ears by now."

Of course, it had—he wanted everyone to know he had me. That he had rescued Meera.

"I can allow Imperator Kormac to take control of you like he's always wanted. I can honor his claim, and send you home to Korteria as his son's bride. Allow him to breed you."

And I'd be a prisoner for life. A slave to Viktor and his Ka. Tortured and worse. I'd never see Rhyan again. I'd never free Jules. Bamaria would be doomed.

"I think we can both agree," he said, "that neither of us like option one."

"I think we can agree that you don't want *him* to have control of me," I snarled. "Nor do you wish for him to outrank you. Option two?"

He smiled slowly. "I can expose the truth. Let everyone know you're a murderer. It would be easy to say you confessed to me. To pull the memories from your mind with my nahashim. We can have you tried before the Emperor's Council, imprisoned along with my son. You may even both be publicly stripped. My son, at least, would be. Then, I suspect Ka Kormac will have no choice but to go to war with Bamaria for your crimes—a war he will win since you're currently lacking an Arkturion. How long do you think it would take Bamaria to fall? Hours? Days? It wouldn't be long before Bamaria went from an occupied country, to a conquered one."

It took all I had not to throw up.

"But, like you, I'm not inclined to support that option either."
The Imperator stood, strolling slowly beside the table until he
stood right behind me. The tower shook again. The wind howled
wildly, and the crystals swayed causing their lights to flicker. I
felt dizzy as he breathed down the back of my neck.

Imperator Hart moved even closer, his body heat and aura
brushing against my own. There was a hissing sound that rushed
past my ear, and then something hot and slimy slid across my
collarbone.

I barely dared to breathe.

"It is time we came to an understanding, you and I," he
crooned. "Time to find a third possibility. I have things I want.
And things I can do. You have the same. I believe we can come
to a mutually beneficial agreement, you and I. *Asherah*."

I focused on my breathing, on inhaling and exhaling. "I don't
know what makes you think I'd ever agree to work with you."

"The fate of yourself, of my son, and your country aren't
enough to sway you? Pretend you're brave all you want. But I
don't think you want this nahashim inside your body, or your
mind. I know what the Examiner from Lethea did to you. I had
Kunda show me, in great detail."

The nahashim slid between my breasts, its tongue poking
below the top of my dress.

By the Gods …

"He used far smaller specimens than this. A nahashim of this
size would hurt terribly, I imagine. But at my word, he will enter
you, and he will extract every memory I need to turn you in for
the murder of Brockton Kormac. And then, I will extract every
memory of my son mounting you. Of your sister's vorakh—oh
yes, I know about that, too. You think I don't know exactly who I
allowed in my gates? I can pull every secret you have out for the
entire Empire to see. And I can make sure that you face every
punishment available to you and yours. Or? I can call the
nahashim back, and you and I can talk terms."

His hand pressed into my shoulder, fingers digging into my flesh to the point of pain, his palm pushing until I could swear, he was touching my bone. My chin quivered, and my breath came short as my body tried to adjust to the pain. But I couldn't. I couldn't. Even with my magic. And he fucking knew it. He shifted, standing before me, as his eyes held mine. The pressure increased.

The snake slid down to my lap, its head bolting up in line with my own, its tongue thrust out as it darted for my eyes. That was where they entered, through the eyelids. I could viscerally remember the awful feeling, the pain and the violation. Its head snapped back and then it lunged. I closed my eyes, feeling its tongue slide against my eyelid.

"Call him back," I said, my throat raw.

He made a soft whistling sound, and I felt the snake slide to my shoulder and back up his arm. He released me, and only when I could hear he had returned to his seat did I open my eyes. My entire body was trembling.

"Good girl," he said.

"So, you make Imperator Kormac's threats somehow go away, and then what? I am forced to serve you instead?" I asked, trying to ignore the hissing of the nahashim still sliding around his neck.

"In a manner of speaking. I will bring you under the safety of my Ka. I will publicly announce my sorrow at Brockton's death, and express my woes that it happened at the hands of his friends. And I will issue a formal pardon to my son, revoking his status as forsworn, so he may remain in Glemaria without threat. I will also announce that he and you rescued Lady Meera, that there is no relationship in violation of the kashonim between you two. Legally, and politically, Imperator Kormac won't be able to touch either of you ever again."

I shook my head. "I'm still supposed to marry his son. I'm pretty sure he'll come to claim me for that alone."

"There will be no wedding. Not between the two of you. I can end that as well."

It was so much of what we most desperately needed. But at what cost?

I shook my head. "Rhyan will never agree to that."

"I'm not bargaining with Rhyan, am I?"

"What makes you think I would agree? That I would want this? That I'd sentence him to such a fate? I'd be merely trading one Imperator's prison for another."

"Your choice to see it that way. But I am prepared to offer you more. A far bigger prize." He leaned closer, his body looming over me, blocking the light from the chandelier above. "Something I know you desire greatly. You agree to serve me, and become one of my Ka. And I will help you get exactly what you want."

"What I want? I want to leave here. I want you to tell the truth about what happened to Rhyan's mother, un-name him forsworn, and then release him and Meera. You think there's truly anything you can offer me beyond our freedom? Beyond our safety?"

"I know there is." His eyes sparkled. "Because I know who the Emperor is keeping locked up inside his palace." He smiled slowly, holding my gaze. "Lady Julianna."

I felt like the wind had been knocked out of me.

Jules.

I shook my head, trying to remember what I was supposed to know, what I was supposed to say. "But she's … she's …"

"Alive? You can cut the act, Lyriana. I know you were made aware." He stroked the top of the nahashiin's head. "*He* told me."

Imperator Hart leaned forward and lifted the lid to another silver tray. This one was also lacking food. Instead, there were a dozen tightly wound scrolls. Letters. Imperator Hart picked one off the top and placed it in my hands.

"Go on. Read."

I unraveled the parchment slowly and gasped.

To my favorite friend in the North—also my only friend in the North (a fact that does not make you any less my favorite, by the way)—

The shock of hearing Jules's voice in my head the other day had been one thing. But to come face to face with her handwriting again was another. To read her wording, her specific turns of phrase. There was no doubt in my mind who'd written this. My heart hurt at the truth of it. At her lightness, the joy she'd once possessed. The letter was dated on Auriel's Feast Day. Two years ago. My birthday. The night of her Revelation Ceremony. The night she was taken.

By the time you read this, most likely you'll be back to your rigorous soturion training.

Jules had kept up a correspondence with Rhyan. She'd written to him the last night she'd been in Bamaria.

"Where did you get this?" I asked, my heart pounding.

"A copy," he said. "We copied all of her letters as they arrived. The originals, sad to say, are gone. My son, in his anger after receiving this one—the last one, burned the others in a fit. I'll spoil the ending for you, but this was the night he learned about you and Lord Grey." He chuckled. "He was absolutely devastated."

My eyes shot down to the end of the letter.

Your not-so-favorite lord, of the mixed colors of black and white, has finally made his romantic intentions known. She hasn't come to tell me yet, but I expect she will soon—they're together now. Officially.

I think this will be a good thing for her.

My chest tightened. The night I'd first kissed Tristan. I remembered running to meet her before the ceremony, telling her in an excited, hushed whisper of what had happened. And all this time, Rhyan knew. Gods. Myself to Moriel. Kenna said Rhyan had spent a year not looking at any girls. And then something happened ...This letter. This letter had happened.

He knew. He knew that very night. After a year of waiting for me, he'd tried to move on. Auriel's fucking bane.

"I stopped in Numeria, briefly on my way to your aunt's consecration," his father said. "I took our little friend here. Imperators have special privileges at the Emperor's Palace, you see. We can access certain rooms, are granted the privilege of guarding copies of the building's layout, and blueprints. Things you might need if you were to say ... attend the Valabellum and attempt a rescue of Lady Julianna."

He made a sharp hissing sound, and suddenly the nahashim was across the table, staring into my eyes. Its blackened orbs filled with blue light, until all I could see was the color blue.

The room vanished. And suddenly, I was slithering down a hall, seeing what the nahashim saw.

Black and white marble shone beneath me, the black scaly reflection was as clear as if I were sliding across a mirror. I slipped beneath a door, feeling the roughened wood slide against my back, the floor cold against my stomach. And then I slid beneath another, and another, until I entered a room. Small, rounded, with multiple doors. A single bed in the center. Jules lay on it. Her skin was lightly tanned, paler than when I'd last seen her. There were marks on her arms, and thighs: bruises, the kind that came from being gripped too roughly.

My eyes welled.

She was thinner than she had been, wearing a long black dress with slits to the tops of her thighs, and a V from her shoulders to her belly that left most of her body exposed. Though revealing, the material was loose. The dress looked too big on her, like she'd once filled it out, but no longer did. Some of the threads at the hem were coming undone. She noticed the snake, and sat up. But there was no sense of fear in her eyes, only a tired, and resigned dullness. Her brown hair fell like a lion's mane around her shoulders.

The vision ended.

A tear rolled down my cheek, and my hands clenched. She was so thin, so pale. Those bruises. And her eyes … she wasn't dead. But she wasn't far from it, either. I had no time to lose.

"I think we can all speak plainly now of what we know," Imperator Hart said. He retrieved his nahashim and returned to his seat across from me, taking another sip of wine. "The stripping of a vorakh's power in Lethea was one of the greatest lies the Empire ever sold. Those in power know better. They are taken to the Emperor's Palace to serve as the *chayatim,* the cloaked ones. The Emperor's most esteemed servants. His spies. They are the ones who keep an eye on Lumeria for him. Lady Julianna has spent two years as his personal slave. She offers insights and visions to the very man who ruined her life." His lips curled. "Amongst the other *services* I hear she supplies."

I was shaking. If I had my weapons on me, he'd be dead. Fuck the consequences. I couldn't take any more of this torment, this grief. But no. No. I needed to breathe. I needed to calm down, to find some control.

I tried to imagine Rhyan was here, telling me to keep a clear head. To do what I had to do to survive, to get us out of here, to focus on the outcome I wanted. See the end.

Partner. Inhale … Exhale … I've got you. It's okay. I've got you.

Hearing his voice in my mind, I took a breath.

"And your plan is what, Your Highness? I agree to become your servant, agree to do whatever you want, and you're going to rescue her for me?" I asked in disbelief. "Out of the goodness of your heart?"

"The goodness of my heart," he scoffed. "Call it that if you will. But no. I will do this as a favor, if you do something in return for me. There is something I want from the capital. Something I believe only you can take. I will provide you and my son all that you need to get it. The blueprints to the Palace, the full layout of the Nutavian Katurium. You'll have access to keys, knowledge of the soturis' schedule, and a group of mercenaries at your beck and call. I will personally assign two of my most trusted men to assist you in planning. I'll even let you in on the secret of which of the Emperor's guards are loyal to me. You will have everything you need to acquire it."

I frowned. "You want me to be your thief?"

"If that's how you want to put it, then yes. Now, are we in agreement?"

My mind was whirling. None of it made sense. What did he want so badly that he was willing to dangle Jules in front of me?

"What am I stealing?"

He slowed, and reached into his pocket, removing a small cloth bag which he passed to me. "I need to know that you will not speak to anyone about what I share with you." He gestured for me to open the pouch.

I did. It was a lock of hair. Ash brown and fine. Meera's. Aemon had left me something similar after she'd been taken by his akadim.

"How did you get this?" I asked.

"How do you think?"

A chill ran down my spine. Kane had a key to her room. "You're threatening her."

"I'm using her as collateral. Should you reveal this to anyone beyond those I approve of—" He made a snipping motion with his fingers. "Agreed?"

I swallowed. "Agreed."

"What I seek hangs in the Great Hall, above the throne where it is guarded day and night by the Emperor's sentries. But during a Valabellum, it is brought into the arena ceremonially. Why else do you think I whispered in the Emperor's ear to host the event?" He smirked, pleased with himself. "That means there is a time where it is changing hands, where it is more vulnerable. That's what you're to steal. I will gift you your freedom for the next month to prepare for the event. Under the roof of Seathorne, you will have access to all you need for the theft. You agree to do this, and I'll give you all you need. You keep it a secret, and Meera gets to live."

"And if I agree to steal this for you, you'll rescue Jules?" I asked, still not believing him. What didn't I know? Why would he offer me anything I wanted when he already had me and my loved ones completely cornered? He could demand this theft without the promise of Jules.

He nodded, but my mind continued to race. Was he after Jules, too? From what I knew about Rhyan's father, he preferred blood oaths for his agreements. But Rhyan had broken his. Perhaps he worried we couldn't be trusted with them. If he thought we'd break them, then giving them to us was a death sentence. We'd be useless when he wanted us alive. He wanted control of Gods and Goddesses. But he had us here, he could simply keep us imprisoned. And if he needed collateral, if he needed to threaten someone I loved, he had Meera. What the hell was this object he wanted?

Gods. I needed Rhyan. Needed to discuss this with him.

I needed time to think.

"What happens to her after? Won't they notice she's missing?" I asked.

"They will. Eventually. I'll leave a decoy. She'll need a new name. Perhaps a new face. Not a problem. You've met Aiden. You've seen what he can do."

"And what about Rhyan," I said carefully. "I assume I'll need his *specific* set of skills to do this."

"You will. Not within the Palace. They have wards to block such a thing, of course. Magic siphoned from others like him have proven invaluable for security. But outside the walls? Yes, we'll need him to spirit Jules away, after I free her."

"Then he is to be seen by your best healer, and freed from prison. Tonight. Or no deal. You will remove his binds, and you will let me see him."

"Remove his binds? And let you see him? Hmmm. That sounds wonderful. For you." He clucked his tongue. "And then what happens when the two of you are alone, and my son is unbound? You vanish? Just as you wished to earlier? You think I couldn't see the plan in bold letters across your face?"

"We wouldn't leave. Not without Meera," I said. "You separated her from me, placed her under guard for a reason. And you've made sure the entire Empire knows she's here. I think you already know you have me locked into Seathorne."

"I do. And I know that you know that. My son, on the other hand? He's impulsive. Bull-headed. Forgive me if I do not trust him. But I'll tell you what I will offer tonight. He will be healed—"

"By your best healers!"

Imperator Hart nodded. "By my best healers. He will be freed from his prison cell, and he will be escorted to a private meeting with you so you can fill him in on his duties. But he will be bound for that meeting. Or there's no meeting. You must explain things to him in order to win his cooperation. During the events of tomorrow, if I feel his behavior proves you've done your job, then, and only then he may have his ropes removed. But that will depend on you. And how convincing you are."

Gods. Either he was bound, his own form of personal hell, or he agreed to live under his father's rule, something that would be equal parts torture for him. If I didn't bring Rhyan into this, it would cost me Meera. And if I did—it might cost me Rhyan. No matter what I chose, someone would be hurt. Every choice felt like a betrayal.

But I had to believe that if forced to pick between the two, he wouldn't want the ropes. He'd play along to help me, to help

Meera, and Jules. We wouldn't stay here forever—no matter what I swore tonight. We'd find a way.

"Once Rhyan is healed and freed and has the chance to see me, his binds will be removed," I said again. "And no harm comes to Meera. Only her guards have a key to her room. Not Kane."

"Kane is Arkturion. He may have any key he wishes."

"Except for one!"

He shook his head. "You have nothing to offer in that negotiation. But you have my word—no harm will come to her."

No harm that would be obvious. No harm that couldn't be hidden under the complex Glemarian dresses she'd be forced to wear.

"I have drawn up a contract for you with rather agreeable terms." He lifted the lid of another silver platter and handed me a scroll.

I unraveled it to see that this contract only included stipulations between the Imperator and myself.

"You are to steal the item I request," he said, reading the points he'd written out. "You may have Rhyan and any other resources you need to complete your missions. You must remain at Seathorne until the Valabellum. You will also resume your soturion training during that time—however, no one knows you have magic. I intend for you to keep it that way. And I will reinstate Rhyan as an heir. He will no longer be forsworn."

"He'd be Heir Apparent again?" I asked.

He made a disapproving sound with his tongue. "Gods, no. That honor goes to my next son. But Rhyan can be an heir once more. I can even allow him access to his old bank accounts."

"How? You had your own men swear he killed his mother. That they saw it with their own eyes." I bit my tongue before I could say that *he*, Imperator Hart, was the true murderer.

"Let me and him worry about those details." He continued, "Now, your reputation, along with his, must be rehabilitated. We must squash the rumors of your affair. This work will begin the moment I make the claims of your innocence in Korteria, and end your engagement to Viktor Kormac."

I shook my head. "And how do you plan to do that? You said so yourself, I am too valuable to him. He'll come and claim me at some point. Fight you on the fact that my engagement to his Ka came first. He may not be able to retaliate against Bamaria with this, but I doubt you wish to go to war with him over me, not when the Emperor is on his side."

"It's easier than you think," he said. "You never publicly accepted the engagement. And even he cannot force a marriage on a noble already betrothed." He winked.

My stomach sank. I didn't need to ask who. He'd been trying for years, trying since I was a baby. I'd be engaged to Arkturion Kane. To Shiviel reincarnated.

I couldn't decide which fate was worse. A marriage to Kane? Or a marriage to Viktor?

I felt nauseated. "What happens after I bring this object to you? Are we released from your service?"

"Released?" He chuckled. "You will find a far better life here than under any other options you now face. You'll need me anyway to keep you safe, to continue hiding Julianna."

Rhyan had escaped before. He'd do it again. And I still had to fulfill my deal with Mercurial. I had to find the red shard. I had to claim it, and use its power. He'd been less than forth-coming about when that would happen, or how. But I knew one thing—it *would* happen.

I looked down at the table, at the edge of the letter Jules had sent to Rhyan. Under her signature, she had written:

Yes! Anything is possible.

She used to say that all the time. But it had been so long, I'd forgotten.

I swallowed roughly and looked up at the Imperator. "If I fail to steal this object for you?"

"Don't," he commanded, and removed the dagger from his belt, passing it to me. "Your signature, and a willing drop of your blood."

"A blood oath?" I asked.

"I think we both know that you're at too high a risk for breaking one, as is my son."

Then what was the catch?

I read the rest of the contract, scanning for discrepancies, for any hidden stipulations. It said everything he'd mentioned. But at the bottom was one more clause—what would happen if I failed to steal what he asked for. The price was Jules. She wasn't an act of goodwill, nor was she the carrot to dangle in front of me for motivation. She was the final collateral. Meera died if I didn't fall in line. Jules died if I didn't finish the mission. He was going to remove her from the Palace no matter what. Our success determined if she left there dead or alive.

"What exactly am I stealing?" I asked. "You still haven't told me. I won't sign unless I know."

"You lost something of great value to me when you broke into the tomb without permission." He took out the red jewel— the key to the moonstone seraphim—and let it roll across his palm. "You owe me. I intend for you to bring me something in return. Go on," he crooned to the nahashim. "Show her."

The snake lifted his head, its gaze on mine. I stilled and once more, blue light filled my vision.

A golden throne sat in the middle of the largest room I'd ever seen. There were dozens of white marble columns that reached for a ceiling too high to even comprehend from the ground. On either side of the Seat were two dozen of the Emperor's soturi, each of them wearing a golden Valalumir tattoo on their cheek.

Through the snake's eyes, I looked above the throne, my eyes traveling up and up the wall. Mounted between the purple tapestries descending from the ceiling, was an old-fashioned shield made of bronze. It was round, adorned with a fiery golden sun. And in its center was an orange crystal.

I stifled a gasp. It was the same shield I'd found in Meera's vision—in my vision. The one I'd seen in the arena. Sunlight shined through the windows, and light from the crystal erupted, filling the entire hall with bright, beautiful orange light.

My heart pounded, the Valalumir inside me was beating its own, rapid rhythm, before the heat spread across my chest, growing hotter and hotter. If my dress were cut lower, he'd see markings of Mercurial's bargain with me coming to life.

And then I knew.

This wasn't just any shield. This was Ereshya's. I knew why Aemon and Morgana would be at the Valabellum.

If Morgana hadn't handed over the indigo shard to Aemon yet, then she would after she was in possession of the shard she'd guarded in her past life.

And when that happened, they'd both be able to tap into their God and Goddess power. They'd be unstoppable. It wouldn't matter who conquered Bamaria, or who was anointed Emperor.

We'd be under the reign of Moriel's terror once again.

If I agreed to this, I'd be handing a shard of the Valalumir to a tyrant. A tyrant who had a God as his warlord. A tyrant with his eyes on the Emperor's throne. But I was going to keep it from Morgana and Aemon. And if we could save Jules, and then find a way to escape, we could go after the red shard, we could find a way to fight back.

My heart thundered.

"Meera won't be harmed. Rhyan is healed and freed from your prisons," I said. "And his binds are removed."

"Sign," was his only response.

I stared down at the contract, and the blade he'd handed me. A scratch pen but no ink was offered next. I was signing my name in blood. Gods. This wasn't a blood oath.

It was worse.

Signing a blood contract was an old practice. It would bind me to Imperator Hart, compel me to follow his orders whenever he was near. Like a blood oath, I'd be bound to what I signed, to any request or order he gave. Compelled to fulfill his every request. I'd be his slave. My free will would be gone any time he was near enough for my blood to sense him.

But there was no other way out. No other option that gave us a chance. That got us to Jules.

Anything is possible.

I squeezed my eyes shut, and pressed the blade into my skin, hissing as the sound of my blood splattered against the parchment. Then I picked up the scratch pen. And signed.

CHAPTER TWENTY-ONE

RHYAN

I was shivering furiously. The cell they'd left me in was a Godsdamned ice box. It didn't matter that I was bound, that the ropes tightened around me were meant to burn. Even they were of no use down here as they barely conjured heat.

I'd been taken to the absolute bowels of the dungeon in Ha'Lyrotz. This wasn't where my father had imprisoned me before. Last time, I'd been placed where my bodyguard Bowen could get to me without issue. Where healers could reach me after I'd nearly lost my eye the night he gave me my scar. The night my father forced the blood oath on me.

The night he'd killed my mother.

It had happened in the Seating Room. Right where he'd tortured Lyriana. Just thinking of it now … Gods, I could fucking kill him.

I resumed my fight to tear through the ropes. It had been hours. I was exhausted, hungry, and thirsty. But I kept going, fueled by my worry for Lyr. Determined to not lose anyone else. Especially not her.

I picked up the speed of my pacing, though the cell was so

tiny, I could barely manage more than a few steps before I hit the wall. So little space made it difficult to work up a sweat or retain any semblance of body heat. And I needed heat, needed energy, if I was going to break free.

A tiny fire flickered in the hall, offering the dimmest light for me to see. Aside from the faint sounds of the flames licking, and the inconsistent drips of water from a nearby pipe, it was silent through the outer labyrinth of halls. I was so far down the lower levels of the dungeons, there weren't even any guards nearby.

I wasn't sure what to make of that knowledge. That even my father doubted my escape. Or that he knew I couldn't leave— that I *wouldn't* leave. Not without Lyriana, not without Meera.

Gods. Fuck. Please, please let them be okay. Let Lyr be all right.

I squeezed my eyes shut, and I turned again, hitting the wall once more. Each of my three walls were made of rough stone, but not sharp enough. If only they could cut the ropes that bound me. But even after hours of rubbing against them, the threads had barely begun to weaken.

I hit my shoulder against the wall and turned. A light burst beyond the bars before the darkness resumed, just as a sudden flash of heat rose up my frozen limbs.

"Thought I'd find you here," purred a feline voice. "Right back here in the very place you hate."

Mercurial stepped out of the darkness of the hall beyond my bars.

The blue Afeya was almost naked, as usual, wearing only glittering sandals that were laced up to his blue knees, and a silver loin cloth. Small diamonds sparkled in the center of each tattooed whorl across his body. He clearly didn't feel the effects of the freezing cold that permeated every damp inch of this place.

My mind flashed. The memory of Kane as Shiviel, followed

by my memory of Mercurial on Gryphon's Mount a thousand years ago.

"No more falcon head?" I asked. "Quite an interesting look for you."

"You remembered? It was stunning, wasn't it? Shame having a bird's head went out of fashion. At least, it did outside of the Night Lands." Mercurial clucked his tongue. "But look at you, wearing the latest trends in binding. Atrocious. Those ropes are all ragged and torn." He lifted an eyebrow. "Not your best look, my lord."

"Don't you mean *not-lord*?" I asked. "Or are you finally addressing me as Auriel?"

Slowly, seductively, he shook his head. "You were once Auriel. He peeks out from behind your eyes. Every now and then, I see it. Sometimes I think he sees me." Mercurial shuddered. "But you are not the same. Not completely. The shifting of shared personalities and lifetimes between souls is not a subject I have time to explain. In any case, I would not presume to address you as what you are not. You seemed so preoccupied with the status of your titles, their relevance, their currency. But soon you'll see exactly what I mean, *Lord* Rhyan, Heir to the Arkasva, High Lord of Glemaria, Imperator to the North."

My old title. At least, most of it. I was Heir Apparent before. I looked the Afeyan up and down, hearing his words echo in my mind, almost like a song. The title I'd been forced to bear. The title I hated.

Lord Rhyan.

"No." I shook my head. "That's not possible. I remain forsworn."

"Are you so sure?" He shimmied his shoulders. "What if you were Heir once again?"

A sinking feeling began to drill deep into my gut. "How? What happened?"

"Lyriana happened," Mercurial said.

I stilled. If Lyr had somehow gotten my title back, it meant she'd given my father something in return. Something that was bound to put her life in danger. My father didn't give anything freely.

My eyes narrowed. "Not Heir Apparent," I asked, clarifying, as if it made a difference. "Just Heir."

"Do you think I made an error?" He feigned offense. "You could ask me for information on the subject. But you know it will cost you."

I glowered. He knew Godsdamned well I wouldn't ask.

Water from the pipe continued to drip as he turned his head, looking behind him. My fingers latched onto a stray thread around my wrist and I began to tug, my hand cramping.

"News of your change in status is on its way to you right now. But oh," he pouted, stepping closer to the bars. His hips swayed sinuously with each step as his violet eyes resumed their intense scrutiny of my face. "Just look at your nose."

"Kindly refrain from mentioning it unless you plan to do something about it."

His lips curled. "There's no need for me to do that either. Someone else is on the way."

"Not Lyr," I said, my voice choked with emotion.

"No." His head tilted to the side in disapproval, violet eyes flashing with anger, looking me up and down. A dirty water droplet fell onto his shoulder and he hissed with disgust.

"She can heal now," I said, my voice low. "Or the light inside her can. But it hurts her, she takes on the pain of those she's healing. And it leaves her drained. Powerless." My hands clenched.

Mercurial lifted his black eyebrows, then tore a loose thread from my binds, and flicked it on the ground. "I'm aware."

"You knew? Of course you did. Did you always know? Did you know putting the light inside her would do that?" I snarled.

"Me? It was you, my *lord.* Your selfishness, your theft, your choices that put us here—that put us all here. You are the one who made the choice that fateful day in Heaven. You are the one who decided to steal a light never meant to survive in this world. And it was you who chose to fall, to allow it to break, to start a war that drowned an empire." A light flashed and then he was inside the cell with me, his face inches from mine as he took up nearly every inch of space that remained. "You may not be Auriel now. But you still are in many ways, and it was *you*, my lord, who put the Valalumir into her heart and melded it to her soul. I simply returned it."

"And who decided to steal Asherah's chest plate?" I asked, my jaw clenching. "It was supposed to end that day. The day she died. I did everything right. I sealed her tomb, I made sure the shards were hidden and locked. Without you going behind my back, none of this would have been set in motion. None of it! So don't fucking pretend that I am the one who brought us here."

"And you shouldn't fucking pretend to have any idea of what you're talking about! You are not Auriel, not yet," Mercurial yelled. "You are the reason Lyriana is imprisoned by your father now, just as much as you are the reason your ex-lover carries his child." He shook his head, his lip curling. "And after all sweet Kenna sacrificed to free you ..."

"Fuck you."

"Oh, my *lord*, you already have. By cursing me to this immortality." Stars appeared along the ceiling, flickering in and out, blinding me with their light and then leaving me in total darkness until spots formed in my vision. "You accuse *me* of theft? But have you returned Canturiel's light? Have you made any true effort in your centuries of lifetimes to fix it?" He laughed. "I didn't think so. I already told you. The two of you do not get to walk away from what you started. It doesn't matter how long ago it was. What lives you were living. I don't care if you're called Rhyan now. If you're called a murderer. Betrayer. Son of the Imperator. Partner. Lover. Lord or not-lord. You will always be Auriel to me. Thief of the Valalumir. Forsworn Guardian."

I gritted my teeth, my body pushing against the ropes until I felt the smallest tear. "Did you just come here to taunt me? Or are you actually here to tell me something useful?"

"I came to remind you of the debt owed by my remembered Goddess. If Lady Lyriana does not resume her quest to uncover the red shard, she will pay the price. And my prices are quite exorbitant, I've heard."

"Well," I scoffed, flexing the muscles in my arms again, "we'd love to be on our way. Jumping when you say jump. Going where you say go. But I'm a little tied up at the moment. As is she. You'll have to talk to my father about that."

Mercurial laughed, the sound haunting, like old bells. "Of course, let me dance on down to Imperator Hart's study and chat. He's so known for his grace and reason. I am sure I can convince him, especially after the bargain he's made with Lyriana." He smirked. "There's no chance of that now. While we're here discussing the lengthy list of your poor choices, thank you, sincerely, for delivering a literal Guardian detection tool right into his hands!" He yelled, the anger permeating every inch of the cell. "Now he has Auriel, Shiviel, Asherah, and Cassarya under his thumb. And he damn well knows it."

"Cassarya?" I said, my heart pounding. "Meera? Lady Meera is Cassarya." I felt the truth of it in my heart. Of course she was. Cassarya was the Goddess known as the observant one in the stories, the one who always appeared with the largest eyes, the one who saw, the one whose visions had been most powerful.

Mercurial rolled his eyes. "Took you long enough."

"We've been a little preoccupied." I exhaled sharply. But just like that, six of the seven Guardian reincarnations had been identified. "That leaves only Hava to find."

There was a shake of Mercurial's head. "You've already found her."

"I have?"

He pressed his lips together. "Once. Others are after her now. You'd be wise to leave this place quickly. It's not good to have too many Guardians under the rule of one man—even if not every Guardian is aware of their identity."

So, Kane had no idea of his true origins. How like my father to withhold such information.

Mercurial lifted his eyebrows. "And your father intends to keep it that way. There's not one man on this earth who should have that much power."

"Like you aren't lining that power up for yourself," I snarled.

"I am no man. I am Afeya."

"Be that as it may, I can't exactly leave right now." I held out my palms, tied down below my hips. "You're not here to free me, you're not here to free Lyriana, or Meera. You would have done that by now if you were."

"Bravo. Your deductive reasoning skills are surely limitless, my lord. Very impressive. But you are correct." His eyes turned to slits. "My magic is still bound. Curse of the Afeya and all." He flicked a non-existent speck of dirt from his shoulder. "I cannot go around offering free favors just to anyone. Not unless they pay."

"Let me guess. You're here to offer me a deal?" I asked.

"I think in this case, you'd be wise to take one."

"And for what price?" But I quickly shook my head. "No. We'll figure it out ourselves."

"Have it your way." He shrugged, and rocked back on his heels. "The stakes are higher than you realize, my lord. I would speak with Lady Lyriana, but I cannot reach her at this moment. Rest assured that my interests lie in my debts. I want her to fulfill her end of the bargain."

"And yet you came to visit me." I watched him carefully through my swollen eyes. "There's something else. Something you're not telling us." I frowned. "And you're lying about your magic abilities. You're not supposed to be able to do any magic unless it's requested by someone. Afeyan magic only works by request. Lyr never paid you for her ankle after her first habibellum. Nor did she ask to be healed. You did that for free."

The Afeya's eyes narrowed, his lips curling viciously upward. "Not free. Not at all. That was paid for. By someone else," he said slyly.

"Someone else wanted her ankle healed?" I asked, suspiciously. "Someone else knew and requested it?"

Mercurial stepped back, his aura suddenly dark and thick like a shield around him.

"Who?" I asked, my hands fisting. "Who!"

"That's a question, my lord."

"Of course it fucking is." Something shifted inside of me. The need to protect Lyriana was overriding my senses. "Go ahead, Mercurial. What's your price? Who wanted her healed? Who wants her tied up in this quest? Who are you truly serving?"

"You have far more to lose than you know when you ask that question. Careful. That information is not the kind even I would dare to trade for."

I stepped forward. "Are you kidding me? You were open for business a moment ago. But not for this?" I was onto something. Mercurial didn't refuse deals. And he didn't offer favors. All this time he'd been fucking with us, and it was on someone else's behalf. "How high is the price?" I asked again.

"There is no price. It's not for sale." His voice darkened. "Do not ask me again," he hissed. "Just be happy that your actions a millennia ago left Shiviel weakened, even unto this day. Thanks to you, he is the only one of you without a vorakh—or access to one as Lyriana is. Otherwise ..." He clucked his tongue. "You'd have been dead long ago. Not even your father would be able to control him now."

My heart thundered at the warning. I still didn't understand, or have the full memory of what had happened. The vision had come so fleetingly when I was upstairs. Lyr had been so scared, and in so much pain. But I remembered being Auriel, and Asherah had saved me from the brink of death. Together, we'd killed Shiviel.

"Not quite," Mercurial said, reading my mind. "It was something far more dangerous that you did to him. In the end it cost Asherah her life. It certainly should have cost you yours."

"What did I do?" My memories of being Auriel were returning, but not quickly or fully enough. Most of what I knew was still sparse, hazy and unclear.

Mercurial tutted. "That's another question." His eyes narrowed.

"She healed me. Healed Auriel, after …whatever it is we did to him," I said.

"Asherah healed you by taking on *Rakashonim*. Just as Lyriana healed you earlier using the same. But she wasn't strong enough. Not then. And certainly not now."

"*Rakashonim?*" I said. "*Your kashonim.*" I rolled the translation around in my head, and then the High Lumerian. The word seemed to resonate in the back of my mind. Familiar, and yet, I couldn't place it. I'd never heard that term before. At least … not in this life. "What do you mean by not now?"

Mercurial shook his head. "That's a question. And not one I will answer today, my *lord.* I am simply here to remind you, as a courtesy, that Lyriana is running out of time. And therefore, you are running out of time. Moriel is growing closer to claiming his indigo shard by the day. And Ereshya is not long from finding hers. Despite the magic you placed upon it, every action you take, and every choice Lyriana makes is leading her to it." He shook his head. "Can you imagine the threat of destruction those two shall pose if they claim them? If they remain unchallenged? If they claim the rest?" His eyes darkened. "You lived through it once before. But Asherah did not survive."

My chest tightened, the visceral memory of losing her still haunted me, days after my dream. And now, the fear of losing her again, of losing Lyr, had become a constant ache in my chest.

"This *Rakashonim*," I said. "Is that what she's using to heal? Is this what she's been drawing on when she calls on Asherah? Is it related to vorakh? You said Shiviel was the only one without vorakh or access to it, so what does that mean for Lyr?"

He shook his head. "You've gotten enough out of me, old friend. You both need to leave here. You're getting distracted. Falling into his plots. Again! My remembered Goddess can have what she wants. But she needs to escape your father, needs to come find me, needs to claim the red shard before the others find theirs. They are too close, and it won't matter how many Guardians you have on your side if you don't have any shards to wield in the coming war."

The Valalumir stars twinkling against the ceiling suddenly went out as the torch in the hall hissed with fresh life.

"How?" I asked desperately. "How do we get out of here? How do we get to the red shard?"

The door at the end of the hall creaked open.

"Godsdamnit! You tasked her with this! You expect her to meet your demands. Give us something!" I seethed.

"Get away from here," Mercurial hissed. He stretched his neck from side to side, the movements snakelike, until his body began to shimmer. Then he vanished, turning to mist as I rushed forward, trying to stop him.

"Mercurial!" I yelled. But the Afeya was gone.

Footsteps echoed in the hallway. Boots splashed through the pooling puddles on the ground. The sound grew louder, the boots coming closer, and my dread began to grow.

I puffed out my chest, grunting under my breath, pushing and fighting. I was desperate to tear through more of the ropes, to break free.

"I so hate to see you like this," my father said, peering

through the bars. His aura, cold and vicious, wrapped around me. "Nose broken, power and body bound. So unbefitting of an Heir to the Arkasva and Imperator."

So, it was true. I'd been reinstated. "Where is she?"

"You will be happy to know that as of tonight, you have received an official pardon from the Glemarian Council. You will no longer be considered forsworn. You will be publicly recognized as my Heir. You will henceforth be known as Lord Rhyan Hart, Heir to the Arkasva, High Lord of Glemaria, Imperator to the North. The title of Heir Apparent that you once possessed will go to my other son, your new baby brother."

I shook my head in disbelief. My title. My *brother.* Kenna's baby.

"All other crimes that you're accused of from the Imperator of the South will be amended, including your absence without leave. We will also put a stop to the claims alleging you kidnapped Lyriana. As for the vile, disgusting rumors of the affair between you two, those are now null, and should no longer be of concern."

"What did you do to Lyriana?" I gritted through my teeth.

But he ignored me, continuing on as if I weren't there. "Now that you are no longer forsworn, you will resume your duties as an Heir, as well as your daily soturion training at the academy. You will be an apprentice. Lyriana will remain your novice, though under close watch. No one knows of her magic—she shall continue as if she has none. That, at least, should feel familiar." He winked. "When not in class, you will be expected in Court, like before."

"Like nothing happened? Are you farther than Lethea? Everyone in Glemaria is just going to, what?" I yelled. "Accept me? Decide to ignore the word of their Imperator and every belief they held for the last year? You swore I was a murderer. Do you expect them to forget that? Forget that your own private guard swore to my crimes? That you obtained the testimony of your Arkmage, and then forced testimony from Kenna? You shared those with every Arkasva in the North."

"New compelling evidence has arisen from the night of your mother's murder."

"New evidence!" I spat. "Pray tell, Father. Is this new evidence the truth? Are you going to turn yourself in?"

"Father? You mean, Your Highness," he growled. "Careful now, you don't want to speak of treason." He cleared his throat. "I need you looking presentable. We're having a special session in the Seating Room tomorrow. I'm sending someone to fix your nose. You'll also need to be bathed," his lip curled in disgust, "and shaved. You'll be offered a new set of Glemarian leathers, one with the proper sigil of Ka Hart. No more of that gryphon-shit thing you were wearing. You fight for us now."

"Where is she?" I asked. I didn't care about this farce of a Council meeting. I didn't care about my titles, or what farther than Lethea story he'd invented to erase my crimes. "What have you done with Lyriana?"

He sighed. "You'll be twenty-three at winter's end. A ripe age to renounce your bachelorhood." He frowned. "I think you've done more than enough courting. We don't need a repeat of last time."

My chest tightened. Last time …

He steepled his fingers below his beard. "It's good for the people of Glemaria to see some stability with you—especially after your wanderings."

I huffed. "What a fucking polite term for exile."

"Rhyan," he said, his aura pulsing, somehow heavier, its weight crushing down on me. "I've entertained you tonight. But I'm going to lose patience soon. And you don't want that. Not after Lyriana pleaded so prettily for you to be healed. Now, most importantly, we need to squash those rumors about you and her. You know the punishment for fucking someone in your soturion lineage. Which is why we will announce your engagement."

"Absolutely not! I left before," I threatened. "You think I won't do it again? That I won't find a way? That I won't hesitate to take Lyriana and Meera with me?"

"You might be surprised at their refusal to go with you— after all, you weren't so good at convincing Kenna to leave with you before, were you? Or Aiden, or Dario. Or," he frowned, "poor Garrett."

"Don't you dare say his name!" My hands clenched.

My father grinned. "You won't leave. Because she won't. Lyriana, you see, understands the importance of the situation. She has given me her word, not just with her voice, but with her blood, to do a great many things to make this work."

No, no.

"She's a smart girl," he said. "She knows I can keep her safe. Keep her away from Ka Kormac. They'll hurt her. You know they will. You saw them, didn't you?" His lip curled. "You saw Brockton Kormac touch her."

"What the fuck could you possibly know about that?"

"Everything," he said. "I know you killed three wolves. I know you left one alive in some misguided attempt of giving her vengeance."

My jaw tightened, my blood boiling with a rage I'd carried too long.

"You made a dire mistake that night," he said. "You should have killed Brockton yourself. But you made your choice, and these are the consequences. The wolves know. And that knowledge means she can be compelled to return to the South. Imperator Kormac will lay claim to her. And he will make sure she is bred, mark my word." He smirked. "It won't be just once. She'll be bred by all of them—again and again. And it won't matter to them who the father is. Lord Viktor. The Bastardmaker. Imperator Kormac himself." He shrugged. "As long as the seed in her belly is wolf. Do you want to see that happen to her? See them share her? Touch her? Hurt her?" His lip curled. "I don't think you do."

"As if what you'll do to her is any better!"

"Lyriana thought so. I made my wishes and desires quite clear. She has willingly accepted my offer to keep her safe from Kormac." He held up a piece of parchment, unraveling it to the bottom. In dark red ink was Lyriana's signature.

No. Not ink.

Blood.

I stumbled back, my shoulder hitting the wall. She was his. He had her. And now, after all these years, without forcing me to utter a single oath of my own, he had me.

"Come now." He clicked his tongue. "This is the best possible outcome. I, like you, have a desire to keep her safe."

"You have a desire to keep her for yourself!" I shouted, my muscles straining. Every single thing inside my body was desperate to break free. To escape. To kill him and end any agreement Lyr had made.

"If that were true, then why would I have betrothed her to another?"

My heart sank. I already knew.

"NO! Not Kane! You know what he is!"

"I do know." His eyes darkened. "And whatever the fuck you know, you best keep to your Godsdamned self." The fact that he was a reincarnated God.

My breath started to come faster. My muscles burned. Every inch of me was shaking, trembling, straining. I was almost there. In my father's taunting, he hadn't realized that he'd given me the rage I needed to push me over the edge. To reach beyond every physical limitation.

I tore right through his fucking ropes, feeling them fall to my feet.

I was at the bars in an instant, pushing my hand through. My fingers wrapped around his neck, squeezing as fucking hard as I could.

"Rhyan," he warned, before he coughed, his eyes bulging. "You're only making things worse. For yourself. For Lyriana." His fingers clawed at my hand, but my grip was iron-clad.

I squeezed harder. I was farther than fucking Lethea. The rage inside me felt like a living breathing thing. A monster tearing through my skin and muscles, ripping me apart from inside. I was no longer myself. I could barely remember my name, only this rage, this anger, this need to hurt him. Destroy him. Destroy his body. Destroy his soul.

Consequences felt small, I could barely remember why this was wrong, or think of a single compelling reason to stop. A reason why I shouldn't end his life right then, right there.

And then a fiery sharp pain shot through my abdomen. I hadn't noticed when he pulled his fingers away. Hadn't heard the sound of metal being pulled from its sheath.

I wheezed and stumbled back, falling onto the cot, my legs crashing against the metal bed frame as I stared down in horror at the dagger embedded in my stomach.

"Look at what you've done," my father snarled. "You stupid, fucking idiot."

My eyes widened, my arms trembling. There was so much blood. More than there ever had been before. I was caught somewhere between a gasp and cough as my whole body shook.

My father reached for his neck, rubbing at his throat and hissing in pain. "Healers are on their way to you now. I'd leave that in while you wait, unless you prefer to bleed out."

Blood coated my hands until it was slipping through my fingers, dripping down my legs.

"You will appear at Court tomorrow. You will say yes to the betrothal of the bride I choose, and you will Godsdamned act like you're happy about it," he yelled. "Especially when Lyriana's engagement to Arkturion Kane is announced. One longing look between you two, one hand held too long, one single fucking moment to suggest you aren't completely enamored with your new bride, and all of this goes away. Everything Lyriana negotiated for you will end. And *she* will pay the price for *your* insolence. I promise you her suffering will reach heights your imagination has never dreamt of. Unless you do exactly as I say."

Something was coming over me. My stomach had been torn in half. I was in agony. Every inch of my body felt like it was being tortured. But somehow, I was sitting up, because some other force was taking over—something greater than me, something bigger. It was ancient and God-like. A memory of a vision of power.

And then I was standing, feeling my weight in my feet, my body almost like a stranger's. I moved to the bars, half-crazed with pain and fear, half led there by a magic and a determination I didn't yet understand.

"I have a message for you," I said, my voice foreign, lower, louder. Full of power.

My father's chin twitched, his eyes widening.

"If you hurt her, if you harm one hair on her head, there will be nowhere safe for you. Nowhere you can hide. Not in this lifetime. Not in the next. I will hunt you to the bowels of eternity. You will not know life free of my wrath. I will hunt, and I will take, in agonizing slowness, every life you're born into, until you know nothing but fear. Until your pain is so excruciating, you cease to exist. *Me sha, me ka.*"

My father had an odd look in his eyes then, and for a second, I could swear he was shaking, looking at me as if he'd never seen me before.

All at once, I felt the power leave me, my body drained. This was the second time he'd stabbed me like this. The first time was when I confronted him in Bamaria, when I'd stolen the key to Asherah's tomb. He clearly meant to make up for last time.

"Be careful," he said, "making promises like that. Even you don't know how many lives you have left, Auriel." His shoulders had hunched, and his breath was heavy as he glared.

I fell back onto the bed, gritting my teeth. "How did you know?"

He stepped back, his face grim in the firelight. "A vorakh told me, when you were still in the womb."

"I was seen in a vision?"

"Many times."

"By who?" I asked.

He chuckled. "Your mother."

CHAPTER TWENTY-TWO

LYRIANA

I stared at the crackling flames in the fireplace. A green wool shawl was wrapped tightly around my shoulders. I was still in my formal Glemarian dress—the dress Imperator Hart had selected. The dress Kenna had laced up. It was tight, and constricting, with far too much material. Everything about it, the boning in the bodice, the thick layers of skirts, felt as much like a prison as Seathorne itself.

The fires rose higher, the heat wafting toward me in thick, warm waves. But I couldn't stop shivering. Couldn't stop replaying everything Imperator Hart had said, couldn't stop feeling the nahashim sliding against my skin, crawling over me. Under me.

Threatening to go inside me.

The wind howled and a nearby gryphon squawked angrily as snow fell against the frosted pane of my window. Beyond the glass, small torches lit the mountains on the horizon.

Suddenly, there was a violent knock on the door, but I remained still, unwilling to answer it. Unwilling to respond, or move. I'd been promised a meeting with Rhyan hours ago.

Promised a respite after being tortured, after being forced to sign Imperator Hart's contract. But instead, I'd suffered a visit from Lord Dario who wanted to be sure I hadn't climbed out the window, or some other inane escape attempt. Then a short while later, I entertained another visit from him in which he shoved half a dozen soturi inside to stare at me and learn the details of my face. The same thing happened a quarter of an hour later. And then a half hour after that.

I was tired of being ogled and stared at, all so I could make a better prisoner, all so the features and the shape of my body could be memorized. Noticed. And if need be, captured.

But the worst part of it all, the most humiliating, and the hardest to bear, was when they took turns lifting the sleeve of my dress so that they might recognize my tattoo. I knew it was just my arm. Nothing intimate. But I couldn't stand to be naked after Vrukshire. Could barely stand to be seen. Even by Rhyan. At least, at first. It wasn't the nudity that bothered me, it was the touching and manipulation of my clothes—the feeling of being powerless, and out of control, even over my own garments. The fear of being exposed and helpless. I'd nearly panicked several times, forcing my gaze out the window, pointedly watching the snowfall as I breathed deeply.

And then, as if that weren't enough, Dario tried to see if the fire would turn my hair red. He'd seen the effect of the sun on me when we'd landed at Seathorne that morning. He'd been quiet about it, but the rumors of my hair's solar transformation were all over Glemaria, and he wanted to make sure the soturi knew damned well if they saw someone in the daylight with my likeness, only with bright red hair instead of brown, that it was still me. And if they saw me with either hair color, I was to be watched, and reported on. And if attempting to escape, restrained.

The knock came again, rougher this time, more urgent. "Lady Lyriana," Dario yelled gruffly.

The door swung open. I squeezed my eyes shut. *No. No. No more.* My shoulders shook, and I pinched the edge of my sleeve, tightening the closure of material around my hand ...

"Lyr!"

I froze.

Rhyan's anguished voice had called out. Not Dario's. "Lyr," he said again. "It's me."

The door closed, and I turned slowly, barely daring to believe what I'd heard. Barely daring to hope that Imperator Hart had kept his word. That I'd actually had one thing go my way since we'd been captured.

Then I saw Rhyan standing in his old bedroom. We were alone.

"Rhyan," I practically gasped his name, tears in my eyes.

"Lyr," he cried.

And then we were both rushing for each other, running, racing, desperate to cancel the space between us, needing to find each other's embrace.

"Partner," he said, his hands on my back, pulling me into him. He buried his face in the crook of my shoulder, and breathed me in, one hand sliding up my spine to cradle the nape of my neck, fingers twisting in my hair. "Are you hurt?" he asked, with deep gasping breaths.

I let out some unintelligible sound as I wrapped my arms around his back, hugging him against me as tightly as I could. Then I sobbed in relief. "You're here."

"I'm here. I'm right here," he said, his voice hushed and desperate. "Gods, I'm sorry. I'm so sorry."

"Me, too." I shook my head. "I'm sorry we're here, I'm sorry I put you through this." The guilt had been gnawing at me for hours. "I should have been faster at the cave, thought quicker—"

"Lyr, no. Shhh, no," he murmured. "That's not your fault. None of this is. All right? We're alive. That's all that matters. Have you seen Meera?"

"No. But, I heard she's in a room nearby, being watched by Aiden."

"Okay. Okay," he said again, almost as if reassured, one hand rubbing up and down my back, before gripping the nape of my neck again.

I let the shawl fall from my shoulders, content to bask in the warmth of Rhyan's hug. I squeezed him even tighter, trying to meld his body to mine. I wanted no space between us, no end and no beginning to our bodies, no distinction. I tangled my fingers in his hair, trying to find the soft curls I loved, but his hair had been cut since I'd last seen him.

Of course, his father would have had him cleaned up. I buried my face against his neck.

A moment passed, our hearts pounding together as if in their own conversation, our stifled gasps the only sound in the room as we simply held each other.

And much as I was content to stay there holding him, and being held by him until I lost consciousness, until I forgot the day we'd had, forgot where we were, forgot we were prisoners, I opened my eyes. Time was a luxury we were not afforded. Kenna had already warned me. Imperator Hart would use nahashim to watch me inside these walls. I could only truly speak to Rhyan before they came. After that, nothing would be private. Not unless we escaped.

And that ... that was no longer an option.

I pulled back, and stared into his eyes, reddened and damp with unshed tears. He smelled clean, like himself, like pine and musk. The scruff across his chin and cheeks had been shaved, his nose no longer broken. At least ... it appeared healed. His skin was smooth, and the overall color of his light complexion looked even, and healthy, though the skin under his eyes was still dark.

Rhyan slid his hands down my arms, his eyes searching me over, frantic with worry. "He hurt you," he said, his accent so thick his words ran together. He tugged my dress off my shoulders, his fingers pushing and prodding my skin.

I shook my head. "I'm okay."

"Lyr." His eyes blazed into mine. He didn't believe me. "I've been so fucking worried." He pushed my dress down even farther. "What did he do to you?"

Shaking my head, I said, "I'm not the one who had a broken nose."

"But Kane—" he said urgently.

"I broke his nose," I said.

"And after?" he asked. "After using your power like that?"

"I'm fine. I promise. It was like the other times. I passed out." I gently stroked the scar up from Rhyan's left cheek to his eyebrow. He leaned into my touch, sighing in relief as I let my finger slide down the bridge of his nose. I watched for any signs of pain or discomfort. "It's healed," I whispered, half expecting to be fooled by another of Aiden's glamours. "Truly?"

He closed his eyes, his nostrils flared, his jaw tightening as his hands found my hips and squeezed. "It's healed."

"Did they hurt you?" I asked.

Rhyan was silent for a moment, the wind howling at the windows, before at last he said, his voice dull, "Mending broken bones … always hurts. And happens slowly when you're bound." He released a long breath. "This is the same place I was in the last time that had to happen." Eyeing his bedroom warily, he swallowed. "Gods. I hate it here."

"I know." I pulled his face down, kissing his forehead, then pressing it to mine, stroking his cheeks. "Did they do anything else to you? Your father?"

His chest rose and fell heavily for a moment. Then instead of answering, his lips found mine and we were kissing, his tongue already seeking mine, his hands on my ass, pulling me against him.

"Rhyan," I gasped.

Before I knew what was happening, he was walking me backward, back to his bed.

"I'll kill him," he muttered, his lips skimming across my cheek to my ear. "Kill him for touching you. For hurting you."

I felt the same way. The same rage was burning inside of me. We didn't have time for this. We needed to talk. But the frenzy of touching him again, of feeling him so solid and hard against me, of feeling him healed, and alive, I couldn't stop. I knew we were about to be separated and I didn't know for how long. I pulled him closer.

I reached for his belt, tugging at the buckle, and sliding my hands beneath the leather of his armor, inside his tunic, my fingers grazing his belly. His skin was cold. I pushed my hands deeper, exploring more of his torso.

His abs tightened, as he let out a cry of pain.

I stepped back. "What the fuck? You are hurt!" I was already reaching for the buckles of his armor beneath the freshly pressed material of his new soturion cloak. I realized then that everything he was wearing was brand new. Black leather over metal, the material shining. No sign of wear or battle.

It was traditional Glemarian armor, the sigil of Ka Hart carved into the torso. No seraphim or moon for Ka Batavia. No sigil representing our kashonim. Our connection. I hated it. I wanted it off, and I needed it off so I could see what had happened. So I could fix it.

Already my palm was heating, the light of the Valalumir glowing from inside my heart. I welcomed the fire, the burn, if it meant he'd be all right.

"Fuck! No!" Rhyan suddenly stepped back, alarm in his eyes. "Lyr, please. Don't!"

My voice darkened, and I could feel my aura flaring in anger, little embers sparking around me. "Rhyan, what happened? You have to tell me."

He stepped back into me, and took my hands in his, keeping

me from reaching for him again. "My father ..." his mouth opened, like he was going to be sick as his chest heaved, "he ... stabbed me."

Immediately, I was struggling against him, trying to free my hands, to touch him, to examine him. To undo and fix whatever had happened.

But he tightened his hold on me, fervently shaking his head. "It's healed. I'm fine, I swear to you. He's done it before, remember? I'm just ... sore."

"If you're just sore, then why can't I touch you? Why won't you let me?"

"Because ..." His chest was rising and falling quickly, as his jaw tightened. "Because, I'm still healing, and I don't want you taking it on! Because it's not a big deal."

"Not a big deal? Rhyan, he stabbed you!"

"I know!" he roared. "I was fucking there when he did it! I'll be healed by morning. I heal fast. It's only taking longer because of the binds—that's it—I promise. I don't want you feeling this —don't want you weakened anymore. Okay?" His voice cracked, his eyes watering. "Partner, I won't budge on that. Now what about you? Tell me the truth. What happened?"

I sniffled. "We negotiated."

He exhaled sharply. Rhyan had told me he'd *negotiated* with his father many times. It was never a simple conversation. He took my hand and our fingers intertwined.

"He showed me your name in blood. That gryphon-shit-Moriel-fucking-bastard. I swear on the Gods. I'm going to get us out of here as soon as possible. Whatever you agreed to, what-ever he forced you to sign, I don't care. It doesn't fucking matter. I'm taking you away from here as soon as I'm strong enough. You and Meera. I swear it."

I squeezed my eyes shut. "You can't." I rubbed my thumb over his palm. "You can't take us anywhere. You're bound. And the only way he'll remove the binds is if you agree to everything

I agreed to. That's the deal. You have to prove your obedience to him. Make him believe it, or he'll keep punishing you."

His lips twisted, and I could almost see his thoughts, hear him say that he didn't care if he was punished.

"No," I said. "I don't want to see you bound. You can't be if you're going to heal. And neither of us will ever have a chance at freedom. You have to play along."

"Fine. Done. I'll agree," he said quickly. "I'll play the game, I'll follow his orders. I'll be the perfect Heir, perfect soturion, perfect—" he swallowed roughly. "Whatever it takes. And once the binds are off, we're gone!"

"No!" I shouted. "We can't go."

His eyes searched mine, his mouth a tight line. "What do you mean, no? Lyr, we can't stay here! Seathorne, as long as my father breathes, is a death trap."

"I mean *no*. We're not leaving. We're not escaping," I said. "Not until the Valabellum."

"The Valabellum? That's in a month! Do you know what kind of damage he can do to you by then? Do to us?" Rhyan's breath came quickly, his chest rising and falling in rapidly as his face contorted with a mix of anger and confusion, one eyebrow lowered. "Lyr. If we stay here, you marry Kane! Do you get that? Do you know who he is? Did you see? Because when he touched you, when the Valalumir lit up again, I had another memory. I saw him, and I remembered. He's fucking Shiviel!"

I shuddered, even though I'd already known the truth of it. "I thought so. I felt it."

He shook his head, the movement frantic. "I can't. Can't let him hurt you. He was bad enough when he was just Kane. He's always been a nightmare. But—fuck." His knees bent suddenly, his fingers violently pushing through his hair before he straightened. "Gods! I spent years trying to prevent this. To stop this. To protect you—" His voice shook.

"I know. I know you did, but you can't now. Not yet. It's not that simple."

"Yes, it is," he gritted. "Whatever oath you swore, we'll find a way to break it."

Shaking my head in defeat, I said, "There's something else I need to tell you."

"What?" He sounded defeated.

I took a deep breath, pulled him back to the bed and sat beside him. Then I told him everything that had happened in his father's tower. Told him about Vrukshire and the interviews Imperator Kormac conducted. Told him that they knew we were there that night—that they knew we'd killed Brockton and the others. That the sole reason they weren't calling for my public arrest was to use me to make a claim on Bamaria. That his father threatened to use the nahashim to go through me and turn us both in for what the Empire would consider far worse crimes. And that the only way to stop my wedding to Viktor Kormac, the only way to keep Imperator Kormac from showing up here with a legion to claim me, was my marriage to another.

Rhyan nodded, his jaw muscles working. I could see he knew some of the details I shared already, or that he'd been close to piecing them together with the way his eyes darkened.

"Okay," he said, when I finished explaining the role Kormac had in this. "But, partner, these are Imperator games. Not ours. We don't have to be his servants to get what we want. We'll run away," he said urgently. "I'll protect you from Kormac, and from my father, I swear. I've been ready to leave with you since Valyati. The plan hasn't changed ..."

The plan to run away. To forget all of this and leave the Empire behind. Rhyan had first promised to take me from danger if I didn't survive the Emperor's test in the arena.

And then again when he learned Arianna was my enemy.

"The plan has to change," I said. "You know that. You know

I won't leave. Especially because there's more to the bargain."
Tears fell down my face. "It's about Jules."

Rhyan's eyes widened, watching me warily. "Jules?"

"He knows she's alive. He told me."

"Of course, he fucking did." Rhyan shook his head in
disgust. "All this fucking time and he kept it to himself."

"He promised to help us get her back."

"Help? Help! My father! Do you hear yourself?" Rhyan leapt
off the bed, and began pacing back and forth. "For fuck's sake,
Lyriana! That's what this is really about? Jules!" One eyebrow
lowered, the muscles in his jaw working. Then he came before
me, falling to his knees. He took my hands into his. "He's not
going to help you save her. He's not going to rescue her! He's
incapable. I swore to you we'd get her back, and I meant it. Look
at me. I've never broken an oath to you. Not once! Lyr, please.
Tell me you still trust me."

I squeezed his hands. "Of course, I do."

"Then trust me when I say my father was fucking with you,
just like Brockton was."

"But Brockton wasn't," I yelled. "That's the thing! He was
telling the truth in the end. He was right about Jules. And your
father showed me proof—he knows exactly where she is. He was
able to get to her. His nahashim saw her in the Palace."

"So?" he roared. "Auriel's fucking bane! It doesn't matter
what his snakes have seen. It's nothing we don't already know,
that we didn't figure out on our own. All it does is bind us to
him, and put us in danger! Showing that to you was nothing
more than manipulation."

"Manipulation?" My voice was ice cold. "You think I don't
know that? That I'm new to this game? I knew exactly what he
was doing! And I know exactly what he is. It doesn't change the
facts. Doesn't change that she's in grave danger."

"Yes, it does, it changes everything. Because binding yourself to him puts you in danger. And I need you safe!" he said.

"I need Jules safe," I sobbed.

He released my hands, moving back to the bed. The mattress dipped as he took a seat beside me. But he was distant now. His body no longer touched mine as he stared toward the fireplace. "Let me guess. He said he'd kill Jules if you didn't agree to everything he wanted." He leaned forward, his elbows resting on his knees, his face turned away. "He was bluffing. He's powerful —too fucking powerful for his own good. But," he growled, "he's second to Imperator Kormac. He always has been. If Emperor Theotis has Jules, that makes her a Kormac pawn, and I can tell you this much: Kormac doesn't share outside the pack. My father does not have access to her."

"Just like Brockton didn't have access to her?" I cried out. "Just like Brockton didn't rape her? Because he wasn't important enough? Only he did. And your father *does* have access to her. He knows *exactly* where she is. I saw it with my own eyes. His snakes can reach her. And you know Godsdamned-well what they're capable of doing under orders. He has spies in there, guards he's paid off. You know it's true. And he can disguise her after—disguise himself going in using Aiden."

A long moment passed, the muscles in his jaw ticking, before he nodded. "Okay, fine," he said, his voice low. "Say he can get to her. Say he has all the access he claims. Why wait? Why hasn't he taken her before now? And why in Lumeria would he offer to help you?" He lifted his hands, his palms raised as if in question. "Threaten her to gain your submission? That I under-stand. But why offer you anything else beyond keeping you safe from Kormac?"

"Because he needed another angle. You told me so yourself, he escalates his threats—he finds new ways when his authority fails, or when pain isn't enough. He knew he had to do some-thing more than just blackmail us. He knows he can't fight you unbound, not unless you're behind bars." I looked uneasily at his stomach. "And he saw what I could do downstairs, he saw the power I can invoke—the kashonim I possess with Asherah."

Rhyan stiffened. "I wish he'd never seen that."

"But he has. There's nothing we can do except use it to our advantage. He knows deep down inside that I have power he can't compete with. Power that he wants to control. He told you he knew years ago. He needs me on his side, needs me to have a reason to want to be here. I almost escaped the Seating Room. I almost had you freed. And he knew that, too."

"He knew," he said quietly. "Lyr, he knew exactly what to offer you."

"Because his fucking snake had been spying on us in the caves. He knew we were going after Jules, knew we needed to infiltrate the Palace."

"Then he should know exactly where the indigo shard is and who possesses it. That was his goal, wasn't it? Take possession, harness its power. It doesn't make sense that it's not his priority beyond controlling us." He sighed, his voice despondent. "Fuck, Lyr! Every move we make can't just be about rescuing Jules!"

"Why the fuck not? You gave me your word! You swore. You swore you never broke an oath!"

"I'm not breaking one now!" he yelled, standing up. He began pacing again, his hands running through his hair in frustration. "Gods. Look, Lyr, please. You're a fucking warrior, and you're smart as hell—that's not in doubt. But I also need you to listen now. Because I know my father better than anyone. You want to rescue Jules so badly that you're making it easy for anyone who can see it, anyone who can sense it, to manipulate you."

"Oh." I stood up, too, crossing my arms over my chest. "I'm so easily manipulated? I just caved and bent the knee over one fucking image? After all I've done, all we've been through? That's what you think? This is just about Jules, and not every other fucking thing I told you tonight?" I walked away, standing before the fireplace again, cold all over again.

A moment later, there was warmth against my back. Rhyan had wrapped his arms around me from behind. I didn't move, didn't soften as he hugged me to him, his hands hot against my stomach. I could feel his breath on my neck, his chest rising and falling against me. "Partner. I'm sorry. "

I didn't answer.

"Forgive me," he said, his voice hoarse. "I didn't mean it."

"Yes, you did," I hissed.

"Lyr. Lyr, just talk to me. Please." He ran his hands up and down my arms, as the fire spat and crackled. "Partner?"

The wind howled and I could feel tears pricking my eyes. Suddenly I was reminded of the other thing between us. I was aware of his bed. Aware of who he had shared it with. I looked back, unable to help myself, then trained my gaze back on the fire.

"Gods," he said. "I used to dream about you being here with me. So many times over the years. But not like this."

"Please," I said, my voice breaking. "Don't."

"Are you trying to punish me?" Rhyan asked, he was so quiet, I wasn't sure I heard him at first. "For Kenna."

My breath came short. "How can you ask me that?" But some small part of me wondered if I was, if that was why I was letting this go on for so long. It felt complicated, like it required a lot of explanation. But maybe some part of me was fighting with him to ease the pain of knowing what was about to come. A month of imprisonment. Of separation. A chance we would fail, a chance we'd lose everything. A chance we'd lose each other.

"Should I punish you?" I asked, my heart pounding.

"You can if you want," he said. "Punish me if you need to. Do what you will. I never should have let him blindside you like that. I should have told you about her."

"You should have," I said, the backs of my eyes burning. "Why didn't you tell me?"

He sighed. "Because, then I'd have to tell you everything else that happened. What I did to Garrett. What happened to my mother. To Bowen. Dario's father. The way I failed everyone. It was— still is—so painful. Lyr, I have secrets. Secrets I've never told anyone. Except you. Just … not all of them—not yet. But I swear to you, I will tell you everything. Because you're the only person I ever trusted to see all of me. Even if I'm still scared shitless of showing you." He pressed me to him, his hands firm against my belly, his nose grazing my neck.

I softened. "You don't have to be scared. Not because of me." And much as I wanted to hear everything from him, and knew he needed to tell his story, tonight wasn't the time. We had bigger problems to face.

As if sensing that, too, Rhyan sighed. "I know. But, when the time's right, I swear it. No more secrets between us." He kissed my neck. "Please. *Mekara.* You're the last person I want to fight with. Especially here, especially now. I'm on your side. But I am scared. Being back here …" His chest rose and fell against me. "It's hell. It's where I lost everything, where I was most power-less to fight back. And the only thing worse is knowing you're trapped here, too. I just—" His lips moved against my skin. "I don't see a way to safety for us by working with my father."

I leaned back against him. "As crazy as it sounds, I truly believe we have to do it this way. Rhyan, I need you to trust me. Trust my plan. Trust my reasons."

There was an old timepiece on his desk that suddenly seemed too loud. Every second, a pebble dropped inside the glass, falling with a clang. Again and again. Each one eating away at my last chance to figure this out with him. At the time that remained between us.

"There's one more thing," I said, reaching back, my hand resting against his cheek. "I'm sorry—it's a lot to cover in one night. But we're running out of time. Your father's nahashim will be here soon."

He held me closer. "Lyriana, I trust your instincts. It's *his* I'm trying to understand. If he's helping you to rescue Jules, it's not for you. It's because he has his own reasons, he wants her for himself."

I shook my head. "She's the bonus—and the collateral. The carrot to dangle in my face while I go after what he really wants. He wants something from the Palace, and he's going to give us everything we need—the blueprints, schedules of the guards, access to their keys. He's offering mercenaries to fight on our behalf. And if we can bring the item to him, he'll get Jules."

"Bring him what?" Rhyan asked, his voice low.

"A shield hanging above the Emperor's Throne." My eyes searched his. "Rhyan, it's the same one I saw in Meera's vision. There was an orange crystal in the center—and when I saw it through the nahashim," I placed my hand over my heart, "the Valalumir lit up again."

His eyes widened. "Ereshya's shard!"

I nodded. "I guess he decided not to go up against Aemon and Morgana—at least not yet. But, since he lost the indigo, he wants the orange in return. He doesn't know that I recognize it, so I think promising Jules was a way to ensure I'd take the theft seriously."

"And if we don't steal it first, Aemon and Morgana will claim a second shard of the Valalumir," Rhyan said dully. "And who knows how quickly they'll find the others. Moriel will return to power. Fuck. Fuck!" He grimaced. "Fucking bastard could have mentioned that!"

"Your father?" I asked.

Rhyan's mouth tightened. "Mercurial. Our old friend came to visit me in the prisons. Nothing useful to say. He went on about you finding the red shard, but said nothing of the orange."

"Did he say anything else?" I asked.

His eyes flew to my heart, then back to my face. "In my memory of Kane as Shiviel, we fought him together. I don't quite know what we did. I mean, what Asherah and Auriel did. It was some kind of ancient magic. Powerful. Whatever it was, it broke Shiviel somehow. Broke his soul, I think. And Kane is weakened from it," he said. "It left him debilitated, permanently. He's not as powerful as he could be, even in this life."

I frowned. "That shouldn't be possible. What kind of magic does that?" I asked.

Rhyan shook his head. "I don't know. But I'm going to find out. Mercurial also told me Meera's identity. She's Cassarya," he said. "So that leaves us with only Hava to find."

"Cassarya?" I closed my eyes. Of course. The observant one. Goddess of the Blue. I could see her suddenly, her silvery white hair, and large blue eyes, hypnotic, and commanding. Something Meera had always quietly been. "I'll have to tell her. If I'm ever allowed to see her."

"You'll see her," he said. "I promise you."

I gripped his shoulders. "I'm sure Mercurial didn't offer any clues as to who Hava is."

"Hava? No," Rhyan said quickly. "No, he didn't." He ran his hands up and down my arms, and kissed the crook of my shoulder. Then he stilled, like he'd realized something. "Lyr," he breathed, his arms around my waist, pulling me toward him. "Are you sure this is the way? If you say it is, I'll do as you command. But by the Gods. Every instinct inside me is shouting to take you away from here."

There was a hiss at the door, and something black slithering in my peripheral vision.

"Your father's nahashim. They're coming," I said.

"Not yet," he groaned. "Not yet."

I shook my head. The hissing was louder now, the snake sliding across the carpet. "It's too late, they can see us."

"So?" he practically growled. "Does it fucking matter? My

father already knows about us. Nothing we do will placate him—
nothing we do will convince him we feel otherwise."

"We have to try. He has to see our effort." Even if it was just
for his own sadistic satisfaction. "He needs to see us jumping
through his hoops. Playing along. Or he'll do worse, you know
he will. We can do this. We have to. To get your binds off."

He gripped the nape of my neck, pulling me back toward
him. "I'd wear them forever and burn with a smile if it meant I
could be near you. But I will do as you wish. As always." He
squeezed his eyes shut, his finger twirling around mine. Then he
stepped back, releasing his hold on me. A long moment passed
as he stared at me. Then he bowed, the movement formal. When
he rose, he looked ready to vomit. "*Tovayah maischa* on your
engagement tomorrow."

"Thank you," I said, my eyes hot with fresh tears.

His mouth tightened. "We shall have a day of celebrations.
You're not the only one who will become betrothed," he said, his
voice choked. "Did he tell you?"

My chest tightened. "What? You? No! To whom?"

He shrugged sadly. "Does it matter? When it's not you?" He
turned around abruptly as the snakes undulated and hissed across
the carpet. "You know, I've been forsworn for a long time. But
tonight, it's the first time I feel like I'm truly breaking an oath.
The one that was most important. Protecting you."

A sobbed welled in my chest, my heart feeling like it was
splitting in two.

"Partner." He looked over his shoulder at me. His jaw
muscles working, his eyes red, his hands clenched so tightly I
could see his veins popping out. Shoulders shaking, he gave me
one final blazing look, like he was trying to memorize me. Then
he turned, and walked out the door.

I stood before the fire, my eyes glazing over as the flames
glowed. A snake slid up behind me. And I kicked it.

CHAPTER TWENTY-THREE

LYRIANA

The next day, as the clock towers finished their hourly call, I was marched to Seathorne's Seating Room. I looked out the looming windows, my heart half-expecting to see ashvan horses, the blue glow of their hooves in the sky. I'd been away from Bamaria for so long, I was starting to feel homesick. There were no ashvan here, no glittering waterways reflecting the sky. No warmth in the air carrying the scent of spices. Just endless stretches of gray skies and gryphon wings blocking the faint light of winter's sun.

Dario stood by my side, my new personal escort, his hand on the hilt of his sword a useless gesture when a dozen soturi lined the hall ready to strike. Not that I had any more plans to escape. Not when Imperator Hart had my name signed in blood, and my promise to do his will. Not when Rhyan's, Meera's, and Jules's life hung in the balance.

The Imperator had already called his Court into session. He had a busy day ahead. Addressing the newly reported akadim threat, Glemaria's participation in the upcoming Valabellum.

Parading Meera around so his people could ogle at the survivor of an akadim attack and praise their Imperator for her rescue.

And he had two betrothals to announce. Mine.

And Rhyan's.

Not to mention, Rhyan's acquittal for having been named forsworn.

Meera's part would be finished by now. I was to be presented next. Then Rhyan would follow. The grand finale.

I could hear the announcements around Meera coming to a close. There was a round of applause, then cheers.

"They're ready for you," Dario said.

I narrowed my eyes. "Really? I couldn't tell."

His hand flew to his heart, his head falling back as if he'd been stabbed. "Pardon me for forgetting that you know how this works. You must know everything thanks to your once noble status." He straightened, adjusting the leather tie around his curls. "But all the same, you better be ready in there. You know what's at stake."

The cut on my skin still burned, and I could still feel the way my blood felt against the parchment as I signed my name.

"I'm ready," I gritted through my teeth, and nodded at the herald. "Go ahead. Announce me."

The doors swung open, and I was hit with the force of hundreds of auras at once—excited, curious, searching. And judging. A wave of dizziness washed over me as I withstood the assault.

The herald called my name, and Dario shoved me across the threshold.

All at once, the noise and laughter of the Court turned to hushed whispers as hundreds of eyes turned to me.

I kept my gaze forward, to the dais, where Kenna stood. Where Imperator Hart sat back in his Seat, daring me to falter.

I wouldn't. I'd signed my name in fucking blood.

And no matter who sat on the Seat of Power in Bamaria, or

who tried to claim it, nothing could take away the fact I was still Lady Lyriana Batavia. The reincarnation of Asherah, Goddess of the Red Ray. A Guardian. A Warrior.

I walked down the center aisle, aware of every eye turning toward me. Aware that Meera was somewhere in the room. But I never took my eyes off the Imperator's. He'd caught me off guard yesterday, caught me weak. I wouldn't give him the chance to do it again.

This was war.

"Your Highness," I said when I reached the front. I curtseyed low and stood, my back to the nobility.

"Lady Lyriana Batavia," Imperator Hart said. "Or shall we call you, Soturion Lyriana?" he asked with a chuckle.

The Court laughed in response—a sort of immediate, expected sound that I assumed they'd been trained to do for decades under his rule. Laugh when he made a joke. Believe him when he lied.

"Come, my lady," he said. "Join us up here on the dais as I introduce you. Lady Kenna shall be your companion." Rhyan's ex-lover. Of course.

But also, my new ally.

"I am honored, Your Highness," I said sweetly, and picked up my sea of green skirts, prepared to step onto the stage. Surprisingly, Dario was by my side, his hand on my elbow, steadying me as I made my way. He waited until I was balanced enough to drop my skirts. Then I stepped to the left, moving respectfully beside Kenna.

She looked my way, concern filling her brown eyes which seemed to ask if I was okay.

I nodded quickly, grateful for her steady presence. But my attention went almost at once to the front row. Meera sat before me. She also wore a Glemarian green gown, her ash brown hair styled like mine. Though she somehow seemed more at ease in the foreign style than I was. Aiden sat beside her, a soturion I didn't know on her other side—her escorts.

I noted right away that his dagger was out. Not noticeable to anyone who sat near him. It was meant for me. A reminder to behave. A reminder that Meera could be hurt with a single blink of Imperator Hart's eyes.

"Lady Meera told you all, so sweetly, of how she was rescued from the akadim," Imperator Hart said, one hand stroking his beard. "Two soturi rescued her. Two brave heroes. One stands before you now. Lady Lyriana Batavia." I kept still, kept my face neutral.

"I know you have all heard the stories," Imperator Hart continued. "Lady Lyriana has no power. No strength. She was found without magic at her Revelation Ceremony." He paused, his eyes scanning the crowd. "This is true. But she is a fighter who benefited from an excellent apprentice. One I myself had a hand in making." He gestured to the herald.

Rhyan was coming.

The front doors opened. Two guards appeared standing shoulder to shoulder, blocking him. Two more soturi marched behind, taking their places as the doors closed.

Everyone in the room began to turn, shifting in their chairs, looking over their shoulders at his entrance. At last, the front guards parted, revealing Rhyan between them.

For a moment I forgot how to breathe. It didn't matter how many times I saw him dressed in his full soturion uniform. My breath caught as he stepped forward, his green eyes blazing, his hair curled just so. I drank in the sight of him. I couldn't be positive, but he appeared unbound, and at least from what I could observe, he wasn't injured. He looked only tired, though his scar was red and angry, like it was new. And from the gasps I heard, and the whispers of the word "scar" suddenly, I supposed it was new to the members of the Glemarian Court.

Then the shouts came. They called him a murderer, forsworn, and then someone from the back of the room called him a whore.

Kenna remained stoic as Imperator Hart stood and shouted, "Enough!" All at once, the room listened. And Rhyan was left to be marched in complete silence down the aisles toward the dais. The only sounds came from the footsteps of the soturi surrounding him.

When he reached the base, he bowed and stood, his back erect. I could feel the ice of his aura. The first time since we'd arrived. So, he *could* access his magic. That meant Imperator Hart was pleased with last night. But he could still be testing us —testing to see if Rhyan would stay in control unbound.

"Your Highness," he said as he rose. He spoke in the clipped, formal way he did when he was concealing his emotions, when his lilt was most suppressed. "Thank you for welcoming me back. I am at your service, and Glemaria's."

The crowd erupted again, even more furious than before.

And again, Imperator Hart's voice rose above, as he gestured for Rhyan to join us on the dais as well.

"No one knows the tragedies that occurred here better than I do," Imperator Hart addressed the Court. "I understand your anger. Your sorrow. For they are in my heart as well. But I swore I had many things to tell you." He stood and wrapped his arm around Rhyan's shoulder. Rhyan's aura seemed to strike out, a painful chill of ice, sharp and violent. And then just as quickly, it was gone. His feelings withdrew.

He was following orders, falling in line.

For me.

His father continued, "My duty to you as your Imperator, as your Arkasva, is sacred. What I tell you now is not said lightly, or without proof. My son, Rhyan, and Lady Lyriana rescued Lady Meera from death. They alerted Arkturion Kane to the threat of akadim at our borders. They are owed our thanks."

"Forsworn!" came one final shout.

There was a deadly look in Imperator Hart's eyes, and then the protester was removed at once by two soturi.

He gestured for everyone to sit, and to remain still, as he tugged Rhyan closer. Only from the vantage point of the dais could I see the way his fingers dug into his shoulder. The fact that Rhyan didn't flinch was a testament to his strength.

"We all know the story of the tragic death of my first wife, Lady Shakina."

Someone in the audience said, "*Ha Ka Mokan.*"

This was answered by several calls of "Remember Lady Shakina," and "her soul freed."

Rhyan looked at me, a sudden flash in his eyes, then he stared ahead.

"I told you all what happened that awful, terrible night," Imperator Hart said. "And until today, I thought I understood the events that transpired. Until today, I grieved for my late wife, for the mother of my eldest."

My throat felt dry. His use of past tense had me on edge. The torches lining the room began to flicker, the flames crackling against the sounds of the wind, and the increasingly familiar sounds of a gryphon flying past.

"My personal guards bore witness to her death. Arkmage Connal, and even my wife, Lady Kenna saw Rhyan's hand wield the blade that took Shakina's life."

Kenna seemed to be still beside me. I wondered if anyone else knew the truth. Did Dario and Aiden? Could Rhyan's life-long friends truly have believed this about him?

His father continued, "In my grief, I learned that even Imperators make mistakes." He let the words hang in the air. "This past year has been one of contemplation. One where I found myself without an answer to an important question: why? Why would my son do this? What would cause one of our academy's brightest and most dedicated warriors to slay his own blood? After all I had taught him, all he learned as a soturion, after swearing an oath of loyalty to me, to Glemaria and his people, how could he commit such an act?" He nodded solemnly. "Now I know. Our eyes had been deceived."

At this, several nobles began to whisper in agitation. Imperator Hart's aura darkened, with a cold, raging violence.

"You may be skeptical. It was Rhyan's hand that took his mother's life. I do not deny that."

I frowned, unable to follow how this was going to lead to a different outcome. Was it all a joke? My eyes met Meera's, who seemed to be silently asking the same question as she watched the Imperator with careful eyes. Observant eyes.

Cassarya's eyes.

"There was something I didn't know," Imperator Hart said. "Something I didn't want to believe. Something that I admit, even *I* was afraid to tell you." His voice was suddenly sad, almost vulnerable sounding. "It was later in her life when it happened, so late she managed to keep it a secret, even from me. Without my knowledge, Lady Shakina developed vorakh."

My mouth dropped. The audience let out a collective gasp. Immediately half the room was rising, their fists raised. It was the kind of instantaneous anger towards vorakh I'd seen countless times in the Barmarian court. The same anger I'd seen in the temple when Jules revealed hers. The same vitriol Tristan expressed when he'd said she had to die.

Rhyan's jaw clenched. His aura was expanding beyond his control, forcing a blanket of ice across the dais, leaving me shivering.

"She managed to hide it from me," his father said. "For had I known, despite the love I bore her, she would have been dealt with at once. The night of her death, a vision took her. She devolved into violence, and attacked me. Because I'd only known her as gentle, her strength caught me by surprise. I thought she was having a fit. But Rhyan saw the truth. He saw her vorakh."

The room was silent, every noble hanging on his every word. They were slowly beginning to sit down, leaning forward, rapt at his story. He truly had them in his palm.

"My son did not hesitate to protect me. Not only did he stop the threat, he accepted all of the blame to protect our Ka. He became forsworn to keep Glemaria safe, to keep his mother's reputation untarnished. He did it for me. He did it for all of you. To keep the Emperor from falsely accusing our country, and you, my people, who I think of as my family, of hiding her."

I nearly gasped. He was taking the fear nobles felt at Ka Azria's story, and turning it on his Court.

"My son has sacrificed everything for Glemaria. For you. And he did so in silence. We do not honor vorakh, do we?"

The crowd shouted, "No!"

"No." His voice darkened. "We stop the threat! And we honor the ones who stop it."

A chill ran down my spine. In seconds, Rhyan's mother had gone from being a beloved leader to a monster. With one lie, he'd convinced the entire country to tarnish her memory.

Imperator Hart grabbed Rhyan's arm, and held it over his head in victory. "My son! He will henceforth be known as Lord Rhyan Hart, Heir to the Arkasva, High Lord of Glemaria, Imperator to the North. I revoke the title forsworn. I absolve you of all charges. Your exile, Lord Rhyan, has come to an end. Welcome home."

CHAPTER TWENTY-FOUR

LYRIANA

Rhyan's eyes met mine, green and wide, and horrified. For a moment, they softened, the way they always did when he looked at me. Filling with his love and his warmth.

And then just as quickly, as if he remembered his role, the game we had to play, he looked ahead at the Court—at the people who'd turned on him, who'd betrayed him and stood behind the lies of their Imperator.

I hated all of them at that moment. Hated how easily they were swayed, how gullible they proved themselves to be. And how fickle. The sound of the nobles cheering for Rhyan—the son they'd turned their backs on—was grating to my ears. As was the sound of their cries. I'd never heard anything so fake. So performative. None of them had believed in him, or stood by him. They didn't deserve him. And they deserved none of my pity.

"I am thrilled to welcome Rhyan home to our academy as a decorated soturion, and back to Court. Of course, as the child of a vorakh, he will never be Heir Apparent. That title remains with my unborn son."

On cue, Kenna grinned widely and stepped forward, proudly showing off her belly. She turned to each side, letting everyone bask in the swell.

"Speaking of continuing my bloodline," Imperator Hart laughed, his eyes dancing with mischief, "Now that Lord Rhyan is home, and a Glemarian once more, perhaps it's time for him to feel the weight of responsibility. To not only carry his part in this, but to shoot his load."

There was a roar of laughter by the men in the room that left me uneasy. The laughs all felt edged with an undertone of violence. Despite Imperator Hart's orders, despite the sharp pain in my temples, I couldn't help but look at Rhyan, at the tightness in his mouth, the muscles of his jaw working. "It is time for Lord Rhyan to marry," his father announced.

It felt like someone had knocked the wind out of me. I knew this was coming. Knew it had to happen, knew we both had to play the game. It wasn't real. None of this was. And yet …

"I am pleased to announce his betrothal. And, who better, and more fitting to wed the Heir to the Arkasva and Imperator, than the beautiful, and intelligent, niece of our own Senator Oryyan."

I blinked, not recognizing the name.

But Kenna frowned and Rhyan's body was somehow both violent and still. His skin paled. I braced myself for the impact of his aura … but felt nothing. Not just nothing, but the complete and total absence of it, a feeling that usually only came when he was bound. The smallest glimpse of his eyes showed me they were empty.

He'd turned his emotions off. Something he'd told me he used to do to survive his father's wrath. Even after he escaped Glemaria and entered exile, he hadn't been able to turn them back on. When he finally had, at first it had only been grief. Then slowly desire. Only with me recently had he been able to begin to feel more, to open up all of his emotions again, to feel love and joy. It killed me to know I'd asked him to do this, that the only way he could get through this was to shut down again.

"Lady Amalthea Oryyan," Imperator Hart said. "Please, join your new Ka, and stand with your groom."

Lady Amalthea had long dark curls with a reddish tint beneath the flames, and she was looking Rhyan up and down with greedy, knowing eyes that had me itching to break another nose. Her dress, Glemarian green of course, looked like it was two sizes too small for her breasts. Her chest puffed out, and there was a look in her eyes that reminded me of Naria.

My gut twisted with a vile feeling, and a sense of distrust, the complete opposite of how I'd felt when I met Kenna. But Amalthea? I wanted to come between her and Rhyan, to push her away.

Control what they see, and you control what they think.

I had to stay calm. Remember she meant nothing in this game. Just some noble his father had picked.

But then Rhyan's fingers curled, and he scratched the palm of his hand.

My heart stopped.

There were very few times he did that—only in his moments of complete distress. The habit had started when he was a boy and the Senator from Hartavia had arranged to get him alone, took his hand, and tried to—

Lady Amalthea placed a silver ring on Rhyan's finger—a ring I assumed had the sigil of Ka Oryyan emblazoned on it.

And then Rhyan slid her ring on, a golden band decorated with silver gryphon wings and the sun.

My chest tightened. And all I could think was *mine. Mine! My* love. *My* ring. *My … Rakame.*

"*Tovayah maischa!*" shouted a noble, his fist in the air. There was a deafening round of applause, followed by more shouts. They were shouting for them to kiss.

By the Godsdamned fucking Gods! No. No. Fucking no.

Rhyan took Amalthea's hand.

I couldn't breathe. My skin was crawling. I could barely imagine Rhyan kissing someone else. If I had to see it happen now—if I had to be in the same room when it happened …

"Kiss her!" The shouts grew louder now, more demanding. "Kiss your bride!"

Rhyan's hand tightened around Amalthea's, and he looked at her with adoring eyes. He leaned in. There were spots in my vision. I was going to be sick. I was actually going to be sick. I could feel it, feel the bile rising up the back of my throat.

Then Rhyan turned his head. His green eyes blazing as they found mine, searing into me. Holding me. He kissed Amalthea on the cheek, never removing his gaze, never breaking our connection.

I swallowed, wincing, and Kenna squeezed my hand. "Stay calm," she whispered. "Just breathe. You're next."

"You tease," Imperator Hart yelled jovially. "A kiss on the cheek? We know you're capable of far more than that."

"He certainly is!" someone yelled from the back. They laughed bawdily, the nobles nearby joining in.

The demands for a proper kiss grew louder, and Imperator Hart's eyes fell on me. He lifted his eyebrows, his lips puckered, clearly asking me if they should kiss. I stared back, my expression blank.

Then his entire face changed—full of the cruelty I knew lived and breathed inside him.

I couldn't look any longer. I turned away.

"All right, you've had your fun," Imperator Hart yelled. "Save your excitement. You'll see the kiss, and maybe more," he waggled his eyebrows, "on their wedding night. We do have the bedding ceremony to look forward to after all." The room exploded with laughter and cheers, until the Imperator yelled, "Right now, I have even more happy news to share with you." His eyes narrowed, offering me a crooked smile. "You must be wondering why Lady Lyriana has been given the honor of standing with us. I shall tell you. She approached me in private, expressing her desire to continue her studies. She has no power, she is weak—but she greatly admires the strength of the Glemarian soturi." He paused, allowing for more applause.

"Of course, Lady Lyriana's request was not for me to fulfill. I am only the Imperator," he chuckled. "I asked Arkturion Kane to meet her." A grin slowly spread across his face, his teeth white against his dark beard. "And by the end of the meeting, our Arkturion's impeccable training was not the only thing making an impression on Lady Lyriana." He waggled his eyebrows again, and even shook his hips.

"For years, our great warlord Arkturion Kane has lived as a bachelor!" Imperator Hart laughed, and the rest of the room joined in, as if Kane's singleness had been some bawdy joke told regularly over drinks. "But today, it is my pleasure to announce their engagement as well!"

I squeezed my eyes, blinking back tears.

Kane appeared, and all at once I was struck again by his appearance. The fact that he was all sharp angles and muscle. Every movement was cruel and harsh as he approached.

And his aura—I could feel its violence. And something else. Something deep, something ancient. Something that called out to the part of my soul that was still Asherah.

He stepped onto the dais and heat crawled across my skin. There were too many people on the stage. Everyone was too close. It was all too much.

He hugged his daughter and kissed both of her cheeks. Kenna went completely still, the way an animal might when noticed by a predator. Then he took my hand and leaned in, his face inches from mine. My stomach churned. His breath was disgusting and hot against my lips as he exhaled heavily. He smelled like meat drowned in stale beer.

"My bride," he growled.

"Do not kiss me," I hissed, unable to stop myself. "Or I swear I'll break another bone."

"Threaten me," Kane said, his voice dangerously low. "And I swear come sundown, I'll start with your sister—and when I'm covered in her, I'll get you next."

I seethed, breathing through my teeth, trying not to take in his scent, trying not to show my fear.

"I'm not interested in *kissing*, anyway." He smirked. "I have other plans for your foul mouth." He tugged me violently to him.

Rhyan turned to his father at once, a grave expression on his face, one I couldn't read. He looked almost like a different person for a second. Like someone I'd known for a thousand lifetimes. Like a God.

Auriel. I could see it. See the hint of the immortal Guardian he once was—my vision flashing. But more importantly, I could see the threat in Rhyan's eyes. Not a warning, but a promise he was prepared to make good on.

Suddenly, his father's aura exploded. A hurricane-like force blew across the dais.

Against my will, my grip on Kane's hand tightened to keep me from falling over. Kenna cried out, stumbling back, while Amalthea took the moment to wrap herself around Rhyan. Nobles began to shout, and many in their seats were frantically adjusting their tunics and dresses, fixing their hair which was in disarray.

"My apologies," Imperator Hart said, his smile anything but apologetic. "I am overcome with excitement to see my son find his perfect match. And for Lady Lyriana to find a union with my closest friend." His eyebrows formed a deep V. "She looks good as a Glemarian, doesn't she? And now, she will be my wife's stepmother, and she will serve as step-grandmother to my son."

By the Gods. He was farther than fucking Lethea.

Suddenly Kane's huge hand was wrapped around mine, his fingers digging into my skin. I was dragged to the center of the dais, and placed beside Rhyan. I trembled, not daring to look at him, knowing I'd crumble if our eyes met. His arm brushed against mine, and a shiver raced down my arm. I could feel his touch in every part of my body.

Imperator Hart produced two rings, one silver and one gold. I wasn't sure how he'd gotten a golden ring with Ka Batavia's sigil. Maybe he'd always had it, had always been prepared for the culmination of his years of scheming. Prepared all those years ago when my mother visited, when I was still a baby. He dropped it into my palm, and a silver ring was dropped into Kane's.

The Arkturion turned me toward him, one hand steadying my elbow as he shoved the ring painfully onto my finger. There were silver gryphon wings, engulfed in flames. The sigil of Ka Gadayyan. I placed the golden ring into his hand. I didn't have it in me to slide it onto his finger. His hand closed around the metal, the nail on his pinky scratching me.

And it was done.

We were engaged, and my engagement to Viktor and all of Ka Kormac was over.

The nobles cheered and clapped as they yelled congratulations, and demands for us to kiss.

It was at that moment when Rhyan's aura returned. A cocoon of cold air wrapped around my body. He released Amalthea's hand, and took a step toward me.

I could see it, see it all play out, as clearly as my own plan to escape had been in my mind. He'd jump to me, free me, and take me away.

He could do it. I knew he could. We'd be gone before anyone blinked. But there were too many guards seated before us. He'd never reach Meera in time.

And we'd never get to Jules, never beat Morgana and Aemon to the orange shard.

The soturion beside Meera seemed to sense Rhyan's shift,

alerted to the subtle threat Rhyan posed. The soldier lifted the blade to her neck, keeping it carefully concealed beneath her ash-brown hair. But I saw. He turned the blade, letting the steel catch the torchlight. His eyes met mine.

I shook my head, my eyes pleading with him to stop.

Rhyan tracked the knife, his jaw tightening as his eyes met mine again. His face fell as he stepped back into place, his aura retreating as he took Amalthea's hand back in his.

Meera's eyes widened, sensing the danger. She turned suddenly to the soturion, her eyes almost glowing. He relaxed, pulling the blade back ever so slightly.

"Now," Imperator Hart said. "We have a busy few weeks ahead. We'll be preparing to attend the Valabellum in Numeria. Planning two weddings. But we shall have an exciting time together as our newly betrothed couples celebrate their engagement across the country."

My heart sank. Of course. Of course, he was going to parade us non-stop, force us into our roles every chance he had. Show off so word reached Imperator Kormac that he'd lost, that Imperator Hart had me. Owned me.

With a clap, servants entered the Seating Room floating trays of wine glasses which were quickly handed out.

"Arkturion," his father said quietly, "might I have a word with your bride?"

"Of course, Your Highness." Kane stepped aside, leaving me alone with Imperator Hart.

"Next time we are before the Court," he said, taking my hand and squeezing, "You will kiss him, and more than that if I desire it. You will do whatever I order you to do. I went easy on you today. On you both. But you signed a contract. Are we understood?"

My nostrils flared, as I glared in response. I would not kiss Kane. I would not do anything of the sort.

But just thinking the thought became difficult. My blood

heated as if in response to Imperator Hart. And despite me being fully aware it was the contract, and not what I wanted, a part of me began desperately to want to agree.

From the corner of my eye, I felt Rhyan watching us.

Imperator Hart leered even closer, and I could no longer resist. I had to agree to his terms, agree to whatever he asked.

"Understood," I said.

His lips curled. "Then drink."

CHAPTER TWENTY-FIVE

MORGANA

The waves lapped against my feet, the tide soothing against the warmth of the afternoon. I slid my body down the sand, digging my heels deeper into it, loving the way it moved and shifted with me. I loved how it kept me cool beneath the sun. Loved these moments alone. I pulled back the hem of my dress, sliding it up my thighs, and then I opened my legs, letting the waters rush toward my center.

My eyes sprung open. There was a hand on my knee, the callused fingers of a warrior stroking my skin. All at once, I shifted into a seat on the bed, eyeing Aemon as I slid away from his touch. He was dressed as he always was, as an Arkturion of Ka Batavia, in golden seraphim armor, and a red cloak.

"I thought you were a king now," I sneered. "Why are you still dressed up in your old role?"

"I didn't know kings had such a strict dress code."

"I didn't know kings betrayed their lovers either," I said.

He furrowed his eyebrows, his aura darkening. "I have not revealed myself yet to the Empire. For my errand, I remained myself in case I was seen. But soon, they will know. There will be no doubt who I am, what I can do. And why they must submit."

"And why must I?" I asked.

His eyes moved to the indigo shard by my side. It was starting to glow, glittering from nothing more than his gaze in its direction. I could see the pull between them. See the strength he could draw from it, the strength he could bring to it.

For the past few days since I'd begun to work with the shard, I'd felt my own power increase. My energy was better than it had ever been since I developed my vorakh. And though the only thoughts that plagued my mind lately were from Parthenay, and my maid, Lissa, the girl I'd taken from the akadim, I'd found I was able to shut them out better than I ever had before. I was finding the same peace I had only previously found in sex.

"Come," he said. "There is someone I want you to meet."

I narrowed my eyes. "Who?"

"A vorakh. A chayatim. She's like Meera. She has visions, so she can't read your mind. But she can show you what she's seen. And what she's seen is of great importance."

"Seems convenient," I said. "Does she plan to show me what you want me to see? Something to change my mind? To make me give you your way?"

"You think I'd stoop so low to get what I want?" he asked.

I gestured around the cave. "This is not proof enough? Dragging me and Meera here against our will? Tricking Lyr?"

"She knows Jules," Aemon said.

I stilled.

"She's seen a great many things that would be of interest to you. You're discerning. You hold the indigo shard. I only left you days ago and already I feel the change in you. The growth in your power. I am glad to see it. It reminds me of the power you once possessed. I await the day you control even greater power. But first, you must see her for yourself. Judge her for yourself. Make up your own mind."

Aemon stood, holding his hand out for me. His aura had calmed but as I reached for the shard beside me, nestled in my blankets, there was a flash of darkness in his eyes. An overwhelming surge of power that I felt down in my bones.

I slowed my breathing. "Perhaps I am not ready for a visitor just yet."

"Do you want breakfast in bed? Do you want me to grovel? Get down on my knees for you?" He raised his eyebrows. "Lick between your legs?"

Lissa stifled a gasp in the corner.

Aemon chuckled. "Don't worry ... Lissa," he said, pulling her name from her mind. "She likes to be watched."

"Leave her alone." I groaned. "I'll come and meet your chayatim." Despite my wariness, I was curious. And hungry to pull any memories she might have of Jules from her mind.

Carefully, I set the shard down, and walked to a pair of tall black riding boots that Parthenay had an akadim procure on my command. Before I could reach for the laces, Aemon was before me, on his knees, staring up with a level of care I didn't think possible as he threaded and tied up each boot. "I told you I'd get on my knees for you."

"And between my legs," I said.

He grinned. "Trust me, kitten, the moment you ask it of me, I will."

Something heated inside me. A spark that reminded me of all the times we'd been together. But I stared ahead. I wasn't ready. I didn't want to remember. Didn't want to forgive. I just wanted to right the wrongs in Lumeria. To free Jules. To free all of my kind. The rest was too complicated.

With the final lace tied, he smoothed his hand over my knee, letting the touch linger between us.

"I know you're still angry with me. I understand. But do you know how many centuries I waited to find you?" he asked.

I reached for the shard, holding it above his head, keeping it tauntingly in his eyeline.

"Considering the poor execution of your plan, I would have waited longer," I snapped.

"I couldn't," he said, the intensity in his eyes somehow amplified as they tracked my movements. "The time had come."

I shook my head. "Sometimes I don't know if you're speaking to me, or the crystal."

"Why can I not speak to both?" he purred. "You are so much more connected than you know, than you remember." He rose to his feet and then reached for a black shawl, reverently wrapping it around my shoulders. "You'll need a crown next," he said. "*Maraaka*. It will look so beautiful atop your raven hair."

A shiver ran down my spine as he called me "queen" and I rested my fingers in his palm. I'd been calling myself queen for days. Acting like one, too. But prancing around a cave of akadim, having only two mortal subjects to do my bidding … it felt like I was playing dress up, a child in an endless fever dream. Hearing it on his lips made it feel real. Made me feel like I was true royalty.

"You like the idea," he said, smiling seductively.

"I like a lot of ideas."

"Stubborn girl." He laughed.

"Lissa, wait here," I said. "Tidy my room, and then have a long breakfast. Eat as much as you want."

"Yes, *Maraaka*," she said, staring at her feet. She hardly ate, despite my best efforts.

"Nice meeting you, Lissa," Aemon purred. Then turned to me, and whispered in my ear, "You don't want her attending you at Court."

"She fears the akadim," I said.

He lifted an eyebrow in surprise. "And you keep her here, still?"

I didn't need to read his mind to know his thoughts about

that. But he shrugged, and led me into the Allurian Pass's stone corridors, down the stretch of hall into the Seating Room.

Torches flickered from every corner of the cavernous walls, and all at once, the grunts from akadim fell silent as they all dropped to their knees in supplication. Hundreds of silver collars around their necks gleamed in the torchlight. I sifted through the mass of bodies, of large extended limbs that ended in claws, ones that still made me want to cower in fear.

But behind them, interspersed were more and more of the *others*. The ones whose eyes remained intelligent, whose bodies were clearly akadim, sharp, and deadly. And yet ... less. Smaller, and not as threatening. The ones who were easier to look at.

Aemon walked me to my Seat. Not truly a Seat. But after a lifetime of referring to it as such, of living in an Empire without kings and queens to rule the twelve countries, the word "throne" still felt foreign to me. Only the Emperor had one. Yet, that was what stood before me. A throne. A throne for a king. For a queen.

I sat down, the shard gleaming in the torchlight. It seemed brighter, its unique aura pulsing with more energy than it had before.

That was from Aemon. Just his proximity triggered its true power, its full essence. And if that was all it took, what hope did I have in controlling it? In standing up to him?

This is only true without the power of the Orange Ray. My shard. The Orange Shard of the Valalumir. You could control both.

I swallowed. That was an Ereshya thought. Not one of mine.

Or was it?

The lines were becoming more blurred.

Aemon's eyes focused on the nightmare of a court he'd assembled.

"Rise," Aemon said at last, his arm lifted.

The akadim rose to their feet, their bodies stilling, muscled arms at their sides as they chanted, "*Maarak. Maaraka.*"

I released the onyx wall in my mind, finally dropping my guard. I had the strangest feeling of being suddenly naked.

Aemon noticed at once, his head jerking in my direction before he returned to facing his monsters.

Why are they different? I asked.

His lip curled as he tilted his head to the side. *Oh, you're letting me in now?*

I shrugged. *I gave into your request. Now I want you to answer one of mine. Why are some of the akadim here smaller and more mortal in their appearance?*

They are not mortal, he thought. *They are anything but. They possess all the power of the akadim you've known your whole life. The same powers and inclinations as the ones who brought you here. They feast on souls. Their claws will tear a man to pieces without a thought. They are just as prone to violence, to giving into ... their needs ... as any other.*

I swallowed, my heart thumping at the description. I'd almost tricked myself into forgetting how awful they were in the last couple of days. Forgetting why I'd pulled Lissa into my quarters. *So what? Those are just miniature-sized monsters?*

Aemon laughed. *They are still far larger than you. And me.*

But smaller than all the other akadim. It's not just that. Their eyes are different, too. They seem ...

Intelligent? he offered.

Yes.

His lip curled. *I've been working on that for a long time. Cultivating a shift in their transformation. I cannot be every-where at once, when I lead my army. I need generals, I need intelligence. The legions must be organized. That's what these akadim are. Extensions of me. They can think. They can plan.*

I'd barely survived the simple-minded akadim who'd taken me. The beasts were barely able to think past their most basic needs. They were incredibly violent. But easily tricked. And in the end, completely controlled by Aemon's orders. If they hadn't been, I wouldn't be alive. Nor would Meera.

But akadim that could think for themselves …

I did that for you, he thought. *For decades, I've tried to figure out how to make them more palatable. Had I accessed the shard sooner, your captivity would have been far more comfortable.*

I glared. *Maybe I didn't need to be captured at all. Nor Meera! Maybe you could have asked—*

Asked Asherah and Auriel to open the tomb and collect it for me? To simply hand it over?

Yes!

Kitten, he purred. *We both know how that would have gone.*

You weren't asking Asherah and Auriel! You were asking Lyriana and Rhyan.

They are the same! The sooner you accept this, the better. Why else did you betray them? Why else did you keep the shard when you could have left with the forsworn?

My nostrils flared. I'd never wanted to betray them. I just understood what had to be done. I was willing to play dirty enough to make it happen. They weren't.

But the longer Aemon looked at me, the more I began to doubt, until I shoved the thought deep into the recesses of my mind.

His lips lifted, and I knew he'd read the thought clearly. Fuck.

We can circle back to that argument again if you want, he thought. *Whether they're different or the same as their past selves. Or I can tell you what makes these new akadim truly stand apart from the others.*

I stared ahead, watching their eyes track ours. They couldn't read minds, but somehow, I still felt exposed, like they could sense what I was thinking, what I was feeling.

Heart pounding, I asked, *What makes them stand out?*

This time a full grin spread across his face. *They can hunt in the sun.*

My mouth opened. Akadim could only hunt at night. That had been the first thing every child learned about the beasts. That had been the key that protected everyone from their evil. The one comfort against the nightmares they threatened. If the sun couldn't hurt them now …

I shook my head. *Aemon, that's too dangerous. Akadim that can think, that aren't bound to the night … they'll go on rampages. Destroy everything.*

Not if they are under my control. Not if they are under your *control.*

Like Moriel had sworn he'd control them a millennia ago. How the fuck were we having the same argument in another life, in different bodies? Were we truly the same?

I could feel my stomach knotting, my heart threatening to pound through my chest, as a bigger question vied for attention. Did I want that control? Everything about this felt evil. Wrong.

And yet … if they could attack in the day, that meant they could travel in the day as well. Akadim that could plan, and organize, were akadim that could hide from soturi. These were akadim who could take legions down. These were akadim that could reach the Emperor. Reach the Imperators. Destroy an Empire.

We don't have the numbers, kitten. Not yet. But … there might be enough to disrupt a Valabellum. Now, is there anything else you want to know?

Did you see them? I asked desperately. *Did you see my sisters?*

I did, Aemon thought.

I turned in my seat, my heart pounding. "And?" I practically shouted, too anxious to think.

He took my hand in his, shaking his head in admonishment.

With a click of his tongue, he thought, *I took the time in my travels to listen carefully. They're safe. They've been taken in by Imperator Hart.*

I frowned. *Then they're not safe.*

The idea of safety is relative for them at the moment. But from what I've heard, our old friend is no longer forsworn. Thanks to Lyriana. She has made quite the deal with the Imperator. Aemon stroked the skin around my wrist. *Does that worry you?*

My throat went dry as I tried to process all of this. The business of dealing with Imperators never ended well. And wasn't that the fucking point of everything I was doing? Ending their tyranny? Freeing those they oppressed? Making life somewhat fucking better in this Godsdamned world? Even if I had to burn it down first.

But if Lyr was entrenched—and so were Rhyan and Meera—to an Imperator who had control over another Guardian. I squeezed my eyes shut. The whole situation was giving me the kind of headache I hadn't had since Bamaria.

You see how necessary the akadim have become? Aemon thought.

I shook my head, closing my mind and thoughts to him once more. "I don't see anything except an empty room to which I was dragged to from my bed." But in the back of my mind, there was the shadow of his response, one I was glad I could not hear. It was proof I was getting stronger—proof I could stand against him. "You promised an important guest," I said, my voice full of irritation as I scanned the room. "Well? Where are they, Aemon?"

Aemon's eyes darkened at my outburst, and throughout the room, I could sense the agitation of the akadim who'd been impatiently waiting for his command. Their annoyance now shifted to me. With a sudden burst of his aura, shadows darkening the cave with an oppressive weight, I realized I'd spoken out loud. Worse. I'd shouted the name no one else here was allowed to use.

"Much as I *love* hearing you say my name, kitten," he said, "do not call me that here again." His finger stroked the back of my palm, but the threat was clear.

"Moriel," I said, the word slipping from my tongue with far too much ease for my comfort. It was as if someone else had said it, someone who had said it a million times before.

Ereshya.

"It's time." Aemon looked ahead. "Parthenay, please, show our guest in."

Parthenay entered the room, her golden Valalumir star shining against her cheek as she gestured behind her. Suddenly, my heart pounded with traitorous hope. Had Aemon been lying to me? Toying with me? Could it be Jules?

But as soon as the chayatim came into view I knew it wasn't her. She was far taller than Jules was, and possessed a frail looking body with long black hair.

She was beautiful, perhaps ten years older than Aemon, but without a touch of gray in her locks. She was gaunt in the same way Parthenay was, a result of having served the Emperor for so long. But Aemon's guest had the frame of someone who had once been curvy, had once been built thicker, sturdier. Her skin looked like it had once been tanned, like she had once come from the South.

There was something familiar about her, something I recognized, though I was sure I'd never seen her before. She had deep set eyes, dark like Aemon's, and full lips. Maybe it was because she was so clearly Ramarian when I'd been deprived of my people for weeks. Or the mere fact that she was vorakh that gave her a sense of familiarity to me.

"May I present, my queen, *Maraaka* Ereshya, reborn," Aemon said. "Lady Morgana Batavia."

The woman curtseyed. "It is an honor to meet you, *Maraaka*

Ereshya, Lady Morgana." She spoke with a smoky voice, deep and powerful. Immediately I could feel the coldness of her aura, the specific kind that came from visions. It was almost identical to Meera's in its feel and its temperament.

"And what is your name?" I asked.

She dipped her chin, before her dark eyes settled on me. "Andromeny," she said. "Your Majesty."

"Andromeny," I said. "A beautiful name. And your Ka?"

She nodded. "Ka Melvik of Bamaria."

My eyes widened. "Ka Melvik?" I looked again at the shape of her eyes, the familiar way her features came together. Dark, and beautiful. Like *his*. The similarities began to jump out at me then, and I couldn't believe I hadn't seen it at once. The coloring, the details—she was so similar in every way, except she was a softer, more feminine version of Aemon. She could have been his twin in so many ways. Except for one marked difference.

Andromeny had a prominent beauty mark, just above her lip.

I turned to Aemon, my heart pounding as I took in his features again, as if for the first time.

He nodded. "Andromeny is my sister. She's the one who told me who I was when I was a boy, she helped me remember. And she helped me control my vorakh. It was she who predicted the birth of every Guardian to be reborn, and many more things, until she was taken to Lethea and forced into the service of the chayatim."

I shook my head. "No one should be taken from their home or forced into servitude. You have my sympathies. And my understanding, Andromeny."

She nodded graciously. "Your Majesty. Thank you."

"When were you taken?" I asked.

"Twenty years ago," she said, her voice sounding suddenly much older, and tired.

"You survived your Revelation Ceremony?" I asked. If she

was Aemon's older sister, she would have turned nineteen thirty years ago at least.

She nodded. "I survived the Imperator's scrutiny that night. As well as the High Lady of Bamaria's—your mother's. But I felt the power of it, I knew what I was. I redirected the magic that night, and tricked them all. They never knew. Not for years."

My jaw dropped. I'd heard so few references to the time when my mother ruled. Even fewer references to those Lumerians who survived the Revelation Ceremony if they already had their vorakh. Most weren't like us—most developed their vorakh later.

"What happened?" I asked. "How was it that you were discovered?"

"I was in a vision, a powerful one. It told me what had to be done. And I listened. I killed two." Her eyes flashed with gold, like a bolt of lightning. "Two mages."

A chill ran down my spine. "Two mages? Killed? In Bamaria?" I asked, too stunned to stop myself.

"A lord and a lady," she said, her aura pulsing with something like agitation. "Nobles. High ranking. Wealthy. They were … in my way. Blocking me, hiding it. I was close. So close," she said, her eyes distant. "So close to ridding the Empire of an ancient evil." Suddenly her gaze focused, and she stared right at me. "To protect my brother, to protect Moriel, to protect my God, but they tried to stop me."

Her voice rose. She was angry, agitated and frantic. Clearly still angry she'd been thwarted. Angry she hadn't finished what she'd begun. But within seconds, her frenetic energy dissipated, replaced with something I could only name as satisfaction.

Andromeny smiled, her lips lengthening into something almost sensual. "When they refused me, I didn't give up. I listened to my vision. I ripped them to pieces."

I barely held in my gasp. Aemon covered my hand with his, his grip steadying me.

I ripped them to pieces.

I knew of only one nobleman and noblewoman who'd died that way. And it had happened twenty years ago. In Bamaria. Aemon held my hand, his grip tightening to keep me still.

She had her reasons, he thought. *Let her show you, so you'll understand. So, you can see the path forward. For all of us.*

Reasons? I stared at him. *She's farther than Lethea!*

Aemon's jaw twitched. *You say that now, but you forget, she's just like Meera. She's just like Jules.* His mouth hardened.

They never killed anyone!

Not yet. Aemon narrowed his eyes. *That you know of.*

I felt sick, and even without knowing a single detail, or having any proof before me, I knew without a shadow of a doubt it was true.

Not Meera. But Jules. That was entirely possible.

Sometimes the end justifies the means. Sometimes it's all one can do to survive a world that has been designed to work against them, he thought.

The backs of my eyes burned.

She's like us, Aemon continued in my mind. *Do not judge. Listen to her. She can help you. Tell you things you need to know. Things to help your cause. Information that will help your sisters.*

And I should believe you on this? When you yourself don't care about helping them.

I care about succeeding. And your sisters are powerful forces in this war, whether we like it or not. Anything can still happen. They may aid us. Or I may destroy them. It all remains to be seen.

And I'm just supposed to be okay with that? I could hear the hysteria in my mind. It was like being Ereshya all over again, hearing her lover tell her that after millennia of fighting against akadim, we'd be allying with them.

So, she's taken lives. So have I! And so will you in the coming war. You're young now. But you won't be for long.

Killing in battle isn't the same as what she did.

Consider this then. Aemon leaned toward me. *Will you accept another millennia of suffering, and slavery? Another millennia of vorakh being taken hostage, stolen from their homes and forced into enslavement under Lumeria Nutavia?*

All I could do was glare back at him, my chest tightening.

You know I won't.

Then calm yourself. And remember that you are queen.

I snatched my hand from his, and stared back at my so-called court, at my assembly of monsters and liars and … murderers. I tried to settle into my throne, to look unaffected, but my heart was still hammering through my chest. More akadim were moving in agitation, still picking up on my emotions. Particularly the smaller ones. The smarter ones. The day ones.

"Do you have any other questions for me, my queen? Any questions I can answer for you?" Andromeny asked. Her voice suddenly sounded innocent. And younger. Icy almost. The way Meera's did.

She's like Meera, I reminded myself. But she wasn't—she couldn't be.

I swallowed. I'd never feared vorakh before, not the way everyone else did. But Andromeny was different. She *had* killed. She had become the very thing we feared Meera becoming. She was the thing Meera most feared about herself. But I tried to push the thoughts down, to regain my composure. I needed to understand, to find my way forward. Maybe I didn't understand. Maybe she had her reasons.

Or maybe, I could help her. Find a way, a path forward for her, so when Meera's time came, I was ready.

I nodded at Andromeny. But I couldn't bring myself to ask about the killings—not yet.

"Did you know I was coming, Andromeny?" I asked instead,

my voice shaking. "Did you know that I would be born, that I was a Guardian?"

She nodded. "Yes. I knew all of that, and more. A lady, a Goddess, and a queen, Your Majesty. May I show you? I see a great many things. Some inevitable. And some that require a different choice to be made, a new seed to be sown for fruition."

I frowned. "You can see possibilities?"

"I can."

"And your visions? How do they appear to you? As symbolic? Or are they more direct?"

"I see paths. No symbols. Just outcomes."

I could hear the thundering beat with each pulse of my heart as I gestured for her to approach. And then I opened my mind to the mage who'd brought forth one of the most vicious vorakh hunters in Bamaria.

The vorakh who murdered Tristan's parents.

CHAPTER TWENTY-SIX

LYRIANA

I pulled my soturion cloak closer as I settled onto the back of the gryphon in the courtyard. Surprisingly, this one had several harnesses attached.

"You mean I could have been buckling myself up this entire time?" I asked, securing the belt around my waist. That would have certainly improved my flight experiences.

"Obviously," Dario said, as he climbed on, and took the harness in front of me. "What, you think we're savages?"

"Well then where were these the other night?" I asked, double-checking that I was secured.

"You tell me," he said, tightening his strap. "That was your gryphon we rode—maybe ask your Lord Rhyan why he didn't provide any harnesses for you, my lady."

Because we'd stolen the gryphon from Aemon. But I couldn't say that.

Instead, I spat, "Sorry, we were a little too busy saving your life."

Artem, the stable master, finished untying the gryphon's rope, and handed it to Dario.

"Are you going to be needing transport for the lady each morning?" he asked, looking me up and down.

"Imperator's orders," Dario said. "She's Rhyan's novice."

Artem nodded. "Not staying in the soturion apartments for training then?" He lifted a bushy white eyebrow.

"No, she's not permitted to," Dario said. "Any more questions, Artem? Or can we start our day?"

"Just an old man being nosy. Have a good day, my lord." He slapped his knee. "My lady. I'll have Lord Rhyan's gryphon ready next," he added, looking me up and down carefully.

Dario leaned forward, ignoring the last remark. It had been unnecessary for him to mention. It didn't concern Dario. He wasn't in charge of Rhyan's escort. I realized, it had been for my benefit.

A clue that Rhyan was near and staying in Seathorne like me. Of course, his father wouldn't trust him in the apartments either.

"Thank you, Artem," I said, hoping to convey that I understood.

He nodded, and our gryphon lifted onto its hind paws, and then raced forward, soaring into the air. The courtyard faded from view just as I made out the shadowy silhouette of a soturion flanked by two guards, stepping outside.

After the toasts and endless rounds of congratulations the day before, we'd all been whisked back to our rooms and locked inside. I sat by the fireplace for hours, practically holding my breath, terrified there'd be a knock on the door.

I expected Kane to show up and make good on his threats. When I wasn't sitting with my muscles tense, I'd been trying to bribe my guard to give me news of Meera. I'd taken my ring off the moment I was alone. It was heavy and uncomfortable on my finger.

The next morning, I received a scroll from His Highness telling me to dress for soturion training and that once I reached the Katurium, I'd be reunited with my armor and weapons. And if I had a good day, and wore my engagement ring like a good girl, I'd get what I needed next.

I stared at the offensive metal as it glinted in the morning sun, and contemplated letting it accidentally fall, letting it vanish into the pine below. But because the Imperator had ordered me to wear it, that thought suddenly seemed ridiculous to me. Even a bit painful.

I sighed. It didn't matter. It was just a ring. And not worth whatever punishment might come next.

A few minutes of silence passed between me and Dario in the sky, before I felt that sudden plunge in my stomach as the gryphon made its descent before the Katurium. I took deep breaths. At least this time I had the protection of a harness.

Once we landed, I unbuckled and slid to the ground as Dario tied the rope to a post. He left me to stare at the Academy. It was massive. Every bit as intimidating looking as I'd imagined. The Glemarian Katurium was far larger than Bamaria's in every way. I could barely see the sky above from where I stood.

"This way," Dario barked, leading me inside.

I took one last look at the imposing architecture and followed Dario through the doors and down a long winding corridor to my new training room. At least this was familiar to me. Musty, and faintly smelling of sweat. In the center, on a pile of training mats, was my Bamarian armor, and my blade. But not my sword, nor my knives. Asherah's chest plate was also missing. And I noted that I wasn't being given new armor—no Glemarian leathers of my own.

This was my first time in a Katurium with my magic power, with my soturion strength pulsing inside me. I could feel it buzzing through my veins. For once, I actually wanted to run. Wanted to exercise. And the one time I'd be able to show my true strength, to race properly against my fellow soturi I'd have to pretend I was still slow and weak.

Because that was how Imperator Hart intended for me to be

seen. And exactly how he planned to keep me. Under his control, unable to fight back.

I bit my lip, trying to prepare for what came next. "Will the rest of my armor and weapons be returned? I assume if His Highness wants me to be an actual soturion of Ka Hart, I'll need a sword at some point." Dario grunted non-commitally.

"What?" I asked. "No sassy come-back?"

His eyes narrowed. He always had something to say.

"Oh wait, it's too early for you. Isn't it? Let me guess," my voice filled with saccharine sweetness, "Nursing a hangover?"

"You know what!" Dario yelled. "Whatever Rhyan told you before, forget it. You don't know me. You don't know anything about me. And neither does he. Not anymore. So maybe, just maybe, for once, shut the fuck up."

"Likewise," I seethed.

His nostrils flared. "I'll be outside. Come out when your armored up. If you even know how to put it on!" He slammed the door.

I punched a mat against the wall. I hated everything about this. After everything I'd been through, everything I'd learned, I was back as a fucking student in a fucking soturion academy.

Then, knowing I had no other choice, I began the process of buckling and tightening each strap of my golden, seraphim armor. When everything was tightened, and my dagger secured at my hip, I walked outside to the track. Hundreds of soturi jogged by me, all taking their positions. Without fail, every single one stopped to look at me.

Imperator Hart had gotten his wish. I was a spectacle on every level. My golden armor stood out against the sea of black leather like a beacon. And the morning sun left my hair a bright flaming red.

But there was something else that made me stand out. At home, there'd been an equal number of men and women who joined the soturi. I'd never thought twice about that. But here, I had to actively search for the women. There were few and far between the men, who seemed to be moving closer and closer to me.

My heart pounded, until Dario grabbed my hand. He'd slammed his dagger into the ground, and jerked his chin for me to follow.

I did, my eyes searching desperately for a glimpse of Rhyan. I needed to see him. To see how he was doing. And to find a way to talk to him.

A moment later, he was there, marching toward me.

My heart leapt at once at the sight of him, my feet already starting to move.

But it was Dario who brought me back, who reminded me of the game.

"That look on your face," he muttered, "better be for your betrothed. Unless you want to have a very, very shitty day."

I froze. Kane was marching right behind Rhyan. Imperator Hart had made it more than clear that I was to convince everyone of my engagement to Kane. And that next time, he'd demand a kiss. And all at once, I could feel myself giving in. My eyes on Kane, my feet taking me toward him. I tried to step back, and immediately, felt a jolt of pain in my chest, running out through my arms.

"My bride," Kane yelled, causing everyone in the arena to turn in our direction.

A cold front from Rhyan blew past me.

"Give me a hug," Kane said, "for good luck before your run."

"Thank you," I said, and bounced on my heels, running to him. I was ready to vomit. Every instinct in my body told me to turn away. To run in the opposite direction. Or better yet, to run to Rhyan. But instead, against everything inside me, I raced into Kane's arms, and hugged him.

He smelled like sweat. Immediately I pulled back, and waved

as if the interaction were over, running back to my dagger and Dario, my fingers tensed. The ring on my finger felt too tight, too small.

But a moment later, my stomach plunged, my body feeling hollow, as a heavy arm was slung over my shoulder.

"Give me a kiss," Kane demanded.

"No," I said, my blood running cold. Imperator Hart wasn't here and without a direct order from him telling me to do it, I wouldn't. I refused. But my heart pounded, painfully so.

"If you want the scrolls Imperator Hart promised you, do it."

The blueprints. The plans to the Emperor's Palace. The only way I could rescue Jules.

I wanted to punch him, to break another bone. But even without a direct order, I knew I had to do as he asked. Because every rebellious thought made me sick. He hadn't said where to kiss him though.

I stood up on my tiptoes, suddenly dizzy, and brushed my lips against his cheek, barely allowing for contact. But it seemed to satisfy the command my blood was forced to obey.

He laughed. "That's how you kiss? You can do better."

Tears were in my eyes—he was pressing so hard on me, bruising my shoulder.

"Arkturion," Rhyan yelled. "Lovely morning to be back, isn't it? I'm ready to run!"

Kane grunted, his hold on me tightening as he looked up in fury at Rhyan. He pulled me even closer then, his eyes holding a challenge for Rhyan who was walking swiftly to us.

Rhyan's eyes sparked, the green blazing so brightly, they almost looked gold in the morning sun.

Kane huffed, his hold on me growing more painful by the second. But he pushed me away. And I stumbled toward Rhyan as Kane headed for the center of the field.

I tried to keep my breakfast down, while I fought the urge to wipe my mouth on my cloak.

Suddenly, there was a cool cloth against my neck. Rhyan was by my side.

"Partner." He shook his head, his aura pulsing.

I blinked back my traitorous tears, swallowing the bile in my throat.

His eyes were roving across my shoulder and collarbone, assessing. He knew. He knew the damage Kane could inflict with a simple touch.

"When it's time for him to die," Rhyan said, his eyes still on my shoulder, "It will happen slowly. Over days." He slid his hand from the towel up the nape of my neck, his fingers pressing against my head beneath my braid. I leaned back, arching into his touch.

"Rhyan," I gasped. "Don't. It's too risky." But still, I pressed against his hand, desperate for any form of contact. For touch that was gentle and welcome, and not Kane's. Not Shiviel's. Not one commanded by Imperator Hart.

"You say the word," Rhyan said. "You say it, and we're gone."

I closed my eyes, biting my tongue before I said yes, before I threw myself into his arms and let him take me away. Because I knew if I did, I wouldn't just let him, I'd beg him.

Shifting my neck, I could feel his own engagement ring, cool and hard against my skin. At last, I pulled away, far too aware of the soturi who watched the exchange.

Dario moved beside us, making a small attempt to block Rhyan's touch from public view.

He glared, "Are you two actually that stupid, or just farther than fucking Lethea? You're supposed to dispel the rumors, not make new ones!" He stomped back to his dagger.

Rhyan's eyes slid up and down my body, stopping where Kane had touched me. "Can you run?" he asked, voice low.

"Just a sore shoulder. I'm fine."

His eyes narrowed, blazing with anger. "Just remember," he said quietly. "You have to be the worst one out there."

I smiled sadly, remembering our first ever run together. He'd said something similar then, trying to get me to focus.

"At least, this time I'm trying to be the worst, and not actually."

He took a step back, his eyes shining. "You'd be the best, if you were allowed to be. The strongest soturion in the Gods-damned Empire. That day will come. But for now, remember, no winners. It's not a race. Don't let them get to you. Don't let them trick you into running faster, or giving up the game. No one out there, not a single one of them is worth it."

Kane called everyone's attention to him, while more soturi watched me from the corner of their eyes.

Dario was suddenly alert, shooting death glares at everyone in our vicinity. His eyes caught Rhyan's, and something passed between them. A second later, Dario moved so I was sandwiched between him and Rhyan.

He was an ass. But at least he took his job as my bodyguard seriously.

The bell rang. Rhyan offered one final anguished look at me, and then he took off. I breathed out slowly, my power dancing through my veins, my feet feeling so light I swore I could fly. I wanted to tear the track up, I wanted to outrace everyone. I wanted to see the smug look on every soturion's face fade away as they ate my dust.

But I took a slow, measured step, and then another.

And I was the worst one out there.

I could barely focus the rest of the day on all the classes I was forced to sit through, and the bland lunch I could barely keep down, while Dario's eyes shot daggers at me across the table.

I'd almost believed I'd get to be alone with Rhyan in the

training room. But a familiar hiss in the corner shattered that fantasy at once.

We were both sweating by the end, second guessing our every move. Trying to perform each exercise, to keep up with Academy guidelines, all while we knew his father's snake was memorizing everything to report back.

When the final bells rang, there was a knock on the door.

Kenna's cousin, Soturion Baynan, held a scroll closed with a wax seal stamped with the letters *H.H.I.H.*

His Highness, Imperator Hart.

Rhyan's eyes widened as he closed the training door behind him. I broke the seal, unraveling the parchment for us both to read.

To Lady Lyriana and Lord Rhyan,

Come to the courtyard immediately following the combat clinic tonight.

A gryphon will be waiting to take you to the Library of Glemaria. There, in a reserved room only the head librarian can unlock, will you find the items we discussed. All information you need will be stored there.

No materials are to ever leave the premises. You must memorize everything you need. I have chosen my men to assist you. They will join you tonight, along with Lady Meera. Use your time wisely. You have only one chance. H.H.I.H.

Rhyan's eyes met mine, the same determination brewing in them that I felt running through my veins—more powerful than his father's command. Then he crumpled the scroll.

CHAPTER TWENTY-SEVEN

RHYAN

I stood outside in the cold, the night like a familiar and unwelcome blanket covering my body. Combat clinic ended a short while ago. And Lyriana had fought. Because, of course, she had. It wasn't enough to parade her before the entire Court, or force her to run in armor that stood out. She was to be a spectacle at all times. The disgraced Heir to the Arkasva, the weak and powerless soturion.

But despite my father's and Kane's attempts to hurt her, she'd done well. More than well. I'd been proud as fuck watching her evade every hit and punch. She'd even managed to knock out one of my old apprentice's snobby cousins. And she'd done it all without revealing her true strength, or her true power. Asherah's power.

My stomach turned as I continued to wait. Because hard as I tried not to, I couldn't help but think of Lyr that moment in the cave, the moment when Dario and Aiden had revealed the truth about Garrett. The split second before she looked to see if I was okay, I'd seen it on her face. The fear. The horror. And there was still so much more to tell her. So much more to reveal. But how could I? How could I tell her the things I'd done? The ways in which I'd failed. The other secrets I'd kept. The secrets I was still keeping. The secrets I'd tucked away about the Guardians.

And about her power. Her *Rakashonim*.

It had killed Asherah. And if Mercurial was right it would kill her again. I needed to understand it. Needed to learn everything I could. When we visited the Library of Glemaria tonight I intended to begin my research.

Asherah had left Auriel behind for another world. I'd be damned if Lyr left me in the same way. Not when I could stop it. Not when I could save her.

I scratched at my palm, then suddenly stopped. The habit was one I'd barely noticed I did, but tonight, I couldn't help it. My *betrothed*'s engagement ring was rubbing against my skin. Another secret I carried. One I did not yet want to face.

The doors to the Katurium opened, finally revealing Dario and a freshly showered Lyr. Her hair was still damp, pulled back into a loose braid that fell over her shoulder. They were both looking annoyed, their arms folded across their chests as they marched toward me.

"To the library then?" Dario asked, his gaze to the sky as a soturion began a descent on a gryphon. The one I assumed we'd be flying.

Lyr was watching the beast warily, but suddenly, she looked at Dario, her eyebrows wrinkled. "I hope you're not too bored all night. I'm sure the library's not your scene. I'd suggest some books for you to read, but—"

"Bored?" Dario asked. "Why would I be bored? Are you trying to insinuate I can't read?"

Lyr smiled sweetly. "Of course not. I'm assuming you have no interest."

Dario snorted. "You really formed quite an opinion there. Well, I hate to break it to you, but I'll be anything but bored. Because I actually am interested in reading. *And*, because I'll be working right alongside you on this little project. Imperator's orders."

Lyr's eyes widened. "You—you!" she sputtered.

"Oh, yes. Me and Aiden." His lips curled into a satisfied smile, one directed at me.

"And you're prepared to do the research necessary?" Lyr asked, advancing on Dario.

My eyes met Lyr's. And I could see the questions in her eyes. Could we trust him?

My jaw tightened. We had no choice.

"Shall we?" Dario asked, gesturing to the gryphon.

Lyr's face hardened, her hazel eyes still on me. I nodded, and moved forward, my guard close behind.

Once we were all buckled into our riding harnesses, we took off into the night. Lyr sucked in a breath, and when Dario wasn't looking, I grabbed her hand, giving her a quick squeeze. Her fingers curled around mine with such intensity, I felt it through every limb. And then, just as quickly, we released each other. But my hand continued to vibrate and pulse with the feel of her, the way it had in the early days of training, when we barely touched each other, when it had been forbidden, and I could recall exactly every part of her body I'd come in contact with. Could recall for exactly how long.

I'd sometimes spend hours reviewing every look between us, and every brush and graze between our bodies. Every adjustment I'd had to make to her form during stretches—I'd feel them everywhere, and I'd play the moments over and over during my endless shifts of guard duty.

Lyriana tensed beside me, as the gryphon's angle shifted, the speed picking up. She glanced at me quickly, and then stared ahead, determined to conquer her fear of flying this way. A minute later we landed in front of the library, exactly at the same time Meera and Aiden's gryphon arrived.

I tried to clear my mind as I stared up at the building. I'd forgotten how large it truly was. How majestic. And how long it had been since I'd last been inside.

Before I was forsworn. Before the tournament.

Before Garrett had died. A lump formed in my throat, the backs of my eyes burning, until I looked at Lyriana.

Her eyes lit up as she stepped back, her neck craning as she took the library in. I felt warmer than I had in hours as my heart seemed to beat faster. I'd seen fear and stress branded into her face for days.

But at that moment, she was just a girl who loved libraries. A girl with stars in her eyes and her first genuine smile in what felt like forever. The girl I'd fallen madly in love with. My own lips curled in response, and I resisted the urge to sneak up behind her, to wrap my arms around her waist and hold her so she could lean back and stare more comfortably.

"This is your library?" she asked, her voice full of wonder.

And fuck, if I didn't swear in that moment to do everything in my power to give her another experience like this. Another chance to see something she loved, something that made her happy, something that made her eyes light up. Something that made her smile.

But just as quickly, my stomach hollowed. Before she could have any more moments like this, I had to ensure she survived. I had to get a hold of the research I'd been silently compiling in my mind for hours.

"I've never seen anything like this before," Lyr continued.

"I've seen pictures," Meera said, "but they don't do it justice. The size, the detail." She shook her head in appreciation. "In person, it's beyond impressive."

I looked at it again, imagining I was seeing the library through Lyr's eyes—as if I were seeing it for the first time. The base of the library was constructed from a series of stone archways. Each arch was several stories tall and could have easily fit several Bamarian buildings beneath it.

Above the arches was the actual library, a series of interconnected towers, each one five stories high. Carvings depicting scenes from the Valya adorned the arches, and right before me was a carving of Auriel holding out his hand for Asherah, but she was just out of reach. Shiviel appeared to be sneaking up behind her, ready to attack.

"The scrolls are all kept at the top in the towers," Aiden said confidently. "The Library of Glemaria was built seven hundred years ago. Even though hundreds of years had passed, there was still concern about the Drowning, about whether or not the tides would sweep the structure away, especially with how close it was to the shore. So, it was built above the arches, which had once been a bridge, allowing for the tide to rise from time to time without affecting the scrolls kept inside. Though the waters don't come close anymore."

"Wow. I didn't realize you'd been assigned the role of history professor in this mission," Dario said.

"What? It's a unique structure and worth mentioning," Aiden said, ignoring Dario's jab.

I opened my mouth, about to defend Aiden. Garrett would have—but … Garrett wasn't here. Because of me. And I'd lost my right to jump in as their friend.

"How exactly do we reach the library part of the unique structure?" Lyr asked, wearily.

"There's a small lift in the northernmost arch," Aiden said. "Follow me."

At this hour there was only one mage controlling the lift— and with the weight of all of us combined, it was a slow ride. As we finally stilled, the doors opened, and we were led through shelves upon shelves of scrolls. We were met by a librarian who already had lamps ready for us to light our way. "Citrine?" Lyr asked.

I nodded. "We use these for light here, and they do allow some torchlight."

Her eyebrows crinkled in curiosity, and then she quickly returned to looking over every section in wonder. I looked, too, watching as the citrine stones cast a warm golden hue across the shelves of scrolls.

We were led through the first tower, out onto a small bridge that led to another tower, and then another before we were finally in the one that contained all the studies, the one I used to frequent with Dario and Garrett when prepping for academy exams.

We were shown into a private study room I hadn't seen before. And from the looks on Dario's and Aiden's faces, they had no idea this room existed either. Our eyes met, our shoulders all lifting in a confused shrug—as if we'd forgotten we were enemies now. For a second, we were just the sons of nobles, at the library for a study session, when we'd rather be elsewhere. Training. Fighting. Partying. Dario would have wondered if he could access the room to bring his latest lover there, while Garrett would be plotting to get Aiden alone in it.

I'd be dreaming about Lyr.

The door closed behind us, and the fantasy shut down. Garrett wasn't here. Garrett wasn't going to be here. Somehow, being in exile, it had felt easier to grieve for him. To understand that he wasn't where I was, because his place was here. It was easier to pretend I'd left him behind, left him safe with Aiden and Dario. To forget the last time I'd seen him.

But the longer I spent here with my old friends, without Garrett, the more his absence began to feel like a living pulsing thing. The more I missed him.

And the more guilty I felt. The more my final secret about him weighed on me.

Our escort remained outside, and as Dario and Aiden took their seats at the long study table, I did my best to push thoughts of Garrett away. I had to focus.

The table was already full of neatly organized scrolls. For a moment, we all stared at each other, no one willing to take charge, or open the discussion.

Then Lyr's eyes narrowed on Aiden and Dario. "What has your Imperator told you?"

"Enough," Aiden said.

"No. Not good enough. What do you know? What do you need explained?" she asked.

"Sounds to me more like you want us to reveal something to you that we shouldn't," Aiden said. "Well, we won't. Give it up now. Your efforts will prove fruitless."

"Fine," she said. "I'll assume you both know nothing, despite the fact that you're here means you must have some level of clearance. So, I'll fill you in. And don't worry, I'll speak very slowly, and use really small words." She glared at Dario.

"Go as slow as you want, my lady." Dario winked, his tone suggestive. "I can go all night long. I'm not under a deadline. But you are. You're the one with a month to fulfill your contract to His Highness."

"So then you know we're going to the Valabellum," Lyr said.

"Myself to fucking Moriel," Dario said. "Yes, we know. We also know we're planning to take the Emperor's big old shield from his throne room, and then spirit Lady Julianna from the Palace."

Lyr stiffened, her eyes darting to me, and then Meera whose eyes widened.

"What?" Meera asked. "We're going to rescue Jules? With Imperator Hart's help?"

"We are," Lyr said gently. "I'm sorry, Meera. I wanted to tell you right away. But I haven't exactly been given any permission to talk to you." Her aura flared with anger, the emotions jutting out toward Dario and Aiden, but quickly, her focus returned to Meera. Meera, whose relationship with Lyr had been rocky for days. "You should have known," she said.

I realized then, if Meera had no idea about the plan, then she still had no idea she was Cassarya, that she was the Goddess of the Blue Ray. And I didn't know when we'd be able to tell her.

Meera took a few deep breaths, her eyes watery.

Lyr reached out a hand to Meera, and squeezed. Dario and Aiden watched the interaction, their bodies leaning forward, as if they were audience members at a play.

"Can you give them some privacy?" I asked.

"No," Aiden said quickly, his voice harsh. "Whatever game this is, whatever madness your father wants, you're still under our watch."

Fuck. Meera deserved to know the truth about Cassarya, and about the shield. Dario and Aiden might know we were stealing it, but we weren't going to tell them Ereshya's shard lay in its center.

"Do you know who Lady Julianna is?" Lyr asked, her voice shaking.

Dario, to my surprise, nodded, his eyes softening. "She's your cousin."

Lyr's face tightened. "We thought she was dead. But she's been the Emperor's prisoner for over two years."

"I know. I'm sorry," Dario said.

Lyr frowned, surprised by his sympathy. I looked away. I wasn't. I knew Dario was harsh on the outside, but the softest of us all on the inside, much as he tried to hide it.

I could feel Aiden's eyes on me, watching carefully. Jules had been my friend, too. They knew I'd had a pen pal for a while with a Bamarian noble but I'd never told them who. And then when her letters stopped, I'd never mentioned it again. And they'd never asked.

Lyr looked away, clearing her throat, trying to get her emotions under control. I could feel her unsteadiness in her aura. "The main mission we've been assigned to complete is to steal this shield. Otherwise, we don't get Jules. Do you know anything about it?"

"We've seen descriptions of it," Aiden offered. "It hangs in the Emperor's throne room, above his seat."

Meera made a noise of surprise. "We're stealing a shield? From the Emperor? From his throne room?" She gestured around the room. "Us and what army?"

"There are several Palace guards currently in the employ of His Highness," Aiden said. "We're also being offered a team of mercenaries to assist with our escape and retreat—should it come to that." He swallowed roughly. Aiden had always been a stickler for the rules. For him to be so calm about breaking them, even if they were under my father's orders, was unlike him. It made me wonder what other things he'd been forced to do for my father. What other cruelties I'd left my friends to endure. What other cruelties they'd been forced to commit.

"Okay," Lyr said slowly. She stared across the table at Aiden and Dario, clearly waiting for them to speak next. But they were silent, unwilling to share information in case they revealed something we hadn't known yet.

"We know about Rhyan's vorakh," Aiden said suddenly, breaking the silence. He spoke quickly, like he was tripping over the words.

"You know what?" I burst out, my heart pounding.

"We know," Dario said. "We've known. We were sworn to secrecy."

I felt my chest tighten. A scar on my back that had been dormant for months suddenly burned as if it had just been carved into my skin. I could feel it then, clear as I had the night I'd gotten it. Feel the blade on my back. Hear the oath spoken into the night.

My eyes met Aiden's, my stomach roiling.

He nodded, something in his expression I couldn't read.

And then he looked away, his attention back on Lyriana.

"You both know?" she asked, looking at me with concern.

"Yes," Dario said. He reached for one of the scrolls.

"Just like that?" I asked, incredulous. "That's how you tell me?" I wanted to throw up. I'd nearly died keeping this secret from them. I couldn't even remember all the times my father had used it against me. Blackmailing me, threatening me, torturing me, forcing me to do his will.

"What do you want from us?" Dario asked. "A Godsdamned coming-out party?"

My chest heaved, and I eyed Aiden. He'd been the one I was most worried about—the one who Garrett—

I coughed, trying to clear my throat. A thousand questions raced through my mind. A hundred different scenarios I'd imagined about the day they'd learn my secret and how they'd react.

Nothing like this reality had ever once entered my imagination.

Aiden pressed his lips together, his eyes red before he shrugged and looked away, fiddling with the scrolls before his seat.

"His Highness told you?" Lyr asked.

"Who else?" Dario said, tapping his fingers on the table.

"We're here," Aiden said. "So you can take our presence for consent and acceptance of Rhyan's situation."

Lyr slammed her fists on the table, rising from her chair. "Situation? It's not a fucking situation. It's part of who he is. And it's fucking amazing. Do you know how many times he's saved my life with his vorakh?"

Aiden's neck reddened. "Now is not the time, my lady, to mention saving lives."

"I think it fucking is," Lyr sneered.

But it was Meera who stood then, her aura icy and powerful. "Lyr's right. Now I don't care if His Highness assigned you to be here or not. But you're going to listen, because what we're planning to do here is save a life. My cousin's, and she is vorakh. What we do in this room determines our success out there, and what happens out there is life and death, especially for Jules. If there's any reason why we can't trust you to help us, then leave. I'll speak to Imperator Hart myself." There was a flash in her eyes—a blue light. Cassarya's.

Aiden stilled.

But Dario's aura flared. "We're here," he said. "That's your answer. Now sit down, both of you. You're upsetting the guards."

"Give me your word," Lyr said. "I want your word that you're going to do everything in your power to complete this mission."

"We can't," Aiden roared. "We can't give you our word. All right?"

"Why the hell not?" she asked.

"Because!" I shouted, and then we were all standing. Everyone stilled, turning to stare at me. "Because," I said, my voice cracking. "They already gave their word to my father." I sat back down, pulling my chair violently in toward the table. "They'll do whatever he asks, and that's it. So enough! He wants a shield, and this is how he's going to get it. Everyone sit down and open your fucking scrolls. We're doing this. We're doing it right. And we start now!"

Lyr sat down next, followed by Meera. Finally, Dario and Aiden joined, everyone adjusting their seats and rearranging their scrolls.

"I think the best place to begin," Lyr said, clearing her throat, "is to memorize the schedule that day, as well as the layout of the Palace. Places marked for chayatim, dungeons, rooms—" she cleared her throat again, "rooms that the Emperor can easily, or secretly gain access to. We need to make a list of every place where Jules might be kept."

Dario shook his head. "We're not going after Jules. We're going after the shield."

"I know. But once she's free, it's our job to make sure she isn't taken from us again."

"Focus on the shield," Aiden said. "His Highness has her rescue set."

Lyr's nostrils flared.

"No shield, no Jules. We need a starting point for the theft." Dario tilted his chin. "Look, I'm in. I'm all the way fucking in. And I don't like losing. So let's study. Memorize the schedule, pick starting points."

At this, Lyriana and Meera shared a look, but both seemed to be in agreement.

Silence filled the room as everyone's scrolls began to unroll. My heart was still pounding. My body still reacting to the knowledge that its secret had been revealed.

But then I thought of Jules. Of her last letter to me. Of the way her friendship had been all I had when I'd returned home from Bamaria, my heart broken over Lyr.

I pushed all other feelings aside. I was getting her the fuck out of there. Whatever else was happening tonight between me and my old friends—it didn't matter. I began to read, my fingers unclenching, and like everyone else, I pored over the maps before me.

Sometime later, Lyr set her scroll down with a sound of frustration. "I have no fucking idea where to start," she said.

"We can mark a few places off-limits though," Meera suggested. "Some are too far, and too guarded for us to hide in. Those make no sense and should be crossed off as possibilities." She pulled her map out toward the middle of the table, and stood, grabbing a few markers from her pack, and blocked off some sections. After a few moments, we all agreed. Meera eyed the map carefully. "Seeing the Palace like this, I think we can narrow down our starting points to half a dozen locations. Here." She set down the first marker. "Here. Here," she placed two more. "And any of these spots along these three corridors." She set the final markers down.

"And there," Lyr said, adding one more.

Everyone leaned forward, their eyes going back and forth between Meera's map and their own.

"This is good," I said. "We can begin planning around these entry points, and cross-reference the guard schedule and locations."

Aiden tapped his fingers against the table. "Lyr's entry point lines us up with most of His Highness's Palace guards." He frowned. "But we have less chances of being seen if we follow this one of Meera's." He pointed to a marker just outside the Throne Room.

"You're sure?" Dario asked.

"We have to look out for the chayatim," Aiden said. "The Emperor's cloaked ones. They'll be able to read your minds, see us coming."

"Won't we have protection?" Dario asked. "The potion that protects our minds?"

Meera put her head in her hands.

"The Imperator has that?" Lyr asked, her voice high.

"Of course, he does," Aiden said. "We can't walk in there with a crime in our thoughts. We'd be caught instantly."

"So, we're using magic that was stolen from a vorakh?" Lyr asked, her voice filled with disgust.

"It's that, or get caught and join your cousin," Dario said.

"Don't you—" Lyr started, but I pushed my chair out and stood.

"No more fighting," I said. "We're here to succeed." My eyes met Lyr's.

"Fine. Are we settled on these two entry points to begin planning?" Lyr asked.

"I think so," Meera said.

"We should still have back up plans in place," Aiden said. "These are ideal, but we should be able to pull this off from any location."

Dario pursed his lips together. "That's a lot of fucking work."

He held up his hands before anyone could argue. "But we need to do it." His lips curled in disgust. "I don't exactly fancy becoming one of the Emperor's prisoners."

I turned to Lyr and Meera. "What do you both think?"

"It makes sense," Meera said. "Aiden's approach is right."

Lyr bit her lip. "As long as we figure it out, and succeed, I don't care how hard we work."

"We're going to succeed," I said, and placed my hand over my heart. "*Me sha, me ka.* And we'll have a plan for after."

Aiden stood up again, walking around the table to see Meera's map at a different angle. "Yes. I think this is a very solid assessment, especially for day one."

"Right, except that all of these locations are literally going to require completely different plans," Lyr said.

"Let's split up then," I said. "We can't all be in one place at the same time. And if we plan from two locations, we have better odds that one will be successful," I said.

"Your odds of succeeding here," Dario pointed to a marker, "are better, because you'll be out in the open." He gestured to Meera and Aiden. "No one would ever suspect either of you. And with so many of the Lumerian elite present, there's guaranteed to be more commotion and therefore more chances for distraction while you make your move."

Meera nodded, her expression thoughtful.

Dario frowned. "I think Rhyan and I need to plan for the more potentially violent mission. Fighting our way in and out."

"And me?" Lyr asked.

"Well, you're the one who has to take the shield in the end. So, you can move between both plans."

"Either way, you'll need me to create a glamour," Aiden said. "Once you have the shield, I can leave behind a decoy. I can also conceal the real one in your possession."

"Okay," Lyr said. "Let's start working. Aiden and Meera, you start here. We'll call this Plan A. And Dario and Rhyan," she pointed to the map, "you start here. Plan B. I'll start with Meera and Aiden, then join you two."

"Me and Rhyan," Dario said. "Great."

I stilled, hearing the unhappiness in his voice. He still hadn't acknowledged that moment in the cave, the moment he'd gone into shock and I'd held him. And from the look on his face, and everything I'd ever known about Dario my entire life, my guess was he wasn't ever going to.

Hours later, when Dario's head was drooping and Lyr was rubbing the exhaustion from her eyes, the clock tower began to ring, announcing midnight.

The doors opened, my guard waiting, along with a few members of my father's personal escort. Once we all left the room, and were searched to ensure we hadn't taken any of our study materials, we were led back through the towers and archways to the entrance.

Once there, waiting for the lift, I pulled a small note out of my belt pouch, and stepped toward the desk.

"I'm interested in any titles that relate to these topics," I said quietly, slipping the scroll across the table.

The librarian frowned, but took the parchment and read.

"Lord Rhyan," one of my escorts scolded. "You're to wait for the lift with us."

"I am waiting for the lift with you," I said. "I'm just doing so over here."

Lyr watched me with a curious expression as the librarian scanned my requests.

"Eye witness reports and histories of Shiviel," she said, frowning. "I haven't been given leave to offer these titles to you."

"I'm Heir to the Arkasva and Imperator," I said, my stomach turning. "I have permission to use the library."

"I—Yes, you do."

"There's no notice that I'm forbidden from such things, is there?"

"No, Your Grace," she said.

"Then please," I said. "Any accounts. Anything related to Shiviel."

She bit her lip, tapping the table, assessing the request.

"And," I continued, "texts on ancient, forbidden magic, magic of the Gods. This in particular, please." I pointed to my note on the scroll, my finger right beside the word *Rakashonim*. The power Lyr was drawing on when she called on Asherah.

"I'll pull some titles for you, Your Grace, they should be ready tomorrow."

But I didn't want Lyr to see them. Not yet. "Can you have the scrolls delivered to my room at Seathorne?" I asked. "Please."

The librarian's mouth tightened. "I—yes. It will be done, Your Grace."

"Thank you," I said. "Truly." Then feeling the glare of my escorts, I moved back to join them in their wait for the lift.

"What was that about?" Lyr asked, her shoulder dangerously close to my arm.

"Research," I whispered. "On Shiviel."

"You're trying to find out what we did to him?" she asked.

My hand found hers beneath our cloaks, and our fingers threaded together. "I'm going to find out everything."

CHAPTER TWENTY-EIGHT

TRISTAN

"Galen, take it," I said, shoving the bag of coins at him.

"No. I don't need it." Galen looked away, staring out at the arena of the Nutavian Katurium. His arms were folded across his chest. He wore no tunic or armor, enjoying the early whisperings of spring and the bright sun.

"Please," I said. "You should at least accept me as your sponsor."

"The Palace is my sponsor," he said coolly.

I sighed. Sure, the Palace was housing him, giving him the arena to train in every day and providing basic meals. But not enough. He needed more, and at the very least I wanted to give him that. But he was so fucking stubborn.

"Why are you offering me this anyway?" Galen pulled on his arms, stretching them side to side before lifting them over his head. A habibellum was happening in the field. Every day there was one as all of the potential soturi for the Valabellum auditioned and fought to earn their roles in the arena. Every day, soturi were being cut and sent home. But Galen kept making it to the next level. "You know that I don't need it. Nor have I ever asked for anything like this from you." His face tightened. And underneath, I detected the smallest bit of resentment.

I sometimes forgot just how much money my Ka had. And how vastly different that level of wealth was from the other nobility. Ka Scholar was on the cusp of such noble status. Since his people mostly stayed in Scholar's Harbor, and most took up posts there in the Library or in the temples, they were not always included amongst the nobility. Nor invited to most events. But I'd never paid attention. Never thought twice about Galen's status. Not until my grandmother pointed it out.

Apparently, Galen had noticed. More than he'd willingly let on in our long years of friendship.

His dark eyebrows furrowed, and he reached at last for his tunic on the bench. Once the next hour was called, he'd be in the next set of trials. These were for the roles of the Guardians. Under no circumstances could Galen be cast. These games were deadly. And the last thing I wanted was to see him harmed. He risked enough as a soturion as it was.

"Last I heard," he muttered, pulling his tunic down past his waist, "you were giving your coin to my enemies."

"Fuck," I muttered. "You weren't supposed to know about that."

"Betting against your best friend. Real fucking nice."

"I'm not betting against you!" I said. "I'm trying to keep you safe!" I gestured towards the habibellum happening before us. "This is a bad idea. People are going to get killed. I've lost too much already." I paused, feeling the familiar pang in my chest. "If she was here …" my voice cracked, "Ha—" I stopped. I couldn't say Haleika, not without crying.

"But that's exactly why I am here!" he snapped.

All the nights we'd spent together grieving, drinking … I had no idea the anger he was carrying deep down. I'd never realized that calm, logical Galen, Galen who hailed from Ka Scholar, would be the one to carry such vitriol.

"Galen, fuck. Come on. I can't lose you too."

But Galen wasn't listening. "I have to do this," he said. "I have to make him see. Emperor Theotis needs to see." His jaw was set and anger was radiating off his aura. "If I can at least look him in the eye, and say out loud what he did, it's worth it. Don't you want that?"

My hands fisted at my sides, my own anger pulsing through me. I couldn't think about it. Couldn't think about it without feeling the horror washing through me, attempting to drown me and push me back into my grief and shock. I understood how Galen felt. I felt it, too. But there was a strategy, a way to do something. And it wasn't this.

Gods. I had enough to worry about. Least of which was what was still happening to me.

I sat back, watching as Galen began to fasten the clasps of his golden Bamarian armor around his chest.

"I need to stretch," Galen said. "If you're going to be like this, then I don't need you here. Don't try to hand me money and claim you support me, not when I know what you're really doing."

"Auriel's fucking bane. I'm not betting against you," I hissed. "I'd never bet against you."

"Then what?" Galen's voice darkened.

I was trying to form an alliance, trying to find any soturi I could bribe, and convince them to make Galen a target. I wanted them to get him out of the trials. If he wouldn't leave himself, if his strength wouldn't fail, then my only option would be to have him disqualified.

The bells rang.

"I want you to be safe," I shouted. "Don't you get it. I've lost enough. I don't … fuck. You're my friend. I don't want to lose you."

Galen looked away. "It's not just me," he said. "His Majesty has been losing his popularity for a long time. Do you know how many people are here who want to see the Emperor be held accountable? How many more wish to see him fall?"

I leapt up from my seat, and gripped his armor, pulling him toward me.

"Fucking listen to yourself," I hissed. "You're speaking of treason."

"I'm speaking facts."

"Fine. Facts. If there's others who want to bring an end to …" I paused. I didn't want to speak treason. I couldn't afford to. My existence was treason enough now. "If others want that, let them then. Let them take care of it. But you? You do nothing."

"I loved her," he said.

"And I didn't?" I said. "She was my cousin. I loved her."

"It's not the same," he said.

I shook my head. "What about Leander?" Her apprentice had been her lover, too. Not just Galen. I couldn't understand why he was so driven when I was still not sure if Haleika had truly returned his affections.

"I don't care. I know she loved me. And I loved her—even if she loved others, even if she loved them more. They're not here. He's dead. It's up to me. Anyway, you're one to talk. Let's not forget Lyriana. And yet, you're going through all the motions— and I mean all of them—with Naria."

Lyr. She didn't love me. Not the way she loved the forsworn. And yet, when I thought about her in danger, or what the Imperator had demanded of me, I wondered if I, too, would have the strength to defy it, to fight back. If the forsworn couldn't do it, could I step up, even knowing where her heart was?

"I've got to go," Galen said. He pinned a flag to his armor. The number forty-four. Then he glared at me. "Just stop. Stop what you're doing. You want to stay out of this mess? Play it safe? Keep the status quo?" He leaned toward me. "Then do it, Tristan. Do it. But nothing changes unless someone does some- thing. And if no one does, there will be another Haleika. Even if

I wasn't the love of her life, it doesn't matter. It's as good a cause as any. Someone has to do something. And it won't be Leander. Or you, or Ka Grey." He stepped back, before I could say anything, and then ran out into the arena with the others.

I sank back against the bench, my gold coins still in my hand. Utterly fucking useless. What good was money if I couldn't use it to help my friend?

The Katurium mage walked out onto the field and new silver circles to bind the fighters were drawn. A few of the soturi I'd spoken to, Galen's competition, walked onto the field, and noticing me, dipped their chins in respect.

I looked away.

"Since when do you take an interest in arena games?" Imperator Kormac drawled. His golden Laurel of the Arkasva gleamed in the sun, as did the golden border of his black robes, as he made his way down the aisle to my bench. The Bastardmaker and about a dozen more wolves followed behind him.

I jumped to my feet, my pulse pounding as I bowed.

"Your Highness," I said quickly. "I'm sorry I haven't seen you in sometime."

"Not since we heard news from the North," he said, and gestured for me to sit.

I did, and then he took the seat right beside me.

"Leave us," he ordered his men.

We were silent as they walked away. Not far. Away enough for us to speak in private. But close enough to remind me of the threat they posed.

"Lord Tristan," he said, "If I remember correctly, you were never exactly told what would happen to you if you failed to bring me Lady Lyriana and Rhyan Hart."

I swallowed. "I remember."

"Well," Imperator Kormac said, draping his arm across my shoulder. His other hand was on my chest. The touch was, I supposed, friendly enough. Not something that would cause anyone to gawk if they walked by our bench at that moment. And yet, my heart was thundering, sweat beaded at my forehead. Because it was anything but a friendly touch. I had the sudden realization that if he wanted to, he could crush me. Right then and there. It didn't matter my station, or how much money I could access. If the Imperator turned on you—that was it.

It's a dangerous thing, my dear, to not have that man on your side.

My grandmother's warning flashed in my mind.

"You should know," the Imperator said, "I've been watching you since you've arrived here."

Now my heart stopped beating. Watching? How closely? Who was watching me? And when? What could they have seen? My stomach twisted violently and every part of me was hot and cold at once.

My vorakh. The visions. I'd had them again since I'd arrived —the same thing each time. The monster who killed my parents. The promise that my parents would regret what I would become. The evil inside me.

My chest tightened as I waited for him to spell it out. To tell me I was damned—that I was next for Lethea.

But no, no. He couldn't know. I'd only had two instances. Two visions. One in the shower, and I'd been sure I was alone. The other came in the middle of the night when I was still in bed. I thought it was a dream, until the repeating images came, and the season's sudden shift into spring did nothing to remove the chill in my bones.

If anything, I'd proven my loyalty to him and to his cause just this morning. It made me sick. I'd had to rush to the bathroom right after, I puked up my guts. But I'd found a vorakh in the Palace, visiting their brother who was competing in the trials. I'd captured them. Had Bellamy and Eric deliver them directly to the Palace prisons before I sent word to Imperator Kormac.

"Watched?" I said, nonchalantly, my pulse thrashing. Galen

was in the middle of a Five and expertly doling out punch after punch. "Surely, beyond today's excitement with the criminal I apprehended, I've not been so interesting to observe."

"You seem to have taken a great interest in these trials," he said, his tone light and conversational, like he wasn't threatening me, like my life didn't lie between his two hands.

"It's the reason we're here," I said. "The Valabellum."

"Not the reason you're here," he snapped. "You could have arrived later, arrived with your betrothed. You came early because you had a job to do. And since that job has shifted, I expected you to pivot. The entire story of Lyriana's engagement stinks of gryphon-shit. And I expected you to find out more. To party, to schmooze, to find out what's really happening in the North. Maybe you can't legally hunt for her in Hart's lands, but I did not intend for you to make daily trips out to the Katurium, to spend hours in the arena and the soturi apartments. You've never done that before. Not even when your girlfriend became a soturion."

I stared ahead, terrified to make eye contact with him. His hands were still on me, and it was taking all of my focus and energy not to shake.

"N-no. But—" I swallowed roughly, my throat constricting. "But this is a unique event. The place to be it seems."

"People don't change. Their interests don't change. Nor do their habits. I pay attention to such things. You've gone years without a shred of interest. Your Ka won't even employ soturi. You've never been one for the games."

I shrugged, the movement awkward, constricted by his hand tightening on my shoulder. "I'm not exactly one for them now," I said. "But, like I said, these are unusual circumstances. A grand event in the Emperor's honor."

"Are you interested in knowing more about what we discovered as we watched you? It seems there's someone in the trials of interest to you. Someone you've tried to sponsor."

I stopped breathing. "Hard to know where to place bets when like you said, I've never been one for the games."

"Galen of Ka Scholar," he said.

My throat bobbed, my entire body still.

He removed his hands and laughed. Though the sound was more like a howl. "Number forty-four. Doing quite well in his trials today, isn't he? I figured you had plans for betting on him to win the final games, to see him get cast into some major role. If you were offering money to support his training, I could only assume it was an investment. Perhaps you were gambling. But then your money patterns changed. You started offering money to his opponents instead. You even began funding alliances. All working against him. The one soturion you seemed loyal to." His mouth was against my ear as he whispered, "At least, after your forsaken cousin, that is."

My throat tightened, and then my chest followed. I could barely breathe. I wanted to get up, to run out of there, to find my room and slam the door and get into bed until this was over. How had I not noticed his spies? How had he realized all of this so quickly?

"How about this?" Imperator Kormac said. He stood, and stepped forward, leaning against the wall which enclosed us in. A jerk of his chin signaled for me to join him.

I did, resting my elbows on the white wall, watching Galen fight. A powerful kick of his leg, and the last soturion in his Five was down. His silver binding broke, and he ran into the fray in the center of the field.

"You want him safe, yes?" he asked.

"Yes,' I admitted.

"He shouldn't be cast in a major role then. And of course, we cannot have him playing Moriel."

"No. Absolutely not."

"Very well. Galen will not make it to the final round. Nor will he appear in the games on Asherah's Feast Day. So long as you fulfill your promise. Lyriana and Rhyan will be here soon with Imperator Hart. Your task still stands, your mission only on pause while they're unreachable. You still must hunt. Not just vorakh—which we thanked you for earlier."

My stomach twisted.

"You will uncover the truth and bring them to me. You will find a way. The minute they are under the roof of the Palace, I expect to know what I need to take back control."

"It will be done," I said.

He smirked. "A shame. Soturion Galen truly is a great fighter. He could have gone to the end. Too bad he won't."

Then he walked away, and I sank back to my seat on the bench, eyeing Bellamy and Eric from a distance, my heart feeling like it would explode. I was a traitor. A traitor in every way. To everyone I loved, no matter what I did. But worst of all, to myself.

CHAPTER TWENTY-NINE

LYRIANA

I woke the next morning with every map of Numeria, of the Palace, and the Nutavian Katurium racing through my mind. I dreamt of the images I'd studied like I was swallowed into the scrolls themselves. As I prepared for training, I imagined myself walking down the waterways, entering the Palace's throne room, and counting my steps across the field of the arena. It helped that I had a detailed mental picture of the layout, thanks to the vision I'd taken from Meera.

With the nahashim visions Imperator Hart had given to me of Jules, and Ereshya's shard, I felt confident in my knowledge of the Palace. How much space we had, how many people could fit inside the hall. Places to hide and blend into the crowd. And just exactly, what moment I'd need to make my move and take the shard.

Kane wasn't present to run morning exercises. A small miracle. Word had reached him of new akadim patterns being tracked in the west. Most likely sent by Morgana and Aemon.

As I ran in the Glemarian Katurium, I closed my eyes and

saw the arena in Numeria. I went over the maps again and again. As I sat through classes, as I trained with Rhyan, I kept going. I replayed everything in my mind over and over.

And when night came, and we reentered the library, I was ready to mark out our plan. I gave Aiden and Meera their orders. From there, we began focusing on the schedule, and then on the Emperor's guest list—understanding each person's exact rank and where they'd be, how close to Theotis and the shield they might get. We also discussed who would be allies and therefore standing together, as well as who might be enemies, and thus, be standing even closer. Then we cross-referenced that with each guard who'd been paid off by Rhyan's father.

Rhyan sat across from me, his leathers shining under the golden glow of the citrine lights. Our eyes continued to meet every few minutes from our opposite corners of the room. He was hunched over the table, his jaw clenched as he planned his moves with Dario. Every so often he stopped to confer with me, and then I'd move over to them, working on the alternate plan. As we ran into snags, or realized complications, the plans began to shift, and new ideas were thrown in and just as quickly tossed out.

In the end, we had gathered what we needed to know. There were three times that seemed primed for our theft. In the dead of night before the Valabellum, at the changing of the guard; in the morning in the Throne Room, just as the shield was taken down for its presentation; and right before it was paraded outside.

But the rescue of Jules, that had my mind occupied. We'd have to take the shield to Imperator Hart at his specified location. And then we'd have the task of getting Jules safely past the walls. Imperator Hart swore no one would know she was missing at first, but if she was seen by the wrong person, she'd be taken back immediately. And no matter how well we prepared to steal the shield, getting Jules out of Numeria felt completely unpre-dictable. Rhyan would most likely need to use his vorakh immediately. He'd be unable to use it in the Palace with their wards up, but outside it was of the utmost importance that he was ready.

What we didn't have was a way to escape Imperator Hart and Seathorne when it was all over.

My contract was going to be invoked the moment we had Jules. The moment we had the shard I'd be commanded to return to his side. And that in turn would force Meera, and Rhyan to comply as well, if he didn't attempt a last-minute blood oath by then.

And as we delved deeper into our plans, we realized something we should have from the start.

The promised mercenaries weren't there to help us. But to attack and capture us if we made any attempt to escape.

There was no plan for such a thing. I never got a chance to speak to Rhyan in private. Dario was my shadow from sunrise to midnight. Then I was locked into my room every night with the nahashim slipping through the door. The only time Rhyan and I were together, away from Dario, was in the training room. And then we had the snakes for company, hissing and undulating as they watched our every move, their black eyes wide, reporting everything back to Imperator Hart.

The way we had structured things, Dario and Aiden were absolutely integral to our success. And yet, they were exactly what would keep us from being free in the end.

My only hope of getting to Rhyan alone, or getting word to Meera, was to go through Kenna, and I wouldn't see her until the weekend—not until we were dragged to our first series of engagement events in Glemaria. But I was dreading each one. Imperator Hart had made it clear through further messages, that I was not only to continue holding Kane's hand, and kissing his cheek like an idiotic, besotted bride, but we were to dance together at each event at least twice.

Rhyan's eyes met mine from across the room. It was nearly

midnight, our last night of prep before we switched into engagement mode. He was scratching his palm again, the silver of his
ring glinting in the citrine light.

I'd almost forgotten about his betrothed. About Lady
Amalthea.

"You okay?" he mouthed, his one eyebrow raised.

I glanced quickly at Dario, poring over a map, and then at
Aiden, debating a passageway with Meera. "I need to talk to
you," I mouthed back. "Alone."

He nodded, his lips tight. "We'll find a way," he said.

Our guards came, moving us from the room, conducting their
daily search and marching us back through the library towers,
onto each bridge, and back to the lift.

There, Rhyan stepped aside again, the movement quick, as he
spoke in a hushed voice to the librarian. He looked back at me,
his eyes filled with concern, then back to the librarian, who he
thanked before rushing to the lift as it arrived.

I watched him carefully as we went down, a question in my
eyes, one I knew he could read. He sighed and nodded, the most
he could do while being watched. But I understood. He'd fill me
in. When we could actually talk.

I woke Saturday morning to an offensively loud knock on my
door. Throwing off my covers, I stalked across the cold floor and
slung the door open, ready to curse at Dario. But Kenna was
waiting for me instead.

"Your Grace," I gasped. "It is wonderful to see you." And I
meant it.

"As it is you, my lady. Today should be exciting. You'll get
to see more of Glemaria, and in turn they shall get to see more of
you. Something our people are very excited for." She motioned
to a trio of mages behind her. They floated in two racks full of
gowns with their staves.

At a quick glance, they appeared mostly green, cut from satin and velvet, but there were a few white numbers thrown in along-side velvet and furred soturion cloaks. At least I wouldn't freeze.

"Thank you. You may go," Kenna dismissed them. Dario started to move into my room, but she held up her hand. "I don't think so. You'll wait out here."

"I'm under orders, Ken."

"To guard her—out there. Now move aside, Dario. We have dresses to try on."

"You hurt me, Ken," he said, placing his hand over his heart. "Assuming I don't want to try dresses on, too."

Kenna laughed, taking his hand in hers. "I'll make it up to you."

He winked. "I'll be right out here. Not trying on dresses, and trying not to cry."

"The difficulty of your life," Kenna said, gliding into my room.

"You're awfully close," I said, once we were alone. Dario was so different from the standard sort of Glemarian stoicism I'd seen in Rhyan and Aiden. Even in my few interactions with Rhyan's uncle Sean, there was a seriousness to their auras, to the way they stood, that Dario seemed to lack. And yet, he was as harsh and cruel as any other soldier I'd encountered.

Kenna shrugged. "Dario's been one of my best friends for years. And ... well, for a time, we were ... more."

"Dario was your lover?" I had so many questions.

"It was quite a while ago. And you can clearly see, he's just as torn up and heartbroken about it as I am." She pulled a green dress out, and laid it over the chaise.

"How? Why?" I asked.

Kenna glanced around the room. "Something to do. At our rank and stations, our choices can be limited. Sometimes it's nice to just be with someone you at least care about, even if they're not ... exactly what you want." She shrugged. "What about this one?" she asked, her voice loud. "A perfect example of Glemarian green, but it would look lovely with your complexion. I think our people would—"

"It's okay," I said. "You can speak freely. No nahashim."

Relief spread over her face as she walked to me. "You're sure?" Her eyes flicked back and forth across the room, her body still.

"Positive," I said. Though my ears were strained, fully ready to catch the exact moment things changed.

"Good. Now tell me, how are you doing?" she asked urgently, her voice low. "How's Rhyan?"

I shook my head. "I don't know. We never get to really talk. I see him every day, but we're never alone. We never have anything remotely like privacy. No ways to really communicate."

"You need to talk," Kenna said decisively.

I folded my hands together. "I was hoping you could arrange that. We're running out of time and we need to figure out our escape. Or at least, begin to discuss the possibility. But I can't get word to Rhyan or Meera about anything, not even to see how they're feeling without Dario and Aiden seeing."

"You're not meant to. But I'm going to look for any openings I can find, any sort of time slot I can bring you two together. Without the nahashim or your guards seeing."

"It's tricky. I can't disobey any direct orders." Every day, I was sent a note, reminding me to follow his command, to continue doing what I was doing. If there wasn't a note, I'd see him in person. He'd pass me in the hall, greet me, and whisper his commands. I never went more than a full day without orders. And each time they came, I felt that same pull in my blood, the same need to follow.

To obey, no matter how much my mind or body seemed to rebel.

I pulled out a dress, pretending to look at it, but there was nothing in me that gave a damn. I shook my head in exasperation. "If the Imperator thinks I'm trying to meet with Rhyan, he'll tell me directly I can't. And then there'll be nothing else I can do. I'll be compelled to listen."

Kenna tapped her chin. "He's probably anticipating that. What about writing? I could try to deliver messages back and forth between you."

I shook my head. "Too risky. How can I trust they won't be intercepted?"

"You'd have to trust they wouldn't, and ... take every precaution, assuming they do."

I groaned. "I could write to him in High Lumerian, but that seems pointless. It's too easily translated. If only I could speak to him directly—" My eyes widened. "The vadati stones. We could use those, and they'd be easier to hide. Can you get them for me?"

She frowned. "I don't know. It's dangerous, and it would take some time. I know where he's keeping them, but I'd need Devon to be away to gain access."

"Of course." I sighed. "And I'm assuming he's not leaving Seathorne anytime soon? At least not before the Valabellum?"

"No." Kenna grimaced. "He's made sure of that. But you'll have more room to move about this weekend. All eyes will be on you, but everyone will also be drinking. A lot. If I find a window, I'll bring you two together and offer as much cover as I can. In the meantime, you may need to simply tell me what it is you wish for him to know. That may be the only safe option."

I closed my eyes. I wanted him to know that we needed to plot our escape. That I had no intentions of remaining a prisoner here, or as Kane's wife. I wouldn't subject myself to that fate, nor him.

I'd told Rhyan the plan had to change, that we couldn't just run away. But maybe it was time to leave the Empire. But only if we could take Meera and Jules with us. I loved him enough to do it. To sacrifice everything. If we had to. If it came down to it. At least, until it was safe enough to fight our way back.

But that seemed too big a thing to express through Kenna. I needed to talk to him face-to-face, to touch him, to hold him.

"Just let me know as soon as you find a window," I said.

Kenna nodded. "And Meera?"

"Yes, for her, too." I still had to tell her so much. Who Kane was. Who she was. And of course, what it was we were truly stealing.

"Shall we pick out your dresses?" Kenna asked. She'd added several more choices to the chaise.

I stared at the gowns and my body felt suddenly hollow. Kane was back in the fortress. His arrival had been announced the night before. He would be by my side all day. By my side while I was forced to wear what was before me. "I guess I have no choice." I eyed the dresses warily. "He didn't send any armor my way, did he?"

Kenna shook her head. "I don't think you'll get that back. Nor your stave. Not before the Valabellum."

I took a deep breath, nodding in defeat and Kenna went to work, turning me into the perfect Glemarian bride.

Just for the wrong man.

And the wrong God.

A few hours later, after being served a private breakfast in my room, and having several of Kenna's maids arrive to pin back my hair and paint my face, I was flown to our first event. A luncheon at the private mansion of Senator Oryyan, followed by a parade through the City of Harton, the only major city in Glemaria. The Library of Glemaria sat on its edge and loomed over the buildings around us.

I stepped down from the gryphon, surrounded by a series of stone buildings and streets. The sounds of a river rushing nearby added to the chatter. Senator Oryyan's mansion seemed to be made up of more window than wall. Green curtains hung before all of them. Dario led me inside, taking me down what felt like an endless hallway lit by silver lamps. At the end of the hall was a dressing room where I'd wait until I was announced. I stood before a mirror assessing my gown. It was made of satin with a velvet corset threaded with silver. Long flowing green sleeves ran past my wrists, and the skirt puffed out so dramatically at my hips, they looked twice their size.

"Your dress needs to be fixed," Imperator Hart said suddenly. He'd entered the room without any warning, his eyes watching me in the mirror. Slowly, he walked behind me, his eyes roving up and down my body as I realized I'd yet to receive his commands for the day. "You look like you fell off a gryphon."

"Your Highness," I said, turning to curtsey. "I'll be sure to fix it."

"Allow me," he said, reaching for my waist and spinning me around to face the mirror. His front pressed to my back. Before I could catch my balance, his hands lifted, gripping the top of my corset.

I sucked in a breath, my heart beating too quickly. His wrists brushed against the tops of my breasts, his fingers pressing into the boning, as he lifted the corset higher, tugging it violently.

My vision blurred.

"Brockton," I cried. "Please. Please. Don't do this. Don't."

"Sorry, Asherah." He slid his blade down my chest, and the thin material which remained—all that covered me—was shredded in half, leaving me exposed. Naked.

I couldn't breathe. I couldn't breathe.

"She looks beautiful, Your Highness," Dario said, his voice too loud for the room. "Her corset is perfectly placed. You truly have an eye for such things."

Imperator Hart stilled, his hands remained on my dress as he watched me in the mirror, watched my chest heave, watched my breath come in short, labored gasps. His hands slid up to my collarbone, his fingers dancing against my skin as they moved to

my shoulders. He pulled me back against him and whispered in
my ear.

"Be convincing today, little slayer." He kissed my cheek and
it was all I could do not to recoil. "I've received word from
Imperator Kormac concerning your canceled engagement to his
son."

"Have you?" I asked, my voice high, my body far too aware
of every place he touched me. A slimy feeling was starting to run
down my neck.

"He is most displeased." He smiled widely in the mirror.

"As we expected," I said carefully.

"Exactly as we expected. You'll be happy to know he has
renounced his claim on you. But he will take you back, despite
the insult, quite willingly. He said specifically to let him know if
you decided you don't prefer the company of Arkturion Kane in
your bed."

I stared ahead, refusing to meet his eyes.

"I know we've told everyone how chaste and pure you
remain—how untouched by my son you are. But you are free to
test out your betrothed's bed anytime you want. Or mine."

"I'm rather traditional," I said.

"Hmmm. Of course. You remain the model of virtue. In that
case, to keep Kormac from beginning any legal claims, we may
have to move your wedding up."

"Oh?" was all I could manage, but my stomach was twisting
and turning, my mind too able to imagine the horrors Kane
would unleash on me. *Please, please. Not before the Valabellum.
Not before I found a way out.* "Surely, such an event will take
time to plan?"

His eyes narrowed. "Not in a hurry to wed?"

"A girl dreams of this day for years." I forced a smile. "I
would want such an event to be done right. And, I would be
honored if the Emperor attended. I believe you would, too. That
would surely end all other claims."

I watched the Imperator's eyes narrow. "He'll be there," he said.

"That's wonderful. I know his schedule is full and will require careful, advanced planning." My heart pounded. "For now, we still have a few weeks of engagement events to attend. The Valabellum right after. It would have to wait until then."

Imperator Hart smirked. "You'd let it wait forever, wouldn't you?" His breath on my neck was too hot, too close. And somehow still, his aura was too cold. "Do not give Kormac a reason to claim you," he commanded. "Because he still very much wants to get inside your ... country." He tilted his head. "You look upset. This little thing you're doing, the way your pulse is racing, your breath catching—is that worry for Bamaria? Or," he whispered, "is that a parting gift from Brockton? Is it my hands on you? Or is it when I ..." he pushed my corset forward, exposing the top of my breasts, "adjust your clothing?"

I felt faint. Could feel the brush of tears against the back of my eyes, hot and burning, pushing forward. No matter how hard I fought against it, I was so fucking close to crying. But I couldn't. I knew if I started, if I let one tear fall, I'd never stop.

I took a deep breath, my skin crawling, and lifted my chin. "Imperator Kormac will have no reason to claim me—not by any action I take."

"I'm glad to hear it. And to ensure that we keep him away, do remember your part in all of this." He gritted his teeth, his mouth even closer to my ear. "Stop watching my son when you think no one's looking."

A shiver ran down my spine. I nodded.

"And while I have you here," he squeezed my shoulders again, hard at first, and then he was crushing them between his fingers, his bones digging into mine.

I bit back a cry, Dario watching us. He'd taken a sudden step forward. His hand on his sword. His aura blaring with something that felt almost protective. His fingers curled around the hilt, the tip of his starfire steel blade glinting in the fire, and then just as quickly, he let his hands fall to his sides as he stepped back. Dario's eyes moved pointedly beyond us to an old painting of a gryphon.

Imperator Hart squeezed me harder and harder until I winced. Another bruise would form there, right in the spot that had just healed from Kane.

"I'm telling you now," he said. "I have given you everything you need. Warrior training. Access to secret materials—maps, and schedules that only Imperators have ever been allowed to see. And I've given you a team to assist you. There's nothing more you need other than to do as you were told."

I nodded again, my face pale from the pain, beads of sweat forming at the nape of my neck. "You've been most generous, Your Highness."

"It brings me great joy to hear you say that you agree. And that you feel the same, hmmm?"

"Yes."

His eyes assessed me through the mirror. "Then stop fucking around trying to arrange private meetings behind my back."

My breath caught. I'd only mentioned that to Kenna this morning. And I'd checked—I'd double checked the room for nahashim. I'd been sure none were in there. How the fuck had he known? Had Dario overheard and reported it? Another guard? Had Kenna been forced to betray me? Fuck. Fuck!

Either way, I couldn't go to her now. Ally or not, she'd been compromised. And even if I dared risk it, I wouldn't be able to form the words to her. I wouldn't be able to disobey Imperator Hart's direct command. Not without immense pain. The blood contract I'd signed made sure of it.

"The lady is a beauty, Dario. She's finally fit to be seen," Imperator Hart said then, stepping back, his voice now jovial and light. Like he hadn't just threatened the shit out of me. He chuckled and winked at Dario, before stepping out of the room. The door closed, and I stumbled forward.

Dario was by my side in an instant. "Are you all right, Lyriana?" he asked, his hands reaching for me, but not quite touching me. "Fuck." His dark eyes scanned back and forth across my shoulders in the mirror. He let his hands fall, his fingers twitching. "Did he hurt you?" He shook his head. "Of course, he did. I–I can get a mage in here, get some ice magic for your shoulders."

Swallowing, I turned around, staring directly at him.

"You're being nice to me?"

He scoffed. "Don't look so surprised. Wait here."

I wrapped my arms around my chest, shivering with the remnants of fear and Imperator Hart's aura.

But for the first time, I began to see why Rhyan and Dario had been friends. He was more like Rhyan than I'd realized. He had the same protective streak. I'd been so quick to write him off —to distrust him because of the cave incident. Because he'd captured us. But I was slowly beginning to understand that no one became a part of Imperator Hart's inner circle unless the Imperator could guarantee his control over them. The night Dario and Aiden caught us, they might have had no choice but to tie us up and bring us back. And all at once, I felt sympathetic to Dario. But still wary. If he was under orders, under a blood oath or a contract like mine, he'd always betray us in the end. It was entirely possible he'd overheard me and Kenna this morning and had no choice but to report his findings.

He returned a moment later, a mage at his side, her stave glowing with a bluish white light.

"Can she see your shoulders, my lady?" he asked, his voice gentle. "Just your shoulders, nothing else."

Our eyes met and I realized he'd noticed my anxiety. He was more observant than I gave him credit for.

I nodded at the mage. "It's fine."

"Do you need help moving your sleeves?" Dario asked.

"I can do it." I slid the material down to my biceps, wincing as I did so.

Dario nodded for the mage to approach.

"This will feel a bit cold," the mage warned. "But it shouldn't hurt, and will soften any soreness you feel."

I sucked in a breath as the ice pierced my skin. "Dario." I found his gaze, needing it as an anchor as the ice continued to burn. "Thank you."

His eyes softened, but then he turned away, his body language that of someone on guard. "You won't have long before they call for you."

I swallowed roughly, my shoulder beginning to numb.

"Can I ask you a question?"

His eyes remained on me, still soft, but wary.

"Is Aiden—" my throat caught, "Is he as protective of Meera as you are of me?"

"He is." Dario looked toward the door. "Please, don't ask me again. It's time."

I closed my eyes, praying she wasn't suffering. At least, I knew that Dario wouldn't hurt me, even if he couldn't yet be trusted. But at the very least, if I couldn't be at Meera's side, Aiden was. And for the first time since our capture, that seemed a comforting thought.

I lifted my sleeves back over my shoulders with Dario's help and walked out into a dining hall full of Glemarians. Immediately, I was given to Kane, who I couldn't help but stare at and hug, and kiss on his cheek. Thank the Gods, Imperator Hart hadn't asked me for anything more.

Kane gripped my hand, his fingers bruising mine as everyone cheered. I swallowed back the bile in my throat as I continued staring at him, unable to take my eyes off his, even when I knew Rhyan had entered the room. I'd always know. I could feel his aura. Feel his soul. But only in my peripheral vision could I catch a glimpse of him, his hand in Amalthea's, his jaw tight and his emerald eyes blazing on me.

When we'd heard enough congratulations, when he'd emptied enough wine glasses followed by toasts, and after I'd danced with Kane for three whole songs, we were led away to the engagement parade and carried through Harton on litters. I managed through the change in venue to catch sight of Meera, dressed to perfection as a noble. Aiden stood by her side, his hand on his stave, his dark eyes looking every bit as eagle-like as his nose. He was guarding her. Her hazel eyes met mine. And for a brief moment, she smiled, a reassuring one. One that only a sister could read. It said both "I'm okay," and asked if I was. I couldn't smile back though, because I was pulled away.

I stopped paying attention after that. Barely noticed the shouts of congratulations from the crowd. I didn't even flinch when we got back on the gryphon and flew to another town. I didn't move when another set of servants arrived in another back room to freshen my hair and makeup and help me dress in a new gown. Identical to the first, but white.

I didn't feel it when Kane took my hand at the next event. Or when Rhyan entered. I refused to give Imperator Hart any other reason to give me orders, or question me.

I had one goal. Prepare for the Valabellum. Get the shield. Get Jules. And so while I was twirled in circles, while Kane's fingers dug into my hip, or when the scent of Rhyan, of musk and pine and something that felt like home, flew past me, I didn't react. I went over maps in my mind. I mentally reviewed schedules. I did the very thing Rhyan taught me to do when I first started training. I imagined the end. I saw the outcome I wanted.

And I rehearsed it again and again.

Ereshya's shard in my hands.

Jules in my arms.

The two of us with Rhyan, and Meera, escaping Numeria.

Escaping Glemaria. Free.

And before I knew it, the engagement events for the weekend had ended. A snake slid into my bed, a scroll in its mouth.

"Miss me already?" I snarled, swiping the scroll from its jaws.

My lady,

I stared dully at Imperator Hart's now familiar writing.

You've done well. If you can do it again this week, I may allow you to see your sister outside of your busy schedule. As a further precaution, Rhyan will be bound at all future events. His power is only needed for training during the week after all.

Prove your loyalty, and I may give him more freedom. H.H.I.H.

P.S. Make sure your gowns are properly fitted moving forward. You don't want to cause men to have an imagination now, do you?

I threw the scroll into the fire, seething. Everything I'd done, everything I'd bargained for Rhyan. All for him to be fucking bound again.

I realized quickly as the days and then weeks passed inside Seathorne's gates, there was nothing else I could do but follow Imperator Hart's orders.

So, I did. I trained, I ran, I didn't show my power. I kept my eyes away from Rhyan's, avoided his touch when he reached a concerned hand for my shoulder after having heard about my latest "discussion" with his father. I pulled my hand from his in the rare moments we had privacy because I was told to, and watched his face fall as we grew further and further apart. I missed him every night, and during the day, even though I always saw him. It was a unique form of torture, being so close like this.

I took small comforts alone in Rhyan's room. Looking at his old things, reading through his old scrolls to help me fall asleep while smelling the lingering scent of him in his blankets. Until the snakes reported that, too. Rhyan's scent had been meant to torture me. The moment it wasn't, it was gone. While I was in training, I came home to new linens, the scent of pine and musk completely replaced with lemon.

Every day I did as I was commanded. I was a loyal Glemarian subject to the Imperator, a puppet on his strings following through on his every written and verbal request to smile and dance and look besotted and turn my attention from those I loved.

And every night, I focused on our prep in the library. In the mornings, I stood guard at the crack of dawn inside our training room, while Rhyan practiced traveling with Dario in his arms, making sure he was strong enough for whatever came at him in the capital. Rhyan practiced jumping back and forth between our room and Dario's, until he was a sweating mess, sinking onto the mat. But he was getting stronger, lasting through more jumps each time.

When the next set of engagement events arrived, I was dressed again in fancy Glemarian-style gowns and paraded through the different towns and into the private homes of select nobility. By then, my third weekend of events, I was used to being forced to dance with Kane, being forced to feel his hands on my waist, on my back and my shoulders, his rough cheek hair against my lips. At least, that was all I'd had to feel.

And when the weekend came to an end, I was left with another note.

I am not yet convinced of your affections for your betrothed.
Try again.
Convince me.

I crumpled the note, too tired to even take it to the fireplace.

The weather warmed in Glemaria the following week— our final week before the Valabellum. Kenna came by my room more often during those mornings, but I didn't dare speak to her out of turn—I didn't ask about Rhyan. I didn't ask about Meera. I talked to her about dresses, and rings, and wearing a lighter coat without fur that weekend, since we were on the verge of spring.

We'd been flown past the border to Hartavia, to a manor owned by one of Rhyan's relatives on his mother's side. His aunt, Lady Sheera was his mother's sister, and her husband, Rhyan's uncle through marriage was Lord Marcus of Ka Telor, a prominent Ka in the North.

At the start of the ball, we went through the traditional protocol of being announced one by one and presented to the nobles. As guests and members of the Ka ruled by the northern Imperator, we entered the ball last. But I was on edge, focused on finding one man in particular. The Senator from Hartavia. Rhyan's childhood abuser.

The first dance of the night was a group number, a traditional Hartavian dance that involved holding hands in large circles, commonly known as the "Dance of the Laurels." I'd ended up in a circle of all women, holding hands with Kenna, as I anxiously looked over my shoulder for Rhyan. But he was sandwiched between Aiden and Dario. As the circle broke apart, the musical notes playing faster, I linked arms with Kenna. The next part of the dance had us skipping in a circle, twirling around each other. But with Kenna so far along in her pregnancy, we performed more of a walk.

I leaned in toward her, noting the Imperator distractedly dancing with Lady Sheera. Kenna looked radiant, her brown hair shining and thick down her back. She'd traded her traditional green gowns for a flowy yellow dress that looked far more comfortable for her condition.

Talking to Kenna about Rhyan, about escaping, about anything not related to dresses and parties had been taken off the table. But Imperator Hart had never forbidden me from this line of questioning.

"The Senator from Hartavia," I hissed in Kenna's ear.

Her brown eyes widened, searching the room. "Where?" she asked.

I shook my head. The music changed and we released each other's arms, turning to link hands, our circular walk moving counterclockwise now. "No. I don't know what he looks like. Is he here?"

Her brows furrowed, but her walk slowed, her free hand going to her belly as if in preparation for anyone asking her why she wasn't dancing harder. Quietly she scanned the room, her eyes searching through the different couples across the dance floor.

At last, she gave me a satisfied shake of her head, relief clear in her relaxed expression. "No. No sign of him."

I exhaled sharply. "Good." Because if he was here …

The notes changed again, returning to the song's start signaling it was time to remake the laurels. This time the circles were mixed and my hand was seized by Kane. He pulled me into the smaller dance when it came again, while Kenna had found a noble woman I thought I'd seen with her a few times before.

When the song ended, the instruments slowed and Kane dragged me against him.

Bile rose in my throat, but I was suddenly dancing close to him, our bodies pressed together, his hand sliding down the curve of my ass. I leaned into the touch, unable to stop myself, even as tears burned behind my eyes. Even as across the room Rhyan's face paled. If I tried to pull away, my stomach hurt, my blood heated.

Soon, the formal dancing ended, and the Hartavian Arkturion pulled Kane aside for some drinks. The night had disintegrated into something more casual, something I used to see at the clubs in the city, when Jules and I would sneak out. It made my heart pang, missing her, wishing I could simply be in the moment, enjoy the music and the dancing. Things I used to love. And I wasn't the only one affected by the festivities. The soturi on guard even seemed to relax, some lowering their weapons, or abandoning their posts as the wine, mead and beer flowed freely.

As I looked around, I realized there was no sign of Imperator Hart. No sign of Kenna. And no nahashim. Dario was even distracted, momentarily talking to a mage he'd danced with earlier. Meera was dancing, still rather formally, with Aiden. And Rhyan? He was dancing with Amalthea.

I saw my opening. I rushed from the room down to a spare hall, my chest heaving. I didn't care if I was punished. I didn't care if disobeying the Imperator's commands caused me physical pain. My stomach lurched the second I stepped foot outside, there was a sharp sting shooting through my guts, and out to my arms. But I couldn't take another second back there—couldn't stand to see Rhyan with someone else. Couldn't stand to feel my own skin knowing it had been touched by Kane's disgusting hands all night. Finally, the emotional and psychological pain of it all hurt worse than Imperator Hart's commands.

Footsteps sounded down the hall, coming closer and closer. I ran without thinking, dashing behind a corner, desperately trying to control my breathing, to silence my emotions, and pull back my aura. The person kept coming, walking faster. From the echo of their gait, I knew they were wearing soturion boots. Probably Dario, realizing I'd left. But I wasn't ready to face him, to face anyone. I needed a moment to be alone, to fall apart. To breathe. I turned around, moving deeper into the corner I'd found, leaning against the wall.

Then all at once, pine and musk filled my senses.

"Lyr? I saw you run out. You okay?"

I squeezed my eyes shut, my stomach twisting. "You shouldn't be here. Your father—"

"You think I fucking care? Tell me. What's wrong?"

I turned, coming face to face with Rhyan. And despite all of my orders, despite the pain reverberating inside of me, I didn't think. I stepped forward, wrapping him in my arms.

He made a muffled noise of surprise, his body still. I pressed my fingers into his back, feeling the sturdy muscles, savoring the feel of this part of him I'd been denied. My hands slid up to his shoulders, pulling him closer. We were both still, just breathing, just holding each other after being denied doing so for weeks.

And then, without warning, something was unleashed. With a growl low in his throat, his hips pressed against mine, pushing me back into the wall. He hardened against me. A gasp escaped my lips. My chest began to heave, my breaths coming short. After so much deprivation, being unable to talk to him, to look at him, to feel him like this, all of him against me, it was almost too much.

Too dangerous.

His father was down the hall. Arkturion Kane. Lady Amalthea.

Rhyan cupped the nape of my neck, as his other hand slid down my back. It was such an innocent touch, and still I moaned, wanting to cry at how starved and untouched I'd been by him. His eyes flashed, desperate, and filled with hunger. His hand moved even lower, squeezing my waist, and hip, until his palm settled against my ass, pulling me closer, lifting me toward him.

"What are we doing?" I asked.

"I don't know. I don't fucking know." He rolled his hips, pushing against me. "But I can't stop."

I was already seeking out his length, trying to pull him closer even as my stomach twisted, even as I cried out, "We have to. We have to stop."

Rhyan hissed through his teeth practically panting. But he stilled at once, his neck red. "Did Kane do anything to you?"

I closed my eyes, squeezing his arms, trying to pull him closer. "Nothing you didn't see. I just—" I winced. "I couldn't take it anymore. I needed to get away. Just for a minute."

"Partner," he breathed against my neck, his voice shaking with emotion.

The backs of my eyes burned. Gods. I couldn't remember the last time he'd called me that.

His grip on me tightened then, possessive, claiming. "I fucking miss you," he growled. I could feel his breath hot against my skin, leaving shivers low in my belly as he grazed his nose against my jaw, finding the crook of my shoulder on my other side. He pulled me closer, inhaling again.

"Rhyan," I panted. "I miss you, too. So fucking much."

His forehead pressed against mine, his lips just inches from my own. I could smell the honey of the mead he'd drunk on his breath. His eyes were screwed shut as he kissed the corner of my mouth.

"You say the word, Lyr, you give the command, the order, and I'll take you from here. I'll take you away. Nothing has changed. I'm still sworn to protect you, to follow you."

My lips trembled, every part of me wanting to melt into his touch, to say yes, to scream it. "You know we can't," I said, blinking back tears. "Not yet. I'm sorry."

"I know," he said sadly, and kissed my forehead. "Fuck."

"Rhyan?"

"It's okay, Lyr. It's okay. But I had to say it. Had to ask. At least, once more."

My eyes watered. "I hate this," I cried. "I hate not talking to you. Not holding you."

"I know." He sucked in a shaky breath, and smoothed my hair behind my ear, his fingers tracing the curve of my lobe. "I feel like … like I lost you, even though you're right in front of me."

I shuddered, hating to know he felt that way.

His jaw worked as he composed himself. "We'll find a way," he said. "We leave in a day for the capital. It's almost over. Then we'll figure it out. We'll find our way back to each other."

Another set of footsteps echoed in the hall and Rhyan pulled back. I felt the loss of his touch everywhere, like I'd been stripped of my clothes and left out in the cold.

"Promise?" I asked, wrapping my arms around myself.

He lifted the cloak of his soturion hood over his head, his face vanishing into the darkness as he stepped into the shadows. A torch flickered overhead, suddenly weakening. It was my aura —my emotions causing it to blink out.

"I swear," he said. Then he was gone.

CHAPTER THIRTY

RHYAN

I laid in my bed back at Seathorne—my last night here. My last night here ever, if I got my way. I'd been unable to sleep after reviewing all the scrolls I'd borrowed from the library. They filled what space remained on the blankets beside me. I'd been poring over them, over everything I could find, everything the librarian had sent me, again and again. I'd been at it for weeks, since the night of our first meeting. I'd read over every text on forbidden magic, on ancient magic, on God magic. And I couldn't find anything that remotely described what Mercurial had told me. I still for the life of me didn't understand what Asherah and Auriel had done to weaken Shiviel. To weaken him to the point that he was altered even now as Kane.

More importantly, I still didn't understand how that had affected Asherah. How it was tied into *Rakashonim*. And how I was going to help Lyr now. Every day, I grew more worried. The closer we got to the Valabellum, the more likely she was to call on it again. If we ran into trouble, if we couldn't get to Jules, or if one of us were hurt, nothing would stop her. I knew that too well.

I'd figured out how to protect her here from my father. I couldn't stop Kane from touching her, from their dances, from the bruises I knew he left on her arms and shoulders, but the threat I'd made had been enough to keep it contained to that. Contained to the dance floor of our Godsdamned engagement balls. It was bad enough as it was, but I knew all too well, it could have been so much worse.

But once we were in Numeria, I had no idea how to keep her safe. Especially from herself.

"Fuck." I pushed the scrolls off the bed, and stood, moving to the window. It was the middle of the night, the sky black, a small drizzle of rain hitting the glass. It was officially too warm for snow.

I traced a raindrop with my finger down the pane, and stared through the window.

Growing up in the bedroom Lyr occupied now, I could see the endless horizon of mountains. But from this new room I'd been shoved into, I had a view of the edge of Gryphon's Mount. Of the white seraphim. And unlike my old room, with its windows that opened to a drop down the mountain, this one was above a small patch of land. Land leading to the statue. To Asherah's tomb. The tomb that had haunted my dreams since we opened it.

This was my last night near it—my last night to see it again. And if it stirred memories for me when I went to it that night with Lyriana, maybe it would do it again, maybe I could learn what I needed to help Lyr. To save her.

My fingers itched. My whole fucking body did. I was bound. But ... I wasn't that far from the landing. I could jump. Peeking down, I mentally calculated the distance. My legs still worked fine. I could do it. I didn't need my vorakh.

Gripping the bottom of the window, I pulled, and with a grunt, it slowly began to lift, leaving behind a creaking sound loud enough to reach the City of Harton.

I froze, listening for any signs of movement in the hall. If my night escort didn't hear that, it was a fucking miracle. I stilled for another moment, my ears perked, but the only sound now came from the rain and the faint squawking of the gryphons on patrol.

Staying by the window, cold mist blew against my face. But when no one barged through my door, and no alarms sounded, I decided to make my move. I slipped on my boots. Then I wrapped my soturion cloak around my shoulders, folding the excess material around my head as I fashioned a hood. A regular belt held the cloak in place.

Then I crawled up onto the sill, swung my legs through, took a deep breath, and jumped. The rain hit my face, pouring harder as I stood up from the landing, my legs wobbling from the impact. There were no torches on the mountain's edge tonight. And no soturi standing guard.

Now that the indigo shard had been removed, and he'd taken back the key, I guessed my father felt it was of little importance to guard.

But I could see its outline clearly. See the white stone shining in the moonlight, see the rain rolling off its sculpted feathers.

My chest tightened, my heart pounding with each step I took, a reminder that she was there, that I'd left her there. And if I didn't do something now, we'd be doing this again.

Thunder rumbled, lightning striking in the distance. For a moment, the white seraphim glowed, its wings appearing to lift and flutter. Just like in my dreams. My nightmares.

And then she stilled as I slid through the mud, coming to stand before her. The backs of my eyes burned, my chest heavy.

The rain pattered down and I took a deep breath, reaching out a hand, my palm sliding across her stone beak. Nothing happened. I closed my eyes, pressing my forehead against the stone. My heart began to pound, my dreams, my memories suddenly fresh in my head. Carrying Asherah up the mountain.

Building the tomb. Sealing it shut. Seeing Mercurial in his falcon head sneaking up on me.

The grief, the sorrow piercing my soul.

A gust of wind blew.

Rakame.

Asherah's voice. Just as it had been in my memories. In my dreams.

I stared into the lifeless eyes of the seraphim. My knees gave out.

"Shiviel," I screamed. "You betrayer."

"You should have known," he said, his eyes darkening. "I betrayed Moriel. Betrayed my God, my Arkturion. My king. Why would I afford you any less courtesy? You, who put us here. You, who could not keep your damn hands to yourself. You, who caused the Council to betray and forsake us."

I gritted my teeth, staring past him. The indigo shard— Moriel's shard—lay in the temple ruins where we fought. It was just out of reach behind Shiviel. And though he didn't touch it, it gave him the edge over me. Made it impossible to fight back. Not that it kept me from trying. Not that anything would keep me from fighting for her, fighting to protect her.

"You have taken the indigo now. But for how long can you hold it against his armies? He can still defeat you," I spat. "He has the other shards."

"He does not have all of them," Shiviel roared. "He does not have mine!"

My hands shook as I tried to hold onto my sword, as I prayed to anyone who would still listen to help me keep up my strength. I wanted to call on kashonim. To call on that thread that linked Asherah's mortal body to mine. That linked her power. Her strength. Her life.

But I wouldn't risk it. I wouldn't risk her. If I died here—died so she could live—I could accept that. I would embrace it.

Still, I struggled. My hands had been burned again. I bore the scars across my flesh from holding the Valalumir in my hands. Of the fires that ravaged my skin when I fell, a thief grasping pure light. Shiviel had delighted in my torture, in burning anew the hands that had once touched Asherah, that had touched a Goddess. The hands that caused us all to fall. Only by the grace of the green shard, my own crystal, did I heal, did I survive at all.

But I was weakening. I didn't have much time left.

"We can take him down," I said again, more as a distraction than anything else. "We could do it. Together."

Shiviel laughed. "You cannot lie to me."

I raged forward, my sword cleaving the air. Cleaving through the brutalizing energy of his aura. But Shiviel easily sidestepped the blow, his blade piercing forward.

I sidestepped, barely escaping his blow. He clucked his tongue, turning the hilt in his hand, the steel gleaming in the fires that surrounded us.

"Too slow, Auriel. Always too slow," he growled. "Are you prepared to fall again? When I'm through with you, you're not going back to Heaven. I'm sending you to hell."

"You forsworn bastard," I groaned. "I'll see you there first."

Regripping my blade, I fought past the way it slipped through my sweaty hands. I could do this. I had to do this. I used all I had left to straighten my body. To stand tall. Then my eyes widened at the sight I wasn't sure I'd see again. Asherah watched from behind a stone column, her red hair gleaming in the torchlight. Her eyes lit with her own fire, her stave drawn.

She'd come. She'd found me.

Her eyes scanned the room, and then she nodded. The blue light of her magic sparked forth, followed by a glow of red. Asherah's red, the light of the Valalumir she still possessed.

Shiviel's eyes widened, his power momentarily weakened.

Asherah rushed forward with a war cry, her stave replaced by a sword gleaming with starfire that she lifted over her head.

"Now!" she yelled, giving the command I'd been waiting for.

I readjusted my fingers along the hilt, my grip finally tight enough, as the fires spread to my sword. Our eyes met, and together, Asherah and I plunged our blades down through Shiviel's body, cutting through his armor, slicing him in half.

Light exploded in the ruins, blinding me.

My body was flung backwards and Asherah screamed in agony, her cries like a knife in my heart.

I was about to hit the ground and then, something caught me. Stopped my fall.

I gasped, rolling over onto the temple floor, not even bothering to look as I crawled to my knees. Asherah. I needed to find Asherah.

She lay on her back, her arms outstretched, her eyes closed, and her chest plate askew. Her sword lay beside her, just beyond her fingertips.

"Asherah," I roared. "Asherah!" I crawled forward, my knees, my hands, everything in agony. But I wouldn't stop until I reached her side, until I pulled her against me, holding her, hugging her. "Asherah! Wake up. Wake up!" I searched for her pulse, the beating of her heart.

She coughed, her eyes slowly opening as she blinked up at me. "Auriel," she said, her voice weak.

I stroked the side of her face, pushing her flaming red locks from her forehead. "I'm here. I'm right here. You saved me. Again."

"Rakame." Her eyes welled with tears. "Always. I'll always save you."

"And I you," I said, my voice breaking. "Mekara. Always."

"Did we do it?" she asked, her hand brushing against my face. I closed my eyes, relishing the feeling of her, and her touch.

I'd missed that—missed her.

But there'd be time for that later. Fires crackled around us, and a strange aura was filling the temple. An uneasiness wrapped around me, a force of wild magic, all at once ancient and new. Gingerly, we sat up, still holding onto each other, assuring still that the other was all right.

Looking ahead, Asherah gasped, taking my hand. And then I saw it.

What we'd done to Shiviel.

He lay on the ground where we'd attacked him, unconscious. His body was whole, but diminished. He was smaller than he'd just been, as if the sword had taken inches from his height. His eyes opened slowly, blinking in horror. They were still yellow. But the fires inside them had vanished. The light that had shone from his skin, from his soul, the markings of a Guardian, of a God, the feel of his celestial aura were gone. He looked ... human. Mortal. Weak.

On the other side of the ruins was another body. Small. That of a young child. This was the source of the unfamiliar energy I'd felt. It was growing stronger, filling the temple, replacing that which was gone. Shiviel's celestial aura had vanished. But the energy that made him who he was—the part of him that I'd known for centuries, that contained his essence and personality, that still existed.

Asherah let go of my hand, and crawled forward, moving slowly, gingerly toward the child. And as I turned my attention to them, I could feel that this body was both Shiviel and not-Shiviel. My old friend, my brother, and fellow Guardian—the God I'd lost in this war, almost felt like they'd returned. And somehow, despite the history I could sense, the child's aura felt as if it had just been born.

I suppose it had. It was a piece of Shiviel's soul that now lived.

Naked and shivering, the child quickly wrapped itself in a discarded blanket, pulling it tightly around their shoulders.

I stared at the cherubic face, the large brown eyes. The child was innocent, so young it was impossible to see if they were a boy or a girl. My stomach turned with guilt. We hadn't known this would be the result. That an innocent would come from our magic. But we'd had to do it—Shiviel had to be stopped, weakened.

The child cried out, then shook their head in disbelief. "I ... I can feel it. My death. My birth. All at once." Their breath came in short, panicked gasps. "It's so much."

"We had no choice," I whispered.

"It must feel so confusing" Asherah said gently. "But you're going to be all right. I swear. You don't have to be alone in this. I know the role I played. And I'm sorry for it."

A tear rolled down the child's cheek as they stared at their feet, poking out from the blanket. Their hands opened and closed in their lap. Eyes widening, they lifted their arms, looking at their skin. Almost pink in its newness. Unscarred, unblemished. Perfect.

"Are you hurt?" Asherah asked. "We can't stay here. But we'll take you with us. Protect you. Can you walk?"

The brown of the child's eyes deepened before their eyebrows lifted into something that felt like surprise, but quickly devolved into anger. They pulled the edges of their blankets tighter around their small body, their hair falling in brown curls around their shoulders. "You said you had no choice. But what is it that you have done? What am I?"

Asherah held my gaze, her eyes watering, before she answered. "You were part of the God known as Shiviel, Guardian of the Yellow Ray. Now you're not. Now you're new."

"New?" they asked, their voice filling with horror. "I'm not new. I can feel it. I'm ancient. I always was. I can feel where you cut ... where you cut me apart. I remember. Remember too much." Again they shook their head. "I can't be new. I've been here for so long. If I were new, I wouldn't have died. I wouldn't have felt it. My death." Their chest heaved, and I began to fully regret what we'd done. Had the price of weakening Shiviel been

worth this? But if we hadn't, he would have destroyed us all. And after his betrayal of Moriel, his power was too great, too uncontained, too wild. Too dangerous.

"You're right," I said. "You are ancient. We were brothers once. We protected each other. And I swear I will protect you now. I will amend this. You don't have to be afraid."

"Why should I believe you?" They spat, and for a moment, their brown eyes fell on Shiviel's body. "I sense memories. Of another world. Another plane of existence. Of light. A light that did not burn." The child shook their head. "But I am not Shiviel. Not anymore. I am ... other." They stared at their hands, before looking up at Asherah. Their eyes flashed with a glowing, yellow light. "What you did, I don't remember. But I know this much. You're unforgiven. You won't survive."

A light flashed. Asherah screamed beside me. Her body glowed, alight with gold, and red. Until she was the flame. She was the fire.

And I was losing her.

I sputtered, coming to, my mouth filled with rain water, my entire body drenched and freezing. The sun was rising, and I turned over on my side, groaning. Fuck. I'd fallen asleep, I'd spent the entire night out here, sleeping beside the seraphim. In the distance, the clock tower began to yell, alerting me to the late hour. Gryphons soared overhead, their wings like dark shadows in the faint morning sun, and in the mountains, lightning struck.

I grunted, attempting to sit up as thunder rumbled and a fresh bout of rain fell in chilled droplets around me. I had to get inside, finish getting ready. We were leaving for Numeria. But I could barely move. My entire body was stiff from the cold and rain. I needed to find paper, to write this down, to remember. Because finally, finally, I'd remembered something else, something new. Another piece of the puzzle.

Shiviel's soul had been split in half. That was why he was weakened. The reason why Kane had no vorakh. Somewhere out there, there was an eighth Guardian. A part of Shiviel who had no idea how they were connected to all of this. An eighth Guardian who could potentially power Kane again— if they were united.

"Pray tell, *Lord* Rhyan, what exactly you are doing outside your room, sleeping out here with the seraphim," my father's voice called from behind me. "Tell me. Now!"

I turned around too late. My father had marched out onto the mount, his personal escort behind him. I was surrounded.

CHAPTER THIRTY-ONE

RHYAN

The wind howled at that moment, the sound almost violent. Rain was pouring down, sinking into my already soaked clothes. All around me, the soturi making up my father's personal escort stilled, their heads turned toward me, their hands reaching for their weapons. I recognized the bastards. Especially the ones who'd been present for my mother's death, for her murder.

"I give you one inch," my father said, "One! And you take a fucking mile."

My teeth chattered, every part of me shivering, and sore. The scent of damp earth filling my nostrils. "A mile? I'm not even off the grounds of Seathorne," I seethed. "What more do you want? I'm here aren't I? I didn't run!"

He stalked closer, reaching for my chin, squeezing it between his fingers as he wrinkled his nose in disgust. "You smell like gryphon-shit."

"Well, at least I'm consistent, Your Highness," I gritted through my teeth. I stepped back from his hold, needing far too much energy to do so. "Now if you give me leave, I'll return to my room and prepare for our journey."

"No," he drawled. "Not yet."

"For fuck's sake," I said. "I'm bound. I'm here. What more do you want from me?"

My father's chin twitched, and he stroked the edge of his beard, before pulling out his sword. I tensed. But he didn't point it at me. He turned it in his hand, stroking the red jewel embedded in the hilt. The key. My key. Auriel's key.

He shook his head, clicking his tongue again. "I don't think you're in any position to act as though you've done all you can. Not while you're doing the absolute least to even pretend you like Amalthea."

My palm itched. But I would not scratch it. I would not move. He had control for this month. I would honor Lyr's agreement, do what she commanded of me until the Valabellum—but not a second longer. I was going to find a way to get us out. Get her away from him.

"What does it matter to you anyway? Your people don't care or notice the way I look at her. All they see is a man about to be wed. They don't notice anything else." I made sure of it. And it had been easy. Turning off my emotions. Being bound, my aura was already gone.

"You are not just a man. You are my son, a lord of Ka Hart! And to this day, you remain an ungrateful, ignorant wretch."

My lips pulled back, baring my teeth. "Remind me again of what exactly I'm to be grateful for? Huh? My mother? My new stepmother? Your *careful* treatment of me all these years?"

"You do realize that I am the one thing standing between you and a permanent position as a chayatim in the Palace. Or worse? You think I didn't keep your mother safe from being enslaved? You think I haven't kept you off the Emperor's radar all these years!"

I wanted to choke him. He'd saved me from nothing. And what he did was not for my sake, but for his. Always, always for his. I could fill a scroll with all the things he'd failed to protect me from. The Senator from Hartavia's advances. The akadim attacks we'd endured. Watching my mother die at his hands. Losing all of my friends. The scar on my face. The first time my heart broke.

"Never enough. None of it is enough for you," he sneered. "What more can I do to knock some sense into your thickheaded skull? Maybe I should stop trying to help. Maybe I should hand you off to the Emperor myself. Wouldn't that be a memorable Valabellum? Watching him strip you of all you are." His eyes narrowed.

"You wouldn't dare," I said. "You know what I am, and we both know what you're trying to do here." My hands clenched into fists. "Enough of this. I'm going inside." I rose to my feet, and stalked toward him. "We both know you won't hand a God over to your enemies."

"A God?" He scoffed. "You're no God now. A God wouldn't be researching endlessly in the library."

My heart was pounding, still thinking of what I'd done to Shiviel. Of the child created from breaking his soul. The eighth Guardian. Kane was less now, weakened. But weren't we all in some way? I'd felt Auriel that day in Ha'Lyrotz, when I made my threat, swore my oath to protect Lyr. But my father always knew too much. And some old worry began to niggle the back of my mind.

And yet, the memories were too strong, the link unweakened even now. Wasn't the fact that he hadn't escalated his treatment of Lyr to something more horrid proof of my power?

I glared. "Research? I don't know what you're talking about."

He tilted his head. "Do you really think I don't know about every single fucking scroll that was pulled for you?"

"I would think an Imperator has more important things to worry about than one soturion's reading habits."

"I know it's related to her. You wouldn't be out here," he pointed to the seraphim, "otherwise."

"I'm brushing up on my history." I shrugged. "Seeing as how I was part of it."

He stepped closer, and without warning, slapped me with such force that I sank to my knees. My hands clenched, but I willed myself still. He couldn't hurt me. Not if he wanted me to steal the shield, to bring him Ereshya's shard. I needed to be in top physical condition, and he knew it. But I couldn't underestimate him either. Just as often as he was ten steps ahead, he'd let his anger get the best of him. His aura was pulled back, his face dangerously neutral. Gods. It was still impossible, even after all these years, to know which version of my father I faced.

"Let's try this again," he said. "And think carefully now before you answer. I have your girlfriend's contract signed in blood. Do you get that? She does what I want. When I want. When I tell her to dance with Kane, she does. And when I tell her to look like she's in love, to smile and hold hands and kiss his cheek, she does. And you're lucky that's all I've asked. I could have just as easily let him fuck her. I could have fucked her myself. But I didn't. Now you tell me what you're up to, or I may not be so nice in the capital where it truly counts." His eyebrows narrowed to a V. "You understand that all I have to say to her is 'get into his bed,' and she'll comply. I can tell her to open her legs for him, again and again, and she'll do it with a whore's smile. I can tell her to moan for him, and I can tell her to lay there while you watch."

My fist was flying before I could stop it. But my father dodged. All at once, his soturi moved forward, but he signaled for them to remain still and resume their posts.

"Do you know what the punishment is for striking your Imperator?"

"Do you remember what I said in the dungeons?" I gritted.

My eyes glanced side to side, noting his voice had lowered. His men stood at the edge of the mount, offering privacy. So, he didn't want them to hear, but still felt the need to make a show of his strength to me.

His lips curled. "Don't hurt Lyriana? Was that it?"

"I meant what I said. You touch her, you die. And not just once." And with my words, I could feel that same fire, that same conviction that overpowered me in the cell.

"I'll take my chances." He stepped forward, reaching for my throat before I could react. Then his finger was tracing my scar, his nail scratching from my forehead to my cheek, pressing in just enough to hurt but not puncture my skin.

I winced, despite myself.

"You'd do well to be more convincing, Rhyan. You look like you hate Amalthea." He glared.

"I do."

His eyes narrowed. "You forget that by looking besotted with your betrothed you protect Lyriana, too. You still have to convince everyone in the Godsdamned Empire you weren't lovers—because that crime can still have you both stripped and killed."

"I'm aware," I said.

"Then let's not have a repeat in the Palace of what you did the other night. Don't think for a second I didn't know where you went off to at your aunt and uncle's. Or who you sought in the dark of the corridors."

"Fine. You caught me. Can I go now?"

"You still didn't answer my question." His chin twitched. "What were you researching?" He reached into his pocket, and a small black nahashim slithered out. "Tell me the easy way."

My throat went dry, and I gave up. He'd do it. And it seemed pointless to fight. He knew too much already. Knew I was Auriel, knew Lyr was Asherah, and Kane was Shiviel. "I've been researching *Rakashonim*."

The last thing I expected was for my father to laugh. He tipped his head back, and clutched his stomach. Even his guard seemed startled by the sudden shift in his mood.

"*Rakashonim?*" he chuckled. The sound was cruel.

I shook my head, completely unsettled. "You know what it is?"

His face was nothing but pure derision. "If you were paying attention, you'd remember I told you about it years ago. She can call on it—I've seen her do so myself. Luckily for me and for you, she's too weak to use it properly. Because when she does muster her full strength, she will do so with such destructive consequences, you won't wish to be alive."

I shivered. "What about her? Can it hurt her?"

"What do you think? She's in more danger from that than from anyone else in this world." His eyes twinkled. "I'm almost tempted to see what she can do."

My gut roiled. "Is that why you let me do my research?" I asked. I knew I'd been taking a risk with the scrolls. I was aware he knew I'd been reading unsanctioned scrolls, aware he could shut down the operation at any moment, and that he'd find a way to punish me when he did so. And yet, for weeks he hadn't.

"The only thing that has ever moved you," he said, "the only thing that ever unleashed an ounce of submission, or duty, or intelligence into your Godsdamned mind, is the idea of her in danger. Yes, I let you do your little research, expecting you to come to the correct conclusion. She cannot be allowed to use that power."

In the distance I saw a gryphon approaching, a carriage on his back—the one I knew my father would ride on to Numeria.

"Now," he said, "you know what to do today when we arrive —when we appear before the Emperor and his sniveling nephew. You do your Godsdamned duty. Convincingly."

I didn't see the dagger until the hilt punched me in the stomach. Right where I'd been stabbed. I sank to my knees, coughing, and gasping for air.

"I might not hand over the power of a God to my enemies," he snarled, forcing my head up. "But there are ways to weaken you still. To be done with you without giving up my advantage." Then he shoved me down, my face hitting the mud. I watched as my father and his men retreated, leaving me alone in the rain.

CHAPTER THIRTY-TWO

LYRIANA

We weren't leaving for another hour to begin our journey to Numeria, but I was too anxious to sit idly and wait. By the late afternoon we'd be in the capital, in the Emperor's Palace.

I'd be in the same place as Jules.

I paced back and forth across the room, letting the remaining embers in the fireplace die out. Rain pattered against the windows. Outside, a gryphon roared in agitation. There was a sudden, sharp knock on the door.

"Come in," I called, not bothering to ask who it was. Dario was almost always the one at my door, standing guard, or announcing guests.

My lock unclicked, and the door creaked open. A few seconds passed, filled with silence. I stepped forward, expecting to see the soturion's figure come into view, but the doorway remained eerily empty.

"Dario?"

The door slammed shut, and my skin turned ice cold.

The fire burned out as every light in my room and outside

vanished, leaving me shrouded in complete darkness. A single golden Valalumir star floated above me, spinning in a slow circle. Then there were two, then three, until the entire ceiling filled with stars.

"Mercurial," I breathed. I took a step back, turning in a circle. "Mercurial, show yourself."

His bell-like laugh cut through the darkness until the stars blew out, one by one, each vanishing with a pop. "So very demanding, my remembered Goddess," he purred.

"Demanding?" I seethed. "I am demanding? How about the demands you've made of me? Or the fact that you've vanished for a month, offering no guidance on how to move forward."

"No guidance?" he asked. "No guidance!" The fireplace filled with crackling flames, and Mercurial's body appeared, lounging on the chaise, his long blue legs crossed at the ankle. His feet were clad in golden sandals that laced to his knees, and the dark whorls across his skin shimmered around the diamond in each center. "I spoke to your remade lord. I told him to leave. But he didn't listen now, did he?" He inspected his fingernails, and blew across them. Suddenly, they were painted with a gleaming metallic blue, one several shades darker than his current skin color.

"An order to leave here isn't guidance. And you didn't speak to me. The one you made a deal with! The one with a Gods-damned light in her heart!" I pressed my hand to my chest.

The Afeya sat up, his eyebrows narrowed. "Yes, well you've been a little difficult to get into contact with lately."

"I thought Afeya could do anything."

He tapped his feet against the carpet beneath him and leaned forward, gesturing around the room. "Believe it or not, I couldn't do this. So, I did the next best thing. I talked to the previously not-Lord. And I warned him. Much good as it did."

"But you're here now?" I shook my head.

"Yes, well I could get here now. The nearness of the big event means Imperator Hart has the potential to make mistakes. He's already made one. Your wards are down."

"Wards can keep an Afeya out?" I said in disbelief. I'd had wards placed on my soturion apartment that he always walked through. But I quietly pocketed that one detail. That Imperator Hart was making mistakes. That meant he was nervous. It also meant he was more dangerous.

"He is nervous," Mercurial confirmed. "He should be. As far as wards keeping me out, that depends on their structure." The Afeya stood up, his hands in front of him, his fingers stretched. "It's like a web, you see." He turned his wrists. "Lots of conflicting contracts and bargains. Coming to you sooner was a conflict of contract. And I don't engage in those. The First Messenger of Her Royal Highness, Queen Ishtara of the Star Court, High Lady of the Night Lands, never breaks a contract. Ever."

"Isn't that how you came to exist in the first place? Breaking an oath?" My stomach turned, uneasy with him here. And even more uneasy with what he was insinuating. Because after all we'd been through, all of our interactions, he still scared me. Still made me uneasy. But not as uneasy as I felt about the ability of my enemies to get in his way or overpower him. It was only months ago that Aemon trapped him in the Allurian Pass.

But I couldn't tell if it was his own Afeyan Queen with the conflicting contract, or Imperator Hart. Both possibilities left me with a sense of dread.

"You know," he said, his hips undulating as he walked toward me, "the Afeya don't take too kindly to the Lumerians that forced them into such choices, reminding them of such. Nor do they bargain with those entering into other deals. Deals that derail their initial agreements. Especially when those deals are contracts signed by blood."

"Considering you have so many plans for me, you could have helped us to avoid this mess."

"Helped?" He smirked, and held out a hand. A silver comb materialized and he began to slide its teeth through his long black locks. "We've known each other for some time now. You should know as well as anyone, I don't simply *help*."

"Oh, trust me. I know that all too well. When I've needed you these past few months, you were nowhere."

"For most of that time, I was a prisoner, trapped by Moriel."

"You know about Ereshya's shard," I said.

Twirling his hair around the comb, he twisted the section into a tight coil. "I'm aware of its existence, and location, yes."

"Then you know I entered this deal to keep it from him. And her."

"Ah. Yes. Keep the shard away from two evil people. By handing it over to two other, *different* evil people." He clapped. "Bravo. Wonderful plan. Except ..." The comb vanished. The ceiling darkened and filled again with glittering stars. "I need you to claim the red shard. The one that actually gives you your power. The one that will not be complete until it's in your hands. The one that's missing part of its light because it's inside you, beating and pulsing and waiting for more. Waiting for you."

"You had your chance, Mercurial." I threw my hands up. "You were freed. You came and saw us. You could have said something. Told us what we needed to do," my voice rose, my anger growing. "You could have given us the information we needed to know over a month ago. Done something so we could have avoided capture, so we could do what you wanted. You knew the Imperator was looking for us. Knew he was close."

"Knew?" Mercurial asked, his voice dangerously low. "Knew." His eyes narrowed into slits, his neck stretching side to side, undulating like a snake.

There was a hiss in the corner of the room, an actual nahashim, sneaking out to spy.

Mercurial didn't break eye contact with me as his arm shot out, his finger pointing at the snake. There was a flash of light, and a scream.

I turned to see the nahashim's eyes were sealed shut. Its body stood tall, shaking, trembling as it made a pathetic sound, fighting against its sudden blindness.

I sucked in a breath, and turned back to the Afeya.

"Do not insult me," Mercurial said, "by suggesting what I do, or do not know. I know everything. Everything! And despite what a burden it is, it doesn't mean I get to share it all with you." He stepped forward, and I took a step back. "Do you think it is my job to hold your hand and lay out every fucking step for you to accomplish what must be done? I have given more to you than anyone I've ever bargained with. And you—you, my lady, my remembered Goddess, you have gotten the most off-track of them all."

My heart was pounding too quickly, sweat beaded on my palms. "Fine," I said, my voice shaking. "I'm the worst you've ever dealt with. What do I do now?"

"Oh no, no, no," he sang, pointing a finger to the ceiling. "That's a question. And I'm afraid you've run out of favors to offer me in exchange for answers. Especially since you are nowhere near completing the one thing I asked you to do. Typical of the most frustrating Lumerian I've ever dealt with. If you had stayed put in Bamaria, if you had not been so easily deceived, and waited for my directions, you would be a Goddess by now. You would be powerful enough to draw on the link you share with Asherah without it killing you. Without destruction. There'd be no question of Moriel, or Ereshya or even Gods-damned Shiviel getting their hands on a shard. You'd have your precious Jules in your arms."

"And where would my sisters be? Maybe I couldn't save Morgana ... but Meera? She'd be under Moriel's compulsion by now. And let's not forget that you're lucky I did show up in the

Allurian Pass when I did." My voice shook with fear. But I had to remember, he needed me. He needed my power. I had something he wanted. I'd done what he couldn't. I'd found the first Valalumir shard in centuries, and I'd helped free him.

Mercurial glared, clearly reading my mind.

"I'm right, aren't I? Wasn't it the power of the shard's presence that freed you from Moriel's prison?"

He leaned back, looking down his nose at me. "Her Royal Highness, my Queen would have come for me. Aemon's no God yet. He isn't Moriel ... he's still mortal. Luckily for you and your sisters. The only thing that has saved you thus far is the very thing that could kill you." He tilted his chin. "Has his formerly not-lordship told you about his little research project at the library? Has he mentioned all the scrolls he's read, or the worry that keeps him up at night?"

"He's researching Shiviel. What we did to him."

Mercurial shook his head. "Is that what he told you?" he sang. "That's not what he's doing."

I froze. I'd seen him stay back each night to talk to the librarians, seen him slide note after note toward them, lists of titles. I'd wanted to ask him about it a dozen times, but I couldn't. And he'd never freely offered me any information. If anything, he'd gone out of his way to conceal the titles in his possession. My throat tightened. More secrets, more things he was keeping from me.

"Ah," Mercurial said. "He hasn't." He pouted. "Looks like I hit a sore spot."

"You know what he's researching?" I asked.

"Of course I know. Who do you think told him what to research? What your little ability to call on kashonim with Asherah is called?"

"You told him? The first night you came to see him here?" Mercurial grinned like a cat.

Rhyan had been with me at the end of the night. He'd told me Mercurial had come by but he'd never mentioned that they discussed my kashonim. He could have—we'd had privacy—the one and only time we had it.

But he'd said nothing.

"There's a special word for what you can do," Mercurial said. "*Rakashonim.* Your kashonim." He snapped his fingers, and there was another flash of light. A second nahashim cried out in pain, its black scaly body flopping onto the floor. "Kashonim," Mercurial said slowly, like I was a child, "is taking on and absorbing all of the power of your lineage. A false lineage created by force, by the letting, and mixing of blood between you and those who came before, those who trained you, and those who trained them. When it's yours, and yours alone … it means just that. *Rakashonim.* Your own personal lineage. Who you once were. Who you still are. It's calling on the full power of your soul."

"My kashonim with Asherah," I said. "I already know all of this."

Mercurial laughed. "Are you sure? It drains you, doesn't it, when you call on it? And not like normal kashonim. How could it be? Strong as your previously not-lord is, and … my most muscular, reinstated lord is *very* strong, one of the strongest in the Empire. But he is nothing compared to the strength of a God. Or … a Goddess. How else did you defeat the Imperator's nine nahashim on your own?"

"Asherah," I said.

Mercurial nodded.

"But it's dangerous," I said carefully, avoiding phrasing it as a question.

"Not just dangerous. It's volatile. Deadly. Especially for you."

I groaned. "For God's sake! You're not going to tell me what it means. Or tell me what to do to stop all of this. I assume you at least want me to get away from the Imperator with the orange shard, so I can track down the red."

"No. I never told you to go after the orange shard."

"But you would have," I said. "I'm going to go after all of them, aren't I?"

Mercurial shrugged. "It's a fair guess."

"Then help me! Help me get the orange shard so I can claim the red."

"I told you. You are out of favors. I will not break your contract with Imperator Hart."

"Then get out!" I yelled.

He tilted his head to the side, refusing to move, his eyes dancing with mischief. "You Guardians always think you're in charge. That you can defy the Council of Forty-Four, that you can do whatever you want—steal lights from Heaven, break them into pieces, drown empires, and still make demands of the Afeya. No. I leave when I want to."

"That's always it! What you want. When you want it. The power you reference is gone—was gone thousands of years ago. And the Council of Forty-Four? What they do even do now? They might as well be a myth."

"A myth? A myth! They are no more myth than you are, *Asherah*—than the Godsdamned light inside your mortal little heart. You would not stand where you are today if not for the Council of Forty-Four! They are the ones who ordered Canturiel to make the light! They are the ones who began the war with the akadim. Who moved the Valalumir to the Hall of Records. Who determined there should be seven Guardians. You don't remember? You were nothing before they selected you. Before they banished you. Before they cursed you! And trust me, if you don't believe anything else I am saying. They are still watching your every move. And still very much in power—when they deign to take action."

"Sounds like Afeya to me."

He laughed. "Do not insult me."

"Fine, they're not a myth. They're still in power. And if that's the case," I looked up at the ceiling, "I hope they're enjoying the show! Just as much as you are." My anger was growing at his nonsense, at his riddles, at his refusal to offer true assistance. "I'm not dealing with the Council now am I? I'm dealing with you. And you sure have a talent for cherry picking when you'll help."

His anger flared into his aura. The flames in the fireplace extinguished with a groaning hiss, then came back to life. "You think I am the one pulling the strings? The puppet master in control of this play, *Asherah*? I am not. I am merely a player, a member of the orchestra forced to play the notes I am commanded. I cannot be any more helpful than I am. And if you do not find a way to fulfill our bargain, I swear to you, you will burn from the inside out."

My body warmed. Heat rising up my legs, and out through my arms. I could feel it rushing through my body, like the nahashim, aware of every place they touched when I'd been examined. Sweat beaded my forehead, and I stared down at my green dress. The bodice began to loosen, the laces in the back sliding open until the Valalumir star between my breasts appeared. It had been pale gold for weeks, not heating or flaring since Kane. But suddenly, the lines darkened with black, then white, then red and back to gold.

"Mercurial," I shouted. "What are you doing?"

The gold outline of the star vanished from my skin, as if the Valalumir had never existed, as if the contract were gone. The heat intensified. Hotter and hotter.

I stumbled back, the pain excruciating. I bit down on my lip, sweat forming all over my skin, my stomach twisting, my breath coming short. I was starting to panic. No. No, I was panicking. The pain. Fuck. Fuck! My knees gave out as I sank to the floor, tears rolling down my eyes until I couldn't take it anymore. I screamed.

"Mercurial!"

The star on my chest was gone. The skin had burned off, and it was just flames now, just fire, roaring from inside of me.

"Mercurial!"

"The red shard. The Red Ray of Light. Asherah swore to protect it. Until she didn't. And it was whole, and it was pure, until Auriel fell. And then the light was crystal. And it could have been whole still. But Auriel took something from it. He took the last bit that existed, the last piece of pure light, pure power, pure Valalumir, and he put it inside you."

"I know, I know!" I pleaded. "Please. Mercurial! It's so hot! It's … fuck!" I looked to the door, contemplating calling out to Dario.

"You think he can help you? He can't even hear you. Now you look at me because I made a deal with you. I returned the light. I gave it back to you. And all you had to do was the very thing you said you would do. Give me your word. Fulfill the oath of a Goddess born over a thousand years ago. And if you didn't, this would be your punishment. I would burn you from the inside out."

"But I'm not done!" I shouted. "I swear. I will claim the red shard. I will! Once I get Jules out. Once I get her back … I'll leave the capital. I'll figure it out. I swear! I'll fulfill my oath. But please," I cried. "Please." I fell forward, tears rolling down my face. A scream trapped in my throat as the flames grew out of me.

Mercurial snapped his fingers.

The heat vanished, the flames gone. Instead, there was a red light flowing from my chest—far too bright for me to look at it. But as I looked back at Mercurial, he'd fallen to his knees, his posture mimicking mine.

A seven-pointed star, a Valalumir, was glowing on his blue body. A reflection of the light exploding out of me.

"That was a reminder," he said. "Not a punishment."

My chest rose and fell in rapid succession, the light shimmering against his own heart as my body shook. "Could have ... fooled ... me," I gasped.

"I warned you that you wouldn't want to know what I'd do if you failed. That wasn't it. That ..." His violet eyes locked with mine, "was simply a taste of what the *Rakashonim* can do to you. Or to others if you push it out. When you call on Asherah, you're calling on a Goddess's power. On a Goddess's strength. You're taking it inside of you, and using it. But you are in a mortal body." Mercurial shook his head. "You've done well so far. You've survived each call on her power. On your power. The true power of your soul. But ... you are not strong enough yet to sustain it. And even worse, you don't even know when you're calling on it. You think you can heal now? That you can take your sister's visions? Remove your lover's exhaustion, and pain?" He clicked his tongue. "*You* can't. That's the light. Not you. That's *Rakashonim*. If you do not claim the red shard, your body will fail and the light inside of you will either destroy you, or it will destroy everything, and everyone around you."

He said you had the potential to unleash more power and destruction than anyone in the Empire ever has.

My lip trembled. "You ... you handed me the chest plate. The very thing to unlock this."

Mercurial's eyes narrowed to snake-like slits. "I did."

I threw my head in my hands. "Why?"

"Someone had to do something. The Valalumir was never meant for this world. And as long as it remains shattered, broken, and unreturned ... you'll be cursed. In every single life. The Council has ensured it. So, play your little games with Imperator Hart. It matters not to me. I have made several arrangements now, been forced to renege on several promises, all because of you. I will come to collect my debt. And you better pray to your Gods," he laughed, "you are successful. I told Lord Rhyan a month ago, you're running out of time, my remembered Goddess. You are the fire. Act like it. Remember it. Control the flame before it consumes you. Before it consumes all of us."

And he vanished, leaving me gasping for breath, my entire body still aching and hot, as I fell to the floor.

THE THIRD SCROLL: VALABELLUM

CHAPTER THIRTY-THREE

LYRIANA

I stared out the window of the gryphon carriage, Glemaria finally fading from view. My chest still ached from Mercurial's visit hours ago. I could barely handle having the bodice of my dress touch my skin. It felt raw and burned, though in appearance everything was soft and unblemished. But despite a strange, questioning look from Dario, I said nothing about my encounter as we left Seathorne.

I'd been forbidden from making eye contact with Rhyan in the courtyard as Artem readied and prepared each gryphon for the journey. I was, of course, separated from him. Meera, too. But I was glad for the isolation. I wasn't ready to talk to Rhyan yet, to discuss that there was yet something else he'd been keeping from me. I'd climbed into my seat quickly, with Dario and several other soturi who would make up our guard in Numeria, and I watched the mountains and the pine trees pass by. The rain finally stopped an hour into our flight, and the weather began to warm considerably as we continued south.

A few hours later, I could see the Emperor's Palace in the

distance. I'd seen pictures of it in scrolls, and paintings in various places, and I knew the map of its interior inside and out. Still, nothing could have prepared me for the sight of it in person. The Palace seemed to cover an amount of land too immense for my mind to comprehend, dozens of courtyards full of suntrees, glittering blue waterways running through them. There were endless rows of columns painted in jewel tones of ruby, moonstone, and onyx. Golden Valalumirs sparkled above entrance ways, and on the roof of the Palace purple flags waved in the wind. I couldn't stop staring.

I'd known that the Palace wasn't particularly tall, only three stories high. It reminded me in some ways of the Grey Villa, Tristan's ancestral home off in the countryside in Vertavia. Not impressive in height but incredibly long in structure. We landed in a kind of courtyard that could only be reached via flight. There were no doors in or out. A white dome of protection was cast, trapping us within the walls. I was led off the gryphon onto a white marble surface in the shape of a circle. In the center was a golden Valalumir, and behind us were ruby-toned columns. Purple tapestries hung from the top of the walls.

Three ashvan horses pulling golden wagons appeared above us, descending into the circle through a small opening in the dome, their glowing blue hooves landing in the center on the painted golden star. Then three soturi, all with golden Valalumirs tattooed on their cheeks climbed down from the ashvan, and circled us.

"Weapons presentation," said the first soturion. He had strikingly thick, blond hair, and began walking around, looking us all up and down. He paused before Imperator Hart and bowed. "Your Highness, Welcome to Numeria. His Majesty, Emperor Theotis, is most eager to see you."

"As I am him." Imperator Hart waved at us. "Go on. Remove your weapons."

I stilled. I'd been prepared for this. Known that part of the game was giving up our arms, and that Imperator Hart would be coordinating the return of them by morning.

Still, it was jarring to see my sword taken by the Emperor's men, to be without the feel of a blade against my thigh, or resting at my hip.

But there were two weapons not included in the presentation. Asherah's armor. And my stave. Imperator Hart had them packed with his personal items.

We were searched more thoroughly by the soturi for any hidden blades, as another dozen ashvan horses appeared in the sky, all pulling golden coaches adorned with sparkling Valalu-mirs. Once the search was complete, we were ushered into coaches. Within minutes, we were out of the courtyard flying over the Palace.

I could make out the Nutavian Katurium in the distance. It was connected to the Palace via a waterway, half a mile in length. Tomorrow it would be covered with Lumerians attending the games.

We landed in another courtyard, much the same as the first, but this one had doors that led into apartments full of windows.

"Your Ka's quarters for the Valabellum, Your Highness," said a soturion, gesturing to the space around us. "Once you have had a chance to wash up, and take some refreshments, you may seek an audience with His Majesty to officially announce your arrival. You have access to visit the Throne Room from your suites."

"We shall," Imperator Hart said. "Tell His Majesty I shall be with him shortly to thank him for his gracious hospitality."

The soturion nodded, and then one of Imperator Hart's guards began directing us to our private apartments.

"Might I stay with my sister?" I asked suddenly.

A middle-aged woman who seemed to be the authority around our living quarters shook her head. "There is no need, my lady. His Majesty's abundance allows you all your own private apartments."

My eyes met Meera's.

She smiled grimly. "I'll be near," she said quietly.

I took a deep breath and watched as once again, Meera was led away from me.

One of the Emperor's servants, a young mage approached Dario and me. "This way, my lady," he said.

We followed the mage to the third-floor apartments I would be staying in. Down the hall was the escort's suite for Dario.

My room was exactly as luxurious and ostentatious as I'd expected for the Palace. And yet, I somehow still found myself staring in awe at the amount of gold and gilded surfaces that surrounded me. The walls had been painted a deep ruby like the outer courtyard columns. My ceiling was a bright white with a black border, and in the center, of course, there was another gilded Valalumir. Gauzy violet curtains blew lazily against the opened window.

"Thank you," I said, dismissing the mage, until I was alone with Dario.

He took a deep breath, his eyes softening as his mouth opened. But there was a sudden rap on the door, and all at once, his face returned to the somewhat harsh, neutral expression he wore when guarding me.

Dario opened the door, and we were greeted by one of the Emperor's soturi.

He was young, in pale golden armor that looked to be one size too large for his frame.

"Lord Dario," he said, handing a small scroll over. "As an active soturion in the Palace, you have been relieved of all weapons. Your noble now has the Emperor's protection, and it is pertinent that you meet with Numeria's Turion at once."

My stomach twisted, but this had been expected and I nodded for him to go ahead.

Left alone in my room, and coming off of recent commands from Imperator Hart, I had no choice but to follow orders and prepare for my first—in person—visit to the Throne Room.

An hour later, Dario returned, announcing it was time for our audience with Emperor Theotis. He led me outside where I joined our entourage. Imperator Hart and Lady Kenna stood at the front, flanked by their guards, followed by Arkturion Kane. There was a row of soturi in their gleaming black leather, but without any swords at their hips or on their backs. I spotted Senator Oryyan walking with his wife and Lady Amalthea. Rhyan followed them, and then two more sets of soturi separated him from Meera and Aiden, and then me and Dario. In addition to our own soturi the Emperor's men were following closely.

I counted each step in my head as we walked, mentally bringing together the pen-and-parchment images I'd kept locked away in my mind with the reality of walking through the long, winding Palace. It took all the focus I had not to look in every nook and corner we passed, to not pray I'd catch a glimpse of a chayatim. Of Jules. I didn't trust my reaction—didn't trust I wouldn't run for her right then and there and screw the rest of the plans.

Instead, I focused on the fact that my memorization of the Palace's size and the number of steps needed to cross it had been precise. Each room was exactly as I'd counted. I slowed as we climbed the grand staircase leading to the hall before the Throne Room. And only then I realized the small flaw in the plan. My heart had already started to pound, a small heat building inside of me. We were near the shield, and already the Valalumir could sense it.

At the top of the stairs, I watched as the pattern on the floor changed beneath my feet from purple to the mix of black and white tile. It was exactly as I'd seen it in the nahashim's vision. Sweat began to bead at the nape of my neck as we were stopped by the Emperor's herald. Our names were collected.

My chest heaved. The Valalumir grew warmer inside me. The large doors opened and the herald began to list off the names of His Highness Imperator Hart's entourage, methodically naming us all and our titles, one by one.

I stepped into the Throne Room, at once overwhelmed and dizzy. The shard called out to me—I was too close. It called out to the light inside me, the part of itself that had once made it whole. Staring at the black and white marble floor, my eyes slowly, carefully began to rise to see the white marble columns that stood every few feet. The golden throne sat on the opposite end of the room from where we stood.

On either side of the Emperor were two soturi, each wearing a golden Valalumir tattoo on their cheek. They looked exactly as they had when I'd looked through the snake's eyes. And then I dared look up. I made eye contact with Emperor Theotis—the man who'd ruined my life. He looked just as I'd remembered, when he'd entered Bamaria only months ago—when he'd forced me into the arena with Haleika, and then forced Rhyan to watch. His thick white eyebrows were drawn together, his white beard trimmed short. His gold and purple velvet robes were draped across the throne, flowing off the dais, but rather than touch the floor, the ends spread across a long purple rug.

Throat dry and tightening, I met his gaze, and despite my near two decades of practice, nothing could stop the expression of disdain I knew was spreading all over my face. This was the man who'd kept my cousin enslaved for years. Who'd allowed her to be raped—if he hadn't been the one to do it himself. This was the man who'd ordered an entire Ka to be murdered. Who hosted games where people would die just to keep us from questioning his authority.

And because, standing on the dais beside him, were two more of the men I hated most in this world.

Imperator Kormac. And the Bastardmaker.

Their eyes, black, beady and wolf-like, sent a shiver running down my spine. I'd forgotten the layers of cruelty inside of them. The endlessly predatory, violent hunger. All at once, I was reminded of Brockton and Geoffrey, Brett, and Trey. They all had the same eyes. The same promise of barbarousness. Exactly like their father.

And standing on the floor, right in front of them, was Tristan.

I hadn't seen him since our break up, since he'd gotten engaged to Naria. He had the strangest look in his brown eyes as we approached the dais. There was a coldness to them I'd never seen before. And in a way I couldn't explain, at that moment, he looked like he was my enemy. He wasn't just standing close to the wolves, but he looked like he belonged with them. Like he was one of them now.

Tristan cocked his head to the side, his neck filling with red as expressions of anger became more apparent in his aura. His energy wafted toward me in a way that was all at once foreign, and yet, all too familiar. Strangely familiar.

My heart pounded harder as the guards flanking me forced me to step forward again and again, moving ever closer to the shield. My chest grew warmer. And at last, when the pull became too strong to ignore, I let my eyes trail up, just as they had in the vision.

The bronzed-shield hung above the throne, the orange crystal glowing in the center illuminated by sunlight streaming through the stained-glass windows. A thousand colors glowed against the walls, and shimmered across the marble floor.

There was a breeze against my heated skin, cool, and filled with salt—wind from another life, another time.

Spots filled my vision, and I saw gold sand stretching on for miles under a bright sun. I held up my hand—Asherah's hand— darker, larger than my own to block the view. In the distance, I saw a blinding light, and the shadow of Auriel running toward me.

The vision vanished as quickly as it had appeared, the breeze gone. I was dizzy as I returned to this body, this life, the fire now burning inside my chest, the flames rising and growing hotter and hotter.

A small golden light began to glow from within, streams of it escaping the top of my bodice. "Dario," I hissed, gripping his arm. "Alert His Highness. I'm unwell."

"What?"

"Tell him. Help me. I'm–" I didn't have the words. We'd never explained to Dario what had happened in the Seating Room that day. Despite him being privy to so many of our secrets he didn't know this one. But he had seen my heart glow when Kane touched me. I stared pointedly down, and Dario's eyes followed.

"Shit." He didn't hesitate. He removed his soturion cloak, and wrapped it around my shoulders while the other guards frowned.

The Emperor was speaking, using that voice of his which was somehow too loud and too quiet at the same time.

I couldn't listen. Couldn't focus. All I knew was I was in the presence of a shard of the Valalumir and my own piece of the light had very much recognized its counterpart.

I could vaguely hear my name on the Emperor's lips, as well as Meera's name, and then the proclamation of everyone's joy that we'd been found safely, and Meera rescued from the akadim.

But as I looked up again at the orange light shining in the sun, I bit down on my lip to keep from crying, to keep from screaming that my heart was on fire. What Mercurial had done to me that morning had been more excruciating than anything I'd ever felt. But it was nothing next to this.

Everyone was ordered to bow. But my knees were already giving out. I desperately clutched at Dario's cloak, trying to hide the light coming from me.

"Your Highness," Dario yelled. "The lady! She's faint."

Imperator Hart at last turned to look at me, just as Rhyan had, his face filling with concern. He was already moving, racing back toward me, pushing past Kane and Amalthea, and the guards standing between us. The floor was rising up to meet me. Someone was shouting my name. And then I saw no more.

CHAPTER THIRTY-FOUR

LYRIANA

"Thought you could get out of attending the ball tonight, did you?" Imperator Hart clicked his tongue. "It's the eve of Asherah's Feast Day. And I thought that you of all people might delight in such a celebration."

My breath came short as I sat up in bed, taking in my surroundings, the golden Valalumir on the ceiling, the ostentatious furniture. Sunset cast a reddish light through the curtains of my window, filling the room with dark shadows.

My apartment in the Emperor's Palace.

I reached for my chest, my heart pounding. I was still wearing my gown, and the fire inside me was gone. The Valalumir was no longer glowing. At the edge of my blankets, spread wide, like it had been used to cover me, was Dario's cloak.

"Your Highness, I'm sorry," I said, not sure of how much he saw. "I ..." I coughed, my throat raw. "I felt faint."

"Did you now?" he asked, his voice dangerously low. "You do realize that was your one opportunity to take in the object you are meant to steal for me tomorrow? The one chance you had to look around and ensure that you save your cousin's life?"

My fingers clenched at my side. "Believe me, I took it in," I said. "I'm as prepared as I can be to do my part. Our deal still stands." Our eyes met. "Are you ready?"

"Am I?" He got up from his chair, and began pacing back and forth.

"I'll keep the shard if you're not," I said. "Or I'll return it to the Emperor himself, if I don't see Jules. And you can try to compel me, order me to hand it over. But these are ancient artifacts, full of more magic than you can conceive of. I wouldn't trust our contract to override such a thing."

He scoffed. "Don't be so sure. My part is simple. I have access, I have power. You don't." He shook his head. "I suppose if anything, you made yourself look frail and weak. Pathetic. Not a threat to the Emperor—not a threat to even the lowest of his servants."

"As you commanded, Your Highness, I've been practicing appearing meek." I gritted. "That should please you."

He turned abruptly, leaning over the bed, slamming both fists into the mattress on either side of me, caging me in. His breath was too close, his aura was raging. "What will please me," he roared, "is seeing you give a convincing performance tonight! And then getting me what I asked for."

I rolled my shoulders back, affecting the posture of a noble, even while laying down. Even while trapped by His Highness. But I kept my chin low. "I know what to do. And I will succeed tonight."

"I've been lenient with you these last few weeks," he said, pulling back. "Perhaps too lenient. So lenient in fact, you decided to run off at the manor and let Rhyan follow you."

I braced myself, expecting a hit, or more yelling. But his aura had shifted to something calm and almost happy. Serene. My heart thundered.

Rhyan had once told me that when his father was calm, when he was kind—that was when he was at his most dangerous.

Imperator Hart stood up, and tapped his chin, his eyes raking me over.

"Well, it seems he followed you. Not the other way around." He shrugged. "He's proven beyond a shadow of a doubt what a liability he can be. Unfortunately, he's made it clear that when we return home, he can never be free of his bonds."

I clenched my jaw, trying to hide the rage and sorrow bubbling inside of me at his words, trying to keep myself from giving him anything more to hold over me.

He made a disapproving sound with his tongue. "I don't do all of this to punish you, you realize? We're in the viper's nest now, surrounded by those who wish you the most harm."

One viper's nest for another, I thought, but kept my mouth closed. I was too tired to fight. I'd save my strength for tomorrow.

"All eyes will be watching you tonight—you and Kane," he said. "It's especially important that everyone remembers that he is the one you are betrothed to. Tonight, you will appear before Imperator Kormac and Viktor, as well as Lord Tristan Grey. Quite a cadre of your previous romantic entanglements in the South. Despite all my efforts and goodwill, the rumors about you and my son still swirl. Do not run out of the room tonight unescorted. Do not give my bullheaded idiot excuse-for-a-son a reason to follow you from the ball. You are at risk here—especially now. Do you think there is anything that will stop Kormac from abducting you? From forcing you into any of his wolf's beds? He can do it. With his uncle here, and my soturi stripped of weapons, you could find yourself on your back before you blink."

My stomach hollowed. "Will you ... will you force the same thing of me?"

"I should," he said. "I should have had him fucking you the entire time. Should have had you myself." He started toward me.

But then suddenly, he stopped. Something almost like fear flashed in his eyes.

He wasn't afraid of me. But he was afraid.

And all at once I knew. It had been Rhyan. Rhyan had done something. Saved me from worse. Just like he always did.

He cracked his knuckles, then stilled, like he was regaining control. "I've announced to my counterpart that a private wedding occurred between you and Kane. It happened just last night. You simply could not wait a moment longer. You snuck out to the Temple of Dawn, had Arkmage Connal officiate, and then," he smiled, "I heard you shared Kane's bed last night."

I shook my head. Even the story made me feel nauseated. But a story was better than reality. "You told this to Imperator Kormac?" I asked.

"And everyone else who was within earshot. Oh, cheer up. Would you rather that I told him you're not yet wed? Would you rather I leave room for Viktor Kormac to make you his own? Enough of his wolves lurk in the corners, drooling with anticipation. It'd be very easy for them to make their move, to grab you, to drag you before a mage."

"No."

He smirked. "Perhaps your little fainting spell earlier today was a result of a pregnancy." His eyes narrowed into slits. "I know that normally such symptoms don't start so soon, but," he shrugged, "Kane is quite virile. And he's had a whole month to bed you."

I swallowed back the bile rising in my throat. It was just a story—not real. Not real.

And it never would be.

"What do you want from me?" I asked. "Tonight?"

"When Kane goes in for a kiss on your Godsdamned mouth —which he will because I have ordered him to—you will kiss him back. You will accept any and every touch of his body against yours. And you will love it. After all, he's supposed to be your husband now."

I could feel my blood heat. Feel the contract between us answering his command. My stomach twisted. I would have to obey. I'd have no choice. Tears burned behind my eyes.

"Yes, Your Highness."

"I've selected a dress for you to wear," he said jovially.

"Oh?"

"You've been most pleasing to me in your Glemarian-style gowns." His eyes ran down my corset, following the material to where it disappeared beneath my blankets. "But tonight, I think we ought to remind everyone where you come from, hmmm? Remind them that the previous Heir to the Arkasva of Bamaria is now mine—a subject of the North. And wed to his Arkturion."

"Of course," I said, pushing back the covers. I wanted to get out of bed before he got close again.

He stalked toward my closet and threw the doors open, thrusting his hand inside, and I waited for him to reveal some garish yet traditional Bamarian styled dress.

But what he pulled out was the complete opposite in every way. He was holding a slinky red dress—if that was even the word for what I saw. The front of the bodice formed a V that would cut to my belly. Hanging from the waist was what could barely be described as fabric—the gown's skirt seemed to be made of scraps. I could already tell I'd be almost completely exposed wearing it, revealing not just the full length of my thighs, but my hips as well. It looked as if someone had tried to design a dress from my country from memory and had forgotten halfway through.

I shook my head. "Is that supposed to be a Bamarian gown?" I asked.

"Did I get the color right? Batavia red?" he mocked.

"It's, um, close, Your Highness. Perhaps if you want to

remind everyone of my Ka and your claim on me, a more exact shade would be better—"

"I think this is perfect," he said loudly. "It's your color, it's Bamarian, and it's—how did you put it? A dress that shall keep men who see you from having an imagination." He winked. "No room for that here. Not much room for anything." He twirled it around.

"Is there no end to your games? To your humiliation?" I asked, watching the material pick up the red rays of the sunset. After a month of this, I was so tired.

Imperator Hart set the thing alleging itself to be a dress on a chaise, his aura once more too calm, too much like something resembling happiness.

"The games end when you actually decide to play. You've convinced no one of a single thing. Neither has my weak-minded son. Ridiculous. I know you find Kane revolting. But Rhyan? He doesn't even have to pretend intimacy when it comes to Amalthea."

"Doesn't have to pretend intimacy?" My stomach sank.

"You didn't know?" He laughed. "He already fucked Amalthea. Two and a half years ago."

CHAPTER THIRTY-FIVE

LYRIANA

My chest tightened and I fell back on the bed.

He already fucked Amalthea.

I remembered the way Rhyan had looked a month ago, on the night he'd been forced to put the engagement ring on her finger, the way he scratched his palm. The way he was still keeping so many secrets from me.

It was kept quiet—but his father had—well, he'd made it known that he was to resume courting.

Kenna's words came back to me, and my stomach sank. Had Amalthea been a part of that *courting*? My hands flexed involuntarily.

But before I could take another moment to process what Imperator Hart had said, servants of the Emperor entered to prepare me for the ball. My hair was curled, my lashes darkened, and that hideous scrap of a dress was forced onto me until they deemed me ready.

A short while later, I was lined up outside of the ballroom, forced to stand in a long, dark corridor, my mind racing. I just wanted to get out of there. I wanted to get Rhyan alone to talk to him.

Instead, I was stuck, waiting, listening to the crackling sounds of the fire in the lamp above me, and Kane's erratic breathing. Ahead, I could see the traditional purple cloth of Ka Elys, though I hadn't seen anyone from Bamaria. They must have been one of the first Kavim presented. It was only after every Ka was introduced that the Imperators and their entourages proceded in. Until then, I was trapped in the Godsdamned hallway with my arm slung through Kane's, my stomach twisting from the contact, and pain erupting in my blood every time I considered pulling away.

Rhyan was behind me, his arm linked with Amalthea's. Imperator Hart's words played in my mind again and again.

He already fucked Amalthea.

He already fucked Amalthea.

I clenched my jaw. Imperator Hart was lashing out. Trying to hurt me. But he wasn't, not the way he wanted to, at least. Not the way he'd tried to hurt me with Kenna. Because all I could see was Rhyan's hurt and distant look, the way his emotions had withdrawn, the way he'd itched his palm.

I could feel Rhyan's eyes now, boring into my bare back. I could always sense his gaze, feel the heat of where his eyes went. But to my surprise, in that moment his aura reached out, like a gentle brush against my shoulders, and then it cocooned me with a cool reassuring breeze. My heart pounded as its familiar, calming sensation wrapped around me, seeking me out. He'd been unbound. And for a second, I felt less naked, less exposed in my dress.

But then the air around me chilled, and a torch flickered out, the hallway darkening. Imperator Hart's aura was pulsating with his displeasure. He'd wanted Ka Hart to be the final Ka to enter before Emperor Theotis—proof he was the more powerful of the two Imperators. But the wolves now stood behind us, ready to be introduced last. All at once, Kane stepped forward, dragging me along with him. I huffed, and straightened, trying to separate my body from his as much as possible. But then Imperator Hart's command played through my mind, and all of my will to avoid Kane's touch vanished as a sharp pain twinged down my arms.

I knew I didn't want this. I knew I wanted to pull away—to shout no, but I couldn't. Because there was only pain if I did. And because I knew Imperator Hart was right. Ka Kormac wasn't going to let me go. Not without a fight.

Kane grunted and I was led through the end of the corridor, then down a grand staircase draped in purple carpeting. Golden lamps jutted out from the walls all around me as I stepped out onto a white marble floor with thousands of golden stars embedded in its shiny surface. Music played softly as hundreds of trays full of wine floated back and forth across the room. Cascades of gardenias fell from the ceiling, creating canopies across the room. Vines, braided with the flowers trailed across the center of each table, while candles flickered between the greens. The scent was intoxicating, almost overwhelming with its force, becoming more potent with each breath I took.

Moving slowly through the room, their heads held high and their eyes slowly taking in the details of each noble's dress and jewels were the Empire's most elite Lumerians. Layers upon layers of fabric in satin, silk, and lace draped across the figures of each woman I saw, all in an assortment of colors representing their Kavim.

My cheeks reddened, and I was suddenly all too aware of how little fabric I'd been afforded, and just how much of my body had been left on display. I resisted the urge to play with my hair, to spread it across the expanse of my chest. The Emperor's servants had curled my long layers, and twisted the locks to fall over one shoulder. I'd tried my best to center the curls across my chest, to conceal the evidence of my contract with Mercurial.

Between that and the low lights, the golden lines of the Vala-lumir could not be seen. But I still felt too on display.

The herald's voice boomed, and I could feel the shift in attention all at once, feel hundreds of eyes fall on me, on my dress, moving from my exposed cleavage, to the sharpness of my exposed hip bone, and then between my legs where the thin cloth just barely covered me.

I swallowed roughly, willing my free hand to remain at my side, to not try and hide or draw any more attention to myself. But I could already feel the judgment in their auras, hear the whispers and the hushed laughter, mixed with scandalized gasps. Nobles were reaching for each other, their fingers pointing to me. And then to the Arkturion at my side. Imperator Hart hadn't just marked me as Glemarian. He'd marked me as his whore. And all the nobility knew it.

I held my chin high, but I was trembling, and beside me Kane made a grunt of amusement.

It felt like an eternity was slowly passing as I fought to remain still, but finally our announcement was complete, and we all moved aside. Imperator Kormac was announced next.

Each name read out by the herald filled me with dread.

Imperator Avery Kormac. Arkturion Waryn Kormac. And then, Lord Viktor Kormac. Brockton's name was notably missing. But I could hear its absence with every fiber of my being. My heart hammered.

The wolves began their descent of the staircase, their silver armor glinting as the flickering flames of the lamps hit each pellet, and the sharpened steel of their blades shined.

"Of course, they're still fucking armed," Dario muttered.

"They're always armed," I said. Clearly, the benefits of having an uncle for Emperor meant that privilege extended to the capital and inside the walls of the Palace as well.

The wolves of Ka Kormac clustered together at the side of the dance floor, standing beneath a flag boasting their sigil.

I'd been so overwhelmed with our entry, so aware of everyone's eyes on me, I hadn't realized that each of the twelve Kavim had a flag. They were all delicately blowing against the soft breezes entering from the windows near each flickering lamp. Without thinking, I began searching through the sigils, my heart pounding as I sought out the one that always made my heart leap—that felt like home. The one I loved most, and missed desperately. A full moon made of silver between golden seraphim wings. Across the ballroom's dance floor at nearly the other end of the room, I found it painted onto a red flag dangling from the high ceiling. The red was perfect, unlike my garish dress. It was Batavia red. A surge of pride rushed through me.

I eagerly looked beneath it to the members of my Ka, searching for the golden Laurel of the Arkasva, and my father's dark hair beneath it.

But as the golden laurel came into view, its leaves glinting with firelight, I saw red hair nestled around it. Arianna's hair. Arianna was Arkasva Batavia.

For just a moment, I'd forgotten. Forgotten my father was dead. That I wouldn't see him tonight. That I wouldn't see him on any night. Never again.

Someone grabbed my hand, squeezing tight.

Meera. Her chin quivered as her eyes fell on the same sight. Arianna in our father's laurel. Standing to her right was Naria in the golden diadem that should have been mine, the title of Heir Apparent that was rightfully Meera's. And holding her hand, wearing that same angry expression from earlier, with a thick golden ring on his finger, was Tristan.

I felt almost dizzy, my knees shaking as the order to kneel came from the herald. Emperor Theotis's consort entered, wearing a shimmery dress that was nearly identical to the one I'd seen her in when she attended the Valyati ball. It felt like a lifetime ago.

The trumpet sounded, its notes reverberating, followed by a

shout of, "He comes! All kneel for His Majesty, Emperor Theotis, High Lord of Lumeria Nutavia!"

Meera released my hand as she sank to her knees, and I followed, my stomach roiling, while I tried desperately to not expose myself as I sat. The dress left me almost no room to properly kneel. I had to stay high on my knees, and keep my legs pressed tightly together, then readjust the straps over my shoulders before they moved too low. Quickly, I made sure my curls covered the center of my chest.

I could have strangled Imperator Hart for a million reasons. But at this moment, I couldn't forgive him for leaving me so exposed. It wasn't just humiliating. It was dangerous. In this lighting my Valalumir mark was still difficult to see. But I didn't trust it would remain concealed. And I would bet that the Emperor and those closest to him were well versed in Afeyan contracts and would recognize the mark for what it was.

A hush came over the room. Emperor Theotis, and his Warlord, Arkturion Pompellus Agrippa, the man known as the Blade, descended the stairs.

Centered on the dais at the front of the room, Theotis began to speak. His voice had the same eerily soft, yet commanding tone it had earlier. But I couldn't hear a word he said. Because as I looked up from adjusting my gown again, I realized that standing straight across the ballroom from me was the Bastardmaker. His black, beady eyes were watching my every breath, watching in particular the space where my dress no longer existed. His hand moved to his blade, his reddish fingers tightening on the hilt, his gaze never wavering.

I could see the accusation in his eyes. Feel it in his aura.

The anger. The hunger. The hatred. *Murderer. Murderer.*

Viktor knelt by his side, his blond hair pulled back by the silver claws of his diadem. One by one, the soturi of Ka Kormac, who'd been allowed to stand guard instead of bowing, turned their gaze from the Emperor to me. Slowly, their legs widened into fighting stances, their hands slid down to their hilts, fingers tightening.

"I welcome you to Numeria," the Emperor said, lifting his arms. "Rise. I thank you all for indulging me on this eve of Asherah's Feast Day. It's been too long since we last honored our ancestors with a celebration such as this—with a Valabellum. With so much change in the Empire, it is good for us all to come together. We recently defeated a new threat of akadim, thanks to the leadership of our Arkturion Pompellus."

Applause broke out. The Blade stepped forward, his keen eyes vigilant and observing, even as he bowed, his red Arkturion cloak falling over his shoulders.

"And," Emperor Theotis continued, "We celebrate the victories won by Imperator Kormac. Thanks to his strength and leadership, the new threat of akadim in the South has been annihilated."

Annihilated? He'd done nothing. Rhyan and I had slain more akadim than he'd ever encountered.

"We have even managed to save the life of one taken by the monsters," the Emperor continued, "Lady Meera Batavia. Step forward."

Meera didn't hesitate. She picked up the bottom of her dress —Glemarian green and cut into the actual style of a Bamarian gown. Her skin glowed in the torchlights, and she smiled, turning and waving to everyone in the room as she glided forward. Only I noticed the frosty shift in her aura when she paused in the direction of Arianna.

The nobles applauded, shouting congratulations and well wishes on her rescue. I could feel that some were genuine with their emotion, empathetic to her ordeal.

But not everyone was happy. Beside me, I could feel the ripple of Imperator Hart's annoyance. The Emperor's words had been carefully selected. Credit was not being given to Devon Hart, the man who'd proclaimed himself her savior and rescuer.

And his hold on Meera was being called into question. Which meant my own was next.

"Imperator Kormac," the Emperor continued, "saw a new threat in the South, and he immediately formed a task force. Because of his brilliant planning and assignment, sending Soturion Rhyan Hart to find Lady Meera, she was found safe, and then graciously cared for after the fact by Imperator Hart."

Meera smiled and approached Imperator Kormac, curtseying before him.

The sight made me sick—and yet, as she rose and turned to face Imperator Hart there was a defiance in her eyes. She was challenging his claim on her.

The small rebellion left a lightness in my chest—but it was short-lived.

Amidst the applause for Imperator Kormac, Meera made her way back to my side, holding Imperator Hart's vicious gaze the entire time.

The Emperor clapped. "Yes. yes. And thanks to Imperator Kormac's efforts, we smoothly transitioned power in the South, and welcomed our newest Arkasva, Her Grace, Arianna Batavia, High Lady of Bamaria."

I bit my lip as fresh cheers erupted through the room. Meera's eyes met mine again. Her mouth tightened, only the smallest reveal that she, too, was affected. But then her noble training returned and her face was once again neutral.

"With our hearts and minds on recent tragedies that have plagued Bamaria, and Ka Batavia, we must acknowledge," Emperor Theotis continued, "that not all have been accounted for. Lady Morgana still remains in captivity."

The room hushed, everyone's aura suddenly reaching out as if poking at me. I could feel their feelings of pity and worry, but also fear and horror. It made my stomach turn to feel so much of it at once.

"And we have still not heard any word from Arkturion

Aemon Melvik. It has been over a month since we sent soturi to locate him. But our fears for his safety grow by the day. And that is why I want to thank Arkturion Waryn Kormac for the great service he has provided in protecting not only his home of Korteria, but Bamaria as well. During these trying times he has been named the acting Arkturion, and I am proud to say the South has never been safer from the threat of akadim."

The nobles cheered and shouted, and the Bastardmaker stepped forward, his hateful beady eyes taking in Meera's slight form as he lifted a fist into the air, accepting his applause. The claps became louder, more excited. He was being hailed as a hero.

But all I saw was a monster. The man who'd given Brockton his eyes, who'd passed on his cruel nature, and his disgusting proclivities.

And worst of all. The man who'd given him free access to Jules.

I reached for the hilt of a sword that wasn't on my hip. Gods, I itched for it. For the chance to run him through, right then and there.

"Now, the South is safe. I commend Imperator Kormac's leadership. But we shall also mention the latest activities in the North under Imperator Hart's leadership." Emperor Theotis's eyes narrowed, his bushy eyebrows coming together. "First, I am glad to see that Soturion Rhyan has delivered Lady Lyriana to safety. We worried about the two of you for quite some time. I thank the Gods you're safe."

"It was my duty," Imperator Hart said, speaking jovially, his arms outstretched. But I could feel the tension he was trying to control. The jealousy and uncertainty in his aura. He wasn't being afforded the credit he so desperately craved.

Good.

"Now," Theotis continued, "I thought for sure Lady Lyriana would return home when found. And return to the arms of her betrothed, my grand-nephew. After all what more could a girl want after such an ordeal, but to be safe in the arms of her intended, and to see her Ka's new Arkasva come into her own?" The Emperor frowned. "But, if I am to believe what I've been told, her heart has been swayed by another?"

"Young love, Your Majesty," Imperator Hart called out. "What can you do? She saw our Arkturion, and got an eyeful of his immense strength, and power." He paused, the innuendo of his words hanging in the air as my cheeks burned. The room was filling with laughter. "It took no time at all before Lady Lyriana found herself ... bitten ... by love."

The laughter was now a cacophonous cackle. Kane came up behind me, his arms wrapping around my waist, his hands pressing into my belly. I stiffened, my pulse racing, and my skin crawling. And from across the dance floor, I could feel the hungry, predatory eyes of Ka Kormac all over me, imagining the circumstances of the lie, fantasizing about doing the same to me.

I shifted uncomfortably, unable to escape. Kane pinched my stomach through the little bit of fabric between us.

"She's not the only one, Your Majesty," Kane said, "who was bitten. Look at her beauty, her youthfulness, her ... pliability." Then before I could react, he spun me in his arms, leaned me backward and smashed his lips against my mouth. I stifled a cry. His breath was rancid, his nails digging into my skin as he pulled me closer, making sure I felt exactly how excited he was right then.

Bile rose in my throat, and my breath came short, but I was determined to keep my lips shut, to not let this go any further. I wanted to get away from him, to push him off. And yet, everything inside me was urging him closer. Even my balance. I was slipping and couldn't find my center. He'd pushed me back too far, forcing me to rely completely on him to keep from falling. If I did, I knew my dress wouldn't stay in place. I'd be exposed before my worst enemies, before the most powerful leaders in Lumeria.

Kane only pressed harder into me. There were black spots in my vision. I tried to turn my head, to break the kiss, even as I was forced to cling to him with even more fervor, to pull his body closer in my desperation to stay standing. The bottoms of my shoes began to slip. And yet, with every attempt to pull my mouth away, my blood heated painfully, and stabbing sensations ran through my limbs.

I hissed, my limbs trembling with disgust, my body desperate to push back, but I was completely, helplessly at the mercy of my blood contract. And my betrothed.

Kane groaned, his lips punishing until I was fighting back the tears in my eyes. Only then he released me, and I stumbled backward, into Meera's arms, coughing back bile. My stomach was roiling. Gods, I wanted to vomit. I wanted to shower, and rip off this fucking dress, and then strangle Kane and Imperator Hart with it. But all I could do was stand there, following orders, and watching as he stepped forward to perform some mindless victory dance. Like I was the prize.

The musicians began to play a tune, each note plucked with a kind of vile humor.

Bawdy laughter crashed against my ears, and my hands were clenched into fists at my side with so much tension my shoulders hurt. Then suddenly I was only aware of one thing.

Rhyan's aura, stormy, and cold, but protective, wrapping itself around me. Hugging me. Holding me.

He stood several feet away, his hand linked with Amalthea's. But his eyes were on me, heavy and pained, his jaw tight. The restraint he was exhibiting was clear in every sharp line of his features. He wasn't outwardly showing any emotion, not even anger, but it was bubbling under the surface. I could feel it with the same clarity I felt my own. And yet, he was holding back so he could comfort me in the only way he could find.

Emperor Theotis signaled for the musicians to halt, and Kane's dance finally ended. "Yes, yes, quite a show. You may return to your Ka, Arkturion Kane. Next time you decide to regale us with a dance, bring your bride."

"Yes, Your Majesty," he said.

The Emperor's bushy eyebrows drew together, his eyes like slits. "Now correct me if I'm wrong, but I hear there was maybe some *quickness* to this betrothal?"

"You could say that, Your Majesty," Imperator Hart said, clapping Kane on the back. "The lady did not wish to wait for … all the benefits, shall we say, that come with marriage, once her feelings were reciprocated."

"Interesting," said the Emperor. "Considering she waited a whole two years for Lord Tristan Grey."

By the Gods. Had he just … My cheeks reddened.

The Emperor looked out into the crowd, a hand over his eyes as if he were searching. "Ah there you are, Lord Tristan." He gestured for him to step forward. "What say you to this sudden development?"

I forced myself to breathe as Tristan complied, walking into the center of the room.

"I was waiting for my true love, Lady Naria, to wake up and see me, Your Majesty." He bowed. "Clearly Lady Lyriana was doing the same, only for a man she did not yet know."

"Yet what about," Imperator Kormac asked, his lips pulled back into a sneer, "the lady's engagement to my son? The only engagement sanctioned by His Majesty, and Her Grace, Arkasva Batavia."

The Emperor grinned, his smile more wolf-like than I'd ever seen.

"That is an important question," the Emperor said. "Perhaps nothing is settled just yet. We must see Lady Meera returned to her homeland at once—now that we can safely see she is quite recovered. We thank Imperator Hart for his hospitality. However, all things come to an end. Lady Meera, please stand now with your Ka."

"As you wish," Imperator Hart said tightly. He nodded at Meera, and she quickly gathered her skirts and crossed the room, making her way to Arianna's side. There they embraced and hugged. A sight that would always leave my stomach twisting.

"Very well." The Emperor clapped. "Speaking of returns, I see that we have been graced with the presence of Soturion Rhyan. But not just Soturion Rhyan, Lord Rhyan once more." He continued to clap. "Am I to understand that our forsworn Bamarian refugee, has been absolved of all past crimes, and is now an Heir again?"

"He is, Your Majesty," Imperator Hart said.

Emperor Theotis watched Imperator Hart for a long moment before he nodded. "Very well. Since that is the case, Imperator Hart, I hope you will control his travels, outside of Glemaria. Do not let him stray so far from home again, hmm?" His eyes flicked to Rhyan, and for a moment, my heart stopped beating. But then he placed his full attention on me. "Now, as for Lady Lyriana. Step forward, my dear. For what in Lumeria, are we to do with you?"

My cheeks heated. I tried desperately to adjust my dress, and retain some level of modesty, as I stepped back into the center of the dance floor. I curtseyed before the Emperor, my eyes remaining on him.

"You look," he said softly, "enchanting. You know, we went years not seeing the youngest of His Grace's daughters. The youngest Batavia heir. Then finally we saw her on Valyati, then again when she fought so bravely in the arena. Now we get to see her dressed up so *elegantly* again tonight." His eyes ran slowly up and down my body. "We've never," he coughed, "seen so much of you, my lady."

The nobles standing closest to me began to giggle.

I breathed in through my nose as slowly as possible, rolling my shoulders back, lifting my chin, and forced my face to remain neutral. I forced myself to forget that my lips were crawling with disgust. Or that my heart was pounding out of my chest.

"Nothing else left to see," shouted a soturion.

Kane was by my side a second later, his arm slung over my shoulder. "Nothing I haven't seen up close," he said.

The Emperor stepped forward, his aura quiet, but commanding. He was displeased. He wasn't interested in these games. It was obvious from his expression that with all the absolute power he possessed, he considered this beneath him.

"Be that as it may," he said softly, and wiped his hands together as if he felt he'd gotten them dirty in this exchange, "you know, no wedding for a member of our ruling Kavim is binding without my presence at the ceremony."

Imperator Hart stepped forward, joining us in the middle of the room. "Of course, Your Majesty. We are well aware. However, we didn't want the *eagerness* of our couple to interfere with the Valabellum." Imperator Hart lowered his chin, and for once, I realized that he might have overplayed his hand. I couldn't decide if I wanted to gloat, or if I was afraid of what it meant for me. Either way, I was stuck in the center of it, and between Imperators, there was never a winner. "Full wedding plans are in place for a later time," he said.

At this, Kane slid his hand around my stomach, leaning into the Godsdamned rumors.

"Well, the lady is young," Imperator Kormac called. "Such creatures are fickle. Perhaps she might still change her mind. She may also wish for a warmer climate in the end as well."

"I can assure you she has adapted most wonderfully to the cold," Imperator Hart said.

"I, myself, have always encouraged our young women to learn to think with their minds," the Emperor said. "Perhaps, before I attend the nuptials, we shall allow the lady to be reminded of her options. And all jokes aside, however humorous they may be, we acknowledge that without my presence as a witness, no such marriage or activities to follow said ceremony, have occurred. Isn't that right, Your Highness?"

My hair blew from the force of Devon Hart's aura.

He bowed, and then stepped back, his hand on my shoulder, his fingers pressing down to my bone.

"Good," said the Emperor. "And now, to celebrate the reason we are all here. To Asherah's Feast Day!" He signaled to the musicians in the corner. "A Voladarim," he commanded.

Everyone began to cheer, and my heart sank. It was a traditional Lumerian dance, one I'd trained in. One I never, ever would have worn this dress for. Voladarim meant the dance of flying bodies. The movements were full of bounces and lifts by the larger partner.

Imperator Kormac crossed the dance floor in an instant, his predatory eyes taking me in.

"You won't mind," he said, addressing Kane, "if the lady starts the dance with me. She is still free to take other dance partners, is she not?"

Kane growled under his breath, but with a clear and obvious nod from the Emperor, Kane released me.

"Lady Lyriana," Imperator Kormac's wolfish grin spread across his face. "You are familiar with the Voladarim, aren't you?"

He knew Godsdamned well that I was. But I smiled sweetly. "I am, Your Highness. I was trained in all dances."

"All dances?" he asked. "Ah, yes. Forgive me. It's been some time since I've seen you perform. It's been months since your journey from Bamaria began." He gripped my waist, and took my hand, pulling me in. "Even longer since your last ball in the South."

I nearly tripped over the hem of my gown, and immediately tugged the waist back up.

"I have been away for some time, Your Highness," I said.

His nostrils flared. "And tell me, did you enjoy your journey?" He took my hand, forcing it onto his shoulder, over the golden border of his Imperator robes. Then he squeezed my waist again as the music grew louder, the beat signaling the steps.

"I'm grateful," I said, performing the opening steps, "that it led me back to my sister."

"Hmmm. Where else did it lead you?" Imperator Kormac took my wrist, and spun me out, before pulling me against him, lifting me, turning me, and dropping me back on my feet.

"Here," I said. "Your Highness."

"Yes, but how was it you arrived in Glemaria?"

My throat was dry. "We stayed very close to the shoreline in an attempt to avoid akadim, keeping east as we made our way to the North."

"And there you found true love and passion with," he smirked, "Arkturion Kane?"

I could feel Imperator Hart's eyes boring into me from behind, commanding me to answer correctly.

"Yes."

Without warning, Kormac spun me again, throwing me off balance until I crashed into him, more than aware that my dress had shifted and was showing even more cleavage than before. Even my hair falling down the center, covering the worst of Mercurial's contract, was doing little to shield me. His eyes dipped, and before I could adjust the fabric, he tightened his hold on me, walking us in a circle.

"I do apologize," I said, "if there was any insult felt by Ka Kormac by my choice. Lord Viktor, of course, is a strong match. But my heart does belong in the North."

He sneered. "I'll bet it does." He turned, looking pointedly at Rhyan, who looked sick as he was dancing with Amalthea.

Rhyan's eyes widened, then he spun Amalthea out of sight. Nearby, I saw Tristan leading Naria into the dance.

"Tell me more of your journey," he said, and pulled me closer, his arms locked around my back.

I had no choice but to wrap my arms around his neck, or lose my balance.

"Tell me about visiting Korteria." His fingers pressed into my back, right over old wounds. I flinched. "Tell me what Brockton said in his final moments."

"I–I'm sorry," I said, sweat beading behind my neck.

"Something the matter?" he asked, his aura suddenly predatory.

"I suddenly feel … a little faint.

"From your gryphon-shit pregnancy?" he asked. "You've blossomed into quite a young woman. But you will not mind my saying, you've not blossomed into a mother. Not yet. I think you feel fine. You're clearly untouched by that animal."

My chest tightened. "How would you know?"

He grazed my cheek with his palm, and it took all I had not to shrink back from his touch.

"You're not bruised." He looked down the cut of my dress, following the V of the red material to my waist. "Your northern Imperator should've known better. Covered you up." He slid his hands down my arms, holding them out for display. "I can tell. I've seen what Kane has done to his lovers in the past. And you're not one of them."

My heart was beating too hard for me to respond.

"Just know this," he said, lifting me again in his arms. He turned in a circle, and set me on my feet. "Whatever Brockton told you in Vrukshire was a lie."

"Vrukshire?" I shook my head. "I'm confused. He told me nothing. Because I—"

"Enough. I refuse to play this game when we both know the truth." He nodded, pressing me against him. "You were there.

And I know exactly what you did. I know what Rhyan did as well. And whatever my nephew said to you, in his final, desperate moments, was a lie, and not to be repeated." He pulled back, just enough for his black eyes to bore into mine.

My breath came short, my lips pulling back into a snarl I couldn't stop. But then I realized—he was afraid. He knew that Brockton had told me about Jules. He knew I carried the Empire's deepest, most deadly secret. That was what had stayed his hand all these months—that was why he'd sent Tristan to hunt me.

"Now, my lady, you end this farce of an engagement, and come back to the South willingly. Or I will drag you there myself, along with Lady Meera. We'll have you both bred within a week—your aunt has already given her blessing. And if by some Moriel-fucking chance that that gryphon-shit Arkturion did get you pregnant—or, more likely, that the forsworn-shit Rhyan did—we'll remove it. We can clean you out. Then we'll start fresh."

"Tell me then," I said seething. "What do you think Brockton told me?"

He bared his teeth. "Nothing at all. Because, as you said, you weren't there."

"Exactly," I gritted.

"Consider carefully. Because, if you had the conversation I suspect you did, you'd be in grave danger. Certain secrets can be shared, but only if you're willing to accept the consequences. When you know too much, you become a liability. As do those around you."

"Meera wasn't there," I said quickly.

"No, no, of course, not. But Lord Rhyan was." He glanced over at him again. "And if you think I haven't figured out exactly how he got there, or how he got you out of the Shadow Stronghold after I locked you in, then you're not as smart as they keep telling me you are. Your little bodyguard is useless to you—as is his entire Ka. Remember Tristan? Your old hunter? One word from me and he'll expose Rhyan. And the Palace is the perfect place to do it. The wards won't let him use his vorakh. It's the one place he can't escape. When secrets are under threat of exposure, everyone is in danger. And you, my lady, are trapped."

The music grew louder, my ears ringing. The Imperator lifted me one last time before dropping me, his hands squeezing my wrists.

"End the engagement and these games, and your true paramour, the one you're actually fucking, lives. Fail, and you'll watch him fall alongside your country." The music ended and he walked away, leaving my heart pounding outside of my chest.

Rhyan started toward me, but Imperator Hart cut him off, reaching for my waist.

"I told you to convince him!" he snarled.

"I tried! It doesn't matter!" I practically yelled. "He doesn't care about that."

"Why? What the fuck did he say to you?" Imperator Hart gripped my arms.

I glared, breaking free from his hold. "He said he's coming to claim me. And, if I don't give in, that's the end of Rhyan. Because he knows. He knows about Rhyan's vorakh."

CHAPTER THIRTY-SIX

TRISTAN

I watched as one Imperator pushed Lyriana away, giving her barely a second to breathe, before the next one was there. She was caught between north and south. Naria dug her fingernails into my palm, and I brought my gaze back to hers. The Voladarim had ended, and another dance had already begun. I twirled Naria, attempting to move closer to the center of the dance floor—to where Lyriana stood. I needed to get near her. Needed to talk to her. Confirm that Imperator Hart's gryphonshit story about her engagement, or wedding, or whatever the fuck he was talking about was a lie. I couldn't believe it. Refused to. Even if we'd never be together, I knew she wouldn't want that. Would never willingly agree to such a thing. The more I considered it, the sicker I felt.

The fact that she had fainted in the Throne Room wasn't helping convince me either—especially with the pregnancy rumors swirling. I desperately wanted word from her own mouth about her condition. I needed to know that she was okay. I had to pray that no matter what else was going on, the forsworn bastard—or rather the previously forsworn bastard—

wouldn't have allowed it. Knowing him, I didn't think he would. But then again, I never thought he'd have his title returned, or that I'd be engaged to Naria. I supposed anything was possible now.

I watched Lyr from the corner of my eye, her cheeks reddened, her hands moving weakly at her sides in a vain attempt to adjust that ridiculous excuse for a dress.

Naria's aura flared with a prickly annoyance and she grabbed my chin, forcing me to look into her eyes. I did, breathing heavily, aware of another aura approaching.

Imperator Kormac sauntered up to us, grinning viciously. He took Naria's hand, pressing a kiss to her palm.

"Your Highness," Naria said sweetly, releasing her hold on me to curtsey low, her breasts practically spilling out of her dress.

The Imperator's eyes raked down her body, and for a moment, Naira's aura flared again—this time with a nervous, shivery sensation. A second later she seemed calm. The way she was when she was with her mother. Pretending to be unaffected, unafraid. I had the sudden urge to step between them. To protect her.

"Your Grace," the Imperator drawled. "I know I've already told you, but you won't mind my saying how deliciously beautiful you look tonight."

Naria smiled, and bit her lip. "Thank you, Your Highness." Her eyes flicked to mine, accusatory, as if I hadn't offered her enough praise. Unless she was trying to communicate something else. I couldn't tell. I couldn't always read her. She was always so closed off.

"Hmmmm," the Imperator said, shaking his head slowly, his eyes still boring into Naria's body. "I hate to break up the dancing. But," his tilted his chin toward me, "might I have a word with your betrothed?"

I tensed.

Naria smiled. "Of course, Your Highness. You may have as many words as you like."

"How generous." He chuckled. "I thank you." He gripped her hand lifting her arm over her head. The position looked painful, but Naria's expression remained unaffected as he spun her in a circle. "Beautiful as ever. Just like your mother." He released her, shoving her back just a little as he did so.

Her mouth tightened, but she nodded and left us alone, grabbing a floating glass of wine as she walked away, heading for Lady Pavi and the members of Ka Elys.

My heart pounded, alone now with the wolf. "Your Highness," I said, and bowed, realizing I hadn't done so yet in this current interaction.

He leaned back, his weight on his heels as he surveyed me. The music swelled, the song changing to a new tune that required additional musicians to accompany the players.

Someone yelled out "*Rapatayim!*"

"Cheers!" came another yell.

Imperator Kormac's eyebrows narrowed. "We're still in agreement, aren't we? That we have a new opportunity for you to bring someone to me. Two someones," he said, and turned his wolfish eyes to Lyr as she spoke intimately to Imperator Hart.

Her mouth twitched into one of her fake smiles.

"They're here," I said, almost defiantly. "I haven't forgotten. But are you sure you still want her? She's …" I shrugged. "She might be pregnant."

"Pregnancy doesn't have to be permanent. And as far I'm concerned, if I didn't see him fuck her with my own eyes, I have a hard time believing that it happened. If she's been fucked, it hasn't been by him."

By Hart. Myself to Moriel. My blood was boiling. I hated thinking about that, hated talking about her like this. Like she was a thing to be traded, like any of these assholes deserved any say in how she lived her life or who she married. Or slept with.

Even if it would never be me.

"In exchange for Galen's safety," I said, my pulse pounding. "I know what you did. And I thank you." Before Imperator Hart's arrival, I'd been in the arena, watching the final practice with those chosen to fight tomorrow. And to my relief, Galen was nowhere to be seen. I'd wanted to go to his apartment to talk to him. To tell him I was sorry he hadn't made the trials.

But I'd been required to appear in the Throne Room. Since I'd captured that vorakh in the Palace, I'd been given special treatment—permission to carry my own stave, and daily invitations to be present in Court alongside Ka Kormac.

"The plan remains," Imperator Kormac agreed. "I made the necessary arrangements. Though, all of this does depend on you. I need you to do your part. I cannot simply take her from Kane's bed, not without causing a huge political headache with the North."

My throat tightened, and I nodded. I just had to keep agreeing. Agree and do nothing. Galen would be safe. He was already disqualified from the games, hadn't been cast in any role. The games were in hours, they'd start in the morning. I'd make a failed attempt at Lyr. And then she would leave with Imperator Hart. I'd just admit my failure and prostrate myself at his feet. I'd deal with those consequences. As long as it meant Galen lived. As long as it meant I didn't lose one more friend to Imperator Kormac's manipulations.

He stepped closer, and suddenly his hand was on my shoulder, just like it had been that day in the arena. "I would, however, like confirmation that that oversized ogre hasn't taken her to his bed. That there's no beast spawn in her belly. It would be in his character as well as Devon's." He shook his head. "But I don't think so. It's just a desperate attempt from Devon to keep one of my subjects."

"If you already know the truth, Your Highness, why do you need me to confirm it?"

"Because," he drawled, his other hand on my belly, "the truth becomes far more believable when she's the one confiding it in an old friend. One just like you. Who else? After all, you also failed to wed and bed her."

My jaw tightened, and his hands pushed against me, reminding me he could crush me.

"You also failed to put a baby in her belly." He licked his lips. "Now that's our job. And what about you? Any luck with Naria yet? Her breasts seem as pert as ever. Not a good sign."

"I've been away," I seethed, staring ahead. "I've been here, and she only recently arrived with Ka Batavia."

Now Kane was dancing with Lyr again. For a moment, she looked sick to her stomach. But then she smiled, this one almost believable, and she began to move her hips, undulating towards the Arkturion. Her eyes closed, her face revealing her embarrassment and anger. What was going on? I knew Lyr. She was never one to follow orders if she didn't agree with them. Even if they came from an Imperator. Especially not an Imperator. She knew how to play the game, to be amongst the nobles and follow the rules. But I'd always seen the disdain in her face when she disagreed with a request.

She continued dancing, and every step she took revealed the full expanse of her leg and hip in that Godsdamned excuse for a dress. Whose idea had that been? Devon Hart's? Fuck. I needed to get her out of there. But then what? If I could prove she wasn't with Kane's child, and I could take her away from Hart, from the North, what then? Hand her over to another Imperator? One who was just as manipulative, just as monstrous, if only more polished?

The music stopped playing and everyone turned to the Emperor. The merriment of the ball's attendees was still palpable, but in the silence I could better sense how many remained on edge.

Auriel appeared at the top of the stairs. Not actually Auriel, but a soturion dressed like him. His entire body was covered in golden armor, and a green cloak. A green mask covered half of his face, concealing his identity. Short golden curls that I suspected came from a wig peaked out from his helmet. There was no clue as to who he might be, or which country he'd hailed from.

"Ah," Imperator Kormac said, finally taking his hands off me. He grabbed a fresh glass of wine and began to sip slowly. "The presentation of the Guardians for tomorrow's final battle. Exciting." I nodded numbly.

Asherah was next on the stairs. She wore a red mask, and a golden helmet. Her hair spilled from it in wild, loose waves, a bright red that matched her soturion cloak. At the bottom of the stairs, she took Auriel's hand. Next was another masked soturion wearing orange. Ereshya. Followed by an incredibly large and muscled soldier in a yellow mask, and cloak. Shiviel. He wore golden cuffs around his wrists that reached his elbows, with yellow crystals embedded down the center representing the yellow shard of the Valalumir.

My heart began to pound. *Too much yellow. Too much yellow.* It was what the vorakh had said that night—when she'd looked at me. Suddenly, I was back in the Villa. My father alive. Swords cutting through the room.

I blinked the images away.

Cassarya appeared next, and then Hava, arriving in blue and violet cloaks.

"Only one more," Imperator Kormac said. "Moriel. The soturion sentenced to die tomorrow."

"Yes," I said, my voice hoarse.

He appeared at the top of the stairs, his features blurry behind the bright flickering lights of the ball. Then the soturion playing Moriel began his descent, his dark face covered by his indigo mask. Indigo colored crystals were alight in his arm cuffs. He had a familiar gait as he descended, and then I felt an aura, one I'd known for years, reach out into the room.

My heart stopped.

The soturi split apart, walking to either side of the dais.

"Does he look familiar to you?" Imperator Kormac asked.

No. No!

The herald shouted, "Your Guardians who will reenact the War of Light in tomorrow's Valabellum. But we honor them tonight on the eve of Asherah's Feast Day, as we commemorate our history and remember that we survived. That we are still here despite the Gods' fall. Tomorrow in the arena, you will see the epic battle play out between Auriel and Asherah as they join forces with Cassarya and Hava. Together they will face off against Shiviel, Ereshya, and then … in the Nutavian Katurium, as is tradition, we shall all witness the fall of Moriel."

"You said he was safe!" I said, my hand shaking so badly, my wine spilled. "You said that he was disqualified." *Fuck. Fuck!*

"Hmmm," Imperator Kormac said. "With the masks and helmets, it's difficult to say for sure who is who. Their identities, you know, are kept top secret from the public. Until the morning when they shall be revealed before all of Lumeria. Once that reveal happens, it cannot be undone. Unless, someone were to interrupt the proceedings between now and then. Remove a Guardian from their post. Replace them with another. Quickly."

The Guardians were stepping forward now. One by one they bowed and curtseyed to the Emperor, falling to their knees in supplication.

"What the hell am I supposed to do?" I asked. "Run across the room, grab their hands and drag them over here? Imperator Hart is right there!"

The Guardians were moving so fast. Each one stepped aside for the next, until Galen was on his knees before the Emperor. He looked up, and the crowd hushed as he called out, his voice booming. "Hail Your Majesty, Emperor Theotis, High Lord of

Lumeria Nutavia." He rose to his feet. "I am about to die, with honor and respect, reminding us all of Moriel's demise, and our success on this most auspicious Asherah's Feast Day. I salute you."

Emperor Theotis's thick white eyebrows lifted in amusement, and he extended his hand, his signet ring catching the light. "I accept your salute, and your bravery, and your sacrifice."

The Emperor's consort clapped.

Galen stepped up onto the dais, his knees bent as he lowered himself to kiss Emperor Theotis's ring.

I couldn't watch. Couldn't bear it. Imperator Kormac had cornered me, was forcing me to act. To again betray myself. No matter what, I'd lose someone else before this was over.

Then it happened. Too quick for me to process what I was seeing.

Galen lunged. Not for the Emperor. Or his consort. But for the Blade. His fist crashed against the Arkturion's cheek, forcing him back just enough to give Galen an opening, a chance to withdraw the old man's sword.

Everyone was screaming. Some nobles rushed forward, while others were running out of the room.

But all I saw was my best friend doom himself, as he pointed the blade at Emperor Theotis, and with a cry of, "This is for Haleika!" he plunged the sword into His Majesty's belly.

CHAPTER THIRTY-SEVEN

LYRIANA

By the Gods! By the fucking Gods. I blinked rapidly, barely able to believe what I was seeing.

Everything was happening at once. Soturi tackled the soldier playing Moriel. Mages were casting protective domes around the Emperor as he was lifted into the air and floated from the room with what felt like a legion of soturi running after him.

The Blade had recovered from his punch and rushed forward to the man playing Moriel. He was already bound, and encircled by the Emperor's men. But with a growl, the Arkturion lunged forward, punching the soturion on the nose. The crack echoed across the room and left me shuddering.

Imperator Hart was on the move, shouting orders I could barely comprehend at Kane as he rushed into the fray. And just like that, I realized the danger we were all in. If there was one assassin, there could be more. Like the Emartis.

My heart began to thunder as I looked for Meera in the crowd. Aiden was already leading her toward me. I could see Rhyan, his eyes frantic as he let go of Amalthea, rushing to my side.

"LYR!" he yelled, but his voice could barely be heard over the shouting coming from every direction.

Dario grabbed my arms and pulled me back as I struggled against his hold. Every fiber of my being was desperate to reach Rhyan. To reassure him I was okay. To reassure myself that he wasn't hurt. I needed to get him. To touch him. To feel him. To pull him out of there.

He pushed soturi out of his way as the man playing Moriel was taken from the room. Orders from the multitude of escorts present were flying back and forth across the floor. There were shouts to protect the Arkasvim, the Arkturi, the Heirs.

Meera and Aiden were close, and I reached one hand for her, and the other for Rhyan. He was about to reach me. Our fingers nearly touching.

And then we were surrounded. Soturi withdrew their swords, each blade pointed directly at us, as they glowered, and moved in. Orders were shouted from the Emperor's men to our escorts and guards—we were to all cooperate, noble, or not. Our soturi had to answer to the Emperor's. And if any of us disobeyed, no matter our station, we would pay the price.

"Hands up," one shouted. "No one moves. No one leaves."

My pulse thrummed as I watched Rhyan still, and then Meera, swords encircling them.

Rhyan's eyes met mine, concern all over his face.

"Steady," Dario whispered. "Steady."

"You, too," I said, "Careful," but my eyes were still on Rhyan's.

A trumpet blared, and the herald shouted. "His Majesty's Second, Lord Emmaron."

A dozen soturi, all wearing the golden tattoo across their cheeks descended the stairs. A white dome appeared, followed by another dozen soturi, all wearing the pale gold of the Emperor's armor.

Lord Emmaron was a middle-aged man, his hair a mix of

black and gray cut short with a thick black beard. He also wore pale purple robes, though without any of the golden trim found on Theotis's. Like Theotis, and the Blade, he was in far better shape than seemed natural at his age, with a thick torso, and incredibly muscular arms.

Reaching the stage, Lord Emmaron stepped up, his protection dome still around him. The mages who'd conjured it were visibly sweating, and I wondered why the Emperor hadn't had one before. The magical protections in this room must have been so extreme, even he had lacked the proper magic needed to fully guard him. Then again, a stave was little use against a sword already embedded in one's belly. I squeezed my eyes shut.

"Bow," commanded the herald.

The soturi who surrounded us remained still and stoic. Their blades glinted in the firelight. They did not move, nor withdraw their weapons. Instead, they jerked their chins to the ground, indicating we were to fall.

Swallowing hard, and again, far too acutely aware of how little dress I wore, I sank to my knees, my belly tightening to ensure I didn't lose my balance and accidentally find myself impaled.

"An assassination attempt has been made on His Majesty, Emperor Theotis, High Lord of Lumeria Nutavia," shouted Lord Emmaron. Spit flew from his mouth as he continued. "He remains in dire condition. Our medic mages are currently with him. We all pray for His Majesty's immediate recovery."

He paused, looking around the room, his eyes slowly taking in everyone, before he continued.

"The would-be assassin has been apprehended and taken into custody. He will be questioned, along with all of the Valabellum's soturi. The Valabellum is hereby postponed until His Majesty's condition is properly assessed and treated." He motioned around the edge of the dance floor where the sigils hung for the ruling Kavim. "All Arkasvim, Imperators, and

Arkturi will follow me. We will shelter in the Throne Room. As of this moment, the Palace's strictest safety protocols are in effect, and we are officially in *Arkchayperam.*"

Not just a lockdown, but preparation for a vote to name the new Emperor.

Imperator Hart looked back at me, his eyes moving slowly across our little crowd, stopping on Rhyan, and Meera. I could almost feel his orders—the need to obey him rushing through my blood. But he couldn't give a direct command. Not now. Not until he was released from the Throne Room.

I watched as he was escorted out, along with Kane, Imperator Kormac, the Bastardmaker, and Aunt Arianna. One by one they left, until the ballroom only possessed clusters of nobility from each Ka, all huddled together around the room.

"All Kavim will be escorted by our soturi back to your quarters, you'll be locked inside until further notice," Lord Emmaron said once the doors had shut again.

Mages stepped forward on command, appearing out of the shadows.

He continued, "Each of you will be bound during escort for your own safety, and unbound once in the confines of your own rooms. Do not expect to leave your quarters before morning. Anyone who does, will be escorted to our prisons."

Someone screamed, and my heart jumped as I expected to find another assassin. Another murder.

But it was just a noble—one who'd never experienced the pain or humiliation of a binding past their Revelation Ceremony. The ropes were black, glittering and smoking as they snaked across the room in every direction, twisting and twining around each Lumerian who remained.

Cries of pain and shouts of indignation raced back and forth across the dance floor.

Only Rhyan didn't flinch as he was bound.

And then I was hauled into a line with the rest of Imperator

Hart's Ka, and marched at a quickened pace through the Palace back into our quarters. Meera was among us—she may have been ordered back to Ka Batavia, but her room remained with Ka Hart. We were all taken to our apartments, and only at our doors were our bindings removed. Dario was left on guard outside of mine, but he wasn't alone. Soturi loyal to the Emperor had stationed themselves down the hall.

The door was slammed shut behind me, then locked. I paced back and forth across the room, looking out the window for any sign of life, or news before changing out of that Godsforsaken dress, and into a pair of sleep pants, and a light top.

I went back to sit on my bed, unsure what else to do or how to pass the time. We were locked in until morning. Until Asherah's Feast Day. Until the games began. But all at once, the direness of the situation settled in. There would be no Valabellum. A Throne Room full of Imperators and every ruler and warlord in Lumeria stood between us and the shield.

We'd never reach the shard, never steal it, not unless the Emperor recovered. Not unless the games were allowed to play out.

And if they didn't, how would we get Jules?

I swallowed roughly, wanting for once, for the Emperor to be okay. To be in good health. Because I needed to go forward with the plan. I didn't come all this way, or get this close to her, just to fail now.

I wrung my hands together, pacing and pacing, until I heard a knock.

But not on the door. On my window. I tensed. I'd left the glass partially open to feel the breeze. And on the windowsill now, there was a hand.

Someone had scaled the building, and was climbing inside.

My heart pounded, as I searched for a weapon. But then I heard Rhyan hiss, "Lyr."

"By the Gods," I said, and rushed over, pushing the glass the rest of the way up.

Rhyan shoved himself over the windowsill a second later. He stood abruptly and slammed the window shut, his breath heavy.

"They're not guarding the courtyard," he said, "seeing as how there's no way out. Except back in. Luckily that's all I wanted. To get to you."

"You shouldn't be here," I said. "It's dangerous."

"I needed to see you." He sounded desperate, pained, but he held back, waiting for me.

I clutched my stomach, already preparing for the pain, for the rise in temperature of my blood at disobeying Imperator Hart's orders. I wracked my mind, desperately going over our last conversation, and I realized I could look at Rhyan, and step toward him. I didn't feel compelled to send him away, didn't feel any pain. There'd been no command about this. No orders against Rhyan alone in my room. Only about Kane at the ball.

I met his eyes, taking in the brilliant emerald green color I'd been denied so much of this past month. And I nodded.

"Partner," he said. That one word seemed to hold the entire universe in it.

And that was it. We raced into each other's arms.

CHAPTER THIRTY-EIGHT

LYRIANA

"Rhyan," I gasped, just as I was swallowed into his embrace, his arms tightening around me, his hands pressing into my back, his fingers tangling in my hair. For a moment, we just held each other, breathing each other in. Our hearts pounding, seemingly as one.

"Lyriana," Rhyan murmured into my hair. "Lyriana." He breathed me in, his aura intensifying. "By the Gods. We're not safe here." His hold on me, already possessive and strong, tightened.

"We're not safe anywhere," I said, thinking of everything that had happened just within the last day. My talk with Mercurial. What Rhyan's father had revealed. My conversation with Imperator Kormac. There was so much happening, so much we had to worry about, to think through.

I pulled back, just so I could look him up and down. I was drinking in his features, the small details in his face I'd been unable to stare at for the past month. The way his cheeks flushed pink against his pale, northern complexion. The dark stubble nearly always present around his jaw. The soft pout of his lips, the way they always looked so damned kissable, and the pattern of soft curls in his hair that I just wanted to run my fingers through.

"Rhyan, we need to talk."

"You're not hurt?" he asked, his eyes searching mine. And I realized he'd been drinking me in, too. "I've been worried. Ever since we arrived—since you fainted. I wanted to come to you. But I—I couldn't." He looked so guilty as he admitted that.

"It was the shard," I said, my voice shaking. "It made the light flare."

"I thought so." He shook his head, but then his hand slid to my belly, rising slowly up the front of my shirt, until his palm rested between my breasts. Over my heart. Over the mark of the golden Valalumir. "Anything?" he asked. "Does it hurt?"

I shook my head. "No. And now that I was near it, hopefully it got that first meeting glow out of the way."

Rhyan's expression tensed, his eyebrows drawing together.

"I can't believe what just happened back there."

"I know." The soturion had struck out of nowhere. But I'd been close enough to the front of the room to see the blade enter the Emperor's stomach, to see the sword push in, and then up.

Exactly what I'd done to Brockton.

Rhyan sighed. "I don't know what we're going to do now."

I bit my lip, the backs of my eyes burning. "I never thought I'd be praying for the Emperor's health."

"Praying?" Rhyan's face hardened. "I'm not. He deserved a lot fucking more than that. After all that he's done. He can burn in hell."

"But the Valabellum—"

"It doesn't matter," he said gently. "Something tells me, whether he lives or dies, it won't make a difference. Even if there's a new Emperor named tonight—Lyr, there's not going to be a Valabellum tomorrow. There's going to be a whole slew of other events coming instead. And a lot more Godsdamned security."

"Who do you think would replace him?" I asked.

Rhyan ran his hands up and down my arms, before settling on my hips. He blew out a sharp breath. "Fuck if I know. It could be any of those bastards." His throat bobbed. "We have to pray it's not my father."

If Devon Hart became Emperor, I didn't know what that would mean for our bargain. I wouldn't have to steal the shield. I knew that much. It would be his by right. He could simply take it, order it to be stored in Seathorne. And Jules would be his— he'd have all the access to her in the world.

And he'd have utter and complete control over me. Over Rhyan.

Just as he'd been planning all along.

My heart pounded now for another reason.

"There's nothing we can do about it now," Rhyan said, quietly. "We're both trapped in these apartments at least until morning. I can't travel, and we can't get past the guards—there's too many. And the Throne Room's off-limits for the foreseeable future."

"Maybe we can still get the shard," I said, hopefully. "After the Throne Room empties."

Rhyan frowned. "Lyr, listen to me. Our plan to steal the shield was risky enough. Our odds of succeeding were slim. And that was after a month of planning. Everything we prepared was based on a specific event with a specific schedule and protocol. With what just happened, there's too many unknown factors to account for." He shook his head. "There's no way we can do this. We need to wait."

I shook my head, pulling back. "No. NO! We didn't just do all of that planning and suffering for a month. Not for nothing." My chest heaved. "Fuck!" Tears pricked my eyes. "I did not just spend a month missing you. Missing Meera, being taunted and tortured by your father. Being fucking touched and kissed by that Godsdamned monster. All so we could fucking fail in the end."

I didn't even realize it until then just how much the end of the mission was keeping me going, giving me the ability to fight through all my moments of misery and disgust. My lonely nights, my constant humiliation and worry—I'd barely handled it, but I had. Because if it meant saving Jules, it was worth it. But if we couldn't even do that ... if it had all been pointless ...

Rhyan's jaw tightened. "I saw. I saw that fucking kiss," he growled, his emerald eyes blazing. His hands made fists at his sides. "And that Godsdamned dress." His chest heaved, and his eyes searched mine for a long moment. And then, just as he sometimes did, when he looked like he was deliberating, carefully weighing his options, he beckoned me even closer. "Come here. Come here to me."

I did. And he reached for my cheeks, his palms sliding down my neck. A shiver ran down my spine, and then his lips were on mine. Soft, and gentle, kissing only the corner of my mouth. It was barely a kiss at first, and then it was more. So much more.

But I pulled back. So much had happened tonight, I'd been able to ignore the sickening feeling in my stomach, and the disgust I felt from Kane's lips on mine. My survival instincts had kept me safe, just as they had all month. But here, while we were in stasis, while everything was uncertain, I suddenly could feel his mouth on mine again. Feel his hands on my body. His unwanted eyes on my dress.

"Wait," I said suddenly, shaking out of his hold.

Rhyan shook his head. "What? Why?"

"I feel disgusting." I wiped at my lips. "I still feel him. Feel him there." I looked away. "You shouldn't have to—shouldn't have to kiss me. Not after him."

"Lyr, let me," Rhyan said. "Let me kiss you. Let me kiss his touch away. I'll kiss every place he touched you. Every place he looked at you. I'll kiss you, and kiss you, until you forget. Kiss you, until you only know my mouth again." His eyes heated.

"That's a lot of kissing," I said, my voice sounding defeated.

"Well," Rhyan's good eyebrow lifted, "It's quite a hardship." He winked. "But I think I'm up for the job. If you want me."

The sound of boots marching down the hall sounded, and my throat tightened, the moment gone. Rhyan stilled, prepared to go back out the window if anyone entered, but the footsteps faded.

"If the Emperor does die," I said quietly, "we could be dealing with your father in charge. Or, we could be facing an Emperor who chooses a new Imperator for the North. Any access we have right now to Jules could be taken away."

"We haven't lost yet," he said. "It's just that our original plan might not happen tomorrow."

My heart sank. "It might not happen at all." I squeezed his hands. "Imperator Kormac knows. He knows you're vorakh."

Rhyan paled. "What? He told you that? Tonight?"

I sighed. "He's holding it over me. Nothing we did the past month—at least nothing I did—fucking matters. Kormac wants me to end the engagement. He says if I go back to Viktor, you'll be safe."

"And you believe him? Gryphon-shit." He pushed his fingers through his hair. "Gods! How many fucking suitors can they force on you?"

I laughed bitterly. "He was worried," I said. "It's not just that he wants to use me to get to Bamaria. He's worried that Brockton told us about Jules. I think he knows we know."

"Fuck. I never thought about that. But if that's true," he ran his fingers through his hair again, "Then he's never been more dangerous."

"Maybe I should take his offer," I said.

"What?" Rhyan shouted. "Lyr, no! I won't let you do that. You are not risking your life for mine."

"What other choice do I have?"

"Not that one. You are not handing yourself over to those Godsdamned wolves! Just give me a chance to think. Let me handle it."

"Just like you've been handling everything else behind my back?" My voice had come out with far more bitterness than I'd realized I was carrying.

His eyes darkened. "What the hell does that mean?"

"I saw Mercurial," I said, my voice cold. "He told me about *Rakashonim*. He told me you've known for a month. You knew that first day we were in Seathorne, and you said nothing to me. Nothing. We had that night to talk, and you could have told me, warned me, shared your concerns, but you didn't tell me." I shook my head, my chest tightening. All at once, I felt like I was coming undone. I'd been so worried for Rhyan, so concerned and upset about our distance, I hadn't had room to fully be angry. To be upset at the secrets he'd kept. But I was. And I couldn't hide it any longer, because all the buried feelings, were now rushing to the surface.

Rhyan paled. "Lyr, I couldn't. You know I couldn't with the restrictions we've had in place."

"Before those!" I shouted. "Maybe you didn't get a chance to tell me about the *Rakashonim* that night. But what about Kenna? Or what happened with Garrett?" I sucked in a breath. "What about Amalthea?" I couldn't stop. Every secret I knew he was keeping was pouring out of me.

Rhyan's jaw was working, his breath heavy. He was silent for a long moment, his aura almost unreadable as it shifted, growing colder and colder, and then seemingly vanishing all at once.

"Who told you about Amalthea?" His voice had hardened, every word he spoke clipped and harsh.

"Your father," I spat. "Who else?"

"Gods." He groaned, low in his throat. "I didn't want you to know. You weren't supposed to."

"What do you mean I wasn't supposed to?" I felt like I'd

been punched in the gut. "What else am I not supposed to know?"

His eyes flashed with anger. But then, just as suddenly, he looked utterly defeated. He walked past me, sinking down onto the edge of the bed, his head in his hands. "I'm sorry." His voice shook. "I'm sorry."

I sat down on the bed beside him, and for a moment we sat in silence.

Finally, he lifted his head and looked at me, his eyes red. "I didn't want you to know," he said, his voice thick with emotion. "And at the same time, I did. But I couldn't tell you. Because I've been afraid. Because I'm a fucking coward."

"That's not true," I said.

"Yes, it is!"

I felt a knot in my stomach form, unprepared for the anguish in his voice. He looked like he was in so much pain, so much agony. It was the same look he wore when Dario and Aiden had captured us, when they'd first mentioned Garrett. Rhyan was making himself miserable. And I realized then, that I cared more about him than I did about any secrets he'd kept. Cared more for him than any anger I'd been holding onto. I'd needed to express it, but that was it. Whatever secrets he'd kept from me in the past, he'd always done so with good intentions. Rhyan did everything with good intentions.

He didn't need to tell me everything just so I could know, or so I could trust him. I didn't need any of that. I already knew his soul. I already trusted him completely. But this month had been harder on us than I realized.

"Rhyan," I said. "Look at me." I cupped his chin. "Look at me." He did. *"Ani janam ra."*

He sniffled, his eyes crinkling. "I know you."

I nodded. "I know you. I love you. And I trust you. You're not a coward. I know you had your reasons. But you can tell me, anything. If it helps, I want you to. And if it doesn't, then don't.

If you're not ready, I understand. But if you are, I'm here. I just, I don't want to be left in the dark. Not when it comes to my safety. Not when it comes to yours. We're partners." Then I pressed my fist to my heart, and I pressed it twice, then flattened my hand. "*Me sha, me ka.*"

Rhyan took a shuddering breath. "Lyr," he said. "You're right. There are things you need to know. I promised I'd tell you. And I think, I think now I'm ready to tell you everything. I think I need to." He bit his lip. "It's just ..." He swallowed roughly, shaking his head. "It's a lot."

I placed my hand on his arm, then slid it down to his hand, our fingers entwined. "We have some time. I'm not going anywhere. Not tonight."

His eyes moved slowly back and forth across my face.

"I promise," I said. "Nothing you tell me will change the way I feel."

And then he nodded, taking a long, deep breath, as if in preparation.

"I know." He squeezed his eyes shut. "Just ... where do I start?"

"Anywhere."

He squeezed my hand. "I've been having dreams," he said. "Memories. Of myself as Auriel. They're ... haunting." His eyes watered. "Each time I see you, I see you as Asherah, and in the dream, it's like ... it's like no time has passed. My love for her —it's like my love for you. Overwhelming. So deep, and intense." He smiled wryly. "But so many times in the dreams, you—she, dies." He looked away, and something in my heart stirred.

"I hear her screaming," he continued. "Almost every night, I climb Gryphon's Mount in my dreams, I build the tomb, I close her in it. Her body. You. And Gods. It's agony. And it's ..." He blew air from his lips. "It's left me scared of losing you. More than I was already."

I rubbed my thumb back and forth across his hand, and he tightened his hold on me.

"So, when Mercurial came to see me," he said, "and told me that your ability to heal, that your ability to call on Asherah is something called *Rakashonim*, and that it's dangerous, it ... it threw me. I've been researching it. Trying to understand. Trying to find answers. I wanted to find a way you could use it without hurting yourself."

I nodded, knowing he'd been requesting additional scrolls at the library. "I thought you were researching Shiviel."

"I was. I am. I've been looking at both. Because in one of my dreams, I realized that it was what we'd done to him that killed Asherah. Or at the very least, was the start of it. It had been too much. Too much magic for her form to hold. Last night, even after all I'd read, I still didn't know what we'd done. When I couldn't sleep, I snuck outside, and walked to the seraphim. Kind of like I do every night, but this time I was awake. I fell asleep at her side, in the rain. I'd had memories there before, so I thought I'd try again. And I was right. I dreamt Shiviel had captured me —Auriel. And you came. Asherah, came to save me. I was weak. But together we—they—"

I squeezed his hand.

His lips quirked. "We cut through his soul, at least that's my understanding. We cut him in half, but his body remained the same. Less, but whole. And from that, a new life was born. A small child."

"What?" I asked. Something stirred in the back of my memory. Brown eyes. But just as quickly, the memory faded.

"It looked like we killed him. But we didn't. I think ..." Rhyan drew in a sharp breath. "I think there's an eighth Guardian out there. One who isn't as powerful. Kane has no vorakh. But I think this one does. And there's something else. Something else I didn't tell you, because—because I wasn't sure. And I'm still not. But no more secrets between us."

"No more secrets," I said.

"When we fought that first night in Seathorne, about my father rescuing Jules, I still maintain what I said. That he wouldn't save her for you—no matter the bargain. He wouldn't do anything to make you happy, or help her. Not unless it benefited him. Mercurial told me Meera was Cassarya. And that left only Hava to find. But then he said something strange. He said I had found Hava. Once."

"He said you found her?" My eyes widened, piecing together what he was saying. "Rhyan." I could feel my heart thundering. His father would only help rescue Jules if it benefited him. Rhyan had only found her once. Hava, Goddess and Guardian of the Violet Ray.

I remembered then so clearly the way Jules always loved the color violet. The way she wore a violet dress that night. The way her hair fell like a lion's mane. How Hava was depicted the same. "Jules?"

He nodded grimly. "I think so."

"Then your father truly will rescue her."

"To control her—to control all of us."

"We have to get the shard. We can't let Morgana and Aemon have it. And we can't let them take Jules for themselves." I'd known from the vision I took from Meera they planned to come for her, too. But now I could see exactly why.

Not because she was our cousin. Because they needed her for their army—to fight against us. Another Guardian. Myself to fucking Moriel. Jules was a Guardian. A Goddess.

"How?" I asked suddenly. "How does your father know all of this?"

Rhyan stared ahead. "Well, Jules is a guess on my part. But a good one based on the evidence. I think … I think my father's actually telling the truth about my mother." His jaw tensed, his eyes reddening. "I never … never saw her with a vorakh. But, for all his lies, sometimes there's a kind of truth inside them. He bound her, drained her, amongst the other things he did. She would have hardly had access to her magic as it was those last few years. But I think she saw us coming, saw what would happen. I don't know if she told him willingly, or if he forced her to detail her visions to him." He shook his head sadly. "But it's the only thing that makes sense, and now looking back at everything ... When she died, she said something to me." His voice shook. "She said that it was right."

"What was right?" I asked gently.

He shrugged. "That she died for me? That she saved me? Maybe that she knew all along how it would end. I don't know. But just before the tournament when Garrett died, she was speaking cryptically. Offering hints. I'd thought she was maybe intuitive, not vorakh, and then I had written the idea off, thinking she'd only known about my father's machinations. I thought she was warning me. But now, I think ... I think she knew more about what was coming than I'll ever understand."

"Jules is Hava," I said, still in disbelief. "And there's another Guardian. A lesser Shiviel."

"Yes," Rhyan said, looking distant. "Gods. To think that Kane could have been stronger the first time he broke my nose. He probably would have killed me."

I remembered what Aiden and Dario had said. That Kane had hurt Rhyan the day before Garrett died. And that Aiden had healed him, that Garrett had been there, too.

"What happened back then?" I asked, my thumb rubbing small circles against his skin.

"I guess now is the part where I tell you the rest of it. All of it." He took another deep breath, his eyes meeting mine.

"Garrett was vorakh."

My eyes widened. "With which power?"

"Mine," Rhyan said bleakly. "Traveling. Remember when I showed you the scar on my back? The mark of a blood oath. I told you it was dormant, because it had been fulfilled, and because—because the author of it's gone."

We'd been on the beach, beside the Guardian of Bamaria. The waves lapping at our feet. Rhyan had just learned that Meera had visions. Learned why I'd been protecting her.

"I remember." Like all blood oaths, his was invisible, and only detected by the feel of raised skin. "What happened?"

"Akadim attacked at the end of summer, the year before I returned to Bamaria forsworn. Everyone was out that night in the fields, drinking and partying. Even me. Then the bells rang. The akadim were close, and our soturi were nowhere to be seen. Dario was pissed, far too drunk to fight. We had no choice but to send him off with Kenna, who ... who I was with at the time." He pressed his lips together, looking unsure if he should continue.

"It's okay," I said. "I promise. You can talk about her." Then I smiled. "I like Kenna."

Rhyan emitted a small relieved gasp, his eyes watering further, and he nodded. "She likes you, too."

I took a deep breath. "So you sent Dario to protect her?"

"And Aiden. Both of them are mages so ..." He gestured helplessly.

"Not great in an akadim fight," I offered.

"No." Rhyan continued. "Garrett and I went to stop the threat. I was still new to killing the beasts. Not as skilled as I am now. One almost got me. One second, I was there fighting for my life, and the next ... I'd traveled to a nearby river. I freaked out when I realized what I'd done. But it wasn't me who'd done it. It had been Garrett. He'd gotten us out of there. He saved my life." He looked down at the ground. "We swore the blood oath that night. Not exactly to keep each other's secret. But, to keep each other safe. To protect the other. I was the only one who knew about him. Not Dario. Not even Aiden. Garrett didn't want him to have that burden. So I kept it for him. Then, during the tournament, while we were in the wild tracking down our gryphons, we were attacked. Near the Allurian Pass." He shook his head. "We were ambushed by akadim."

"By the Gods," I said, shifting closer to Rhyan, my heart was pounding.

"I thought we were okay," he cried. "I really did. Garrett killed one and we escaped, and tried to warn the others. We had to fly back to the arena. It took hours. And Garrett," his chest heaved, "he was quiet the whole time. Barely saying a word. He was forsaken ... turning. And just—" Rhyan wiped at his eyes. "Silently dealing with it. Accepting his fate." He swallowed. "Inside the arena, it was getting dark. He'd be akadim at sunset —he had maybe minutes. That's when he told me. He wanted me to ..." His shoulders shook. "Asked me to ..." But he couldn't go on. He was filled with too much emotion.

But I understood. "You had to kill him," I said. "To save him."

Rhyan nodded. "And to fulfill my oath. To protect him, to keep him from becoming a bigger monster."

I held Rhyan to me, and his arms wrapped around my waist. But then he pulled back, like he had to keep talking.

He'd kept the secret for too long, and now that he'd started, he had to finish.

"My father threw me in prison after. He wasn't happy. He wanted me to win. But not like that. What happened in the arena destroyed me, but he was only concerned with the political ramifications. He brought me out the night he wanted me to swear the blood oath. The night he killed my mother. He was going to kill me. But she—she came between us. And then, after I rotted in prison for some time, Kenna showed up. She brought the key, gave it to my escort. To Bowen. He smuggled me out. But he didn't make it. He died." He'd been speaking in an almost rushed-trance-like state. But his voice cracked on the name of his old guard. "Just as I reached the border, Dario's father found me.

I was escaping on gryphon-back—one Artem had provided for me. And when we were attacked, the gryphon—" His jaw clenched.

"The gryphon killed Dario's father?" I asked. "Not you."

"It makes little difference. Still my fault he's dead. My fault the others are, too."

"Rhyan, no. No. Listen to me. None of this is your fault." I wiped at the tears now falling freely from his eyes. "You didn't know that any of that would happen. You weren't trying to hurt anyone. You were just trying to escape, to survive. And you had to make impossible choices."

"Whatever it is, it's the reason why ... why Dario and Aiden hate me."

I pushed one of his unruly curls back with my fingers, then traced my palm down his cheek. "I don't think they do," I said softly. "I think they're hurting. I think if they knew ... I think they'd understand." I remembered Kenna's words, that they loved Rhyan, and that she believed they would work it out. And I believed it too now, especially when I considered those small moments when Dario's guard had slipped. "I think they'd forgive you. More importantly, I think they want to."

"I've been distant from them. For a long time. Even before everything with Garrett happened. After the solstice that one year, the year we ... you know."

I nodded. "I know."

He made a low guttural sound in his throat. "Fuck. I was so in love with you that summer. So completely lost. I still feel ill when I think about hurting you. But I don't regret it. Because I did what I had to—to protect you. When I came home, I thought I'd never see you again, never step another foot in Bamaria. And I was okay with that, or I thought I was, at least. I thought I could stand it. But I was miserable. I missed you. And I was lonely. So fucking lonely. I kept to myself for a year. I wouldn't court. I didn't want to. I didn't want anyone. Only you." His eyes flashed. "Because it was always, always you. And I didn't want to talk about it. Not to anyone. But then … well?" He laughed bitterly. "A son of Devon Hart can't be celibate." He spoke, mocking the cadence of his father. "People talk. I had no choice. I had to start … *courting* again. So I did. Whoever my father pushed at me. Nobles, visiting dignitaries, their daughters."

I swallowed, realizing he'd moved on to another confession. A deeper one.

"And with all those nobles, you … you didn't want to …?" I couldn't finish. What he was describing sounded a lot like rape. "Not with any of them?"

Rhyan swallowed, quiet for a long moment, his gaze distant, his jaw clenched. "No," he said at last. "No. I didn't want to." His eyes reddened, and his mouth tightened. "I mean, I was never … never overpowered. Nor hurt, not physically. Any single one of them, all of them actually, I could have fought off without breaking a sweat, even when I was bound. Easily. I just … didn't." His throat worked. "I didn't fight back. Didn't say no." His voice cracked. "I let it happen. All of it. Because I was numb. Because I thought I had no choice. Because I didn't care. Until Kenna. Once there was Kenna, it stopped. She saved me."

My chest hurt, my own tears falling. "Thank the Gods for Kenna, then."

He sniffled and nodded. "Amalthea was the first one. The worst one. I was … so fucking wasted. And I didn't—I didn't want her. Didn't want to. But …" He shook his head sadly. "After my father's threats … and … well … I'd found out that day about Jules being taken. And I knew, knew about you and Tristan. I was a wreck."

"And what about Amalthea?" I asked angrily. I thought of all the times he'd scratched his palm when she was near, the way he'd shut his emotions off around her. The way she pressed herself against him, forcing so much bodily contact. Because it wasn't foreign to her. "Did she know?" I seethed. "Did she know you didn't want to?"

Rhyan looked miserable. "I don't know, Lyr. Maybe. I don't … can't really remember. I was so damn drunk."

"That should have been enough," I yelled. "When I see her again …" My hands trembled with a rage I hadn't known I could possess.

"Don't," Rhyan said, his voice now soft. "Don't. She's not worth it. It's all over now. No matter what, I'll never touch her again, and I'll never let her touch me. I'll never let another. No matter what my father says." He shifted on the bed, his face raw with emotion, but there was something else. A lightening to his aura. A sense of having shared some of his burden with me.

I shifted too, our knees touching, our hands clasped.

"Lyriana. Lyr." He sighed. "It doesn't matter anymore. Because I'm yours. I was always yours. All of those years went by and I never forgot you. Never went a day without you in my mind, without you being at the forefront of my desires. And I'm sorry. I'm sorry I didn't tell you all of this before. I'm sorry you had to find out these things the way you did. I'm sorry if any of it ever hurt you. Or made you question me. Even if only for a moment. I'm sorry I was too afraid to tell you before now. Because I'm with you. Only you. I've seen the look in your eyes. The hurt I caused from my own damned cowardice. I'd do anything to take it back. To erase all your pain from the past month. So if you need to mark your territory, do it. Do whatever you want to me." He sank to the floor, kneeling before me.

"Rhyan?" I asked.

"Take me," he said, his voice almost desperate. Begging. "Take me for all I am. You want to claim me? Mark me? Do it. Scratch me, scar me. I don't care. Your touch is the only one I've ever wanted. The only one I've ever needed. And I'll take it in any way I can. While we have tonight. While we're trapped here. Remind me. Remind yourself, after all I told you. After all these secrets, and all we've been through. I'm yours. Gods, Lyr. I'm fucking yours. I always have been."

My heart was swelling with love for Rhyan, and somehow breaking all at once. I knew him. I knew his soul. I kept thinking we'd reached the height of intimacy, of knowing each other. But somehow, I felt even closer to him, now that I knew all of his secrets. And I realized something else with a sudden, burning hunger.

I needed him.

But the desire inside me wasn't what he was describing.

I rose to my feet, taking his hands in mine, and he stood with me. I expanded my aura, pushing out my warmth, my love, letting it entwine with the cool soothing nature of his. I could almost feel it, our energies joining and crackling around us. Hot and cold, the sun and the moon, coming together into a perfect combination. At last, I shook my head. "No. Rhyan."

His face fell.

My eyes searched his. "I don't need to claim you. Nor mark you. It's not your body that's mine. It's your heart, it's your soul. Just as my heart, body, and soul are yours. In this life, in every life. Forever. *Rakame*."

He was breathing heavily then, emitting an emotional sigh of relief. And then our bodies were coming together, pressing closer to match our auras. His eyes were hooded now, darkening and hungry with desire.

I ran my fingers through his hair. And suddenly nothing else seemed to matter. Not Kane. Not Amalthea. Not the Emperor's death, or anyone else here. Not even the threat of me using *Rakashonim*. Just me and Rhyan for these next few stolen hours. They were ours. Just ours. And I was going to take them.

His father's orders wouldn't touch me here, there was no blood compulsion pulling me away, telling me to stop. I was free. Here, alone with Rhyan, at last, I was free. Free to do this with him. And I wasn't going to waste a single second.

I pressed a soft kiss to the corner of his lips, the way he'd done to me, and lightly tugged at the curls at the nape of his neck, drawing his mouth closer, slanting it across mine.

"It's you," I said, my lips moving against his. "You need to take your power back." I stepped away from him, reached for the hem of my shirt and pulled it over my head, tossing it into the corner. His eyes watched hungrily, taking in my bare breasts, gazing intently as they rose and fell with each of my quickened breaths.

His eyes only shifted when he realized my hands had moved to the waistband of my pants. His gaze was searing, burning through me as they carefully followed my movements, watching as the material slid down to my ankles and I kicked them aside. I was left in nothing but my underwear, tied at my hips.

Then I sat back on the bed, my legs spreading wide. "Rhyan," I breathed. "Claim me."

CHAPTER THIRTY-NINE

RHYAN

Rawness clung to my body, to my soul. I'd never been more naked or exposed, even though I was fully clothed. Even with my armor secured around my body.

But, finally, finally, I'd done it. I'd told her everything. My every last secret, my every last shame. And she hadn't run. Hadn't balked at my truths. At the things that made me *me*. At the things that made me hate myself. Doubt myself. Doubt that I deserved her.

But telling them to Lyriana, watching her accept my words, accept me … something had shifted inside. Permanently. The past didn't feel as heavy as it had. It still stung. Still fucking hurt. And yet, it felt lighter. Like Lyr had taken some of it on. Had burned through the pain. Had healed me, transformed me with the fires innate in her. This wasn't from *Rakashonim*. Not from any magic or piece of light. It was her. Just her.

My soulmate.

But all thoughts of my confession subsided as I took her in then, nearly naked, sitting on the bed. Her skin was gleaming in the light. I couldn't take my eyes off the tantalizing length of her legs wide open for me. Her breasts—Gods, her breasts. I never tired of the sight of them. Or any part of her.

For a moment, her cheeks reddened, and she looked almost shy. I recalled the one night I'd been able to properly see her naked, to simply stare at her entire body, and know it was on display just for me. The first night we'd been together. It had been too long. Too Godsdamned long since that night. Since the last time we'd lain together. Since the last time I'd been inside her. A month.

I was so fucking hard, straining against my pants. My belt felt too constrictive, and my breath was already heavy.

I started forward, barely holding myself back from pouncing on her. Had I been naked I would have. But I was still in my formal attire. I had no weapons on me, but the harsh leathers and metals of my soturion uniform were everywhere.

So I paused, standing before her and reached for her thighs, my hands sliding up and up her smooth, silky skin, all the way to the curve of her hips. I drew my eyes down between her legs, feeling myself somehow harden further. Her gaze followed mine with a stifled gasp escaping her lips. Her stomach rose and fell, her breathing intensifying as I continued to look at my fill, scenting her arousal.

A growl rumbled, low in my throat as I lifted my gaze back to hers. My hands started to slide toward her inner thighs. But then I reached beneath her, cupping her ass, and in one swift movement, I lifted her up. She made a startled sound of surprise as her body connected to mine, her legs wrapping instinctively around my waist, her ankles locked behind my back. I squeezed her ass, while simultaneously pulling her closer.

"You're mine," I whispered, almost too overcome to speak. "Mine."

"I'm yours," she said.

"No one else's," I commanded.

"No one else's," she repeated.

"Take off my armor," I said, my lips seeking her neck. My tongue darted out, licking and suckling, before I bit down. Her thighs squeezed around me in response, her hips lifting, trying to rub herself against me. I bit down again, feeling once again something primal and ancient brewing between us.

"Take it off," I said, my voice guttural. I felt her hands moving quickly to my shoulders, deftly unbuckling and undoing each clasp as I continued to lick and kiss her neck, determined to cover every inch of the delicate skin. When I felt my armor loosen, I held her with only one hand, and helped her push what remained of the leathers from my body, letting them fall. Together, we began to unwrap my cloak from my shoulders, until we reached for my waist at the same time. We both attacked the buckles and clasps of my belt until it too fell to the ground with a thud, and at last only my pants and shirt were between us.

Then we were kissing, my lips hot against hers. I couldn't wait, couldn't take it slow. I'd missed her mouth, been denied this too long, and already my tongue was seeking hers. Her mouth opened to mine, and she returned my kisses with just as much fervor and passion. I sucked her tongue into my mouth, desperate for all of her, delighting in the way she moaned against me. But I needed more of her, more contact.

I turned so the backs of my legs lined up with the bed and sat back without breaking our kiss. And then both of my hands were on her breasts, cupping and squeezing, greedy to feel them after so much deprivation.

Lyr gasped in pleasure, her chest rising and falling, her breaths coming heavier as I fondled her, kneading the swell of her curves, feeling their weight in my palms, before stroking her already sensitive nipples. I never tired of the way they felt, the way they hardened to my touch. The way they tasted.

Only then did I break the kiss.

"Do you know how fucking beautiful, you are?" I growled. "Or how much I missed these." I gave them both a sharp squeeze, forcing her nipples to poke out between my fingers. She whimpered.

"Every night since we've been captured, I thought of these." I squeezed again. "I dreamt of these. Touching them. Licking them." And then I bent down, sucking one hardened nipple into my mouth.

Lyr cried out, reaching for my shirt, lifting it over my head. I released her breasts just long enough to help her remove it. But then I was back, my lips fastening over her other nipple, my free hand taking the other between my fingers, tugging gently, then squeezing until I heard that sound she made— the one that was so uniquely her, the one she only made when she couldn't hold back her pleasure. I fucking loved it. Loved teasing it out of her. And then I did it again, eliciting another cry. I kissed between her breasts, over the Valalumir star that glowed faintly against her skin.

Her fingers were in my hair as she writhed against my ministrations. And Gods, I loved her like this. Loved seeing her lose control.

But then her hands were back at my waist as I cupped her chin, seeking out her mouth again. She was unlacing my pants, stroking my erection through them. And for once, I let her. In all the times we'd been together, most of our shared intimacies had focused on her. On her pleasure before mine. On me taking care of her. I'd loved all of it, hearing her, watching her, even feeling her take her pleasure turned me on more than I could explain. But it was always about her. Because that's how I'd wanted it. And before tonight, I couldn't articulate why.

Something I hadn't understood before became clear with my confession. She'd been right about taking back my power, about claiming her, marking her. Being able to choose, to decide to be with her for no reason other than it was what I wanted, what I freely desired. With all my father had put me through, all the Godsdamned *courting* with Amalthea and all the others, I'd tried to drown my memories with alcohol, I'd been passive. I would lay back, let them do what they wanted, take their pleasure. It wasn't that I didn't feel any of it, my body always responded. But not my mind. It was easier to focus on their orgasms over mine. Because none of it had been wanted. Because it was easier to lose myself when I did, easier to go numb, to forget I was there. Forget they weren't Lyr.

But something had shifted inside me. I was ready now. Ready for her to give me what I wanted. Something I'd been waiting for. Something that for so long, much as I desired it, hadn't been welcome. Not until her.

She was still stroking me, teasing me, making me jump against her. I cupped her ass again, and stood, then as if she understood perfectly my intentions, she released her legs, coming to stand shakily before me, her hands pulling at what remained of the laces of my pants.

"Take them off," I said. "On your knees."

Her face flushed with shock, and then with excitement, her eyes brightening as she nodded, sinking to the floor. My pants and what I wore underneath went with her. My cock sprung free, proof of my desire already beaded at the tip.

Lyr licked her lips, looking up at me with more hunger in her eyes than I'd dared dream of. Gods, she'd be the end of me.

"You've wanted this," I said, my voice low and curling around the words.

"Yes," she said, her hands sliding back up my bare legs.

I twitched. Fuck. She hadn't even touched me there yet— not naked. But every second those hands were coming closer and closer, until she slid her palms up to my hips, her eyes on my cock, doing exactly what I'd done to her. Gazing, taking me in. My breath caught, and I jerked as she let out a breath against the head.

"Tell me how you like it," she said breathlessly. One hand wrapped around me, the other cupping my balls.

I closed my eyes, tilting my head back, my heart ready to burst. "I like it …" I swallowed, my throat tightening. "Every way. Any way." I reached for her hair, my fingers digging into her scalp, drawing her closer. "As long as it's your Godsdamned mouth doing it."

A wicked smile spread across her lips, her cheeks pink, then she leaned in, kissing the head, her tongue darting out to lick slowly up and down as she squeezed.

"Fuck," I growled.

"Like that?" she teased.

"Just like that."

She licked again, her fingers sliding up and down, and then without warning, she took me into her mouth.

It was all I could do to not fall back against the bed, to not close my eyes, overwhelmed with the pleasure she was tugging out of me with every suck, every pull, every touch of her hands, her tongue, her mouth.

Gods.

My breathing came short, harder, and faster. My fingers were tangled in her hair, and soon I was the one making the noises, losing control, my hips moving without my realizing it, needing to push into her, to go deeper and deeper. She took me without question, moaning around me. It was too good. Too fucking good. I was already on edge, and another night, when we had more time, when a tomorrow was promised, I'd be content to stop here, to spill into her mouth. But not tonight. I needed more, needed to be inside her.

I pumped my hips, pushing myself somehow even deeper, suddenly taking control again, until I was hissing through one final thrust. The last one I knew I could manage without coming. Lyr's lips closed around me, sucking hard.

"On the bed," I said, barely able to form the words. "Now."

Lyr complied immediately, and with a pop from her mouth, I was released. She crawled up onto the blankets, taking a seat and gazed up at me, her hazel eyes sparkling with lust, and desire, and love.

I bent down to kiss her, and my tongue moved slowly, stroking hers with long, languid caresses before I bit down on her bottom lip.

"My turn," I said, and flipped her onto her belly. I nudged her up to her knees and then sank to my own at the edge of the bed, gripping her thighs and pulling her ass right into my face. My fingers slid through the ties on either side of her hips. A second later her underwear was gone.

Lyr squirmed, and I tightened my hold on her legs, pressing my face into her center, breathing her in.

"Rhyan," she cried out, then stopped, as soon as my tongue touched her folds.

"You liked tasting me, didn't you?" I growled. "You liked that a lot."

"Yes," she gasped.

She was dripping wet with arousal, it was already running down her leg, and the scent and feel and taste of her was heady. I pressed tiny kisses to her inner thighs, lapping up everything I could find while she shuddered. And then, I found her lips, and I sucked and teased, kissing and licking closer and closer to her center.

She started to buck, pushing back against me carrying her weight on her elbows. But I didn't stop. Nothing could stop me from this. I loved feasting on Lyriana. Loved the taste of her more than I could explain. I'd told her she was my favorite meal. And I'd meant every word.

"Rhyan, please," she begged. "Please."

Finally, I fastened my lips around her center, and she cried out, cursing and mewling, her entire body trembling. Her own arousal was running down my chin from this angle. But through it, I held onto her legs, keeping my mouth moving against her until her tremors subsided. Her back arched, and she lifted herself up to her hands as I crawled back onto the bed behind her. I was on my knees and reached for her belly, pulling her up to rest against me. Her head fell back on my shoulder, her mouth still opened in an O shape.

My cock stroked beneath her folds and I lifted my hips, just enough to apply more pressure, thrusting back and forth.

She reached down, rubbing me between her legs while I sought out her breasts.

Angling her neck, she turned her head and her lips found mine, kissing me deeply.

"You ready for me, Lyr?" I asked, pulling back to push one finger inside her, immediately she began to move, and I pumped two fingers inside, and then a third. "Oh, you're fucking ready," I said, low in my throat.

Her only response was to squeeze around me.

I pulled my fingers out. "Arch your back for me, partner."

"Like this?" she asked huskily, one hand reached behind my neck as her ass pressed back. We were perfectly lined up.

"Just like that," I said, and gripped my cock, teasing her folds once more, coating myself in her arousal. I pressed the head in, moving slowly, carefully until we were joined. We'd barely done this a handful of times, and I knew she was still getting used to taking me.

She sucked in her breath, while I hissed, trying to remain as still as possible, allowing her to adjust. She felt so fucking good, squeezing me so tight, it was like torture, but I breathed slowly, stroking her center, and kissing her neck.

"All right, Lyr?" I asked, ready to burst.

"Mmmhmmm," was all she could manage, but when her breath softened and I felt her wiggle, testing her movements in this position, I knew she was ready.

I gripped her hips, pumping into her, slow and deep, moving carefully at first, but soon my rhythm picked up, and Lyr was immobile, her body against mine as I thrust again and again. It wasn't long though before her soft moans turned into cries, and then a slew of curses.

"Rhyan, I'm going to … going to …" But she never finished. She tightened around me, fluttering and pulsing as she cried out, her body jerking forward, pushing her back onto all fours.

I went with her, still thrusting, still trying to hold myself back. But soon she was grinding her hips, pushing back into me as I reached for her hair, pulling it over her shoulder. "Give me your mouth," I demanded, kissing her again.

When she tightened around me, bucking, I knew I was done for, and pulled out, flipping her onto her back.

"Lyr," I said, pushing back inside. "Fuck." Her ankles locked behind me, her nails digging into my back.

"Come for me," she whispered.

And that was all it took. Three more strokes and I grunted, spilling into her. My entire body shook, every part of me trembling and pulsing as my pleasure came and came and came. I was cursing and calling out her name, yelling it over and over again. It had never lasted this long, never been this good.

"Lyr. Lyr. Lyr."

I was lost, so far gone, so fucking in love with her.

When I finally settled, I buried my face in her neck, hugging her to me. She kissed my forehead, holding me inside her still, before drawing soft lazy caresses with her nails up and down my back. I smiled, loving that this was something she liked. And it was a good thing because I was reluctant to pull out, loving it myself, loving being this close to her. I closed my eyes, content for once to simply be with her, in her arms. Content to simply be.

"I love you," I whispered.

"I love you, too."

I lifted my head, looking into her eyes, awed at how beautiful she looked just then, her hair wild, her cheeks flushed, her lips swollen from my kisses.

Her entire body glowing as if the Valalumir had lit up inside her. "You're smiling," she said.

I grinned even wider, feeling almost silly. "I can't stop." I laughed, and stroked her cheek.

"I love it when you smile. You don't do it enough, you know. But you look so fucking handsome when you do." She leaned up to kiss me, then laid back, her hazel eyes sparkling with flecks of gold. "Even better. You look happy."

I grinned so wide it almost hurt. "I feel happy," I said. And I meant it at that moment. Happiness, even brief fleeting seconds of the emotion, was something that for years had felt impossible. Happiness had felt like a feeling that was not meant for me, not made for me. Like I'd been born wrong and didn't have the ability to feel this thing that everyone else seemed to come by so easily, this thing that everyone else had, that everyone else sought. But for this moment, it was like I'd been let in on the secret. Let in a door that had always previously been locked.

Nothing in my world was right. The horrors still existed. The past. And what I knew lay outside this room was still there. This small cocoon of love and safety and joy we'd built for ourselves was fleeting. But at this moment, none of that mattered. Only Lyr did. Only the pounding of my heart, the light in my soul, and the way my body never felt so perfect as it did when it was holding her.

"I think I am happy," I said. "At least, I am, when I'm with you."

"Do you mean that?"

By the Gods. She looked so full of joy when I said that, I thought my heart would burst. I took it back, I never felt more perfect than when I made her look like this. Forgetting her cares, her worries.

"Of course," I said, kissing her jaw, and her cheek. "When I'm with you like this, it's like everything bad just kind of falls away. And when I think about what we have to face, all the trials ahead, I don't know. With you like this? It all feels more bear-able. Like we can win. Like we can do this. Together." And maybe it was just the post-sex glow, but right then I truly believed what I was saying. I felt stronger, more capable. I kissed her again. "It feels like just knowing you're by my side, I can handle anything. Fight anyone. I love being with you. I love everything about you." I brushed a loose strand of hair from her face. "You make me so happy, Lyr. Always. Always when I'm with you."

Her smile faltered. "And when you're not with me?" she asked, her voice suddenly small.

I sighed, my grin now rueful. "I'm working on that."

She nodded, pulling my face back to hers, kissing me again with a maddening kind of slowness. Like we did have forever. And I wished to the Gods we did. I could have stayed in that kiss all night.

"What about you, partner?" I asked, as we took a breath. "Are you happy?"

"When I'm with you," she said, kissing the corner of my lips. "Always."

"And when you're not with me?" I asked.

"I'm also working on that," she said, her voice shaking.

And I knew the spell was ending. Reality was sinking back in.

"Do you want to practice," I asked, gently drawing back from her. I was softening inside her and overly sensitive.

She let me pull out, but wrapped me in her arms, holding me close. "No, don't go. Not yet. You spent too many nights away from my bed. And anyway, I still need my apprentice here. For a different kind of practice."

"Well," I teased. "I can never abandon a novice in need. Especially when they require further lessons."

I knew I should leave and return to my room. But something

inside me kept me on the bed, kept me from moving. An unwillingness in my soul to leave her side.

"Let's stay happy then," I said. "I'll practice with you here, a little while longer. *Mekara.*"

"*Rakame.*" Lyr nodded, and I rested my head against her breast, letting her stroke my hair, until my eyes closed.

Sometime later, I woke to a gentle breeze rolling through the window. A promise of spring. Lyr's naked body was illuminated by the moon. She was on her side, snuggled up against me, the blanket having fallen to her hip. I reached out and stroked her arm, then slid my hand between her breasts, to her beating heart. The Valalumir pulsing inside.

We'd dozed off, though by my estimates of the moon's position in the sky, no more than an hour had passed.

I took a deep breath, drinking her in.

Gods, she was so fucking beautiful. I knew I needed to sleep, either that or leave. But I couldn't stop watching her. She looked so peaceful like this. Unaware of the trials that lay before us. She looked happy. The way I was happy when I was with her. The way I always wanted to see her.

But the feeling was weakening. I felt all too aware at that moment of what might come next, and I had the urge to scoop her back into my arms, to hold and protect her. To promise every God and Goddess who still listened, to plead with the Council of Forty-Four, or whoever the hell was in charge, to keep her safe, to swear that if it came down to it, this time, they'd take my life over hers.

Lyr stirred suddenly. Her eyelashes fluttered, her eyes opening, and she shifted, looking me up and down, her breathing even and slow.

We didn't speak. We were beyond communication by then. One look from her, one nod and that was all it took. She reached for me, and rolled onto her back, pulling me on top of her, her legs already open.

I pushed myself up onto my hands, keeping my weight off her, as she wrapped her fingers around me, stroking, and squeezing, before guiding me inside.

I was fully sheathed in one thrust, both of us gasping, our eyes steady on each other's. I pulled back, tilting my pelvis just so, and when I pushed back in, she moaned. I did, too.

I kept that angle as her hands found my back, her fingernails digging into me. And then I pumped into her, again and again. We were unusually quiet, like a spell had been cast over us. We both came quickly, keeping our eyes wide open, watching each other writhe and squirm.

"Marry me," I said suddenly, still pulsing inside her.

"What?"

"Marry me. Just … marry me." It was impossible of course. Everything about our fates forbade it. But I didn't care. I'd marry her in secret. I was done pretending, done trying to live any other way. And I was more than fucking done with the men she was forced to entertain.

She grinned. "You do remember that we are already soulmates?"

I laughed, but a tear rolled down my cheek.

"Rhyan." She wiped it away.

"We are soulmates," I said. "I fell from Heaven for you. Tracked you down life after life, and I'll continue to find you after this one ends. I'll find you again. I'll always find you, always know you. But I want more in this lifetime. I want all of you. You told me to claim you. And I'm not done. I want to make you mine in every way I can. Not just in every life, but in every form. And I want you to do the same to me. I want you to have complete and total possession of all I am, and all I have. Because I'm yours. Because I'll always be yours."

Lyr grinned, her eyes sparkling with tears. But before she could answer, bells began to ring, in the distance, the sound soft at first, then it grew louder, more insistent, the pattern revealing itself in precisely timed notes. It wasn't the hourly call, nor was it the threat of akadim.

It was a death bell.

For the Emperor. He'd passed.

I squeezed my eyes shut, my pulse racing. May his soul never know a moment's peace.

Lyr sat up, her eyes widened, understanding.

I sighed, pulling back the blankets and looking over her one last time. Trying to memorize her every last feature. I wanted to remember her like this. The way she looked right at that moment. Naked, beautiful, happy, loved.

Then I climbed out of the bed, and reached for her hand, resigned. "Come on," I said. "We need to be dressed. Anything can happen now."

CHAPTER FORTY

MORGANA

The sound of the bells ringing was like music to my ears. The bells announcing the Emperor's death. His fucking Majesty, Emperor Godsdamned Theotis was dead. Jules's kidnapper. Her rapist. The monster who enslaved my people. Who terrorized my country. My family. My Ka. Finally. Dead. Gone. Rotting in hell. The sound of those bells would now be my favorite tune.

Gods, I could fucking dance. The sun would rise in a few hours, making the Palace shimmer and sparkle as the waves crashed in the distance. I was never one for sunrise, or sunset. Never one to take a deep breath in the morning, or night. Or ever.

But this morning, this morning I could. This morning, I looked forward to it.

"I told you," Andromeny said. "I told you he'd die tonight. That there'd be no Valabellum."

My throat tightened. Joyous as I was to see the Emperor's fall, Andromeny still left me uneasy.

"You were right," I conceded. "And Ereshya's shard lies within."

Don't you feel it? Aemon asked, his voice like a caress in my mind. *Feel your power growing just being near it?*

I closed my eyes. And I did. I felt its call, its spell. It had a unique signature that I could feel even from here, and a flash of memory returned to me. A large bronze shield. The orange shard embedded inside its center, the rest of the crystal concealed by the metal around it. I'd made it myself after the Drowning. And it had kept me safe through many battles.

Until it hadn't.

Are you ready? Aemon asked. I stood and turned to face him. He was dressed in his Arkturion armor, golden seraphim wings at his shoulders, a red cloak flowing behind his back. Behind him, hiding in the shadows, were his most trusted akadim.

How do I know she's not lying? I asked.

Kitten, is this not proof enough of her visions? You've seen the possibilities. Seen the potential outcomes. Your sister remains in grave danger. She plans to take the shard for herself. When she combines that with the light already inside her, the light she can't control, it will be too much. You've seen it. Seen her fall. If you do not claim the shard yourself, she will die.

Andromeny is sure she plans to use it? I thought.

Why ask me questions you already know the answer to. You've seen in her mind. Lyr will go after it, and use it for herself. And it will kill her.

And Jules and Meera? I asked.

We can make them safe. But we need to work together.

I turned around, staring back at the Palace, rubbing my hands up and down my arms.

The visions Andromeny had replayed in my mind. The outcomes, the potential threads of fate. There were some still uncertain. But she'd never doubted this, even though I had. How could the God Moriel kill the Emperor? How was it possible, when Moriel didn't exist in his original form anymore? When his current incarnation had been nowhere near the Palace?

And yet, the Emperor was dead, by Moriel's hand. Even if it was merely someone dressed up as Moriel.

My heart pounded, and I looked at the sleeping gryphon off to the side, his body nestled between the trees. My private carriage was attached to his back. And inside was the indigo shard, glowing even more powerfully than before.

If Jules is freed from the Palace, and Meera escapes from Imperator Hart, I thought, *if those are guaranteed, we can work together.*

You won't bargain for Lyr? Aemon asked. He sounded amused.

But I remembered what Andromeny had shown me. The danger she faced. And the threat she posed. Not just to herself. But to all of us.

I took a deep breath, and headed for my gryphon. I was growing tired after flying all night. And being back in the world, beyond the caves, the voices were returning, my vorakh reactivated, even with the power of the shard at my side. I wanted to sleep for a few more hours, to cultivate my strength. Lissa gestured to me that my bed was ready.

Lyr sealed her own fate, I thought. *And I won't follow.*

CHAPTER FORTY-ONE

TRISTAN

Galen had killed the Emperor. Galen had killed the Gods-damned Emperor.

Fuck. FUCK! I was trying to save him, to protect him. What the hell had he been thinking?

I paced back and forth across my room, replaying it over and over in my mind. Why was he so fucking stubborn? So sure that this was the right thing to do? It was just going to get him killed, like I'd known it would. I didn't think he'd succeed. I never imagined.

But I should have. There was a reason he'd kept winning the trials, kept moving through to the next level.

I wasn't surprised he'd made it to the Valabellum. That he'd gotten a role. But Moriel—Moriel always died. And no matter what happened now, whether they went through with the games, and placed him in there to seal his fate, or they tried him for murder, he'd die. And not just die, he'd be tortured.

My best fucking friend in the world, and he wouldn't listen, wouldn't let me save him.

I had to figure something out. Find a way to help him. But how? Fuck. How could he fucking do this?

There was a loud banging on my door. And then another that came with so much force, my room shook.

Eric and Bellamy were at the door at once. They'd been allowed to remain and guard me, but they were weaponless, their staves gone since we were sent into lockdown. Our true guards now were the Emperor's, or Numeria's I supposed.

We had no Emperor now.

"Who's there?" Bellamy asked.

"By Order of the Senate, and Emperor, High Lord of Lumeria Nutavia, you will open this door at once." I paled. I knew that voice. The Bastardmaker.

Throat constricting, I nodded, and straightened, pushing my hair back, willing my breath to even.

The Bastardmaker strolled in, his black beady eyes surveying my room. "The Emperor has called for your assistance at once," he said.

"The–The Emperor?" I asked. "But … the bells."

"Theotis is gone," he confirmed.

"A new one's already been elected?" I asked.

"Of course. We had to act fast with assassins in the Palace."

"But the bells only just rung. He just—"

"Are you an idiot?" the Bastardmaker asked. "You think the bells ring the moment he stops breathing? That they're some marking of the exact time of death? They're a Godsdamned announcement. We ring them when we're ready. When we already have a new Emperor to take control, to bring order to this mess. And he wants to see you now. Alone."

Bellamy's eyebrows furrowed with worry, and he stood holding his ground. He was supposed to come with me. But nothing about tonight had been protocol. An Emperor had been assassinated. And we all knew if the Bastardmaker wanted to, he could end Bellamy's life in a matter of minutes, legal or not.

"It's okay," I said. "I'll come."

The Bastardmaker turned on his heels, his red Arkturion cloak flying behind him, and he walked out the door. As I followed, I reached automatically for my belt, my fingers itching to wrap around my stave. It was instinct, something I did whenever I faced an enemy. Whenever I felt threatened. I wasn't stupid enough to try and fight the Bastardmaker, but the security I felt in having it on me was reassuring. Even if the reassurance was thin.

The walk through the Palace felt endless, and for a moment, I feared he was taking me to the dungeons, to imprison me on some technical offense.

He could. He fucking could. They'd been watching me all along. And maybe I'd been wrong that I'd been safe, wrong that my secrets had remained hidden. Maybe they knew I was vorakh. Maybe it was because I'd failed to bring them Lyr and Rhyan.

Maybe, it was because I was friends with Galen. Friends with the Emperor's killer.

But then we abruptly turned direction, and headed up the stairs to the Throne Room. I watched as the tiles on the ground shifted from purple to a mix of black and white.

More guards than I'd ever seen were at attention before the entrance, while inside there were hushed, angry voices deep in conversation.

"Let us pass," the Bastardmaker demanded.

All at once the rows of soturi parted, and we were permitted inside. All of the Arkasvim, and all of their Arkturi were present. Standing on the dais beside the throne was the Blade, his face stoic.

I found Arianna's face in the crowd. But she looked disinterested in me. Slowly, I began to do a headcount, quickly spotting every Arkasva I could find. The North were easily spotted and accounted for. Ka Kether of Sindhuvine, Ka Lumerin of Aravia,

Ka Sephiron of Eretzia, Ka Taria of Hartavia, and Ka Valyan of Payunmar. And there, standing at the head, his beard neatly trimmed, was Imperator Hart of Glemaria. They all stood before the dais, all wore their golden Laurels of the Arkasva.

So Hart hadn't been named Emperor after all.

Still, on the dais, the throne remained empty, and above it that shield I'd seen earlier seemed to glow, the color of the stone in the center haunting. I'd been drawn to it since the moment I'd laid my eyes on it, and felt almost as if I were falling into a trance. I'd been terrified of a vision coming on me, especially after I'd brought a vorakh to justice, but that shield was something else.

I quickly glanced at the other side of the room, where the southern Kavim had gathered beside Arianna. There was Ka Maras of Lethea, Ka Zarine of Cretanya, Ka Daquataine of Damara, and Ka Elys of Elyria.

A door opened from behind the throne, and our new Emperor emerged.

Imperator Kormac.

He stepped out onto the dais and sat down on his throne, his black Imperator robes now replaced with the purple of the Emperor.

"Bow," shouted the Blade. "Bow before your sovereign, His Majesty, Emperor Avery, High Lord of Lumeria Nutavia."

No. No.

The Bastardmaker slapped my back and immediately I sank to the ground, my knees hitting the floor with a bruising speed.

Everyone around me, all the Arkasvim, and all the Akrturi followed suit. Only the Blade and rest of the soturi on guard remained upright, their weapons in their hands.

I didn't know if an election had taken place, or what decisions had been made here, but I knew one thing. No one, except those few who were loyal to Ka Kormac, was happy about this.

"Rise," Emperor Avery said. "We shall commence with my

anointing at once to secure the safety of this Empire, just as my predecessor advised me to do in the south when I ruled as Imperator. I made safe our borders, I ended the akadim threat, and I swear to you all, I will end this one as well. Now, as is customary, you will all remain here until morning."

I looked around, all the Empire's rulers looked miserable, and though they had their Arkturi beside them, their eyes were moving warily to the armed guard that surrounded them. They were just as much prisoners here as we were. For once, it was good not to be Arkasva. At least I'd gotten some privacy in my room.

At least, I had. Now I was a prisoner as well.

"Lord Tristan," Emperor Avery said. "Thank you for coming. I require your assistance in a most urgent matter. Follow me." He rose from his throne and again walked behind the dais through a door that appeared suddenly.

The Bastardmaker urged me ahead. I looked back at everyone else, sweat beading at the back of my neck. I didn't want to go. I didn't trust him. I didn't trust any of this. Elections couldn't happen this fast, transitions of power took time. The Emperor's Second should have been installed as the ruler until a proper election could be held. At least a month should have passed first, a true transition.

But he'd done the same thing months ago in Bamaria. He'd removed Lord Eathan, the rightful replacement of Harren Batavia, and placed Arianna in the Seat of Power. And as I glanced at her, at my country's Arkasva and High Lady, at my future mother-in-law, I pleaded with her through my eyes. Begged for protection, for safety and amnesty.

But her expression was cold as she stared ahead, acting as if she barely knew me.

We vanished into a long hall that fed back outside the Throne Room. I watched carefully as the Imper—, the Emperor led me around a corner. Before us stood a simple black door.

"Pay attention," Emperor Avery commanded. "Very few have permission to enter here."

I nodded, not sure what else to do. He knocked on the door, but not with a normal knock. This had a very specific rhythm. A series of beats.

"It's the opening beats to the Voladarim. Do you know it?" he asked.

My throat was dried out. "Of course."

"Musically inclined?" he asked, one eyebrow raised.

"What?" What in Godsdamned Lumeria was happening right now?

"Just a question. It's code to enter back into this room. Do you know it?"

Numbly I nodded. "Yes."

The black door opened, and a soturion stuck their head out. "Your Majesty." A middle-aged man, completely bald, poked his head out. "Are you ready?"

"One moment. Close the door. I'm having Lord Tristan learn the code. Answer the door, if he gets it right."

"Of course, Your Majesty." The door slammed shut and the Emperor pushed me forward.

"Well?" he demanded. "Knock."

I did, playing the song on the black door.

The Emperor scoffed and I stepped back, terrified I'd done it wrong. But the door opened and the same bald soturion gestured for us to enter.

I walked into another hallway, nearly black with darkness save for only a few lamps lit at the end. The further we walked, the narrower the hall grew, and I was forced to walk behind the newly made Emperor.

"We're doing an interrogation," he announced. "Obviously, we've apprehended my uncle's killer." Galen.

"Of course," I said neutrally. "Protocol."

Emperor Avery laughed. "Yes. Protocol."

He stepped aside, revealing a large, dimly lit room. There were no windows. No furniture. Several mages appeared to be huddled together in a corner. Something about them was strange. They were all thin and wearing blue cloaks with hoods over their heads. Their faces were downcast, and they remained shockingly still. The Emperor reached for a torch and lit a series of lamps that brightened the room at once.

I gasped. It was painted bright yellow.

Too much yellow. Too much yellow.

You've birthed evil. You'll regret it when he grows. When you see inside his soul like I have. When you learn what he is!

My heart began to pound, the emotion of fear a palpable sensation.

But with the brighter lights on, my gaze fell on the one person in the room who was not in a robe. He wore almost nothing at all. His clothes had been torn off, his hands chained above his head. Only his short-pants remained, but they'd been ripped up, and looked like they would fall soon. Across his back was blood, so much blood, dripping and oozing from over a dozen cuts made from a whip—the kind used on soturi. The kind that had been used on Lyr.

I was ready to avert my eyes. My stomach turned, threatening to bring everything I'd eaten back up. I couldn't stand the sight of blood. Couldn't look. It was too familiar, too close to what I'd seen that night. The night the vorakh tore my parents apart.

But as I started forward, I stopped just as quickly. I had no idea what to do. I had a stave, but no allies, and a soturion blocked the only exit. I might fight my way free, but then what? I didn't know how to escape the Palace.

"Your friend isn't being too cooperative," Emperor Avery said.

"Not answering questions, Your Majesty?" I asked.

"No. He's answered. We simply don't agree with his answers."

He stalked forward, pulling a key from his belt. And before I could react, he punched Galen in the head.

He groaned again, spitting blood at his feet before Emperor Avery freed his right arm.

"Turn," he commanded, and dragged his arm around, chaining him once more against the wall, but now he faced out. His eyes were bloodshot. His nose was broken, his body covered in sweat.

Our eyes met.

Galen shook his head. "Tristan had no idea. No part," he said wearily, like every word he said hurt.

"Let's see for sure." The Emperor then crossed the room again, coming before the mages in robes.

They all seemed to shrink in his presence, remaining still and silent.

Then he pointed at one, a woman, barely out of her teenage years from the looks of it. She stepped forward and walked to Galen, standing right before him.

"Remove your hood," Emperor Avery commanded.

She did, glancing back at once. Something pricked the back of my mind. I'd seen her before.

"Go on," the Emperor said.

The mage nodded, her eyes on me, before she turned back to Galen. "Did Lord Tristan work with you?" she asked. She practically spat my name.

Galen sniffled. "No."

The mage didn't react to his answer, she simply watched him, staring with intent.

"Again," Emperor Avery commanded.

"Did Lord Tristan work with you? Assist you in any way?" asked the mage. And once again, I could feel the vitriol in her voice as she said Tristan.

"He had no idea," Galen said, sounding exhausted. His head drooped forward, and he coughed in pain. "He tried to keep me out of the games."

The mage continued to stare. "Well?" Emperor Avery asked. "Truth?"

"Yes, Your Majesty," the mage said.

"And all of you?" he asked, pointing back at those who remained huddled together.

"We hear the same," said one voice, small and almost childlike.

I looked back and forth between them in bewilderment.

Emperor Avery came to stand by my side as the female mage asked Galen another question.

"Mind reader," the Emperor said, pointing at her.

"What?" I nearly jumped. "But that's—they're ... vorakh," I hissed.

He nodded. "Yes. They are. I think we almost came to an agreement before, you and I. Your friend's life for Lyriana's and that bastard son of Hart's."

I shook my head. "But ... but you saw him, saw him kill—" I cut myself off. This wasn't going to help Galen. But how could it hurt him? He *had* killed the Emperor, and everyone had been a witness.

"Everyone knows it was the soturion playing Moriel." He shrugged. "He was masked. Only a few know his true identity. A little asking around will tell me how big a problem it is. Perhaps the killer switched clothing with him at the last moment. Who's to say? He could still walk free."

My heart pounded. "He could?"

"If he can offer more information, someone else who might have helped him. I'm in a forgiving mood tonight. I lost my uncle. But I've gained an Empire."

I shivered. His uncle had been murdered right in front of him. But he felt no remorse. No guilt. Not even a hint of sadness.

Fuck. If I didn't know better, I'd almost bet he put the knife in Galen's hand. Told him the moment to strike. He'd wanted this outcome. And he hadn't cared how it came about. And the more I thought about it, the more I wondered how Galen had gotten his chance. Kormac had chosen him to be Moriel—to get back at me. But how had he managed to get to the Emperor? To get so close. Surely Theotis had more protection to guard against such a thing—didn't he?

I thought of how Galen told me that he wasn't the only one who wanted the Emperor gone. And Kormac had been spying on me. What would have prevented him from spying on the soturi, from uncovering any assassination plots. And then not stopping them?

But that would mean ... No. No.

Was I farther than Lethea? Had Kormac set Galen up?

Swallowing, I stared back at Kormac. "I don't understand. Why are you telling me this?" I asked. "Why bring me here?" I looked uneasily at the mages. The vorakh. "What is their purpose?"

All at once their attention was on me, their auras full of hatred.

And they should hate me, I realized. I was one of them, and the biggest traitor of all.

Emperor Avery grinned. "Them? They're all here because of you. This is what becomes of them. Lethea is for testing. To better understand the depth and scope of their talent. If strong enough, they come here to serve at the Emperor's pleasure. At my pleasure now. They're known as the chayatim, the cloaked ones."

I shook my head, not believing him. Sure that this was some sort of trick, or nightmare. "They're not stripped?" I asked. "Not locked up?"

"No. Some are, but most are useful. And we hate to throw away valuable resources." He smirked, his face more wolfish than I'd ever seen. "I sent for these chayatim specifically. Just for you. Don't you recognize them?"

"No, of course not," I said quickly, fearing he was casting me as one, that this was all some big joke, his sick and twisted way of telling me that he knew my secret.

But then the mage before Galen turned around again, looking me full in the face, and then I did recognize her.

It was two years ago. I caught her in the fall. I'd recognized the look of pain on her face, the migraine she had, and the way her eyes had darted so carefully from person to person in the city. She was aware of who I was— what I did. And the moment her eyes caught mine, she ran. I knew instantly, and chased. She was bound barely moments later.

And now she was here. A servant. Not stripped. Not imprisoned. At least, not in the prison I'd imagined.

She was thinner than when I'd last seen her. So much thinner, and as she looked back again, I realized more details I hadn't noticed before. The sallowness of her skin, a bruise on her right cheek, just beneath the golden Valalumir tattoo marking her as one of the Emperor's.

You'll regret it when he grows. When you see inside his soul like I have. When you learn what he is!

She was here because of me. My fault. I did this. I'd sentenced her to this fate. And the others. All the others.

The bile rose in my throat again.

I heard the door open and the bald soturion marched down the hall, his hand on another mage's shoulder. A chayatim.

A cloaked one.

Not one of mine. Please, Gods, I couldn't face another.

"Here it is," said the soturion, slapping the mage across the face, throwing her onto the floor. She landed right before me and the Emperor.

I stepped back in disbelief. This was what we were doing? This was where we were sending all the vorakh? To the Godsdamned Palace, to be beaten and perform mental interrogations —all while the rest of the Empire believed them dead?

The mage grunted, her hood falling off her head revealing long brown waves. Thin arms and legs protruded from the cloak, all bruised and full of small cuts in various stages of healing.

Her chest heaved as she pulled herself up to her knees.

Then she turned, wiping the blood from her mouth. She seethed. "I heard you were promoted tonight. *Tovayah maischa.*" She spat.

The Emperor chuckled. "Do you think I brought you in here for that?"

"You tell me," she said, her voice shaking.

There was something familiar about her, but my mind was blank.

"Tell you? Tell you! Your Godsdamned job is to see. To know. And you didn't see this!" the Emperor yelled. He was suddenly gripping her chin, and dragging her across the floor. He slapped her hard across the cheek, and her head snapped toward me.

Her eyes flashed, revealing a familiar hazel color. And then all at once, I saw the recognition in them. She knew me.

And I knew her. She was someone I'd believed to be dead the last two years.

Jules. Julianna. Lady Julianna Batavia.

By the fucking Gods.

She looked away at once, pretending the exchange hadn't happened.

"What do you want?" she asked. "Not my congratulations. My sympathies?"

"I want you to do your job. And if you can't do that one, then we'll settle for the other."

She shuddered visibly, but only for a second. It happened so quickly I wondered if I'd imagined it. Because now there was a firm, yet resigned look on her face. "I told you I saw his death coming this year. I can't help it if I didn't know it was tonight. That's not how this fucking works."

"Language, pet."

He dragged her to her feet, his eyes boring into hers, his mouth curled back. I'd always thought he had a wolfish energy, a match for his sigil, for the beast on all of Ka Kormac's armor. But it wasn't until this moment I saw the animal he truly was. The monster.

I'd sold my soul to a demon, and I'd never known.

Too much yellow. Too much yellow.

Suddenly the Emperor was reaching for Jules's breast, squeezing hard.

But she remained still, unmoved, almost as if nothing was happening. Emperor Avery's eyes raked down her body, pulling her cloak aside to reveal a bare shoulder, and then another. A loose black gown covered her underneath, but just barely.

By the Gods—what the fuck was happening? Was he about to—was he going to—No. No. No.

I couldn't process this, couldn't be seeing this.

"It works," he roared, "how I say it works." Then he shoved her back on the ground and pointed at Galen. "Now get over there, and start telling me what you see next." He pointed at the rest of the group, still in their place, still, and silent. "And you lot. You tell me if she's telling the truth."

Somehow, despite all of that, Jules rose gracefully to her feet, and lifted her chin. Her shoulders rolled back as she carefully walked to Galen.

"Now, Lord Tristan," Emperor Avery said, "Here's the deal. I need more information. I'll probably need to suck him dry. Wear him out until I learn everything. Who he spoke to. Where he got the idea. All of it. But since it seems you require greater motivation, and because I'm bringing you in to serve me here in the Palace, I'll release him. As a favor. But only if you do what the fuck I asked for."

I was still watching Jules. Still in shock. Slowly, I looked back to the Emperor and nodded.

"I understand why you failed before. Devon Hart has been a thorn in my side for decades. But we have a unique opportunity here. He and his oaf of an Arkturion remain in the Throne Room. His quarters are locked. But as Emperor, I possess the key. I will give it to you, and this." He produced a scroll made of solid gold, the Emperor's sigil engraved on the side. He handed both items to me.

I stared down, feeling their weight in my hands.

"This marks you as my messenger. Any request you make to any servant of the Palace must be obeyed so long as you hold this. It must happen tonight. I want Lyriana and I want Rhyan. You should be motivated to get him. It's a unique chance. Do you know how he escaped with Lyriana from the Shadow Stronghold all those months ago?"

"No, Your Majesty."

He chuckled again. "Well, this should please you. It was vorakh."

I frowned at once, my nostrils flaring. "Then he's a danger to all of us."

"Except here," Emperor Avery said. "The Palace is warded against that. Now that I'm above Devon, and Rhyan cannot escape, this is our chance."

"Bring Rhyan and Lyriana," I said. "In exchange for Galen."

"Exactly."

"Do you mind my asking?" I said quickly. "Why haven't you sent for them yourself?"

"I can," he said. "Easily. But when one works for the Emperor, a certain level of trust must be maintained. Let's call this your initiation."

Something told me he was lying. That he couldn't just get them. Devon Hart might be in the Throne Room, but politics didn't just end overnight with brute force. He knew that. I was still his pawn. But I considered his words as my eyes took in Galen's bruised and bloodied body.

"Galen will be free. And I'll have a position in the Palace?"

You've birthed evil. You'll regret it when he grows. When you see inside his soul like I have. When you learn what he is!

"You will. I've found your skillset very valuable. We'll be needing to add to our ranks. I spoke with Lyriana earlier."

From the corner of my eye, Jules looked back, her body stiff. Then she turned back to Galen.

"Lyriana knows that we're aware of her forsworn lover's secret. Go to him first, and bind him. Show her. Tell her my offer stands. If she comes to me willingly, we'll release Hart back to his father."

"And if she refuses?" I asked.

"It doesn't matter. It doesn't matter what she agrees to. You will bring them both to me."

Jules looked back again, her eye catching mine, a small shake of her head. She was asking me not to bring in Lyr.

Emperor Avery growled in his throat, impatient for me to agree.

I placed the golden scroll in my belt.

"Am I to go alone?" I asked casually. "Hart may not be able to travel within the walls, but he remains a formidable soturion. As is Lyriana. Might I bring my own escorts?"

The Emperor scoffed. "My men will back you up." He pulled a vadati from his robes and ordered three soturi to meet me at the door.

My jaw clenched, but I nodded.

"You have an hour," he said. "Don't be late."

"It will be done," I said, staring at the vorakh I'd helped capture. I thought of all the times Lyr had lied to me, the hatred I bore for Rhyan fucking Hart. The way I was fucking certain now that they'd betrayed me, humiliated me. And I smiled at the Emperor. "When I return, I'll have them both."

CHAPTER FORTY-TWO

LYRIANA

I was fully dressed in my soturion uniform, minus my actual weapons. I had on my Bamarian armor, but I was still missing Asherah's chest plate. And my stave. Those were all stored with Imperator Hart's personal items.

I sat on the edge of my bed, my entire body tense. Rhyan lay his hand on my shoulder, squeezing the back of my neck, his thumb and forefinger kneading my muscles. My heart was pounding. I had a strange feeling. Something was wrong.

"I can stay," Rhyan said, cupping my cheeks. He'd been dressed since the bells rang, ready to return to his room.

Only he hadn't.

I bit my lip. "What if you're seen?"

"I can climb back out the window. The second we hear anything at the door, I'll be gone."

I nodded.

I couldn't tell how much time had passed. It felt like the time we had together was going far too quickly.

But then there was a commotion and yelling outside my door. I opened the window.

"Wait," Rhyan said, his entire body alert. "Something's not right."

"I will go in by myself," shouted a voice outside. "I am the Emperor's lawful messenger, and you are to obey."

"And I," roared Dario, "am the lady's personal escort! You go in, and I go with you."

"Guards," said the first voice. "Seize him."

"Dario!" Rhyan hissed. He looked ready to bolt through the door and fight for his friend.

My door swung open and Tristan entered. Alone.

"Lady Lyriana," he said, his voice overly loud. "I come on behalf of His Majesty, Emperor Avery, High Lord of Lumeria Nutavia." He slammed the door shut behind him, his stave pointed at me.

Several things happened at once.

First, I realized what he'd said. Emperor Avery. Not Emperor Theotis. There was only one ruler with that name. Which meant Imperator Kormac was no longer Imperator. He was Emperor. Like Rhyan's father feared. Like I'd always feared.

A sinking feeling washed over me. A sense of absolute dread.

And then Tristan realized I wasn't alone in my room.

Just as Rhyan lunged for him.

The two seemed to growl simultaneously and crashed into each other, tumbling to the floor, wrestling, and punching.

"You touch her, and I'll kill you," Rhyan hissed.

"Godsdamnit!" Tristan punched. He started reaching for his stave but Rhyan knocked it from his hand. "Forsworn bastard." Tristan rolled out of Rhyan's hold, grabbed the stave, and started to chant. Black ropes began to form.

"No!" I was across the room in seconds, diving for the stave and wrestling it from Tristan.

I shook off the spell, and pointed it at both of them, still tangled up and fighting. Tristan threw a punch, catching Rhyan's ear, just as Rhyan kneed him in the stomach.

"Get up," I snarled. "Both of you."

Rhyan glared, his chest heaving, his aura full of fury. He slammed Tristan on his back, pinning him to the floor.

Surprisingly, Tristan surrendered. "Been a minute," he said casually, sucking on his lower lip. It was bleeding. "I know we used to joke about being happy to see each other, but I didn't expect you to throw yourself on top of me so easily."

"Shut your mouth," Rhyan said.

Tristan coughed. "I'm pretty sure Lyr wanted you to get up." He let his hands fall open, making it clear he was no longer fighting.

"She wants *you* to get up, Lord Grey, and I'd be careful trying to tell me what you think she needs."

"Auriel's bane," I said. Rhyan snapped his head toward me, and I knew it was for more than my use of the expression. "Sorry," I said quickly, then I lowered my voice. "I want you both to get up."

Rhyan's mouth tightened, accepting my decision. But instead of moving, he forced Tristan's hands up over his head, holding them in place with one hand.

"What in Lumeria?" Tristan shouted.

Rhyan told him to shut up, then to me, he said, "Keep the stave pointed at him."

"I'm not armed," Tristan said, but now he was speaking more urgently, losing all of his bravado. "Other than the stave. That's it. You're wasting time. She can't even use it."

"That's what you think," Rhyan said. "We know you're the Imperator's little pet. You always have been. Now tell me who else is coming, and she won't hurt you."

"It's just me," Tristan said, now struggling to get up. His mouth was twitching, and his eyes darted back and forth between us, wild and scared. "For now, at least. And he's not the Imperator anymore. He's Emperor, and a lot more dangerous. If I'm not back in front of him within the hour, more soturi will come for you. You're both in grave danger. I'm here to warn you." He swallowed. "And to ask for your help. Please. Otherwise, Galen is dead."

"Galen?" I asked. "What do you mean? Isn't he in Bamaria?" My stomach turned.

"And what does that have to do with us?" Rhyan asked.

"Emperor Avery sent me personally to bring you both before him. In exchange for Galen." Tristan glared. "Are you enjoying yourself, Hart? Or can I get up?"

Rhyan snarled, but sat back on his knees and stood, freeing Tristan.

He got to his feet, keeping his hands apart, to show he had no weapons and wouldn't fight. But his eyes were on his stave still in my hand. He frowned, looking quizzically at me. "You can use that?"

I stepped forward. "A lot has changed since we last saw each other." I flicked his stave at a torch, and blew out the light. "Threaten either of us, and that's you." My grip tightened, and I lifted my arm, the point aimed at his heart.

Tristan cocked his head to the side, his neck red. "Things have changed." His eyes narrowed on Rhyan. "Though it looks like some things remain the same."

My heart pounded.

"Listen," Tristan said, holding both of his hands up higher in surrender. "I don't want to hurt either of you. I swear. I'm here because the Emperor sent me. And if it's not me, someone else will come. I'm asking for a truce. For your help, because the soturion who killed the Emperor tonight was Galen."

I gasped. "Galen! Galen was Moricl?"

Tristan's chest heaved and he nodded grimly. "He entered the trials to try and get close to the Emperor. He … He wanted revenge for Haleika. I was working to get him out, or at least have him cast in some lowly role so he'd be safe. But when I never found either of you, Kormac ensured he became Moriel—

as revenge. He's promised to keep Galen's identity a secret and to free him, but only if Lyr breaks her engagement to Arkturion Kane. And Rhyan is brought before the Emperor on charges of being vorakh."

"NO!" I yelled.

"Fuck!" Rhyan spat. "Fuck!" He ran his hands through his hair. "No. Absolutely the fuck not. I'm sorry about Galen. I am. I always liked him. But I am not sending Lyr to Kormac."

"You don't understand. I don't want to do that either. I wouldn't endanger her, but this is happening, and it's better if I bring her in, than someone else does."

"Fuck you," Rhyan said. "I've already seen you do that, and I know exactly how this game plays out."

"Like last time?" I shivered. "When you were the one to bind me?"

I'll do it.

Tristan's words the night of my Revelation Ceremony still haunted me.

"No," Tristan said, but his voice had softened.

"What is this?" Rhyan asked. "You try to get our sympathy over Galen, bring Lyr in on the pretense it will hurt less if it's you? Gryphon-shit! I'm not giving her up to Kormac. You'll have to kill me first."

"Then I'll die beside you," Tristan said.

"What?" Rhyan looked truly startled.

"Just fucking listen to me. Please!" Tristan took a deep breath, looking like he was desperately trying to regain his composure. "I have no intention of handing her over, or you, Rhyan."

I blinked. I couldn't remember ever hearing Tristan refer to Rhyan by his first name.

"I was sent here for you two, and given three guards, loyal to the Emperor. They're waiting outside right now to escort us back. Help me. Help me fight them. Then we can retrieve my escorts. They're loyal to me. We'll all go back to where they're keeping Galen. And we can fight. There's only one soturion at the door, and a code to get in. And I have it. We could do this."

"What the fuck are you talking about?" Rhyan asked. "You expect me to believe this? We go in with you, and fight to what? Free Galen? And then end up prisoners of the Emperor? This whole thing sounds like a poorly planned trap."

"It does," I said, slowly. "But it doesn't need to be. None of this is new information for us. Well, Galen. But we've known the rest. We knew he wanted us, knew Tristan was sent to hunt us on his behalf. He could have tricked us with some other reason to go with him. Or just simply demanded it. There's no reason to tell us this. Why else would he leave the guards outside?"

"Exactly. Lyr, trust me. Please," Tristan begged. "We don't have much time."

"Where's the room?" Rhyan asked, his mouth tight.

"It's off this hallway, behind the Throne Room," he said nervously. "I've never seen it before. It's not open to the public, or even most nobles. Some kind of interrogation room."

My eyes met Rhyan's, and I thought of all the maps we'd studied all month.

"Is it to the west?" I asked.

Tristan's mouth fell open. "Yes."

"We've seen it," I told Rhyan. "It has a long corridor leading into some open space that wasn't identified. The one with no windows and only one door. It isn't marked on the public maps. But on the Imperator's, it is."

Rhyan's eyes widened. "Shit. You're right, Lyr."

"And the Throne Room? I asked. "Will it still be full with all the Arkasvim?"

"All but our new Emperor," Tristan said.

"The Emperor's in this interrogation room? Alone? Anyone else in there?" Rhyan asked. "Any other guards?"

"There's vorakh," Tristan said. "Mind readers. He called them ... called them the chayatim."

I stilled. "The chayatim? You've seen them?" I started forward. "Tristan, tell me everything."

But he wasn't looking at me. His eyes had grown distant, afraid. His aura flared. I'd felt his aura a thousand times before when he mentioned vorakh. It was always accompanied by anger, by hatred, something ugly and full of grief.

His aura now, though? It held none of that. It was sadness. Guilt. And fear. A nauseating level of it.

"The vorakh—the chayatim, they're ... they're the ones I caught and arrested," he said, his voice breaking. "I never knew. They don't end up in Lethea. They're not stripped of their vorakh. Nothing is what they told me, nothing is what they promised." He wrung his hands, sounding hysterical. "They're all here. Serving the Emperor. Suffering. Because of me." There was a scuffle outside, and a distant shout.

But Rhyan shook his head, focusing on Tristan. "I'm sure you feel real fucking guilty about that, Bamaria's great vorakh hunter."

Tristan's eyes had reddened, and I remembered the way he looked the last time I saw him. It was his first acknowledgement of my pain over Jules, the first time he'd seemed to understand it.

"Rhyan," I said, and shook my head.

"I thought I was doing the right thing," Tristan said, almost in a trance. "I truly did. But my whole fucking life is a lie. I know what I am. What I've become. What's inside my soul." He shook his head, tears in his eyes. "Turns out I'm the thing I always fucking feared. I'm the monster. And I am sorry. If I can free them all, if they'll even accept my help, I'll do it. Please. Do you believe me, Lyr?" Tristan asked suddenly, sounding desperate.

My heart pounded as his words sunk in. I felt his aura, saw the truth in his eyes. The unbridled pain. "I believe you," I said.

"For the record, I don't trust you," Rhyan added.

Tristan looked like he was going to be sick. "I get it. But there's something else. You're ... you're probably going to think I'm farther than Lethea, I feel like I am after what I just saw, but there was someone else in there. Someone I wouldn't have believed I was seeing if it wasn't for the other chayatim. I didn't even recognize her at first."

Someone else? Her? My heart stopped. "Who? Tristan! Who did you see?"

"Jules," he said.

"You saw Jules?" My voice shook, my pulse pounding. I could swear I heard my blood flowing in my ears, and everything in my body was heating up. I needed to know everything. Know he was telling the truth beyond a shadow of doubt. "With the Emperor? She's in there now?"

The stave suddenly wasn't enough for me. Not for this. I closed the window behind me, and turned around, pulling my arm forward. I slid up one of my leather cuffs. And then, I slammed my arm back. My elbow smashed through the glass. I grabbed the nearest shard before they all fell from the window. It was a thick one. Nice and sharp. Then I sprinted across the room for Tristan, locking his arms behind his back. I pressed the glass to his neck, putting just enough pressure behind it to let him know that I was deadly serious. "You're going to tell me everything you know right now. Where is she?"

Rhyan's eyes widened, and if he was shocked at my sudden violent shift in this interrogation, he didn't say. He just took a step back, giving us some space.

"Godsdamnit, Lyr!" Tristan eyed the glass nervously from his peripheral vision, and his breath caught. "I'm telling you the truth. She was in there. I saw her. One of the vorakh is questioning Galen now, reading his mind. They're torturing him, trying to get as much information as they can," he spoke quickly, his words rushed. "And when Jules was brought in, the Emperor was furious. Her visions weren't detailed enough, or accurate enough for him, or something. I'm trying to remember. She said she knew the Emperor would die this year, but not when."

I gasped, "What else?"

"He was mad Jules hadn't known it was today that he'd die, I think, or mad she hadn't seen more, or knew more? I don't fucking know. But he ... he hurt her. And I don't think it was the first time." He froze. "He looked like he was going to ..." Tristan looked green. "But he pushed her in front of Galen with the mind reader questioning him. She was supposed to use her vorakh, I guess to see what else would happen."

I tried to listen, to understand everything he was saying, and everything he wasn't saying. But all I could think about was the fact Tristan had seen Jules. He had actually seen her. And that Kormac had hurt her. He fucking hurt her. I already knew he had. He'd hinted as much over the years. Brockton had confirmed it. So had my visions of her. But hearing it from Tristan, hearing it was happening now, in the Palace, in the fucking building I was in at this very moment—my decision was made.

"Lyr," Rhyan said, a warning note in his voice. "Lyr. Wait. We need to think this through first. We need more details."

"Rhyan, no." My entire body went still. Even my heart felt like it had stopped beating. "We're not doing this again. Jules is here. Right now! And for the first time, we have a way to get to her. We know exactly where she is."

"What about—?" His jaw tensed. "What we originally came here to do?"

Steal Ereshya's shard. And hand it over to his father.

I shook my head. "Fuck it."

Rhyan's lips quirked, and he nodded.

"Does this mean you'll help me?" Tristan asked. "Get Galen and Jules? And the others, if they're willing?"

"You have my word. Because of Lyr. I swear to you, I'll do all I can to get Galen out. And the others," Rhyan said. "But you need to know right now, our priority is Jules. And Jules alone. And mine? It's Lyriana. If anything happens to her, or this turns into a trick at any point, I will kill you. We do this, and then your men better be fucking ready to cover our backs."

"They will," Tristan said.

"Now you swear," Rhyan said, one eyebrow furrowed in concentration. "Convince me we're on the same side."

Tristan groaned. "Be fucking serious, Hart. What the hell else can I give you now? It's not like I have time to convince you, or anything I can hand over."

"Then think very fucking fast," Rhyan snarled.

"Rhyan!" I warned. I didn't care if he fully trusted Tristan or not. I did. I could see the change in him. I could feel it. He was telling the truth.

"Partner, just … wait," Rhyan ordered. "Let him prove himself to me."

A minute passed, and Tristan began to grow more agitated. Finally, he shook his head, like he'd given up. "Fine. You want proof. Proof I'm on your side. That I'm with you? That I'm one of you? I'm …" He slammed his mouth shut, and almost looked like he was swallowing bile. Then his nostrils flared, his face filled with determination. "I'm vorakh," he said, his voice trembling. "I'm vorakh, Rhyan. Like you." He took a deep breath. "Okay? Me, too. And you … You're the first person I've ever told."

Rhyan blinked rapidly, just as I yelled out.

"What?" I looked Tristan up and down as if I'd see physical proof. "No. But you …? Which one? Since when?"

He looked absolutely miserable, his shoulders slouched forward into the most un-Tristan-like posture I'd ever seen. "The worst of the three." His voice was hushed. "The worst for me."

Because his parents had been murdered, torn apart. By a vorakh. By one in particular. "Visions?" I asked.

Tristan nodded. "It started a few weeks after you left. I don't know. It just happened. And I can't make it stop. And now, Gods, Lyr, I've seen what I've done. And I ... we need to get Galen out. And Jules, and everyone else we can. But now! We're running out of time."

"I believe him, Rhyan," I said. "We know all we can. Enough of this. We know the room, we know the blueprint. We're going."

Rhyan nodded slowly, his nostrils flaring. "Partner. Do me one more favor first?"

I eyed him carefully, on edge. He was my soulmate, and he had just asked me to marry him, and I wanted to say yes, as impossible as it seemed. But I hadn't forgotten our argument that first night in Seathorne—at his suspicions of our enemies manipulating me with Jules. I knew he was still considering that idea, wondering if Tristan was doing the same.

Rhyan stepped forward, slowly looking me up and down. "I want you to pick up that glass again for me. And hand him back his stave. I assume we'll need to appear bound for this plan? To come as captives to the Emperor? Go ahead." He held up his hands. "Use a glamour and fashion some ropes for me."

He snarled, "You dare to bind me for real, and she cuts you."

"Deal," Tristan said without hesitation.

I nodded to Rhyan and handed Tristan his stave, holding the glass shard to his neck.

He cast the ropes, covering Rhyan's body in them.

"Well?" I asked.

"Perfect," Rhyan said. "I don't feel a thing. Now bring me the shard, and he can do yours."

A moment later, we were both glamoured with ropes. Rhyan still clutched the glass in his hand.

"Lord Grey," Rhyan said. "I meant what I said. Anything happens to Lyr, anything at all, it's over."

But before Tristan could answer, the scuffle I'd heard earlier had returned. Louder. There was a fight happening outside. Soturi were yelling. Someone smacked against the wall, and I could hear the unmistakable sound of flesh hitting flesh. And bone.

"Wait for my signal," Tristan hissed, and opened my door.

Dario was in the middle of a Five. He'd broken free of whatever hold they'd had on him. And now he looked like he was fighting every single soturion in our hall.

Already there were three knocked out unconscious. He didn't even have his weapons. Just his own pure, brute force.

He swung a punch at his opponent and another kick. "You boys have been away from the arena too long," he growled.

"Told you he was dangerous," Rhyan said, and sprung forward, no longer needing Tristan's signal. I was next, flinging myself at the first soturion I saw. He was so startled, he never noticed my fist.

He went down, and immediately, I went in with another punch. Breaking noses was apparently my specialty now.

Rhyan's opponent fell, his head smacking against the wall. He turned, the false ropes flying off him and vanishing as he raced for two more soturi. Someone came up behind me, and I spun hitting before thinking.

From the corner of my eye, Dario kicked a tall soturion, who loomed over him, and suddenly something blue flashed in his hand. A vadati.

I dodged a hit, and then another, ducking under my opponent's arm and running. I turned at the last second, and raced back for him, jumping and kicking him square in the chest. He stumbled back, and I used the opportunity to run behind him. Another jump and my arms were around his neck, choking him out.

A minute later, all of the Emperor's soturi lay strewn across the floor, unconscious, some bleeding, some with broken bones. But by the looks of it—all alive. "What the fuck is going on?" Dario asked, retying his hair. He stood for one second, taking us in, and then he slammed Tristan against the wall, his hand around his throat. "What do you want with them?" He looked him up and down. "You're Lord Tristan, aren't you? Imperator's lap dog."

"Emperor's now," Tristan coughed.

"Dario, let him go," I said. "We're going with him."

"The fuck you are."

"Dario," Rhyan said. "I am so sorry for what I've done. For what's between us. More than you know. But—" He cracked his knuckles, preparing to fight.

Dario shoved Tristan aside. "For fuck's sake, Rhyan! I'm not in your Godsdamned way. Whatever the fuck you're doing now, I'm coming with you." He held the vadati to his mouth. "Aiden," he said. "Get to Lyr's room. Bring Meera."

I froze. "Why do you want Meera?"

"You don't want to leave your sister behind, do you?" he asked. "I mean, she's part of the plan. Isn't that what's happening? I figured we have to accelerate our timeline. And then … it's not like we'll be able to come back here for our things, or anyone. We need to be together, and stick together."

"We're not doing the plan," Rhyan said. "It's off. This is something else."

"Fine, then I'll come as Lyriana's escort."

"Dario, enough. Stop. We need to go," Rhyan said. "And I don't want to fight you on this. Tell Aiden to protect Meera, and that I'm sorry."

"Fucking hell," Dario said. "You can tell him yourself."

Aiden appeared, rushing down the hall with Meera right behind him. He was carrying a large leather satchel that looked almost too heavy for him.

"Courtesy of Lady Kenna," he said, tossing the satchel on the ground.

Our weapons were inside. Our blades, our daggers.

Asherah's chest plate. Even my stave.

"Are you going after the shield now?" Aiden asked.

"Change of plans," I said, still stunned.

"Okay, well grab your weapons everyone, and someone tell me what the fuck we're doing." Aiden looked terrified, the way he'd looked when the akadim attacked, but his face was full of resolve.

"We're leaving," Rhyan said.

"Wait, " Dario said suddenly, looking exasperated. "Rhyan, before you try to argue with us again, we know. We know fucking everything. About Garrett, about your mother ..."

Rhyan paled. "You do?" he asked, his voice shaking.

"Fucking hell. Of course, we know. How could we not? We know you. Okay? Look, the contract your father made Lyriana sign," Dario said. "We have one, too. We can't disobey direct orders, unless more than a day has passed. That's why we couldn't say anything. But he messed up. Forgot to give us our orders today with everything going on."

Rhyan's breath caught. "You ... you don't blame me for Garrett? Or ... my mother? Your father?"

Dario's jaw clenched. "No. We don't. I mean, look, I'm pissed as hell at you. And you deserved those punches. It was your hand. And then right after, you left and never came back, never even fucking wrote. We'll talk it out later, when we have time. Okay? But we're with you now. *Me sha, me ka.* On my life." He pressed his hand to his heart.

"And mine, too," Aiden said quietly. "I swear. We're ready. Whatever this is, whatever we're doing, we're at your command."

Suddenly Rhyan was moving toward Aiden and Dario and all three were hugging.

"Heartwarming. Really," Tristan said. "But we're on the clock right now and that clock is running the fuck out of time."

Rhyan's eyes were red, but he stepped back, nodding in agreement.

While everyone gathered their weapons and I clasped Asherah's chest plate around my neck, I filled them in. Told them we were going after Jules, which room it was on the maps, and that after we were escaping to our original rendezvous point. We were abandoning the shield completely. And to get close to Jules and Galen, Rhyan and I were going to pretend to be bound and allow ourselves to be handed over.

"You had three guards," Aiden said quickly. I could see his mind racing, tracking all the details we'd just fired at him.

Tristan nodded.

Aiden pushed his auburn hair back, and his eyes turned to slits, his face showing an expression of deep concentration. "I can't hold this for too long. But long enough to get us inside the interrogation room. Long enough to take them by surprise."

He pointed his stave at his chest, and his features distorted until he looked like an older, paler version of himself, with darker hair, and a beard. His blue mage robes were replaced with a green cloak, and the pale golden armor of the soturi who served the Emperor. A golden Valalumir tattoo appeared on his cheek.

He'd glamoured himself into a Palace guard.

Tristan's jaw dropped, but Dario clapped. "Yes! Yes, this is perfect. Do me now!"

Dario was changed next, his features following a similar distortion, though Aiden turned his hair blond at the last second, and he moved onto Meera. She looked a bit unsettled, taking on the appearance of a man, while Tristan seemed simply shocked by the whole thing. He clearly had never seen Glemaria's Apprentice to the Master of Spies at work. I was just glad this time that he wasn't using his glamour magic against me.

Finally, Rhyan and I were changed. We still looked like ourselves, but instead of armor, it looked like I was in a sleeping gown, my hair mussed as if I'd been pulled from bed. Rhyan was in a simple tunic and pants. And most importantly, we appeared bound. Aiden brushed sweat from his forehead, his entire body tensed.

"Follow me," Tristan said.

We exited our quarters and entered a long hall with soturi standing every few feet. I sucked in a breath with each one we passed. Finally we came to an empty hall I recognized from earlier.

"How did no one hear the fight back there?" I hissed.

"I cast a silencing spell," Tristan said. "I didn't want any other soturi to be alerted, and I didn't really know how this was going to go. Particularly with Hart."

I glanced at Rhyan, but he only shrugged. "I mean, he's right." Then Rhyan slid closer to me as we rounded a corner. "Lyr, when we get in there. I need you to do me one more favor," he said, his voice low.

"You're calling in an awful lot of these," I teased, willing my stomach to stop turning.

But then Rhyan's good eyebrow furrowed, his face serious. "You can't touch Jules. At all. You can't be the one to rescue her, no matter how much you want to be, and you can't heal her. Not until we're outside the Palace."

I shook my head. "But—"

"Hava," he whispered. "She could be Hava. I don't know for sure, but if I'm right, you know what will happen to you." His eyes dipped to my chest.

I sighed. If Jules was Hava, the Valalumir would activate. I'd be incapacitated. And we might not escape.

"Swear," Rhyan said. "Swear you'll let me do it. You'll wait."

I squeezed my eyes shut, my heart pounding, every inch of my body rebelling. But he was right. "I swear."

"Good girl," he said, and reached out to squeeze my hand.

I stared down at the floor, at the purple tiles, their color darker and more jewel-toned in the night. I focused on taking deep breaths, on the weight of the invisible weapons at my hip. I imagined the maps, seeing my visualizations for the past month match the layout of the floor and rooms around me.

My heart started to pound harder when the tiles changed, turning to their black and white pattern. We neared the Throne Room, just as before, and I could feel the sudden warmth in my chest. The recognition of another piece of the light, of the Valalumir.

"It's down this hall," Tristan said quietly, but I already knew that. "And around the corner. We have to get inside first. There's a long hall leading to where they are. No one makes a move until we're there."

"Only one guard?" Dario asked. "You're sure that's it?" He sounded suspicious.

"That's all there was when I was there, half an hour ago," Tristan confirmed.

Rhyan looked skeptical, but we had no way of knowing if that was still true. I didn't think Tristan would lie. But Kormac could have easily shifted how many guards were on duty.

Unless what he was doing was truly meant to be kept secret. I knew the room. It was in the blueprints Rhyan's father had shown us. And only those. Which meant most nobles didn't know it existed. And if he was Emperor now, he'd want to keep it that way. Unless … unless it was simply because something horrible was happening in there. Something he didn't want the others to see.

"Ready, partner?" Rhyan asked, his voice barely above a whisper.

The door Tristan had described, that I'd seen pictures of, was now in view. And behind it was Jules.

"I'm ready," I said, a fire burning inside me. It wasn't my power, it wasn't *Rakashonim*, or the Valalumir, or my contract with Mercurial. It was the anger that had been burning inside me since I'd heard those two simple words.

She's alive.

I thought I'd be more nervous. More afraid. But I wasn't. I was furious. And I was getting Jules back no matter what.

We stopped in front of the door, and I turned around, seeking out Meera. I spotted her easily despite the disguise. I knew the way she held herself, the way she stood.

There was no need for communication. We both reached for each other's hands. Her eyes watered—or rather, the tough, middle-aged soturion's eyes watered. Then she nodded, her chin firm. I could feel her aura, watery and sharp. And full of vengeance.

"Wait," Meera commanded. "Everyone listen to me now. If Kormac's in there, he has more than just the safety of the room and the guard protecting him. He has chayatim. Mind readers. They may all be under a blood oath, or a blood contract. No matter what you see in there, ignore it. You need to think like your role, not just act your part. You need to think about it with every thought. You need to be the soturion loyal to him, following his orders, and happy to do so. If the vorakh sense otherwise, they'll alert him. And he'll call for backup before we're ready."

I gasped. She was right. And of course, after being around Morgana so much, this was second nature to Meera. This was what Arianna had done. How she'd evaded anyone learning the truth for years. That and the elixirs made of stolen power from the chayatim. Imperator Hart had ordered us all to drink before we arrived at the Palace, carefully hiding our plan regarding the shield. But we had no protection against our thoughts around what we planned to do now.

"Control what they see," I said.

"Control what they think," Meera murmured.

Everyone nodded, faces grim. We approached the door.

Tristan knocked with a swift combination of beats.

A minute seemed to pass, and then it opened. A bald soturion poked out his head, and eyed Tristan up and down. He wore the Emperor's armor. But I knew a Kormac when I saw one. His eyes were beady, his mouth wolfish and cruel. "Tell His Majesty, Lord Tristan said it's done." The soldier nodded, and the door closed.

My heart started to pound. And then the door opened again.

The soturion nodded at Tristan before eyeing me up and down. His lip curled into a sneer. "This the one he wants?" he asked. "Batavia?"

Tristan stiffened. "Yes. Lady Lyriana."

"Pretty," said the soturion, reaching a dirty hand to touch my hair.

I immediately shifted back to evade his fingers.

Rhyan tensed, his aura flaring for a brief second, but he had enough sense to remain still. He was, after all, supposed to be bound. He shouldn't even have an aura. But the guard was focused solely on me.

He reached again, this time touching my hair.

"Get off," I said, willing myself not to fight back.

"You like to play, huh?" His hand began to trace lower, getting caught in my locks, and heading toward my shoulder.

"Do you mind?" Tristan asked coolly. "She's for the Emperor. He's waiting for me."

"Go," the soturion said, and ushered in Tristan with me and Rhyan behind him. Aiden and Dario followed, but Meera was stopped at the door. "You, soturion. Wait out here. Don't need three inside for this."

Meera's eyes widened, and I looked to Tristan quickly. I didn't want to leave her behind. Or alone. But I didn't know what to do. If her glamour failed being too far from Aiden, or if the guard got suspicious of her in any way, it was over. But if Tristan fought him on this, on some random soturion that he didn't know, that would raise alarm bells, too.

We had no choice. We had to keep going.

But Tristan's stave was suddenly out, black glittering rope spilling from the top.

"What the fu—?" The soturion was screaming, his body bound, but I couldn't hear a word he said.

"Silencing spell," Tristan said. "Come on. We all go."

Rhyan lifted one eyebrow, almost looking impressed with Tristan.

"One more thing," Rhyan said, and his fist moved so fast, I barely saw. But it connected to the soturion's throat. The soldier's eyes rolled back as he collapsed, soundlessly to the floor in a heap of pale golden armor.

"Two more things, actually," Aiden said. And the soturion's body vanished, looking like it was simply part of the wall.

We all stopped, looking at each other nervously. We were all inside. And past the guard. But then a scream of pain down the hall had us all walking forward, and then running. A scream that pierced my heart and my soul. Because I knew that voice. It was Jules. It was Jules screaming.

CHAPTER FORTY-THREE

RHYAN

There was a long dark hall, with barely any light. The corridor was so narrow I had to run behind Tristan—uncomfortable, since he didn't move fast enough. But I tried to focus on how this was exactly like the map we'd studied— Lyr was right. The hall opened up into a large windowless room, painted an unnervingly bright yellow. It reminded me of Shiviel. Of fucking Kane.

I felt Lyr behind me, moving faster, trying to get ahead, but I was determined to block her, to be the first one inside the room in case Tristan had been wrong. Or … had betrayed us. But now that we were inside, she couldn't hold back.

I heard Jules's cry of pain, and I was ready to kill.

But Lyr, Lyr's heart was breaking. She screamed, the sound was gut-wrenching.

"JULES!"

Imperator Kormac wore the Emperor's purple robes as he stood in the corner of the room, the torch lights flickering and casting shadows on his wolfish face. And there she was. Jules was in his arms, bruised and bleeding. I bleakly took in the sight of Galen, half-naked, beaten and chained to the wall. The chayatim huddled on the opposite side of the room, their blue mage robes hooded over their heads to conceal their faces.

But mostly, I saw Jules. My friend. My confidante. The one person I'd opened up to when I was alone that summer, and then again the year after that fateful solstice. She was the first person who'd been there when my heart had broken, the first person who knew the truth of how much I loved Lyr.

Jules looked just as Lyr had described after seeing the visions taken by my father's nahashim. Too pale. Too thin, her hair disheveled. Her eyes haunted and pained. She wore the same robes as the chayatim, but her robe had opened, falling off her shoulders. Her dress underneath was black with a deep V that dipped to her belly—dirty and ragged, and far too big for her. Her face was blotchy, and her arms bruised, her chest red. My fingers tensed. I was going to kill Avery Kormac.

One of the chayatim's heads jerked in my direction. Then more followed.

I did fucking hate him. That was no secret. But I couldn't do anything about it now.

My hands were tied.

Jules was silent though, her eyes immediately fixed on Lyr. I knew she didn't see me. Not yet. Nor anyone else. She wouldn't understand that Meera was here, too. That we were all here. For her. To save her. She jerked from the Imperator's hold, still putting up a fight, even if she knew she couldn't win it. But he pulled her back suddenly, and slammed her against the wall.

"NO!" Lyr yelled as Jules's head cracked. She paled, looking faint. But her eyes were open and she was still breathing. She wore a look of absolute pain. But there was defiance in her eyes. I couldn't even comprehend what she'd been through these last few years. And a part of me didn't want to. But one thing was certain. She wasn't the same Jules I'd met before. She was stronger, a survivor, a fighter. And by the Gods, and every oath I'd ever sworn, she was about to be free.

"Lady Lyriana," our new Emperor drawled. "I guess the secret's out. Too late."

Lyr practically growled, hardly holding onto her glamour—her bindings. She was moving too much, losing control. I could see it in her eyes. She wanted to run at him. Murder him. One of the chayatim looked up at her suddenly, their eyes narrowed. I had to do something.

"I see some congratulations are in order," I yelled suddenly, trying to get the Emperor's attention onto me. Let him attack me instead. I needed him to leave Jules and Lyr alone. I could only imagine the games he was ready to play, the way he wanted to torture them both. "*Tovayah maischa* on your promotion. Your Highness. Or I suppose, it's Your Majesty, now?"

But it didn't work. Jules was still struggling, still fighting back. She looked woozy, and unsteady on her feet, and the Emperor gripped her arm, squeezing. She snarled, but he held her aside, his strength too much for her to fight back against. Suddenly, her eyes closed, her injuries overwhelming her.

Lyr made a distressed sound beside me, and I willed her to be strong, to be still. For just another minute.

"Lord Rhyan," he said. "As obstinate as ever. You need to bow before me. All of you do. Or have you forgotten?"

I eyed Tristan carefully and he nodded, bending over. We all followed suit. I could have sworn the Emperor's eyes moved behind me. To Mee—, I mean to that one soturion whatever the fuck his name was. He was an odd one. Probably didn't even know how to fucking bow. He probably curtsied. Farther than Lethea.

I swallowed, and stood, and the Emperor, fortunately, had his eyes on me. Good.

Jules suddenly came to, looking more focused than before,

like she had a sudden burst of strength. She lunged for the Emperor, with no weapons, only her own inner strength and will.

"LYR! LYR! Get out of here! GO!" Jules roared.

The Emperor whirled around and slapped her across the face. The cracking sound made me run forward. But Tristan stopped me.

I was two seconds away from ending this. From being fucking done. Except for one thing. I knew the Emperor had a vadati on him. And I knew he'd call in the Bastardmaker, and then my father. We couldn't afford another visitor. Especially not them.

Three chayatim looked up at me.

"You little bitch," the Emperor snarled, and slapped Jules again.

"Why don't you punch me," I shouted. "You know you want to, that you've been salivating at the idea. Punishing your rival's son. Humiliating him. Letting Devon know that you won. Go ahead."

The Emperor smirked. "Lord Rhyan, I will greatly enjoy seeing you suffer."

"Why wait?" I asked. "Start now. You have every reason to. You know I was there. In Vrukshire. I was there when Brockton died. I saw him defeated, like he was nothing. Pathetic. He begged at the end. And he gave you up, told us about Jules, whining for life. And you know what else I did? I killed the others. Your nephews? I can't even remember their fucking names. They were weak. Pathetic. None of them are worth remembering."

The Emperor wrapped his hands around Jules's throat.

"Trying to save this whore?" he asked.

I looked around the room. The chayatim may be onto us, but they were silent. And I was pretty fucking sure they didn't have vadatis.

I wasn't waiting for Tristan's signal any longer. And from the look on Lyr's face, neither was she.

I ran forward, punching the Emperor in the face.

"What the fuck!" he roared, and swung at me, but already he was going into his belt pocket, pulling out the vadati.

Fuck!

The chayatim started running at us, not to fight, I realized. But to get out, and sound the alarm. Soturi would fill this room in an instant.

"Stop them!" I screamed. Lyr and Dario immediately went for the chayatim. Meera and Aiden running, with their staves pointed.

The glamours fell at that moment as Aiden switched his focus onto binding each chayatim he could. But I could see he was getting tired. The bindings were no doubt weak. And the chayatim were determined to get out. Lyr and Dario had their hands full, fighting and pushing back.

"GO," I roared at Tristan, my chin jerked at Galen.

Then I dug my heels into the ground, my teeth grinding together. I'd been itching for this fight for a long, long time. I withdrew my sword just in time to deflect the Emperor's. He swung back, and again steel clashed as I shifted to the left.

I prepared to strike again, when suddenly, the vadati lit up, glowing bright blue.

"Waryn," the Emperor roared. "Get in here. NOW!"

"Avery," the Bastardmaker replied. "Coming."

Fuck. Fuck!

We had to end this now. We had no time.

"DARIO!" I screamed. He was at my side within seconds. "Fuck the chayatim! Guards coming. We need to go!"

I swung at the Emperor again, and this time, I struck, slicing into his arm. I managed to hit the one place he wore no armor.

Dario was by my side a second later. There was something like an explosion beside me.

Tristan had freed Galen, and had hoisted him over his shoulder.

The Emperor's face contorted into something I'd never seen before. He was going to kill us. All the masks of civility were gone. Then his eyes widened.

A dagger flew at his face, the hilt smacking him between the eyes.

"You know it's the pointy side that kills," I said, as the Emperor sank to his knees and fell, his body landing on an unconscious Jules.

"Yes, well, small chance we don't get out of here—I think the criminal charge is less for knocking the Emperor unconscious," Dario said, already pushing his body back.

"Go," I ordered. "Help Tristan with Galen."

I reached for Jules, lifting her into my arms. Her eyelids opened, her eyes moving slowly without focus.

"Jules? Jules!" I yelled.

Suddenly her gaze focused on me.

"Rhyan?" she asked, her voice cracking.

Tears began to fall. "Hi, friend," I said. "It's me."

She started to cry, her lip trembling. "You can't be here."

"Well, I am, and I'm getting you out."

She shook her head quickly. "No. No I can't. It won't work." Then something seemed to break down in her aura and face. Like she was no longer seeing me. "I was right," she cried, she sounded hysterical. "I was right. I was fucking right." She was sobbing now.

I was already making my way out of the room with her, down the dark corridor, all while quickly counting to make sure that everyone was there. Meera, Aiden. Dario with Tristan and Galen. And at the front, leading the charge out was Lyr. She knew the maps better than anyone. She knew the way out. "Aiden," I roared. "Do something."

Lyr knew where to go. But we could only handle so many

fights while carrying two injured. If Aiden could disguise us again, we had a much better chance.

"On it," he yelled. And Lyr's form, and then Meera's shifted to men, wearing the Emperor's pale golden armor.

"I was right," Jules said again.

"I know, Jules, I know you were," I said gently, trying to calm her. I didn't want to scare or upset her. She seemed like she was barely hanging on after her beating, and I didn't know in what other ways she might have changed. But I couldn't have her screaming in the halls, alerting guards where we were. Or slowing Lyr down when she heard her cries.

We burst from the room, and turned, running away from the Throne Room.

I caught sight of a soturion down the hall when I rounded the corner.

"Faster," I hissed.

We raced down what felt like an endless corridor, until we reached another, and then burst into a stairwell, hidden behind a door. It was one used by servants that led down to the kitchens. Lyr looked back up at me, her face anxious, and I nodded, urging her to keep running, to go faster, and to not look back.

She did, picking up her speed, running at a pace that made me so fucking proud. The issue though was quickly becoming Aiden, Tristan, and Meera. All mages. None trained to run.

We reached the bottom of the stairwell, and then another. Windows allowed moonlight and the glimmer of nearby moon-trees to enter.

Windows meant outside. There was no door here. We still had too far to go to get out. Meera was tiring. Everyone was, but if we reached the bottom floor, we could escape out the window. I was sure they were warded, and there were guards outside—but right here according to all the schedules, they were on rotation, because there were no doors.

We'd never make the rendezvous point. But we didn't need to. We were all here.

We just needed a way out. And we had one.

"Lyr!" I called out. "Bottom of the stairwell. All the way. To the window. Go!"

"You sure?" she asked.

"Yes!" Meera shouted. "Yes. I remember. There are stables nearby."

Gryphons. Fucking gryphons. Of course. My heart leapt, and I swore, even though I was exhausted and all my muscles were burning, I felt light. I felt energized.

Because suddenly, I felt hope. A memory of escape once before, of fleeing on gryphon-back, of getting to safety in the middle of the night.

We were going to do this. We were going to get out of here.

I clutched Jules closer to me, trying not to rattle her. She was still crying, still mumbling "I was right, I was right," and wincing in pain with every bump and jostle.

My legs were burning. My arms ached, but I kept going until we were all crowded at the bottom.

I gave Aiden one more look. He let the illusion of our armor fall again. But he was exhausted, and I didn't know how much more magic he could muster.

Meera stepped forward instead and looked at the window. "I've got this," she said, and pointed her stave at the glass. "*Lumir dorscha!*" she yelled. Blue light burst from her stave. And suddenly, the faint buzzing that we'd grown so accustomed to, stopped.

She'd undone the wards.

There was another noise starting. It was a few rooms away from us. It sounded like a bell. A warning bell. Someone knew, and they would be heading this way any minute.

Meera wiped sweat from her forehead, and then she pointed

again, gripping her stave tightly, slowly turning her wrist as she muttered to herself.

The glass shattered, spilling like rain across the floor.

"Meera!" Lyr yelled, her voice full of emotion and pride. Everyone began climbing up to the sill and then out. I was last with Jules, hoisting her higher in my arms, and careful we didn't touch any broken glass.

I barely dared to breathe as I touched down on the dirt outside.

But already I could hear the soturi running from within, yelling. Meera wasn't moving fast enough. Taking down the wards had weakened her. And neither was Tristan while he supported Galen. Out in the open now, we'd be an easy target once the soturi came close enough.

"RUN!" I roared. They did, everyone picking up their speed. But they were still moving too slowly.

We weren't going to make it all the way to the stables.

Unless …

"Dario," I said, "Here, take her. Keep everyone heading for the stables!"

He'd barely scooped Jules from my arms when I vanished, my stomach tugging and my feet touching the ground before a set of opened stall doors. I slipped on some straw, slightly dizzy and looked quickly around me. I needed a gryphon that looked friendly and docile. The first one to make eye contact with me, a medium sized beast with bright silver eyes, won.

I ran to him, cooing and stroking his beak. "You're a good boy, yes you are. You're a good boy."

The gryphon eyed me up and down, pushing his beak into my hand. Bending his leg, he brushed his talon back and forth across the dirt. Curiously at first. And then … shit.

He bit my hand. Bastard.

I backed away, eyeing the other gryphons. Shit. Shit! I needed to be fast and convince one to trust me. I was good at this, but that didn't mean I was tame and sweet talk a gryphon in under-a-minute-good. Especially if they could sense my nerves.

I passed a silver winged one, who was too haughty to even look at me.

So I raced further down the row of stalls, my pulse pounding until an angry squawk caught my attention. One I'd heard before. I ran at once, skidding to a halt at the end of the row when I saw a flash of bronze wings.

"No. You're here?" It was our gryphon from the Allurian Pass. "Okay, friend. You remember me, and you like me. Ready?"

He closed his eyes, pushing his beak into my hand, a satisfied sound rumbling low in his throat.

I slashed the rope tying him down. My stomach tugged, and I was on his back.

"*Vra*," I screamed. "*Vrata mahar!*"

He was still for a few seconds, and I wondered if he didn't understand the command. I'd told him to run, not fly. We needed to be low so everyone could get on.

"*Vrata mahar!*" I yelled again. And this time, he burst through his gates and took off.

I saw everyone running towards us and directed the gryphon straight at them.

Behind them, soturi were starting to swarm into the courtyard from the Palace.

"Stay!" I demanded, and then I was gone. Back on the ground.

I grabbed Lyr, my stomach tugged and we were on the gryphon. Another tug. I grabbed Meera. Tug. We thudded into a seat beside Lyr. She scrambled off my lap to her sister.

Tug. I took Galen from Tristan's arms, lifting him high. Another tug. I was getting dizzy. But I laid Galen down beside Meera, and she pulled him against her. I jumped again, reaching for Tristan. He looked startled as I hugged him, but I only tightened my hold and winked, then the tug came. I released him on the gryphon. I looked down, trying to catch my breath and saw Aiden was climbing up.

Only Dario and Jules were left behind. And they weren't alone. A dozen soturi were right behind them. And in a minute, I knew they'd catch up. There were shouts now coming from every direction. We were going to be surrounded. Dario had to run fucking faster.

Seeing this Lyr yelled, screaming at them to hurry. She was calling out Jules's name, her voice panicked. Then a soturion caught up to them, he was right on Dario's heels. Jules cried out, turning back to see them.

Lyr started to rise to her feet on the gryphon's back. I jumped. My boots slamming into the ground, my knees wobbling and my vision going black for a second. Fuck. I'd jumped farther than this plenty of times, and all while holding Lyr. But I'd never completed so many jumps in such a short period of time.

"Give her to me," I screamed, wrenching Jules from Dario's arms. His jaw tightened, like he was reluctant to let her go. Boots running on the ground began to sound in every direction. Then he nodded.

"Can you fly?" I asked, already moving with him. I didn't trust myself just then. I was getting dizzy.

"Of course," Dario said, running ahead. His speed was remarkable now that he was unencumbered and he reached for the gryphon's feathers climbing up.

Holding Jules close, I jumped again, the last time tonight. My eyes met a guard's as my stomach tugged. I saw his eyes widen as we vanished. My vorakh was exposed.

A second later we were on the gryphon, just as Dario reached the gryphon's back, took a commanding hold of his feathers, and settled near his head.

"Everyone's on?" Dario asked tersely, his eyes moving frantically around. He'd lost his leather tie and now his curls were flying loose everywhere.

"We're all here," Lyr yelled. Our eyes met, her hazel eyes watery, and she nodded, turning back to Dario. "GO!"

"*Vra! Volara!*" he yelled, and this time the gryphon listened at once, turning and starting his run.

"Anyone who can use a stave," shouted Aiden, "should get on that. Now! They'll be throwing wards and protective domes at us with all they have."

"I was right," Jules said again.

There was a blast—someone taking down a ward. And then another.

I pushed Jules's hair off her forehead, and adjusted her in my lap, supporting her head.

"What? What were you right about?' I asked. I couldn't tell if this was something to do with a vision, or if she was simply hysterical from what had happened. It reminded me almost of what my mother had said when she died.

It was right.

Then Jules looked up at me, her eyes suddenly clear. She was lucid. She knew where she was, and who I was.

"About this. I told you," she said. "I told you." She was nodding her head vigorously. "You said it was impossible. But I knew. I knew we'd see each other again."

My heart pounded, remembering the last time I saw her. She said as much. I hadn't believed her—I never planned to return to Bamaria. And then she'd said something to me, the same thing she used to write all the time in her letters.

Anything is possible.

My eyes watered and I nodded. "You were," I said, my voice breaking. "You were right, Jules. You were so fucking right."

She sniffled, and closed her eyes.

And then the gryphon's wings expanded, a gust of wind blowing against us. There was one final burst of light—Lyr's stave glowed. Blue light exploded, a burst of magic raining down. It was the kind of magic only an Arkmage could command. But it had been all Lyr. The final ward standing between us and freedom had been demolished. We passed through it with ease, and flew into the night.

Away from the Palace. Free.

CHAPTER FORTY-FOUR

LYRIANA

We were silent for the first hour as we escaped. I no longer felt the fear I once had of flying like this. It was hard to feel fear of any kind after what we'd just done. After all we'd achieved.

But the weight of it could not be unfelt. We had attacked the Emperor of Lumeria. Avery Kormac, the leader of the wolves, of the soturi occupying my country. And we had just freed and taken two of his most valued prisoners. A chayatim. And Emperor's Theotis's murderer.

We'd left Imperator Hart behind, disobeyed, and escaped from our blood contracts. Evaded arrest for vorakh. And by now, everyone knew it.

At least, everyone who had the power to hunt and hurt us knew it. They'd be after us. Probably for forever, until we died, or we left the Empire for good. I didn't know what to do. I couldn't even imagine what would come next. But I didn't regret what we'd done at all. I only regretted leaving Kenna behind. She'd become a friend, and now she was alone with those monsters. But Dario had assured me she wouldn't have left with us, even if we'd been able to reach her in time.

I tried to bask in our victory. We were free, we had escaped, and we had Jules, and that was all that mattered.

I sat near the gryphon's head silently with Aiden. The air was cold, but refreshing, as we flew south. I could feel, even from here, the temperature rising. And in the sky, the stars were twinkling wildly. I took a deep breath, and turned back to see my friends, my family, all working together to bandage and wrap everyone's injuries. Tristan and Meera were diligently tending to Galen's wounds with the limited first aid supplies we had in our belt pouches. I couldn't help but grit my teeth. I wasn't allowed to use my full healing ability—not yet.

Rhyan and Dario were working on Jules, crouched behind me. Beside me, Aiden was desperately trying to stay awake. He'd been nearly drained from all the glamour magic he'd used, and our takedown of the wards. He was on the lookout for more. But we hadn't seen any other gryphons or ashvan for most of the past hour.

I turned back and watched anxiously as Rhyan wrapped Jules's hand in a piece of Dario's cloak that he'd ripped off.

As if sensing me, Rhyan looked up. Our eyes met and a thousand messages seemed to pass between us. Love. Gratitude. Concern. Memories of our bodies tangled in bed, burning together. Rhyan whispering he loved me in the dark. Calling me his soulmate. Growing so overwhelmed with emotion, he'd asked me to marry him.

I smiled, and looked away. Because he was coming between me and the one thing I wanted right now. The one thing I'd wanted since the night of my seventeenth birthday.

Jules.

I was going to be farther than Lethea if I didn't get to see her soon, if I didn't get to touch her. If I didn't get to heal her. My hands practically itched with the need. She could be fine now. Awake, calm, without pain. I didn't care what it did to me. I'd take it on. For her, I'd do anything.

And I wanted to heal Galen, too. Desperately.

Suddenly, I felt Rhyan's arm around my shoulder, his body pressed to my side. His body heat was a welcome contrast to the cold of the night sky.

"Partner," he breathed, and hugged me to him.

All at once, I buried my head against his chest, and made a noise that was dangerously close to a sob.

He stroked my back and kissed the top of my head. "It's all right. We're okay. Everyone is okay."

"By the Gods."

"Look at me," he said, tilting my chin up. "You fought so fucking bravely tonight. It's because of you we got everyone out."

"That was you," I said.

"It was both of us. And everyone else here." It was true. Everyone had played their role.

I looked back over my shoulder. Dario was wiping a cloth against Jules's forehead. He looked reverent as he did it. Caring. So unlike the Dario he usually showed me. But this wasn't quite the empathetic Dario I knew either. This seemed like something else. Something new.

Rhyan followed my gaze, his jaw tensed.

"How is she?" I asked, turning back in his arms.

He squeezed me. "I think mostly in shock," he said. "I don't know. What the Imperator—I mean, Emperor—did to her tonight was awful. But nothing she won't recover from. It's more about what else happened for the last ... well, while ... I don't really know what she's been through. But I think that's going to take some time. She's going to need your patience."

He took my hand. "We're well into Cretanya now. Luckily, we avoided the hourly ashvan. You remember the inn we stayed at before? The one that Sean's in-laws own?"

"I remember," I said.

"We should stay there tonight," Rhyan said. "We're close.

We need to land now. Everyone's exhausted or injured. We'll be as safe there as anywhere else. And I'll feel better getting off the gryphon. We got lucky considering the ashvan patrol and the other gryphons in the capital. One inventory in the stables and they'll know which gryphon we took. They'll be searching the skies for us, covering it."

We're going to have let him go," he sighed sadly. "We're too far south for the gryphon anyway. It's not his weather."

"He's a good gryphon," I said sadly, realizing we'd have to let him go.

"And you said you didn't like flying on them," he teased.

I laughed. "Well, it grows on you."

"It does."

A minute later, Rhyan told everyone to hold on, and began directing the gryphon's descent.

We landed in the forest, not far from the park by the inn. Galen was still passed out, sleeping off his injuries. Aiden quickly removed his robes and spread them on the ground. Then, Tristan and Aiden lifted Galen into the robes. Dario descended, Jules in his arms. She was also fast asleep. I started toward him, but held back, instead taking Meera's hand, and hugging her as Rhyan said goodbye to the gryphon. He shooed him away, and looked ready to cry when the gryphon finally spread his wings. I pulled out my sword, standing guard, as the gryphon took off into the sky for the final time, without us. He was free. There was only a single torn rope dangling from his back leg as he flew toward the mountains and the cold. It was just like Rhyan's tattoo.

Rhyan jumped then, vanishing into the inn to get us all rooms.

Suddenly, Jules opened her eyes, staring up at Dario.

"You're awake," he said, his voice husky with exhaustion. "How are you?"

"I can stand," she said at once. She sounded anxious as she struggled to get out of his arms.

"Oh, of course, my lady." His accent was always thick. He was one of the Glemarians who never seemed to try and hide it or speak in the more formal way of Court, the way Rhyan's father did. But just then, Dario's accent felt even heavier. He frowned, and then helped Jules to stand.

She swayed, not totally steady on her feet, but she wore a look of determination that I hadn't seen in ages.

Our eyes met, and for a moment there was nothing else. She was staring at me, not speaking and I swore my heart stopped. She stepped forward, that same force of determination in her step. And then another. Like she was coming toward me.

My arms lifted unconsciously ready to run and hug her to me.

Suddenly Meera moved, running between us.

"Jules," she said, attempting to wrap her arms around her.

But Jules stepped past her, shaking her off, and I realized she was looking past all of us.

"Is that Auriel's Flame?" she asked.

Meera folded her arms across her chest, her face full of hurt. My arms were aching with the need to hug Jules. Then I fully heard her question. Auriel's Flame? What in Lumeria? I looked over my shoulder, half expecting to see a fire, or an apparition. But there was nothing, just the city of Thene.

"Jules?" I asked. "What do you see?"

She looked at me like I was farther than Lethea. "The inn," she said, almost impatiently. "We're in Thene?"

I nodded, surprised she knew that when she'd just woken up.

"The inn," she said confidently now. "It's called Auriel's Flame."

I didn't even know that, and I'd stayed there for almost a week with Rhyan. Then again, I'd never exactly walked through the front door. We'd been trying to hide that we were together from everyone, even those Rhyan trusted. But Jules had never been here. I would have known if she had. I would have come with her. My first time was with Rhyan, and Jules had never traveled outside of Bamaria without me.

There was no way she could know Auriel's Flame.

"How—" I started to ask, when she waved me off.

"Because I've been here before," she snapped. "And I stayed at this inn."

"When?" Meera asked. "I don't remember us ever—"

"After," Jules said, her voice terse. "It was after. Okay?" She shook her head. "Gods." She was getting angry. Her agitation and annoyance was palpable, radiating through her aura.

I wanted to cry. I never imagined if we reunited that it would be like this. I needed to hug her. Was she mad I hadn't yet? I doubted Rhyan could have properly explained to her all that had happened to me and why it meant I couldn't touch her until we were safe. I still felt awful about it. But then Meera had just gone to her. And Jules had pushed right past her.

"You had a chance to come here while chayatim?" Dario asked gently. "Lady Julianna?"

"No," Jules said, her eyebrows narrowing. "Of course, not." She folded her arms across her chest. "I was a prisoner of the Emperor's. They don't take you out to stay at inns. I escaped."

"You did," I said, my voice high. I took a step toward her. "What happened?"

"I was caught," she said flatly, and looked away.

Rhyan suddenly appeared beside me, and stumbled. I grabbed his waist, supporting his weight before anyone noticed.

He took a deep breath, getting his bearings, but kept his arm around me. "We got lucky," he said. "They had two rooms available. We'll need to split up, four in one, four in the other. Cal and Marisol said they could bring some extra cots and blankets in for everyone. So we should be comfortable, but some of us will have to share. They also have food—Marisol's scrounging

some hot plates together right now. She's very excited every-
body's here."

"Who are they?" Tristan asked suddenly. He'd been quiet
since the escape, his focus completely on Galen. He'd helped us
fight the wards as we flew beyond the Palace grounds and into
Numeria. But then he'd been silent, staring only at Galen. I knew
he was worried about our friend. But I also suspected that he was
attempting to face the reality of what he'd done tonight. Sacrificed his Ka, his wealth, his status. He'd given up everything.
For Galen.

For Jules.

And for other vorakh.

Gods. He was vorakh, too. For the first time since his Revelation Ceremony, he wasn't hunting them. He was the hunted one
now. Poor Tristan. I wanted to talk with him about it. But that
was a conversation that would have to wait.

"Cal and Marisol own the inn," Rhyan said. "My uncle Sean
is married to their granddaughter."

"We can trust them," I said quickly. "They've hidden Rhyan
many times before. And me, too."

Tristan's eyes met mine, his jaw clenching. The gravity of
what I'd just said sinking in. He knew Rhyan and I were
together. There was no way he couldn't, especially after tonight.
We weren't exactly hiding it anymore. But there seemed to be
something about openly admitting we'd spent more than one
night together here that made the knowledge feel like something
more. A confirmation of sorts. Especially in Tristan's eyes.

At last, he pulled his gaze from mine, his mouth tight, his
hand on his belt. "Fine. Let's get inside." He signaled to Aiden,
and once more they picked up Galen.

"Are you okay to walk?" Dario asked Jules.

She answered by marching pointedly away from him and
heading for the inn. Quietly, we all left the forest, traipsed
through the park, which was completely abandoned at this hour,

and then made our way to the street and the alley to remain discreet.

Then for the first time in all of my visits and stays, I walked through the front door.

An elderly man was behind the front desk, with a face exuding warmth and kindness. Cal, I assumed. I hadn't met him during my previous stay since Rhyan had kept me hidden. But I'd heard his voice multiple times when he'd come to check on Rhyan or bring food to the room. Rhyan always ordered enough for both of us and pretended it was all for him. But I had a suspicion that Cal had seen through that. Marisol, too.

"Welcome, welcome," Cal said jovially. He lifted his arms, his eyes sweeping over everyone. "Here are your room keys." He handed them both to Rhyan, then looked again to the rest of our group. "We are so happy to have you all. Any friends of Rhyan's are welcome at Auriel's Flame at all times." He paused. Suddenly, his mouth opened, his eyes falling on Jules. There was something dangerous in the way he stilled. He'd recognized her

I started forward on instinct, ready to defend her and fight Cal no matter how nice he was.

"By the Gods. Sweetheart." He paled, like he'd seen a ghost. "You're back. You're all right."

I stilled, looking back and forth between them.

Jules shrugged. "I guess. I'm alive. Hopefully I leave this time under different circumstances."

Cal frowned. "I hope so, too. How is your fr—"

Jules shook her head. "No." Her eyes darkened, and she walked away from Cal, her entire body turned toward the staircase. She didn't look back.

I wanted to apologize. It was so unlike Jules to ever be rude or cruel or short with anyone. At least, it was so unlike the Jules I had known. I was beginning to understand that she would be different, that I would have to get to know her all over again after so much time apart—after she'd lived a life I knew nothing about. And I didn't know how to feel about that. How to approach her.

Cal looked down at his desk. Not from embarrassment at being slighted by Jules, I realized. But because he was sad. There was a tear in his eye, and the emotion was pushing itself out of his aura. He reached for Rhyan's arm and whispered, "When she's ready to hear it, will you tell her I'm sorry for her loss. *Bar Ka Mokan.*"

Rhyan frowned, one eyebrow furrowed. "I will, Cal." Rhyan looked at Jules, confused, then turned back to the old man. "We better get up into our rooms. Safer that way."

Cal nodded. "Of course. Marisol will be up soon with food, so don't be alarmed—it's most likely us knocking."

"Thank you, Cal," I said. "We really appreciate it."

The old man grinned. "It's our pleasure."

A few minutes later, we had all gathered into one room so we could decide how we'd split up.

I of course wanted to stay with Jules and Meera. I knew Tristan wanted to be with Galen, and Aiden and Dario would want to stay together. And there was no question, Rhyan was going to stay with me. Though it was tempting to do an even split of boys and girls, this was a natural four and four. And so, it was decided. Aiden and Tristan would continue caring for Galen while Dario stood guard.

As for us, Jules and Meera could rest, while Rhyan and I remained alert.

The boys, minus Rhyan, reluctantly shuffled out of what we'd decided would be our room, and they took the second key next door.

Then Rhyan and I were alone with Meera and Jules.

"I want to sleep by myself," Jules said right away. "I can take the floor if it's a problem."

"There's no need for that," Rhyan said.

We had two beds. And only three of the four of us planned to sleep. At least I knew that was what Rhyan was thinking. He was going to sleep though at some point—whether he wanted to or not. He needed it.

"You can take the first bed, Jules, and Meera can have the other. Rhyan and I are staying up, and if we need to rest, we're used to the floor."

She folded her arms across her chest, eyeing the two matching beds.

I bit my lip.

"Jules, uh …" Rhyan started. "Are you … are you okay with me being here? I could … if it makes you more comfortable, stand guard outside."

She turned around, a sudden look of panic on her face, as she looked at me and Meera. Her eyes flashed then she looked only at Rhyan. "Stay. I'm just going to sleep anyway."

"Do you … do you want to get cleaned up?" I asked gently.

She scoffed. "Into what? I'm not putting this shit back on after showering. And I will not sleep naked."

I swallowed roughly, and saw Meera's eyes water.

"We'll find new clothes for you," Rhyan said. "As soon as the stores open."

She nodded. "I'm going to wash my face, and then I'm going to sleep. Please." Her eyes fell on Meera, and then lingered on me, her expression harsh. "Don't disturb me."

"No one will, you have my word," Rhyan said. "*Me sha, me ka.*" He pressed his fist to his chest.

"Thank you," she said, her voice terse.

"I'll, um, be in the hall for a little while," he said, pushing his hand through his hair. "Give you all some privacy to do whatever you want and get into bed. You can take your time. I'll knock before I enter."

Rhyan headed for the door, and my stomach twisted. I felt like I was on the verge of a panic attack. I didn't know what was going on. But I suddenly couldn't stay in that room. Not alone, not without Rhyan. I followed him outside. My heart was pounding, my stomach twisting. The room felt too small, the ceiling too low. I couldn't breathe. I had gotten what I wanted and I still couldn't breathe, I felt like I had that night two years ago. Watching Jules be taken away from me, right before my very eyes and I couldn't do anything. I had to be still, quiet. I couldn't reach out for her.

Just like I couldn't reach for her now.

"I need to talk to Rhyan," I said, and closed the door behind me. Then I pressed my back to the wall, my knees shaking, and closed my eyes.

"Partner?" Rhyan's aura swept over me, and I looked up. He leaned against the wall beside me, reaching for my hip. "What is it?" he asked. "What's wrong?" His eyes moved toward the door. "Don't you want to …?"

I shook my head. "I need you," I said, my voice shaking. "I need you. Can you—can you take us away from here? Please? Just for a few minutes? I can't … I can't stay here."

He frowned, his eyes moving and back and forth across mine quickly. "You sure?"

My chest started to heave, my breath coming short. "Please. Now!"

"Okay. Okay," he said, and wrapped his arms around me, pulling me against him. My stomach tugged, and the inn's darkened hallway vanished.

My feet touched down on the roof of the main temple in Thene. I could see the entire city from there, the stars twinkling above, and fire torches lit every few feet along the streets. They were mostly empty, but a few soturi were on duty, standing guard, and a couple of mages appeared to be arriving to work early. Not far from the inn was a stable of ashvan horses. A few were running in the courtyard, tiny blue lights exploding with each step their hooves took.

I clutched Rhyan to me, as he caught his breath, and recovered from the jump. When he was steady, I sank to my knees. He came with me, catching me, holding me against him. He sat back, and settled me in his lap, face to face, with my legs wrapped around him. He carefully pulled his soturion cloak around me, both of our hoods lifted to conceal us.

And only then, alone, and nearly invisible, in the middle of the night, at the top of the city, with his arms tight around me, his scent in my nose, the heat of his body radiating toward mine, I sobbed.

Rhyan didn't speak. He just let me cry, let me expel every withheld emotion of fear and stress I'd felt all night long. All winter. Ever since I heard the words "She's alive." It was pouring out of me like I was a broken floodgate. And I couldn't stop.

He rubbed my back, and made shushing sounds, rocking me until I ran out of tears.

"I know," he said softly. "Shhh. I know. That was a lot."

"It's not just that. I don't know what to do about Jules," I cried.

Rhyan brushed my hair behind my ears. "I don't think anyone knows, not even her. But you saved her, and you can't forget that—you did that. Okay? That's enough for tonight. You don't have to know what to do next. I don't know if there is anything you can do. Certainly not tonight. Let her rest. She's away from the Palace, away from the people who hurt her most. They can't do it anymore. That's what's most important."

I sniffled. "She's ... she's so different. She feels like a stranger. And I know it's stupid. Of course, she would be. And I know it's only been a couple of hours but ..."

"She *is* different," Rhyan said. He spoke like it was fact, like it wasn't a bad thing. He pressed his forehead to mine. "She was always going to be different. No one can go through what she has and stay the same."

I shook my head. "I feel like I barely recognize her."

"Maybe. But from what I've seen tonight, the Jules I knew, she's still in there. Deep down. She's still Jules, Lyr. She always will be. She's just a different version. I'm not going to push her to come out. Not for a while. She needs to rest and adjust to her new circumstances. Give her time. I think she's in shock."

"She'd been to the inn before. She said she escaped. But all she said when I asked what happened, was that she'd been caught."

Rhyan sighed. "I imagine she's still afraid of going back. Afraid of not only that happening, but what they might do to her if she does. I remember feeling the same way when I left Glemaria. Like my father or his men were waiting for me around every corner, like I could go back at any moment, and when I did, it would be worse. She's already had that happen." He shook his head sadly. "I can't even imagine." He stroked my hair. "I don't think she's going to be able to relax for some time. Not until she feels safe. Only then will she start to heal. But she will."

I swallowed, understanding. "You're right."

"Should we go back?" he asked. "I know you don't want to be separated from your family for too long. Especially now."

And I knew what else he wanted. He wanted to be reunited with Dario and Aiden. To finally talk and clear the air now that he knew they weren't against him.

"We should," I said. "We should also check on everyone else, make sure they're settled. But," our eyes met, "can we have one more minute? Just me and you."

"As many as you want," he said. "You know I'm at your command, Lyriana. Always."

Our lips met in a fierce and passionate kiss, like we'd picked up from where we were earlier in the night. My body was humming, remembering the ways in which Rhyan had taken me. The way he'd pounded into me, and how we'd both lost control.

"We need to go back," I said suddenly, gasping for breath, as his hands slid up my sides.

"I know," he said, but he was moving against me, his hips lifting. "Gods, I still want you."

I had a sudden tightness in my stomach. Like a warning. It would be a while before we were alone again. Privacy had been difficult when it was just us and Meera. Now, we were on the run with six other people. If we were alone again, it wasn't going to be anytime soon.

"Take me," I said. "Here. Now. Quickly."

His green eyes flashed.

I was on my back the next second, as I undid my belt, and Rhyan fumbled with his. Buckles came undone in a flurry, and we kicked off our boots, slid off pants and underwear, just enough to access each other.

It wasn't like the other times. There was no build up, no finesse, no taunting or teasing. It was rough, and hard. We weren't focused on pleasure or playing together. This was something else entirely. Some kind of animalistic need to join, to remember what we'd done, to revel in the fact that we'd survived the night. That we were alive.

Rhyan grunted, slamming into me. I was tight, not fully prepared for him for once. But I didn't care. I met him, pushing back thrust for thrust.

"Fuck," he groaned, almost immediately. He was already jerking inside me. He wasn't going to last long. But I didn't need him to. That wasn't what this was. This was primal. This was need. A desperate connection. An escape from all the death and danger we'd faced.

And then he was spilling into me, his face contorted into a mixture of pleasure and pain, with sweat beading his brows, the ends of his hair curling.

His chest rose and fell and he took short, labored breaths as he buried his face in my neck, and groaned. "Sorry," he said. "You didn't get to—"

I hugged him tight, then pulled his face to mine and kissed him. "I didn't need to. I promise. This was what I wanted. I wanted you. Just you."

But the moment he pulled out, my anxiety began to grow. Rhyan and I dressed in silence, and then stood up.

"You know, partner," he said, his voice quiet, "you never answered my question." *Marry me.*

"What question?" I teased, wanting to keep the moment light, to hold onto this just a little while longer. "From what I remember of your exact phrasing, it sounded like a command."

He nuzzled my neck. "Me? Command you? No. I am utterly at your mercy."

"Hmmm. Then what would you call it?"

"Begging," he said.

I took his lower lip between mine, biting playfully, then licking and kissing him. "My answer was yes before you asked."

A wide grin broke across his face, his eyes sparkling and the look of happiness had returned. "I was hoping you'd say that." He kissed me again, and this time it was long and slow.

When he pulled back his expression was serious. Our hands entwined, and his finger stroked over mine— right where his ring might go. Then he lifted me into his arms, and I felt the familiar tug as the lights of the city blinked out.

We returned to the corridor outside our rooms, and Rhyan pressed me against the wall, stealing one last kiss. Then we knocked on the door, and Meera called out to say that we could enter. We'd just missed Marisol and Cal, but the effects of their visit couldn't be missed. The room was full of plates of fresh fruit, jugs of water, bowls of stew, hot loaves of bread, scrambled eggs, fried potatoes, and a small platter of assorted cakes. It was enough to feed us all breakfast three times over.

Meera had made herself a small plate, slowly taking small bites. But Jules was fast asleep in her bed.

"Did she eat anything?" I asked.

Meera shook her head sadly. "She will. She needed to rest more."

I watched her anxiously. My stomach rumbled, but I felt too nervous to eat. Rhyan, however, moved to the table and began assembling a plate, and handing it to me.

"Eat, partner," he said. "You need sustenance."

I looked at Jules, Jules who was so thin. Jules who wasn't herself anymore. Who hadn't even touched the food.

He set the plate down, took a fork, and pushed into the eggs, before holding it to my lips.

"There's more than enough for her. Not eating won't change the fact that she didn't. Eat. For me."

I opened my mouth and accepted the food.

"Good girl," he said. "Eat more. You need to be fortified for whatever comes next."

He handed me the fork, and I did, as he did the same.

"What is going to be next, do you think? Going on the run? Claiming the red shard for Mercurial? Or ..." Shit. I froze.

"What?"

"The shield," I said. "Your father and Kane can't touch it now, but ... it can't stay in the Palace."

Meera nodded. "I've been thinking. The shard may be the very thing that is allowing so much magic to work in the capital. It's the only place we know of that can ward against traveling."

I considered. That made a lot of sense—I had to believe they knew what they had on their hands—what else could they be using it for?

"Even if it's not in the hands of the Emperor, it's still a danger. Morgana and Aemon are going to try and claim it." Meera's aura flashed with worry.

"They'd be in possession of their own shards." And we had none. And a lot more people to protect.

Rhyan shook his head. "This is a conversation for tomorrow. Tonight, we eat, and we rest."

Meera finished her plate and soon fell asleep, but I stayed awake with Rhyan, watching over three of the people I loved most in this world. And when the sun came up hours later, I was still up. Still watching.

Until there was a loud, violent bang on the door.

I stilled, my eyes meeting Rhyan's. "Cal?" I whispered.

But Rhyan shook his head violently. "No," he mouthed, his hand already reaching for me.

I pressed myself against the door, trying to hold in my breath as I looked through the peephole.

The hall was full of nahashim.

CHAPTER FORTY-FIVE

LYRIANA

"Rhyan," I whispered, my voice barely audible, my entire body still.

He was already at my side, his hand on the small of my back. I stepped away, our hands clasping together as he looked through the peephole. I watched as his eyes narrowed, his shoulders tensing.

"They're small," he said, his jaw working as he brandished his sword. "We can take them."

"There's so many. They can still bite us," I said, a tremor in my arm. I still remembered the feel of their venom. The absolute spread of paralysis, the fear of being unable to move, unable to stay awake or in control. And then being taken by Brockton.

Rhyan's nostrils flared, looking back out, before he said decisively, "They can, but they can't move us."

"What's wrong?" Meera asked. Her voice was sleepy, but her eyes were alert and she was already slipping out of her bed.

Jules groaned and sat up, the blankets falling from her thin shoulders. Immediately I felt her panic.

"They found us?" she asked. "Kormac?" In the daylight I

could clearly see the golden tattoo on her cheek. She turned her head abruptly, her eyes wide as she looked back and forth between us and Meera. "He's here? He's here for me."

"No." Rhyan held out his hand, as if to stop her from fearing. "It's my father. He sent nahashim."

Jules stilled, her face pale. "Same difference. Gods, I knew it. I fucking knew it." She squeezed her eyes shut. "There's no escape."

Meera was across the room in seconds, sitting beside Jules, and pulling the blankets around them. And to my surprise, Jules softened, actually letting Meera hold her.

"Yes there is, Jules. We did escape. And we're not giving up."

"Meera's right. We're going to fight them," I said. "We've done it before."

Jules's eyes narrowed, perhaps taking in my armor and weapons for the first time since we'd rescued her. I could see the questions in her eyes, and the shock. In that moment, I could feel the full weight of our two years apart, of the separate lives we'd lived without any knowledge of the other.

"Lyr will kill every last one before she lets them come for you. As will I. Dario, too," Rhyan said. "Hang on." He vanished.

"Dario?" Jules asked suddenly, her eyes widening at the place where Rhyan had been. He'd traveled with her already and in front of her, but I could see now how much she'd missed when she'd been in shock.

"He's the soturion who helped you last night," I said. "He's a strong fighter. One of the best."

"I know who he is," Jules said. "Rhyan can just ... vanish like that?" she asked.

I nodded. "His vorakh."

At this a tear fell down Jules's cheek. She shook her head, and then buried her face in her hands. "I can't. I can't go back. Not again."

"You're not," I said fiercely. "There's no way in hell I'm letting them take you. Over my dead body are you going back."

Her eyes met mine then, and for a second, I swore she believed me. Like she understood. But then she wiped her tears with the palm of her hands, and scoffed, before she curled her knees to her chest, resting her head against them.

Rhyan reappeared beside me with Dario in his arms. "Keep the door locked," Rhyan ordered. "Push anything you can against it to keep them from sliding in. Don't open the door, or the windows, not even a crack, no matter what."

"Got it," Meera said.

Rhyan turned to me and Dario, his breath already heavy. "Ready?"

Dario held two swords in his hands, and a fierce grimace. "On my life."

Rhyan wrapped his arms around Dario, his emerald eyes on me, holding my gaze, and then they both vanished.

A second later, he was back. My eyes met Meera's and Jules.

"We're going to stop the threat. Just hang on." I nodded, trying to give them confidence, any kind of reassurance that we'd protect them, that they were safe.

Rhyan's hands tightened around me, my stomach tugged, and we landed in the hall. I didn't even stop to think, or assess what was before me. I ran, my sword slashing at anything that moved. I cut down the first nahashim I saw, then the second. A third undulated toward me, its fangs dripping with venom. With a yell, I lopped off its head, watching its body collapse. Rhyan had two medium-sized nahashim on either side of him. And one was racing toward me.

Dario ran interference, but immediately he was surrounded by the remaining snakes. Still he fought back easily, expertly spinning away from their fangs. The nahashim were too young and too small to be much of a threat. At least on their own. But together, they were a force to be reckoned with. He spun, stabbing and decapitating heads, narrowly avoiding a bite to his thigh, before kicking the snake against the wall. He sprinted across the hall, and a second later, the snake's head had been flattened beneath his boot.

They were falling easily.

Too easily.

My stomach turned, that anxiety I'd felt earlier returning. The largest of the nahashim we faced, the only one who might be worthy of dragging us away, slid back down the hall, his body slithering away from the fight, but his eyes were focused, taking in everything. I'd been around them enough to know what was happening. He was recording the vision and leaving to report back.

"It's a trap!" I yelled.

Rhyan looked at me in horror, and I could see he'd realized it, too.

"We need to get everyone out. Now," I said.

The second that one snake found its way back to Imperator Hart, he'd be here. And it would be fast. I'd seen what those nahashim could do. They could fly. They could travel, and there was no telling how close he was already. He'd most likely started tracking us the same hour we escaped.

Rhyan crossed the hall, took my hand, pulling me against him, and I was back in the room with Meera and Jules.

"We need to run," I shouted. "Now! Get your shoes on, leave everything else behind."

Rhyan vanished, and I checked the peephole. The remaining snakes had retreated. They'd only shown themselves to draw us out—to confirm we were here.

Several minutes passed and Rhyan returned, his face red with exertion.

"I took everyone else," he said breathlessly, "back to the woods. We'll hide out there, find some caves, maybe a wild ashvan or gryphon can get us further." Then he moved toward me, his arms open, but I shook my head.

"Jules and Meera first."

His brow furrowed, his mouth opening in protest, but he snapped it shut and reached for Jules.

"Hold on tight," he said, and they were gone.

"Is it like last time?" Meera asked.

"Yes. One escaped, I'm positive it's going to Rhyan's father."

"Shit," Meera said.

Rhyan returned, stumbling toward the wall. He was using up so much energy and he'd barely slept in twenty-four hours.

"Take her," I said. "I'll run and meet you there."

"Lyr!"

"Go! I'm just as fast." I opened the door, tearing out of the room.

I flew down the stairs, jumping the last few steps and landed in front of a shocked Cal, and the woman I presumed to be Marisol.

"Is everyone all right?" Marisol asked.

"Imperator Hart is on his way. He knows we're here. I'm the last one to leave. Run, if you have to. Please. Be safe!" I yelled as I raced through the door. "And, thank you!" I pumped my arms, running down the alley and across the street, dodging a soturion standing idly before a bakery. Then I made my way to the park, into the woods where Rhyan was standing next to Meera. He was still recovering his breath.

"Go!" I yelled, taking his hand in mine. "Everyone stay together. Keep running straight ahead."

"There's woods maybe a half mile away we can vanish into," Rhyan said. "And draw him away from Cal and Marisol."

"And then what?" I asked.

"West. To the human lands," he said. "As far as we can get."

I looked anxiously at Galen. Sleep combined with the magic of his soturion strength had worked miracles the last few hours. But he was still injured, still running too slow, like the mages.

"Partner," Rhyan said, his voice full of emotion. In that one word, he seemed to convey a hundred things unsaid. A thousand promises of what was to come between us. An oath of strength and love, and a future of fighting together.

I pulled him against me, my lips meeting his in a quick, fierce kiss, trying to say just as much. To tell him I knew, I understood, that I loved him. I wanted him to know with one brush of my lips that we had so much ahead. And I didn't care where we went next. As long as we went together.

I let go of his hand. "Take Jules," I ordered, and reached for Meera. It was the only way we could make up for their lack of speed.

Rhyan's mouth tightened, but he did as I asked, urging Jules forward.

I yelled for Galen to help Tristan, and Dario to help Aiden. If the soturi used their strength to push the mages along, we could make it. Vanish into the woods and hide. Ambush any more nahashim that came along. And fight Devon Hart.

But the moment I thought of him, he appeared, running behind us.

"GO!" I screamed, my legs running faster. Meera was falling behind, her feet stumbling, unable to match my speed. Rhyan picked up Jules, racing with her in his arms. And I scooped Meera up into mine, racing ahead.

"Stop!" The direct command left a sharp chill running down my spine. But I kept running, willing my feet to run faster, to let all of my training catch up to me.

"Stop at once!" Imperator Hart roared. "Lyriana, Aiden, Dario! Freeze!"

My blood heated, pain shooting down my arms and legs. I couldn't hold onto Meera, I couldn't take another step.

"No. No!" I cried out, the pain intensifying. I tried to move my legs, but I couldn't. Meera climbed out of my arms, tugging my hands, trying to pull me forward.

"Come on, Lyr." She pulled harder. "Come on! Fight back."

But I couldn't. Every attempt to move, to rebel was instantly stopped, the pain like shards of glass cutting into my every nerve. He'd never ordered me like this before—so directly, with so much force.

A tear rolled down my cheek. "I can't. I can't move."

"No. NO!" She squeezed my hands.

"Run," I urged.

Meera shook her head. "I'm not leaving you!"

"You have to! Go. Get everyone else out."

Rhyan was already turned around, racing for me, urging Jules to run ahead with Tristan and Galen. Dario and Aiden had already frozen in their tracks, their faces twisted with pain.

Imperator Hart was gaining on us. Nearly within reach. And he wasn't alone. Five giant nahashim slithered behind him. The same size as the ones I killed in Vrukshire. The ones that had required me to call on *Rakashonim* to defeat.

"Keep running!" Rhyan roared. "All of you! Go!"

"Lady Lyriana!" Imperator Hart ordered. "Lord Dario, Lord Aiden. Turn, and face me. Drop your weapons. Hands above your heads."

Aiden and Dario lifted their arms and slowly, my limbs burning, I turned and did the same, until my entire body stilled, unable to move. Only the subtle rise and fall of my chest as my heart pounded. I felt as if I were trembling inside, but on the outside I was frozen. I was completely at his mercy.

Imperator Hart's eyes danced, his hands on hips as he rocked back on his heels.

"*Himai*," he ordered. His nahashim slithered forward, their fangs exposed and dripping with venom, ready to attack.

"Rhyan, run!" I screamed, praying he listened. I could handle being taken, could handle whatever came next. If it meant Jules and Meera were free. If it meant Rhyan was safe.

"LYR!" he roared.

No. No.

"I'll kill you," Rhyan seethed. His voice louder, closer.

His father shook his head. "You fight me, you come near me, and my nahashim will bite every inch of Lyriana's flesh on my command. You can't fight both of us. So be smart for once."

The snakes were already on us. One sliding in a circle around me, its scaly skin coming closer and closer.

"Oh fuck," Dario spat.

Suddenly the snake's tail wrapped around my leg, and then it continued to circle, coiling its body around me, its hiss sounding as it slid around and around.

I couldn't move my head, but I could see Asherah's chest plate from the corners of my eye, the red diamonds gleaming inside each star. Asherah's blood. My blood. My hood had fallen back and in the sun my hair was bright, fiery red.

"*Ani petrova kashonim—*" I started, my voice shaking.

"Lyriana, you call on *Rakashonim*, and you're dead," Imperator Hart shouted. "Keep your mouth shut."

I stopped, thunder pulsing in my ears, my blood raging.

"Now, we can all return to the capital, and I can try to appeal to the Emperor on your behalf. Or we can do this the hard way. Your choice, Rhyan." Aiden yelled out in pain.

Rhyan was beside me, his face pale.

And then I began to feel the squeeze of my own nahashim. My breath came short, and I was starting to panic. I couldn't move, couldn't fight back,

"Lyr," Rhyan said, like my name was a prayer.

"Rhyan," his father said. "Walk away. Or you kill her faster." He held his hand out, his wrist twisting. "You kill them all." He growled, the sound low in his throat.

Dario yelled in pain, and the snake wrapped around me,

brought its face to mine, its mouth opened wide. The other two snakes had vanished from my sight, but I had a feeling I knew their targets—Jules and Galen. The Emperor's prisoners.

Rhyan vanished.

I held my breath, forgetting the snake wrapping around me for a moment while I waited for Rhyan to reappear. I could already see his sword running through his father's belly in my mind. But would it be enough? The snakes already had their orders.

And then he reappeared, his sword flashing behind his father.

Imperator Hart called out, his next command on his lips.

Rhyan wasn't going to fight him. I realized it too late. He was going to stop the threat—remove the command from the nahashim, by removing their commander. Removing our own paralysis. His arms wrapped around his father.

I tried to scream. But I couldn't make a sound. Imperator Hart's eyes widened, just as Rhyan's gaze found mine.

They both vanished.

"What the fuck!" Tristan yelled.

But suddenly, Dario gave a battle cry. I could move my arms again but just barely. I was still pushing through the pain of disobeying my orders, and the nahashim was still wrapped too tightly around me. Imperator Hart was gone, but his command was still in effect. And it would be until he was too far for my blood to sense it. But as the nahashim's muscles flexed its scaly body tightening around me, I realized it didn't matter. The snake had me.

I coughed, trying to breathe, trying to shift my body, to escape and reach my weapons.

Galen yelled, his hands wrapped around Aiden's nahashim, his fingers puncturing the scales.

"Lyr, fight!" Meera cried, her stave pointed.

"Trying. It's too tight … can't … breathe." The panic was rising, and I could see it in Meera's face, too.

"Lyr!" Tristan yelled. "Lyr, I'm coming!"

"Meera!" Jules yelled suddenly. Her voice changed. There was something commanding, and ancient in it. "Control them," she ordered. "Now!"

I stopped, unsure what she meant. Even Jules looked taken aback, as if she wasn't sure what she had just said.

But Meera's eyes widened, the light catching in their bright hazel color. And then she blinked, revealing her eyes were now alight in the glow of blue. Coldness seeped against my skin even with the snake tightening its hold against me, it's scales as hot as fire.

Meera looked distant, lost almost. And I feared the worst, a vision.

Until she lifted her arms, a gust of wind blowing through her hair. This wasn't vorakh—at least no vorakh I'd ever seen. Her eyes weren't rolling back. They were focused, intense and glowing with the blue of a vadati stone.

The blue I associated with Cassarya. Guardian of the Blue Ray. By the Gods.

"*Ani Cassarya, nahashim. Ani petrova ra shah. Nahashim, ani turio, teka.*" Meera's voice rang out, foreign, almost otherworldly. Like it was her voice and Cassarya's mixed together. That commanding look I'd seen her wield so often these last few weeks—it was the Goddess. And she had just demanded the snakes fulfill their oath to her and kneel.

To my shock, they did, their bodies slinking down as if in shame, their mouths closed, their fangs now hidden.

I started to dimly recall that Cassarya had always had a close connection with the nahashim. I associated them so much with Lethea, and then Imperator Hart, I'd forgotten their origins.

Cassarya had been the observant one, the one with big eyes who could see far more than the other Guardians. The snakes had always protected Cassarya. And because of her, they'd protected all the Guardians when we'd fallen.

"*Vra*," she commanded.

And then all at once, the snakes slithered away.

My arms slowly began to feel like my own again and I could take a step without pain. Imperator Hart's orders were loosening —which meant wherever Rhyan had taken him, it was far enough to break the hold. Aiden and Dario started to shake off Imperator Hart's orders behind me.

Slowly, everyone came together, looking a little stunned, and huddled in a circle, as Meera seemed to finally come back to herself.

"Are we … um … going to talk about what just happened?" Galen asked. He looked slightly afraid of Meera.

"Later," Aiden said. "I don't think I really want to know, not just yet."

Then we were silent until Jules was the one to ask, "Where's Rhyan?"

Now that the threat was over, and I'd had a minute to calm down, my pulse was rising again, worried. He'd gotten his father away—far away enough from us to undo his command. And I was sure wherever they were, he was fine. He was stronger than his father, a better fighter. And he was unbound—at full strength. When he was like that, he was undefeatable.

But his strength also depended on his energy, on how far he'd traveled and how quickly he could recover. He couldn't jump too far at once, and not while carrying his father. He might not have known how far he had to go to save us, and might have made several jumps. I could see that happening. As we got safer, he would grow weaker.

My stomach was twisting, and more worries plagued my imagination with every second he did not reappear. He could have traveled to the wrong spot—and been seen by soturi. Or he could have stumbled when they'd landed—just enough for his father to get the upper hand.

But even if that happened, Rhyan would fight. He'd get

away. He'd come back. Of course, he would. He knew exactly where we were. We just had to give him time.

"It takes a little for him to recover, right?" Dario asked. "When he ... travels?"

I nodded. "He needs some recovery time usually."

"How long does that take?" Tristan asked.

I shook my head. "Um. Depends how far he went."

"And what happened to him when he got there," Dario said, his voice darkening.

The backs of my eyes burned.

"He'll be okay," Aiden said. But he didn't sound convinced.

Still, I nodded vigorously. He would be. "We'll just give him some time. Wait here. The nahashim are gone. And it was just his father, no other soturi. So ..."

"What about the Emperor?" Jules asked.

"Um." My voice shook.

"Lyr, I want to find Rhyan, too," she said. "But ... we can't assume Imperator Hart was working alone. They never fucking are. Kormac wolves could be marching on Thene right now. And it wouldn't be the first time."

"You're in charge," Dario said. "What do you want to do? We can keep running, get Jules and Galen out of here. Or wait for him?"

"We just need to give him time. Just some time." I blinked back tears.

It was Tristan who took my hand then. "Lyr. We can't stay out here." He turned to the group. "Does anyone know the area? Well enough to hide?"

Slowly, everyone shook their heads.

"What about the inn?" Tristan said.

"Tristan's right," Meera said when I still didn't respond. "We can't remain exposed. But Rhyan will know to go to the inn. He'll look there."

I felt sick. I finally had an idea of how Rhyan had felt when

I'd done this to him the last time we fought nahashim. I'd let go of his hand, had failed to jump. But at least that time, we could still communicate. This time there was nothing. Too many unknowns.

"Come on, Lyr. Let's get everyone inside. He'll find you."

Shakily, I let go of Tristan's hand, and in silence, we all trudged back to Auriel's Flame. Out of the park, we separated, everyone careful to keep their hoods up, their faces down.

Cal and Marisol were standing in the entrance, both holding staves, looking ready to fight despite their age.

"You're back," Marisol said, her eyes immediately scanning our faces. She frowned. "Rhyan?"

I was going to cry. "He's not back yet. He um, went ahead."

Marisol smiled. "He'll be back, dear. Don't fret."

Cal's face hardened. "We'll be on the lookout for him. Don't you worry."

We all ended up back in one room. everyone taking a seat. No one was in the mood to talk, and I was grateful because I didn't want to talk to anyone. I'd taken a spot by the window, staring out at the streets of Thene. Waiting for Rhyan to return. I knew I wasn't likely to see him walking up to the inn. He'd appear suddenly. But I couldn't help it. I kept watching, holding my breath with every soturion cloak I saw.

I was on hyper alert. Every sudden sound, every creak of the floorboard, or step or gasp made me jump. Ready to catch Rhyan when he returned. Hours passed slowly. Jules and Galen, both still injured fell in and out of sleep. And Marisol and Cal came and went with lunch and then some snacks as a pre-dinner.

Then suddenly, a sense of cold filled the room. A sharp, familiar cold. The one thing I'd spent the past two years fearing the most. The cold that came from a vorakh. From a vision.

Tristan tensed at once, his eyes alert and predatory.

I looked at Meera, anxiety drowning me, my instinct to help

her, to hide her had immediately kicked in. I practically growled at Tristan before I remembered, he was one of them.

He had visions, too. But it wasn't Meera.

It was Jules.

She didn't do what she'd done the last time. She didn't look like she was in pain. Nor out of control. She wasn't fighting an invisible opponent or screaming in fear. Not the way Meera often looked. Jules just closed her eyes, her body perfectly still. She seemed almost calm as she leaned her head back, her brows furrowed.

"Jules?" I asked. "Are you ... are you okay?"

She twitched, her breath catching, her eyes moving rapidly back and forth behind her eyelids.

"Jules?" I asked again.

She gasped, her eyes startling open. She looked out of breath, then sat bolt upright. "He's been captured. They have him in the Palace prisons. They're marching him out to the Nutavian Katurium. Instead of the Valabellum, they're going to strip him for possessing vorakh."

"Strip him?" Dario shouted. "Actually fucking strip him!"

"No," Aiden said. "No. No one's been stripped here in ... No."

I had gone still. My heart stopped beating. My brain stopped thinking. I felt like everything in my body was shutting down. I was cold. Numb. Not fully there. Not breathing.

They're going to strip him.

I couldn't wrap my brain around it. Stripping was the worst punishment that could be doled out to a Lumerian. So vile because they were so rare on land. I'd only ever heard of them happening in Lethea. To vorakh.

But Rhyan was vorakh. And the games were canceled. And knowledge of the chayatim's existence had been exposed. Emperor Avery had only been on the throne a day, and he needed to prove his worth. Prove his power. Prove to Imperator Hart that he had won. That his secrets would not be exposed.

I looked around the room half-expecting to see Rhyan again because he had to be here, he had to have escaped. He did have vorakh and he was strong, so strong. The strongest soturion in the Empire. A God reborn.

But he was gone. He'd been captured, and he was going to be … going to be …

My thoughts felt distant, like they were coming from someone else, some other mind, someone more coherent, someone still in the room. Because I wasn't. I wasn't here. If Rhyan wasn't here, then neither was I. Because there's no way I was hearing what I just had.

There was no way that Rhyan had just sacrificed himself to save us. To save me. Because the world couldn't be that cruel. Because Rhyan couldn't have that fate. Because he deserved better. He deserved the world. Because we were going to have more. We were going to be married.

I saw him fighting in my mind, surviving each time, escaping, winning.

And now, I was supposed to believe his strength had suddenly failed? That he was locked up?

If they actually went through with it, he'd lose all his power, all his magic. And he would … he would die. In the worst, most painful way imaginable.

I still remembered Kunda Lith, the examiner from Lethea—the way he'd explained magic when I was terrified and half-naked in my cell. The way he'd explained stripping still haunted me.

Magic exists in physical form within the body. Inside your muscles and bones. It's why you feel like crawling out of your skin when you're bound, why stripping almost always kills. The magic must be extracted from every inch of the flesh, and the process— painful, yes—causes organs to shift from each other. I am close to finding a method that will allow the Lumerian to live, though I can't yet deny the pain.

"Lyr? Lyr?" Someone was calling my name. But I didn't recognize the voice. It sounded far away and distant. Then they called me again, their voice louder.

I whirled on my heels, turning toward Tristan and reaching out a hand, wrapping it around his neck.

"Lyr!" he yelled. "It's me. It's Tristan!"

I released my hand, and he reached for his neck, coughing. "Lyr, you're scaring me. You're scaring everyone," he said.

I looked down. My hands were shaking, my entire body was shaking. I tried to still, but I couldn't.

Jules stood up, and walked over to me. She placed one hand on my shoulder.

At once, my heart began to warm, to glow. The light of the Valalumir lighting up, heating from her touch. But this time, it didn't hurt. I was too cold, too far gone to feel the pain. I realized in that moment the idea of losing Rhyan hurt far more than any fire or flame ever could. I was dimly aware of the pain, of the sensations I felt when Kane had ignited the red light inside me. It would never hurt me again. Nothing would. Not like this.

I looked into Jules's eyes, and said softly. "He was right about you. You're Hava."

She frowned. "Lyr? What are you talking about?"

"Meera will explain. It's related to what she did with the snakes." I swallowed. "Is it happening now? Where is he?"

Jules took a deep breath. "I was trained to see clear visions of what will pass. But my timing," she shook her head. "It's not always accurate."

"So there's a chance it hasn't happened yet. That it could be stopped?" I asked.

Jules nodded.

"Lyr," Meera said. "What are you going to do?"

"I'm going to go get him," I said.

Dario stepped forward. "You're farther than Lethea. You can't just go get him in the capital."

But I could. I could. I felt the light still inside me. And I touched Asherah's chest plate, felt her blood—my blood—running through my veins. My connection to my power, my ancient Goddess self. I didn't care what Mercurial or Imperator Hart said about my strength. I was doing this. I may have pretended I was weak in the arena, but I'd been training my ass off with Rhyan. And I'd been practicing my magic in my mind.

"Yes I can," I said, my voice cold and hardened.

"Lyr, wait," Tristan said. "We need a plan. Decide who should go with you."

"No one is coming with me." I yelled. I held up my hand before he could protest. "Galen is wanted for murder. Tristan, you yourself aided his escape. Jules is an escaped chayatim. And now Imperator Hart knows that Dario and Aiden have betrayed him. Meera is too big of a pawn in all of this. It's impossible. Not one of you can return to the capital."

"And you will?" Dario asked. "You're guilty of everything you just said, not to mention wanted as a bride by both Emperor and Imperator. Your face is too known, and so is your hair. It's a dead giveaway this far south."

"They'll have to catch me first."

Dario nodded, and cracked his knuckles. "Well then, it's decided. Let's go. I'm coming with you. I'm your bodyguard."

"No," I said. "Once I get Rhyan, and free him, he'll travel with me away from the Palace. He can only handle one person at a time. I can move faster if I'm alone. If you're there, you risk your life and slow us down. I'm not the the one who needs protection now. Everyone else I care about and love is in this room. And I know Rhyan feels the same." Though there was one notable exception for me. One sister I could not reach. But there was nothing I could do about that now.

I looked out at all of their faces, not memorizing them,

because I would return, and I would see everyone again and I would have Rhyan with me when I did.

"I need you here, Dario," I said. "You're the only one strong enough. I need you to protect everyone—Rhyan would want that, too, and you know it. We'll find you when this is over. If you have to run from here, leave a message for where to find you with Cal and Marisol. But if Jules is right, it won't take long for me to return."

"I don't like this," Dario said.

I snarled, "I don't really give a fuck. And I have no time. He could be walking out right now. And I need to get there first." I already had my plan for how to get there. When Rhyan and I had been on top of the temple, I'd spotted ashvan stables not far from here. I would go there first. I'd steal a horse and I'd ride straight to the capital, straight to Rhyan.

Dario's eyebrows drew together. "You can't hold back if you do this. Everyone is the enemy. You'll have to kill. Are you sure you can do that?"

I thought of Brockton. Of his final moments. Of my sword pushing through his belly. And how I wished I'd had more time, that I'd done more. These were the same people. The ones who hurt Jules. The ones hurting my love. And I knew if the roles were reversed, they wouldn't hesitate to kill me.

I tightened my belt around my waist, checking that my weapons were exactly where I could reach them. My stave, my dagger, my knife, my sword, my Valalumir stars on the bottoms of my belt straps. And Asherah's chest plate, which would be crucial when I made my move.

I reached for the doorknob, "I'm going to get him the fuck back. And everyone who stands between me and him will pay. Every last one of them. If they hurt him, and I find them, if they come between us, they'll wish they'd never been born."

CHAPTER FORTY-SIX

LYRIANA

After a month of holding back, of pretending I was slow, of forcing myself to remain docile and feign weakness, I was flying through the streets, my boots barely touching the ground as I took each step.

I'd been bitter, hating that I had wasted all of my newfound strength and power in the arena. But now? Now I could feel it crackling through my body, coursing through my bloodstream, alive and powerful. As if all the speed I hadn't utilized the past few weeks had been saved up to assist me now. I dodged past stunned mages on the street, and a soturion who didn't recognize me with my hood up. I'd tucked my hair back, lest anyone see the fiery redness I was hiding in the sun.

When I saw the stables, I slowed. They were official stables of the ruling Ka in Cretanya, Ka Zarine. I slid against the wall of buildings behind me, trying to find the best way in. I not only had to steal a horse, but I had to get it to trust me.

Rhyan was better at that.

The thought immediately made my heart pang.

But I pushed the thought down. I couldn't be weak now. Couldn't hesitate. Every second counted.

The gates to the stables were closed and inside I could make out about three stable hands working. They seemed to be feeding the ashvan. Two on the end further from me, and one nearly at the entrance.

I drew my hood down, and then considering further, I took my dagger, and sliced off a strip of my cloak, and tied the material around my mouth and nose as a makeshift mask. Then, keeping the dagger in my hand, I stepped into the courtyard, empty unlike last night, and slowly pried open the door. The two handlers on the other end didn't notice, but the third one, the one closest to me, looked up right away.

He was young, barely a few years older than me with curly hair. His eyes brightened and immediately he said, "Morning. Can I help you?"

I saw the moment it happened, the moment he took in my mask and the blade in my hand and his face fell. His mouth opened to yell, but I was on him in a second, my hand around his mouth and my blade to his neck.

"You make a single sound," I hissed, "I will slit your throat. I need an ashvan. Now." I pushed the blade into his skin, not hard enough to draw blood, but enough to tell him I was serious. He trembled, his aura actually stinking with his fear. I almost felt bad. But I couldn't allow myself to think about it. Not until Rhyan was safe. "You are not going to send for help. You're going to take me to your fastest horse, and I won't hurt you. Blink once if you understand." He blinked.

"Good. You have thirty seconds. Choose wisely. You give me a dud, my associates will know, and you'll be dead within the hour," I bluffed.

He blinked again. And I hadn't even told him to comply that time.

"Good boy," I said, "Go. Quietly."

His eyes widened, as if he was unsure what to do, but with a shove from me, he started walking, moving quickly, as best he could with my hand around his mouth, and a knife to his throat. He stopped before a stall housing a moonstone ashvan with a golden mane.

"Fastest?" I asked.

He nodded vigorously.

"Saddle," I said.

He nodded again, and pointed. She was already saddled up, which meant she was going to be pulled for soturion duty soon. Perfect.

"Take her out," I ordered, and I removed my hand from his mouth. "One sound from you that's not coaxing the ashvan to me, and you die."

The stable hand was sweating now, his curls sticking to his face. He placed both hands around the horse's face and spoke quickly, his voice shaking, but hushed.

"You'll be … you'll be okay," he told the ashvan.

We took the horse toward the front, and I realized there was going to be a moment when I couldn't threaten the stable hand, when I had to climb onto the ashvan and leave before he screamed. Then I heard Rhyan's voice in my head, ordering me to protect myself before we left our cave.

If you need to defend yourself—strike first, think later.

I felt awful doing it. But once we cleared the threshold, I took the hilt of my dagger, and I slammed it onto the back of the boy's head. His eyes closed and he collapsed. I dragged back inside the stable doors and closed them behind me, then without looking back I climbed up onto the horse, settled into her saddle, stroked her, grabbed her reins, and kicked.

"*Vraya. Ya!*"

She took off at once, picking up speed with a loud whinny, blue sparks shimmering around her hooves. Then I felt the horse lift up onto her hind legs. I tightened my grip, and we took off, running at an angle that left my heart pounding. She raced up the buildings in front of us, and then over them, rising higher and higher.

I quickly assessed which way we were heading and steered us north, straight for Numeria. I kept my gaze forward, urging the ashvan on. The wind was blowing brutally into my face, and the air was chilled despite the sun. But I only looked ahead, only thought of Rhyan. And if my horse slowed, I yelled until we sped up. I didn't relent until I reached the city.

We descended just beyond the border to avoid being seen by patrol. I had just one task to complete. Find out where in the capital he was.

I moved further into the city. The sparkling waterways were overrun with nobles and Lumerians, all speaking in a mix of northern and southern dialects. I hadn't been around such a mix of people like this since Auriel's Feast Day. As promised, the Valabellum had drawn Lumerians from every corner of the Empire. But that was good, because when I had Rhyan, we could vanish more easily—get lost in the crowd.

And the other good thing—they were all heading in one direction—to the arena.

I breathed a small sigh of relief. Rhyan hadn't been stripped yet. If he had been, if it was over, they'd be walking away. There'd be the sort of mass exodus, the kind one saw after games in the arena or habibellums attended for entertainment.

I walked a few more steps, keeping pace with everyone, letting the ashvan take a short break.

"To the arena!" a soturion shouted, bumping into me. I immediately pushed back and shoved him onto the ground.

"What the fuck?" He was Ka Kormac based on his armor. He scrambled to his feet, clearly hellbent on revenge. "The fuck are you looking at?"

But I didn't answer, I just kept walking, pushing until I vanished into the crowd. As I walked, I mentally went over the map of the Palace. Was Rhyan in the dungeons? Or did they have him in that interrogation room where Jules and Galen were? There was a huge difference in location. The interrogation room would be near the Throne Room, toward the front of the Palace away from the arena. But the prisons on the opposite side of the grounds meant a much shorter walk to the Katurium.

"The forsworn bastard," someone shouted into the crowd, pulling me from my thoughts.

More calls came.

"Heard he killed Theotis."

"He'll get his."

Assholes. I ducked my head down, making sure my hood remained up and tightened the mask around my face. I'd put my cloak on over my armor to conceal that I was Bamarian.

But right then someone noticed. "Your cloak's on wrong," a Palace Turion barked at me. "The armor goes on top. Stop and fix it, soturion. Now."

I sped up, walking faster, my hands tightening on the ashvan's reins.

"Hey! I gave you an order! Stop!"

I froze, unsure what to do. I didn't want to draw any more attention to myself. I pushed my shoulders forward, trying to look cowed.

"Why are you masked," he asked, circling in front of me, his eyes narrowing.

"I got cut in training," I said, looking down. "Nasty scar. My boyfriend said it's too ugly to look at." I sniffled.

The Turion rolled his eyes. "Fix your cloak," he snarled, then moved past me, shouting at everyone to keep order, and not to push.

My stomach was in knots but I walked behind him, wondering if he had any valuable information.

"Full crowd," he muttered, as he came upon another soturion. This one was Glemarian.

I pulled my hood further down my forehead. If anyone was going to recognize me, it was one of them. Especially after I'd been paraded around all month.

"The whole fucking Empire's here," said the Glemarian soldier.

"I heard he did that to you?" the Turion said, pointing to the Glemarian's eye.

"Aye, he did. Fucking bastard. Don't matter. He's not getting away with it this time. His father's got a hundred soturi outside his cell. I'm heading back there now. We're about to bring him out. The Imperator wants everyone there. The Emperor, too." He laughed. "Like he can escape. The forsworn bastard's been bound to hell and back, at least three times. And every part of his body's chained."

The Turion laughed. "Good. I'm looking forward to it. It's been ages since I've seen a stripping."

"As am I," said the soturion. "I'll take my leave. See you out there."

The Turion nodded and walked ahead.

Fuck. He was in the prison. I couldn't tell if the soturion had exaggerated or not. But Imperator Hart had done double bindings on Rhyan before. A triple one for today made perfect sense. And knowing how strong he was, it was easy to believe there were a hundred soturi guarding him.

Another shout of someone calling him "forsworn" came and I stormed out of the crowd, pulling the ashvan with me.

Away from the waterway, I climbed back on, steering her toward the trees.

A horn blew. "Prisoner walk begins at the top of the hour! Please, make your way inside quickly!"

I searched for the nearest clock tower. That was in twenty minutes. I threw my hands on my head in frustration. Think.

Think!

My heart was pounding. I'd survived so many impossible

situations. My first habibellum powerless. The fight against Haleika in the arena. The nahashim in Korteria. I'd always found more strength, more power. Suddenly, my mind cleared, and I knew what I needed to do. The warnings didn't matter. Nor did the consequences. I either left here with Rhyan, or I wasn't leaving at all. I had to go get the shard.

"*Volara*," I commanded, and once again we took off.

The Palace was in view, and thanks to my memorization of the map and blueprints, I spotted the windows of the Throne Room with ease. The stained-glass windows were alight beneath the sun. I pulled the reins around one wrist, and I grabbed my stave with the other. I directed the ashvan forward, blue sparks flying out behind us. My heart was pounding, but I urged her on and we flew over the walls, and the gates.

"Hey!" a soturion yelled, and I could faintly hear a horn being sounded. An alarm. But it was drowned out by the sounds coming from the arena. Shouts of excitement were growing louder. I could hear Rhyan's name being called, and then more insults.

They were bringing him out.

I pointed my stave at the windows. And then I released the spell, blasting through the glass panes, again and again and again.

"Bring her down!" came a shout. "Bring her down!" Soturi were gathering at the front wall, and more were marching out from the Palace. But not enough to stop me.

"GO!" I screamed and we flew through the shattered windows, my entire chest heating at once.

The shield was in view above the Throne. Its power called out to me, the Valalumir beating with my heart. A dozen guards were running across the black and white tiles. Another dozen mages ran behind, their staves drawn. Leftovers from the *Arkchayperam.*

"*Dorscha*," I commanded.

The ashvan whinnied in distress as blue light almost hit us. Another mage was shooting a binding spell up. But we moved just in time to avoid the rope.

Suddenly there was another ashvan below, bronze with a silver mane. Riding on his back was the Blade. Lumcria's Arkturion.

"*Vra!*" He roared and suddenly they were flying up to meet me.

I withdrew my sword, and urged the ashvan forward. Our swords clashed in the air and my hood fell back, revealing bright, fiery red hair.

"Lady Lyriana Batavia." He shook his head. "You'll be next to be stripped for this."

I tightened my grip and again, our swords met. I pulled back and charged, stabbing but the Blade narrowly avoided me.

"Oh wait," he said. "You have no power. There's nothing to strip." His arm lifted, and too quickly came crashing down.

I screamed and my ashvan, seeing the coming threat, backed up and neighed in distress.

We were close to the wall, and two more ashvan below were gearing up to join us.

"Wait," the Blade ordered. "On my signal."

I felt for the wall behind me, realizing we'd lined up exactly where the shield hung.

I reached for it, my heart heating, hotter and hotter.

I couldn't get it, it was being held too tight by rope.

The Blade was shifting his ashvan, preparing to charge.

I turned my back, using my sword to cut the ropes behind it. My blood began to buzz, my chest on fire, flaring with the heat. But this time it spread through my limbs, pushing out of my fingers. The shield started to drop, and I pulled it up, shocked at its weight, but thanks to my training, able to withstand it. And for a moment, a sense of awe and wonder pulsed through me. I held another lost shard of the Valalumir. But the moment was gone almost instantly.

The Blade's sword was coming for me, just inches from my face when I blocked the hit.

I felt the reverberation of the starfire steel against the bronze in my hand.

He looked shocked, and spat. "You bitch."

"I have more power than you know," I seethed and kicked my ashvan forward, racing back out the windows.

"Oh no you don't," the Blade roared. "*Vra!*"

I held up the shield, and turned the ashvan, bright orange light radiating from my hand. Blue sparks were covering the Throne Room, flickering in and out of light with each step the horses took.

But the Blade hadn't given up. I could see his sword, the point coming straight for me.

I thrust the shield in front of me, blocking his hit. There was a blast of orange light that nearly blinded me, and then I turned, and without thinking, I thrust, and I stabbed.

The Blade's eyes widened as my own blade cut through his stomach, finding the one small spot in his armor that let me pass.

His mouth opened in horror, and blood spilled out, his hands releasing the reins of his ashvan. His entire body was aglow in the orange light of Ereshya's shard. He tilted to the side, and fell.

The mages on the ground immediately started throwing spells again, now that the Blade wasn't blocking their target.

"*Volara!*" I roared, steering back toward the broken window.

We were almost there, just a few more steps and we'd be outside.

"Now!" came a shout.

The ashvan jolted suddenly.

"Come on," I begged, we were practically at the window. Almost there.

But we were falling. I looked back and saw a sword buried in her right flank.

I made a wheezing sound as we landed. The horse took most of the fall, but every part of my body ached. And I was slow to roll off her, and to stand. My vision blurred, but then just as quickly, everything seemed to right itself.

The heat was growing inside me, strengthening me. It was pulsing through my very being.

I held up my sword, preparing to fight my way out. I recognized some of the faces I saw now. Guards who'd been at Theotis's side. Who'd protected him. One who I was sure had been chasing us when we escaped. A dozen soturi lifted their swords, their eyes fixed on me. Some of the mages had run from the room, calling for help, not trusting their magic in a soturion fight. But half had remained, and I could see their staves glowing, ready to bind me.

I reached for mine, ready to shield myself against their magic. When all at once, their eyes widened, and their staves rolled onto the floor as if they'd been smacked from their hands.

"The fuck?" one said. And then all at once, they turned, as a door on the other side of the room creaked open.

A mage walked through, her movements slow and mesmerizing. Long shining raven hair fell to her waist from beneath a blue mage's robe. She wore an orange gown with a deep V that cut to the golden belt at her waist. It was Bamarian styled, the fabric draped across her curves, and exposed lightly tanned skin. A deep indigo light cast its aura around her. A light I knew. Had known for centuries. It came from the indigo shard which she held in her hand like a scepter.

Like a queen.

Morgana.

The mages were fumbling for their staves, while the soturi looked stunned, their fighting stances widening, their eyes moving back and forth between us as if they didn't know who was the threat. Two soturi had vadati stones, glowing in their hands. Then all at once, the stones turned white.

The door closed, and a buzzing sound vibrated through the room. Wards. We were trapped.

Morgana came to a halt. Her dark eyes wide, her mouth tight as she took me in.

"Lyr." She shook her head. "I thought I heard you. You have something I need." Her eyes swept across the shield. "Again."

"Morgs?" My voice shook, my heart hammering, even as I tightened my grip. "Morgs, what are you doing?"

"Seize her!" shouted a soturion, snapping out of his daze. "Seize them both!"

I stepped back, my sword lifted and Morgana flinched, but then she held up the shard, sunlight catching the crystal and spiraling its light across the room.

She shook her head, slowly, and removed her hood. "No one will be seized today. Not by any of you." She snapped her fingers, and the door opened once more. Three men entered the Throne Room.

I stepped back at once, my pulse pounding, my stomach twisting with fear. There was something terrifying about them, but I couldn't put my finger on it. They were taller than any man I'd ever seen, looming well over a foot taller than Morgana. Their arms bulged with muscle, exuding strength and violence, and their fingers ended with long, tapered nails. Their teeth were so sharp they extended past their lips. It was almost as if … No.

I stepped back again. And at once, all three lifted their faces revealing red glowing eyes.

Akadim.

No. No.

This wasn't possible. It was day. This couldn't be happening. My eyes were playing tricks on me. They were too small anyway. And whatever kind of evil they were, they couldn't be with Morgana. Morgana wouldn't, she wouldn't … *Maraaka Ereshya.*

She would.

The doors closed behind Morgana with another snap of her fingers, trapping us inside. The buzzing grew louder.

"You're warded in," Morgana said. "There's no escape. I'm sorry it comes to this. But all Empires must fall. Even ours."

A soturion flung his dagger at her. The blade flying straight at her face.

I yelled out.

But Morgana merely moved the shard in front of her, and the blade turned around, flying back at the soldier, piercing him in his gut.

He fell to his knees, crying out in pain.

"Remember," she said, "That you were part of the oppression. Of the suffering. None of you who served him, who subjugated and tortured Lumerians on his orders can claim innocence. I want you to know, as you die, that this was always the fate you deserved."

Then she turned to the akadim looming behind her. All three were wearing silver cuffs around their necks, the marking of demons loyal to Aemon, sharing his blood, and his strength.

"*Himai,*" Morgana said.

The akadim attacked.

CHAPTER FORTY-SEVEN

LYRIANA

I backed away, holding up the shield and my sword. My legs widened, my knees bent.

An akadim grabbed the nearest soturion, and within seconds had torn out his throat.

Blood spattered against the wall.

"MORGS!" I screamed.

I inched further back, trying to line myself up with a column. I didn't know where to start. Who would defend me, and who would let me die. I could only watch in horror as the akadim, tore through the room, grabbing whoever was nearest, biting down on their necks, and shredding through them. They were falling one by one, too quick for me to process, too quick for me to react. I'd fought larger akadim than this—and I'd done so with far less strength. But seeing Morgana now, seeing her control them, command them, it was too much. I couldn't move.

Another soturion fell and finally I snapped out of it.

"Call them off!" I yelled. "Call them off!"

But Morgana remained unmoved. She stood there, still as a statue, watching me, as blood filled the white tiles of the Throne

Room. Scream after scream came as I watched death come nearer.

My eyes welled with tears, and something inside my heart broke. The pain in my chest, this feeling twisting in my gut was far worse than it had been when I'd learned what Arianna was. When that first betrayal had caught me off guard.

Because this time, I had known. I'd known a month ago when the akadim had called her their queen. I just hadn't wanted to believe it. Had been unable to accept the true horror of it all.

Because a part of me had been holding on. Holding onto my sister, desperate to believe she was still good, that this wasn't her, that this was temporary. Because deep down, I thought she'd come to her senses, thought she'd come back to us. Because I loved her, and I thought she loved me.

Outside, I could hear the chanting, the shouts getting louder, more excited. Another horn blew. The energy of the crowd, the auras, it was palpable, violent and hungry. Rhyan was outside. My chest tightened. He was in the arena. And he was out of time. Fuck. Fuck!

"Morgana," I said, eyeing every locked door. "Please! Let me pass."

She shook her head. "No." Her eyes raked across the expanse of the shield, of the orange shard pulsing within. "You know what I'm here for."

I shook my head. The shouts were growing louder, reaching a fever pitch, the excitement full of a bloodlust I could sense from even here. No. No.

"Morgana, please! You know what's happening out there! Please! It's Rhyan. Gods, if any part of you is still my sister, let me go! Let me go to him."

She remained still, blinking slowly, her dark eyes taking in all of the death that filled the room. And then one of the akadim ripped off the belt of the last soturion to fall, and presented it to

Morgana. A set of golden keys jingled and she placed them in her pocket.

"It's because he's vorakh!" I yelled. I knew that's what this was. The keys. The chayatim. She was going to release them all. And I wouldn't stop her. But I wouldn't allow Rhyan to be the cost.

"You came to save them?" I shouted. "Save him!"

"Give me the shield, and you can save him yourself."

"I need it. And I need to go. NOW!" A thousand soturi stood between me and him. I needed every advantage. I had no ashvan, no vorakh. Only me and whatever strength I could draw on from Asherah and the Valalumir. I needed everything.

"Don't you get it?" Morgana hissed. "This is bigger than him. Bigger than us! It's about all the vorakh. I won't damn them all for one life. But you would. That's the difference between us. Look what they did to Jules. And look at everyone in this room. They did that. They hurt her. And they are allowing for more hurt—for what's happening right now outside. And what makes me sick to my stomach—is they used vorakh to do it. Used our own powers against us, took us, stole our magic. It ends now. The shield is mine by right. And you know it."

"What's done here is evil," I said. My throat tightened with emotion. My gut gnawing at me. "But you think Aemon— Moriel—is any better? Do you think if I hand this to you, he will be reasonable? Kind?"

"What does kindness have to do with suffering?" She shook her head. Her aura pulsing with sharp anger. "I did what I had to. And you're being an idiot. Hand over the shield! I still hold the indigo shard. I haven't given it to him yet. Trust me."

"But you will?" I asked, my heart thundering, someone outside had amplified their voice—they were reading off a list of Rhyan's crimes, riling up the crowd to accept and revel in his condemnation.

Morgana stepped forward. "Look around you, Lyr. I

command the akadim now. Think about it. Did a single one come near you? No! Are you hurt by any of them or me? No. I'm your sister!"

"That's not what happened last time. You tricked me!"

"I did what I had to." Morgana's voice shook, and for the first time in what felt like forever, she seemed to show true emotion. Then her face righted, her lip curled into a sneer. "I am not your enemy. Who did hurt you is the one who tore our family apart, the one who has made life in Lumeria a living hell. And the Empire," she pointed to the window, "is the one who is about to strip your lover. Not me. I'm here to end this. To free the vorakh. I'm done playing their games."

"So am I," I said.

Her eyes narrowed. "Then hand over the shard."

"I'll give you the shield," I said, the feeling in my gut had sharpened. Intensified. The shield felt like it was pulsing in my hand. Growing more powerful, more aware of its connection to Morgana. To Ereshya. But that meant growing closer to Moriel, too. "If you give the indigo back to me. A trade."

Morgana's lips quirked up, her face almost sad. "Lyr, you have nothing to bargain for. I hold the power here. Not you. Decide. The shield? Or Rhyan's life."

The horn blew again, the sound in a raging battle against thunderous applause. The reading of the crimes had come to an end. The sound was replaced by the chant of "strip him" emanating from the crowd.

"Gods." My chest heaved, my entire face warm. The three akadim, the ones who could come out now in daylight, walked behind Morgana, waiting for her command. Their eyes reddened, and they looked at me hungrily.

My hand tightened on my sword, but I tried to keep my focus away from them. "How? How do I get to him and save him on my own? How without extra power?"

"Bring the shield to me. Hold onto it, and put your hand on

the indigo shard. I will give you strength. Enough to fight. Use it, and call on Asherah. That's all I can offer."

The crowd was growing wild. My heart pounded. A warning flared in the back of my mind. What would happen if Aemon took control of the shards. If he called on *Rakashonim.*

If Moriel were unleashed again.

I didn't care. I was going to save Rhyan.

I raced across the room, and held out my hand, reaching for the shard. "I touch it first," I said. "Or no deal."

Her eyes narrowed, but she could read my mind, she knew I spoke the truth.

As soon as my hand was against it, the shard began to glow, the crystal filling with pure indigo light. In the sunlight there was no mistaking the color.

I closed my eyes. Just like in the vision I'd taken from Meera, I saw pure orange light and indigo mixing together. I imagined the light flowing through me, into me, strengthening me. And I imagined the red light, the original shard of the Valalumir in its purest form, inside my heart.

All at once, my body began to warm. Aches and bruises I'd been ignoring, hunger in my belly, strains in my calves—they vanished. The shield felt lighter in my hand, and then everything felt lighter, as if I could fly. My blood began to heat, pulsing and buzzing through my veins—it was a power I could feel in my bones. A strength unlike any other I'd known.

I opened my eyes, meeting Morgana's. The shield began to pulse, the shard as well. The room was a mix of orange and indigo light and nothing else. It was emanating from Morgana and pouring into me. She stumbled back, and the lights vanished, leaving my body vibrating, my sight clear, as well as my mind.

"Now!" Morgana said. "Go! Now!"

I relinquished the shard and the shield. *They're yours,* I thought. *Thank you.*

In the back of my mind, was the thought *I love you.* And a prayer that she loved me, too. That this wasn't another betrayal.

But she only shook her head. "I know," she said, her eyes red. "Now run!" The door opened. And a wall of soturi stood ready to attack.

I ran from the Throne Room down the hall, sliding through their ranks, my feet barely touching the ground, my legs moving so fast I could barely see them. They yelled, calling after me. But I was down the stairs in an instant, my vision going back and forth between what was in front of me and what I'd memorized. I could see it so clearly, see the path to the arena. Soturi screamed behind me, calling for backup to the Throne Room. I knew the moment they realized how many had died. That the Blade was gone. And suddenly, all of their attention was back there, and not on me. Back on a Throne Room that I knew Morgana had once more locked.

I kept running until I found a window that would lead to the courtyard and then out to the field before the arena. I ran, straight for the glass, my body smashing it to pieces as I leapt and braced for my feet to hit the ground. Not a single piece of glass had cut me. I was untouched, and I wasn't stopping. An alarm began to ring, but I was already running ahead, moving faster and faster.

I reached the outer wall. A soturion stood on guard. I lifted my mask back up without missing a beat.

"Hey! Slow down!" he yelled, but I kept going, running faster. "Drop your weapons!"

I entered the inner hall.

"What are you? Fuck! Stop her!" he screamed.

A soturion rushed at me from the left, but I was ready. My fist swung, hitting him square in his eye. He doubled back and another one came, catching my fist again. I felt someone from behind and revved up my arm, before elbowing them in the chest with enough force they stumbled. I kept running, moving through the corridors. Anyone in my way wasn't for long. I punched a mage in the face, and knocked another soturion to the ground. After that, everyone stood back, allowing me to pass, seeing me for the threat I was. And then seconds later, I was outside in the stands of the arena. The Nutavian Katurium was just like in my vision and arranged just like the other Katuriums, with surrounding stadium seats and an open field.

In the center was a dais, and on top of it was Rhyan.

I froze, shocked at seeing him like this. He was nearly naked, his skin red, and covered in a mix of sweat and long thick welts, all bleeding. He'd been tied up to a tall golden pole. Kunda Lith, the examiner, stood beside him. Emperor Avery, the Bastard-maker, Rhyan's father and Kane all watched on the dais behind him.

Rhyan's head had fallen forward, his dark curls, bronzed in the sun were matted down with blood and sweat. His shoulders jerked suddenly, his body pushed against the pole. He looked like he was barely hanging on to consciousness.

Kunda pulled back his arm. It looked like a long shining nahashim had wrapped itself around his wrist. It was thick and scaly. The stripping whip. A weapon I'd only ever read about before. One I'd never expected to see. Not outside of my nightmares.

Blue light pulsed around Kunda's hand, its eerie glow flowing like a damn had burst down his wrist. The magic pushed itself out the remaining length of the whip which was long and flowing in the air behind him. He reared his arm back, and with a snapping sound that tore through my soul, he struck, the whip coming down on Rhyan's back.

NO!

I leapt over the benches and the gates. My feet touched down inside the arena, as a burst of blue light flowed out of Rhyan, running back up the whip, to Kunda's hand.

An elderly soturion serving the Emperor in pale gold armor turned, his dagger pointed right at my chest.

I gutted him, watching him fall, holding swords with both hands in front of me, daring anyone else to touch me. The crowd was starting to shift, their attention leaving Rhyan, and focusing on me.

But on the dais Rhyan's entire body shook, as the whip remained connected to him. He roared in pain, his hands shaking in their bonds, his entire body twitching and jerking. But the whip held onto him, drawing out his power. Stripping him of his magic.

I watched in horror as he slumped over. Then Kunda pulled the whip back. The moment it left Rhyan's body, a scream tore through him. Through me. Rhyan's magic was glittering and shining, a ball of light at the end of the whip, pulsing above Kunda's hand. The audience clamored with excitement, shouting, cheering. Kunda deposited the magic into a black box.

Rhyan's body convulsed, his muscles contracting, his eyes following the magic as it vanished from his sight. He looked for a second like he was trying to hold back, to regain control, and then he threw his head back and howled, a sound I'd never heard from him before.

A hundred soturi stood between me and the dais.

It wasn't going to be enough to stop me.

My surroundings went out of focus. The bloodthirsty Lumerians celebrating the violence. The soturi surrounding me, their starfire swords glinting with fire.

I could only see Rhyan. Only see his pained expression as my sword connected to another and another. As my fist met flesh, and I dodged kick and punch and blade.

More were coming. Attention was on me. Rhyan was no longer the spectacle. I felt the subtle shift of the wolves turning their predatory eyes on me. Of Imperator Hart realizing I'd come back. Still, I only saw Rhyan. My hands tightened on my swords, and I continued to swing and scream, racing forward, taking down anyone who stood in my way.

Ducking to avoid a swinging sword, I reached for the leather straps of my belt, pulling off one of the sharpened Valalumir stars. And then I stood, my mask falling off my face, my soturion hood blown back as the evening sun turned my hair to bright, fiery flames. I threw the star straight for Imperator's Hart throat.

He moved at the last second, his eyes like daggers. And I pulled out another, just about to cut through Kunda's heart. But it was the fucking Bastardmaker who pushed him aside, taking the hit in his arm. He growled, but it wouldn't be fatal.

There were more shouts now. My name being called. I was being referred to as forsworn, as a criminal, as a traitor to the Empire. I was to be arrested. And I would be next, publicly stripped.

And only then, my name on the lips of Emperor Avery fucking Kormac, did Rhyan suddenly rally, and lift his head, realizing for the first time, I had come back for him. And that I was almost there.

It was time. Time to call on Asherah. To call on *Rakashonim*. To make the final push as the remnants of light from the Valalumir, and the indigo and orange shards dancing with the red in my heart, began to fade. Damn all the consequences.

"Ani Asherah!" I said, making sure there was no question whose strength I needed. "I call upon her blood, I call upon myself. Help me now."

A mage appeared before me, bindings shooting forth from their stave. My sword came down and slashed the rope in half.

I ran forward, almost at the dais.

"Ani petrova rakashonim, me ka el lyrotz, dhame ra shukroya, aniam anam. Chayate me el ra shukroya. Ani petrova rakashonim!"

All at once, the diamond centers of the Valalumir stars around my neck began to glow, and for once the flames danced outside my chest. I saw fire in the corner of my eyes, fires that engulfed my aura. Power surged inside me, rushing from my head to my toes, bursting through my fingertips, igniting with every breath I took.

They were running from me now. Emperor Avery and the Bastardmaker were being taken from the dais, rushed out of the arena. Lumerians were screaming in terror. My name was being shouted along with cries for help.

"Protect His Majesty!" someone screamed.

"Guard His Highness!"

Ashvan started to descend from the sky, pulling carriages. Escapes for the elite.

I moved past the rest of the soturi on the ground—those brave enough to still fight me.

One final soturion, a member of Ka Kormac, wearing a wolf pelt reminiscent of the Bastardmaker's rushed for me, a sword in each hand. I pressed mine together, and before he could strike, I rammed both blades through his belly.

His eyes widened, his mouth opening as blood poured down his chin, and then he fell.

Only Kunda remained on the dais with Imperator Hart. Kane emerged from behind him. I took another star and I threw it at his face. He screamed as it cut through his cheek, and he fell from the dais.

Kunda was turning, getting ready to run.

"Finish it!" Imperator Hart screamed. Then his eyes met mine, a dark gleam of victory inside them. "Lyriana! Stop! Drop your weapons. Now!"

The familiar flow of blood through my veins came along with the pain of the blood contract. My body stopped, wanting to freeze and obey, to listen to him as it had been forced to for the past month. And then, fire burned through me.

I raced forward, closing the distance between me and the dais.

Whether it was the Valalumir lights or Asherah's power, I

didn't know. But the contract had just been burned out of my body.

"The final one!" Rhyan's father shouted, his voice urgent. I could feel the fear in his aura now. He knew what I was, he'd feared it for some time. But he still had control over the Examiner. "End it. Kunda, now!"

"NO!" I screamed. "I will kill you!"

But with a pained look in his eyes, Kunda let the whip fly.

I reached the dais, jumping up and running straight for the Examiner. He held his hands up and I shoved him, hard enough for him to fly off the stage and onto his back. A loud crack sounded as he landed. His eyes closed.

The stripping whip was still attached to Rhyan's back and he was still screaming, and crying, as if a knife were stabbing him again and again. I reached for the whip, determined to pull it off him, to use my healing to keep it from hurting him, but his father got there first. Grabbing and yanking it off. The strip detached and then Rhyan made a sound that shouldn't have been possible to make. It was primal, and ancient, and pained, and scared, and something inside of my soul cleaved in two. There was a second where I had to decide whether to fight Imperator Hart and claim the box full of Rhyan's magic, or go to Rhyan. To save him.

I was at the pole a second later as Imperator Hart ran from the dais toward the waiting ashvan, pushing a scared soturion to the ground. Kane ran behind him, looking back just once, a promise of death in his eyes, his face bloodied and swelling.

I sheathed my swords, eyeing our surroundings. We were alone for the moment, but not for long. I pulled out my stave, letting it slide from the leather scabbard Rhyan had gotten me, and pointed it to the sky, uttering the incantation needed for a protective dome. White light burst from the end, and spiraled in sparkling waves around us. We were inside, and we were untouchable. But not for long.

Blood covered Rhyan's body. His muscles were twitching

and contracting. He'd collapsed against the pole. The distinct pungent smell of sweat clung to him, as well as something coppery and metallic. His blood. But there was more.

I scented vomit. And the other scent in the air came from a small pool of liquid by his feet. He'd wet himself, too.

None of it mattered to me. I reached out my aura, trying to warm him, to comfort him.

But that was the moment when I realized ... I couldn't feel his calling back to me. There was no cold, no sensation of a comforting night, as quiet and soft as freshly fallen snow. There was no balm to my heat, no balance to my fires, no softening to my pain.

Rhyan's aura was gone.

That final strip had taken all of his magic.

I sank to my knees, ripping off my soturion cloak and wrapping it around him, trying not to hurt his back, but it was impossible. He'd been whipped within an inch of his life. There was no part of his body uninjured, or that wouldn't cause him excruciating pain if touched. I remembered how it felt when I'd been whipped. How my back had been torn to shreds. Everything that touched it hurt—and now Rhyan had that same feeling, only it was everywhere.

I focused my energy on my hands, letting any healing power I had flow through me as I reached for what appeared to be a clean spot on his shoulders. The magic flowed at once, and his breath slowed. Just a little. I could feel his pain then, feel the whip. Feel my skin breaking open, my muscles bruising.

Shit. I bit back a cry. And I poured more energy in.

"Lyr?" Rhyan asked suddenly, his voice was raw and scratched. Slowly, he opened his eyes, red and bloodshot. There was something in them—the loss he'd endured, and the trauma evident in the strange color they now had. Like the light inside him, the glow behind the emerald color, the connection to his essence, his soul, was gone. There was vomit mixed in with the blood on his chest. A pool of it on the ground beneath him, just below where his head had fallen. "Are you ..." he coughed, making a horrible retching sound, and blood dribbled on his chin, "you're really here?"

"I'm really here, Rhyan," I said, biting my lip to keep from crying, from screaming. I was taking on his pain. But it wasn't enough. It wasn't fucking enough. None of his wounds were closing. "I've got you. It's all right. It's over now. It's going to be okay. I'm going to protect you."

"You're here," he said again. But I could barely hear the words. He was so weak, he didn't even sound like himself. Every part of him was shaking and his skin was so cold despite how red it was. "You shouldn't be."

"Not your decision right now."

I was distantly aware that there was an attack on the dome around us. Mages striking it with their magic. Soturi thrashing it with the swords. Everything was bouncing back, but I could feel the brunt of the hits, and I knew we were running out of time.

Rhyan tried to hold onto the cloak, to cover himself, but he was too weak, and let it fall. I picked it back up and wrapped it around his shoulders again, and reached beneath his arms, pulling him back to his feet. The moment his heels were on the ground, he stumbled forward, falling to his knees and crying out in pain.

He was so injured that he looked ready to faint. His eyes rolled back in his head, and I reached for him again, pouring more energy into him. It was starting to drain me. I could feel the barest hint of exhaustion creeping through my aura, into my body.

Not yet!

Once more, I got him to his feet, and this time, I supported all of his weight with my hands, pulling him against me, and hugging him, knowing it would pain him. But it had to be done. I couldn't let him fall again.

He made an animalistic sound, some kind of pitiful mewing that ended in a cry. "Sorry," he breathed.

"It's okay," I said. "You're going to be okay. We're going to fix this. I swear."

He shook his head, the movement labored. "Don't make promises you can't keep. It's too late," he said. "Too late."

"No. No! It's not. Because we're together. I'm going to get you out of here, I just need you to stand for me. Okay, Rhyan? Can you do that for me? Just keep leaning into me. Put all of your weight on me, it's okay. I've got you. We're getting out of here."

"I can't. I … I can't. Lyr." His voice broke on my name, and he shook his head. "It's done. They've taken it. Taken it all." He started to sob.

"No, they haven't! They haven't. Because you're still alive!" I yelled. "You survived!" But he wasn't listening. "I'm going to heal you," I said, letting more of my aura reach him, imagining the red light in my heart pouring into his aura.

Bring his magic back, I commanded it. *Bring it back. Heal him. Heal him.*

Every inch of him was shaking, trembling. He eyed my cloak warily. It was paining him, every piece of the material that touched him hurt him, and I couldn't stop it. Couldn't undo it. I wasn't sure my magic was doing anything anymore to soothe him.

"I'm sorry. Sorry about the cloak. I know it's hurting you. But we need to keep you covered. Okay? I'll get you cleaned up as soon as I can. I promise. I'll make the pain go away. And I swear on all the Gods, no one else will hurt you. No one else will lay a fucking finger on you. I'm going to take care of you, Rhyan. I swear!"

He stared at the ground, his eyes closing.

"Rhyan! Hey! Hey! You look at me. Stay with me." I saw the effort it took for him to barely lift his head. I couldn't ask any more of him. Not until we were safe and I could heal him fully.

I reached for his knees, and swept my arm beneath them. With a surge of energy rushing through my legs, my thighs shaking, I lifted him up, cradling him against my chest.

His head fell against my shoulder with a groan. My calves burned. I was strong enough to hold him, but he was so big that it was impossible to get a comfortable angle. I leaned back, and with a grunt, moved his arm around my neck for extra support.

He made a wheezing, pained sound.

"Partner," he said, his lips moving against my armor. "I'm dying. Leave me. Get out of this place, away from my father. Emperor. Before he returns. Before ... before the magic runs out."

"No." My vision blurred with tears. "You're not dying! It's just a rope! Just a fucking rope." My voice shook, as I climbed down from the stage. I just had to keep my focus, keep the dome strong, keep it going until we left the arena, then I'd find us a horse, and we'd be out of here. I just had to keep going. Keep walking. Keep holding Rhyan. He wasn't going to die. I wouldn't let him.

"Always ... stubborn." Rhyan's face fell, but his eyes met mine. "I love you." He flinched as I stumbled onto the field.

"I love you, too." I readjusted him in my arms, my chest heaving with exertion. "Gods. You make this look so easy."

Despite the pain he was in, he managed to curl his lip into the semblance of a smile. "It was."

I ran. The soturi around us were starting to give up on breaking into the dome, as were the mages, and we began to move faster, moving inside to one of the enclosed stalls. A row of benches lay ahead of us, and a low stone ceiling provided some shade from the sun.

We were going to make it. I was sure of it. Rhyan had been stripped, a process said to be nearly impossible to survive but he'd survived. We were doing the fucking impossible. And we were going to keep doing it, no matter what the cost. Someone shouted in the distance. "Prisoners escaped!"

My stomach twisted, but then they began running away from us, out of the Katurium.

And I remembered the keys Morgana had taken from the dead soturion.

She was freeing the vorakh, creating just enough of a distraction, that there was hope. That we could sneak out.

"It's the vorakh," I told Rhyan. "They're being freed."

"How?" he croaked.

I bit my lip, not wanting to tell him, but knowing I had to. "Morgana. She ... I gave her the shield. She's using it to free them all."

"They have two shards now?" he asked.

I nodded, becoming more unsure of my decision.

But before I could say anything, I heard a scream. A chilling, terrified, pained sound. I turned toward the field, still full of hundreds of Lumerians trying to escape.

My stomach dropped. Aemon was walking across the center of the arena, and behind him were two dozen akadim. Another dozen were already in the stands, attacking whoever was near.

Rhyan's eyes widened. I could see the moment he realized what he was looking at, the shock in his face, his mouth falling open. I didn't know what was going on, or how they'd come to be. These akadim were smaller, just like the ones that had been with Morgana. They were just as fierce as the others we'd faced, just as fast, just as strong. And there were too many. Lumerians were being cut down left and right.

"It's day," Rhyan said, blinking rapidly like maybe what he was seeing was a result of his injuries.

I nodded. "They're different. They're evolving."

And if anything, they were more violent, more calculated. I could see it in their movements. They coordinated, plotted, and attacked together, capturing one person and handing them off to another.

I refocused on the protection spell, until I remembered.

Akadim were impervious to magic. And Rhyan had none. We had to get out of there.

But the only exit from the row we were in was full of people, all jammed together. And I was starting to lose my energy, my magic was burning through me. I couldn't carry Rhyan, and keep the dome enforced, and fight at the same time.

"Put me down," he croaked.

And since we couldn't move yet, I did.

He leaned his head back against the wall, his entire body drenched with sweat. His breathing was rapid, but his chest barely rose and fell with each gasp. I pushed his hair off his forehead.

"You can't stay with me," he said, his eyes now on the field. On Aemon. On the akadim. "Fight."

"I'm not leaving you," I cried.

"Lyr, you need to. It's okay. I'll find you, I swear. In the next life."

"Rhyan. I'm only going to say this one more time. So you fucking listen to me, because I am in charge. And you promised to follow the chain of command." I pressed my forehead to his. "Rhyan My Godsdamned Hart. You're not dying." I gripped his cheeks in my hands, and I could feel the warmth in my chest again, feel it start to spread. "Don't you dare give up! Swear! Swear to me right now that you'll live!"

"I can't," he said, his voice cutting through the screams behind me. "I'm at your command. Always. But I can't … break an oath. Not to you."

"Then don't break this one."

"Lyr. *Mekara.*" He shook his head. "Even you can't heal me now."

"Anything is possible," I cried. "Just hold on. You're alive.

Rakame. Your soul is mine. You're my soulmate. Mine in every way, and I do not release you."

"How?" he asked suddenly. "How did you do this? Get here? It didn't seem ... possible." He coughed.

"*Rakashonim,*" I said.

"Lyr." He shook his head. "No."

But then our row started to clear.

I swallowed and prepared to pick up Rhyan again. "We're leaving."

But just as I grabbed his waist, his eyes widened, and something like clarity came over him. "They'll all turn. Like Garrett. It won't end. They can come out in the day. They're loyal to Moriel. We'll be overrun. Innocent people ... they'll die. I couldn't save him."

"Garrett?" I asked.

He nodded. "I'm too weak to fight. But if I do this ... I can make it right this time. Not just for Garrett. But for Haleika. Leander. I know it haunts you, too. You can stop it. And I ... I can save you."

An akadim growled, and started down the row coming for us.

I tossed Rhyan over my shoulder and I leapt onto the bench, climbing up to the next row, grunting with exertion. And then I laid him down and withdrew my sword, placing it in his shaking hands.

"I'm going to stop the threat," I said. "Wait for me." I pulled his fingers around the hilt. "Rhyan, you still know what to do with this! Use it."

Then I leapt down to the first row and ran for the akadim. With a cry I jumped into the air, my feet kicking its chest. I launched myself back, just barely landing on my feet and brandished my sword. I could feel the pop of the protective dome ending, and a sudden feeling of whiplash and exhaustion. The *Rakashonim* was starting to burn through me. I'd already used more than I ever had. And I wouldn't last much longer.

I spun on my heels and my sword sliced through the akadim's arm.

He spat, and I drew my arm back ready to wield again. I feinted and then slashed, hitting the same spot. These beasts were smaller than the ones I was used to, but their skin was just as tough, their muscles just as thick.

He started to walk back, his red eyes boring into me. For a second, my vision blurred, and it looked like there were two of them. But then it righted itself. Only I stumbled again, the sword in my hand suddenly feeling heavy. The akadim ran and tackled me to the ground, his claws around my neck.

I screamed, feeling his nails digging into my skin, my air cut off.

I kicked and twisted my hips, but I wasn't getting anywhere. Suddenly, he stood, still choking me, and held me up, my feet dangling on the ground. I couldn't fight back. Couldn't do anything.

He leapt over the gate onto the field, running with me as I kicked and punched his hands, desperately trying to get him off me. I closed my eyes, drawing on my energy and kicked. It was enough. He released me.

Another akadim came. I spat, both hands on my sword, and I ran him through. Another was nearby, ripping open the tunic of a mage. I raced for them, screaming, and managed to cut off its arm, and then I pulled my blade back, and took off its head.

More soturi were on the field now, fighting the akadim.

The demons at last were beginning to retreat.

I saw the silhouette of Aemon leaving the field, the remaining demons marching behind him.

Alarms were ringing everywhere now. Warning bell on top of warning bell. But I could only assume the retreat meant one thing.

Morgana had succeeded. The vorakh had been freed.

My chest heaved, and my knees buckled, as I dropped my

sword, the tip of the blade pushing into the ground. I leaned on the hilt, seeing stars, my vision darkening. There was a fire in my chest. Too much power. Too much. I was too weak. Too spent. The *Rakashonim* was taking its toll.

I fell to my knees.

But Rhyan was in the stands and he was waiting for me. And with everything happening, we had an opening. We could get out. I would recover, and I would heal him, and I'd find a way to restore his magic.

Thinking of him, of my love, and all we'd promised, all we had to look forward to, I got back on my feet, and I ran for the stands, my arms pumping furiously. I reached for the wall, and hoisted myself up. And then again onto the benches.

"Rhyan!" I yelled, climbing up the next row. My feet slammed down, and I reached automatically for him.

But he wasn't there.

His blood smeared the white stone. And my cloak covered in his fluids was on the floor.

I grabbed it, my hands trembling. Underneath the cloth was the sword I'd left him.

"Rhyan!" I screamed. "RHYAN!" I picked up the sword, and climbed to the next set of benches and the next. I raced down the row, and then back, climbing the next and the next, and then I ran down again, my eyes searching, moving rapidly to every seat, every inch of floor space, every possible corner he could be tucked into.

"RHYAN!" I jumped back over the wall and into the arena. My heart hammered, the panic at full throttle now. Where was he? Where the fuck was he? "RHYAN!"

Mercurial appeared on the opposite side of the arena, leaning casually against the wall of the stadium. His body was blue. But for once, he wasn't fully human. Instead of his beautiful face with his feline features and long hair, he had the head of a falcon.

Something shifted inside me. A memory. His old form. He

used to appear that way. Popping in and out, always with the head of a falcon. I gasped, feeling a punch to my gut. And suddenly, I saw an ancient temple in ruins. And Auriel, weak and fighting against Kane. Not Kane. Shiviel.

And then my heart cracked, and my vision went blank, pushing me from the memory, back into the arena.

Mercurial watched me curiously, his falcon head snaking side to side as he stretched his neck.

Lost your lover? His voice purred into my mind.

Where is he? I demanded. I kept running. He had to be near. "RHYAN!"

I see you've called on Rakashonim. Again. You were warned. It's burning through you now. Slowing you down. It killed you once before. But you risked it again. Bad girl.

Go fuck yourself, I thought. *Where is he? Where the fuck is he? Tell me! Now!*

He shrugged his shoulders, and held his blue hands out, his palms lifted to the darkening sky.

An akadim attack in the day. Mercurial made some kind of clicking sound, followed by a whistle in my mind. *Not even back in my day did I think I'd live to see such a thing. I told you that this wasn't your fight—this wasn't the course to take.*

Where is he!

You didn't listen to me, my remembered Goddess. And now, you will lose everything.

He vanished.

Help me, Mercurial! I screamed in my mind. *Fuck! Help me. Anyone! Asherah! Auriel! Please. Bring me to Rhyan. Bring me to Rhyan. Bring me to Rhyan. Show me where he is! Show me!*

And then someone listened. Because I saw him. On the other side of the arena. He was in the arms of an akadim. Too weak to fight back. The monster bit down on his neck, a hand over his bare chest. When he pulled his claws away, a black shadow formed across Rhyan's skin. White light emanated from Rhyan's heart. The akadim was eating his soul.

I screamed in horror, and pulled my arm back, willing all I had left inside of me to aim true. And I threw the sword, the blade flying at the beast. I missed.

I was running before I could think, screaming, trying to scare it away. But my *Rakashonim* was running out. Spent.

More light poured out of Rhyan, and his head fell back, his eyes closed.

One more time. Just one more time, I had to call on Asherah. I just needed enough to get to him, to stop this.

I began to chant. And this time, the words flowed from my lips without effort, almost as if I weren't speaking at all.

"Ani petrova rakashonim, me ka el lyrotz, dhame ra shukroya, aniam anam. Chayate me el ra shukroya. Ani petrova rakashonim!"

The fire in my heart exploded. My entire body was engulfed in flames. I was in agony as I roared Rhyan's name, the energy burning through me. I ran forward, my arms pumping at my sides, my legs moving faster and faster, my heart pounding. Lightning flashed in the sky, thunder crashing. And then I felt that familiar tug in my stomach, and suddenly, the Katurium was gone.

I slammed down onto uneven ground, slipping and sliding forward, searching for Rhyan in front of me, my sword withdrawn, ready to slay the demon.

But he wasn't here.

And I wasn't in the Katurium, or even outside of it.

Sand. I was in the sand. I fell to my knees, feeling a heat I hadn't felt in months bear down on me.

The waves of the ocean were lapping at my feet.

I stared at the horizon, the sky a thousand colors as the setting sun glowed bright red instead of gold.

No. No. No!

What was this? Was this a vision? A memory? Had I traveled on my own? Or was this just a fucking trick of Mercurial? I searched anxiously around me. The beach wasn't too far from the Palace. I could still get back, still run. Still find him again and save him. But how? How had I gotten here?

Your Rakashonim. I warned you. Mercurial's voice was in my mind. And then he laughed, the sound ringing and cruel.

My heart shattered.

A few yards away stood the black statue of a gryphon that stood three stories tall, watching the ocean. A statue that was unique to one country.

The Guardian of Bamaria.

I was home.

CHAPTER FORTY-EIGHT

LYRIANA

"NO!" I screamed. "NO!"

Wind blasted as the ocean tides began to rise, roaring against the rapidly darkening sky.

"BRING ME BACK!" I roared as the waves crashed, leaving foam against the shore.

There was no answer.

"Bring me back now! Mercurial! Godsdamn you. Mercurial! I'll make a deal!" I yelled. "We'll bargain! Just bring me back. Let me heal him! Please! I'll give you anything you want. Mercurial!"

But there was still no answer. Not from Mercurial, nor any other Afeya who might hear me.

I started running for the Guardian before I knew what I was doing, rage pulling me forward. I felt farther than Lethea, no longer in control, barely conscious of what I was doing.

But I could still feel the new burst of *Rakashonim* burning inside of me. Still feel its power. It was waning, but it was there. And I was going to use every last bit of it. Until I passed out. Until I had no choice.

I was shaking, on fire, my heart ripping in two. Just before I reached the black onyx statue, I pulled out my sword, and with a primal scream I smashed it into the stone, the blade slicing through to the hilt. Then I punched the gryphon, all my strength in my fist. And I punched again. Raging and grieving, yelling Rhyan's name, over and over, until my knuckles bled.

I stepped back, tears blurring my vision, and I kicked again.

A loud groan came from inside the structure.

I jumped back.

There was another groan. The thick sound of moving stones interrupted the rhythm of the tides.

I pulled out my sword, resheathing it at my hip. The sound intensified, louder, like thunder. And then I watched in shock as the Guardian's head slid off its neck, and fell into the water.

My eyes widened. I ran for the front, climbing up on its talons, to look inside, my heart pounding. The Guardian of Bamaria had always been unique. A gryphon in seraphim country. And in Glemaria, the land of gryphons, they had a seraphim. Asherah's tomb, built by Auriel himself. Was it possible, was this …?

I looked down, expecting to see more. But there was nothing. Just more solid rock. Whatever small semblance of hope I'd had was gone. I didn't know what I expected, but I was done expecting anything to go my way. To work out.

I ran to the water, my legs getting soaked as I slipped on the sand, and stepped further into its depths. Until I reached the head of the statue. It was bigger than me, and carried a weight I couldn't conceive of. But at that moment, it didn't matter. I reached for the black stone, and I hefted it over my head like it weighed nothing.

"I defy you," I screamed into the sky. "I defy you all! Every God. Every Goddess. All of Heaven. The Council of Forty-Four! You all have power! I know you do! And I served you! I honored you. I sacrificed for you. And I was fighting back! Fighting the fucking demons that you unleashed on us!"

There was no answer.

Only a rage growing inside me, a darkness I'd never felt.

"Then fuck you! Fuck all of you. I am Asherah reborn! I guarded your Godsdamned light for fucking centuries! And this! This is how you repay me! You've taken everything!" I roared. I threw the gryphon's head into the ocean with a strength I knew shouldn't have been possible.

It was the *Rakashonim*. I was getting used to it, and I was starting to wonder if all the warnings I'd been receiving about not using it, about it hurting me, were just a misdirection. That if the true fear was that I could hurt everyone else.

I pushed the waves back, my mind imagining them retreating further and further from the shore. They listened and I didn't know why, whether it was because I was more powerful than ever, or fueled by my grief, or this new understanding. But the waves continued to retreat, the head of the gryphon floating away. I stepped into the damp sand, further and further, all the while the water continued to recede.

Lightning struck and thunder rumbled. There was an eerie stillness to the air.

I could sense the water gathering, coming together. It couldn't retreat forever. I could feel it in my fingertips, feel it in my toes. I was going to cause a tsunami.

And I wasn't going to stop it.

I held up my hands and I screamed at the sky. I could feel my power, feel it pushing out of me. Volatile. Destructive.

"You see what you've done! Do you see? I lost my cousin! My sister! My home! My country! You took my mother before I could walk. And you killed my father! You let the monsters survive! You let rapists win! Demons can walk in the sun. But Rhyan loses his power? His life!" My voice broke. "After all you've done to him. Done to me! He served you, too! He was good, and he was pure, and he was mine! After all he suffered, it didn't break him! He still loved! But you took him anyway! So you know what? I don't care anymore. I tried to do the right thing. But if this is the life you've created, and these are our fates, then I'm done! I'm done. I'm on fire and I don't fucking care. Let it burn me. Burn me from within. Let it burn everything. I'll take everything down if I have to. Do you think I fucking won't? I'll destroy this island. I'll destroy the rest of the Godsdamned Empire. And when I'm done, it can join Lumeria in the bottom of the fucking ocean."

Lightning struck again, and again. The thunder crashed.

The waves began to rise, rolling, thrashing and returning back to the shore, returning to me, to the land. The air stilled, and I could feel the force of the destruction looming.

Then a bright golden light shimmered in the blackening sky.

"Wait!" said a voice. Familiar. "Wait."

The light continued to grow, and I had to cover my eyes to block it. To keep it from blinding me.

I stumbled backwards.

"Release the waters. Now. Do not destroy this world. Remember who you are. You are Goddess of the Red Ray of Light," said the voice.

I didn't want to listen. I didn't want to care. But then the light touched down in front of me, and took shape.

The shape of a man. He looked so familiar, with eyes that were a bright brilliant green.

Every part of him glowed with light.

"Ani janam ra," he said, and only then did I realize he'd been speaking in High Lumerian the entire time. I'd been translating unconsciously. But that phrase, that one phrase, "I know you," had pulled me back.

"Rhyan?" I asked, tears streaming down my face.

"Release the waves, *Mekara,*" he said. "Release them. Trust me."

I deflated. The power was leaving me. And I released my hold. All at once, I felt dizzy and weak. The *Rakashonim* had finally ended. My power was drained.

"It's done." I started for him then, and froze. The light was lessening and more of his features were coming into focus. His hair curled the way it always had, but it was golden, and his eyes were a brilliant shade of green, but not Rhyan's green. His face was similar in structure, the features reminiscent of Rhyan's, but they weren't his. His normally pale skin was tanned, golden.

I stepped back. "You're not Rhyan."

He smiled sadly, and reached out a hand to mine, clasping our fingers together. Then his glow subsided completely.

"No, I am not Rhyan. Not at the moment."

I froze, my heart thundering. "What do you mean not at the moment? Who are you?"

Then he smiled, his eyes raking me up and down in a way that felt oddly familiar, like something Rhyan would do. He squeezed my hand, and then released me, his chest rising and falling rapidly. He was out of breath, his face turning red. It was so like Rhyan after a jump. He fell to his knees, his hands opening and closing in his lap.

I gasped.

It was the exact same thing I'd seen Rhyan do when he was first remembering his past life. The same exact movement and position I'd seen of Rhyan in my dream all those months ago. I'd been in the temple and he'd fallen.

I can cool you with my waters, I'd said in the dream. *You don't have to burn.*

"You're the fire," said the stranger, taking Rhyan's words out of my mind. Then he shook his head in disbelief. "I didn't think it was possible. Didn't think I'd make it in time. It's not allowed anymore." He swallowed roughly. "It's been ages since I was down here. Since I took physical form."

I stepped back. "Where's Rhyan?"

"Numeria currently. At least, that's where his body is."

I shuddered, a sob racking through my chest.

"But," the stranger said, "his soul is somewhere else. Not of this realm. That's why I think I could do it." He nodded. "Yes. That's why I'm here. How I took form. Returned."

"Who are you?" I asked, my voice shaking.

Shakily, he rose to his feet and bowed, his green eyes blazing. "I am Auriel."

CHAPTER FORTY-NINE

RHYAN

I can't breathe. I can't breathe.

That's the first thing I realize as I come to, alone in the woods. I can't fucking breathe. And yet, somehow, I'm still alive. I'm still alive. My chest is moving. But I'm not breathing. This is something else, something dark.

I can feel it. Feel the lack. The lack of my beating heart. Of the air flowing through my lungs. Of the blood pumping through my veins. All that kept me alive. All that made me mortal. And all that made me *me*. None of it's here. None of it's happening. Gods. Nothing about this is right. It's like I'm pretending to breathe. Pretending to be alive. Pretending I'm human. Pretending ... I'm not a monster.

But I am. At least, I'm about to be.

Anything else I do is a lie. A cowardly way to avoid the truth. Every breath is a myth, and every rise and fall of my chest is a falsehood.

So I stop. I stop all of it. I make my chest remain still. I stop breathing. I stop moving. I don't even blink. Don't even flinch. And seconds go by, and then a minute. And then another. And

I'm still not breathing. Still not moving. And it doesn't hurt. It doesn't fucking hurt. It should. I should be in agony, I should be desperate, in pain and gasping for breath.

But I'm not. I don't need any of it. And that—that is fucking with my head more than anything else ever could.

Because not breathing feels the same to me as breathing. Not breathing feels just as natural.

And why wouldn't it? I'm forsaken. *I'm* not natural. Not anymore. And I never will be again.

The finality of it all snaps me from my frozen state and I rake my fingers across my face, nails cutting through my skin, pushing through my hair. When that's not enough I'm punching myself in the chest, and the shoulders. Anywhere I can reach just to fucking *feel* something, to make myself breathe, or sigh, or gasp. Anything.

But I can't.

Already, I've forgotten. I've forgotten how to breathe. Forgotten what it's like to need to. But how? How is that already gone? No. No. It can't be. Not yet. I'm not dead yet.

I try to stick out my chest, but that's all I do. I'm not ... I'm not breathing.

Suddenly, I can feel the panic rising up inside me. A hurricane brewing in my belly. The need to run, to hide, to scream, to cry.

I'm not alive. Not alive. Not alive.

But I'm not dead. I'm forsaken. In between.

Turning.

I can still feel it behind my eyes. The sensation of hot, wet, burning tears is there. I know it is. But it's just a memory— the ghost of what I once felt. Like a lost limb that I swear I still have. I don't cry. I can't. I don't ... I don't think akadim do that. Don't think they have the right emotions. Or heart.

Or soul.

Sunset's approaching. The sky is a vibrant purple and blue.

As I gaze out, I can see the sun is a shimmer of gold on the horizon through the trees.

Fuck. Fuck.

I have minutes. Minutes before I finish the transformation. Before my body elongates. Before my fangs descend, my nails stretch into claws. Minutes before I'll no longer be me. It'll be quick. I've seen it happen. I know that much.

And then a tear does fall. One single tear. Perhaps my last. Because I don't want to be gone. I don't want to die. I don't want to be … one of them.

Right at that moment, I remember Garrett. The fear in his eyes. The horror of when he realized he was forsaken. That he would change. That he would lose himself and become a monster. I remember what he said, the desperation in his voice.

Let me die as myself. While I'm still me. While I still feel. While I still love.

I had to kill him. Had to stop the threat. But in the end, even killing him hadn't been enough. Because he'd still turned. He'd become the monster we'd spent years training to kill.

I still see it. Still see his face in my dreams. In my nightmares. I can't forget. How he changed, how he was different when I found him again. When I fought him as an akadim in the wild at the Bamarian border. It wasn't him anymore. He wasn't Garrett. He wasn't my best friend.

He remembered who he was though, remembered me. But that was it. He had no soul. He had no heart, only colorless, empty memories of our friendship, of a life that he had twisted. And the things he'd done as an akadim … The people he'd hurt … Gods. Gods!

That's going to be me. Unless I can act fast. Unless I find a way to end myself. But what kills a forsaken? Garrett had still been breathing before he died. Why? Why not me? Was less of his soul taken? Or is it just because I'm too close to the transformation?

I don't know what to do. If I can't breathe, I can't drown. I can't suffocate.

Can I stab myself in the stomach?

Can I even find a fucking weapon?

I kick at the silver moontree in front me. I'm barefoot. Naked. And despite that fact, despite losing all of my strength, all of my magic from being stripped, when I kick this tree, it moves. This tree with its thick silver trunk deeply embedded into the ground, the tree that's hundreds of years old bends to my will.

My strength, it's already too much.

Then, there it is, between the trees, in the dying sun. I see a flash of fiery, beautiful, red hair.

Batavia red.

Lyriana.

No. NO!

I have to get away from her. I have to run. Because I'm almost done. Almost a monster. And if she's near me, and if I hurt her …

Suddenly, my gums are on fire and everything inside of me starts to burn. My skin is stretching, my bones are aching. The fangs are filling my mouth as the sky darkens. It's happening. It's happening.

And I can't stop it. Can't do anything to stop it.

Except die. Except get away from her, get away from the girl I love. I have to put distance between us. All the distance I can muster.

It's all I can do. The only way I can stop the threat.

Stop myself from doing the one thing that will destroy my soul again.

"*Rakame*." Her voice is in the air, smooth and ethereal. Beautiful. Ancient and new.

"Ly–Ly—" Fuck. My mouth is so dry, I can barely speak. And I don't know how anymore. My teeth are foreign to me. My jaw feels disfigured. "Lyr," I finally gasp, forcing out the word. "*Mekara.*"

"Rhyan," she says and steps out from behind the tree.

"No!" I yell, backing away. "Don't! Get out of here. Get away from me!" But as I look at her, truly look at her, I'm suddenly on my knees, my hands opening and closing into helpless fists as her light shines. She's alive, and beautiful, and glowing. And my heart's breaking. She's too full of life. Too full of love and beauty, and all that's good in this world—all that was good in mine. She's too bright. And it's not glowing just from her chest. From the Valalumir inside her. It's everywhere, it's under her skin. And it's too fucking bright.

Brighter than the brightest star in Heaven. Brighter than the sun.

"Lyr, please," I cry. I can't see her face, not with the light she exudes. I wish I could. Gods, I wish I could gaze upon her one last time. Alive. With these eyes. "Please. Kill me. Kill me before I'm a monster. Before I change. Before I hurt you."

"No," she says. "Rhyan. Look at me. Rhyan, look. I am not Lyriana."

And it's at that moment I obey and gaze upon her face, and see her beauty. Her otherworldly beauty. The beauty of a Goddess.

"Not Lyriana, yet," she says.

"Asherah?" Her name rolls off my tongue with ease, and for a moment, I almost swear I can breathe again. That my chest rises and falls, that blood flows through my veins.

But in the end, it doesn't. I'm still forsaken.

She steps forward, her body glowing, still too bright. Something like an aura of red flames encircles her. She doesn't even seem real. She definitely doesn't belong in this world. She never did.

"Can you kill me?" I ask. "Can you end this?"

"No," she says sadly. "I cannot. Even if I had the power.

Even if I had physical form, I would not. You are of Auriel. Eternal. A Guardian. My love. You are the vessel of his soul, and you are his future, as much as he is your past. You are connected. You are not him. But I love you as if you were. I could never harm you."

I shake my head. "Please? Please! If you love me, then you must. You must find a way. I'm dangerous. To you. To *her*. To your future. I'm dangerous to everyone."

"No. You are not. For you're not gone."

"Not gone!" I cry. "Where am I then if not here? My soul? I'm forsaken! My soul was torn from my body. Eaten. Destroyed!"

"It's not gone," she says. "Of course, it's not. Never. It can never be gone. Not truly."

Nothing new was ever created. Nothing ever destroyed.

But I fear those are just words from the Valya. Just words written by men who fear death and pray for eternity—the eternity we once had, the eternity we lost when we fell.

I shake my head. "If I'm lost, then," I say dully, and rise to my feet, my legs shaking. "Can … ?" I step forward. "Can you help me find the pieces? Can you heal me?" And for a moment, something like hope shudders through me with the tiniest spark, and I remember our past together so fucking clearly. An eternity flashes in my mind. I remember meeting Asherah, losing her, being captured and her finding me, saving me—saving Auriel.

But she frowns, and shakes her head. Her eyes water. "I cannot heal you. I am sorry."

"Fuck." My voice breaks. "What is this then? Why am I seeing you? What are you doing here?"

"Because you called out to me in your heart. Because you needed someone. Because you're alone. I'm here because you're dying. And because I'm sorry for it."

At this I do cry. Falling to my knees, to my hands. I'm on all fours, primal, naked. Broken like an abandoned child. As angry and scared and helpless as the soul we tore from Shiviel centuries ago.

Somehow, the human part of me is winning, fighting back. Desperately going for its final breath. Clawing at life. The sobs are racking my body. My chest hurts and I don't know if it's because I'm crying too hard, or because I can feel the absence of my soul and it's killing me. Actually fucking killing me. Nothing has ever hurt worse than this, than the missing of my soul, of my essence. My humanity.

"Get up," she commands. "Sit with me." She kneels beside me, her arms outstretched.

I do as she says and sit, and she moves closer to me, wrapping her arms around me. But not really. She's not really here. I feel her somehow, but not physically. She's spirit only. Light. Maybe less, maybe nothing more than an illusion. A dream to comfort me in my final moments. But even if that's all this is, I'll take it. I let my head fall against her chest. Pretending it's real. Pretending I feel her.

"You'll hold me?" I ask, already calmer.

"Of course I'll hold you. I'll always hold you, *Rakame*."

"Will you stay with me while I'm still Rhyan? Until I'm not? Until the end?" I ask.

"Until the end," she says.

I wrap my arms around her, through her. Truthfully, I'm holding myself. I'm still sobbing. But my tears have stopped. And so have my breaths. The sky is darkening. Nearly black. The sun is gone. There's a foul, cold chill in the air. Far too cold for spring. My last sunset, my last view of the sun, my last time feeling. This really is the end.

"Where is she?" I ask, my voice hoarse. "Where's Lyr? Is she …" My stomach knots. And then this is what becomes the worst pain of my life, worse than the missing of my soul. Missing her. "Is she safe?"

"She's safe," Asherah says, her translucent fingers running

through my hair, smoothing down my tear-streaked face. "She was sent away."

"Was she captured?" I ask, already afraid my father has her, or our new fucking Emperor.

"No. No man of the Empire holds her now. She was sent away by a higher power. Away from you." Away from me.

I close my eyes, my head falling forward. Of course. Because I'm the threat. Because I wouldn't stay away from her dead or alive. Because she wouldn't stay away from me. I can already see it. She would have come for me. She would have called on *Rakashonim* to heal me. She was trying to get to my side back there, trying to reach me. And it was good she didn't. It would've killed her. And if somehow that didn't, then once I changed, I would kill her. And I can't live with that horror.

Gods, I want Lyriana. I miss her. I need her. I want to see her. I want to kiss her and hold her, and hug her. I want to plunge inside her, and fuck her until I forget. I want to talk to her and taste her and lay in her arms and weep. And most of all, I need her to hold me.

But she's safe. And that's all that matters. She's away from me. My Lyr. My partner. My love. My soulmate. She can't get to me now.

"Thank the Gods," I croak.

A harsh wind blows, and Asherah's form fades, almost like she's a light flickering out.

"I'm sorry," Asherah says. "I came to be with you. So you wouldn't be alone. But I cannot hold this form any longer. I'm not supposed to come here anymore. Not when the other part of me still lives."

"I know."

"Rhyan, you'll forget soon, forget what makes you, you. You'll forget a lot from your life, not the details, not the history, but the meaning. The way things felt. You'll forget what was important. Yet, if you can remember anything, remember this. Don't give up."

Don't give up? But it's already too late.

"Remember. *Ani janam ra*," she says.

And she's gone.

And I scream.

Because it's agony. Because I'm dying. Because I'm changing. Because my body is expanding and growing and I can see the tears in my skin, and feel myself ripping apart. A monster is cutting through me, becoming me. I can feel my jaw swelling and my fangs cut through my tongue and my chest is pushing itself out and out and out. Like I'm searching. Searching for my soul. Growing big enough to fit something that feels infinite back inside me.

But it's gone. And I'm empty.

It's too late. My body's on fire. And it's dying.

No.

It's dead. As am I.

I already know it before I look down at myself, at my destroyed, and newly made form.

I'm akadim.

And I'm alone.

I rise, and everything looks clearer. I can see in the dark, as if it were day. There's no light. But I don't need it anymore. Everything looks different, because I'm seeing the trees from a new height. The ground is farther away than I remember. The sky is closer.

"Don't give up," says a voice in the air. It was familiar until a moment ago.

But now, I can't … can't remember. Can't remember who spoke to me. Can't remember who was here. Whose touch still feels like a ghost on my skin.

I just remember a girl. A girl with hair that shone red in the sun. A girl with gold specks in her eyes. A girl who's too far away for me to reach. A girl who causes an ache and a hunger to burn inside me. I want to find her.

"Don't give up," the voice says again.

I growl. Because I find her voice grating. And I'm hungry. I am so fucking hungry. More hungry than I've ever been. And all at once, I feel it. The need to feed, the need to hunt. I need blood. I need life. I want to eat. I want to drink. And I want to fuck.

I stalk through the forest, and I find a deer. It's dead before it knows it. And Gods. The blood makes me feel alive. Makes me want more. But I'm not satisfied. It only makes my hunger deepen. I can already tell from this feeling that I will never feel satisfied.

I scent the air, my sense of smell unlike anything I've ever experienced. I can detect everything now, every note. I can smell the ocean in the distance, the salt in the air, the fish in the sea. The nearby droppings of a deer, and another rabbit. I can smell the ants, the worms, the earth. Everything.

But there's something else. Something I want far more. Something I hunger for with a burning, bleeding desire.

There's a girl nearby. A mage. In her twenties. I can tell all of this from her scent. And I want her. I need her. I must feed.

Because by the forsaken Gods, I'm starving.

Before I know it, I'm running, scenting her in the air. Smelling jasmine and incense. Something familiar. Something feminine. I'm fast, and getting faster, moving quickly, seeing more life, smelling more scents, getting closer, and closer.

Jasmine.

Incense.

Blood.

Sweat.

I turn the corner, burst through the trees into a clearing, lit in the faint moonlight. And there she is. All alone. Dark hair and dark eyes.

I growl, my nostrils flaring.

"Stop," she commands.

"No." I lick my lips, slide my tongue around the sharpness of my fangs.

But there's something strange about her. She's powerful. Magic.

Doesn't matter. Magic can't touch me. I remember that much.

"On your knees," I say.

She chuckles. "Funny. I was about to tell you the same."

Then I see it, a bright orange light glowing behind her. Something awakens in the back of my mind.

Orange light. It meant something. It was important. But I can't … can't remember.

It doesn't matter now. I rush forward, determined.

And the light blinds me.

"You will serve me," she says. "And in return, I will protect you, and I will provide for you."

"Don't need protection," I roar, and continue forward, my eyes closed. I'll still kill her. Even if I can't see her.

But then I black out. My knees hit the ground with a sharp thud, and I open my eyes. From here, I can see directly into hers. And they're more familiar.

"I know you," I say.

"You remember?" she asks, pulling out something silver.

It glints and shines against the moontrees.

I do. And I don't. But at that moment, I have a vague memory of wanting to die. Of a girl. Of red hair and the sun. And a need. A need to end it all.

I'm so confused. Maybe this is for the best. Maybe this sword will end my life. End my hunger. And in the back of my mind, I think there was a reason for it. A purpose.

But as she moves the metal closer, I see it's not a sword. Not a blade, not even a weapon. It's a collar, with a crystal in the center.

She extends her finger. It's covered in a metal nail, one sharp enough to cut, and I watch hungrily as she slices the nail through her skin, letting her blood bubble and drip into the stone. My stomach rumbles.

"Now you," she says.

I cannot for the life of me understand why I listen. Why I don't reach out and lick the beads of blood, or bite down on her arm. But I hold out my hand, and she cuts me. Mixing our blood together. The crystal is glowing, red. Bright red. I vaguely recall armor. Kashonim. Sharing power and strength. And then it's around my neck.

I shake my head in frustration. "I knew your name. I know I did. Why can't I remember?"

"You're still new. Still recovering from the transition. It's disorienting at first, but your memories will return in time. I'll help you when they do. I'll help you sort through them, because I know you."

I nod, reassured. "What do I call you?"

She smiles, and places a crown on her head. "Ereshya."

TRAITOR OF THE DROWNED EMPIRE

THE STORY CONTINUES IN THE DROWNED EMPIRE
SERIES, #5

APPENDIX I: THE EMPIRE OF LUMERIA

There are twelve countries united under the Lumerian Empire, Lumeria Nutavia. Each country is presided over by one of the Twelve Ruling Kavim. Each country is governed by an Arkasva, the High Lord or Lady of the ruling Ka.

All twelve countries submit to the rule and law of the Emperor. Each Arkasva also answers to an Imperator, one Arkasva with jurisdiction over each country in either the Northern or Southern hemispheres of the Empire. In addition to the Emperor's rule, twelve senators, one from each country, fill the twelve seats of the Senate. A senator must not belong to the ruling Ka of their country.

The roles of Imperator and Emperor are lifelong appointments. They are not passed onto family members, but must instead be elected by the ruling Kavim. Kavim may not submit a candidate for either role if the previous Imperator or Emperor belonged to their Ka.

Imperators may keep their ties to their Ka and continue to rule in their own country, but an Emperor will lose their Ka upon anointing and must be like a father or mother to all Lumerians.

Empiric Chain of Command

Emperor Theotis, High Lord of Lumeria Nutavia The Emperor rules over the entire Empire from its capitol, Numeria. The Emperor oversees the running of the Senate, and the twelve countries united under the Empire.

Devon Hart, Imperator of the North
The Imperator of the North is an Arkasva who not only rules their own country, but also oversees the rule of the remaining five countries belonging to the North. His rule includes the following countries, currently ruled by the following Kavim:

Glemaria, Ka Hart

Payunmar, Ka Valyan

Hartavia, Ka Taria

Ereztia, Ka Sephiron

Aravia, Ka Lumerin

Sindhuvine, Ka Kether

Avery Kormac, Imperator of the South
The Imperator of the South is an Arkasva who not only rules their own country, but also oversees rule of the remaining five countries belonging to the South. The sitting Imperator is also nephew to the Emperor. His rule includes the following countries currently being ruled by the following Kavim:

Bamaria, Ka Batavia

Korteria, Ka Kormac

Elyria, Ka Elys (previously Ka Azria)

Damara, Ka Daquataine

Lethea, Ka Maras

Cretanya, Ka Zarine

The Immortal Afeyan Courts*

The Sun Court: El Zandria, ruled by King RaKanam

The Moon Court: Khemet, ruled by Queen Ma'Nia The Star Court: Night Lands, ruled by Queen Ishtara

Afeyan Courts are not considered part of the Lumerian Empire, nor do they submit to the Emperor. However, history, prior treaties, and trade agreements have kept the courts at peace, and working together. They are the only two groups to have shared life on the continent of Lumeria Matavia.

APPENDIX 2: THE BAMARIAN COUNCIL

Each of the twelve countries in the Lumerian Empire includes a twelve-member council comprised of members of the nobility who assist the Arkasva in ruling and decision- making.

The Bamarian Council includes the following:

Arkasva: Arianna Batavia

Master of the Horse: Romula Grey

Arkturion: Waryn Kormac (until Aemon Melvik returns)

Turion: Dairen Melvik

Arkmage: Kolaya Scholar

Master of Education: Shanna Kasmar **Master of Spies**: Sila Shavo

Master of Finance: Trajan Grey

Master of Law: Kiera Ezara

Naturion: Dagana Scholar

Senator: Janvi Elys

Master of Peace: Brenna Corra

APPENDIX 3: TITLES AND FORMS OF ADDRESS

Emperor: Ruler of all twelve countries in the Lumerian Empire. The Emperor is elected by the ruling Arkasvim. They are appointed for life. Once an Emperor or Empress dies, the Kavim must elect a new ruler. The Emperor must renounce their Ka when anointed, but no Ka may produce an Emperor/Empress twice in a row.

Imperator: The head of the hemisphere. The Empire always has two Imperators, one for the Northern hemisphere, one for the South. The Imperator will also be the Arkasva of their country. They have jurisdiction over their hemisphere, and act as a voice and direct messenger between each Arkasva and the Emperor.

Arkasva (Ark-kas-va): Ruler of the country, literally translates as the "will of the highest soul." **Arkasvim** (Ark-kas-veem): Plural of Arkasva.

Heir Apparent: Title given to the eldest child or Heir of the Arkasva. The next in line to the Seat of Power or First from the Seat.

Arkturion (Ark-tor-ree-an): warlord for the country, general of their soturi/army.

Arkmage: The ruling mage of the country. Ethical disputes over the use of magic are brought to them. They lead the seven Watchers of the Light, and maintain the temple as well as the country's collection of Valya scrolls. They are granted a stave which allows them to exert the power of ten mages and preside over important holidays, rituals, and ceremonies.

Chayatim (Kheye-ah-teem): Cloaked ones, vorakh who have been enslaved in the Palace to serve the Emperor and Lumerian elites.

Lady: Formal title for a female or female-identifying member of the nobility.

Lord: Formal title for a male or male-identifying member of the nobility.

Soturion: Soldier, magically enhanced warrior. A Lumerian who can transmute magic through their body. May be used as a form of address for a non-noble.

Turion: Commander, may lead legions of soturi. Must answer to their Arkturion.

Mage: A Lumerian who transmutes magic through spells. A stave is used to focus their magic.

Apprentice: A soturion or mage who has passed their first three years of training. As an apprentice, their time is divided between their own studies and teaching the novice to whom they are bound. This is done to strengthen the power of kashonim, and because of the Bamarian philosophy that teaching a subject is the best way to learn and master a subject.

Novice: A soturion or mage who is in the beginning of their learning to become an anointed mage or soturion.

Your Majesty: Formal address for the Emperor or Empress. Previously used for the Kings and Queens of Lumeria Matavia. It can also be used for the King and Queen of the Afeyan Sun and Moon Courts.

Your Highness: Formal address for Imperators. The term of address has also been adopted by the Afeyan Star Court.

Your Grace: Formal address for any member of the ruling Ka who is in line to the Seat of Power, including the Arkasva. A noble may only be addressed as "Your Grace" if they are in line to the Seat.

APPENDIX 4: GLOSSARY AND PRONUNCIATION GUIDE

Names

Lyriana Batavia (Leer-ree-ana Ba-tah-via): Previously third in line to the Seat of Power in Bamaria.

Morgana Batavia (Mor-ga-na Ba-tah-via): Previously second in line to the Seat of Power in Bamaria.

Meera Batavia (Mee-ra Ba-tah-via): Previously first in line to the Seat of Power in Bamaria (Heir Apparent).

Julianna Batavia (Jool-lee-ana Ba-tah-via): Cousin to Lyriana, Morgana, and Meera.

Naria Batavia (Nar-ria Ba-tah-via): Heir Apparent, first in line to the Seat of Power in Bamaria.

Arianna Batavia (Ar-ree-ana Ba-tah-via): Current Arkasva and High Lady of Bamaria.

Aemon Melvik (Ae-mon Mel-vik): Warlord of Bamaria, Arkturion on the Council of Bamaria.

Parthenay (Par-tha-nay): Previously a chayatim, or cloaked one serving the Emperor, Parthenay is a vorakh who can read minds and serves Aemon.

Rhyan Hart (Ry-an Hart): Forsworn and exiled from

Glemaria. Previously was first in line to the Seat of Power (Heir Apparent).

Tristan Grey (Tris-tan Grey): A noble of Bamaria, previously linked to Lyriana Batavia, he is now engaged to her cousin, the Heir Apparent, Lady Naria Batavia. Tristan is also the grandson to two members of the Bamarian Council.

Galen Scholar (Gay-len Skal-ar): A Bamarian of the prominent Ka Scholar, Galen is a soturion previously romantically linked to the deceased Haleika Grey. He is Tristan's best friend.

Theotis (Thee-otis): Current Emperor of Lumeria Nutavia. Theotis was previously from Korteria, and a noble of Ka Kormac. His nephew, Avery Kormac, is the current Imperator to the Southern hemisphere of the Empire, and Arkasva to Korteria.

Avery Kormac (Ae-very Core-mac): Nephew to the Emperor. As Imperator of the South, he rules over the six southern countries of the Empire, as well as ruling Korteria as the Arkasva.

Devon Hart (Deh-vawn Hart): Imperator of the North, he rules over the six northern countries of the Empire, as well as ruling Glemaria as the Arkasva.

Aiden DeKassas (Ai-dan Deh-cah-sus): A Glemarian mage who grew up beside Rhyan and became one of his best friends before becoming Apprentice to the Master of Spies, and part of Imperator Hart's most trusted circle.

Dario DeTerria (Dar-ree-yo Deh-tair-ree-yah): A Glemarian soturion who grew up beside Rhyan and became of his best friends. His father was previously Master of the Peace on the Glemarian Council, and he currently serves Imperator Hart.

Kane Gadayyan (Cain Gaw-die-yan): Arkturion and Warlord to Glemaria and the North.

Names (Gods and Goddesses)
Asherah (A-sher-ah): Goddess, Guardian of the Red Ray.

Original Guardian of the Valalumir in Heaven. She was banished to Earth as a mortal after her affair with Auriel was discovered.

Ereshya (Air-resh-she-ah): Goddess, Guardian of the Orange Ray. Original Guardian of the Valalumir in Heaven.

Shiviel (Shiv-ay-el): God, Guardian of the Yellow Ray. Original Guardian of the Valalumir in Heaven.

Auriel (Or-ree-el): God, Guardian of the Green Ray. Original Guardian of the Valalumir in Heaven. He stole the light to bring to Earth, where it turned into a crystal before shattering at the time of the Drowning.

Cassarya (Cah-sar-ree-ah): Goddess, Guardian of the Blue Ray. Original Guardian of the Valalumir in Heaven.

Moriel (Mor-ree-el): God, Guardian of the Indigo Ray.

Original Guardian of the Valalumir in Heaven. He reported Auriel and Asherah's affair to the Council of Forty-four, leading to Asherah's banishment, Auriel's theft of the light, and its subsequent destruction. He was banished to Earth, where he allied with the akadim in the war that led to the Drowning.

Hava (Ha-vah): Goddess, Guardian of the Violet Ray. Original Guardian of the Valalumir in Heaven.

Names (Afeya)

Afeya (Ah-fay-ah): Immortal Lumerians who survived the Drowning. Prior to this, Afeya were non- distinguishable from other Lumerians in Lumeria Matavia. They were descended from the Gods and Goddesses, trapped in the mortal coil, but they refused the request to join the war efforts. Some sources believe they allied with Moriel's forces and the akadim. When the Valalumir shattered, they were cursed to live forever, unable to return to their home, be relieved of life, or touch or perform magic—unless asked to do so by another.

Mercurial (Mer-cure-ree-el): An immortal Afeya, First Messenger of her Highness Queen Ishtara, High Lady of the Night Lands.

Ramia (Rah-me-yah): Half-Afeyan librarian.

Zenoya (Zen-oy-ya): Half-Afeyan librarian.

Places

Allurian Pass (All-or-ree-an Pass): Mountain cutting through the western border of Glemaria and the non-magical human lands. Marks the edge of the Lumerian Empire, and is the only way to enter the non-magic lands through Glemaria.

Aravia (Ar-ay-vee-ah): Country in the North on the southern border of Glemaria. Ruled by Ka Lumerin. It contains a vibrant system of caves.

Bamaria (Ba-mar-ria): Southernmost country of the Lumerian Empire, home of the South's most prestigious University and the Great Library. Ruled by Ka Batavia.

Cretanya (Creh-tawn-yuh): One of the northernmost countries in the South of the Lumerian Empire, ruled by Ka Zarine. Known for its city of Thene and vibrant night life.

Elyria (El-leer-ria): Historically ruled by Ka Azria, rulership has now passed to Ka Elys, originally nobility from Bamaria.

Damara (Da-mar-ra): A Southern country known for its strong warriors, ruled by Ka Daquataine.

Glemaria (Gleh-mar-ria): Northernmost country of the Empire, ruled by Ka Hart. Imperator Devon Hart is the Arkasva and Imperator to the North. Rhyan Hart was previously first in line to the Seat.

Hartavia (Har-tah-via): A Northern country that borders Glemaria, and maintains a close relationship with Imperator Hart.

Korteria (Kor-ter-ria): Westernmost country in the Empire. Magic is least effective in their mountains, but Korteria does have access to starfire for Lumerian weapons. Ruled by Ka Kormac.

Lethea (Lee-thee-a): The only part of the Empire located in the Lumerian Ocean. Ruled by Ka Maras, this is the country where criminals stripped of powers, or accused of vorakh are sent for imprisonment. The expression "Farther than Lethea" comes from the fact that there is nothing but ocean beyond the island. Due to the Drowning, the idea of going past the island is akin to losing one's mind.

Lumeria (Lu-mair-ria): The name of the continent where Gods and Goddesses first incarnated until it sank into the Lumerian Ocean in the Drowning.

Matavia (Ma-tah-via): Motherland. When used with Lumeria, it refers to the continent that sank.

Numeria (New-mair-ria): The Capital of the Lumerian Empire, home of the Emperor, and location of the Palace, and the Nutavian Katurium. Numeria is located in the center of Lumeria and not considered part of the North or South.

Nutavia (New-tah-via): New land. When used with Lumeria, it refers to the Empire forged after the Drowning by those who survived and made it to Bamaria—previously Dobra.

Vrukshire (Vrook-shire): The fortress of Korteria, ruled by Ka Kormac.

Prominent Creatures of the Old World Known to Have Survived the Drowning

Seraphim (Ser-a-feem): Birds with wings of gold, they resemble a cross between an eagle and a dove.

Ashvan (Ash-van): Flying horses. These are the only sky creatures that do not possess wings. Their flight comes from magic contained in their hooves.

Nahashim (Naw-ha-sheem): Snakes with the ability to grow and shrink at will, able to fit into any space for the purposes of seeking. Anything lost or desired can almost always be found by a nahashim.

Gryphon (Grif-in): Sky creatures that are half-eagle, half-lion.

Akadim (A-ka-deem): The most feared of all creatures,

akadim are literally bodies without souls. They kill by eating the souls of their victims.

Terms/Items

Bind/Binding: A spell that ties a rope around a Lumerian to keep them from touching their power, or restricting their physical ability to move. A Binding is temporary, and can have more or less strength and heat depending on the mage casting the spell.

Birth Bind: Unlike a traditional Bind, a Birth Bind leaves no mark. It is given to all Lumerians in their first year of life, a spell that will keep them from accessing their magic power when it develops during puberty. The Birth Bind may only be removed after the Lumerian has turned nineteen, the age of adulthood.

Dagger: A ceremonial weapon given to soturi. The dagger has no special power on its own, as the magic of a soturion is transmuted through their body.

Ka (Kah): Soul. A Ka is a soul tribe or family.

Kashonim (Ka-show-neem): Ancestral lineage and link of power. Calling on kashonim allows you to absorb the power of your lineage, but depending on the situation, usage can be dangerous. One, it can be an overwhelming amount of power that leaves you unconscious if you come from a long or particularly powerful lineage. Two, it has the potential to weaken the mages or soturi from whom the caller is drawing strength. It is also illegal to use kashonim against fellow students.

Kavim (Ka-veem): Plural of Ka (see above). When marriages occur, either member of the union may take on the name of their significant other's Ka. Typically, the Ka with more prestige or nobility will be used thus ensuring the most powerful Kavim continue to grow.

Laurel of the Arkasva (Lor-el of the Ar-kas-va): A golden circlet worn by the Arkasva. The Arkasva replaced the titles of King and Queen that were used in Lumeria Matavia, and the

Laurel replaced the crown, though they are held in the same high esteem.

Mekarim (Mee-kah-reem): Soulmates.

Mekara (Mee-kah-rah): Term of endearment, translates to "My soul is yours."

Rakame (Rah-kah-may): Term of endearment, translates to "Your soul is mine."

Rakashonim (rah-ka-show-neem): Link of power to one's soul, allows you to absorb the power of your own life lineage and past selves, but can be too volatile for the mortal body to sustain.

Seat of Power: Akin to a throne. Thrones were replaced by Seats in Lumeria Nutavia, as many members of royalty were blamed by the citizens of Lumeria for the Drowning. Much as a monarch may have a throne room, the Arkasvim have a Seating Room. The Arkasva typically has a Seat of Power in their Seating Room in their Ka's fortress, and another in their temple.

Stave: Made of twisted moon and sun wood, the stave transmutes magic created by mages. A stave is not needed to perform magic, but greatly focuses and strengthens it. More magic being transmuted may require a larger stave.

Vadati (Va-dah-tee): Stones that allow Lumerians to hear and speak to each other over vast distances. Most of these stones were lost in the Drowning. The Empire now keeps a strict registry of each known stone.

Valabellum (Val-la-bell-um): A traditional arena game in which soturi battle over the course of the day in honor of Asherah's Feast Day to reenact the story of the War of Light. In the final battle, soturi play the roles of the seven banished Guardians. The game ends when the fighter playing Moriel dies.

Valalumir (Val-la-loo-meer): The sacred light of Heaven that began the Celestial War, which began in Heaven and ended with the Drowning. The light was guarded by seven Gods and Goddesses until Asherah and Auriel's affair. Asherah was banished to become mortal, and Auriel fell to bring her the light. Part of the light went into Asherah before it crystalized. When the war ended, the Valalumir shattered into seven pieces—all lost in the Drowning.

Valya (Val-yah): The sacred text of recounting the history of the Lumerian people up until the Drowning. There are multiple Valyas recorded, each with slight variations, but the Mar Valya is the standard. Another popular translation is the Tavia Valya, which is believed to have been better preserved than the Mar Valya after the Drowning, but was never made into the standard for copying. Slight changes or possible effects of water damage offer different insights into Auriel's initial meeting with Asherah.

Vorakh (Vor-rock): Taboo, forbidden powers. Three magical abilities that faded after the Drowning and are now considered illegal: visions, mind reading, and traveling by mind. Vorakh can be translated as "gift from the Gods" in High Lumerian, but is now translated as "curse from the Gods."

ACKNOWLEDGMENTS

First of all, I want to thank you if you've read this far. Being able to write the fourth book in a series (or the sixth if you've read Rhyan's previous "novellas"), is such a privilege. I've been waiting to get to this moment for over a decade—yes, I've always known we were going to end up here, and now that we have arrived, everything is about to get a lot more interesting. Thank you for trusting me this far, I'm honored and more grateful than you'll ever know.

Of course, I would have never gotten here without you, Sara DeSabato! I literally cannot thank you enough for being there from the start when I was working on early drafts of these books in grad school, for being one of my best friends, and then becoming the most amazing developmental editor ever! Thank you for helping me overcome every fear I had about this, and also for just helping me shape every idea into what it needed to be to tell the story I always set out to tell. Also, I'm so glad whiteboard sessions are back.

Marcella Haddad, a million thanks for staying on top of my mental health, being the best in-person assistant at events, my best friend, my favorite person to road trip with, my sister, and of course the one who unlocked the way I would approach the ending when I'd had it in my head for so many years that it felt too hard and big to write. I'll never forget sitting down at the café with you and telling you everything I was planning to do, and then watching as you simplified it into an outline that made sense to me. And then receiving confirmation from my dad that we'd gotten it right when Enya began to play.

Corporate, thanks for constantly caring and for the regular conference calls. I'm so excited for our upcoming corporate retreats and travels.

Asha Venkataraman, thank you for being my beta reader and still being one of my best friends after all of these years. I'm so glad we've been getting to see each other more despite living on opposite ends of the country!

Dylan, Blake, Hannah, and Dani, because I will always thank you for existing and being a part of my life.

Taryn Fagerness, thank you for helping the Drowned Empire books find new homes and reach new readers. So excited for what's to come.

Natasha Qureshi, thank you for believing in the books and bringing me onto the Hodderscape Team!

Molly Powell, and Sophie Judge, thank you both so much for stepping in and taking care of the books, and working with me as I finished Warrior during one of the toughest phases of my life.

Andy Ryan, I can't thank you enough for coming through with the copy edits.

Stefanie Saw, and Saint Jupiter, again for amazing cover designs for our indie covers.

Steve Kuzma, thank you for keeping the digital empire safe.

Drowned Empire Arc Readers and Forsworn Mayhem members, I will always be so so grateful to you for reading the books and sharing your excitement.

And of course, thank YOU for reading!

Love,

Frankie

ABOUT THE AUTHOR

Frankie Diane Mallis is the bestselling author of the romantic fantasy *Drowned Empire* series. The books became number-one bestsellers on Amazon in Greek and Roman Myth in their debut year, and have gone on to become number-one bestsellers in historical fantasy. She lives outside Philadelphia, where she was previously an award-winning university professor. When not writing or teaching, she practices yoga and belly dance, and can usually be found baking gluten-free desserts.

Visit www.frankiedianemallis.com to learn more, and sign up for the newsletter. Follow Frankie on Instagram (@frankiediane), and on TikTok (@frankiedianebooks).